Oh where to start!

This story has been a long time in the telling. Its central characters lived separately in my head for a number of years before I found the confidence to connect them and set them free.

For the language purists out there I'll humbly apologise now. "Stronger Within" is largely set in the USA and, while I have endeavored to use the correct American terminology for everyday items e.g. cell phone not mobile phone, sidewalk not pavement, it is written in UK English. If the s's instead of z's offend then I'm sorry.

I'd like to take a moment to thank my "infamous five" alpha readers. This book wouldn't have come into existence without your love, support and encouragement.

To my beta readers who swept in like the literary cavalry at the end, thank you for your support and attention to detail.

To my writer "fairy godmother" a huge thank you for your support and technical assistance with the final cover design. You were a life saver!

The Celtic dragon knot is a recurring theme through the ongoing tale of Jake, Lori and Silver Lake. I'd like to thank my artistic friend from the bottom of my heart for the wonderful gift of the original artwork. (There's a rock 'n' roll story there too but that's one for another day)

To all my family and friends, thank you for putting up with me throughout the birth of "Stronger Within". It was a long and at times painful labour of love.

And finally, a personal thank you to YOU for picking up this copy of my "book baby".

Love and hugs to you all

Coral McCallum   10 April 2015

Cover Artwork –

Cover photograph – copyright CMC Photography

Celtic Dragon Knot- created by Fiona Knox and gifted to the author.

Stronger Within

Coral McCallum

ISBN: 151176709X
ISBN-13:978-1511767095

With a long sigh of complete contentment, she felt the tension melt from her shoulders. Her first tentative steps onto the beach since last summer. It felt good to be home. It was late afternoon and she could feel the last of the spring sun's warmth on her skin. She was also acutely aware of Mary's eyes on her, as she watched from the sun deck. No going back now. After all, she had made it this far and it felt good to be outdoors. She adjusted the grip on her crutches, making sure the broad base plates didn't sink into the soft sand and slowly headed across the beach towards the ocean. Once on the hard packed surface, she felt more stable and her confidence began to grow. The waves rolled in gently beside her, but she was careful to stay beyond their reach. Tasting the salt on her lips, she smiled and headed along the shoreline towards the boardwalk.

The beach was quiet, with only a few families packing up after an afternoon at the shore. It had been unseasonably warm all week and everyone was making the most of the bonus sunshine. Small seabirds were playing in the shallows, rushing backwards and forwards twittering merrily. After about a hundred yards, she stopped to watch the waves, listening to their rhythmic flow. Hopefully by summer, when the water would be warmer, she would be able to enjoy swimming in the ocean again. Hopefully…

Oh, it was good to be home; good to be back by the ocean.

Step by carefully placed step, she kept wandering along the sand towards town. She drank in all of her surroundings; the birds, the shells, and an occasional abandoned sand castle. Lost in her own thoughts, she immersed herself in her private beach world.

It was the throbbing pain from her leg that brought her back to the real world. She had been stupid. She had walked too far. With panic and fear rising in her chest, she headed up the beach towards the boardwalk that ran parallel to the shore. If she could get onto firm ground and rest for a while, maybe she could recover enough strength to get back to the house. Mary had warned her to be careful, had warned her not to try to go too far on her first day out. The boardwalk seemed to be a mile away, even though it was, in reality, only a few short yards away. As the sand got softer her crutches dug further in, despite their broad base plates. The left one sank into a particularly soft patch. Suddenly her leg gave way and she crashed onto the beach.

For a few moments she lay there, tears welling up in her eyes, terrified that she was hurt. Gingerly, she manoeuvred herself into a sitting position.

"Shit!" she yelled out to the world. "Shit!"

Her crutches lay just within arm's reach and she dragged them over towards her. Getting back to her feet was going to be a challenge. One that looked impossible in the current situation. There was no one in sight and Lori felt a sharp stab of fear in her chest. As she sat figuring out how she was going to get up without falling again, she was unaware that she was being watched from the shadows of boardwalk.

Jake watched her from the distant vantage point of the boardwalk. He had headed for the beach after the end of his shift at the pizza parlour. It had been a rough day and he had decided to walk off his black mood before heading to meet the guys. The last thing they needed was him turning up in a foul mood, stinking of tomato sauce and cheese. He had walked to the south end of the promenade and had just turned back when he saw the girl walking down on the sand. It was the sun catching the golden highlights in her hair that had attracted his attention. He never noticed her crutches at first. Watching from a distance, he had kept pace with her, then stopped to watch as she turned towards the boardwalk. When he saw her stumble, he regretted not following his instincts and going down to walk on the sand with her.

"Shit," he muttered. "Shit."

There were no breaks in the fence nearby, so he jumped over the wooden palings into the dune grass and ran towards her, sand immediately filling his shoes. By the time he was close enough to call out to her, she was sitting up and looked to be unhurt. He almost turned away, but decided against it and continued to walk down the beach.

"Hi," he called out. "Are you ok?"

She was sitting rubbing her thigh and there were tears on her cheeks. Her pale complexion suggested she hadn't been outdoors much recently.

"Hi," she replied with a weak smile. "I could do with some help."

"Figured," he said, sitting down on the sand beside her. "Are you hurt?"

"No, not really. It was my own stupid fault. I came too far and wasn't paying attention. I lost my footing."

"Can't be easy walking the beach with crutches," he observed. "How far have you walked?"

"Less than a quarter of a mile. I was fine when I was down on the wet sand, but I began to get tired. I was trying to get up to the boardwalk. I figured if I got onto solid ground, it would be easier to walk back."

"Let me guess," observed Jake. "You've not been out much with those sticks?"

"No," she confessed. "I haven't."

A single tear ran down her pale cheek. She reached up to roughly brush it away, embarrassed by her show of emotion, but only succeeded in leaving a smear of sand in its place. That was the final straw. Burying her face in her hands, she sat and sobbed. Months of pent up frustration flowed down her cheeks in a river of tears. Hesitantly, Jake put a comforting arm around her shoulders and held her as she wept.

"Hey," he whispered softly. "It'll be ok. I'll get you home safely."

"I'm sorry," she sniffed. "I don't usually sob all over complete strangers."

"Well, I don't usually go around picking up fallen angels on the beach either."

She smiled at his weak attempt at humour.

"I'm Jake by the way."

"Lori," she replied.

"Well, Lori, let's get you up on your feet and up onto the boardwalk."

"Thank you."

Gauging that she didn't weigh much, Jake handed her the crutches, told her to hold onto them then lifted her up into his arms. She was even lighter than he had guessed, so carrying her up the beach to the nearest pathway was no challenge. Once back up on the boardwalk, he sat her down on the first bench they came to.

"You sure you're ok?" he asked, as he sat beside her.

"Yes, thank you. I honestly don't know what I would've done if you hadn't come along."

"You'd have figured it out eventually."

"I guess. Either that or Mary would've come looking for me," admitted Lori, brushing sand off her jeans.

"Mary?"

"Yeah, she's my housekeeper. It was her idea that I take a walk. I've been sitting on the deck all afternoon gazing out at the ocean. She told me I needed to venture off the deck sometime and that today was as good a day as any. She'll feel so bad when she hears I fell," she explained.

"Who's going to tell her?" Jake said with a wink. "I'll walk you back. You don't need to tell her that you fell."

"Thanks."

Stiffly and with more than a hint of nerves, Lori got to her feet and repositioned her crutches. Her leg was screaming at her and she knew it would be hard to keep news of her fall from the ever watchful Mary. As they began to walk along the sandy boards Jake observed how carefully Lori walked - watched the determination in each step and sensed the pain that was etched into her pale face. She had the bluest eyes, he had ever seen, but there was a deep sadness cast through them.

"Pardon my asking but what happened to you? I'm thinking the crutches are a very recent addition to your wardrobe."

"And you'd be right," she confessed, pausing to look up at him. "I had an accident just before Christmas. I broke my leg quite badly. I came down here about six weeks ago. This is the first time I've been out on my own since the accident."

"And you thought a walk on the sand was the smartest place to start?"

Lori laughed. Jake thought it the most beautiful musical laugh and joined in.

"I guess not, "she giggled. "So what brought you out this far?"

"A shit shift at work. A foul mood."

"And scraping a dumb blonde off the sand wasn't in the plan?"

"No, but I'm glad I was there to rescue you," he admitted. That wonderful laugh and those sad blue eyes were having a strange effect on his heart. A weird but wonderful effect. It had been a long time since he had felt that way. "Where exactly am I taking you when we run out of boardwalk?"

"Fourth house past the end. If that's ok?"

"Not a problem, li'l lady."

They walked on in silence for a few minutes, the end of the boardwalk drawing closer and neither of them really wanting to reach it. Surreptitiously, Jake watched her steely concentration, drank in her fragile beauty and breathed in her light, floral perfume. It had been a very long time since someone had had such an impact on him. A long time since he had bothered to look, if he was honest with himself. Between each painful step, Lori subtly surveyed her rescuer. He would make a fantastic model for a life drawing. His long sun bleached blonde hair fell carelessly down over his shoulders, almost reaching the middle of his back. She guessed from the tiny lines around his twinkling hazel eyes that he was a little older than her and his height dwarfed her small frame. There was something genuine about him. A rough diamond found in the sand? A friend? Lord, she could use one!

Deciding to take a risk, Lori said, "When we reach the house, will you come in for a coffee or a beer? It's the least I can offer."

"I'm not sure," began Jake glancing at his watch. "Oh, what the hell! The guys can wait. Beer sounds good."

It may have only been a hundred yards, but by the time they reached the end of the boardwalk, Lori was drained and exhausted. Her arms were trembling; her palms sweaty. The thought of the final walk along the soft sand filled her with dread.

"Hey, Lori," began Jake softly. "If you don't mind me saying, you look wiped out. Would it be too presumptuous of me to offer to carry you the rest of the way?"

"A bit, but I'm not in a position to decline," she admitted, her eyes filling with fresh tears of frustration at her own admission of weakness.

With ease, he scooped her up into his arms and headed across the soft sand.

The fourth house on the right stood out from its neighbours with its low white picket fence and generous sun deck. Its enclosed garden had been recently landscaped and a large cushioned sun lounger sat centre stage on the deck. Perched on the edge of it was a small, motherly dark haired woman. As they came to the open gate Jake set Lori down on her feet and guided her into the safety of the garden. She breathed a sigh of relief – home at last!

"Where in Lord's name have you been?" cried the older woman, leaping to her feet. "You've been gone for over an hour!"

"Jake meet Mary," introduced Lori. "My housekeeper and surrogate mother."

"Pleased to meet you," snapped Mary sharply. Her concern for Lori was written all over her face. "I've been worried sick, Lori."

"I'm sorry, Mary," apologised Lori, as she eased herself down onto the sun lounger. "I walked further than I meant to. Jake kindly offered to see me safely home."

"You fell didn't you?"

"I told you she would know," said Lori, glancing up at Jake. "Yes, I stumbled, but Jake arrived to rescue me. I promised him a beer for his efforts. Would you be so kind as to fetch us both one?"

Muttering under her breath, Mary stomped back into the house through the patio doors. Lori laughed that wonderful laugh again and gestured to Jake to pull over a chair from the table. Gingerly she slid herself back and lifted her throbbing leg onto the lounger. The relief at being off her feet was written all over her face.

"I recognise this house now," mused Jake looking round about. "I worked on it when it was re-modelled about four years ago."

"Three", corrected Lori. "Are you a builder?"

"No," declared Jake, shaking his head. "I was the manual labour for the summer. I loved that sun room when it was finished. If I ever hit the big time, this is the kind of house I want to own."

"Thanks. My parents bought the original house when I was a little girl. When I inherited it, after my dad passed away, I had it extended. I've always felt this was home, but could never spend enough time here. Work always kept me away."

She paused to reflect for a few moments, lost in a memory of a previous life. With a wistful smile she added, "Now it looks as though I'm home to stay."

"So what line of work kept you away from the beach?" asked Jake, stretching his long denim clad legs out in front of him.

"I was an art buyer until last year. I travelled a lot. What do you do when you're not rescuing people?"

"I'm a frustrated rock star," he confessed with a smile. "I work here and there to pay the bills. Just now it's a few shifts a week at the pizza place on the boardwalk. Really rock 'n' roll!"

Both of them were laughing when Mary returned with their beers. She slipped two painkillers to Lori then left them to chat. There was plenty of time left to chastise her charge once her new friend had left. Deep down, she was just relieved to see the girl home in one piece and even happier to hear her laughing. There had been precious little of that in Lori's life recently and it was good medicine. The housekeeper retired to the kitchen to prepare dinner and to keep a watchful eye on them from the safety of the house.

As the sun set behind them, the sun deck lights came on and dusk settled over them. Draining his beer Jake glanced at his watch. "Damn, I'm late."

"Sorry," said Lori. "I didn't mean to keep you late."

"It's alright," he replied, getting to his feet. "I need to run. I'm late for rehearsal. Sorry to leave in such a hurry."

"No, it's me who should be apologising," said Lori, starting to get to her feet.

"Stay where you are," said Jake warmly. "I'm just glad you're not hurt. Glad we met. Maybe, when you feel up to it, you can come and see the band? We have a regular slot on a Friday night twice a month at one of the bars in town."

"I'd like that," said Lori softly. "And thank you again for rescuing me."

"My pleasure li'l lady," he said with a smile. "And thanks for the beer."

With a wave, he was gone in a few short strides down the path and onto the sand.

It took longer than he had anticipated to get back along the boardwalk and into town. By the time Jake reached the band's rehearsal room, he was almost an hour late. Band rules about timekeeping meant a twenty dollar fine. Rules were rules and he would pay up without complaint. After all, it was the first time he had been late for about six weeks. A record for him.

"Nice of you to join us," called Paul, the band's drummer.

"Sorry, something came up," apologised Jake, lifting his guitar. As he plugged it into his amp, he added, "Where are we at?"

"Full set run through for Friday night," answered Grey firmly. "I spoke to Joe at the bar and he's promised us two one hour sets. He's got a beer promo night on so we get a half hour extra."

"And beer?" asked Jake hopefully

"Only if we buy it ourselves," said Grey. "I tried. If Jeannie is behind the bar, she might sneak us a couple. No promises."

With the rehearsal schedule set, the band settled down to their full run through. They had been playing together for almost five years and had a small, but dedicated local fan base. All of them had hopes of hitting the big time; of getting a support slot on a big tour. None of them were full-time musicians. Rich, the other guitarist, came closest. He was a music teacher at the local high school.

It was after ten thirty before they called it a night. Once outside, they agreed to meet up again on Thursday for another run-through, then went their separate ways into the night. Jake wandered slowly back to his apartment, his head full of ideas for his own songs and more than a few thoughts of the beach. Once home, he settled down with his acoustic guitar and began work on his own compositions, playing into the small hours.

Back at the beach house, Mary had insisted on helping Lori to bed immediately after dinner. Throughout the meal, she had scolded her charge on her foolhardiness and elicited a promise that she would be more careful the next time she ventured out. Lori listened patiently to the motherly lecture, allowing her thoughts to wander back to Jake. All of a sudden she felt like a love-struck teenager. Yes, he was attractive in a haunted kind of way, but she was too old to confuse gratitude at his rescue with feelings of attraction. Or was she? Shortly before nine, Mary ran out of lectures and headed home, leaving Lori alone with her teenage thoughts. The day's excitement had taken its toll on her. She was completely exhausted and every inch of her ached. Her leg had eased to a dull throb after a further dose of pain relief. Was this the way her life was going to be from now on? Ruled by pain relief schedules and controlling well-meaning housekeepers? Eventually, she drifted off to sleep. Her first nightmare-free sleep since her accident. She was still sound asleep when Mary returned at breakfast time the next day.

"Hey!" called a voice from the beach.

The interruption broke her concentration and she laid down her sketch pad and pencil. It was a voice that had filled her head for two days. "Still thinking like that love-struck teen," she muttered to herself.

"Hey!" she called back. "Come on in."

A few seconds later, Jake appeared up the path looking every inch the rock star. The wind off the ocean had tousled his long blonde hair and his tight black t-shirt and slim fitting jeans set off the look. He sat down on the empty chair beside her at the table and glanced at her discarded half-completed sketch.

"That's good. Very good," he commented.

"Thanks," she blushed. "I'm just doodling."

"Well, it looks like good doodling to me," stated Jake matter-of-factly. "I just wanted to see if you were ok. I hope you don't mind. I came along the beach just to be sure you weren't face down in the sand."

She laughed. There was that sound that had filled his head since their first meeting. He smiled.

"I've been a good girl," she said coyly. "Mary has seen to that."

"Ruling you with a rod of iron?"

"Something like that," admitted Lori with a giggle. "She's gone to the food store so I escaped out here."

"So, are you ok after the other day?" asked Jake, concern written all over his face.

"I'm fine. I was sore yesterday, but I'm ok today. I might think twice about walking the beach for a while though," she said. "I was just thinking about fetching a coffee. Would you like one?"

"If it's not too much trouble," he replied.

"You can help," said Lori, picking up her crutches and getting to her feet. "Come on."

He followed her into the house and through the sun room towards the kitchen. It felt strange being back in the house he'd left as a newly-finished undecorated shell. The coffee pot was ready and the aroma filled the kitchen.

"The mugs are in the cupboard over there," said Lori, nodding towards the stove. "Do you take cream?"

"Yeah and two sugars," said Jake, opening the cupboard.

A few minutes later, they were both back outside on the desk with their coffee and some cookies that Lori found in the pantry. They sat in silence for a few minutes, listening to the waves crashing in on the beach. It felt as though there was a storm approaching.

"I was wondering," began Jake, sounding almost nervous. "If you would like to venture into town with me sometime. We could go for a beer or something."

His words blurted out all wrong and he suddenly felt like an awkward sixteen-year-old asking a girl out on a date.

"I'd like that," she answered with a smile. "I haven't been into town since I got back. It would be good to get out of here for a while."

"Great. When?" asking Jake, sounding more like his adult self-assured self. "I don't want you getting in trouble over this."

Lori laughed again, "I'm a big girl. I can decide if I'm going out or not. How about Saturday afternoon?"

"I'm working till three," said Jake. "But I could pick you up after my shift?"

"Stupid question," began Lori, seeing a potential flaw in the plan. "Do you have a car? I don't think I could walk that far yet."

"A truck," replied Jake. "Will we need to clear this with Mary?"

Lori shook her head. "No. She's not my mother. Beside she finishes at two on a Saturday. I can be trusted to behave for a few hours now. What she doesn't know won't hurt her."

"You're scared of her," accused Jake jokingly.

"Just a bit," confessed Lori. "But don't tell her."

"My lips are sealed," he said, as he took another sip of coffee. "So what do you do stuck out here all day?"

"Not a lot. My physical therapist comes out once or twice a week. Mary helps me with the exercises the other days. I read. I listen to music. I sketch a bit. Daydream a lot." She paused, then added, "It was easier in a way when I was really sick. Now I feel stronger, I'll admit I'm finding that I get bored quite quickly. It's so frustrating not being able to do the things I would usually do."

"I don't think I'd cope like this," confessed Jake. Immediately the words were out, he regretted them. It had sounded insensitive. If his comments stung, Lori never let it show.

"Before," she began. "I'd have agreed with you." Then changing the subject asked, "How did rehearsal go the other night? Were you in trouble for being late?"

Jake shook his head. "The guys were fine. They are kind of used to me being a bit late. Time keeping isn't one of my strong points. Another slot tonight, then the gig's tomorrow. Should be a good night."

"Where are you playing?"

"Bar in town. There's a beer promo night so we get to play longer. Not quite Madison Square Garden but it's a start."

"Don't tell me," she mused. "Vocals and guitar?"

"Got it in one, li'l lady," he laughed, with a mock bow. "There's four of us. We've been together for a few years. You never know there might be a scout in the crowd."

"Do you write your own stuff?"

"Sometimes. Not often enough," he muttered.

"Oh, sore spot," commented Lori. "Sorry."

Jake shrugged, "Someday…. yeah… someday."

From the front of the house they heard the sound of tyres scrunching on the gravel. Mary was back.

"I'm out of here," said Jake, getting to his feet. "I don't want her growling at me."

Lori laughed, "Mary's fine. Chill."

"No way!" he stated, draining his coffee cup. "Three thirty on Saturday. Be ready."

With a brief smile and a mischievous wink, he was gone and,

by the time Mary came through the sun room to say she was home, there was no sign of him other than the empty mug on the table.

♪

Saturday dawned grey and misty with a strong chilly breeze blowing in from the ocean. As she lay in bed, Lori gazed out of the window down towards the beach. An early morning jogger trotted past in the distance down on the sand, a dog keeping pace with him, as he headed south. It was just after eight thirty and she could hear Mary preparing breakfast in the kitchen. She sighed and sank back into the pillows. There were butterflies fluttering in her stomach already as she thought ahead to her afternoon date with Jake. Mary was due to finish at two so that would give her plenty of time to get ready before he was due to arrive.

"I hope this mist lifts," she grumbled, as she swung her legs stiffly over the side of the bed. During the night, her nightshirt had ridden up and she stared down at her skinny thighs- one soft and blemish free; the other disgusted her. The scars were still red and angry, the skin discoloured and puckered. Roughly, she pulled the nightshirt down and reached for her crutches. With a grimace, she pulled herself to her feet and made her way down the hallway to the kitchen.

"Morning," called Mary cheerfully. "Coffee's hot."

"Morning," replied Lori. "What's new out in the world today?"

As she settled herself at the table and buttered her bagel, Lori half listened to Mary delivering her download of the morning's news. The housekeeper always listened to the local radio station in the car on her way over to Lori's, so, by the time she pulled up outside, she knew everything that was going on in town. If the radio had missed anything, she heard of it in the bakery when she stopped off for bagels or Danish pastries.

"Did you catch a weather update?" asked Lori casually. "Is that mist meant to burn off?"

"The guy on WGMD said it should clear by lunchtime," answered Mary. "Why? Are you thinking of venturing out?"

"I had hoped to go out on the deck later," said Lori, flushing slightly at the white lie. "I might do some sketching."

"No sketching until you complete your exercises, girl," stated

Mary, trying and failing to sound stern. "We need to get you built up and steady on those feet."

"True," Lori agreed. "Give me five minutes to finish my coffee, then I'll get dressed."

Lori's morning dragged by as she tried to focus on the stretching exercises and light strength work. The pain and effort was going to be worth it in the end, but for now it didn't feel that way. After four months of treatment she was beginning to have her doubts. The mist had lifted by the time she was showered and dressed and the sun was breaking through. Together the two women ate lunch out on the sun deck, then Lori suggested to Mary that she finish up early.

"Would you mind?" asked Mary, obviously keen to depart sharply. "I have an appointment at the salon over in Lewes to get my hair coloured."

"On you go. I'll be fine," assured Lori.

"If you're sure…"

"Go!" insisted Lori with a laugh. "Before I change my mind."

"Thanks. There's a chicken salad set out for your dinner. I've left it covered in the refrigerator," said Mary, clearing the lunch dishes from the table. "I'll be back to tomorrow around lunchtime to check you're ok."

"You're meant to have Sundays free," commented Lori. "I'm a big girl. I'll be fine. Take the day off. If I need you, I have your number. I'll call."

"I don't know," began Mary, concern etched all over her face.

"You need a day off. You've more than earned it and I promise to be sensible."

"And you'll call if you need me?"

"Promise."

"If you're sure. I'll load the dishwasher before I go," relented Mary. "And I'll be back first thing on Monday. Remember Jo will be over on Monday at nine for your therapy session."

It took another half an hour for Mary to satisfy herself that the house was in order and that Lori was safe to be left alone. As she finally drove away, Lori let out a sigh of relief. Freedom for a whole day and a half. The first time she had been left on her own for so long since the accident. It felt liberating! Once she was sure Mary had really left Lori went back indoors to get ready for her outing with Jake. She had struggled to decide what to wear. Jeans or a skirt? A dress? Eventually she opted for a dress, figuring it would be easier for her to move around in. She had purchased several long summer maxi dresses to hide her legs and she opted for a pastel floral one, finishing the outfit off with her white Converse- no heels allowed- and her short denim jacket. As she brushed her hair back into a loose ponytail, she felt butterflies of excitement building.

"This is pathetic," she said to her mirror reflection. "I'm worse than a kid. It's only a trip into town."

She had just put the finishing touches to her makeup when she heard a truck crunch over the gravel in front of the house. By the time she had made her way down the hallway to the front door, Jake was already on the porch. His long hair was still damp – signs of a recent shower- and he too seemed to have taken care with his wardrobe. Behind him in the driveway she could see a black Dodge Ram pickup truck parked under the tree.

"Your chariot awaits," he declared theatrically.

"Hi, Jake," she smiled, stepping out onto the porch, pausing to pull the door closed behind her.

"Hi," he replied. "Are you still ok with this?"

"Of course! I've been looking forward to it," she said. "And to seeing you," she added silently to herself.

"Ok. Let's go then. The local metropolis awaits you."

Getting into the passenger seat of the truck proved to be a challenge, but Jake swept in and lifted her up into the seat. He slid her crutches in behind then handed her the strap of the seatbelt.

"I hope you're impressed. I even cleaned out the truck for you," he said proudly. "It's not usually so tidy."

"I'm honoured. Thank you."

As Jake turned on the ignition, the stereo burst into life and the cab was suddenly filled with very loud hard rock music. He reached to switch it off, but Lori stopped him.

"No worries. It's fine with me," she assured. "Is this the kind of stuff your band plays?"

"Yeah," said Jake reversing out into the narrow road. "Depending on where we're playing, it can get a bit heavier. We do the occasional acoustic set too."

"How did last night go?"

"We've played worse," he replied. The gig of the night before hadn't gone as well as the band had hoped. The beer promo had not drawn a big crowd and the bar owner cut their set short. A crowd of brewery executives had requested a karaoke session instead of live music. Jake had been beyond furious and stormed off home, not even pausing to collect his cut of the fee.

"So what's the plan for this afternoon?" she asked, changing the subject.

"Well, I'll try to park near the beach patrol office. If you feel up to it, we can walk along the boardwalk or through town. I'm easy. It's up to you," he said. "There's plenty of places to stop at if you get tired. Later we could maybe grab some dinner?"

"Sounds good to me," said Lori, watching the scenery go by. "This is the first time I've been this far from the house in almost seven weeks."

It only took them a few minutes to drive into the heart of town, but finding a parking space proved to be more of a challenge. The tourist season had still to start, but the town was busy. Jake circled round a few blocks trying to find a space near the boardwalk. Finally, he found one two blocks further north than he had hoped for in Olive Avenue.

"Do you have any quarters?" asked Jake, rummaging in his pocket for some change.

Lori opened her purse and found six coins for him, "How long will these give us?"

"An hour and a half. Not long enough," he muttered. "Ok, I've got another three here. It'll have to do for now. We'll need to get change and I'll run back to top up the meter."

Lori manoeuvred herself out of the truck while Jake went to feed the parking meter. She gazed around, drinking in the scenery, glad to be free from the house for a few hours. A few moments later, Jake was back.

"We've struck gold," he declared grinning. "There was an hour already on the meter."

"So, as long as we feed the meter before seven, we'll be in good shape?"

Jake nodded. "Let's go!"

Together they walked down the street towards the boardwalk. Now that the earlier mist had cleared, the sun was out and it was a pleasantly warm spring afternoon. The boardwalk was busy with families and kids on skateboards. As another two whizzed passed them, Jake felt Lori tense up beside him.

"Don't panic," he said, leaning towards her. "I won't let you fall."

She smiled up at him trying but failing to disguise her nerves. As they reached the town's famous taffy shop, she paused to look in the window.

"I used to love when my dad brought me here," she reminisced. "We would walk along the sand from the house and come in for a bag of salt water taffy. He'd then take me along to the amusement arcade before we walked home. Happy days."

"How old were you then?" asked Jake casually.

"About ten I think. We came here every summer for July and August. Are you from here?"

"No. I'm from Dover. I moved down here after college and just kind of stayed. I guess I've been here for about fourteen years."

They moved on silently, both lost in their own thoughts. Lori headed off the boardwalk and up the town's main avenue. She paused occasionally to look in the boutique windows.

"Can we go in here?" she asked when they reached a small clothes boutique.

"Your wish is my command, li'l lady," he joked, opening the door for her.

The shop was small and more tasteful than most of the t-shirt and beachwear shops on the avenue. It was quiet with gentle classical music filling the store. Behind the counter sat a small white haired lady lost in the depths of her book. As the door closed behind them, the wind chimes above it tinkled and she raised her head.

"Miss Lori Hyde as I live and breathe!" she cried excitedly. "I haven't seen you in far too long!"

"Hi, Miss May," greeted Lori warmly. "I couldn't pass without saying hello."

The old woman was tiny when she stood up, but she hurried round from behind the counter to hug Lori.

"My dear," she sighed. "What happened to you?"

"I had an accident last December. I'm fine, really. I came back here to recuperate at the house," explained Lori, deliberately avoiding going into detail. Jake moved to stand closer to her, almost as if to protect her from more awkward questions. "Oh, Miss May, this is Jake."

"Pleased to meet you, ma'am," said Jake, shaking the little old lady's hand.

"Likewise," said the tiny woman.

"Miss May was close friends with my parents," explained Lori. "I've known her forever."

"Lord, I know I'm old, dear," laughed the old woman. "But forever is a bit of an exaggeration!"

They exchanged pleasantries for another few minutes. Lori treated herself to a couple of white summer tops, then they politely said their goodbyes and returned to the spring sunshine outside. As they made their way up the street Lori's eyes were everywhere, drinking in all the sights and lives of the ocean front town. This was what she had missed during the last few bleak months. To actually be here and to be walking around town felt like a dream come true. Spotting an old favourite haunt across the street, she asked Jake if they could cross over. He felt her tense up beside him again as he guided her safely across the street. More ghosts of her accident, he guessed. Once across onto the other pavement Lori turned towards a small skateboard shop. Its window was filled with boards and t-shirts.

"I used to buy my band T-shirts here as a teenager," she explained, studying the array of rock band shirts in front of her. Suddenly she spotted one and turned to face Jake, "Silver Lake?"

He blushed and nodded. She laughed at his embarrassment.

"You never told me you were on a shirt?" she giggled. The artwork on the shirt was good and there was no mistaking Jake in the photo on the printed cotton.

"Rich got a batch made up for us by the school he teaches at," said Jake, still flushed with embarrassment. "One of the seniors designed the logo for us a few years ago. I'll get you one if you really want one."

"I'd like that," she said shyly. "I've designed a few in the past for bands. I like that kid's style. Strong lines."

"Any of yours in there?" asked Jake, pointing at the display. Then he had a flash of memory. "Mz Hyde? You're Mz Hyde?"

"Guilty as charged," confessed Lori with a laugh, as she

moved away from the window. "There's a couple of my designs in there."

"What ones?" he asked, scanning the display.

"I couldn't possibly say," she teased. "Let's go and get a coffee and I might tell you."

He followed her back towards the boardwalk, still shocked to discover her "rock identity". She had designed album artwork and band logos for more than a few of the bands on his iPod. Several of them were world famous. To look at her, Jake would never have identified Lori as being as much, if not more, into rock music as he was. This revelation began to make him wonder what else she wasn't telling him.

The nearest café was back on the boardwalk, beyond the pizza place where he worked. Jake kept his head down as he passed the door, his heart already dreading his next shift the following night. Once they were safely past, he suggested turning back off the promenade onto Wilmington Avenue to a café there. It was one of his favoured stop offs on the way to work and he wanted to share it with her. By the time they reached the café there were lines of pain etched into Lori's pale face and she was failing to disguise her fatigue. There were a couple of tables outside still free and she lowered herself onto a seat with obvious relief. Once he was sure she was alright, Jake went inside to place their order. While he was out of sight, Lori quickly swallowed two painkillers in an attempt to relieve her discomfort and thereby allow her to prolong the outing, at least until the quarters in the meter ran out.

A few minutes later, Jake returned to sit beside her, promising that their drinks would be brought out shortly.

"You ok?" he asked, unable to hide the concern in his voice.

She nodded silently, but her face told a different story. "I just need to rest for a few minutes," she admitted. "You have no idea how pathetic I feel being like this. I feel like an old woman."

"Nonsense," replied Jake. "You just need to take it slowly. You'll be chasing me along that beach by the end of the summer."

"I hope so," she said with a sad smile.

"Now, about this art buyer line you fed me the other day?" he challenged playfully.

"I worked as an art buyer in New York for two years," she replied trying to keep her face straight. "But I specialised."

"In what, may I ask?" enquired Jake playing along.

"Rock memorabilia," she confessed with a giggle.

Jake threw his head back and laughed. At that moment the waitress appeared with the tray with their coffees and two Italian pastries.

"Ok, you win," conceded Jake, adding sugar to his latte.

"Uncle Jake!" cried a child's voice from behind Lori. "Uncle Jake!"

A whirlwind of blonde hair came flying into Jake's lap in the form of a little girl of about five. She threw her arms around his neck and hugged him tight. Her adoration of him was obvious for all to see.

"Becky!" called a male voice from behind Lori. "Stop strangling him!"

"Hi, Grey," said Jake, gently peeling the adoring Becky from round his neck. "She's just happy to see her Uncle Jake."

"Uncle Jake," began Becky. "Will you come to the beach and play Frisbee with us? Please!"

"Honey," said Jake gently. "I'm having a nice cup of coffee with my friend right now. Maybe later?"

"No! Now!" pleaded the little girl. "You throw better Frisbees than Daddy does."

Lori laughed, causing Grey to turn and take note of her. He glanced at Jake, then turned back to Lori, "I apologise for my daughter."

"No need," said Lori. "She's adorable."

"I'm Grey by the way," he introduced. "A friend of Jake's, in case you hadn't guessed."

"Lori," she replied. "Why don't you join us?"

Jake shot her a dark look, but Grey was already pulling up a chair.

"We'll sit for a minute," he said. "But I promised this young lady some Frisbee throwing."

Jake had repositioned Becky on his knee so that he could reach his cup. He had hoped to keep his friendship with Lori to himself for a while before introducing her to his friends, but, now that Grey had seen them together, there was no hope of keeping this quiet. Grey, the band's bass player, was the only member of the band who was married with a family. He had made repeated attempts over the years to set Jake and the others up on dates. Usually dates that ended in disaster.

"Jake," began Lori, picking at her pastry, "If you want to go down onto the beach for a while that's fine with me. I'd hate to see this little princess disappointed."

"Please, Uncle Jake," pleaded Becky again. "Just for five minutes."

"Are you sure you don't mind?"

Lori shook her head. "Not at all. Might be fun."

"I'm sorry," apologised Grey. "We've barged in on your date."

"Nonsense," said Lori. "Our plans have been quite flexible so far. Haven't they?"

"I guess so," agreed Jake somewhat reluctantly. "Here's a suggestion though, Becky. Why don't you and your daddy go on ahead and Lori and I will catch up when we've had our coffee?"

The little girl looked from Jake to her daddy, who was nodding, then back to Jake. "Ok, I suppose so." She clambered down from his knee and added, "But don't keep me waiting too long."

They all laughed at the serious expression on her face.

"I promise," said Jake, then turning to Grey he asked, "Where are you headed?"

"Just across from the Turtle," replied Grey, getting to his feet. "Don't rush. We'll be there for a while. Sandy's preparing dinner and told me to keep Becky out for an hour or two. Don't think I'll last that long, but I better try."

"Ok," said Jake. "We'll wander down when we're finished here."

"Right, Becky, come on. Let's go. Say goodbye," instructed Grey firmly.

"Bye, Uncle Jake. Bye, Uncle Jake's friend." And she skipped off down the street towards the beach. Her father just smiled and shook his head as he followed her.

"Is he in the band?" asked Lori, once they were out of earshot.

"Yeah," answered Jake. "Bass player. I've known him for as long as I can remember. He's a good guy. Cute little kid too."

"Oh, she's adorable," agreed Lori. "But a handful, I imagine."

"Wait till you meet her mom," muttered Jake, as he bit into his pastry.

Neither of them rushed their coffee and cake, both content to idly chat about this and that and to watch the world go by. To Lori it all felt so refreshing and "normal" that for a while she forgot all that had happened and simply relaxed. Despite her protestations Jake insisted on paying the bill, then helped her back to her feet. The painkillers had kicked in and she felt ready to head to the beach. When they reached the boardwalk, they turned right and headed for the nearest path down to the sand. Beside the entrance to the path was an empty bench. Lori insisted she would wait there for Jake while he went to play with Becky and Grey. He was reluctant to leave her sitting on her own, but Lori insisted he should go.

"I don't have the wide bases for my crutches with me," she explained, sounding a little embarrassed. "I'll just sink in that soft sand and I don't want to fall in front of your friend."

Jake conceded defeat and promised to be back in a few minutes. He loped off down the narrow path towards the beach. With the sun settling lower in the sky, Lori settled back on the bench, lifted her face towards the sun and closed her eyes. Feeling the warmth settle over her filled her with hope and reassurance. Her earlier butterflies had long since settled and, for now, being here felt like the most natural thing in the world. She stretched her legs out in front of her, feeling her muscles starting to rebel against the exercise she had put them through. Being back out in the "real world" felt good and reminded her of why she had returned to Rehoboth instead of staying in New York City.

There were fewer folk around than there had been when they had arrived, but she sat casually people watching. In the background, she thought she could hear Jake and Becky down on the sand. She could hear him laughing and the squeals of the little girl as they played. It brought a smile to her lips. If the local fans could see their "rock star" now.

"Penny for them?" broke in a voice beside her.

"Hi," she said, sitting upright and squinting into the sun. "Grey?"

Jake's friend nodded and sat down beside her, "Jake asked me to check you were ok. He told me about those," he said, pointing at her crutches. "Guess they don't go with sand too well?"

Lori smiled, but never had the chance to reply before Grey

continued, "Breaking your femur's a tough one. I've done it."

"You have?"

"Yeah, playing football in college," Grey explained. "Snapped clean in half. Took about three months to get back on my feet. Never played football again."

"It's not fun," admitted Lori with a sad smile. "It's been four months since my accident."

"And you're still in this shape? Shit," he muttered with a hint of embarrassment.

"It wasn't exactly a clean break," said Lori. "I think there were four or five pieces. The surgeon told me I was lucky not to lose my leg. It was touch and go for a few days apparently. I'm a bit like the bionic woman. All pins and screws and a large titanium rod."

Grey paled at the very thought of such an injury. "I'm sorry," he muttered quietly.

"No, I'm sorry," said Lori. "I'm not looking for sympathy. I'll heal. It's just taking longer than I'd hoped." Then changing the subject added, "Sounds as though they're having fun."

"Well, Becky is," laughed Grey. "I think Jake is about worn out."

Lori laughed, "He'll get over it."

"I was going to get them an ice cream. Would you like one?" said Grey standing up.

"Please," replied Lori. "I'll come with you if you like."

"Good," agreed the bass player. "But I don't think you'll be much help carrying them back."

Lori laughed and got stiffly to her feet, "Well, if I can't carry them, I can pay for them."

Ten minutes later the four of them were back on the same bench eating small tubs of ice cream. The little girl was sitting on Jake's knee quite happily enjoying the vanilla ice cream with sprinkles. Conversation had almost ceased while they were eating and to any passer-by they looked like a happy family group. Before she had finished the ice cream, Becky climbed off Jake's knee and handed the tub to her daddy.

"I'm done," she said plainly. "Is it time to go home?"

Grey checked his phone for the time and muttered a curse under his breath. "It sure is, honey. Time to say goodbye to Jake and Lori."

"Bye, Uncle Jake," she said with a wave. "Bye, Lori. Thank you for the ice cream and the sprinkles."

"Bye, Becky," replied Lori smiling at the little girl.

Once Grey and his daughter were gone, Jake and Lori sat quietly finishing their own ice creams. The afternoon hadn't exactly worked out as Jake had planned, but from the relaxed look of contentment on Lori's face he judged it to be a success. As he scraped the last of the ice cream out of the tub, Jake remembered the parking meter. His watch said it was just leaving six thirty. Time was literally running out on them and he had no more quarters. Lori too had finished her ice cream. He took both the tubs and dumped them in the nearest trash can.

"I'll need to go back and feed the meter," he said, as he came back over to the bench.

"How long do we have left?" asked Lori, stifling a yawn?

"About twenty minutes," replied Jake. "And I've no more quarters. Sorry."

Deciding it was now or never, Lori said, "We could just go back to the house."

"We could," agreed Jake. "But I had hoped to buy you dinner."

"You can still buy dinner if you insist," said Lori struggling to her feet. "We can get take out."

"Not really what I had planned," Jake admitted. "But if you're sure. As long as it's not pizza."

Lori laughed. "No pizza."

They debated the choices for dinner as they strolled back along the boardwalk and by the time they had reached the truck they had agreed on fish. There were several choices of fish restaurant between town and the house and they agreed to stop at whichever one had space outside. Luck was on their side and Jake got a prime parking space outside his favourite place. While he went in to pick up the food, Lori waited in the truck. Once Jake was out of the cab, she cranked up the volume on the stereo a few notches and enjoyed some good old fashioned hard rock in the form of Black Sabbath. In the centre console, between the seats, there was a pile of CDs. She lifted them up and browsed through them while she waited. There were a few of her favourites in there and a few that were missing from her own collection. Perhaps, if she asked nicely, Jake would loan them to her sometime.

"Lord, it's busy in there tonight," commented Jake as he climbed back into the driver's seat a few minutes later. "Can you hold these?"

He handed her two bags of food and a bag with a six pack of beer. She raised one eyebrow at him.

"To wash down the fish," he explained, with a wink.

She laughed and accepted the bags from him.

It only took five minutes to drive back to the house, but by that time the sun had set and it was almost dark. The porch light came on automatically, lighting their way in. Lori asked Jake to take the food through to the sun room while she fetched some cutlery. Soon they were settled on the couch eating out of the cartons, drinking beer and listening to some soft rock on the music channel. When their meal was done Jake carried the empty cartons out to the trash while Lori found some snacks for them to nibble on. It was a relaxing end to a nearly perfect day and Lori was savouring every minute of it.

"Thanks for today," she said softly, as Jake handed her another beer. "It's been good for the soul."

"It's been fun," he agreed as he opened his own beer. "Not how I had it planned out in my head, but it's been good."

"Here's to more like it," said Lori, raising her beer bottle in a theatrical toast. "Here's to friendship."

"I'll drink to that."

It was almost midnight before Jake took his leave. They had laughed and chatted the evening away; compared taste in music, movies and books and generally got to know each other a bit. As she relaxed in his company, Lori had stretched out on the couch while Jake had moved to lie on the floor in front of her. He sprawled across her oriental rug like an oversized puppy. By the time he rose to leave, Lori was struggling to keep her eyes open. She started to get up, but he stopped her by planting a gentle kiss on the top of her head.

"Stay where you are," he said softly. "Is it ok to leave the truck? I don't want to get stopped."

"Of course," she replied with a yawn.

"I'll go back along the beach. I'll pick the truck up sometime tomorrow."

"Fine," acknowledged Lori sleepily. "Mary won't be back until first thing on Monday."

"I'll come back for it in the morning. I need to shift some gear for Grey before work."

With another gentle kiss delivered to the top of her head, he was gone out of the patio doors and into the night.

Bright sun was streaming into her bedroom and across the bed when Lori finally roused herself from sleep. She had slept soundly and dreamlessly all night, but was still shocked to discover it was after midday. It had been years since she had last slept so late. Gingerly she sat up and swung her legs out of bed, again pulling her nightshirt down sharply to hide her ever present scars. She had expected to feel stiff and sore, but was pleasantly surprised to discover she felt good. The house was completely silent and empty. That too felt good. Slowly she wandered into the *en suite* bathroom to shower.

When she finally made her way down the hallway towards the kitchen, she glanced out the front of the house. Jake's truck was gone. A wave of disappointment swept through her. Secretly she had hoped to see him again today. *C'est la vie.* Preparing coffee and brunch posed a few challenges as her crutches kept getting in the way. Hesitantly Lori put one of them aside, tested her balance and calculated that she could cope with one. Having a free hand made life easier and she soon had the coffee poured and had taken the chicken salad that Mary had prepared out of the fridge. Deciding to go for the easy option, she ate her meal at the small kitchen table while browsing through the local newspaper. She stumbled across an advert for Silver Lake in the entertainment section. There was a small local charity event coming up at the end of April and they looked to be the headline act. It was an outdoor event to be held at Surfside Park and she silently hoped Jake would invite her along.

Pouring herself a second coffee, she carefully made her way out onto the sundeck. As she set the mug down on the table, she noticed something on the seat of one of the chairs that was pushed in against the table. Sitting down first, she reached under the table and pulled out a flat pizza box. She opened it to find a folded piece of paper and a Silver Lake T-shirt inside. Laughing, she read the note- "Dinner 7:30 Wednesday. Be ready. J x"

Smiling, she folded the note and slipped it back in the box.

Lori was outside on the sun deck with a coffee and her

sketchpad when Mary arrived the next day. It didn't escape Lori's attention that the housekeeper was quick to notice that there was only one crutch beside her. The glowing smile on the older woman's face said it all.

"Morning," she called brightly. "Good weekend?"

"Hi," replied Lori, without looking up. "Yeah."

"Are you remembering Jo's due here in a half hour?"

"Sure," said Lori, looking up from her sketch pad. "Sorry, I was just trying to finish this bit before she got here."

"Ok," answered Mary, looking a little hurt. "I can take a hint. I'll call you when she arrives."

"Thanks. Mary," said Lori, then feeling a bit guilty added. "How was your weekend?"

"Lovely, thanks. I'll not lie. It was nice to have some time off," she admitted.

"Well," began Lori. "Maybe we could do the same this weekend?"

"Let's see how you behave this week," joked Mary. "But it would be nice to have some time to catch up with my family."

"I'll behave," Lori promised. "Make plans for your weekend. From now on, you finish at noon on Saturday. Same pay though. The deal was to care for me as I needed you."

"Thank you, but that's way too generous, Lori," Mary protested shrilly.

"Not at all. You earn every cent I pay you."

"Thank you."

While the housekeeper tided away her coffee cup, Lori continued with her sketch. She had been playing with a design since the day before and it was starting to take shape. It had been a long time, over a year, since she had felt the urge to design anything. Now she could feel the beginnings of a new surge of inspiration emerging. Maybe it was time to return to being Mz Hyde, a professional name she had retired almost three years before. Just maybe.

"Lori, good morning!" called a cheery voice from the patio doors. "Time to stop doodling."

With a mock groan, she laid down her pencil. "Morning, Jo. I'd love to say I was glad to see you."

"How do you feel about going through your paces out here?"

suggested the physiotherapist. "It's a beautiful morning after all."

"Fine by me," Lori agreed. "It might as well hurt like hell out here."

Jo laughed as she glanced down at Lori's sketch pad, "That's great! I never knew you were an artist."

Closing the pad over, Lori responded, "You never asked. I've done some design work before. I just felt like trying to do something to move on."

"Moving on is good," Jo agreed. "And I see you've moved onto one crutch."

"I couldn't carry my coffee out here using two."

"Fair point. Let's see how you are and if I think you're ready to just use one," stated Jo firmly. "You can't rush this, missy."

The physiotherapist worked with Lori for the next forty five minutes. She put her through resistance and stretching, some strength work and then offered her a massage to finish with. Jo had worked with many patients who had suffered similar injuries but had to admit Lori's was an extreme case. There was muscle wastage and muscle loss. There was some limited nerve damage and a lot of scar tissue to keep supple. On the plus side, Lori seemed to have turned a corner in her rehabilitation and was showing signs of improvement.

"What's his name?" asked Jo, as she finished her massage routine.

"Pardon?" said Lori, sitting up and staring at her therapist.

"Mary might not have guessed, but I saw you at the coffee shop. I was inside with my husband and the kids. So who is he?"

"Jake," said Lori, blushing, then, before she realised it, she was telling Jo all about her beach walk and fall and rescue and the date with Jake.

"I thought it was him," said Jo when Lori finished her confessional tale. "I've seen his band play a few times. Have you heard him sing?"

"Not yet," replied Lori softly. "It's very early days."

"Relax," laughed Jo. "I'm not about to tell tales on you. He seems a nice guy and, Lord knows, you deserve to have some fun, girl!"

"Thanks, Jo," sighed Lori with a smile. "One step at a time."

"Exactly," agreed the therapist. "I'm out of town at the end of this week, so I'll be back next Monday. Same time."

Lori nodded.

"Fine. You're ok to use just the one crutch about the house. If you are out and about, use two. Be careful if you go back onto the beach. You were lucky you never hurt yourself when you fell. Remember, it is still very early days for you," cautioned the physiotherapist. "When did you last see a doctor?"

"Before I came down here."

"Too long. I want you to make an appointment at the medical centre. It won't hurt to get checked over."

"I'll call and make an appointment after you leave," promised Lori, secretly dreading the thought of yet more time spent with doctors.

"Make sure you do. I'll be checking up on it. Enjoy the rest of your day," said Jo warmly. "I'll see you on Monday."

Silver Lake met up on Tuesday to rehearse as usual. As he entered the rehearsal room, on time, Jake was praying that Grey wouldn't mention Lori. He wasn't ashamed in any shape or form of his friendship with her, but it was all so new that he wanted to keep it private for a while longer. It wasn't to be.

"Hey, Jake!" called Paul. "Who's Lori?"

Jake shot a dark look at Grey, who smiled and shrugged. "Becky told him not me."

"She's just a friend," muttered Jake.

"A friend?" echoed Rich coming in at his back. "Not what I heard."

"Guys," said Jake with a frown. "Leave it. Please."

Grey came to his defence. "Let's leave him be. She's a lovely girl. She'll see sense soon."

The others laughed while Jake's mood darkened a shade. Soon they were settled into rehearsing a new number to add to their set. It was a frustrating session with more stops than starts. Both Rich and Jake had issues with their amps and tuning. After almost an hour, Jake unplugged his guitar, "I need a break."

"Same here," agreed Rich. "I'm ready to smash that shitty amp."

"Fine. Ten minutes, guys," said Paul. "I'll go get us a drink from across the street."

Jake wandered over to the battered couch that sat at the side of the room. His acoustic guitar was lying beside it.

"Don't you let me down," he muttered under his breath as he settled himself to play. Without giving a thought to the others, he began to play a song he had been writing at home. Within a few bars, he was lost in his own thoughts as he tried to focus on the music from memory. It was a slow rock ballad in the making, but it had the potential to be his best composition to date. He began to sing some lyrics he had been toying with but stopped after the first verse.

"Hey, don't stop!" called Rich sharply. "That sounded awesome."

Jake looked up and realised they had all stopped what they were doing to focus on him. He felt himself start to redden at the unexpected praise.

"It's not finished," he muttered. "I'm just playing with it."

"You got any more like that?" demanded Grey. "This could be a turning point for us."

"One or two," said Jake laying his guitar down. "I wasn't sure they were right for us."

"Sounded right to me," stated Rich. "Play it again."

It proved to be a pivotal point in their rehearsal and when Paul came back with their beers they made Jake play the piece through again. His vocals added a haunting, slightly tortured edge to the gentle melody. After another run through, Grey joined in on bass. Together they worked on the song until after eleven, all of them enjoying a new-found enthusiasm for the rehearsal.

"I'm done," yawned Rich. "I've got classes tomorrow. How about we meet tomorrow night for a couple of hours?"

"Sorry, I've got plans," said Jake, as he packed his guitar in its case. "Unless we meet early. I can do four till six."

"No can do," said Grey. "I've got Becky till Sandy gets in at seven."

"How about Thursday night then?" suggested Rich? "Usual time?"

They all muttered agreement as they headed out into the dark.

"Hey Jake," called Rich, as he got into his car. "Can you finish the lyrics for Thursday?"

"I can try, but I've got work tomorrow and Thursday. Two

early shifts."

"See what you can do."

Slowly Jake walked back to his apartment with chords and lyrics flying round and colliding in his head. When he got in, he dumped his guitars on the couch and fetched himself a beer. Taking a chug from the bottle, he sat down with his guitar to work on the lyrics for a while before bed. All too soon he was immersed in his creative world and by two in the morning the lyrics were done. When he realised the time he lay back on the couch and sighed. He had to be at work for eight and wanted to go for a run before his shift.

"Well, four hours sleep will have to do," he said to the empty room as he turned off the light.

Lori was still putting the finishing touches to her makeup when she heard Jake's truck pull into the driveway. A glance at her watch told her he was dead on time. She smiled and wondered if he had stopped off along the road to time his arrival accurately. As before, he was on the porch by the time she made her way to the front door.

"Come in for a minute," said Lori opening the door. "I'm not quite ready. Sorry."

"Is it safe to come in? Is Mary here?" asked Jake, faking fear.

Giggling, Lori said, "She left at five. Go on through to the sunroom or the lounge. Your choice. I'll just be a moment."

"No rush. There's plenty of time," said Jake warmly. "I'll wait in the lounge, if that's ok."

The room was adjacent to the front door and Lori indicated he should take a seat. She promised to be back shortly and headed off back down the hallway.

With a cream leather suite and dark mahogany furniture, the lounge was far more formal than the sunroom. There were several framed photos on the sideboard, including Lori's high school and college graduation photos. He was still admiring them when she returned. She looked stunning. Her long blonde hair was loose and she was wearing a black sundress with her short denim jacket.

"You look fabulous," complimented Jake warmly.

"Nonsense," murmured Lori blushing. She had never been very good at accepting compliments. "I've got something to give you before we go."

"Oh," said Jake, looking curiously at her.

"It's next door. Follow me."

The house's layout was open plan and the space next to the lounge was Lori's study and indoor work space. Her drawing board took up one corner and there were two desks – one neat and organised; the other piled high with papers and books. On the drawing board was a sketch and it was this that Lori went to pick up. It was the design she had been working for the last four days.

"I thought you'd like this," she said, handing it to Jake. "It's my way of saying thank you for your help last week."

"You didn't need to," said Jake admiring the design. "It's awesome."

"It was good therapy for me," admitted Lori with a smile.

The design was a detailed circular Celtic knot design. Around the outer edge Lori had completed a different smaller, more intricate pattern that included the band's name. She had tried to keep to the lines of the band's current logo as far as she could.

"Will you sign it?" asked Jake, immediately embarrassed for asking.

With a smile Lori autographed the piece with her distinctive Mz Hyde signature and passed it back to him. "If the band wants to use it, I'm ok with that. If you want to use it as a beer mat, I could get upset," she joked lightly. "Now, did you not mention dinner?"

"Thank you," said Jake softly, blown away by the gift. He flashed her a grateful smile. "I mean it. Thank you and yes, I did mention dinner."

It was a beautiful spring evening and dusk was settling over the town as they drove out towards the Coastal Highway. From the passenger seat, Lori drank in the scenery, noting all the places on the outskirts of town that she intended to revisit as soon as she was back on her feet and independent again. She took special note of the outlets as they passed, trying not to listen to the "Sale" and "70% off" signs that were screaming out to her. Once they were about five miles from the centre of town, Jake turned off the highway and into the parking lot beside a steakhouse. He parked the truck next to the entrance, then jumped out to come round to help Lori down from her seat. With some reluctance, she allowed him to lift her down like a small child. He passed her crutches to her then, once she was steady on her feet, escorted her inside.

A small older woman stood at the desk just inside the door, "Good evening folks. Do you have a reservation?"

"Yes. Power," said Jake. "Table for two."

He felt Lori suppressing a teenage giggle beside him and tried to ignore it.

"This way," said the waitress, lifting two menus and a wine list.

Soon they were seated by the window at a corner table. The

---

waitress lit the candle in the centre of the table, then rhymed off a list of the evening's specials. Having taken their drinks order, she finally left them alone. They smiled at each other and then Lori burst out laughing, "Is Power your real name?"

"Yup," said Jake. "Blame my dad."

"It's a cool rock name," she giggled. "What a pair we make. Jake Power and Mz Hyde!"

Her amusement and laughter was infectious and Jake soon found himself laughing along with her.

"I still can't thank you enough for the design," he said, reaching over to touch her hand. "No one's ever done anything like for me."

"It was my pleasure," answered Lori, taking his hand. "This last week has been good for my soul and it's down to you. No pun intended, but that fall was just the jolt I needed."

"Were you struggling that badly?"

She nodded, not trusting herself to speak. There were tears in her eyes as she finally answered, "I can't talk about it all just yet, but yes, I was in a bad way. Not just my leg and physically, but in my head too. You made me laugh. I guess that was what I needed. You've shown an interest in me without prying. I appreciate that."

Before Jake could respond, the waitress returned with their drinks and asked if they were ready to order.

"Can we have a few minutes, please?" asked Lori politely.

"Of course. I'll be back shortly."

Picking up the menu, Jake asked what she fancied to eat. Together they debated the choices. Neither of them felt like an appetizer so focussed on the entrees. The steakhouse was not the cheapest restaurant in town and Lori guessed Jake would insist on paying the check. She opted for a mid-priced small fillet mignon while Jake chose a 16oz prime rib. Before she could argue, Jake ordered a bottle of Pinot Noir.

"My dad always says you need a nice red to wash down a good steak," Jake commented, sensing her unspoken protest.

"I'd have to agree with him," Lori said with a smile. "First wine since last December."

The tea light candle on the table guttered and went out. It was growing late and they were the only diners left in the restaurant.

The waitress put their check on the table and offered to re-cork the wine so they could take the remainder of the bottle with them.

"I think we'd better take the hint," said Jake.

"How much do you need for the tip?" asked Lori, reaching for her purse.

"I've got this," he assured her.

"And I'm getting the tip," she stated firmly. "How much?"

"Twelve would cover it," he relented, taking some bills out of his wallet.

"There you go," she handed him fifteen dollars. "I'm going to the ladies room. I'll see you back at the truck."

"Be careful."

"I'm fine, Jake," she assured him.

When she came out of the restaurant a few minutes later, Jake was standing waiting for her beside the truck. He was smiling and looked every inch the rock star with his tight black jeans, loose black shirt and long blonde hair. Everything about him was the polar opposite to her previous boyfriends. Well, it was time she had a bit of fun she guessed, as she reached the truck. As he lifted her up onto the seat, he leaned forward and kissed her gently on the forehead. She lifted her face and brushed a gentle kiss onto his cheek.

"Thanks for dinner."

"Pleasure," said Jake, closing the door gently.

Lori noticed the half full bottle of wine was sitting in the centre console storage box. She also caught sight of a guitar case behind the driver's seat.

When Mary pulled into the driveway the next morning she was mildly surprised to see a truck parked in her usual spot under the tree. She didn't need to be told who the owner was – Miss May had met her at church the previous Sunday and told her about Lori's visit to the shop. Once inside, Mary went about her usual morning routine in the kitchen, then went through to the sunroom to tidy up. She only just stifled a scream as she found Jake sprawled out across the couch sound asleep. There was a discarded pair of jeans and a shirt on the floor. His guitar was propped up in the corner. Silently she slipped out and went in search of Lori. As Mary entered the bedroom, Lori was just getting out of bed.

"Morning," greeted Mary, her tone sharper than she had intended.

"Morning," said Lori with a yawn. "Did I sleep in or are you early?"

"A bit of both," answered the housekeeper. "I didn't know you were having a guest over last night?"

Lori blushed, then threw her a puzzled look.

"He's still here," stated Mary, folding her arms across her ample chest. "Out cold in the sunroom."

Lori burst out laughing at her housekeeper's motherly dressing down. Here she was almost thirty years old, getting a lecture about having a friend over. The older woman struggled to see the humour in the situation and demanded an explanation.

"Jake took me to dinner last night," Lori explained. "When we got back he came in for a drink. The waitress had insisted we take our bottle of wine home from the restaurant. We got talking. We opened another bottle from the store in the basement. It got late and I said to Jake to lock up when he was leaving. He was playing his guitar when I went to bed about two."

"And how much did you have to drink?" demanded Mary, staring at her intently.

"Relax," said Lori, getting to her feet. "I had two glasses of wine, maybe three. No more. Yes, I know it doesn't go with my pain meds. I haven't taken any since late yesterday afternoon. No, I didn't get drunk. I just had some fun with a friend."

Mary relaxed a little.

"We talked. He played some music. That was it," stated Lori. "Now I better go and wake sleeping beauty. Would you mind putting the coffee pot on?"

"Harrumph," muttered Mary as she turned on her heel and headed back to the kitchen.

Still laughing, Lori made her way down the hallway and through the lounge to avoid the kitchen. Trying to be as quiet as she could, she made her way into the sunroom. Exactly as Mary described, Jake lay along the larger of the two couches. He had dragged a blanket over himself, the fleecy one she kept for snuggling into if it was cold. Carefully, she bent down beside him and ran her fingers through his long hair, clearing it off his face.

He stirred slightly in his sleep. Trying not to giggle, she laid a hand on his bare shoulder, not surprised to find his shoulders and back tattooed. She traced the outline of one with her finger and he stirred again.

"Good morning, sleepy head," she whispered in his ear before she kissed it.

He opened one sleepy eye without moving, "Wha'?"

"Good morning," she repeated and stepped back, sensing imminent movement.

Suddenly realising where he was, Jake turned to face the back of the couch instead of getting up. His head was pounding and his back was aching from a night sleeping twisted on the sofa.

"Shit," he muttered into the fabric of the couch.

His pounding head was suddenly filled with Lori's musical laughter. She had moved to sit on the edge of the other settee and was enjoying watching him squirm.

"Oh shit, I'm sorry," he said, rolling over and sitting up. "What time is it?"

"I think it's around nine," giggled Lori. "You ok?"

He nodded as he ran his hands through his hair, "I'm really sorry."

"Stop apologising," said Lori warmly. "I'll get you a coffee while you pull yourself together. I don't think Mary is ready to see you in your boxers."

"Shit, is she here?"

Lori nodded, "She found you out here."

He cringed and shook his head. "No. Please tell me you are joking?"

"No. She found you. I think she got quite a fright," laughed Lori. "Don't worry. She'll be fine. We're not kids."

Jake just stared at her with a look of complete and utter embarrassment. How could he have been so stupid? After Lori had gone to bed, he had kept on playing his guitar for a while, trying to work out something new. He'd finished the wine and felt a little drunk. He remembered getting undressed and lying down on the couch to sleep, but he was sure he had set the alarm on his phone for seven o'clock. If he got up early he had figured he could slip out before Lori was awake. His cell phone lay on his shirt. He checked and found the battery was dead. By now Lori had left the sunroom and gone through to the kitchen. He quickly pulled on his jeans and his shirt, then followed her through. She was sitting at the table with a coffee and a cinnamon bagel. Another mug was sitting opposite her along with a large glass of orange juice. Over at the stove Mary was cooking eggs and bacon.

"I really am sorry," he said, sitting down at the table.

"Will you stop apologising," said Lori then added, "There's no harm done. How's your head this morning?"

"I'll live," he replied, downing the glass of orange juice.

Mary placed a plate of bacon and eggs in front of him and cleared away the empty glass, "Best cure for a hangover is to feed it. You gave me quite a start this morning, young man."

"I'm so sorry," he apologised yet again.

"Lori's right. No harm done. Now, do both of you want to come clean about what's been going on around here for the last few days?" teased Mary, some of the usual warmth creeping back into her voice. "Whatever it is, it's been good for Lori."

While Jake ate his breakfast, Lori explained about their outing into town, the note and the T-shirt and finally last night's dinner date. Unable to keep up the charade of being angry, Mary too confessed that she had met Miss May, who had told her that she had seen the couple in town on Saturday afternoon. They agreed that there would be no more sneaking about and no more secrets.

Once the meal was almost over and Jake was on his second mug of coffee, he said, "Do you mind if I leave the truck here till after work?"

"Not at all," said Lori. "What time do you finish work?"

"Around eight tonight," he replied. "I've got an eight hour shift."

"Why don't you come back here for dinner? No pizza, I promise," suggested Lori hopefully,

"If you don't mind, but I can't stay late. I promise I'll go home by ten."

Lori laughed, "Be careful what you promise."

He swallowed the last of his coffee, then rose to leave, "Thanks for breakfast, Mary."

"Not a problem, son," she said warmly. "Just give me a bit of warning next time."

"I'll try," he promised. "And thanks again."

"See you tonight," said Lori softly. "Dinner will be ready at eight thirty."

"I'll be here."

After Jake left, Mary reminded Lori that she had an appointment at the medical centre at midday. She had not forgotten, but had tried to push it to the back of her mind. Over the last few months she had had her fill of doctors, but she had promised Jo that she would go. Once she was showered and dressed, she came back through to the kitchen to find the housekeeper. The older woman had agreed to drive her out to her appointment. The medical centre was outside town and they had to pass the outlets to get there. Lori suggested that on the way back they stop for a late lunch and a little shopping. Those "sale" signs were still calling to her. Much to her surprise, Mary readily agreed but only if Lori wasn't too tired after her visit with the doctor.

Shortly before noon Lori found herself sitting in the small waiting room. She was nervous. Her palms were clammy and she could feel her heart racing. Mary had insisted on waiting out in the car with her book, leaving Lori to face her fears on her own. Visits to the doctor filled her with dread and it was twice as daunting when she had never met the doctor before. If she could have run away there and then she would have. She smiled at the irony of it.

"Miss Hyde," called a warm voice from the doorway. "Let me help you through."

"Thanks," she said. "Dr Brent?"

"Guilty as charged. Jo's told me a lot about you. It's a pleasure to finally meet you," he said, guiding her into his office. "Take a seat, please."

Once she was settled, he sat on the edge of the desk and asked her to tell him, in her own words, about what had happened to her, about her surgeries, her recovery and about her recent fall. It wasn't a tale she could tell without tears, but, when she was overcome by her emotions, Dr Brent gave her time to recover her composure before encouraging her gently to continue. He didn't rush her. He just listened until she was finished. Once she had told her tale, the doctor said he had arranged for a fresh series of x-rays to be taken and to run some routine bloods. He phoned for a nurse to come and fetch Lori and escort her through to the radiography suite. It took almost an hour to complete the x-rays and blood work and then she found herself back in the original waiting room. Her leg was starting to ache after all the bending and stretching into various positions for the x-rays. She was rummaging in her bag for some pain killers when Dr Brent called her back through to his office.

"How are you feeling?" he asked, taking a seat at his desk.

"A bit sore," she confessed quietly.

"Understandable," he nodded, opening his desk drawer. "Take two of these if you need to."

He passed her a bottle of Advil.

"Thanks," she said helping herself to two of the white pills while the doctor fetched her some water.

"I see from your records you've been prescribed some strong opiate pain medication. Do you still use it?" he asked, as she passed the bottle of pills back.

"I've cut the doses right back," answered Lori bluntly. "I'm not a Vicodin junkie if that's what you're getting at."

"Glad to hear it. Stick to Advil if you can cope on it," he replied. "Now let's take a look at your x-rays."

He turned his computer screen round so she could see the fresh images for herself. Lori turned away. Looking at the x-rays was hard for her.

"Some impressive hardware in there," commented Dr Brent. "That's a lot of carpentry."

"I know," she sighed, glancing up at the mess of screws and plates and the ever present titanium rod.

"Well the good news is that it looks to be healing nicely, slowly but nicely, and you don't appear to have rearranged anything when you fell. Usually at this stage in the recovery I would be talking to patients about when we can look to remove some of the metalwork. I'm sorry to say that it looks like you may have yours long term. There's still a degree of healing going on there, especially around the point of impact."

She nodded with reluctant acceptance.

"Right, let's get you up onto the couch and I'll take a closer look at how your scars have healed."

The doctor helped her onto the couch and she focussed on the ceiling while he assessed the extent of the scarring to her leg. He tested the range of movement she had achieved and seemed genuinely pleased with her progress. Carefully he helped her down and back over to the chair.

"I'm not able to work miracles, Miss Hyde," he said quietly. "You're healing well, if a little slowly. Your scarring is extensive, but the scars themselves are not hindering your recovery. There's minimal loss of skin sensation in your thigh area and some muscle loss, but I'm confident that in time you will be able to walk unaided, but possibly only for short distances. A lot of what happens from here on in is down to you."

Lori looked at him and nodded. There were unshed tears in her eyes.

"Stick with the physical therapy regime. Try to minimise the use of pain meds if you can. It's going to be a long slow road, but you are getting there," he said in an attempt to reassure her. "I'm going to be totally honest with you. If your initial orthopaedic surgeon hadn't been as skilled, we would be talking prosthetics now."

"I know," whispered Lori, as a single tear slid down her cheek.

"Hey, there's no need for tears, Lori. Your therapist has a great programme worked out for you. She'll get you through this," he promised. "I have a lot of faith in her."

Lori looked up and smiled weakly.

"I should have," added John Brent. "She's my wife."

"Your wife?" echoed Lori, her eyes wide in surprise. "Jo never said. She's been fantastic. So patient with me. It's the time this is all taking. The lack of progress. It's frustrating."

"I know," said the doctor. "I'll speak to her about increasing the intensity of your rehab plan, but this isn't something we can force. Ok?"

"I'm ok," she replied. "I get it."

"I know you do. Now I'm going to get my secretary to make a follow up appointment for you for six weeks' time. We can reassess then."

Mary was totally engrossed in her crime novel when Lori returned to the car. As they pulled out of the parking lot she asked Lori how the appointment had gone. Calmly Lori explained what John Brent had said, then burst into tears. By the time they had pulled off the Coastal Highway into the outlets' car park Lori had calmed down and sobbed out all of her frustrations. As they headed across to the food court, Mary put her arm around her shoulders and whispered, "You'll get there, honey. You've come such a long way already."

"Thanks, Mary," she said with a smile. "Let's get some lunch. I'm hungry, then I'm ready to shop."

After a brief lunch of a slice of pizza and a soda, the two women spent an hour or so shopping round the Midway and Bayside sections of the outlet complex. Lori listened to the call of the "Sale" and "70% off" signs and treated herself to a few new items for her wardrobe. Even Mary succumbed to the call of the "sign" and purchased a few bits and pieces. A little retail therapy proved to be good for both of them. They made a brief stop at the food store as they drove back to the house. At the sight of Jake's truck still parked in the driveway Lori smiled. Only a few short hours before he would be over.

Once they were inside Mary chased Lori into the sunroom to take a rest for a while. The day's exertions had left her looking pale and drawn and the housekeeper was concerned at just how much it had taken out of her charge. Over the weeks she had grown very fond of her mistress and protective in a motherly fashion. Feeling every inch of her ache, Lori retreated to the sunroom without complaint. She opened the patio doors to allow some fresh sea air to filter through, then stretched out on the couch. Casually she ran her hand up and down her injured thigh and sighed. The day had taken it out of her both physically and emotionally and her leg was throbbing. She adjusted the cushions about her, placed one under her knees, then lay back and closed her eyes. Within seconds she had drifted off to sleep; a thankfully dreamless sleep. An hour later Mary came through and reluctantly wakened her to explain what she had prepared for dinner and to say goodbye for the day. Sleepily Lori listened to the instructions about turning on the oven and taking things out the refrigerator ahead of time. The housekeeper added that she had made a jug of homemade lemonade and that it was chilling in the fridge.

After the older woman had left Lori went to freshen up and change before Jake arrived. She was back in the sunroom with at least an hour to spare and felt at a bit of a loose end. Spotting Jake's guitar still propped up in the corner, she decided to do a quick sketch of it to pass the time. Pausing only to turn on the oven for dinner, as instructed, Lori focussed on the drawing. Art was a good escape from the day, allowing her to banish everything else from her mind. She was so engrossed in the sketch that she never heard Jake approach across the sun deck and gave a start when he called "Hello" from the doorway.

"Hi," she said, dropping her pencil. "How was your day?"

"Don't ask," he growled, flopping down on the couch.

"That good?" she sympathised softly.

"Something smells good," commented Jake. "And it doesn't smell like pizza."

Lori laughed as she stood up stiffly. "It's chicken. Mary's special recipe. I think you've won her over."

Jake smiled, "Do you need a hand with dinner?"

"Probably," admitted Lori, adjusting her grip on her crutch. "Come through and keep me company while I figure it out."

Between them it took only a few minutes to serve the meal and to settle themselves at the kitchen table. Mary had laid two places in the dining room, but neither of them felt like being so formal and agreed to sit in the kitchen instead. Ever the gentleman, Jake stepped in and offered to serve while Lori poured their drinks.

"So tell me about your day," he said, taking a seat across from her.

"I had pizza for lunch," she teased with a cheeky grin.

Jake groaned.

"No, seriously, I did," giggled Lori before adding. "I had a doctor's appointment out at Beebe Medical Center then Mary and I stopped off at the outlets on the way back for a couple of hours."

"I thought I saw you eyeing up those sale signs last night," laughed Jake.

"I deserved a treat after the trip to the doctor."

They ate in silence for a minute or two. Jake was keen to ask if she had got a good report from the doctor, but felt he couldn't pry too much. He knew from the little she had let slip over the last few days that her accident was a taboo subject for now. Before he found the right words to ask, Lori explained what the doctor had said to her. Jake was silently relieved to hear she had not suffered any further injury after her tumble on the beach. Feeling a bit braver, he risked a question, "Tell me to but out if you want, but how much metal work did they pin you together with?"

Lori paused for a few seconds before replying, "A lot. I've a photo of my x-rays on my phone. I'll show you after dinner. My phone's through in the sunroom."

"You don't have to if it makes you uncomfortable," said Jake, reaching across the table to take her hand.

"I know I don't," she replied. "But it might help both of us."

"Well, only if you are sure," said Jake. "I don't want to upset you and ruin this."

Lori giggled. "This?"

Jake blushed and looked down at his plate, suddenly feeling like a clumsy tongue-tied teenager again. "Well, I hope "this" is the start to an "us"."

"Me too."

When their meal was over and the dishes loaded in the dishwasher Lori fetched them both a beer. They took their drinks through to the sunroom. Her discarded sketch caught Jake's eye and he smiled in approval at the image of his guitar emerging from the page. He had had that guitar since his eighteenth birthday and had spent a long time pouring his heart out into its strings over the years.

"It's not finished yet," said Lori settling herself on the couch and reaching for her mobile phone.

"Can I keep it?" asked Jake hopefully

"Not yet," she replied. "It's not finished and there's a price."

"A price?" he asked curiously.

Lori nodded, "You need to play for me."

"Deal," agreed Jake with a twinkle in his eyes. "I'll play when the drawing's done."

"No, tonight," teased Lori. "Or I won't finish it."

"*Touché*," laughed Jake, reaching for his guitar.

"No, wait a minute," said Lori, stopping him. She handed him her phone. "You wanted to see. There you go."

"You sure about this?" he asked, taking the phone from her.

She nodded, then whispered, "Look at it please, before I change my mind."

Jake turned the phone over in his hand and looked down at

the image on the screen. The photo of the x-ray was not quite what he had been expecting. He had thought he would see a couple of screws and the rod she had mentioned, but the picture in front of him was more metalwork than bone. The rod went down the centre of the bone, a plate also ran more than fifty percent of the bone's length and he counted at least eight screws.

"That's some sculpture," he said, handing the phone back to her, unsure of the right thing to say.

"Well, now you know," said Lori sadly, returning the phone to its home screen.

"Might be best to stay away from big magnets," he joked quietly, not sure how she would react to his weak attempt at humour.

Much to his relief she laughed. He moved over to kneel on the floor in front of her. Putting his hands on her knees, he said seriously, "I appreciate you trusting me enough to show me that. And it doesn't change a thing."

"Thanks," she said with a smile. "Now how about you keep your end of the bargain?"

Jake stood up and went over to lift his guitar. Sitting down on the opposite couch, he began to pick out a gentle melody and was soon lost in the song he had been working on the night before. Softly he began to sing. His voice was husky and quite haunting. Soon Lori too was engrossed in his music. When he finished a few minutes later, Jake sat with his head bowed, his hair falling in front of his face, feeling strangely self-conscious all of a sudden.

"That was beautiful," breathed Lori. "Will you play some more?"

Jake nodded and began to play a well-known rock song that was part of the band's standard set. He played three more songs for her, then laid down his guitar.

"No more," he said with a yawn. "It's getting late."

Lori started to protest that it wasn't that late, but realised she too was tired. She watched Jake lay the guitar lovingly in its case, snapping the catches shut, then he fished the truck keys out of his pocket. Slowly she walked him to the front door.

"Can we catch up tomorrow?" he asked.

"Sure. I've got a therapy session in the morning, but I'll be done by midday."

"I've got work till eight again. I'll come over after that if it's ok," he said, brushing her cheek with a gentle kiss. "Now get to bed. You look wiped out."

"Night, Jake," she called into the dark as he loped off the porch towards his truck. Lori watched as he backed out of the driveway, then closed the door.

Next morning, Lori wakened at five thirty. The sun was coming up and she could hear the birds in the trees over near the lake. Suddenly she felt claustrophobic in the house and needed to get out in the fresh morning air. Without stopping to shower, she slipped on her yoga pants and a sweatshirt, pulled her hair back into a messy ponytail, then wrote a note to Mary – "Gone for a walk on the beach. Lori x". Having left the note on the kitchen table, she headed out of the back door. It was a glorious spring morning and the sea air was cool and fresh. Lori hadn't stopped to put shoes on and the soft sand was icy cold on her feet. Slowly and carefully, she made her way across the sand towards the ocean. As before, when she was down on the hard packed wet sand, her confidence grew. Even the ocean was calm and small waves lapped ashore beside her. She had only gone about a hundred yards when she spotted a pod of dolphins playing just off shore. There were about ten of them, as far as she could tell. It looked as though they too had decided to enjoy the fresh spring morning. Mornings like this were good for the soul, she thought.

As she stood gazing out at the ocean, her mind began to drift over everything that had happened since her accident. Gradually, she began to appreciate how far she had actually come along the road to recovery. Her whole life had been on hold for four months. Maybe meeting Jake was the sign for her to relax about things a bit and enjoy living. She thought back to the previous evening and to the songs he had played for her. He showed real promise. Although she had only been on the periphery of the music world, Lori recognised real talent when she heard it and she had heard it last night. Talent not just as a musician and a singer, but as a songwriter too, she suspected.

Her own talents- what was she to do with them, she wondered. The few raw sketches she had completed recently had reminded her of how much she loved to draw and design and create. Jake's delight at the Celtic design she had drawn for him had been heart-warming. Maybe it was time to resurrect Mz Hyde and to put some feelers out for some work. She could easily work from the beach house without the need to return to New York.

Her laptop had lain in its case, dormant for weeks – her business emails untouched for months. At last she felt ready to begin to pick up some of the tatters of her old life.

The dolphins had begun to move south and to swim further out from the shore. Lori watched them until they were out of sight, then slowly headed back up the beach towards the house. As she walked, she strayed closer to the edge of the water and the occasional small wave washed over her feet. The water was cold, really cold, but it felt good. An early morning jogger was heading along the hard packed sand towards her and, as he drew closer, she realised it was Jake. His sweatpants were soaked around the ankles where he too had strayed into the waves. His long hair was tied back in a loose ponytail and he had his earphones in. When he spotted her, a huge smile broke out across his face and he picked up his pace to catch up with her.

"You're out early!" Lori called, as he approached.

"What?" shouted Jake, pulling out one ear bud.

"I said, you're out early."

"I could say the same thing," countered Jake, grinning. "But at least you're still upright on the sand this time."

Lori laughed. "So far," she said, then added, "I was watching the dolphins."

"Yeah? I usually see them if I'm out at this time. Anyway, I was going to call you later. I need to cancel tonight. Sorry."

"Oh," replied Lori softly. She hoped her face didn't give away the disappointment she was feeling.

"I got a text from Rich late last night. He's managed to get us two free studio slots. A friend of his works at a small recording studio and occasionally gets us a free stint. We've got about eight hours tonight and tomorrow night. Graveyard slots," he explained, obviously excited at the thought of studio time. "Anyway, Rich has contacts through the high school where he works and he's got us a couple of guys to record some tracks. It's too good to pass up."

"Of course it is," agreed Lori, smiling at his childlike enthusiasm. "Do I get to hear the end result?"

"Maybe," teased Jake. "The rough plan is to try to get a handful of songs recorded so we can sell a few CDs at our gigs. There's a charity event we're playing in a couple of weeks. If we could sell some at that it would be good."

"I get it," said Lori, sharing his enthusiasm.

"If we get the stuff together," he began, hesitantly. "I was thinking, if you didn't mind, that I could share your design with the band. It could be our first album cover."

Lori threw back her head and laughed at his awkwardness about asking. He sounded like a little boy asking for permission to take something precious into Show and Tell at school.

"And if I say no?" she teased, trying to feign seriousness.

"If you don't want me to...."

"Jake, I'm teasing. The design is yours. Go for it. If I can help in any way, you just need to ask," she assured him warmly. "Now walk me home and tell me what you hope to record."

Together they walked back towards the beach house and Lori listened while Jake talked animatedly about the pros and cons of the different tracks they could record. He explained that they had had a few practice sessions in the studio over the winter, but hadn't had the opportunity to record before. Jake went on to add that Rich could get some CDs produced cheaply and quickly. His enthusiasm and passion was infectious. By the time they reached the path to the house, Jake was convincing her they could reach the top of the Billboard 100 with their first release.

Still laughing, Lori asked, "Do you want to come in for some breakfast?"

Jake shook his head, "I need to finish my run and then get to work."

"You sure?" she asked, hoping he'd change his mind.

Gently he kissed her on the forehead, "Sunday. Make me breakfast on Sunday, Mz Hyde."

"Deal," agreed Lori, smiling at his use of her professional name. "Now, run!"

With a wave, he jogged off along the beach, back towards town, taking long easy rhythmic strides. She smiled as she watched him, still feeling refreshed by his passion for his music. Once he was out of sight, she headed up the path towards the house.

When Jo arrived for Lori's physiotherapy session, Lori was out on the sun deck with her laptop and a mug of coffee. She was so engrossed in the screen that she was oblivious to the therapist's arrival until Jo coughed politely. Looking up, Lori blushed, "Sorry. I was catching up on my mail. Four months' worth."

"No worries," said Jo, taking a seat. "How are you today? Mary says you were out on the beach earlier."

"I'm good," replied Lori, switching off the laptop. "Really good actually. Watching dolphins play just after sunrise is a beautiful start to the day."

Jo laughed and said, "I couldn't agree more. Now how did it go with the doctor's appointment?"

With one eyebrow, raised Lori answered, "I'm sure you know, Mrs Brent. You never said you were a doctor's wife?"

"Sorry," apologised Jo. "We don't discuss patients at home, but, yes, John was very impressed with you. We've had a chat about the way forward and I've revised the rehab plan."

"So, what does Plan B look like?"

"Well, we need to build up some stamina as well as the stretching and resistance work while keeping up the strength work. The first goal is to lose the crutches when you're indoors and be comfortable on one outdoors," began Jo.

"I'm barely comfortable on two outdoors!" protested Lori sharply, nerves starting to flood through her.

"I know, so we need to work on that. How long had you been on crutches before you came down here?"

"About ten days," replied Lori quietly. "The clinic in New York kept me on the walker until my hip and wrist fully healed."

"Your hip and wrist?" queried Jo. "There was nothing in your case file about any other injuries other than your leg. And you never mentioned them."

Lori shrugged and murmured, "Maybe you should call them."

"Or," suggested Jo, "You could tell me what happened?"

"Someday. Maybe," said Lori bluntly. "But not today."

Sensing the girl's stress and anxiety at the prospect of recalling the accident, Jo backed off, but not before asking her to expand on the details of the hip and wrist injury.

"I fractured my right wrist and suffered a pelvic fracture on the right side. They put some kind of mesh wire support in my pelvis to allow the bone to knit better," explained Lori quietly, without looking up.

"Thanks, Lori," said Jo warmly. "I'll call the clinic when I get back to the office. They should have sent me the whole file. And, in hindsight, I should have asked you before now."

There was a moment's awkward silence before Jo said, "Let's go for some stamina work today. We're going for a walk along the beach."

"Sounds good to me."

Once they were across the soft sand and onto the firmer damp surface, Jo asked Lori to pass her one of the crutches. Nervously, she handed one over and they continued their walk slowly along the hard packed sand. As they walked, the physiotherapist apologised for distressing her earlier.

"It's ok, Jo," said Lori, stopping for a rest. "I'm sorry too. I just can't talk about it much yet. Some wounds are still too raw."

"Did you get any counselling in New York?"

"Some," admitted Lori, with a sigh. "The police sent someone to talk to me too."

"I could arrange more sessions for you here," suggested Jo. "It might help."

"I'll think about it," agreed Lori. "But, I think, I'm ok for now. Jake's good therapy and I've been doing a little exploration about going back to work."

"Work?"

"I was, well, I am, a freelance artist," explained Lori. "That's what I was doing when you arrived. Checking through my business email box."

"An artist?" echoed Jo curiously. "What kind of art?"

"Album covers and graphic art for the music industry mainly," answered Lori. "I've been playing with a few designs over the last few days. It's been fun."

"You'll need to show me some of your work sometime," said Jo, handing her back her second crutch. "Back to two for a while."

"Are we turning back?"

"Not yet, unless you want to. How's the leg holding up?"

"I'm good," replied Lori, settling herself back onto both crutches.

By the time they returned to the house almost an hour later, Lori was limping heavily. The physiotherapist told her to lie down on the sun lounger and she put her leg through a short but intense stretching routine. She finished their session with a deep muscle relaxing massage.

"Rest for at least an hour," she instructed. "I'm going to call that clinic and fill John in. Depending on what I find out, he may call you in for another appointment next week."

"Dr Brent knows about the pelvic injury," confessed Lori. "It showed up on the x-rays."

"Typical," muttered Jo. "Ok. Have a quiet weekend and I'll see you on Monday. Usual time."

"Monday," agreed Lori, through a yawn. "Looking forward to it."

When Mary brought her lunch out an hour or so later, Lori was sound asleep. The housekeeper let her sleep on.

Claustrophobia, and a degree of cabin fever, was setting in by the early hours of Sunday morning. Silver Lake had been locked away for five hours and had three to go. The bass and drum tracks had been completed, leaving Grey and Paul hanging about playing poker and helping where they could. Work on the guitar tracks had been slow and, at times painful, but at last they were almost there. Both Rich and Jake were flagging, the lack of sleep catching up with them. They knew time was running short and Rich was conscious that he wanted to leave Jake enough time for the vocal tracks. Finally, shortly before three in the morning, Rich declared he was done. He practically threw his guitar onto the settee in the corner, then walked off to get some air.

"Let's take a short break," called one of the guys from the booth. "Back in fifteen."

In his heart of hearts, Jake knew if he took a break now he wouldn't start again. He was almost spent and no amount of caffeine could keep him going much longer. He laid down his electric guitar, acutely aware that he had two tracks to go, and picked up his beloved acoustic instrument. Casually, he played and sang for himself, the two newly composed ballads he was working on. It was relaxation enough for him. Soon, he was lost in his music and the recording studio claustrophobia was banished from his mind. Just playing and singing for the sheer pleasure of it was good for his soul. None of the band interrupted him. No one broke into his psyche. When he finished, he laid the acoustic guitar back in its case and picked up his dark red electric instrument.

"Ready?" he called out to the booth.

"Still recording. Keep playing."

Jake resumed from where they had left off, totally unaware that his acoustic jam session had been recorded.

Despite his lack of sleep, Jake nailed the vocals at the first time of asking and they finished up five minutes before their six o'clock deadline. Grey and Paul had bailed out and gone home. Rich was asleep on the floor, with his head resting on his guitar case. Satisfied that his presence wasn't needed any more, Jake lifted his cases, grabbed his leather jacket and was heading out the door, when one of the recording gurus gave him a shout. He stopped and turned back. The guy tossed a USB stick to him.

"First cut," called the other guru. "Rough but it is all there. We'll get the final cut to Rich by Wednesday night."

"Thanks. Night, guys," muttered Jake, pocketing the flash drive. "Or morning. Or whatever."

He was dead on his feet. He hadn't slept since Friday. Blindly, he drove out to the beach house, abandoned his truck under the tree, and then crept round the side to the sun deck. It was too early to waken Lori, so he lay down on the lounger and was almost instantly asleep.

Even though she had kept herself busy all weekend with her business email clear out and the beginnings of the resurrection of Mz Hyde, Lori had counted the hours until Jake was due to arrive. Before she had left on Saturday, Lori had asked Mary to take her food shopping, as she wanted to be sure she had everything for a perfect Sunday breakfast. With the refrigerator fully stocked, the housekeeper had left her to wait patiently. Over the last few days, Lori had been sleeping better, less nightmares disturbing her, so it was almost eight when she woke. While she showered and washed her hair, she sang to herself, feeling happy and relaxed for the first time in a long time. Even as she massaged the oil that the surgeon had recommended into her scars, she kept singing, determined that nothing was going to destroy her good mood. She dressed casually in a soft pair of well-worn jeans and a vest top, then went through to start up the coffee machine. As she passed the front door, she spotted Jake's truck parked outside. Immediately, she guessed where he was.

Out on the sundeck, Jake was curled on his side snoring softly. His leather jacket was draped over his shoulders as a make-do blanket and his hair was straggling over his face. Quietly, Lori went into the sunroom to fetch a proper blanket. Carefully, she spread it over him. The lounger was in the shade and it was still cool out. Jake stirred slightly, but remained asleep, as she lifted off his jacket and snuggled the blanket round him. He looked so peaceful. Leaving him to sleep, she went back indoors to fetch herself a coffee, then came out onto the deck with her laptop to do some work while he slept.

It was after midday before Jake finally stirred. The squeaking of the lounger's springs caused Lori look up from the computer screen in time to see him stretch and yawn. He reminded her of a cat stretching itself out in the sun. He sat up slowly, pushing his hair out of his face, then looked round as though he didn't know where he was.

"Afternoon, sleepy head," said Lori coming over to sit beside him.

"Morning," he yawned.

"No, afternoon," she corrected. "When did you get here? I found you out here about eight thirty."

"Not long after six," Jake explained. "I didn't want to wake you, so I came round here."

"You ok?" asked Lori, concerned by the dark shadows under his hazel eyes.

"Nothing a shower and some coffee won't cure. It's been a hell of a long weekend. I did two ten hour shifts at the pizza place and two all-night studio sessions. I'm getting too old for that shit."

Lori laughed, "Go take a shower then and I'll make some lunch."

"You sure you don't mind?" asked Jake.

She shook her head, "Make yourself at home. There's clean towels in the cupboard in the bathroom."

"Thanks," said Jake, helping her to her feet before getting up himself. "God, my back's killing me. You need to get a more comfortable lounger, li'l lady."

Lori giggled and confessed it wasn't the best for napping on. Together they went indoors and, while Jake went out to his truck to check if he had a change of clothes in his gym bag, Lori went into the kitchen to fix them some lunch. She had her iPod plugged into the dock in the kitchen and switched it on while she prepared some tacos and a salad for them. It took several trips through the house for her to transport everything out to the table on the sundeck but she was pleased with herself that she managed it without spilling or dropping anything. She could hear the shower running and Jake singing in the bathroom. It made her smile.

She was sitting at the table, sipping a beer, when he finally walked through from the sun room. His long hair was hanging damp around his shoulders and he was stripped to the waist, his clean t-shirt clutched in his hand. Lori tried and failed not to stare at his half naked body admiringly.

"Thanks," said Jake, sitting beside her at the table. "I feel almost human again."

"Not a problem," said Lori, still studying the tattoo on his left shoulder. "Sorry, I shouldn't stare."

He shrugged and declared, "Signs of my misspent youth."

"They're well done," said Lori, nodding approvingly.

"Go with the territory, I guess. My own personal art gallery."

"So," said Lori changing the subject. "How did it go in the studio?"

While they ate their lunch, Jake filled her in on the details of the recording sessions. He seemed confident that Silver Lake had accomplished all they could have hoped for in the hours that they had available. It was a relief that none of their egos had got in the way and he was happy that they had pulled together as a team. Briefly, he outlined the plans for the next couple of weeks leading up to the Surfside Park gig.

"What's the next step?" asked Lori.

"I don't know. We hope the radio station that's sponsoring Surfside will pick up on our stuff and maybe we can get some air time."

"Have you ever approached any of the agencies or record companies?" she asked, casually.

"This is the first we've had a professional demo to take to them. We need to talk it through as a band. I want to push it, but Grey has commitments here. Rich has his teaching job. Paul might be up for it."

A plan was forming in the back of her mind, but she didn't want to over-step the mark.

"When do I get to hear the result of all your hard work?"

Jake reached into his pocket and pulled out the flash drive, "Now, if I can use your laptop. It's only the first cut."

"Sure," said Lori, keen to hear Silver Lake's first recording. "Let's go inside and I'll hook it up to the theatre sound in the sunroom."

Ten minutes later, they were both listening to the recording. As far as Jake knew, there were only four tracks completed, but the file marked "SL" looked to have six in it. He was critical of the music as he listened to it first time through then stopped dead when his solo acoustic piece filtered through the speakers.

"What the...." he began.

"Shh," said Lori. "This is great."

He was shocked to find the second acoustic track recorded. Part of him was anxious as to how the rest of the band would feel when they heard it, but a bigger part of him was thrilled to hear how solid it sounded. They played the tracks through again. This time, Jake was less critical, but was also making mental notes of bits he would change next time he played the pieces. When silence filled the sunroom again, Lori decided to push her luck and asked if she could keep a copy of the file. Jake shook his head and politely refused. "I'll bring you a finished copy as soon as I get one, Promise. I can't give you this without the guys approving it all. Band politics."

She understood and, reluctantly, passed him back the flash drive.

"Do you need to work today?"

"No," said Jake. "My next shift isn't till Tuesday night," then added, "I don't know how many more I can cope with."

"If you can't be a full time rock star yet, what do you want to do?" she asked, curious to learn the answer.

"Teach music," he replied, without hesitation. "I did music in college and took my teaching diploma, but have never managed to get a job. I did a few supply slots for a year after college and that's been it. I've done some private tuition, but not a lot. It doesn't pay enough to pay the rent."

"Could Rich not help you out with something?" she asked. "He teaches, doesn't he?"

"Yes," Jake replied. "He's mentioned me to the principal. There might be an opportunity for some part-time stuff. He's looking for help to run an out-of-school group too. I'll wait and see what happens, but it's pizza till then."

Lori laughed.

"So what are you going to do for work?" asked Jake, seizing the opportunity to quiz her.

"I'm not sure yet," confessed Lori. "I've been going through my business emails and there's a couple of projects I hope I can explore. I can't do the memorabilia bit for now as there's too much travelling involved with that. I don't want to leave here either for now."

"Can you do the artist bit from here? The Mz Hyde stuff?"

"If I can get the commissions, I think so," she said hopefully. "I'll need to get some of my stuff sent down from New York but that's no big deal. My studio is all set up in my apartment in the city."

"I didn't realise you still had a place in New York," he commented.

"It's a long story for another day," said Lori, closing the door on the conversation. "Do you fancy taking a walk on the beach?"

They spent the rest of the afternoon down on the beach casually chatting and getting to know more about each other. As they walked, Jake noticed that Lori seemed more confident than on their previous outing and steadier on her feet. She spotted the dolphins off shore and they stopped to watch them for a few minutes, before continuing on their way. The beach was busier than the previous weekend, with more families out on the sand and more fishermen spaced out along the water line. All of these were signs that the summer season was nearly upon them and that the tourists were making their way back into town. By Memorial Day at the end of May, the town would be swamped again.

"Can we head back?" asked Lori quietly.

"Sorry. Have I dragged you too far down the beach?" said Jake with some concern. "You should've said sooner."

"I'm ok but I can feel my leg starting to protest," she admitted. "I'd feel happier if we turned around."

"Of course."

When they finally reached the house, the pain was etched into her face. Lori excused herself and headed straight to the bedroom in search of some pain medication. It was tempting to take something stronger, but she stuck to the over the counter drugs and silently prayed they would take effect quickly. Back in the sunroom, Jake had switched on the TV, selected a classic rock channel and fetched them both a beer from the fridge. Lowering herself onto the couch beside him, Lori apologised for being so pathetic.

"Stop being so hard on yourself, li'l lady," he scolded. "Now why don't you stretch out and I'll sort some dinner for us?"

"Mary's left a lasagne in the refrigerator," said Lori. "You could heat it up. I think there's some garlic bread in the freezer."

"That I can manage," agreed Jake. "Do you want to eat indoors or out?"

"Let's stay in," she said, as she lifted her leg onto the couch and eased it out straight. "If you fancy some wine, there's a bottle in the cupboard next to the front door. I got Mary to move the wine rack up from the basement."

"Red?"

Lori nodded.

After their meal was over and the dishwasher loaded up, Jake said he had to leave. He could tell that Lori wanted him to stay a while longer, but he confessed, somewhat awkwardly, to having some chores to do at home, including his laundry. That made her laugh and she reluctantly agreed that they should call it a day. Together they debated what to do the next day. Lori had her usual Monday morning session with Jo so Jake agreed to come over at lunchtime and maybe take her out for a drive in the afternoon.

Once his truck had pulled out of the driveway, Lori settled herself in the study for a couple of hours at her drawing board. Listening to the Silver Lake demo tracks had sparked a few new ideas and she wanted to make some rough sketches. She paused only to fire off a quick email to one of her girlfriends from New York. It had been a couple of months since they had caught up, so Lori invited her down to Rehoboth for the weekend, deliberately choosing the weekend of the Surfside Park event. She left her emails open on the screen while she sketched and, just before she was ready to call it a day, Maddy replied that she would love a weekend at the shore.

The two weeks in the run up to the Surfside event saw a few milestones for Jake and Lori. Their relationship continued to blossom slowly. Neither of them wanted to rush it and ruin a good thing. They used the time to become more relaxed in each other's company and to learn more about their pasts. Lori's accident was still a tale off limits, but she did open up a little more about her life in New York. As good as his word, Jake brought her a copy of Silver Lake's finished CD as soon as he got his hands on it. She was impressed with the results and shared in his boyish delight when the radio station sponsoring Surfside agreed to add it to their playlist. After a bit of persuasion, Jake had agreed to get her tickets for the charity gig. He was worried it would be too long a day for her and he pointed out he wouldn't be free to spend much time with her until after the band had played. In an attempt to allay his concerns, Lori explained that she had a friend coming down for the weekend and that Maddy would look out for her. Eventually he relented and promised to try to secure some privilege passes for them.

The biggest milestone for Lori came at the start of the week. When Jo arrived for their therapy session, she brought two walking canes with her.

"Time to move on," she said, handing them to Lori. "Let's see how this goes."

Lori was hesitant at first, feeling vulnerable and unbalanced. Patiently Jo explained to her how to adjust her way of walking, convincing her that the canes were as strong as her crutches, and with practice Lori was soon coping well. Jo caveated the progression by advising that she stick to her crutches if she was alone down on the beach. Her aim, she declared, was to get her down to one cane by the 4th of July. It was a challenge Lori accepted.

The two canes, that Jo presented her with, were plain black. With a streak of artistic rebellion, Lori had Jake take her out to the hardware store to purchase some primer paint then she spent the next two evenings customising them with her own designs. The end result was fabulous and, when Jo returned on Friday morning, she could only agree it was an improvement and that they were now more suited to Lori's character.

"I've a present for you," said Lori, as Jo was leaving that day. "Silver Lake are playing at Surfside tomorrow. Jake gave me two extra passes for you and John. If you fancy going along that is."

"Thanks," said Jo, with obvious delight. "Are you going?"

Lori nodded. "I'm having a house guest for the weekend so we are both going."

"Well, maybe we will see you there. I think that Beebe has sponsored one of the afternoon acts. One of the nurses, if I remember right."

"I'll look out for you," promised Lori. "I'm not sure how early we'll go along. I'll see what Maddy wants to do."

It was early evening before Maddy finally roared up into the driveway in her black Mustang. Anxious in case her friend missed the house, Lori had been sitting on the rocking chair on the front porch watching for her. The car door opened and Maddy stepped out into the driveway. She was a vision in black- short spiked hair, shaved at the sides, skin tight black mini skirt, black and purple corset style top and her customary spike high heels.

"Lori!" she screamed in delight at seeing her friend.

"Hi," called Lori, from her seat on the porch. "How was the drive down?"

"Lord, it took forever," called Maddy bringing her holdall, appropriately black and purple zebra stripes, out of the car. "I left the city at two."

"That's about right, I'd guess, for Friday evening traffic," said Lori. "Come on in. Dinner's almost ready."

"You're looking fantastic," complimented her friend. "Some colour in your cheeks. Such an improvement on that white skeleton I visited in the hospital."

Lori laughed as she got to her feet and led her friend through to the guest bedroom. She left her to freshen up and went back to the kitchen where Mary was finalising dinner. In return for staying late, Lori had given her the whole weekend off. The housekeeper was keen to leave, as she was going to stay at her sister's in Lewes to get away from the Surfside event. Her apartment was near the park and she had declared she could not face a whole weekend of noisy music and traffic chaos.

"Thanks for staying late," said Lori warmly. "I really appreciate the help."

"I heard your friend arrive," stated Mary. "Is she some kind of a rock chick? What's with that noisy car?"

"Sort of," confessed Lori. "You'll meet her in a minute or two. Can we eat out on the deck?"

"I've already set the table and lit the lanterns. I'm guessing you girls will be out there till after dark."

"Thanks. What would I do without you?"

At that they heard the click of Maddy's heels on the hall floor as she came towards the kitchen. Quickly Lori introduced her to Mary then, before the shock of her Goth appearance caused the housekeeper to have a heart attack, led her out to the sun deck. In the early evening light it looked fabulous with the table set for dinner and the candles and lanterns lit.

"This is beautiful," declared Maddy, walking to the edge of the deck to get a better view of the beach.

"Now can you see why I came down here? It's a good place to recover," replied Lori softly.

"And you seem to be recovering well," added Maddy, her concern for her friend apparent in the warmth of her voice. "I've been worried about you."

"I'm getting there," sighed Lori. "Slower than I like, but I'm getting there. It's been a long journey."

"And a tough one, I'll bet," added Maddy, hugging her friend.

"Enough talk of that," Lori stated. "I'm not spoiling our weekend with maudlin talk."

"Lord, you sound like my grandmother!"

Both girls laughed and went to sit at the table. Just as Lori had poured them some wine, Mary brought their meal out, then said her goodbyes. As they ate, Maddy filled Lori in on all the girlie gossip she had been missing. She brought her up to date on the work projects she had in the pipeline for the next few months, which included several overseas trips, then finally showed off her two new tattoos - one on her ankle and the other at the side of her right eye. It had grown dark while they had chatted and caught up with each other's news, not that Lori had had a chance to contribute much to the conversation.

As Maddy refilled their wine glasses she asked what the plans were for the weekend.

"Well," began Lori slowly. "I've left tomorrow fairly fluid during the day, but I've got us tickets to a local charity music festival for tomorrow night. I thought we could head over there about five."

Maddy raised one well waxed eyebrow and enquired, "Is this a business or pleasure music thing?"

"It's whatever you want it to be," countered Lori, stifling a giggle. Her friend had seen straight through her subterfuge. "Just go along with an open mind and listen. See if you hear anything you like."

"Is there anyone I should be listening out for in particular?"

"Yes," admitted Lori. "But when you meet them don't say a word about this."

"Now I'm curious, girl. Tell me more."

Briefly Lori explained about Silver Lake, the demo and suggested that if Maddy liked them as much as she did, then perhaps she could spread the word about them when she got back to New York.

"I can't promise anything," cautioned Maddy. "I'll listen to them, but if they're shit I'll tell you straight."

"I know you will," laughed Lori. "Just don't tell them who you are. As far as Jake knows you're my friend. Just here for the weekend to check up on me. Ok?"

"Ok, girl, I'll play along," agreed Maddy with an impish grin. "But you owe me one."

"I owe you more than one."

It was getting late, but the girls were still sitting outside putting the world to rights when Lori heard footsteps on the path. A few seconds later, Jake appeared, looking a little tousled, as he loped onto the sun deck.

"Sorry to barge in, ladies," he apologised, flashing them both a smile.

"Want a glass?" asked Lori, indicating the newly opened bottle of wine.

"Maybe one. I can't stay long," he said. "I'll grab a glass from the kitchen."

When he came back to join them Lori introduced him to

Maddy.

"Pleased to meet you," he said warmly. "Are you ladies still coming to Surfside tomorrow?"

"We were talking about that earlier," explained Lori. "I thought we'd come along about five."

"Probably a good call. All the kiddie stuff will be done around three, then there's the high school band on at four. We're on at eight to finish it all off. The fireworks display is scheduled for nine thirty."

"Do you want to meet us after you play?"

"If you're up to it," said Jake. "We were planning on going out for a few beers in town. You can show Maddy here the beach night life."

The girls laughed and agreed it sounded like a plan as long as Lori felt up to it.

"Oh, before I forget," said Jake reaching into his back pocket. "Here's a parking pass. I got a spare one for you so you can park in the performers bit. Thought it might help. Call me when you arrive and I'll come out and find you."

"Thanks."

Jake stayed for a few more minutes before declaring he needed to go. He stood up, drained his glass, kissed Lori on the forehead, then bid his farewells and slipped off into the night. Once he was out of earshot, Maddy declared, "So that's the attraction to Silver Lake!"

Lori blushed, but didn't reply.

"If they play as well as he looks then I might be able to help," teased her friend.

As Maddy guided the Mustang along a very crowded Lakeview Street towards the VIP parking area, they could hear the high school band finishing up. There were teenagers hanging about the entrance to the designated car park at the corner of Grenoble Place. A parking attendant guided the girls down towards a place near the boardwalk. While Maddy parked the car, Lori called Jake to say they had arrived.

"Hi, li'l lady," he said, answering on the second ring. "You here?"

"Yup. Just parked two slots up from the boardwalk. Are you

able to meet us?" asked Lori hopefully.

"Not for about half an hour," answered Jake. "Your passes will get you into the guest area beside the stage. Come up the boardwalk and enter that way. I'll come and find you."

"Ok, no rush," said Lori. "We'll see you in the VIP area."

It took Lori a minute or two to lever herself out of the low slung car and another to steady herself. This was her first big outing with only the canes for support and she was nervous. She just hoped it didn't show to Maddy.

"We've to head along the boardwalk to the VIP area," explained Lori. "Jake'll meet us there in half an hour."

"Ok, lead the way, girl," said Maddy, slinging her large scarlet bag over her shoulder. "I'm ready for some rock music!"

As they neared the boardwalk entrance to the festival site, the girls noticed that there were small groups of teenagers hanging about, most of them wearing Silver Lake T-shirts. They moved aside to let Lori pass and several of the boys wolf whistled at Maddy. The two friends looked at each other and laughed. As they showed their passes to the security guard, Lori whispered to Maddy," I bet they think it's you who's the girlfriend of the band."

Maddy laughed, "The night is young, girl!"

They made their way through the crowd that had already gathered in the guest enclosure towards a small beer tent. Lori had spotted a few tables and chairs over to one corner so headed over there to find a seat while Maddy fetched them a drink. Each of the tables had "reserved" signs on them but she was relieved to see a notice on two that said "Silver Lake"- two that were in the sun for now and had a great view of the stage. With a smile, she sat down, thinking Jake really had put a lot of thought into this. The band had been helping to set up the event for the previous two days, so she guessed he had pulled a few favours to make sure she was safely seated in full view of the band. People were piling into the area, but she didn't recognise any of them. On stage, a young boy was playing an acoustic country set. He looked to be about sixteen and had a pleasant enough voice to listen to.

"Lori!" squealed a child's voice from the crowd.

She turned to see Grey's little girl, Becky, coming running towards her. The little girl stopped beside her and blurted out in excitement, "I'm going to see my daddy play his guitar on the stage."

"Hi, Becky," said Lori, smiling at the little girl. "Are you excited about that?"

The little girl nodded furiously, "Mommy said I could stay up for the fireworks too."

"Rebecca!" yelled a harsh woman's voice. An angry looking woman was heading towards them.

"That's my mommy," whispered Becky, looking a little scared.

The woman had reached the table by now. "Do not run off in this crowd or we are going straight home, young lady," she snapped sharply.

"Sorry," whispered Becky, tears welling up in her eyes.

To break the tension, Lori said, "You must be Grey's wife? I'm Jake's friend. Lori Hyde."

"Sandy," said the little girl's mother. "Nice to meet you. Grey said he had met you a couple of weeks back."

The woman sat down at the other reserved table and handed a carton of apple juice to Becky. Taking the carton, Becky clambered up on the chair next to Lori. "Are you here to see Uncle Jake?"

"I sure am," replied Lori. "My friend Maddy is here too. That's her coming over. The lady with the shiny red bag." She pointed towards Maddy, who was threading her way through the crowd with two plastic cups of beer.

When Becky spotted her piercings and tattoos, she whispered to Lori, "She looks scary."

Lori was still giggling at Becky's reaction when Maddy set the cups down on the table. Quickly Lori introduced them all then settled back to listen to the boy on stage. She could sense her friend scanning the crowd in the enclosure as though she was searching for someone. Force of habit, perhaps thought Lori sipping her beer. Part of Maddy's job was scouting for new acts, but also to be on the lookout for rival scouts.

"You ok?" she asked when the country act was done.

"Yeah," said Maddy. "Thought I saw JJ at the bar. Must've been someone else."

JJ was a professional rival and an ex-boyfriend, so it explained the edge to her friend's mood.

"Relax," said Lori. "You're at the beach. Chill."

At that moment Becky wandered over to stand beside Maddy and stood staring at her pierced ears. Her mother was busy talking on her phone, oblivious to her young daughter. The little girl counted the hoops through Maddy's ears.

"Wow, that's a lot of earrings," she said with a child's innocent seriousness. "Mommy says I can get my ears pierced when I'm ten."

Children were not the Goth's favourite things and she just stared back at the child, unwilling to be drawn into conversation.

"Show Becky the tattoo on your foot," suggested Lori.

Reluctantly Maddy slipped off her shoe to reveal a beautiful butterfly design inked along the edge of her foot.

"And I can't imagine your daddy with a butterfly tattoo," said Jake, appearing through an opening in the crowd beside them. He scooped the little girl up into his arms. She flung her arms around his neck, squeezing him tight. Shifting her weight onto his hip, he leaned over to hug Lori. "You girls ok here?"

"Fine. How's it all going?" asked Maddy casually.

"So, so. Depends on what you are here to listen to. We've been helping the kids set up and helping to keep the instruments in tune if nothing else. One girl was so nervous earlier that I went on to play with her," Jake replied. "It's all a family thing till after six. That kid was the last "family act". There's a band from Lewes on in a minute, then a nurse from Beebe, then us."

Sandy had finished her phone call and nodded over to Jake, "Where's Grey at?"

"He said he'd be right out. He's setting up the kid from Lewes' bass for him. It's their first gig."

"Can you watch the kid till I grab a beer?" asked Sandy, getting to her feet. "You ladies want one?"

Both girls declined and before Jake could say anything Sandy was gone into the crowd. It was obvious to all of them that she did not want to be there or to be hanging out with her daughter. The little girl snuggled in tighter to Jake as she watched her mother disappear into the crowd. Jake gave her a kiss and whispered something to her. She kissed him back.

Jake sat down beside Lori, with Becky still clinging onto him, and stole a mouthful of her beer.

"I can't stay out here for long," he said. "If Sandy doesn't come back, can you keep this little princess safe?"

"Of course," said Lori, sensing his concern.

"Thanks. I'll fill you in later."

The band from Lewes were out on stage playing a mix of EMO and punk. Not Lori's taste at all but she could see they were young and keen. Maddy had her unimpressed face on and turned her back on the stage to continue her people watching. A couple looked to be heading their way and she pointed them out to Lori.

"That's Jo and John," said Lori, glad to see some familiar faces. "My physical therapist and my doctor, believe it or not."

"Hi," called Jo brightly, as soon as they were within earshot. "Thought we'd say hello before Alice comes on."

After another quick round of introductions, the couple took a seat for a few minutes and exchanged pleasantries about the event. There was no sign of Sandy returning nor of Grey coming out to join them all. As the EMO band began their last number, Jake got up to go.

"Becky," he said seriously. "Stay with Lori till your dad comes over for you."

"Ok, Uncle Jake," promised the little girl. "Where did mommy go?"

"I'm not sure, honey. I'm going to have a look for her on my way backstage. You'll be fine here with Lori and Maddy. I promise."

With a quick wave, he was headed across the enclosure towards the backstage area. Jo and John also took their leave and re-joined their friends before the nurse from the medical centre took to the stage. The sun was sinking in the sky, bathing the crowded VIP area in a red glow. Maddy suggested she go and get them another drink before Silver Lake were due out on stage and wandered off into the crowd towards the beer tent. The nurse, Alice, appeared on stage and started her set. She was the best act that Lori had heard so far. The girl had a strong voice and ably performed half a dozen rock classics from Cher and Tina Turner. The crowd had now gathered tighter towards the stage and Lori guessed there had to be about six or seven hundred folk there. Part of her would have preferred to be in the crush down at the front rather than sitting here. She could feel her own excitement building at the thought that there were only a few short minutes left until Silver Lake were due on. Maddy returned with their drinks plus a can of cola for the little girl and a large bag of French fries for them all to share. Alice finished her set with River Deep Mountain High and left to a huge appreciative cheer from the growing crowd.

The stage went dark and Lori could just make out the shadows of a couple of stage crew scurrying about setting up. A gradual chant began in the heart of the crowd. "Silver Lake, Silver Lake, Silver Lake, Lake Lake". Lori glanced over at Becky, who was kneeling up on her chair, leaning on the back and gazing longingly up at the stage. The crowd's chants grew louder until the sound of the bass track from the band's opening number began to ring out. With an explosion of drums and lights, the band were suddenly there. Jake had changed his clothes and stood in the stark spotlight in skin tight ripped jeans and a black vest T-shirt. He had his guitar slung over his back. Grabbing the mic stand with both hands, he launched into their first song. Gone was the soft, haunting, melodic voice that Lori had heard in the sun room. In its place was a strong, powerful, rock vocal. She stole a glance at Becky, who was totally bewitched by the sight of her daddy and her Silver Lake uncles out on stage. After their first three numbers, Maddy tapped Lori on the knee and gave her the thumbs up. Her appreciation of the band's talent was obvious.

Up on the stage, Silver Lake felt as though they had come home and were in their element in front of the small crowd. Jake looked out from the stage and drank in the sight of all the adoring fans faces staring up at him, getting a kick out of a small group of girls down at the front who had a homemade sign saying "Jake, we love you." When he looked over to his left, he could see Lori in the VIP area. Beside her, Becky was totally focused on Grey. He moved across the stage and whispered to Grey, "Switch sides with Rich," and pointed to the little girl.

"Good evening Surfside!" he roared from the stage. "You're looking beautiful tonight."

The chant of "Silver Lake, Silver Lake" started up again and he just stood and smiled for a few seconds, savouring the moment.

"OK. Time for you guys to join in," cried Jake. "You all know this Bon Jovi classic, so let me hear you sing with us."

He had the small crowd eating out of the palm of his hand.

They cheered; they sang; they clapped when told to. The band played a good mix of their own material plus some favourites from Led Zeppelin and Guns N Roses.

"OK. There is a special young lady here at her first ever gig," called out Jake, blowing a kiss towards Becky. "Sweet Child O' Mine."

The little girl was almost jumping off her seat as Grey, Rich and Jake all moved over to the left hand side of the stage to play to her for just a few moments.

"Daddy, I love you!" she screamed towards Grey. With a smile, Lori hoped he had heard her.

The band played another couple of numbers, then Jake ducked off stage to switch guitars. He came back on to a huge cheer and he waved to the crowd for quiet.

"Surfside, let's take this down a bit for a moment. This is a new one for us. This is "Stronger Within," he said, then added, "Lori, this is for you."

It was the song he had sung for her in the sun room; the first song she had ever heard him perform. Gone was the rough, rock voice and the soft, husky, haunting vocal had returned. His range was fabulous and he nailed all the notes. The acoustic melody rang out crystal clear across the crowd. It was perfect. A moment that would live with Lori forever. No one had ever sung just for her so publicly.

Up on the stage Jake was playing and singing with his eyes closed. He didn't want to see the rest of the crowd for this song. In his mind, he was back in the sunroom, playing just for Lori. Lost in the moment, on stage, in front of almost a thousand people, he realised he had fallen in love with her.

When the song was over Lori got to her feet and blew him a kiss. On stage he played along, pretended to catch it and blew one back to her. The crowd cheered and the moment was gone. Paul struck up the beat on his drums and Jake dashed to switch guitars again before rushing headlong into their final three numbers.

Shortly after nine thirty the last notes faded out into the night to be replaced with the thunderous cracks and bangs of the fireworks display. Sometime during the fireworks, Sandy reappeared at the next table. She looked the worse for wear and a vodka bottle was poking out of her bag. Her daughter made no move towards her, content to stay safely seated between Lori and Maddy. As the last of the fireworks went up, Silver Lake made their way through the guest enclosure, beers in hand. When she saw her daddy, Becky flew into his arms, her adoration plain for all to see. Jake flopped down into the seat beside Lori and put his arm lazily across her shoulders. Together they watched the last colourful specs burn up. Once the fireworks were over, the floodlights came on and the crowd started to make their way home.

Someone had sent over another round of beers for the Silver Lake table. The band, still high on adrenaline, were all talking at once about this chord and that rhythm or this missed vocal. Paul, the drummer, only had eyes for Maddy, who was flirting outrageously with him. Becky had climbed up onto Grey's knee and was fast asleep with her head resting on his chest. All of them agreed the gig had been their best so far. The CDs and remaining T-shirts had sold out. One of the "suits" from the local radio station had asked for a meeting with them to discuss playing at a few more radio station events.

"Guys," said Grey quietly. "I'm going to head. I need to get this little girl home to bed and I guess I better take Sandy too." He glared over at his wife, who had passed out across the table.

"Let me give you a hand," offered Rich getting to his feet. "If you can drop me off, I'll call it a night too."

"Thanks, buddy," replied Grey, more than a little embarrassed by the situation. "Lori, thank you for taking care of my baby girl tonight. Appreciate it."

"My pleasure, Grey," said Lori, genuinely meaning it. "Bring her over anytime. She's adorable."

He nodded and waved as he turned to go. Rich shook Sandy awake and half carried her towards the exit.

"Well, I'm going into town for a few beers," declared Paul. "Maddy, are you coming?"

She looked at Lori hopefully.

"On you go," said Lori. "Have some fun."

"Are you guys coming?" asked Paul, as he finished off his beer. "We'll head along the boardwalk to the Turtle."

Suddenly Jake wanted some quiet time with Lori before the buzz of a bar. Hoping he wasn't overstepping the mark, he said,

"You go on ahead. We'll catch up later. If we're not coming, I'll call you."

"Ok," agreed Paul, putting his arm around the Goth's tiny corseted waist. "Come on, Maddy, let's rock 'n' fucking roll."

Watching them disappear off towards the boardwalk, Lori commented, "I hope he realises what he's doing."

Jake laughed, "She'll be fine. Paul will look after her."

"It's not her I'm worried about. It's Paul I'd be concerned about!" she declared with a giggle. "Will Maddy's car be ok here tonight?"

"Should be fine. Rich is parked across from her. We don't need to be clear till noon tomorrow," he replied. "Now, do you feel up to a slow walk along the boardwalk or would you rather go home?"

"A walk sounds good. I'm stiff after sitting all night."

The boardwalk was still busy with teenagers and young couples. A few of the kids stopped Jake and congratulated him on a great gig. Some of the girls asked for autographs. He took it all in his stride, keen not to offend any of them, but also made it clear that the show was over and that this was his private time. As they walked, Lori asked what was going on with Grey and his wife. Jake shrugged and admitted it wasn't good. His friend was talking about kicking her out, but didn't want to lose his little girl. It was all a bit of a mess he explained and added that Grey was embarrassed and angry about the way Sandy had abandoned Becky earlier on. When they reached the centre of town, they stopped to get a burger and fries. Like a teenage couple, they sat on one of the white benches eating their meal and watching the world go by.

"You do know you were great out there tonight," said Lori softly. "You really come alive on stage."

Jake blushed and lowered his head to stare at his feet. "I enjoy it. I enjoy seeing others enjoy what I do." He paused, then added, "I'm glad you enjoyed it."

They sat in silence for a few moments more, then he helped her to her feet and they continued down the boardwalk towards the Turtle, a sports bar popular with the younger crowd on a Saturday night. Lori struggled with the stairs up to the bar room, but declined Jake's offer of help. When they entered the crowded room, they quickly spotted Paul and Maddy at a table and while Lori went to join them, Jake went to fetch them a drink. He got stopped by more fans on his way back to the table, much to his embarrassment.

"Jesus, I just want a few quiet beers now," he muttered, passing round the drinks. "Show's over for the night."

"Goes with the territory, darling," declared Maddy loudly. "All part of the rock 'n' fucking roll show."

"I guess," he agreed reluctantly.

It was almost midnight when Lori said she would need to head home. She insisted the others didn't need to call it a night on her account. Much to Paul's great disappointment, Maddy said she would share a cab home with Lori. She placated him by suggesting they meet for lunch next day, when she came back into town to fetch her car. The guys both agreed, promising to call to invite Rich and Grey too. Lori phoned for a cab to meet them on the corner of Wilmington Avenue, then allowed Jake to help her down the stairs back to the boardwalk. Her leg was screaming at her and even standing was hurting like hell. Once the two girls were in the car, she let her guard down a bit and sat rubbing her thigh, tears of pain silently gliding down her cheeks.

Maddy put a comforting arm around her friend, "You should've said sooner that you needed to leave, honey."

"I know," sighed Lori. "I'll be fine when we get home. It's all so frustrating. I hate being like this."

"I can't imagine how hard this is for you," said Maddy, showing a soft side that Lori had rarely seen.

When the cab pulled up at the beach house, Lori paid the fare, then had to ask Maddy to help her out of the back seat. Her legs were shaking as she stumbled the few short yards to the front door. She only just reached the bedroom without falling and collapsed on the bed in a heap, blinded by tears. Her friend came hurrying in behind her, asking what she could do to help. Thankful for the assistance, Lori directed her to the bathroom cabinet and a bottle of Vicodin. Still hearing her doctor's warning about using such strong drugs echoing round in her mind, she quickly swallowed two pills, washing them down with a glass of water that Maddy had brought from the kitchen. Refusing to accept any more help, Lori said she was going straight to bed.

Bidding her goodnight, Maddy pulled the bedroom door closed behind her. Lori slipped off her shoes and her jeans, then slid under the covers. Sleep came in seconds, the drugs working their magic on the pain, melting it away for a few blissful hours.

Back at the Turtle, Jake and Paul sat on with another beer, then Jake suggested they head back to his apartment for a few more. As they meandered through the streets, his friend asked him about Lori and the artwork she had done for the band's CD. When Jake had shown the design to the guys, he hadn't told them who had done it, other than it had been designed by Lori.

"Maddy let slip that Lori's done a fair bit of professional design work," said Paul. "Do you think she'll do any more for us?"

"She's already offered," replied Jake before adding, "Not a word to the others. Lori's Mz Hyde."

"What?" shrieked Paul, in disbelief. "I bought framed prints of four of her covers for my lounge last year. They cost me a month's wages!"

"The very same," said Jake with a grin. "Not what you expected?"

"Not at all," stated Paul, shaking his head. "So what's with the canes and the leg thing?"

"Some kind of accident in New York last Christmas. She smashed up her leg pretty badly. There's enough metalwork in there to rebuild the Brooklyn Bridge. I don't know the details. Subject's off limits, but she showed me a photo of her x-rays," Jake explained. "I'm no doctor, but it looked as though she was lucky not to lose her leg." He paused, then added, "She's a special person."

"It's a long time since you've fallen for anyone," observed Paul. "Why this one?"

"I don't know," shrugged Jake, reaching into his pocket for his keys. "It's just different. Feels right."

"You look happy, so it must be right," agreed the drummer. "No more moody, mean Jake at rehearsal. And you nailed it on stage tonight."

"Shut up," said Jake, playfully slapping him on the back.

After a few rushed phone calls and text messages, they all met for lunch at Hooters next day. Grey was the last to arrive with Becky in tow. Over lunch, they all reminisced about the Surfside gig, with the band members tearing their performance to shreds then rebuilding it again. Maddy threw a few observations into the discussion, but, after a dark look from Lori, was careful not to give too much away about her knowledge of the inner workings of the music world. While the adults chatted, Becky used the kid's entertainment pack to keep herself amused. After a time, Lori noticed that the little girl was quieter than usual.

"What are you drawing?" she asked softly, leaning over to take a look.

"Daddy and my Silver Lake uncles," replied the little girl seriously. "But I can't draw the music."

With a flash of inspiration, Lori showed the little girl how to draw a variety of music notes. Soon the page and several napkins were covered in their doodles.

"Having fun, girls?" enquired Rich, lifting one of the napkins.

Lori laughed, "Yes. Do you want to keep that one?"

"A Lori original," he teased grinning mischievously. "Will you autograph this original artwork please?"

Without realising what she'd done, Lori signed her flamboyant Mz Hyde signature and passed it back. Rich looked at it, then at her then at Jake.

"Mz Hyde?" he asked, eyes wide. "THE Mz Hyde?"

Lori smiled and nodded slowly.

"Jesus!" cried Rich. "You did our album artwork!"

"Yes," replied Lori. "I did. That's what you do to help out a friend or to say thank you or both."

"I paid a fortune for a signed print of your last album artwork!"

"Well, you better take good care of that napkin, then, Rich," said Lori softly, mischief twinkling in her blue eyes. "It's an original."

The others laughed and the playful banter continued for another hour or so. Maddy excused herself and left the table to go to the ladies room, pausing *en route* to settle the table's bill. When she returned, she thanked them all for a great weekend, but apologised that she had to go. She had collected her car before lunch and it was now parked across the street and the time had ticked down on the meter. There were protests from the members of Silver Lake about her buying their lunch, but she joked that they could return the favour and buy her dinner when they were all rich and famous. Jake and Lori walked her out to the car. She hugged them both then hugged Lori again, squeezing her tight.

"Take care of her, Jake."

"I intend to," he promised, putting his arm around Lori's shoulders.

"And you take care of him," added Maddy with a wink. "I'll be in touch when I get back from my trip. I'm away till mid-June, if all goes to plan."

"Call me when you get back," said Lori, sad to see her friend leave. "Keep in touch."

They stood and watched her reverse the Mustang out of the parking space and then roar up the avenue on her way out of town.

"Do you want to go back in?" asked Jake, giving Lori a hug.

"Not really," she confessed, looking up at him. "Can we go home, please?"

"You struggling today?" he asked, concern filling his words.

"A bit," she admitted. "But I really just want you to myself for a few hours. We could go for a walk? A short walk."

"Sounds good to me," he agreed, leading her towards where his truck was parked.

As they drove back towards the beach house, with the cab filled with the gentle strains of country music, Jake suggested they spend the rest of the afternoon down on the beach. It was a warm afternoon and he commented that he felt like a swim in the ocean. Much to his surprise, Lori agreed, saying she had beach chairs in the garage and possibly a fishing rod of her dad's if he was interested. It had been a while since he'd been fishing and Jake was tempted. While Lori went indoors to change, Jake opened up the garage to search for the beach chairs. His gym bag was in the back of the truck and he decided to change into his shorts in the garage rather than trailing into the house. Once he had changed, he gathered up his clothes and beach gear and headed round to the sun deck. The patio doors were open and he stepped into the sun room, calling out to Lori.

"I'll be out in a minute," she called back. "Can you fetch towels from the cupboard in the bathroom?"

"Sure," said Jake, heading barefoot through the house.

"There's some beers in the fridge you could lift," called Lori from the bedroom." And I think there's some tortilla chips on the counter."

"On it, li'l lady."

In the bathroom, he found a pile of brightly coloured towels and grabbed four of them. On his way back through, he lifted four beers and the bag of chips.

"Lori!" he called. "I'll go down and set up. Will I come back up for you?"

"No," she replied. "I'll be ok. Go on out and I'll catch up."

In the bedroom, Lori stood in front of the mirror. She had changed into a black one piece swimsuit and found a sarong to tie round her waist. It only just covered the scarring on her thigh. It would have to do, she thought, as she lifted her crutches and headed out to meet Jake.

He had set up the chairs and towels on the soft sand just out of reach of the waves. As she walked barefoot across the warm sand, she watched him strip off his T-shirt, revealing his tattooed, well-muscled body. She was smiling by the time she reached him.

"What are you grinning at, li'l lady?"

"You," she giggled.

Jake gave her a hug, then turned and ran into the surf. She watched as he ran out through the shallows, then dived into a wave and swam strongly out into deeper water. Another large wave broke over him and Lori was relieved to see his blonde head surface a few seconds later. She watched as he swam in a ragged easy circle, then turned to body surf back in on the waves.

"Woo hoo!" he screamed, as he walked back towards her. "Christ that felt good."

Laughing as she passed him a towel, Lori said, "I'll take your word for it."

"You should come in," he said, rubbing himself dry.

"I don't think so," she said, very carefully sitting down on the spread out beach towel, taking care not to let her sarong ride up.

Jake flopped down on the towel next to her. He rolled over onto his back, folded his arms behind his head and sighed. This was the life. He closed his eyes and allowed himself a few minutes to drink in the sound of the waves and the warmth of the late spring sun. Beside him, he was aware of Lori moving into a more comfortable position and attempting to stifle a groan as the movement obviously caused her some discomfort.

"You ok?" he asked, without opening his eyes.

"Yes," she lied. "Just a bit awkward to get comfortable. I'm fine now."

They lay on the sand lazily chatting about this and that, music, film and books, discovering more that they had in common with each other. After a while Lori grew too sore to continue lying on the sand and, with some help from Jake, she moved up to sit in one of the chairs. He came and sat beside her in the other canvas chair, stretching his long legs out in front of him.

"I should've brought my guitar down," he said, digging into the soft sand with his toes.

"Relax," said Lori, reaching over to take his hand. "Tell me the story of this body art."

"It's a work in progress. And a bit of an addiction, I guess."

"Tell me about them. I'm curious," she encouraged. "Start with the sword on your back."

"Good place to start," he nodded, with a smile. "It was the first one when I was about eighteen or nineteen. Hurt like Hell for what felt like forever. I got the dragon on my shoulder as a twenty first birthday gift from my girlfriend at the time. The Grim Reaper came along a couple of years later. I gave the guy some guitar lessons to pay for it. The two tribal ones down my sides were an act of rebellion at turning thirty. Now they hurt!"

"And the two on your calves?" asked Lori.

"The dagger was with some money I made giving guitar lessons a couple of years ago. The Maori face came along the same way about the same time."

"So what's next?" asked Lori curiously.

"Come with me next weekend and see for yourself," he invited with a cheeky grin. "It won't be anything major so it won't take long."

"Ok," she agreed. "I'll watch you squirm."

Jake laughed and agreed he probably would flinch a bit. He passed her one of the beers and they sat gazing out into the ocean. The surf had calmed down and the breakers had been replaced with small gentle waves that meandered their way ashore.

"Come on," coaxed Jake, encouraging Lori to her feet. "Time to dip a toe in the ocean."

"I'm not sure," began Lori hesitantly.

"Trust me," said Jake, putting his arm around her waist. "I won't let you get hurt."

Keeping his arm around her waist, he led her into the shallows then took her hands. It took a few minutes, and for a few small waves to go by, for her confidence to grow. Lori couldn't deny that the water felt good. Gradually, Jake led her out a little further until the water was just above her knees. He could see the fear in her eyes but was also picking up on her inner determination to overcome it. The waves were growing a bit stronger as the result of the wake from a boat that had gone past further off shore. Out of the corner of his eye, Jake saw a much bigger wave coming towards them. Instinctively he scooped Lori up into his arms and turned his back to the oncoming wave. She let out a cry as the wave broke over Jake's back, drenching them both.

"Lori," gasped Jake, spitting out salt water. "Are you ok?"

"Yes," she replied, her voice wavering. "Just wet."

He carefully carried her back up the beach and laid her down on the towels. Her sodden sarong had ridden up round her waist. Before she could pull it down, Lori saw Jake catch his first glimpse of the scars on her thigh.

"Not as pretty as your body art," she said quietly.

Jake knelt beside her and gently traced his finger over the thick purple scar that ran the length of her thigh. She flinched at his touch. Slowly he bent forward and delivered light feathery kisses along the length of the scar. He kissed each of the smaller knotted scars in turn, then kissed her softly on the cheek. There were tears in her eyes as he moved closer and kissed her tenderly on the lips, tasting the salt from the ocean.

"They are a part of what makes you you," he whispered gently. "And nothing to be ashamed of."

"They're ugly."

"Nothing about you is ugly," he argued, kissing her again. "You are the most beautiful person I've ever met."

"Now that's cheesy," she giggled, before kissing him back.

"Cheesy but true."

"You're not so bad yourself," said Lori, with a hint of mischief.

"Such flattery," laughed Jake. "Now are you sure you're ok?"

"Wet but fine," assured Lori, covering her thighs with the damp sarong. "Why don't you go for another swim while I dry off in the sun, then we can head home?"

"Deal," grinned Jake. "I won't be long."

Lori propped herself up on her elbows as she watched him lope down the beach and dive back into the water. Subconsciously, she reached to finger the scars then sighed. It was almost a relief that Jake had seen them. Another barrier removed from between them; another step on her way to the acceptance of things. She watched him swim another ragged circle out in the ocean and smiled. There was something special about Jake. As she watched him swim ashore, Lori realised she had fallen in love with him and she suspected he felt the same way.

Jake ran up the beach to re-join her, sending a spray of sand over her as he dropped down onto the towel beside her.

"Do you have a BBQ?" he asked randomly. "And some coals?"

"Yes," she replied. "I think there's some coals in the storage box."

"And burgers?"

"Mm, not so sure about that bit."

"I fancy a BBQ," declared Jake. "You?"

"Fine by me, but you might need to run out to the Giant for some burgers and rolls."

As the sun set a few short hours later, Jake stood over the BBQ grill cooking burgers and a couple of pieces of chicken. He took a swig out of his beer bottle and glanced over at Lori. She had stretched out on the lounger and had dozed off in the last rays of sunlight. While he had been out at the food store, she had showered and changed into a plain deep red maxi dress. The folds of the material were now draped over her, her blonde hair was spread out around her face and to him she looked like a sleeping Disney princess. Once the food was ready, he went over and knelt beside her, kissing her gently on the forehead. As she stirred, he kissed her full on the lips, allowing his tongue to gently caress her lower lip.

"Time to wake up, sleeping beauty," he said with a warm smile. "Dinner's ready."

With a yawn, she sat up and sleepily made her way over to the table. As she sat down, Lori commented that the sea air had worn her out.

"I guess you've had a pretty full on weekend," said Jake, passing her a burger.

"True," she admitted. "It's been a while since I've had a "normal" weekend. I've loved every minute of it."

Grinning, as he bit into his burger, Jake said, "So let's plan the next one."

"Well, you said about the tattoo thing," began Lori. "When's that booked for?"

"About five on Saturday," he replied. "I've got an early shift on Saturday and finish at four. Then a late on Sunday starting at four."

"No gigs?"

He thought for a moment, then said, "Shit. Yes. A wedding in Dewey Beach on Friday night."

"What about during the week?" she asked between bites. "Do you have a day off this week?"

Jake shook his head, "Because I was off this weekend, I'm in twelve hours Monday and Tuesday then half shifts Wednesday and Thursday. Both lates. Punishment I guess."

"When do you get to rehearse for the wedding gig?"

"I don't," he muttered, with almost a growl.

"Oh, ok," she said, focussing on her burger. "I guess this is it until Saturday, then unless you want to run over for breakfast Wednesday and Thursday. I've got therapy on Wednesday at ten."

He shrugged, "Let's play it by ear if that's ok?"

"Its fine," she assured him. "I've got a few things to set up work wise this week too. I've decided to resurrect Mz Hyde officially. I put the feelers out last week for some commissions and there may be a couple of projects I could be tempted by."

"I loved the look on Rich's face at lunch when he realised," laughed Jake, his mood suddenly lightening. "Priceless."

"It was funny," she agreed with a giggle.

When their meal was over and the BBQ coals had crumbled to ash, they moved indoors to the sun room. It was growing late and, much as he wanted to stay, Jake said he really had to make a move. Before he left, Lori made him promise to drop by on Wednesday. He relented but said it would need to be early. Gently he kissed her on both cheeks, then the forehead and promised to call her. He slipped out through the patio doors and was gone into the darkness. A few moments later, she heard the engine of his truck give its throaty growl and he was gone.

On the drive back into town, Jake twice nearly stopped and turned back. The thought of not seeing Lori for three days was eating at him. She was such a beautiful, fragile person in so many ways, but then the persona of Mz Hyde showed a core of steely determination. Those scars had spoken volumes to him of what she must have been through. By the time he parked outside his apartment, he had lyrics and a new melody swimming round in his head. All the gear from Surfside was still in the back of the truck and it took him three trips up and down to the apartment to move it all. The lyrics and melody were growing louder in his head, positively screaming to be let out. A glance at his phone told him it was after eleven. Sleep could wait a couple of hours. He grabbed his acoustic guitar and his notebook and sat working out the song. Both lyrics and music flowed effortlessly from his mind into the guitar. He scrawled the lyrics onto the first blank page in his battered notebook, then added a title – "Lady Butterfly." He played and sang it all through another few times making minor tweaks and lyric changes before he was satisfied. Just before three thirty he played it through a final time, recording it onto his phone. Content with the result, he laid down his guitar and crawled off to bed.

All day Monday and Tuesday, Lori was restless and fidgety. She had finished setting up her workspace next to the lounge and accepted two small projects with lengthy deadline dates. Her drawing board was covered in doodles and half started ideas, but she couldn't settle on one theme. The first project was for an album cover for an established rock band based on the west coast. She had been sent some video footage of the band rehearsing the album tracks to help her get a feel for the material she was to illustrate. It was a band she had worked for before when she designed their logo. The other project was a different venture, a new direction for her, and involved designing the dust jacket for a fantasy novel. Again, she had been given a synopsis of the book and the first couple of chapters. The theme was obvious – swords and dragons and a princess, but she was trying to see beyond that.

Before she finished for the evening on Tuesday, Mary came through to the study with Lori's cell phone and a glass of wine. She sat both down on the desk and said simply, "Call him. I'll see you in the morning," then left. Taking a sip of wine, Lori smiled to herself. Maybe Mary was right and that she wasn't focussed because she was moping about like a lovesick teenager. Instead of calling, she sent Jake a text message. "J breakfast on the sun deck 7.30 T x" then turned back to her drawing board. A few moments later her phone chirped like a cricket – "Make it 7 and you've got a deal J x"

"Deal." She messaged back before turning her attention back to her work.

As she sipped her wine, she continued to doodle and play with some ideas. Gradually a theme began to emerge and she focussed on the task in hand. The drawing for the book cover took shape as she created depths to the folds of material. In front of her, she had a clear image of the folds of the princess' velvet dress. In the dark shadow folds, she brought themes from the story to life in miniature. Totally engrossed, her wine forgotten, Lori worked away, painstakingly teasing life onto the piece of paper in front of her. As the light grew dimmer, she reached over and switched on the desk lamp. The shadows it cast over the drawing added to the atmosphere allowing her to create a little dark menace to an otherwise pretty, delicate piece. By midnight, she had cramp in her hand, but was satisfied with what she had produced so far. Her glass of wine still sat on the desk half full.

When the alarm rang out wakening her next morning, Lori could hear rain pounding down outside. Definitely not a morning for breakfast on the deck. *C'est la vie,* she thought as she wandered through the sun room. She unlocked the patio doors and slid one open slightly, then went through to the kitchen to start breakfast. Trying to move about the kitchen to set the table and use her canes was frustratingly impossible. Swearing under her breath, she leaned one cane against the table and tried to continue using just one. Eventually she had the table set and the coffee pot on. She had just sat down at the table, with a glass of juice, when she heard the squeal of the patio door opening.

"Morning!" called Jake from the sun room.

"In the kitchen," she called back.

His wet shoes squeaked on the wooden floors as he made his way through the house to join her. When he walked into the kitchen, she saw instantly that he was drenched. His hair was dripping and his grey T-shirt was stuck to his chest.

"Wet out?" she teased tossing him a towel.

"Slightly," admitted Jake as he dried himself off. "I don't mind running in the rain. It's good for cleansing the soul."

"Does your soul need that much cleansing?"

"You'd be surprised," he muttered, taking a seat. "No Mary?"

"She won't get here till after eight. I hope bagels and coffee will do," said Lori, passing him a glass of juice that she had already poured for him. "If you want bacon, I'm afraid you'll have to cook it yourself."

"You ok?" he asked, sounding concerned.

"I'm fine," she replied. "Morning's aren't great if I'm honest. Takes me a while to get moving."

"Bagels are good," he said, before draining his juice glass. "I saw you'd been working. Sorry, I peeked on my way through."

Lori scowled at him disapprovingly, then shrugged, "It's a start. I made some progress last night. How's your week been?"

"Shit," he declared bluntly. "I'm waiting for a call from Rich about teaching some classes till summer break. If he gets me into school, I'm quitting the pizza place."

"I wish I could help," she said softly.

Jake reached over to lift a bagel from the basket in the centre of the table. "Maybe you can."

"How?" asked Lori, suddenly curious.

"Rich's been raving about you to anyone who'll listen. He's planning to ask if you'll talk to some of the students at the school. Seniors, I think."

He got up to fetch them both a coffee. "If you don't want to do it, that's ok. No one's going to be offended, but those kids will be disappointed."

"Talk to them about what?"

"Art. You. Getting started," said Jake, pouring the hot liquid into the two mugs Lori had left out on the counter top. "He was on the phone last night while I was on a break. He might drop by after school."

"I'll think about it," conceded Lori quietly. "Not really my thing."

"Don't let him pressure you," warned Jake, adding half and half to his coffee. "Rich can easily get carried away with an idea."

"I won't," said Lori, as she buttered her cinnamon bagel. "So is anything else new? Any feedback from the weekend?"

Jake went on to explain, between mouthfuls of bagel and coffee, that the radio station, who had sponsored the Surfside event, wanted them to play three more events over the summer. All three would be paying gigs and they could have their own merchandise stand. Already they had pulled resources and committed to another run of their CD plus a fresh batch of T-shirts. Once he was talking about the band, the dark cloud that had hung over him all week lifted. His hazel eyes gained an extra twinkle as he told her about the new song he had worked on, after he had left her on Sunday. They exchanged email addresses and Jake promised to mail her a copy of the music file. Both of them were on their second coffee when Mary arrived. She entered through the back door, muttering and shaking water off her umbrella.

"Good morning, one and all," she declared brightly.

"Hi," said Jake, still wary of the matriarchal older woman.

"Where's your truck?" she asked, as she slipped off her rain jacket.

"I ran along the beach," explained Jake. "The rain doesn't bother me."

"Mad boy," she muttered, as she went through to start tidying up the sun room.

Both of them laughed, then went back to their breakfast. All too soon it was time for Jake to leave. Lori walked him through to the sun room. It looked as though the sky was growing lighter and that the rain was easing off a bit but it was still wet out.

"I'll ask Mary to run you back into town," offered Lori.

Jake shook his head, "I'll be fine. I'll walk back along the shore."

"You sure?"

He nodded, then wrapped his arms around her slender waist. Gently he held her close for a moment or two.

"I need to ask you a favour," he began. "Can you make your own way into town to meet me on Saturday?"

"Sure," she agreed. "What time and where?"

"Meet me outside of work about four thirty," he suggested.

"OK. I'll be there."

With a gentle kiss, he took his leave and jogged across the deck into the rainy morning. Suddenly Saturday afternoon felt like a lifetime away to both of them.

By mid –afternoon, the rain had cleared, the clouds had burnt off and the sun was shining. At the first glimpse of the cloudless sky, Lori decamped from her study out onto the deck for some air. She brought her sketch pad and her iPod, hoping that by listening to the music of the band, she was to design for, she might get a flash of inspiration. Earlier, she had emailed photos of her rough draft for the dust jacket off for approval. She had forwarded them on with a degree of nerves – the first official design work that she had completed for almost two years.

The cushions for all the chairs were still damp after the rain. Having spread them along the railings to dry in the sun, she went back into the sunroom for the blanket. Quickly she folded it up as a makeshift cushion and settled herself at the table. Before she became too engrossed, Mary brought her out a juice, then asked if she could finish for the day. The housekeeper had been quiet all day and now explained that her sister was ill.

"Do you need a few days off?" asked Lori, seeing Mary's concern and worry in her eyes.

Mary shook her head, "A few shorter days might help. Can I start at ten and finish at three for the rest of the week till I see how she is?"

"Of course," agreed Lori warmly.

"Thank you, Lori," said the older woman, giving her a brief hug. "I'll be honest. I'm worried about her."

"I'm sure she'll be fine with you looking after her. Now go," said Lori, with what she hoped was a reassuring smile.

"I'll see you in the morning."

"Go!" chastised Lori smiling.

As she drank her juice, Lori played with a few Celtic knot designs, then, almost subconsciously, began to work on a small butterfly design. The delicacy of it absorbed her as she drew in the detail of its gossamer wings, then added some swirls to the wing tips. Carefully, she added in some colour – blues and a tiny hint of yellow. When it was done, she surveyed the design and smiled. An innocent but pretty bit of fun. Still smiling, she turned the page and began to gather her thoughts again for the album artwork. A loose screw lying on the sundeck caught her eye and gave her the flash of inspiration she had been searching for. Visions of nuts and bolts; cogs and gears filled her head and she began to formulate a plan.

The crunch of car tyres out the front distracted her some time later. She paused and listened as she heard the engine stop, then the door slam. Suddenly she remembered that Jake had said Rich might drop by.

"Lori!" called a male voice from the side of the house. It was Rich.

"Out back!" she called back. "Come on round."

A few moments later, the tousled dark hair of the band's guitarist appeared round the side of the house. He had come straight from school and was wearing dark chinos and a white shirt, open at the neck. He was carrying a large folder.

"Hi," he said, removing his sunglasses. "I hope you don't mind me dropping by."

"Not at all," said Lori, closing her sketch book. "Can I get you

Coral McCallum

a coffee or a beer?"

"Any soda?" asked Rich, setting the folder down on the table.

"Sure, it's diet. Is that ok?" asked Lori, getting up.

"As long as it's cold and wet."

"Take a seat. I'll be back shortly."

"Need a hand?" he offered.

"No. I'm good, thanks."

Lori returned a few minutes later with two bottles of diet coke and a bag of pretzels. As she sat back down, she winced – a sharp stab of protest from her thigh, suggesting that one cane wasn't enough. If Rich noticed, he politely ignored her discomfort.

"How was school?"

"Good actually," he said. "Most of the kids are keen so that helps."

"Pity you couldn't get a post for Jake," commented Lori. "He was over earlier. He's so pissed off at the pizza place."

"I know and it's a total waste of his talents," agreed Rich. "Trust me, I'm working on it. Even if I can get him two or three days a week it would pay more. Hopefully I'll get confirmation this week from the principal."

"Fingers crossed," said Lori then, deciding to tease him a little, asked, "Have you framed that napkin art work yet?"

He laughed, then confessed he had actually bought a frame for it. Lori blushed at the thought of her music note doodles on a Hooters napkin being framed.

"I had no idea you were Mz Hyde," Rich confessed. "Turns out I was the last to know."

"It's not something I broadcast," explained Lori. "It was a side of me I had retired for a while, but she's back in business now."

"I guess it's an easy thing to work on while you recover from your accident," Rich mused, taking a handful of pretzels.

"I hope so," she said quietly. "Jake said you wanted to ask me a favour."

All of a sudden Rich seemed shy and embarrassed. He started, then stopped what he was planning to say, stumbling over his words. Lori stared at him, then stated calmly, "You want me to talk to the kids at the school."

"Yes," he sighed, relieved that she had cut to the chase. "The school has a small senior class who are keen to pursue careers in

96

graphic art and design. We've had a few guest tutors in over the semester and I was hoping you could spare a couple of afternoons to work with them."

"I have no experience of teaching," she said, "But, if it helps you out, I'll give it a go. What kind of things have your guests done with them?"

"Glad you asked," he said, reaching for the folder he had brought.

Rich talked animatedly about the examples he had brought of the art students' work. Some of it was quite impressive and showed originality. Lori browsed through the test pieces for a few minutes, then closed over the folder.

"Would it be possible to talk to the art teacher first?"

Of course. You'll love Linsey. She's great with the kids. She'd be honoured to talk with you," he gushed excitedly.

Lori giggled and he paused.

"And you happen to like this Linsey?" she teased.

"That obvious?"

Lori nodded.

"Sorry," apologised Rich, fidgeting with the leather cord bracelet he wore.

"Ok," began Lori. "Give her my number. I'll talk to her and we can take it from there. I might even put in a good word for you."

"Thanks," he said, with genuine relief.

Lori scribbled her phone number on a piece of scrap paper that Rich passed to her then, as an after- thought, added her email address.

Downing the last of his soda, he rose to leave, "Thanks again, Lori. I appreciate it."

"Happy to help," she said genuinely.

"Great. I'd better head," he said. "I've got test papers to mark. Really rock 'n' roll."

"Well, if it pays the bills," she said with a sigh. "I've got work to finish off too."

"Anything exciting?"

"Some album artwork for a band from Sacramento," she replied cryptically. "Sorry. Can't name names."

"The ever discrete Mz Hyde," teased Rich. "Take care, Lori.

Get Jake to bring you along to rehearsal sometime."

"Perhaps," she agreed, reaching for her sketch pad. "Have fun grading those papers."

After Rich left, she worked on for a couple of hours pulling together an intricate design of bolts and cogs. It took on an almost natural 3D form and that gave her inspiration to draw some more of it from a different perspective to enhance the 3D effect. She was having fun with the piece and was reluctant to stop for the evening, however, it had grown chilly now that the sun was setting. When she retired indoors, she put the Silver Lake album on via her iPod filling the house with loud music while she prepared her dinner. Having eaten her salad alone with another bottle of soda, Lori decided to retire to bed for the evening with a book.

The boardwalk was crowded on Saturday afternoon as she made her way along towards the pizza parlour. Lori had asked the cab driver to drop her off one block south of the main avenue so she could stretch her legs a little before she met up with Jake, plus she was fifteen minutes early. It was a damp, hazy day but that hadn't deterred folk from visiting town for the weekend. Most of the benches were occupied and she couldn't find a spot where she had agreed to meet Jake. Eventually she found an empty bench near the bandstand. Quickly, she rummaged in her bag for her phone and sent him a text message to say where she was. As a last minute thought she'd stuffed her small sketch book into the bag too. She was still flicking through it, reflecting on the draft designs for the album piece, when Jake flopped down on the bench beside her.

"Last shift over!" he sighed, with a huge grin.

"Did Rich get the go ahead?" she asked excitedly, almost dropping her book.

"Called last night," said Jake, putting his arm around her shoulders. "Three days a week till summer break, then full time from September with a bit of luck."

"Brilliant news," she declared, kissing him on the cheek. "Congratulations."

He pulled her into his embrace and kissed her full on the lips, his tongue gently, teasingly caressing hers.

"No more fucking pizza," he sighed, as he moved away from her. "No more late shifts."

Lori laughed and ruffled his long hair. "You'll need to cut this if you're going to be Mr Power, music teacher."

"No way!" he exclaimed, knocking the sketchpad off her lap. "The hair stays."

He bent down to retrieve the fallen book. It had landed open at the butterfly design.

"That's pretty," he observed, handing the book back to her. "Would make a nice tattoo."

"Thanks. I was just doodling the other day," she replied, putting the sketchpad back into her hobo bag. "I hadn't thought of it as a tattoo design."

"Speaking of body art, we'd better make a move. Danny will be waiting. Are you ok to walk a few blocks?" he asked, as he helped her to her feet.

Lori nodded and they set off up the main street. As they walked away from the boardwalk it grew quieter and less crowded. The tattoo parlour was a couple of blocks up from Hooters restaurant. A wind chime jangled as Jake pushed the door open and a surprisingly clinical smell hit them. Inside the shop there were three chairs, resembling vintage dentist chairs, a long low bench seat running along one wall and two private cubicles screened off at the end.

"Jake?" called a hearty voice from the back room of the shop.

"Hi, Dan," called back Jake. "I've brought a friend to watch. Is that ok?"

"Sure," said a tiny, bald man emerging from the rear of the shop. He was wearing jeans and a pristine white vest T-shirt. Almost every visible piece of skin on his arms was covered with designs.

"Danny, meet Lori," introduced Jake. "Lori, this is Danny, ink artist extraordinaire."

"Pleased to meet you, princess," said Danny, bowing theatrically. "Been in the wars I see."

"Pleasure," said Lori, suddenly nervous of this strange diminutive tattooed man. She turned to Jake, "So now will you tell me what you're having done?"

"Not yet," teased Jake, removing his denim jacket. "Dan, did you get the design onto the transfer ok? I don't want this smudged. It has to be crisp lines."

"Yes, boss," said Danny, stretching on a pair of dark coloured surgical gloves. "Choose your throne, if you please."

Jake settled himself in the middle chair, while Lori sat on the bench opposite. This was a whole new experience for her and she watched with childlike curiosity as Danny swabbed then shaved Jake's inner right forearm. The ink artist explained to her that the skin had to be prepared as though he were about to perform surgery. Next he aligned the design transfer, checked with Jake if he was happy with the position then they debated for a few minutes before finally agreeing the exact angle. Swiftly and skilfully, he drew on the design with a fine marker pen. In complete fascination, Lori watched him draw out the design, then focus on the lettering that went underneath. When he was finished the hand drawn outline she saw it was a line of music with the words "Stronger Within" written in script underneath.

"Happy?" Danny asked Jake. "Speak now or forever hold your peace."

"Keep it as crisp as that and I'm happy," said Jake, with a wink over at Lori. "You're not squeamish are you, li'l lady?"

Lori laughed. "After all I've been through, are you kidding?"

"Just checking," he replied, with a warm smile. "Come over here and watch if you like."

"I'm fine here," she assured him. "I can see just fine. It's fascinating."

Danny had a tray laid beside him with the paraphernalia required to complete the tattoo and had loaded up the ink cartridges. Picking up the hand held tattoo gun, he checked Jake was ok and happy to proceed one final time. Jake nodded and relaxed back in the chair with his eyes closed. The ink artist worked accurately and carefully, pausing to steady his hand every few minutes. He worked in complete silence, his entire focus on Jake's forearm. Both men appeared oblivious to Lori's presence. Realising this she brought out her sketch book and began a sketch of Jake as he reclined on the "throne". She rarely drew people and had never done portraits professionally but it didn't hurt to practice for pleasure now and again. Silence reigned over the tattoo parlour, apart from the buzz of the machine. Throughout the entire procedure, Jake never flinched and lay back with his eyes closed looking the ultimate picture of calm. Eventually Danny was happy with his work. He turned off the gun and laid it on the tray beside him. Before speaking to Jake, he removed the used needle disposing of it into the yellow sharps bin beside him. Carefully, he cleaned up the fresh tattoo and wiped Jake's arm down with antiseptic.

"Want to inspect it?" he asked, poking Jake in the ribs.

"Sure," said Jake sitting up. He gave the fresh tattoo the once over, rotating his wrist to ensure the lines stayed straight and nodded in silent approval.

"Want a closer look, li'l lady?" he asked Lori.

She moved over to inspect Danny's work and was impressed with the accuracy and sharpness of the design. Small drops of blood were beginning to ooze through the fresh ink. Just as she was about to comment on this, Danny applied a warm, damp towel over the area.

"Ok, Jake, are we photographing this one for my art gallery?" he asked hopefully.

"No," replied Jake, fishing his phone out of his pocket. "Lori, can you take a photo of it for me please?"

He passed her his phone and, when Danny removed the towel, she took a few quick shots of the freshly tattooed design then passed the phone back to Jake.

"Can I take a photo with my phone?" she asked.

"No," said Jake bluntly, much to her surprise. "Maybe later."

Swiftly Danny covered the fresh tattoo with a white dressing and taped it in place. "OK, Jake," he said, passing him a folder with the bill and aftercare instructions. "You know the drill."

Jake nodded, "I should do by now."

He drew a wad of notes out of his back pocket and handed them over. Danny pocketed the cash without counting it.

"Lori," began Jake, carefully putting his jacket back on over his arm. "Show Dan your butterfly design."

Obligingly, she opened the sketch book at the picture of the delicate blue butterfly. Danny nodded approvingly, "That would work well. Love the lines of it. Did you design it?"

"Guilty as charged," said Lori, slipping the book back into her bag.

"Well, I'll tattoo that for you anytime, princess," he offered. "Would look good on an ankle or the inside of your wrist."

"I'll think about it," said Lori, adjusting her grip on her canes.

"Right, let's go," declared Jake, opening the door for her. "Till next time, Dan."

"Next time, Jake,"

The street outside was quiet when they emerged from the tattoo parlour. Both of them agreed they were hungry, so Jake guided them towards the nearest restaurant.

"Seafood ok?" he asked.

"Perfect," agreed Lori. "And will you explain the tattoo over dinner?"

"Maybe," he teased. "Stings like hell right now."

"I'll bet," she said softly. "I'm not sure I could do that."

"Your butterfly would look good inside your wrist," he commented. "But it has to be your choice. Ink isn't for everyone."

"I think you've enough for both of us and then some," she declared, as he held the restaurant door open for her.

"For now, yes," he agreed, with a mischievous wink.

They had to wait for a table, but were finally seated at a small table near the rear of the restaurant. A group of teenagers were at the table in the centre and they kept glancing over at Jake and Lori. The attention made him uneasy, but he conceded that it went with the Silver Lake territory. It made him wonder if he could handle fame and fortune if the band ever made it. Sometimes he doubted it; sometimes he craved it, especially when he was on stage. Before their meal arrived, Lori prompted him for an explanation about his choice of new artwork. Without looking up, he said simply, "I wrote the music for you. I played it for you first. It just felt right to wear it and see it every time I play."

"I'm flattered," she replied, totally lost for something more appropriate to say.

"Each of my tattoos tells a part of my life story. That one is for this chapter," he added quietly. "Call me a romantic fool if you like."

"No, I get it," she said softly. "It's one of the most extreme displays of affection I've seen though. I'm honoured."

Jake reached across the table and took both of her hands in his, "I've fallen in love with you, li'l lady."

"Likewise," confessed Lori, then added, "And it scares me a bit."

"Likewise," he admitted, with a smile. "But it's a good kind of scared."

It was getting late by the time they had paid the bill. Without a word of complaint, Lori let Jake call a cab to get them back to the house. As they waited for the cab to arrive the table of teenagers came past them. One of them, a long haired boy, paused and asked, "Are you that guy from Silver Lake?"

"Guilty," said Jake, a little more bluntly than he intended. "You were right down the front at Surfside weren't you?"

"Sure was," said the boy obviously impressed that Jake recognised him. "You guys are awesome, man!"

"Why, thank you," said Jake, noticing the cab pulling up beside them.

The teenager was rummaging in his pocket and pulled out the receipt from their meal, "Can you sign this for me?"

Lori passed him a pen from her bag and he scrawled his autograph across the check. "Need to go. Take care."

"Thanks," said the young fan, staring at the autograph.

As she climbed into the cab, Lori started to giggle. Jake clambered in beside her, gave the driver the address then sat muttering about autograph hunters. The more he muttered, the more Lori giggled.

"Christ, we were only out for dinner. I wasn't even playing."

"Chill," she said. "It goes with the territory. You'll need to get used to it, if the band ever really takes off. You need kids like that to get you where you want to be."

"Harrumph," Jake mumbled, hating to admit she was right.

"Plus," added Lori. "I can sense a sudden interest in music amongst teenage girls on the horizon when you start at the high school. Are you ready for that?"

"I guess," he relented, with a long sigh. "Don't you ever get that kind of attention?"

"Occasionally," she answered. "When I've been at events in New York or the like. You just need to paint on that Disney smile and go with the flow. Even though inside you are screaming to be left alone."

Jake laughed, "That about sums it up."

Once back at the beach house, they settled on the couch in the sun room to watch a movie. It was one they had both seen before which was just as well because they had missed the first twenty minutes. Lori had just returned from the kitchen with a bowl of popcorn for them to share when Jake's cell phone rang. The rattle of "Sweet Home Alabama" was cut short as he answered the call, "Grey, what's up?"

The colour drained from Jake's face as he listened to his friend. Lori watched with concern, praying that nothing was wrong.

"Bring her here, Grey," said Jake. "I'm at Lori's and I've not got wheels." Quickly he gave out Lori's address.

He glanced over at Lori and shook his head slowly, indicating that something was wrong, "See you in a few minutes. I'll wait out front and watch for you."

Stuffing the phone back in his pocket, he turned to Lori, "Sandy's been in an accident at a bar in Dewey Beach. The police have just called Grey. Sounds serious. He needs me to watch Becky for a few hours, I couldn't say no."

"Of course not!" exclaimed Lori. "What was Sandy doing over at Dewey Beach?"

"Lord knows" sighed Jake, with a look of disgust. "She's a drinker. You saw that for yourself. If it wasn't for Becky, Grey would have bailed out a long time ago."

"Hope she's ok," said Lori quietly. "For his sake."

"We'll find out soon enough."

A few minutes later, she heard the crunch of tyres outside. Jake had gone out to sit on the porch to watch for his friend. When she heard Grey's truck, Lori went out to see what was going on. She stayed on the porch while Jake lifted a sleepy Becky out of the passenger side, exchanged a few words with Grey then slammed the door shut. Snuggling Becky into his shoulder, Jake watched as his friend sped off into the dark, heading for the emergency room. The little girl was wearing her pjs and was clutching a small, well-worn rag doll.

"Come on, princess," said Jake quietly to her. "Lori's made some popcorn. Want some?"

"I want my daddy," she said with a sob.

"He'll be back real soon," promised Jake, hugging her tight.

Once back in the sun room, none of them could concentrate on the film. The popcorn lay untouched. The little girl had cried for a few minutes, then settled on Jake's knee. When Lori looked over, she was clutching the doll tightly under her arm and fingering Jake's long hair. Her other thumb was firmly in her mouth. Soon Becky was fast asleep, her tousled head resting on Jake's chest.

"What did Grey say?" asked Lori, once she was sure the little girl was sound asleep.

"Not much. Seems like Sandy started a fight in a bar. Someone's pulled a knife or maybe a broken bottle. All he knows is that she's been stabbed," he replied, keeping his voice quiet.

"He said he'd call when he knows more."

"Doesn't sound good," said Lori sadly. "Do you want to wrap Becky in the blanket on the other couch? She looks as though she's out for the night."

"Please," agreed Jake with a smile. "She's a dead weight on my arm and it's starting to hurt."

Soon the little girl was snuggled up in the soft fleecy blanket on the smaller couch and both of them were cuddled up together on the other one, anxiously waiting for Jake's phone to ring. Neither of them knew what to say so they sat in silence, the TV still playing in the background. At some point, Lori dozed off leaning against Jake's shoulder. He sat staring at the TV without really seeing it, her head resting on his shoulder. Shortly after one in the morning his phone finally rang. Jake answered it after one ring before it would waken Becky. As soon as he moved, Lori stirred and sat up.

"Grey?" he said, getting up and walking through towards the kitchen.

Lori watched him go then decided to follow him. She could hear him on the phone as she limped through the dining room, but couldn't make out what he was saying. As she entered the kitchen, Lori heard him say, "Shit, I'm so sorry, buddy. I'll wait here till you're done."

Silence for a moment as he listened, then he replied, "She's asleep. She'll be fine. We've got her."

Finally, he said, "We'll see you when you arrive. Drive safe."

Ending the call, Jake turned to Lori, took her into his arms and just held her tight. She looked up into his eyes and saw nothing but sadness.

"She never made it," he whispered hoarsely. "He's lost her."

"No!" cried Lori softly in total shock at what she'd heard. "How?"

"He's a mess," began Jake sadly. "Something about it being a broken bottle. It caught an artery. Before the paramedics could stop the blood loss she went into cardiac arrest. She was gone by the time he got there."

"What now?"

"He's still with the police but said he should be here in about an hour. We've not to tell Becky if she wakes up. He needs to tell her himself."

"Poor little mite," said Lori, thinking of the pretty, little girl sleeping innocently in the sun room. "What a mess."

"Sure is," muttered Jake. "Do you mind if I make some coffee?"

"I'll make it," said Lori, lifting the jug to fill the machine.

"I'm going out front for some air," murmured Jake. "I just need a minute."

"On you go. I'll call you if Becky wakes up."

Death was a cruel visitor and seldom a welcome one, thought Lori as she made the pot of coffee. She could hear Jake pacing up and down in the driveway, his feet crunching on the gravel, but guessed he needed time on his own. Although she had only met Grey's wife once, her heart went out to him and especially to Becky. Quietly she went through to check on the little girl. She was still curled up on the couch, her thumb firmly in her mouth. Satisfied, she was ok, Lori returned to the kitchen, lost in her own thoughts. She was sitting at the table with her coffee when Jake came back in. He poured himself a mug, then sat across from her in silence.

"You ok?" she asked softly.

"Yeah, I'm fine," he said, with a sigh. "It's just so surreal. I only saw her the other day. She brought Becky in for a slice of pizza. I just wish Grey would get here. It's him I'm worrying about."

"He'll be here soon. I checked on Becky. She's still sound asleep," reassured Lori. "What do you think will happen now?"

"I don't know," admitted Jake. "Sandy wasn't from here. Don't know what family she has. She was from out west. Grey's local. His mom lives in Lewes and he has a sister in Chicago."

It was almost three in the morning when they finally heard Grey's truck pull up outside. Jake flew out of the house to greet him while Lori fetched another mug from the cupboard and topped up the coffee pot. A few minutes later, the two friends came back into the house. She could see from his eyes that Grey had been crying. Gently she hugged him and whispered, "I'm so sorry."

"Thanks, Lori," he said, emotion catching in his voice. "I'm sorry to land all of this on you."

"Nonsense," she replied. "Can I get you a coffee or something stronger?"

"Coffee would be good," he sighed, taking a seat at the table. "Where's Becky?"

"Asleep in the sun room," said Jake, sitting beside his friend. "She's fine. Let her sleep."

"What am I going to tell her?" said Grey with a sob. "How do I tell her that her mommy isn't coming back?"

"You'll find the right words," reassured Lori, putting a hand on his shoulder.

"I just don't know what to say to her."

"Lori's right," said Jake. "You'll say all the right things when you have to."

"Lord, I hope so," sighed Grey, wiping a tear from his cheek.

All three of them sat and chatted around the kitchen table. Grey explained to them all he knew about what had happened. He was thankful that the police weren't pursuing anything. Sandy had started the fight and had smashed the neck off the beer bottle. In the struggle, she had slashed another woman across the cheek. When the woman pushed her away, she had fallen and landed on the broken bottle in her hand. It was sheer bad luck that she had cut herself so badly, but it appeared to have been a massive heart attack that had killed her a short while later. The paramedics had worked on her, but there was nothing they could do and she had died in the ambulance before they reached the hospital. The other woman was in the emergency room receiving treatment for her slash wound. When he was all talked out, Grey asked if he could stretch out in the sun room until Becky woke up. Lori fetched him a blanket from the hall cupboard and a pillow from the spare room. With his head lowered and shoulders hunched over, he retreated to the sun room to be with his little girl. Jake and Lori were left alone in the kitchen.

"You should go and get some sleep, li'l lady," said Jake, noticing how pale she had become.

"So should you," she replied, reaching out to take his hand. "Come on. Let's go to bed for a couple of hours."

Sitting on the end of the bed in Lori's room Jake felt out of place and awkward. This was not how he had envisaged spending his first night with her. Once in the bedroom, Lori had excused herself and gone into the en suite bathroom. He could hear running water and the sounds of her brushing her teeth. A few minutes later she came back into the room. She was wearing her Silver Lake T-shirt and three quarter length pyjama bottoms. Propping her canes up in the corner, Lori limped across the room and climbed into bed. Jake still sat, fully clothed, at the end of the bed.

"You can sit there all night if you like," said Lori softly, "But you need some sleep too."

Standing up, he pulled off his T-shirt then slipped off his shoes and socks and finally his jeans. With all the awkwardness of a teenage virgin, he slipped into bed beside her.

"You sure about this?" he asked anxiously.

"About this? No. About sleep? Yes," she replied sleepily. "I've set the alarm for eight just in case."

"If you're sure," said Jake, settling down beside her.

As he lay on his back, staring up at the ceiling, Lori wriggled over and laid her head on his chest. "Hold me, please," she whispered. He wrapped his arm around her and held her until they both drifted off to sleep. Before the alarm went off a few short hours later Lori wakened. Beside her Jake had rolled over onto his side and was snoring gently. Reaching over, she cancelled the alarm, then glanced at the clock – it was just after seven. She thought she could hear the sound of the TV coming from the sun room. After a few minutes deliberation, she got up, collected her canes from the corner and went to investigate. When she entered the sun room, she saw that Grey was still asleep, but that Becky was sitting on the rug watching cartoons.

"Morning, princess," said Lori quietly as she sat on the couch. "You ok?"

Becky nodded, then whispered, "Daddy's still asleep. Shh."

"So is Uncle Jake," replied Lori. "He's snoring."

The little girl giggled.

"Why don't you switch off the TV before you waken your daddy?" suggested Lori, her voice barely above a whisper. "And we can go into the kitchen for some cereal."

"Ok," agreed Becky, pressing the red button on the remote. "Do you have any Lucky Charms?"

"Let's go and find out."

The girls went into the kitchen and Lori closed over both doors so that they wouldn't waken the sleeping males. There was a tiny portable TV on top of the refrigerator and Lori turned it on to the cartoon channel to help keep Becky amused. Her supply of cereal turned out not to include Lucky Charms but the little girl was happy to settle for a bowl of Cheerio's. While she sat munching contentedly on her cereal, Lori busied herself clearing out the coffee maker and setting it up for a fresh pot. As the coffee brewed, she rinsed out the three mugs from the night before, ready to use when the guys awoke. When Becky was finished her cereal, she politely took the bowl over to the sink, then asked if she could have a drink of milk. Lori rummaged in the cupboard and found a glass from her own childhood with Elmo and Cookie Monster on it. Quickly she rinsed it out, then filled it with milk for the little girl. She had just sat down with her own coffee and toast, when Jake came stumbling into the kitchen wearing only his boxer shorts.

"Morning, ladies," he said with a yawn.

"Morning," said Lori with a smile. "Coffee's hot. Grey's still asleep."

"Morning, Uncle Jake," said Becky, jumping down to give him a hug. "What happened to your arm?"

In all the commotion Jake hadn't yet removed the dressing from his new tattoo.

"Let me get my coffee and I'll show you," he replied, pouring himself a mug of coffee then adding some half and half and sugar.

He came over and sat between the girls, took a mouthful of coffee, then carefully peeled the tape off the dressing. Taking great care not to disturb the fresh tattoo, he lifted the dressing off. He had expected it to look angrier than it did. Resisting the temptation to touch it, he turned his arm round to show Becky.

"Those dots look like the music you showed me how to draw!" she squealed in delight. "Can I touch it?"

"Not till it's healed, honey," said Jake, admiring his new body art. "Do you like it?"

"Yes," said the little girl, nodding furiously. "It's not scary like the other pictures."

"It looks sore," observed Lori. "But it's nice."

"I'm scared of the bad man on his arm," stated Becky bluntly. "He's ugly."

Glancing at the image of the grim reaper, Lori couldn't disagree, no matter how well it was inked.

"It's not as ugly as that skull your dad has on his arm," muttered Jake, feigning being upset.

At that moment the other kitchen door opened and Grey stumbled in, rubbing sleep from his eyes.

"My skull tattoo is not ugly," he said, forcing a smile.

"Morning," said Lori. "There's coffee in the pot."

"Thanks," said Grey, helping himself. "I hope this young lady has been behaving herself."

"Of course I have," stated Becky indignantly. "Lori made me some Cheerio's and gave me milk in her special glass. Look, it's got Elmo on it."

"She's been fine," added Lori warmly. "Can I get you guys something to eat?"

"Not just now, thanks," said Grey. "Guess it's now or never."

He turned to Becky and asked her to come back through to the sun room so that he could talk to her about something important. Both Jake and Lori watched sadly as he led the happy little girl out of the kitchen. Not wanting to eavesdrop, Lori declared she was going for a shower. Jake came through to the bedroom a minute or two later to get dressed then returned to the kitchen. He could hear Becky crying then heard Grey begin to sob. It was breaking his heart to see his friend so distressed and grief stricken. Not knowing what to do or if he should go through to comfort them, he took the coward's way out and remained in the kitchen watching cartoons on the tiny TV screen. With her hair still damp, Lori came back into the kitchen about half an hour later to find Jake engrossed in Tom & Jerry. She hugged him from behind as he sat on the kitchen chair. Taking her hand, he guided her round and sat her on his knee. Gently he kissed her.

"You've been amazing with them. Thank you," he whispered

into her damp hair.

"I've not done anything," she disagreed. "At least not anything you couldn't have done on your own."

"Should I go through there?" asked Jake, completely out of his depth with the situation.

"Maybe," said Lori. "I don't know."

Both of them were spared the decision as a few moments later Grey came back into the kitchen with Becky trailing behind. He was pale and strained looking; the little girl was quiet, her face all red and blotchy where she had been crying.

"I'd better head home," he said sadly. "I've folks to call and shit to sort out."

"If we can do anything to help, you just need to ask," said Lori warmly. "I mean it, Grey. You aren't alone in this."

"Thanks, Lori. Appreciate it."

Jake got up and embraced his friend.

"Thanks, Jake," said Grey. "I'll call later. Thanks for everything."

"Bye, Lori," whispered Becky sadly.

Reaching out to hug the little girl, Lori said, "You can sleep over here anytime, honey. I'll keep the Elmo glass handy for you to use."

Becky gave her a sad smile, then followed her daddy out to the truck, her rag doll tucked under her arm.

Jake and Lori sat on in silence in the kitchen for a few more minutes, neither of them knowing what to do or say. Nothing seemed appropriate; nothing seemed important. Eventually, Lori suggested they go for a walk to get some air. Jake shook his head.

"If you don't mind, I'll head home for a few hours. Get a change of clothes," he said. "I'd better try to see the guys too till we see what we can do to help here."

"Ok," said Lori, sensing his need to be on his own. "Why not invite them over here later? We can do food or whatever you think is right."

"Might be a plan," he agreed. "Let me talk to them. I'll try to be back here after lunch. You should try to get some more sleep. You look wiped out."

"I'm fine," she assured him. "Go and do what you need to do. I'm not going anywhere. If the guys are coming over, you might want to get some beers. There's not many left."

He nodded, kissed her on the top of the head, and then headed off through the sun room to walk back along the beach.

Once out on the sand, Jake walked slowly back towards town. A strange mix of emotions were brewing up inside him, mixing in with the guilt that he felt for leaving Lori at the house. He needed to get them straight in his head on his own though. Death scared him. Even if there had been no love lost between him and Sandy, he cared for Grey like a brother. He had sat back and watched her hurt and embarrass him time after time over the years; watched her abandon Becky to his care, to anyone's care, so she could party and drink. It angered Jake that part of him was relieved, almost glad, that she was gone out of their lives for good. He knew that deep down Grey still loved her, but he had listened to his friend unburden himself about the mess his marriage was in, more times than he cared to recall. Then there was Becky. Such a beautiful, innocent little girl didn't deserve to have to deal with this. As he walked, kicking the loose, soft sand up in front of him, Jake thought back to how effortlessly caring Lori had been with the little girl. She had naturally cared for the child without overstepping the mark. She had subtly cared for Grey too.

With a heavy heart and a confused mind, Jake sat down, watching the waves roll in and the sea birds play. He looked down at the fresh tattoo on his forearm, hearing the music in his head. The tattoo, the music and the lyrics- they all represented Lori to him. He thought back to the day he had met her, not far from where he was now sitting. How would he feel if something or someone took her away from him? What if his moods drove her away? Lying next to her in bed the night before had seemed the most natural thing in the world to do. Neither of them needing the complication of sex in their fledgling relationship, but both of them needing the comfort of each other. It certainly wasn't the image he had pictured in his head of the first night in her bed. Perhaps the reality was better. A fresh wave of guilt washed over him as he thought of her alone back at the house. With a deep sigh, he hauled himself to his feet and continued his walk along the beach, up onto the boardwalk and back towards his apartment.

The small apartment felt lonely and unwelcoming when he

entered it. Throwing his jacket down on the couch, he wandered through to take a shower. Once under the hot jet of water Jake began to feel his maudlin mood shift. By the time he came back through to the living room, with a towel round his waist, he felt more like himself. On his way through to the tiny galley style kitchen, he flicked on the stereo and filled the apartment with the sound of Guns N Roses. Without realising it, he began to sing along as he made himself some coffee and tidied up the mess from the previous day's breakfast. Totally engrossed in the song, he almost never heard the hammering at his door. Adjusting and tightening the damp towel round his waist, he opened the door to find Rich in the hallway.

"I just heard about Sandy," he said, pushing past Jake. "Shit!"

"Did Grey call you?" asked Jake, closing the door behind his friend.

"No, Paul did. He's up in Dover at his sister's. He's heading back later. Grey called him," explained Rich. "Said you'd taken care of Becky last night."

"Yes. Well, Lori did," began Jake then he filled the guitarist in on the details of the night before.

"Now what do we do?" asked Rich. "What do we say to Grey?"

"We carry on," stated Jake bluntly. "We do whatever Grey needs us to do. You say what feels right to say. He was hanging in there when he left Lori's this morning. If anyone gets him through this it will be Becky. We just need to take our lead from him."

"I guess."

"Look, I don't know if it's the right thing to do or not, but Lori's suggested we all go over to her place later. I think we should go," suggested Jake. "Let's take some beers. I'll bring my guitar. We can BBQ and toast life. Who knows, maybe Grey will join us."

"It's as good a plan as any," Rich agreed. "But go easy on the beer. Remember, you have a meeting with the principal at nine tomorrow."

"Looking forward to it," said Jake, unable to hide his grin. "First time in the principal's office for a while."

Back at the beach house, Lori had fetched herself another

coffee before heading through to the study. She turned on her laptop and called up her email account. It had been a day or two since she had checked them and, by the time she had deleted the junk, she was pleasantly surprised that there were only a dozen left that needed her attention. One jumped out at her. It was from Maddy and the subject heading was "Silver Lake idea". Quickly she opened it. Typically Maddy, it was short and sweet. "I can get them into the studio in New York. Full team. Full support staff. Only free date is week of June 10th. Should be a few strategic folk recording in the studio next door. It will cost. Call me if you want it set up. M "

Reaching for her cell phone, Lori hit Maddy's contact details. The phone rang out for several rings before her friend picked up the call.

"Maddy here."

"Hi," said Lori. "I got your mail. What's the deal?"

"Well, hello," replied her friend. "How's life in beach paradise?"

Quickly Lori filled her in about Sandy's death.

"Shit, that's tragic," said Maddy, sounding stunned by the news. "Maybe we should abandon this idea."

"No," disagreed Lori. "What's the deal?"

She listened while her friend explained there had been a last minute cancellation by an A-listed band. The whole team were on standby as she had promised to fill the vacant slot. A cancellation fee had been paid, but anyone taking the slot would still need to pay part of the costs. The best she had been able to negotiate was fifty percent off, but that still ran well into five figures.

"You know they can't afford that kind of money," stated Lori.

"But you can," countered Maddy. "They need never know. It's your call."

"That's a bit presumptuous, Maddison," she chastised softly. "If they ever found out….."

"You haven't told Jake, have you?" challenged her friend.

"Look, Maddy," began Lori. "I haven't told him much about my private affairs. I haven't told him much about New York, apart from the fact I still have an apartment there."

"Ok. Ok," protested Maddy. "I get it. Do you want the slot or not?"

"Yes," stated Lori firmly. "Send the bill to David. You know the address. If you breathe a word of this to the guys, I'll never forgive you."

They spent a few minutes working out the "story" and agreed on a plan – the cancellation had led to a "free slot" with a full production team. It was simple. Loosely the truth – the slot would be free for Silver Lake. Details of the opportunity had to come via Maddy. There could be no direct involvement on Lori's part.

"That bit's easy," giggled Maddy. "Paul gave me his number. I could innocently call him."

"You never did anything innocently in your life, girl!" declared Lori, laughing.

"Ok, leave this bit up to me. Remember to act surprised," cautioned her friend. "I need to run. Duty calls."

"Thanks, Maddy," said Lori. "Take care."

"You too. See you soon."

Temperatures were starting to climb into the low eighties by mid-afternoon – warm for the first week of May. Lori was trying to relax for a while before Jake arrived with Rich but she was fidgety and couldn't get comfortable. She had tried working earlier, but her head wasn't in the right place for it. Her book also lay discarded beside her on the deck, its tale unable to hold her attention. Every time she tried to settle to something, her mind was flitting between worrying about Grey and Becky, to wondering if Maddy had called Paul yet. If she had, how would the guys react? Would they want to go? Was this chance really what they all wanted, especially now? Only time would tell, she figured. In a final attempt at relaxation, Lori lifted her iPod from beside her book, snuggled her earphones into her ears then lay back on the sun lounger. Carefully, she stretched her leg out, gently rubbing the length of her scar through her flimsy summer skirt. Now that she had been moving about more and doing more strength work with Jo, she could feel an improvement in the muscle bulk and tone. With a sigh, she wondered if she would ever be free of her canes; would she ever be back to normal. Time would tell on that one too.

As she listened to some gentle country rock music, she must have drifted off to sleep. The next thing she knew, Jake was bent over her kissing her gently.

"Wake up, sleeping beauty," he whispered, kissing her again. "You have guests."

"Sorry. I must have slipped away," she murmured sleepily.

"Stay where you are," said Jake warmly. "You still look tired. Rich and I have this under control."

Rubbing the sleep from her eyes, Lori sat up and greeted her other guest. She saw from the pile of bags on the picnic bench that the boys had been food shopping for BBQ supplies, including beers. Both guys happily took control. Jake busied himself lighting the coals while Rich fetched her a beer.

"I could get used to this," declared Lori with a giggle, as she accepted the beer from him. "Thanks."

"We'll even serenade you later," Rich joked, indicating the two guitar cases by the patio door.

"I'll look forward to it," said Lori then added. "Is Paul coming over?"

"He should be here about four," replied Jake, taking the top off his own beer. "He's on his way down from Dover. I spoke to Grey. He said he might drop by but he's still sorting stuff out."

"How did he sound?"

"Surprisingly ok," Jake admitted. "There's only so much he can do as it's Sunday."

"I guess," agreed Lori, unplugging her headphones from her iPod and rolling them up. "Rich, do you want to plug this into the dock in the sunroom?"

Soon the three of them were sitting relaxing with a beer and with the gentle strains of Lynyrd Skynyrd filtering out across the deck. Inevitably, they ended up talking about Jake's new job and Rich's plans for the music department. There was only a month of school left before the summer break, but he felt it was enough time to pull together an end of term concert. The guys bounced ideas around while Lori sat quietly enjoying the normality of a Sunday afternoon BBQ. An engine roar from the front of the house disturbed their tranquillity, as Paul raced up in his beat up old Mustang. It was his pet project and the car spent more time in pieces in his garage than on the road.

"Hi guys," he called brightly as he ran round the side of the house. "Guess who just called me?"

"Who?" asked Jake, handing him a lite beer.

"Maddy," announced Paul, sprawling himself out on an empty chair. "She has a business proposition for us."

Both Rich and Jake stared at him. "What kind of business proposition?" asked Rich curiously.

"A week in a Manhattan recording studio with full production support for free. All we need to do is get there and play."

His announcement was met with stunned silence.

"She says the studio had a cancellation and she's talked them into giving us a shot at it. The other studios are booked out solid. She said it would be a good chance to be heard by the right people," he continued enthusiastically. "We've got seven full days from June 10th."

"Maddy? Where does she fit into this?" asked Rich, not really believing what he had just heard.

"I can guess," said Jake turning to look at Lori suspiciously. "Maddy wouldn't happen to be short for Maddison would it, Mz Hyde?"

"I believe it is," replied Lori with a smile.

"And she wouldn't happen to be Maddison Addison by any chance? Jake continued. "A&R empress and tour manager to the stars?

Now it was Paul's turn to look on in disbelief as Lori nodded, "Yes, I believe she would be."

"And she just happened to get an invite to visit you over the Surfside weekend?"

Lori nodded again, trying hard not to giggle, "But she really is one of my best friends from New York. We've been friends for years."

"I'll bet!" exclaimed Jake. "I don't know whether to hug you or murder you for your deviousness, Mz Hyde!"

"I'll make that decision for you," laughed Rich rushing over to hug Lori tightly. "Did you know about this, Mz Hyde?"

"Not really," confessed Lori. "Yes, I wanted her to hear you guys play. I had no idea if she would like what she heard. She obviously liked it when she's offered you this chance. I didn't ask her for any special favours."

"Are you sure?" asked Jake, trying to feign anger and failing miserably.

"I promise I didn't," said Lori seriously. "So, are you going to go?"

There followed several minutes of heated debate amongst the three musicians as they tried to agree their schedules, budget for travel and general logistics of the whole New York thing. About the only aspect they agreed on was that if Grey couldn't go, then none of them would go without him.

"Can I make an offer that might help?" interrupted Lori eventually.

"Of course," replied Paul. "All help gratefully received in sorting this out."

"You could stay at my apartment. It's not too far from the studios and I can get guest parking for a couple of cars without too much trouble. Assuming Grey wants to go and wants to take

Becky along, then I'm sure I can keep her amused while he works on the bass tracking."

"I never knew you had an apartment in Manhattan!" exclaimed Rich loudly. "Will there be room for all of us?"

"I'm sure we can all squeeze in," she assured him, hesitant about revealing too much about her city home.

"Lori," began Jake, "Are you sure?"

"If you guys agree to go then it's the least I can do to help you out. Hotels and parking aren't cheap."

"Thank you," said Rich before his band mates could say anything else. "So are we agreed? As long as Grey says yes to this then we go?"

They agreed and immediately Paul and Rich began discussing playlists and music. Only Jake remained quiet. He busied himself at the BBQ, putting some burgers on the grill. As she watched him from across the sun deck, Lori was worried that he was angry with her; worried that this was all a bad idea. Slowly she made her way over to stand beside him, forgetting to use her canes to assist her. Balancing herself by leaning on the small table beside the grill, she reached out and put a hand on his shoulder.

"Are you ok?" she asked softly. "Are you mad at me?"

He looked round and smiled at her, "I'm not angry, li'l lady. I'm just blown away by all of this. It's the chance of a lifetime and you've been instrumental in handing it to us on a plate. I'm trying to figure out how I- how we –can ever repay you."

"This chance is on me," she replied, hiding the truth in her carefully chosen words. "Carpe diem"

"What?"

"Seize the day," she translated. "If this weekend has taught us nothing else, it's about living for today. You're the one that's made me pick myself up out of the depths of self-pity. Without you, I'd still be acting like an invalid and dwelling on what ifs."

"I love you, Lori," he blurted out, then blushed red right down to the neck of his T-shirt.

"Likewise," she replied, putting her arms round his waist. "Now can you do something for me?"

"What?"

"Help me over to that chair before I fall."

"It's the least I can do, li'l lady."

Once the burgers had all been cooked and devoured, Rich and Jake's conversation returned to music and the expectations of the school. While they debated what Jake could, and what perhaps he best not, bring to the music department, Paul helped Lori to clear away the leftovers and to load the dishwasher. By the time they returned to the sun deck, the two guitarists had picked up their guitars and were working on a melody. Soon Paul was drumming along on the edge of the table. It struck Lori just how relaxed and comfortable the three musicians were in each other's company. They were so engrossed in the music that none of them heard the car pull into the driveway.

"Hope there's a beer left," called a voice from the side of the house. It was Grey.

After a fresh round of condolences and expressions of sympathy, he joined them in a beer. His face was strained, but Lori was glad he had made the effort to come over.

"How's Becky?" she asked, as she passed him the bag of tortilla chips that they had all been nibbling on.

"Kind of quiet," he admitted. "My mom's with her at our house."

"When's the funeral?" asked Paul, not being one to beat around the bush.

"Friday, I think," began Grey. "But in the circumstances, it's a private family only affair. I know you guys are like my family, but her mom wants it this way. It's probably for the best."

There were several nods from the group and then an awkward silence settled upon them. Suddenly Paul let out a yelp, "Shit! We've got a gig on Friday night."

"Dammit," muttered Jake. "So we do. At that new bar in Lewes."

"No way I'll be there," said Grey, stating the obvious.

"Ok," began Rich, taking calm control. "We have two options. Cancel or play an acoustic set?"

After a quick debate and a lot of persuading by Grey, they agreed to call the bar, explain the situation and confirm if they were ok to do an acoustic set.

"I think the guys have forgotten to tell you something," Lori prompted, giving Jake a nudge in the ribs.

"Ouch!" he squealed, rubbing his side. "That hurt, girl!"

"Lori's right though," said Rich with a smile.

Suddenly the penny dropped and they all realised that they had forgotten to tell the Grey about the studio offer in New York. All too soon they were all talking at once and bombarding the stunned bass player with information and ideas.

"Slow down, guys," he snapped sharply. "This is all happening too fast. I don't know what I'm doing tomorrow, never mind next month. I need some time here."

"Sorry," apologised Jake, feeling a wave of guilt wash through him for stressing his friend out even more.

"Well, book it and, if I can't go, get Maddy to find you a new bass player," he snarled, getting to his feet. "I'm out of here."

As they watched him storm off round the side of the house, Lori urged Jake to go after him. They could all hear heated raised voices, but not exactly what was being said. Slowly things seemed to calm down and, about ten minutes later, they heard a car drive off. A fresh surge of guilt and remorse swept over all of them, including Lori. They had all acted insensitively to his grief and general heightened emotional state. Their only hope was that Jake had managed to calm him down and smooth things over. Eventually Jake came back round, running his hands through his hair and shaking his head.

"It's ok," he said, sitting back down beside Lori. "He'll be there as long as he can sort himself out by then and as long as Becky is ok. He made it crystal clear that she comes first."

"Thank God," sighed Rich. "We're idiots for even mentioning it."

"That was my fault," apologised Lori quietly. "I'm sorry for interfering"

"Look, no one's to blame," said Jake, taking Lori's hand. "He's fine about it. Let's just give him his space for now. I'll talk to him at the end of the week."

Draining the last of his beer, Paul stood up and declared, "Right, I'm out of here too. I've got work early tomorrow. Usual time on Thursday night?"

The others agreed to meet up to run through an acoustic set at the rehearsal hall as long as the gig was still on. As Paul made his move to depart, Rich got up to leave too.

"I'll see you at school, Mr Power," he joked with a wink.

"Night, Lori. Thanks for tonight."

"Pleasure," she said with a smile.

Once the others had left, Jake cleared up the rest of the BBQ stuff and made sure the grill had burned out. Satisfied that everything was tidy and safe, he went over to sit on the sun lounger next to Lori.

"I need to head too," he apologised, putting his arm around her shoulder. "I've got stuff to get ready for school."

She giggled at the thought of him in the principal's office. "Don't forget your apple for the teacher."

"Very funny, li'l lady," he said, trying not to smile. "I'll call you after school."

"I'll be thinking about you," whispered Lori, snuggling into his shoulder. "I hope the kids are gentle with you."

"Me too," he said. "It's been a long time since I've done any classroom teaching. Almost ten years."

"You'll be great."

Gently he kissed her, then said he really had to make a move. She followed him round to the front of the house and watched from the porch as he drove off towards town.

Overnight a storm moved in and the week started wet and thundery. The storm lingered over town for three days. Trapped indoors, Lori began to feel like a caged animal. She turned her attention to her work and managed to finalise the book jacket design by Tuesday afternoon. The finished piece looked good and Lori hoped it represented what the author and their team were looking for. A flutter of nerves passed through her as she pressed "send" on the email with the JPEG files attached. Her second commission was proving to be more of a challenge. Her nuts and bolts theme seemed to fit, but none of the concepts she devised felt right. That special "Mz Hyde" touch was missing from it and it was beginning to frustrate her as much as the weather.

It took until Wednesday morning for her financial advisor, David, to get in touch via email to question the invoice for studio hire. As she read his email, Lori began to laugh as she visualised him having a fit in his ivory tower at her sudden frivolous expenditure. He had been her father's best friend and his accountant for over ten years before his death; he had been her accountant and adviser ever since. Until she had inherited her father's estate and firm when she turned twenty eight, he had kept her on a tight rein. Old habits died hard and he still questioned every four figure sum she spent. A five figure sum was sure to trigger a heart attack. Quickly she typed up an appropriate response, explaining the background and bulleting projected additional expenditure for that week. She instructed him to have her apartment readied, the kitchen stocked, a daily cleaner hired for the week and for three parking spaces to be reserved. As an afterthought she asked him to have her car serviced and ready for use. After she hit send on the email, Lori sat waiting for the phone to ring. He didn't disappoint and her phone rang less than ten minutes later.

After she had chatted with David for almost half an hour, Lori gave up on work for the day and went through the house in search of Mary. Her housekeeper had been quiet and distracted all week as she continued to fret about her sister. Lori found her sitting at the kitchen table with her head in her hands and her cheeks wet with tears.

"Hey," said Lori gently, putting a hand on the older woman's shoulder. "What's wrong?"

"I just don't know," replied Mary with a sob catching in her voice. "I just don't know how she's going to cope."

"Who? Your sister?"

Mary nodded and explained that the tests had shown that her sister had a mass in her stomach that the doctor suspected was cancerous. Surgery had been scheduled for the following week to remove it.

"Mary, you need to be with her," said Lori sitting down beside her.

"I know," she admitted. "But what can I say to her? What can I do?"

"Just be there," answered Lori. "Ok, no arguments here. Take some time off. At least until after her surgery. I've told you, family comes first."

"But I've things to do around here for you," protested Mary. "This is my job."

"And it will still be your job when you come back," reassured the younger woman firmly. "Now, please, take whatever time you need and we can work this out together."

"You shouldn't pay me if I'm not here working for you," muttered the housekeeper. "I'm not taking charity."

"Mary, it's not charity. It is an authorised leave of absence," stated Lori bluntly. "Let's leave things flexible. You take the rest of this week off and all of next week. Call me next week to fill me in on how things are and we can work out a short term reduced schedule from there. Does that sound like a plan?"

Mary nodded and wiped fresh tears from her cheeks. "You're an angel, Lori."

"Nonsense. Now get your stuff together and go to your sister."

"And you're sure you'll be ok here?"

"Yes," replied Lori, feeling inside that this might be a challenge. "I'll be fine. I can always call you, or Jake or Jo if I'm stuck."

"Thank you," sobbed Mary, hugging her tight.

"No need," said Lori quietly.

The housekeeper insisted on preparing lunch before she left.

Having watched her depart via the back door, Lori sat on in the kitchen eating her chicken salad and listening to the rain pounding down outside. Apart from the noise of the rain, the house was silent. It was a relaxed, calm silence. A cricket chirp from her cell phone interrupted it a few moments later.

"Will be over after school. J x"

"Looking forward to it. L x" she responded, then as an afterthought added a love heart.

There were still a few hours until school came out for the day and, with nothing better to do, Lori picked up her sketch pad, settled herself in the sun room with some music on and began to doodle a few simple designs. As she doodled a repeating Celtic knot design across the page, she began to think back to her conversation with David and the whole New York thing. Was she really ready to return to the city? Could she cope with it? Lord, she hoped so. Then she began to think about getting behind the wheel of her car again. Was she even fit enough to drive? There was only one person who could answer that. Reaching for the phone, she called John Brent's secretary and made an appointment for the following week. She was due to go back to see him soon anyway and it would give her peace of mind to talk to him. Since her last visit she knew she had made good physical progress and mentally she was stronger too. When she stopped to think, life was actually pretty good. The thought made her smile.

By the time Jake arrived at the house, she had doodled her way through six pages of her sketch book, covering the pages with a variety of Celtic knots and tribal designs, ultimately ending up back at her cogs and gears/nuts and bolts theme. While she made them both a coffee, Jake told her all about his first few days at the school. His enthusiasm and passion for the job was apparent the minute he began to talk. Such a change from the sultry Jake, who had worked at the pizza place. Already some of the kids were asking about private guitar tuition over the summer and one group of boys even wanted him to help set up a band. Eventually he paused and asked her how her week had been and Lori got the chance to fill him in on the progress she had made with work and also about Mary's leave of absence.

"Will you be ok here on your own?" he asked obviously concerned.

"I'll cope," said Lori then added. "But I do need to ask one favour. Linsey from the school wants me to come in for the day next Tuesday. I've also got a late afternoon medical appointment. Can you take me to the school, then out to Beebe?"

"Sure. She told me you were coming in," said Jake. "Is there something wrong when you need to see the doctor?"

"Just a routine check-up," she explained. "But I want to see if he will clear me to drive again. My car's in New York so if he gives the ok, I can bring it down here."

"Are you sure?" asked Jake. "It's at least a four hour drive."

"We can work that bit out nearer the time," said Lori then changing the subject asked after Grey and about the gig planned for Friday night.

"I called him last night. He's holding up ok. Well, as ok as anyone would," he replied. "Said he'll be glad once the funeral is over."

"It's the period of hanging about in between that's the hardest," agreed Lori, remembering the deaths of both her parents and feeling Grey's pain and grief.

"About Friday night," began Jake a little nervously. "Do you want to come along?"

"Sure, if you want me to," said Lori delighted at the thought of hearing him sing and play again.

"Wouldn't have asked if I didn't want you to be there."

"Can I ask another favour?" asked Lori a short while later.

"Sure, but I'm not promising to grant it," he teased.

"Can you take me into town or to the outlets? I need out of the house for a while," she confessed. "The walls are closing in on me!"

"OK on one condition," agreed Jake. "You let me buy you dinner."

"Deal," she laughed. "Let me get myself together, then we can go."

It had been twelve years since Lori had been in a high school and she felt more than a little nervous as she followed Jake into the building on Tuesday morning. The high school on the outskirts of Lewes served a wide area and was far bigger than the exclusive Manhattan school she had attended. Several students shouted a greeting to Jake as they walked along the main hallway towards the elevator that would take them up to the art department. As they walked, he explained that art and music were adjacent departments and shared a teacher's base station. When they reached the elevator, Linsey was coming along the other corridor.

"Morning," called out the art teacher cheerfully. "You must be Mz Hyde. I'm Linsey Bergman."

"Lori, please," she corrected. "Pleased to meet you."

"I'm so glad you could come in for the day at such short notice. The students are really looking forward to it," gushed Linsey, as they entered the small lift.

"Be gentle with her, Linsey," cautioned Jake, putting a protective arm around Lori's waist.

"Oh!" exclaimed the art teacher. "Are you…. eh…together?"

"Soul mates," said Jake playfully. "Just make sure Mz Hyde here doesn't over do it."

"Of course," promised Linsey, with what she hoped was a reassuring smile. "Rich said you were down at the beach recovering from an accident. I hadn't realised you weren't fully fit yet."

Trying to hide her discomfort at talking about herself, Lori replied, "I'm fine. It's just taking longer for my leg to heal than I'd planned. I'm fine to be here for the full day. Mr Power is just being over protective of me."

They had arrived at the third floor and the doors opened, allowing them out into the art/music corridor. From the signage, Lori noted that the art department was to the left and that music was down at the far end to the right. With a quick kiss on the cheek, Jake left her with Linsey and headed off to his first class. Taking a deep breath to steady her nerves, Lori followed the art teacher along the corridor to the first art room. It was a large bright room with four tables in the centre floor space and several smaller work stations along the back wall. It was far more modern than any art room she had been in and a far cry from the one in her old high school.

"I've split the day into three workshops," explained Linsey, handing Lori an agenda of the day. "The first students are in the ninth grade. The junior group will be the middle set and the seniors will be last after lunch. Is that ok?"

"Are we doing the same workshop three times?" asked Lori, leaning against one of the tables to take some of the weight off her leg.

"That's up to you," said Linsey. "What did you prepare for this?"

"Well," began Lori nervously. "I had prepared a short talk about what I do and what I've done, then I thought we could let the students do a small piece of design work that I could critique. We can do the same talk three times if that works for you."

"Works for me," agreed the art teacher. "Do you want a coffee before the first invasion?"

"No thanks, but a water would be good."

Afternoon classes began at one thirty and by then Lori was starting to tire. Over lunch with Linsey, Rich and Jake she had taken two Advil to relieve the ache that was growing in her leg. When she returned to the classroom, Lori confessed that she would need to sit down for this session.

"Are you ok?" asked Linsey, mindful of Jake's warning to be gentle with her guest.

"Just a bit sore," confessed Lori before adding, "I badly smashed up my femur and it's pretty much held together with metalwork. I'm just a bit sore from standing for most of the morning. I'll be fine in a while."

"We can cancel if this is too much for you?"

"Nonsense," dismissed Lori with a smile. "I'm enjoying this."

A few minutes later the group of senior students began to filter into the room. There were twelve of them- eight girls and four boys. As before Lori gave her pre-rehearsed presentation, then set the class the design challenge. She asked if there were any questions before they got started

"How do you get started on a design?" asked one of the girls.

"Well, if it's for album artwork I'll listen to the band's work. If there's a theme through the tracks I'll try to pick up on it. If it's a book cover, then I read the story and follow the same theory," answered Lori.

"Have you ever failed to come up with an idea?" asked another student.

"Sometimes," she admitted honestly. "Sometimes I've turned

down a commission as it didn't feel right. Others I've done the opposite and approached the band or artist with an idea or a draft design."

"Did you really do Silver Lake's artwork?" asked one of the boys. "Mr Power said you gave it to them as a gift."

"Yes," answered Lori, blushing slightly. "Sometimes it is nice to help out a friend."

"Ok, guys," interrupted Linsey sharply. "You know the task. You've got an hour to come up with a design as per the remit on the board."

Her pain medication had finally taken effect and Lori felt comfortable enough to move around the art room using only one cane, leaning on the tables for occasional support. As she surveyed the class' work, she was really impressed with the designs that four of the students had come up with, especially the work of one of the boys. He had come in and sat at the back of the room and appeared to be disengaged from the whole workshop, but when Lori went over to look at his design it blew her away. The paper in front of him was already covered in expert graffiti art and he was quietly working on the shading.

"That's great," she said softly, leaning on the desk for a moment.

He looked up at her, but said nothing. This struck her as odd, but she calmly moved on to the next student. Linsey had noticed the lack of response from her student and went over to speak to him, but next thing, he had leapt to his feet and charged off out the door. His design lay discarded on the floor.

"Sorry," said Linsey to Lori after the class was over. "I should've warned you about Brad. He's a gifted artist. My best student. When I told him you were coming in he was the first to tell me he was a fan of yours, but he's mildly autistic and a bit unpredictable."

"I wondered," said Lori, relieved to learn that it wasn't her who had offended him. "Do you have any more samples of his work?"

"Yes. His portfolio is still in the drawer," replied Linsey. "Why?"

"That kid has real talent. I could make a few recommendations to some contacts if you think he would be ok with that. I can think of a few places that would be interested in his work," offered Lori warmly.

"Let me talk to him first," suggested the art teacher. "That might be too much for him to cope with. I'll talk to his mom too."

"Of course," agreed Lori. "Give him my number and he can call me or his mom can call."

"Thanks," said Linsey with genuine warmth. "Today's been great. Have you enjoyed it though?"

"More than I thought I would," Lori admitted. "If you ever need me to come back in, just give me a call."

From outside the art room a voice called, "Mz Hyde, are you ready?"

"Almost," called Lori, lifting her bag onto her shoulder. "Can I take this?" She had lifted Brad's discarded design.

"Of course. He will be flattered that you want it."

"Thanks," said Lori, putting the piece of paper into her bag. "Now I need to make a move. Doctor's appointment."

"Come on, Lori," called Jake. "We're tight for time."

They made it across from the school to the medical centre with a few minutes to spare. As they drove across town, Lori filled Jake in on her afternoon and the incident with Brad. He knew of the senior student, but hadn't taught him yet. By all accounts he was also a gifted musician, but had so far skipped Jake's class. When they arrived at Beebe Medical Center, Jake dropped Lori off at the front door, then went to park the truck. Slowly she made her way through the building to Dr Brent's office. There were a few other patients in the waiting area. Hoping to avoid any well–meaning enquiries from strangers as to why she was there and what had happened to her, she sat in a corner seat away from them all. The waiting part made her nervous and Lori was relieved when Jake walked through the door and came to sit in the empty chair beside her.

"I hate the smell in these places," he whispered, taking her hand in his. "You ok?"

She nodded, then added, "I hate the waiting."

"I'm sure it won't be long," said Jake softly, not feeling convinced that they wouldn't be there for a while.

Lori looked at him, forced a weak smile, then sat back and closed her eyes. It was the first time Jake had seen her look scared and he knew better than to try to talk to her. She was holding his hand tightly. He gave it a gentle reassuring squeeze.

Half an hour later they were still sitting there and both of them were getting restless. Several of the patients had been called and had left, only to be replaced by several more.

"Miss Hyde!" called the receptionist at last.

Lori got stiffly to her feet and, with a quick glance back at Jake, headed off towards the doctor's office down the corridor. The door was open and as she walked in she tried to muster all her remaining confidence and inner strength.

"Afternoon, Lori," greeted John Brent, getting up from behind the desk. "You're looking well."

"Thanks," she replied abruptly

"You ok?"

"Yes, I'm fine," sighed Lori, immediately feeling guilty for being sharp with him. "I just hate waiting. It makes me nervous."

"Sorry you had to wait so long. It's been a busy clinic today. The spring weather always brings me a plethora of new broken bones," he said with a mischievous smile. "Start of skateboard season."

Lori laughed and relaxed a little. "Explains the ankle and elbow injuries out there."

"Keeps me in business," joked the doctor. "Now, how have you been? Jo's very pleased with your progress. She's hoping to sign you off her list soon I think."

"I've been good," began Lori then she explained to the doctor how she felt she was getting on, expressed her frustration again at the lack of strength in her leg and her annoyance at still having both canes and her general exasperation about how slowly things were improving.

He listened attentively, then asked her to pop up onto the couch. After a thorough examination, he was happy with her range of movement, a little concerned that there wasn't much muscle gain as yet but generally he was satisfied that she was improving.

"Thanks, Lori," he said, helping her down. "Let me double check a few things with Jo about her treatment plan. I think you should be steady enough to shift down to one cane or no cane around the house only. If you push your limits that bit further it might let you see a bigger improvement. At the end of the day, it's what you feel comfortable with. I don't want you to risk a fall. A bad fall and you will be back in surgery."

"I wanted to ask you something," began Lori nervously. "Am I ok to start driving again? I'm going to New York with Jake and the band for a week next month and was hoping to bring my car back here."

"Is it an automatic?" asked the doctor.

"Yes," replied Lori, hoping this was the right answer.

"Then I'm sure it will be ok. Maybe not make that drive yourself though. Why not rent a car here for a while and see how you feel driving again?"

"I had thought of that as an option," she agreed. "I promise to split the drive from New York with Jake. He wouldn't let me drive all that way anyway."

"Then, yes," said John with a smile. "Go for it."

"Thank you."

"How do you feel about going back to the scene of the crime?"

"A bit apprehensive," admitted Lori quietly. "But it needs to be done some time."

Nodding in agreement the doctor said, "Just be careful, Lori."

"I will," she promised.

"Fine. I don't need to see you back here till the start of September," he declared. "If you've any concerns before then please give me a call."

"Thanks," she said, rising to leave. "Who knows, I'll maybe see you around town or on the boardwalk."

"Perhaps."

As soon as they were back outside, Lori let out a long sigh of relief and her mood visibly lightened. When Jake asked what the doctor had had to say she filled him in on the discussion and then explained about her plan to bring her car back down from the city. As she announced that she intended to lease a car for the next few weeks, she could sense his concern.

"I need to do this," she stated as they reached the truck. "I need a bit more independence, especially with Mary being away more."

"I guess," relented Jake reluctantly, as he opened the door for her. "I'll just worry about you."

"Then come with me to collect a rental car later in the week," she suggested, then adding, "I'm not about to rush out and lease a sports car. I couldn't get in and out of it for a start!"

That made Jake laugh as he climbed into the truck.

"Let's go and grab something to eat," he said. "And we can discuss this further, li'l lady."

"Yes, sir," she joked, then laughed at his serious expression. "Lighten up, Jake. You're acting like my dad would have."

"I guess," he conceded. "I just don't want to be spending more time around hospitals if this all goes horribly wrong."

"Me neither," agreed Lori, reaching out to touch his denim clad thigh. "But you can't wrap me in cotton wool either. Let's go and eat before we argue over this."

"Deal," he said, starting the engine.

After a quick bite to eat, they headed back to the beach house. As they pulled up outside, Jake apologised that he couldn't come in.

"Why not?" Lori asked with obvious disappointment.

"You'll laugh," he muttered.

"Try me?" she said, guessing what he was about to say.

"I've papers to mark," he confessed as she giggled. "And I know it's really rock 'n' roll!"

"Are you sure?" she said. "I've a bit of work to do too, so I would leave you in peace to correct your papers."

Jake shook his head, "Not tonight, li'l lady. You're too big a distraction."

"Ok," she sighed sadly. "Tomorrow?"

"Tomorrow," he agreed. "But I have a rehearsal at eight."

"Do you have classes tomorrow?"

"Only till lunch. I'll be over about two," he promised. "Try to behave yourself until then."

Climbing out of the truck, Lori called back, "I'm going in to look into the rental car thing. I'll see if I can get a deal on a Ferrari or a Porsche."

"You dare!" he laughed. "I'll see you tomorrow."

"Night, Jake," she called, as he drove off.

Shortly after lunch the next day a local car rental firm dropped off her rental car. Despite teasing Jake about leasing a sports car, Lori had elected a much more sensible Honda SUV. As she signed the paperwork and accepted the keys another truck pulled up into the driveway. It was Grey and Becky, who was waving furiously from the front seat. As soon as her daddy had turned off the engine, the little girl jumped from the cab and ran over to hug Lori.

"Hi, Becky," said Lori, bending to hug her. "This is a nice surprise."

Hearing the other door close, she called out a greeting to Grey.

"Hi," he called with a sad smile. "Hope its ok to just drop by like this."

"Of course it is! Go on through while I finish this car rental thing," said Lori, handing the signed paperwork back to the rental car man.

Grey and his daughter went through to the sun room and by the time Lori joined them, Becky had the TV switched on to the cartoon channel and was sitting cross legged in front of it.

"Coffee?" asked Lori warmly.

"Please," said Grey. "I'll help you make it. Becky, wait here."

The bass player followed her through to the kitchen.

"You ok?" asked Lori with genuine concern.

"I guess. Highs and lows," he admitted as he took a seat at the table.

"It's early days yet," said Lori softly. "It's only been just over a week."

"I know," he sighed, then added. "I hate to admit it, but it's almost a relief that she's gone. Does that make me evil?"

"Not at all. Jake had said life wasn't exactly paradise."

"Christ, you can say that again!"

When the coffee was brewed, Lori passed him a mug, fetched the sugar and half and half, and then sat down at the table opposite him.

"How's Becky coping?"

"Better than me," he confessed, stirring his coffee. "She's had her moments but she never did hit it off with her mom. My mom's been spending time with us but she left this morning. It was Becky who asked if we could come over here."

"You know you are both welcome here anytime."

"Appreciate that," said Grey warmly. "There was something I wanted to talk to you about."

"What?" asked Lori, taking a mouthful of her coffee and wondering what the bass player was about to say.

"The New York thing," began Grey quietly. "Is it for real?"

"Yes," said Lori, almost with relief. "As far as I know, it's all set up. The guys have agreed to stay at my apartment and Maddy has set up the studio arrangements."

"And you'd be ok looking after Becky while I'm in the studio?"

"Of course. There's plenty to keep us girls amused while you're working. She'll be fine with me for a few days," assured Lori. "It's been a while since I've been back to New York. It might help me if I have Becky to focus on. I'm kind of nervous about going back."

"Why? I thought you lived there?"

"Most of my life," said Lori gazing down into her coffee mug. "But I've not been back since my accident. I've a few ghosts to lay to rest."

"The accident was in New York?"

Lori nodded, but didn't offer any further information. Changing the focus of discussion, she explained that her apartment was in the Upper West Side so they would be central for all city's main attractions. "Even FAO Schwartz and the American Girl store," she joked.

"And this studio session just happens to come free for us?" he enquired sceptically, raising one eyebrow.

"Maddy's sorted all of that out," said Lori without a word of a lie. "The only bits she can't secure are a record deal or the networking angle. That's up to you guys."

"But the right folk to be networking with will just happen to be in a studio next door?"

"Such cynicism," laughed Lori. "But most likely. If they aren't, then I can maybe, just maybe, make a few well-placed introductions."

"No one has ever done anything like this for me in all of my forty plus years on earth," said Grey seriously. "I don't get it. Why?"

"It's the pay it forward thing," she explained. "Jake's helped me. Now it's my turn to help him and, in this case, all of you."

"So now I have to do something to repay you?"

"No, you just pass on the "good turn" to someone else. It doesn't have to be me."

"I like that theory," he said with a smile. "Feels like the new start Becky and I need right now."

As May moved towards June, life around the beach house took on a new relaxed routine. Most days saw Lori working to finish off the album artwork commission during the morning, then she would either have a therapy session with Jo or go for a walk along the beach in the afternoon. Three days a week, Jake came over straight from school to spend some time with her. Initially, when he saw the rental car in the driveway, he insisted she take him out for a short drive just to satisfy himself that she was safe to be back behind the wheel of a car but she quickly convinced him that she was. As the date of their trip grew closer, the band upped their rehearsal schedule, meeting three and four times a week. Twice a week these sessions ended up being held in Lori's basement as it meant she could keep an eye on Becky while Grey put in the time with the band. She could feel their excitement about the trip building. Their focus and determination to make the most of the opportunity impressed her. At the weekends Jake would stay over with her, often sitting playing his guitar and writing into the wee small hours.

The night before they were due to leave for New York, they all met up at Lori's for a BBQ and a last minute planning session. School had finished a few days before, so Jake and Rich had been put in charge of packing up all the band's gear and stowing it in Lori's basement ready to be packed into the back of one of the trucks. They had already worked out who was travelling with who - Rich and Paul were going in Rich's truck with half the gear, Grey and Becky were travelling together and Jake and Lori would transport the rest of the equipment. If it all went according to plan, on the way back Paul would drive Jake's truck while he and Lori followed in her car.

After they had eaten their fill and the BBQ was burning down, the band lay sprawled across the sun deck-all except Jake, who had been dragged down to the beach by an over excited Becky. Paul was lying on his back on the deck staring up at the cloudless early evening sky, "I've never been to New York. I'm nearly thirty five and I've never seen the Statue of Liberty."

Rich laughed and confessed neither had he.

"I can't believe it's tomorrow we head off," said Grey, sipping a lite beer.

With a quiet smile at their childish excitement, Lori asked, "Ok, what have you forgotten to pack? There has to be something."

"Don't think so," commented Rich. "But you're right. We're bound to have forgotten something."

"Well, I'm sure whatever it is, we can source a replacement," laughed Lori, as Jake came back up onto the deck carrying Becky on his shoulders.

Lifting his daughter down, Grey declared it was time they were heading home. The little girl started to protest, but, after a stern look from her father, she fell silent.

"We'll see you tomorrow," promised Lori. "You and I are going to have fun while the boys work. What do you want to do first?"

"Dance on the big piano in the toy store," declared Becky emphatically.

"We'll see what we can do," said Lori. "Grey, you've got the address ok?"

"Sure have," he confirmed. "See you all tomorrow in the Big Apple."

With all the gear loaded into the back of the two trucks, they left Rehoboth before ten the next morning. The roads out of town were quiet and they made good time as they headed towards the New Jersey Turnpike. In Jake's truck he had some Lynyrd Skynyrd playing on the stereo and was happily singing along to "Tuesday's Gone." Beside him Lori was trying to relax but was obviously anxious about heading towards the city. In an effort to get her to relax, Jake asked about her apartment and her plans for the week.

"My dad made his money from property," she said, opening up for the first time about her father. "He helped me to choose the apartment when I was about twenty one. I lived there after I finished college."

"Are you sure there's room for all of us?"

"Plenty. There's four bedrooms so we're good." she said then, as an afterthought, added, "I assumed you would be ok sharing with me."

"Anytime, li'l lady," he replied with a grin. "How far is your place from the studio?"

"Well, the studios are on 28th Street and the apartment is 82nd. It's a fair walk. You'd be best getting a cab downtown," she explained. "Maddy has reserved two parking spaces for you to get your stuff in and out on Sunday and next Saturday, but its tight four hour slots each day I believe."

"It'll be fine," said Jake softly. "I just can't believe this is actually happening. What if we mess up?"

"You won't," she said warmly. "I trust Maddy's judgement. She's not about to risk her reputation. She has to have seen something in the band that's worth this. Relax and just go with flow."

"That's rich coming from you," he declared. "You haven't relaxed since you sat in that seat nearly two hours ago!"

Lori laughed that beautiful musical laugh of hers and confessed that he was right.

"I'll be fine when we get there. It's just been a while. Almost six months."

A couple of hours later, as they emerged from the Lincoln Tunnel into the madness and mayhem of the Manhattan traffic, both of them were on edge. Despite the thousands of miles he had driven over the years, Jake was inexperienced when it came to city centre driving. Calmly Lori directed him up town through the melee of yellow taxi cabs, and eventually, to the underground garage beneath her apartment building. As they had driven through the city, the sheer scale of the place, the buzz and the height of the buildings had blown Jake away, making him feel like a real country boy blown into the big smoke. When he had parked the truck in the space that the garage attendant directed him to, he breathed a sigh of relief. While they were getting their holdalls out of the back, Rich pulled into the garage behind them, with Paul in the passenger seat. He was directed to the space beside Jake's truck. Rolling the window down, he called out, "Jeez, that traffic is fucking crazy!"

Lori laughed, "Welcome to New York!"

"I think I'll walk everywhere," muttered Rich, as he climbed out of his truck. "That traffic is insane!"

Trying not to giggle, Lori led the way through to the elevator that would take them up to the lobby. As they walked through the garage, she spotted her own car sitting in its usual spot waiting for her. She resisted the temptation to point it out to Jake. Once they exited the elevator in the main lobby, Lori was greeted warmly by Charles, the duty concierge for the building.

"Welcome home, Miss Hyde. Lovely to see you back," he said with a broad toothy grin. "Do you and your guests need any assistance?"

"Thanks, Charles, but we're fine," answered Lori politely. "I am expecting two more guests shortly. Can you make sure they find their way up?"

"Certainly, Miss Hyde," he promised, pressing the button on the next elevator for them.

The doors opened to reveal a spacious elevator with a deep pile carpet. The three would-be rock stars looked at each other, suddenly wondering what kind of apartment Lori owned. She entered a six digit code into the control panel, the doors closed and they were on their way up. From the display Jake saw there were fifteen floors plus a penthouse suite. As the elevator glided past fifteen, he too was wondering where she was taking them. Soon the doors opened and the four of them stepped out into a private marble floored lobby with two ornately carved oak doors at the end. Entering another code into a digital pad, Lori opened one of the large doors and led them into the apartment.

"Home sweet home," she said brightly, walking through to the living room and dropping her handbag onto the couch.

"Wow!" exclaimed Rich, as he walked over to the window and looked out over the city.

"Make yourselves at home."

"Where will I put the bags?" asked Jake, gazing round at the sheer size and luxury of the apartment.

"Put them in the hall for now," said Lori. "Let me show you all where everything is."

As she turned to leave the lounge area, Lori explained that the kitchen and dining room were straight ahead. A broad oak staircase led them down to the bedrooms. At the foot of the stairs, Lori suggested Rich and Paul take the two bedrooms to the right then she led Jake towards the master bedroom.

"What about Grey and Becky?" asked Jake.

"They can have the room next to us. It has its own en suite," said Lori. "I told you there was plenty room for everyone."

"And you weren't kidding, li'l lady," he said, as she opened the bedroom door and showed him in. "This place is stunning."

"Thank you."

The master bedroom was more traditionally furnished than the living area with a large Colonial style four poster bed as the room's centre piece. The rich dark red curtains and bed spread complimented the antique style of the room. Lori stopped in the middle of the room and gazed round, taking in all the familiarity. Her hair brush and perfume were still on the dressing table where she had left them. A novel sat on the nightstand, half read.

"You ok?" asked Jake, taking her into his arms.

She nodded, then buried her face in his chest. He held her as she sobbed quietly for a few minutes.

"I'm sorry," she whispered without looking up. "It feels weird being here."

"I understand," soothed Jake quietly, running his hand through her hair. "You've done the hard bit though. You've come home."

"I guess," said Lori pulling away. "Time to start a new chapter here."

Jake sat down on the bed, sinking into the plump duvet. He looked round, noting the en suite and walk in dressing room. Never had he dreamed of staying in such a luxurious room.

"Lori," he began, "Can I ask you something?"

"Of course. What is it?"

"You said you moved here after college. How could you afford this as a first apartment?"

"The bank of daddy," she replied, a little embarrassed by the question. "He saw it as a good investment and it has been."

"Smart man your dad," mused Jake, with an appreciative smile. "And a wealthy one it would seem."

"You'd have liked him," said Lori wistfully. "Now, let's go back upstairs and you can help me to fetch everyone a drink and a snack."

By the time Grey arrived with Becky an hour later his fellow band members were stretched out in the living room watching the sports channel on TV. While the boys watched the baseball game, Lori showed Grey and Becky to their room. The little girl skipped and danced down the stairs and along the hall, squealing with delight when she saw the room she was to share with her daddy. There were two queen sized beds in the room and on one sat a brand new American Girl doll.

"Is she for me?" cried Becky, hugging the doll.

"She sure is," said Lori, glad that she had thought to get the doll delivered. "I thought we could take her with us when we go to the American Girl store."

"Can we?" squealed the little girl.

"Of course," said Lori then turning to Grey she said, "I hope you don't mind."

"Not at all, Lori," he said, just happy to see his daughter so happy and excited. "This is some place you have here. A veritable palace."

Lori blushed, then admitted that it was quite nice to be back for a few days.

"I just hope the guys treat it with respect," added Grey. "This is one hell of a way to pay it forward for Jake scraping you up off the sand at the beach."

His comment made Lori laugh. "It's just somewhere for you guys to crash while you're here. Nothing special. I'll leave you to unpack. Come upstairs when you're ready."

When the baseball game on TV came to an end, the band began to discuss what to do for dinner.

"Sorry to interrupt," said Lori. "But I've taken the liberty of booking us a table for dinner."

"What time for?" asked Paul. "I'm starving!"

"I booked it for seven so we've an hour or so to wait. I can call and see if they'll bring the reservation forward."

"Seven's fine," stated Jake, shooting Paul a dark look. "Do we need to change?"

"No," she said. "Everyone's fine as they are."

"So where are we off to?" asked Rich curiously.

"The Hard Rock Café," replied Lori with a smile. "A bit cheesy I know, but I thought it would be a fun place to start."

"Sounds good to me," laughed Rich. "It's in Times Square isn't it?"

"Sure is. So you can all experience some of that too."

Times Square was crowded when they got out of the two cabs that had brought them downtown. Seeing the four guys' faces filled with childish delight at their surroundings brought a smile to Lori's face. All of them were talking at once and pointing to this and that. Grey had lifted Becky onto his shoulders and was pointing to the big Toys R Us store on the opposite corner. The little girl's eyes were wide with amazement at the scale of the whole thing going on around her. Carefully they made their way through the crowds to the Hard Rock Café. They entered under the huge neon lit guitar, walked through the gift shop and down to the restaurant. The restaurant welcome area cum mini rock museum was dimly lit. Lori walked up to the meet and greet desk and said she had pre-booked a table for six in the name of Hyde. The hostess apologised that there would be a short ten minute wait and that they would be called as soon as their table was ready. She advised Lori to keep an eye on the board announcing the tables being called.

"Ok, boys," she said, as she walked back over to join the others. "You've got ten minutes to play in here."

"Yes, mom," joked Jake as he headed off with Rich to browse the displays.

Only Becky stayed with her, holding on to her hand nervously. The little girl seemed unsure of the dark surroundings and the crowds of people milling about the small enclosed space. After a few minutes the guys wandered back over and then posed beside the wall of guitars taking photos with their mobile phones. As their name reached the top of the board, they headed through to the restaurant, stopping only for a souvenir photo to be taken. Their waiter showed them to a large table at one side of the restaurant, took their drinks order and left them with the menus. Around them on the pillars were video screens showing the rock videos that went with the songs being played. From the happy childlike faces seated round the table, Lori reckoned she had made a good choice for dinner.

"Maybe someday it will be our video on the TV," joked Rich as he gazed round.

"I hope so," said Lori. "But who will be donating their guitar to the memorabilia collection?"

"Paul," said Jake and Grey together, laughing at the drummer's expense.

The good humoured banter continued all through dinner. Seeing them all relaxed and happy in each other's company helped Lori to relax about being there. The waiter had given Becky a kid's entertainment pack and she was quietly colouring in a picture while the adults chatted around her. When the meal was over, Grey called the waiter over to ask for the bill.

"Sorry, sir. It's been taken care of already."

"Lori?" said Grey quite firmly.

"Tonight's on me, boys," she replied with equal firmness. "Welcome to New York."

After they had all thanked Lori and protested that she shouldn't have done that, the group took their leave. On the way out, they all stopped to play tourist in the gift store, buying T-shirts, key-rings and lapel badges. Once back out in the crowded street, Lori felt her nerves return. It had been a long day, an emotionally draining day, and her leg was starting to ache. As the guys started to head towards the toy store at Becky's insistence, Lori called Jake back.

"What's up, li'l lady?" he asked with concern.

"I'm going to head home," she said softly. I'll get a cab. Will you guys be ok to make your own way back?"

"I'll come with you," offered Jake instantly.

"No, you stay out for a while," insisted Lori. "I could do with a couple of hours to myself. Do you mind?"

"No," replied Jake warmly. "I understand. I think."

"Thanks," she said with a smile. "Here's the guest card to get back in. Please don't lose it. I'll see you back at the house."

"We won't be late," promised Jake, kissing her forehead.

"Take as long as you need," said Lori. "I'm going this way to get a cab. Have fun."

Once back at the apartment, Lori kicked off her shoes in the living room and left her canes lying against the couch, then wandered through to the kitchen in search of some pain medication. As she had hoped, she found an old strip of Advil in a drawer with two pills left. Pouring herself a glass of water, she quickly swallowed the two tablets. "Home", she thought looking round. It had been home for almost eight years, but it suddenly felt as new and alien to her as it did to the boys from Silver Lake. She wandered back through to the lounge and out onto the terrace. The view over the city always took her breath away. As she leaned on the railing, gazing out over the rooftops, her cell phone rang in her handbag indoors. She got to it just before it cut to voicemail. It was Maddy.

"Hi," called her friend brightly. "I just wanted to check you were all set for tomorrow."

"Hi yourself," said Lori, wandering back out onto the terrace. "As far as I know they are all ok for tomorrow. Is it ten o'clock they've to be there?"

"Nine would be better," admitted Maddy. "Time to hang about and mingle if you get my drift."

"I hear you, girl," laughed Lori. "I'll tell them."

"Ok" said Maddy. "I've had a change of schedule. I'm back in town on Tuesday night till Thursday morning. I'll go straight to the studio."

"Am I to tell them?"

"Best not," admitted Maddy. "I've a plan, but I'm still trying to tie down the final detail."

"Who is it?"

"Can't say," teased Maddy.

"Let me guess," giggled Lori. "You just happen to have a meeting scheduled for late Tuesday with Jeff that you will be strategically late for so that he will be tempted to kill time by tuning into the studio sessions."

"Close, but it's not Jeff," laughed Maddy. "I thought Jason, the English guy, would be a better option. He's just dropped two acts, both rock bands, from his books so there's an opening there."

"Loving your style, Maddison," declared Lori. "Will you have time for a quick lunch with me or dinner on Wednesday?"

"No promises, but I can maybe do lunch. I'll call you nearer the time."

"Look forward to it."

"Need to run," said Maddy. "Press event to cover. Bye!"

"You work too hard, girl!" laughed Lori. "I'll see you soon."

Putting her phone into her pocket, Lori limped back indoors.

Her studio workspace was situated just off the living room and she naturally drifted in there. Everything was just as she had left it - a design sitting half-finished on her drawing board. Casually she fingered her pens and pencils that were scattered over the desk then she returned them one by one to their correct place. She removed the design from the board, tempted to tear it up and destroy any links to the day of her accident but she couldn't do it. Instead, Lori slipped it into one of her many slim storage drawers. She replaced it on the board with a brand new sheet of paper – a fresh start.

A glance at the clock on her phone told her it was almost ten. Running her hand through her hair, she decided to take a shower before the band got back. Once down in the bedroom her melancholy mood continued. Safe in the knowledge she was alone in the house, she stripped naked in the bedroom in front of the full length mirror and surveyed her reflection. The Lori staring back at her was thinner than the Lori from last December. Her scars though looked less angry, as though they were finally starting to fade a bit. The surgical scar on her right hip had healed to a thin purple line that was slowly fading to silver. It was the ones on her thigh that remained particularly unsightly. With a wistful sigh, she entered the bathroom and turned on the shower.

When she came back into the bedroom a few minutes later wearing a soft towelling robe, Jake was stretched out on top of the bed. He was still fully clothed, but had removed his shoes and socks and was slowly wiggling his toes.

"Sore feet," mused Lori. "Must be those hard city blocks."

"Or worn out sneakers," he conceded.

"Is everyone else back too?" she asked, brushing the knots out of her wet hair.

"Yeah," replied Jake. "Grey's putting Becky to bed. Rich and Paul said they were going to watch some TV for a while."

"Maddy called," began Lori innocently. "She suggested that you get to the studio for nine tomorrow."

"Ok, we can do nine," agreed Jake before commenting. "This is all happening so fast."

"You nervous?" she asked, coming over to sit on the bed beside him.

"A bit. Scared of making a fool of myself," he admitted. "I've chased this dream since I was fourteen. What if we're not good enough?"

"You'll be fine," she assured him softly. "Just go in tomorrow, relax about it and play like you always do."

"I guess," he sighed. "Will you come with us in the morning?"

Lori shook her head, "No. Becky and I are going to the Natural History Museum. It's only a couple of blocks from here so it's an easy first adventure for us."

Jake looked disappointed.

"We'll drop by later in the week. You're here to work remember."

With a smile, Jake sat up and hugged her, "But we can play a bit too."

"Yes," agreed Lori, kissing him on the nose. "But the work comes first, rock star."

"Slave driver," he teased.

"I'm going upstairs for a drink," said Lori getting to her feet. "Do you want anything?"

"I'll come up with you," he said before adding. "Can I make a suggestion, Lori?"

"What?"

"Don't go up in your robe. Please."

Silently agreeing that this was a good idea she slipped into some yoga pants and a baggy well-worn Mickey Mouse T-shirt.

"Better?" she asked.

"Much," agreed Jake, putting his arm around her waist as they headed upstairs.

Silver Lake arrived at the recording studio shortly after nine, as suggested, on Sunday morning. There followed a chaotic hour of moving gear and getting set up in Studio B- home for the next seven days. Much to Paul's surprise a drum kit, set up identically to his was already waiting in the studio. There was a post-it note stuck to one of his hi-hats – "Maddy x". It made him smile and helped to settle his nerves a little. While Grey and Jake took the trucks back up to the garage at Lori's apartment building, Paul and Rich familiarised themselves with Studio B. Around ten, their technician and sound engineer both arrived carrying coffee cups and nursing hangovers. A few minutes later Grey and Jake returned, breathless from running up the stairs. Once all the pleasantries were out of the way, Jack, the sound engineer said, "We've had some basic instructions from Maddison about the plan for this week. The suggestion is that you spend today getting to know this place and deciding what you are going to record."

"We've worked that bit out already," said Rich, pulling a crumpled piece of paper out of his pocket. "We figured we could get ten tracks done in five days with a bit of luck and effort."

"Ambitious," mused Jack, looking round at the four eager faces hanging on his every word. "But, it may be possible."

"How many do you think we'll do?" asked Grey solemnly.

"Four most likely. Six at a push." Jack replied bluntly. "But if you are prepared to put in the hours, let's aim high. Bench mark eight, but stretch target of ten."

He moved over to a whiteboard on the wall that was already gridded out with black tape. Briefly, he took the band through his tried and tested system as per the grid format. Tossing a marker pen to Rich, he said, "Write up your ten in order of preference."

After a bit of debate and reprioritising they had their ten tracks listed on the board.

"Ok," said Jack. "I'll be about till eight. Todd here will be with you till you finish. If you all want to stay till next Saturday, he'll be here. If you take a break so does he. Get it?"

They nodded in unison.

"Great. I'll leave you to it for a few hours. If you need

anything, ask Todd. If you are short of instruments, we have a store room you can borrow from. When Jim your producer arrives tomorrow be ready for him to change everything you rehearse today."

And with that he left the room. They all stared at each other for a moment, then Rich said, "You heard the man. Let's rehearse."

"Ok, let's do it in the order of the board for now and see how far we get," suggested Jake, suddenly wishing he was at the museum with Lori and Becky.

By lunchtime they had run through the ten numbers twice. Nerves had got in the way for most of the morning, but, by the end of the second run through, they were all focussed on the task in hand. So far Todd had said very little. He had interrupted them a few times to change leads or amps, but hadn't engaged any of them in conversation.

"I'm going to McDonald's," he declared around one thirty. "Anyone want anything?"

They agreed to break for half an hour for lunch. While Grey and Rich went with Todd to get their burger order, Jake went to explore. He wandered past Studio A noting the "recording in progress" sign on the closed door. Studio C was also closed – "rehearsal in progress". The lounge on the upper floor was empty. It was a huge space with several large couches, a bar at one end, a large glass fronted chill cabinet filled with bottled water and various juices. Along one wall were framed photos of the bands and artists who had used the studio. There were a handful of gold discs on display too.

"Hey," said a voice from behind him.

Jake turned and found himself face to face with the lead singer from the English rock band, Weigh Station. He had been a huge fan of theirs for a long time and could barely return the greeting.

"You in Studio B?" asked the singer, casually.

"Yes," he replied, then offering out his hand. "Jake Power from Silver Lake."

"Dan Crow," said the older man, shaking his hand firmly. "First time here?"

"Yes," nodded Jake. "Does it show?"

"A bit," admitted Dan, lifting four bottles of water from the chill cabinet. "Enjoy. Relax. Have fun. That's what it's all about."

"We'll try."

"Might stick my head in later to hear you," said Dan as he headed for the door. "Need to keep an eye on the up and coming opposition."

Still somewhat star struck, Jake lifted four bottles of water for the band and returned to the studio. The boys were back with lunch. When Jake told them who was in the studio next door, they were as star struck as he was. With a mutter Todd put his lunch trash into the bin and declared that Weigh Station were assholes to work with. Silently Jake wondered what he was making of the four of them.

Three hours later the band were on their fifth run through and struggling a bit with the bass on what was now "No. 8". As Grey was getting ready for a temper explosion, the door opened and Jack strolled back in.

"Winning?"

"No," growled Grey sourly.

Jack raised his eyebrows, but said nothing.

"Ok," said Rich calmly. "From the top again."

The sound engineer reclined on the battered leather couch that sat in one corner and listened. For the next hour and a half he sat and listened as they ran through all ten songs again. This run through went smoother than their previous attempts. It wasn't perfect and there was one moment of nervous hilarity when Jake forgot the lyrics mid song, but, apart from that one lapse, they were all happy with how it had gone. More than happy with the improvements they had made during the day. As the final chord faded out of "No. 10" the sound engineer got to his feet.

"Take a break, boys," he instructed. "I have to say, I'd expected you would be shit. One of Maddison's charity cases that she throws our way now and again. I was wrong. You guys are shit hot."

"Thanks," said Jake with a broad grin. The relief at hearing the sound engineer's approval was written all over his face.

"Right, guys," began Jack firmly. "Plan for tomorrow. Be here for nine. Warm up. Caffeine fuel yourselves, if need be. I'll be here by ten. Todd will be here early. I'll call Jim before I leave tonight and chat things through with him. And, Mr Power, rest that voice for tomorrow. No more vocals tonight. It's going to be a long, tough week for you."

"Are we ok to do another run through without vocals?" asked Rich. "I want another shot at a couple of bits."

"Up to you guys," Jack shrugged. "I'm out of here. See you in the morning."

And he turned and left.

"Look, it's almost seven thirty," began Grey with a yawn. "Take your guitars home. We can play a bit back at the apartment. I need to see my little princess."

"Sounds like a plan," agreed Jake, feeling the day's efforts in his forearms and shoulders. "We can work on the acoustic tracks for an hour or so tonight."

"You definitely calling it a day?" asked Todd hopefully.

"Yeah," yawned Paul. "I'm hungry anyway."

As they were packing up, Jake sent a text to Lori to say they would be back shortly. She replied to say she would sort out dinner if they hadn't already eaten. Both Jake and Rich packed up their acoustic guitars and elected to leave everything else where it was. Day One was over and they were all worn out but still on an emotional high at the praise from the sound engineer.

When they came out of the elevator and into the apartment, Becky came flying out of the living room and threw herself into Grey's arms. He scooped her up into his embrace and listened attentively as she told him all the different things Lori had shown her at the museum. From the kitchen, Lori called that dinner was waiting for them. She had set the dining room table and had her iPod playing some soft rock in the background. Jake dumped his guitar case in a corner and went through to the kitchen, suddenly desperate to see her. She was standing at the counter with her back to him. Jake came up behind her and wrapped his arms around her tiny waist, nuzzling into her neck.

"Good day?" she asked hopefully.

"The best," he said, hugging her tight. "We meet the producer and start recording tomorrow. How was your day?"

"Good fun," replied Lori, turning to face him. "The museum was a big hit with Becky."

"I could tell," he laughed, indicating towards Grey, who was still being regaled with tales of dinosaur bones and giant whales. "Do you need a hand here?"

"There's two lasagnes in the oven that you can take through plus some garlic bread," she answered.

"You didn't cook did you?" asked Jake, feeling guilty if she felt she had to cook dinner for them all.

"No. I ordered in from a little Italian restaurant a few blocks away," admitted Lori. "Seemed the easiest option. I had no idea when to expect you back."

Soon they were all seated round Lori's large rosewood dining table, all desperate to talk about their day. They were suddenly transformed into four enthusiastic teenagers that had had all their Christmases come at once. In between tales of this track and that solo, Becky told them all about the natural history museum. The band gave her a fair hearing, glad to see the little girl so happy and talkative. Once their meal was over and the table had been cleared, Rich and Jake went back to work on the acoustic stuff. Paul declared he was going to find a ball game on TV and Grey led Becky downstairs to bed. The two guitarists were camped out in the dining room gently working out the chord progressions and melodies that had felt clunky and awkward a few hours earlier. With the kitchen tidied up and the dishwasher stacked, Lori poured herself a glass of wine and sat at the table listening to them play. Eventually Rich was happy enough to call it a night so he poured himself some wine and went to join Paul in front of the TV for the last two innings of the game. With a smile over at Lori, Jake continued to play. He was fiddling with a melody line, then paused and began to play a song she hadn't heard before. Quietly, almost whispering, he sang the lyrics. The softness gave the song an ethereal, ghostly quality that contrasted beautifully with the strong guitar. When the song was finished, he sat staring down at his guitar, his hair falling carelessly over his face.

"That was beautiful," complimented Lori. "Amazing."

"Thanks," he said, lifting his head. "Just something I've been playing with for a few weeks."

"Is it on the board to be recorded?"

He shook his head, then got up to put his guitar back in its case. "No. They've not heard that one."

"We have now," said Rich and Paul from the doorway. "If

there's time it goes on the board and you perform it exactly like that."

"I don't know," began Jake hesitantly. "There's already seven of my songs on there. You guys have other stuff that we could add too."

"It's going on the board," declared Grey from the hallway. "Band decision. No arguing. What's the name?"

"Lady Butterfly," he admitted reluctantly.

"Definitely in the top ten," said Rich. "We can debate on what to drop tomorrow."

"Do I get to voice an opinion here, folks?" asked Jake.

"No!" came the immediate chorus of his band mates plus Lori.

"There's no point in even trying, is there?" he asked.

"No," replied Lori. "We can't all be wrong, so chill a bit about it."

"I guess," he surrendered, pouring the last of the wine into a glass for himself. "Ok, we add it on. Nothing comes off the list. We tell Jack that it's eleven tracks not ten."

"Deal," agreed Grey. "But you do "Lady Butterfly" as a solo. That just blew me away."

As Jake started to protest, the others over ruled him again. Tired and embarrassed, he excused himself and, carrying his glass of wine, wandered through the apartment and out onto the terrace. He needed a few minutes in the evening air to clear his head. Sensing his need for solitude none of them followed him out. Having set his glass down on the table, Jake stood at the railing, gazing out over the city. The sounds of cars, horns and the occasional siren filtered up from the streets spread out below. He missed the sound of the ocean waves. Missed the smell of the ocean. Missed the screech of the gulls. It's only for a few more days, he thought to himself running his hands through his hair. From behind him, he could hear the ball game finishing up on the TV. It was getting late and the sensible part of him knew he should head in to bed but the selfish part of him needed a few more minutes in the stuffy night air. Leaning on the railing, he gazed out at the skyline.

"Penny for them?" whispered Lori, wrapping her arms around his waist.

He jumped, startled by her soundless appearance beside him.

Casually he pulled her round into his embrace. Her subtle floral perfume filled his nostrils and he leaned forward, burying his face in her long blonde hair.

"I'm sorry," he whispered hoarsely. "I'm a jerk."

"Nonsense," she replied. "I understand. I think."

"It's been a long wonderful day," sighed Jake. "Guess I'm just tired."

"Me too," confessed Lori. "I brought out some more wine. Want to sit for a while with a glass?"

Jake nodded and allowed her to lead him over to the small glass table and wrought iron chairs. As she topped up his glass, Lori said, "I used to come out here all the time to think. I'd listen to the city and lose myself in my own thoughts. I'd feel safe up here in my own tiny corner of the world."

"This is a fabulous place," answered Jake, "But I miss the ocean."

"Me too," she admitted sipping her wine.

"We'd best not stay out here too long. I need to be up early and I want to go for a run first thing," said Jake, running his fingers up and down the stem of the glass. "I need to stretch my legs a bit."

"Well, the park's only two blocks over. You can do a loop through part of it," suggested Lori. "Nothing more New York than jogging round Central Park!"

Jake laughed, "I guess."

They both sat quietly for a few minutes, then agreed it was time to end this wonderful day. Hand in hand, they walked back indoors. The apartment was quiet- everyone else had already gone to bed. Once down in the bedroom Jake casually stripped down to his boxers before wandering through to the en suite bathroom. Lori sat at the dressing table brushing and plaiting her hair, then she too undressed and pulled her Mickey Mouse T-shirt over her head. She went to lift her yoga pants then paused. What was there to hide? It was a warm evening, despite the air conditioning – the T-shirt would do.

When she climbed into bed beside Jake a few minutes later she snuggled down and laid her head on his chest, listening to the slow steady beating of his heart. The tattooed dragon on his shoulder appeared to be staring at her and she giggled.

"It's like being watched," she confessed, fingering the tattoo's bright eyes.

"Go to sleep, li'l lady," murmured Jake sleepily. "He's protecting us."

By eight thirty the next morning Silver Lake were back in the studio, armed with hot coffee and bagels from a nearby deli. True to his word, Jake had risen before six and gone for a five mile run round Central Park. It had been good for his soul and even before the caffeine hit, he was firing on all cylinders ready to go. Todd wandered in around nine and quietly set up the live room with the necessary amps and mics needed for recording. He had just finished setting up when Jack arrived accompanied by the producer.

"Morning, boys," he called loudly. "Let me introduce you to the boss. Dr Jim Marrs. Your producer and musical wizard."

"Hi, guys," said the tall slim man standing to his right. "I've heard great things about you. I'd like to hear them for myself. Todd, are we ready to go?"

"Yes, Doc," said Todd, saluting the producer.

"Ok, let's make some music," declared Jack. "Start from the top of the board. We'll tell you when it's time to stop and start. It's going to be a long day."

Back at the apartment the girls were having a lazy breakfast of Cheerio's in front of the TV. Becky was glued to Sesame Street and even Lori had to admit to herself that she was enjoying the nostalgia trip as she watched the show. They were booked for a day at the American Girl store and Lori was keeping half an eye on the clock to make sure they weren't late. When the programme was finished, she asked Becky to go and put her shoes on and to bring her doll with her.

"Where are we going?" asked Becky when she was ready.

"Well, I thought we would spend the day at the American Girl store," began Lori with a smile. "This doll needs some accessories and some clothes."

"And a hairdo?" asked Becky, jumping up and down with excitement.

"Maybe," said Lori. "Let's see what happens when we get there."

It was almost eleven when the cab pulled up outside the

American Girl store on Fifth Avenue by which time Becky was almost bursting with excitement. Having paid the fare, Lori got herself out of the cab, placing her canes carefully, then waited while her little charge clambered out. The little girl practically bounced onto the pavement clutching her doll tightly. When they entered the store, they were met by a smiling young assistant, who welcomed them warmly.

"Morning," said Lori. "We have a booking for the day package. The name's Hyde."

"Of course, Miss Hyde," replied the assistant. "If you'll follow me."

Still bursting with excitement Becky asked, "How did they know we were coming?"

"I planned this as a surprise for you when I bought your doll," explained Lori, smiling at the little girl. "She'll get her hair done. We'll have some lunch, then you can choose some new things for her to wear."

"Wow!" exclaimed Becky. "Thanks, Lori!"

"Come on, miss," laughed Lori. "Let's have some fun."

Work in Studio B progressed smoothly all morning, thanks to a constant supply of coffee and more than a little luck. Under the concise direction of Jim Marrs, who preferred to be called Dr Marrs, they had run through all ten songs on the board while he had recorded them just as they were. He explained that he preferred to take that approach and build on things from the bare bones. They had a couple of takes at some of the tracks and the whole morning was interspersed with occasional moments of madness, forgotten chords and lyrics. At one point, Grey had been playing the bass line for track six when the rest of them were playing track five, but, on the whole, it had been a productive session.

"Ok guys," called Dr Marrs. "Break for lunch till I listen to this. Go and get some air. I can see this being a late night."

After a quick lunch at a nearby Thai restaurant, Silver Lake walked back to the studios. The sun was shining down on them and they all agreed that life didn't get much better. When they re-entered the studio it was empty. While they were waiting for the others to return, Grey added track eleven onto the bottom of the board.

"Guess I'd better run through it," muttered Jake, lifting his acoustic guitar from its stand.

He settled himself on a stool, with his back to everyone, and began to play the melody line to Lady Butterfly. Soon he was lost in the song, singing and playing with his eyes closed, oblivious to the world around him. When he was finished, there came a round of applause from behind him. Unbeknown to him Dr Marrs, Jack and Todd had returned just as he had started to play.

"From the top again, Mr Power," called out the producer. "I don't know where that came from but let's get it recorded now. Just as you played it there. That's your show stopper."

After only two takes, Lady Butterfly was recorded. No frills; no fancy effects – just the bare song; acoustic guitar track and Jake's haunting vocal. While he worked on it, the rest of Silver Lake sat back in the control room and watched in awe. All of them agreed with the producer, there was something special about that track. A certain spark of musical genius.

Once track eleven had been ticked off on the board, Dr Marrs called on Paul to come into the live room to start on the drum tracking. This left the others free for a few hours to do as they pleased. Jake stayed in the control room to offer moral support while Rich and Grey headed off upstairs to the lounge. Recording the drum tracks proved time consuming and to Paul seemingly never ending. Four hours later they only had four of the tracks recorded and the drummer was losing patience. Eventually he threw his drumsticks in the corner and yelled, "Fuck it! I need some air!"

Ok," snapped back Dr Marrs sharply. "Go for a walk. Be back here in half an hour ready to work your fucking ass off."

"Whatever," growled Paul, as he stormed out of the studio, slamming the door behind him.

"Is he often like that?" the producer asked Jake.

"No. He's usually pretty laid back about stuff."

Shaking his head Dr Marrs sent Todd off in search of Grey, declaring they would make a start on the bass tracks while Paul calmed down.

It was after midnight by the time the band crept into the

apartment. All four of them were completely wiped out and there had been a tense silence during the cab journey back up town. Jake was surprised to find the lights still burning in the living room when they walked in. While the others headed into the kitchen to find some food, he went through to see Lori. She was lying on the couch, half asleep, watching an old John Wayne movie. On the other couch, Becky was curled up with her doll fast asleep.

"Hi," whispered Jake, sitting on the floor in front of her. "You're up late."

"I know," she said with a yawn. "Becky fell asleep and I couldn't get her down to bed. I didn't want to leave her up here alone."

"I'll go and get Grey to carry her down," said Jake getting up. "How was your day with her?"

"Good," said Lori sitting up. "I took her to the American Girl store."

"You're spoiling her," cautioned Jake, as he helped her to her feet.

"Just a bit," conceded Lori. "It's fun. And she deserves a few treats."

Putting his arm around her waist, Jake led her through to the kitchen where the rest of the band were gathered, snacking on an open bag of tortilla chips and fruit juice. Lori leaned on the counter for support as Jake poured them both some apple juice.

"Grey," said Lori. "I'm sorry I couldn't get Becky to bed. She's asleep on the couch through there."

"No worries," said Grey warmly. "I really appreciate you looking after her for me. I hope she behaved today."

"She's been great," said Lori smiling. "It's a pleasure to spend time with her."

"She's hard work," countered Grey. "And don't try to tell me she isn't. I better get her to bed. I'll see you guys in the morning."

"Night," came the chorus as he left the room.

"I'm off to bed too, guys," said Lori with a yawn. "Night."

"Night, mom," called Rich and Paul in unison, their mouths full of tortilla chips.

"I'll be down in a minute," promised Jake.

Taking her glass of juice, Lori limped her way out into the

hallway and down to the bedroom. When Jake finally followed her a short while later he found her already fast asleep in bed.

A blinding headache drove Jake out of the studio late on Tuesday afternoon. The thundery weather outside had affected him all day and after eight hours in the studio his head was pounding. Todd had thrown him a strip of painkillers as he walked out of the live room, heading for the lounge. Once upstairs, Jake helped himself to a bottle of water from the chill cabinet, then wandered over to the large black leather couch that faced the window. He swallowed down two of the Aleve then washed them down with some water. Setting the bottle on the floor, he stretched out on the couch and closed his eyes. He hoped a few minutes peace and quiet would lift the headache enough to allow him to return to work. Voices entering the lounge roused him some time later and, as things came back into focus, he recognised Maddy's voice as one of them. The light from the window had a dusky glow to it and a look at the clock on his phone told him he had been asleep for two hours. On a positive note, his headache was almost gone.

"I'm so sorry for being late, Jason!" gushed Maddy. "Traffic from JFK was a nightmare."

Jake then heard an English accent reply that he had only just arrived.

"Let's grab a drink," said Maddy. "I've got those papers ready for you."

From his reclined position, Jake saw her feet appear round the edge of the couch then heard her squeal.

"Jesus Christ, Jake!" she squawked. "You scared the crap out of me!"

"Sorry, Maddison," he apologised sleepily.

"So you should be," she declared, realising this was actually quite fortuitous. "Now why are you napping up here? I thought you guys were recording in Studio B?"

"We are," he said, sitting up and stretching, feeling his back stiff from lying so long on the couch. "I came up here for some peace. Blinding headache. Guess I fell asleep. I'd best head back down."

"You ok?" asked Maddy then said, "Oh pardon my manners.

Jake, this is Jason Russell. Jason meet Jake Power from Silver Lake."

The two men shook hands.

"Maddison's been telling me about your band," said Jason.

"All bad I assume," joked Jake, flashing them both one of his smiles.

"On the contrary, all very encouraging," replied Jason warmly. "I'd be interested in hearing what you've been working on?"

"Sure," agreed Jake, glancing over at Maddy for approval. "Come down to the studio."

"Later, Jake," answered Maddy. "I'll bring Jason down after our meeting. Give me about an hour."

"Fine," replied Jake, lifting his water bottle. "I'll tell the others. Oh, does Lori know you're in town?"

"I called her earlier," said Maddy. "We're having lunch tomorrow."

"She'll be glad to see you," nodded Jake. "I'll leave you to it."

"See you in an hour or so," Maddy promised, relieved that her plan was sliding nicely into place.

"Oh the long lost Mr Power!" declared Jack, as Jake re-entered the studio a few minutes later.

"Sorry, guys," apologised Jake shrugging his shoulders. "I fell asleep upstairs."

"How's the head?" called out Rich, with some concern in his voice.

"Better," said Jake, running his hand through his hair. "I can think straight at least."

"First time for everything," joked Paul.

"Yeah, very funny," muttered Jake then added, "I met Maddy upstairs. She said she'd be down in an hour."

Both the sound engineer and the producer looked surprised to hear this and Jack asked who she was meeting upstairs. Quickly, as he picked up his guitar and got plugged back in, Jake explained that it was an Englishman called Jason Russell. Knowingly the sound engineer nodded over to Dr Marrs. The producer gave him the thumbs up signal in return.

"Hey," said Grey, noticing this silent exchange "Is there something going on here that we should be in on?"

Dr Marrs laughed. "Maybe. Looks like Maddison is scheming. We'll see when she comes in. Now back to work. Guitar tracking. Jake, you're up. Track four if you please."

By the time Maddy and her English "friend" entered the studio Silver Lake were totally engrossed in the task at hand. A quick look at the whiteboard indicated to her just how much work they had put in over the first three days. It was impressive to say the least. Dr Marrs called a halt to the recording and greeted her warmly, then shook Jason's hand, "Long time no see, Mr Russell"

"Evening, Jim," he replied coolly. "Looks like this pet project of Maddison's is going well. She wants me to listen in for a while."

"Not a problem. Take a seat," invited the producer turning back to the window to the live room. "Rich, track four from the top if you please."

Rich was on form and nailed tracks four through to seven at the first time of asking. His fingertips were throbbing after playing all day and his wrist was stiffening up. Massaging his wrist, he asked for a break. The producer agreed and called Jake back up to do his part for tracks six and seven. Maddy interrupted the producer, smiling sweetly, "Do you have any vocals recorded that Jason could hear?"

"Maddison, you know my rules," replied Dr Marrs sharply. "The answer's no."

Sensing her plan drifting off course, she tried a different approach, "Do you have time for the band to even run through one track for us?"

"Bit hard, Maddison," he replied. "Rich just went out with Paul to get dinner. Only half a band here. Look for yourself."

"Maddy," called Jake, trying to diffuse the situation. "While we wait for dinner arriving, I could play a couple of acoustic versions for you. Doc, is that ok?"

Getting angrily to his feet, the producer declared he had fifteen minutes to do whatever the hell he liked as he was going for a coffee. As the door slammed shut behind them, Maddy apologised for causing trouble.

"Wouldn't be like you at all, Maddy," commented Jason with a smile. "Apologies for the interruption, gentlemen."

"It's been a long day" confessed Jake as he switched guitars.

"Guess everyone's feeling it a bit."

From his seat on the battered couch in the corner beside Todd, who was restringing one of Rich's guitars, Grey called out, "Hey, Jake, play her track eleven."

Perching himself up on a stool, Jake settled to play while Jason and Maddy came in to join them. All the technology was switched off- no amps, no mics- just him and his guitar. Closing his eyes, he began the first chords of Lady Butterfly. Within moments his haunting vocal was filling the live room, stirring deep emotions in his small audience. When the song was done, without a word to the others, he launched into an acoustic version of track three, also known as "Flyin' High." It was a total contrast of style. This one was harder, heavier and vocally powerful and strong. Reclined on the couch, Grey was nodding with approval at the impromptu performance Jake had given. As the last notes faded away, Maddy came forward and gave him a hug.

"Awesome, Jake," she whispered in his ear.

"That was quite something," said Jason calmly. "Quite something indeed."

"Thank you," acknowledged Jake humbly.

"Well, Mr Russell," began Maddison, changing tack. "Are you going to buy me dinner?"

"Subtle as ever," he declared. "Yes, I'll buy you dinner. Plenty to discuss tonight after this."

"Thanks again, guys," called Maddy as they turned to leave. "I'll see you all tomorrow. I'm meeting Lori here to go for lunch."

"Night, Maddy," called Jake, as he put his guitar back on the stand.

"Night," called Grey. As the door closed, he turned to Jake and asked, "What's that woman up to?"

"Lord knows," laughed Jake. "But I suspect we'll find out soon."

"She scares me," muttered the bass player. "Let's go and see if the others are back with our dinner yet."

During the cab journey from the apartment to the studio, Lori had tried to explain to Becky that they might not be able to have lunch with the band, but if she promised to be very quiet, they could perhaps visit the studio. Although the little girl had been perfectly behaved all week, Lori was a little anxious at taking her into the studio. If she was honest, she was a little anxious about visiting herself, but also excited at the thought of lunch with Maddy. The late morning traffic was congested and it felt as if the journey down to 28th Street took forever. Eventually the cab pulled over out of the stream of traffic and stopped outside the studios. Once inside the building, Lori led Becky towards the elevator and they headed up to the top floor lounge to meet Maddy as arranged.

The lounge was deserted when they arrived. Becky settled herself down on the couch and asked if she could watch TV. Lori passed her the remote control, then sat down beside her. Quickly she sent a text to Jake to let him know that they had arrived. Silver Lake knew the girls were coming down, but had not promised to be free to chat. There was still a lot of work to be done, and now that they had reached midweek, it felt a though time was running away from them. A cricket chirp came from her phone.

"Be there in 10. J x"

The little girl had found a cartoon channel and was happily watching Scooby Doo. She was totally engrossed in the show when her dad slipped silently into the lounge a few moments later and crept up on her.

"Boo," he whispered in her ear.

"Daddy!" she shrieked, throwing herself at him.

"Hi, Angel," said Grey, hugging her tight. "I've missed you this week."

"Me too," said Becky

"Hi, Lori," said Grey, sitting down on the opposite couch with his daughter glued to his side. "Is this young lady wearing you out?"

"Not yet," laughed Lori. "We're having a quiet day today. Lunch here, then we're heading home."

"You don't need to keep taking her places. She can watch TV for a day or two," said Grey. "I feel bad that you're running all over the city with her."

"Trust me," commented Lori with a smile. "I'm not running anywhere!"

"Sorry, bad joke," apologised Grey, looking a little embarrassed. "Anyway, Jake sent me up to fetch you both."

"Are we going to see the studio?" asked Becky excitedly.

"Yes, but we have to be very quiet," warned her daddy. "The guys are working. Uncle Jake's doing vocal tracks."

"What's that mean?" she asked curiously.

"He's singing," explained Lori, getting up from the couch. "And they are recording it."

Down in Studio B Jake had been working on the lead vocal tracking for four hours. There had been several false starts and a few fits of laughter as he forgot lyrics mid-song. So far it was all taken in good fun, but he was beginning to get exasperated with himself. As Lori and Grey crept in, he was just starting on Stronger Within. He was standing with his back to them, totally unaware that they were there; totally oblivious to the fact that Lori was listening intently to the lyrics he had written for her. His voice rang clear and strong, no lyric fluffs and after three runs through Dr Marrs was happy. As Jake removed his headphones and turned round, the first person he saw was Lori.

"Ok," called the producer. "Let's break for lunch. Be back by two."

Without a word, Jake came over and took Lori into his arms holding her tight. She snuggled into his chest and allowed herself to be held. Gently he tipped her chin up and kissed her passionately with no thought to the fact they were being watched.

"I love you, Mz Hyde," he whispered softly.

"Ditto," she whispered back.

Keeping a protective arm around her, Jake guided her out of the studio.

"Where are we going?" she asked.

"Lunch," he replied with a grin. "Maddy called and left a message to say we were all to meet her at the Thai place along the street. Any idea what she's plotting?"

"What makes you think she's plotting?"

"Because it seems like she always is!"

Lori giggled, "Plotting is her speciality."

The Thai restaurant was busy with office workers out for lunch when the band walked in. From a large table in the centre of the restaurant Maddy was waving at them. Spotting Lori she came rushing over to hug her friend, enthusing about how well she looked then she introduced Lori to the gentleman seated at the table.

"Lori, this is Jason Russell from JR Management," she said theatrically. "Jason, this is Mz Lori Hyde."

"Pleasure," greeted Jason, shaking Lori's hand. "I've admired your work for a while Mz Hyde. Perhaps we can talk business sometime? I've a few projects I would like to offer to you."

"Thanks. I'd be interested to hear about them," said Lori taking a seat. "What brings you to New York?"

"Maddison," he replied succinctly. "She's been setting up appointments for me all over the east coast."

Realising what was going on, Lori asked, "And have you found what you were looking for?"

"I believe I have," said Jason smoothly.

Over lunch, they all chatted like old friends talking about everyday events, anything except music. Becky held court for a few minutes as she told them about visiting the American Girl store, then Lori explained that they planned to go to Central Park zoo the following day then over to FAO Schwartz. The four members of Silver Lake bemoaned the fact that they had seen very little of the city so far and gradually the conversation turned naturally to their progress in the studio.

"Any plans for after you've finished recording?" asked Jason casually.

"Try to get a record deal or a support slot on a tour I guess," replied Rich.

"Do you have any management behind you?"

"Not as yet," admitted Rich. "Up until now we've looked after ourselves."

"Smart answer," chimed in Maddy with a suspicious looking smile.

"I'd like to talk to you about letting my company manage you," said Jason calmly. "Perhaps we can meet up tomorrow or Friday. I fly back to London on Friday night."

The band exchanged glances and nods, then Jake said, "Why don't we meet for breakfast tomorrow and we can take it from there?"

"Fine with me," agreed Jason. "Meet me at my hotel at eight. I'm staying at the Crowne Plaza."

"Deal," stated Grey before anyone butted in.

It was well after midnight when the band returned to the apartment. With a few grunts of "good night" they all crawled off to their separate rooms. The light was still on when Jake crept into the bedroom and he found Lori sitting up in bed reading. She put the book down as he collapsed onto the bed.

"I'm beat," he groaned. "I'm too old for this shit."

Lori giggled, "Sounds like you're just getting started, rock star."

"I know," he sighed. "Doesn't feel real."

"Oh, it's real alright," she commented. "Maddy has this covered. She'll be there tomorrow to keep you guys straight."

"I'm kinda glad to hear that," Jake admitted, as he hauled off his T-shirt. "We're out of our depth here. Way out!"

"She'll look after you," reassured Lori softly. "I spoke to her after you left the restaurant. Jason's a decent guy too, as far as I've heard."

"Do you not know him?"

"No," she admitted. "But I trust Maddy's judgement here one hundred percent."

"Guess we've no choice," he said with a yawn.

They chatted quietly for a few minutes about the progress the band had made that day and their plans for the last three days of studio time. They were on schedule to finish on Saturday and the producer was confident they would get all eleven tracks completed by late afternoon. Everything was coming together nicely.

"Is the plan to travel home on Sunday?" asked Lori.

"Grey and Paul need to be back for work on Monday," replied Jake. "I'm not sure about Rich."

"I thought maybe you and I could stay on for a couple of days," suggested Lori hopefully. "Play tourist perhaps?"

"Sounds like a plan. Will be nice to have you to myself for a while," agreed Jake pulling her closer to him.

"I was going to book a table for dinner for Saturday," continued Lori. "A sort of celebration dinner."

"Celebrate our freedom from Studio B?"

"That and my birthday," she confessed quietly.

"Your birthday?"

"Yes," nodded Lori. "I'll be thirty on Saturday."

"Why didn't you tell me?" accused Jake.

"I just did," she replied. "Now it's late. You've a big day ahead of you. Get some sleep."

"Night, li'l lady."

"Sweet dreams," she replied as she rolled over to her side of the bed.

Time was running away from Silver Lake as they remained locked away in Studio B. Recording ran like clockwork and, despite their lack of studio experience, Dr Marrs declared they were among the most professional and dedicated musicians he had had the pleasure of working with. He had joined them for their Thursday morning breakfast meeting with Jason and Maddy, wanting to ensure that negotiations went fairly. As a precaution he had brought along his ex-wife who was a lawyer. By ten o'clock Silver Lake were signed to JR Management with the promise that this was only the start for them; by ten thirty they were closeted away in the studio for another fourteen hour session. Friday had started even earlier than usual and it was almost dawn before they crawled back to the apartment for a few brief hours of rest.

While the band continued to work day and night, Lori and Becky kept themselves amused. Their trip to the zoo was fun, but short as the little girl was more interested in going to visit the toy store to play on the Big Piano. After a quick lunch at McDonalds, Lori gave in and led them over to FAO Schwartz. She videoed the little girl dancing on the famous Big Piano and sent it to Grey. Becky's delight at the experience made Lori smile with pride. It was heart-warming to see the little girl fully restored to her happy, carefree self. If Becky was happy it made it so much easier for Grey to accept that Sandy was gone. Lori had done her best to make sure the little girl would have plenty of happy memories of New York to take home to the beach. On Friday she took her clothes shopping for an outfit to wear to dinner on Saturday. Unable to decide on just one outfit, they left Macy's with two bags full of new clothes for the little girl.

When she awoke on Saturday morning, the instant ache from her leg warned Lori it was going to be a tough day. She was fully aware she had pushed herself to her limits every day during the week and now her battered body was starting to protest. There were some painkillers in the drawer of the nightstand beside the bed and she swallowed two before even attempting to get up. As she lay back, waiting for the medication to take effect, the bedroom door opened and Becky bounced in.

"I'm hungry, Lori," she declared, climbing up onto the four-poster bed.

With a weary sigh, Lori replied, "I too, honey, but can you wait a few more minutes? My leg's really sore today. I've just taken some medicine to help with the pain, but it will take a few minutes for it to work."

"Why's your leg sore?" asked Becky directly. The little girl had never asked her about her leg or why she walked with a cane or canes so the question came as a bit of a surprise.

"I had an accident a while ago," began Lori trying to keep it simple. "And I hurt it very badly. It's not fully healed yet. We've been out and about a lot this week, so today it's a bit painful."

Looking confused Becky asked, "What kind of accident?"

"A bad one," said Lori simply, not wanting to talk about it to the little girl any more than she would talk to anyone about that day. "I broke the big bone in my thigh. The doctors had to put the bone back together again with some metal pins and screws."

"Where are the pins and screws?" asked the little girl curiously.

"Inside my leg," explained Lori. "I had surgery to get it fixed. Well, several surgeries actually."

"Did that not hurt?"

"Yes, it did," said Lori softly. "But the nurses gave me medicine so that it wouldn't hurt too much."

"So why's it hurting today?"

"Well, began Lori, sitting up a bit. "My leg isn't very strong yet and if I walk about on it for too long it gets sore. We've had a busy week and I didn't rest it as much as I should have, so today it's very sore."

"Is it my fault?" asked Becky quietly, tears welling up in her eyes.

"No!" exclaimed Lori, reaching out to hug her close. "Not at all. Don't cry. I'll be fine in a little while, but we will have to have a lazy day today."

"Ok," nodded Becky, a look of disappointment crossing her face. "Can we maybe go to the park later if you feel better?"

"Let's see after lunch," relented Lori.

By early afternoon, after a morning of lying on the couch

watching cartoons and another two painkillers, Lori felt ready to face the world. She told Becky to go and fetch her shoes, then went to get herself ready for a short trip over to the park. Although it was only a couple of blocks over to Central Park, Lori decided to take a cab to the east side and to take Becky to see the Alice In Wonderland statue then head over to the lake where they raced model boats. It was also handy for a trip into the toy store if the little girl suggested it. Half an hour later the taxi dropped them off near the Metropolitan Museum of Art and Becky skipped her way along the path into the park. It never ceased to amaze Lori how trusting and accepting of the world around her that the little girl was. She was happily singing one of the songs from Barney and Lori found herself tempted to join in. Part of her was sad that this would be her last outing with her little friend for a while. Spending time with her had been refreshing and, she had to admit to herself, exhausting.

Around the same time in Studio B the last of the backing vocals had been recorded and Dr Marrs declared they were done. It was a huge relief to realise that they had finally finished all eleven tracks. All of them were exhausted but knowing that the hard work was finished for now, gave them a new lease of life. That morning Jake had brought his truck down to the studio, thankful that Jack had managed to secure a safe parking spot for the day. Once all their guitars and bits and pieces were safely stowed away in the back of the truck, Silver Lake returned to the studio one last time to say their goodbyes. Shaking Dr Marrs hand, Jake invited them to join the girls and the band for dinner later. All of them politely declined, declaring it had been a long week for them too.

It was almost four o'clock when Silver Lake all piled into Jake's truck to drive back to the apartment. The overly crowded streets and one way system kept Jake focussed on his driving as he headed uptown. Cursing under his breath, he longed to be back on the familiar roads around Rehoboth. When they finally arrived back at the apartment block's underground garage, he breathed a long sigh of relief.

"Will the gear be ok down here?" asked Grey.

"Garage is manned 24 hours a day," replied Paul as he

climbed out. "I got talking to the doorman guy the other night. No one's going to touch it. You have the golden protection of Mz Hyde over both trucks."

"Golden protection?" echoed Jake, unsure as to his friend's meaning.

"What are you getting at?" quizzed Grey with a frown.

"You guys don't know?" replied Paul, glancing round at his bandmates. "She owns the whole fucking building."

"What?" snapped Jake sharply.

"Lori owns the building," repeated Paul slowly and deliberately. "Ask the door guy if you don't believe me."

"Makes no difference to me," muttered Jake, heading towards the back of the truck.

He opened up the back of the truck and lifted out two of his guitars, slammed the lid shut and headed towards the elevator. Behind him, he could hear the guys still talking, but he had meant what he said. Money or no money, it was Lori he was in love with and no amount of money was changing that. As they all piled into the small elevator, after a subtle nudge from Grey, Paul apologised for acting like a jerk. Once again band harmony was restored.

As soon as they opened the door to the apartment, the band could hear the girls singing Barney songs in the kitchen.

"Daddy!" shrieked Becky, as she saw Grey enter the room.

"Hi, honey," he said, hugging her tight.

"Beer?" offered Lori, opening the fridge.

Beers in hand, the four musicians spilled out onto the terrace to chill for a while before dinner. It was still hot out and, after a week of being shut away indoors, it felt good to feel the sun on their skin. Even the stuffy city air tasted heavenly to them. Slowly conversation turned to plans for their departure in the morning. It had been agreed that Paul would drive Jake's truck back to Delaware and leave it at the beach house. Grey announced that they would be leaving early as his mother was expecting them for a family lunch. There were protests from Becky, who didn't want to go home at all, but, between them, Grey and Lori convinced her that Grammy was waiting to see her fancy new American Girl doll. Paul and Rich debated whether to play tourist for a while and eventually decided to visit the Empire State Building in the morning and head off around lunchtime.

"What's your plan, Jake?" asked Rich, draining the last dregs of his beer from the bottle.

"We'll hang around here for a day or two," answered Jake, sitting with his arm casually draped over Lori's shoulders. "Probably be down Tuesday at some point or maybe Wednesday."

"You know you're all more than welcome to stay on," invited Lori, secretly hoping they all said no.

"Think your man wants you to himself," stated Grey, with a wink.

Lori flushed bright red.

"Enough," chided Jake, also blushing.

"Come on, Becky," called Lori, getting up from her seat. "Time to get dressed for dinner. Let's leave the boys to enjoy their beers."

"Hey," said Jake. "Do we need to get all fancied up?"

"A clean shirt and non- ripped jeans should do you," replied Lori. "But we girls want to look our best."

Taking Becky by the hand, she disappeared indoors. Once downstairs in the bedroom, Lori helped the little girl dress in one of her new outfits. She chose a pretty pale blue sundress with daisies round the hem. To complete the outfit, Lori had bought her some sandals with daisies on the front, a small handbag in the shape of a daisy and two hair elastics with daisies on them. Once the little girl was ready, she sat on the bed and let Lori brush her hair and put it up into two ponytails.

"Thank you, Lori," she said, admiring in her reflection in the full length mirror.

"My pleasure," replied Lori warmly. "Now are you going to wait here until I get ready?"

Becky nodded and climbed back up onto the bed. Positioning herself with her back to the little girl, Lori stepped out of her jeans and pulled off her vest T-shirt. Her own new dress was hanging on the back of the door. As she limped over to lift it from the hanger, she caught a glimpse of Becky in the mirror. The little girl was staring wide eyed at the scars on her leg.

"It's the scar where the doctor put the pins in to fix my leg," explained Lori quietly.

"There must be a lot of pins in there," said Becky still staring.

"Can I touch it?"

The directness of the question caught Lori off guard and she could only nod silently. Slipping off the bed, Becky came over and ran her small warm hand over the full length of the surgical scar then gently fingered the other smaller rougher scars to the side.

"The doctor that made these wasn't very good," said Becky seriously. "The big one's all smooth and soft. These are all lumpy and bumpy."

Recovering some of her composure, Lori explained, "The smaller ones were caused by the accident not the surgery. No doctor made them."

"Oh!" said the little girl, not fully understanding. "Do they hurt?"

Lori shook her head, "Not any more, honey."

Turning away so that the little girl wouldn't see the tears in her eyes, Lori slipped the sea green maxi dress over her head and sighed as its silky material slid down her thighs, covering the scars once more.

"Have I done something bad?" asked Becky quietly. There were unshed tears glistening in her eyes.

"No, honey, you haven't" reassured Lori, hugging her tight. "I haven't shown those scars to too many people. I don't like them. They remind me of a very sad time. You definitely haven't done anything wrong."

"Has Uncle Jake seen them?"

"Yes," said Lori. "Now can they be a secret between you, me and Uncle Jake for now?"

Becky nodded.

"Thank you," sighed Lori, praying that the little girl would keep her promise, but also feeling guilty for asking her to keep secrets.

Sitting down at the dressing table, Lori quickly brushed her own hair up into a loose ponytail, applied a little make-up, treating Becky to a touch of lip gloss in the process, then slipped her feet back into her white Converse sneakers.

"Are you not going to wear some pretty shoes?" asked the little girl. "There's lots of shoes in your closet."

"Well," began Lori, "Most of them have heels and I still can't wear heels. It hurts my leg. Let's take a look for some flat pumps though."

The little girl opened the wardrobe doors and rummaged through the pile of shoes lying in the bottom. She found a pair of flat silver ballet pumps and insisted that Lori wear them. Laughing at her determination Lori changed her footwear then asked Becky to find her a silver bag to match.

"Happy, Little Miss Bossy?" she teased.

"You look like a princess," said a husky voice from the doorway.

"And how long have you been standing there?" Lori asked, as Jake stepped into the room.

"Long enough," he replied, then turning to Becky added, "Your dad's looking for you."

Without argument, the little girl skipped out of the room. Once she was safely out of the door, Jake pushed it closed then stepped over to where Lori was standing.

"You look beautiful, birthday girl," he whispered as he began to kiss her with a slow, gentle passion. "Happy birthday, Mz Hyde."

They stood kissing for a few moments. Through the thin material of her dress, Lori could feel Jake's passion hardening and stepped back just a little.

"Hey, slow down, rock star," she whispered softly.

"How am I meant to resist you, Lori?" he asked. "You're beautiful. You'd stir the loins of a corpse with that sexy look of yours."

"Nonsense," she giggled, suddenly feeling like an embarrassed teenager. "I just don't know if I'm ready."

"And I'm not about to rush you, li'l lady," he assured her hoarsely.

"I'm sorry, Jake," she apologised, a catch in her voice as tears welled up in her eyes.

"Sshh," he soothed, hugging her close. "Now how about letting me get showered and ready too?"

Lori nodded and stepped out of his embrace. Lifting her cane and her bag, she left the room, closing the door behind her.

Half an hour later they were all hanging about the living room waiting for Jake. Eventually they heard his feet on the stairs and he wandered in wearing tight black jeans and a black shirt, open at the neck. His long hair, still damp from the shower, had been pulled back at the nape of his neck and tied with a length of leather cord. Rolling up his shirt sleeves, he asked if they were all ready to go.

"It's you we are all waiting on, Uncle Jake," stated Becky bluntly. "Twenty bucks in the pot!"

The others laughed. Grey reached over to pick up his daughter, drew her a dark look before declaring, "Out of the mouths of babes, Jake. What can I say?"

Still giggling, Lori picked up the phone to call down to the concierge, "Evening, Charles. It's Lori Hyde. Can you get me two cabs, please? We're headed out to Amarone."

Putting the phone back on the cradle, she turned to the others, "Let's go, guys. Time to celebrate."

By the time they reached the foyer there were two cars waiting for them. After a quick debate, Paul went in one with Grey and Becky while the others got into the second car. It didn't take the drivers long to navigate through the early evening traffic towards Hell's Kitchen. Jake helped Lori out of the car while Rich insisted on picking up the fare. Confidently she led them into the Italian restaurant, her favourite in the city.

"Miss Hyde," welcomed the maître d', "Lovely to see you again. Table for six?"

"Yes, thanks," she replied. "It's lovely to be back."

"I've reserved your usual corner table," he said, leading the way through the restaurant.

Once they were all seated, he took their drinks order, then left them to browse the menu. The four band members all looked at each other as they tried to decipher the Italian menu. Noticing a growing confusion among the members of Silver Lake, Lori quietly recommended a few dishes from the extensive menu that she hoped covered all tastes. She also reassured Grey that they would prepare a simpler dish for Becky if she would prefer that. When their waiter came back over a short while later they all placed their order with a mock confidence that made Lori giggle.

"Sorry, boys," she apologised. "I didn't intend to make you feel uncomfortable there."

"No harm done," said Rich with a smile.

The wine waiter approached with the two bottles she had

selected from the list. Lori nodded her approval and asked him to pour. Once they all had a full glass, she proposed a toast, "To the success of Silver Lake"

"To rock'n'roll," declared Paul theatrically.

"No," corrected Jake warmly, "To Lori. Happy Birthday, Mz Hyde."

She blushed, then added, "To health, wealth and happiness."

While they waited for their starters to arrive, Becky produced a gift bag from beneath the table and gave it to Lori.

"It's from all of us," she said with a smile.

Lori carefully opened the small bag to reveal a long slim black jewellery box. She opened it to find a silver charm bracelet with three guitar charms, drumsticks and two music notes. It was perfect.

"Thank you," she said softly. "Can one of you help me to put it on?"

Jake obliged by helping her with the catch before producing a second small gift bag, "And this is from me."

Inside the bag she found a second small black box, squarer in shape. She opened it to find a delicate silver chain with a treble clef hanging from it. There was a small diamond in the tail of the treble clef.

"It's perfect," she whispered, kissing Jake on the cheek, "I love it."

"Put it on, Lori," squealed Becky, clapping her hands.

Again, Jake assisted her, kissing the nape of her neck as he fastened the clasp. "I'm glad you like it."

"Thank you," said Lori again. "I never expected presents. You're all too kind."

"Nonsense," stated Grey. "It's the least we could do after all you've done for us this week and for Becky."

"It's been a pleasure."

From across the restaurant, the maître d' spotted the birthday celebrations and quietly slipped off to the wine cellar. Just before the party's main course was brought out from the kitchen, he came over with a bottle of champagne.

"Compliments of the house, Miss Hyde," he said with a smile. "And happy birthday from Amarone."

"Thanks, Marco. This is too kind."

"Nonsense."

"Can we save it for dessert, please?" suggested Lori.

"Of course," he replied and retreated from the table as the waiter arrived with their meal.

Champagne and gateau provided a delicious end to a wonderful meal. All the stresses and strains of the studio seemed a long way away as Silver Lake laughed, told stories and joked with each other through all three courses of dinner. As the champagne bubbles lowered Lori's guard a little, she told a few tales about her exploits with Maddy and the rest of girls club. Before they knew it, their meal was over and it was getting late. At some point, Becky had climbed up into her daddy's knee and fallen asleep with her head resting on his chest.

"I'd better get this little girl home to bed," he said, cradling her in his tattooed arms.

"Time we were all making a move," agreed Jake, reaching for his wallet.

Lori put a hand on his arm. "Already taken care of."

"You shouldn't have to pay for your own celebratory end of recording dinner," she countered with a mischievous smile. "You can buy me dinner tomorrow night, rock star."

"Deal," he said, kissing the back of her hand.

"We're going to head up to Times Square," announced Paul, pushing his chair back. "Let our hair down a bit."

"Don't let it down too much, boys," cautioned Grey.

"We'll behave," promised Rich, with a wink to Paul. "Thanks for dinner, Lori."

"Pleasure," she replied softly. "Jake, can you ask the waiter to call us a cab?"

Once back at the apartment, Lori went to open a bottle of wine while Jake put on some music. Grey had carried the still sleeping Becky downstairs to put her to bed. The little girl had barely stirred during the drive back uptown. With the gentle strains of some country music filtering through the house, Lori carried the wine through to the lounge. She had left her cane lying propped up in the hallway and Jake resisted the temptation to reach out and help as she limped across the room, a mix of determination and pain etched across her face. Setting the bottle and glasses down on the coffee table, she asked him to pour.

"You ok?" he asked, passing her a glass.

She nodded before replying, "Just over did things this week."

"Have you taken something for the pain?"

"Yes, mom," she teased. "I'll be fine in a few minutes."

Before Jake could reply, Grey came striding back in, "She's still sound asleep. I think you've worn her out this week, Lori."

"I think they've worn each other out," Jake observed, handing the bass player a glass of wine.

"We've had fun," said Lori, stretching out on the couch. "It's hard work having fun."

"You've spoiled her rotten," stated Grey. "I don't know how to repay you. Thank you just doesn't seem enough."

"Don't be silly," smiled Lori. "I had as much fun treating her as she's had getting presents. After what you've both been through, she deserved a little spoiling."

"You're an amazing woman, Lori Hyde," said Grey, raising his glass to her.

Lori blushed and took a sip from her own glass. The painkillers she had taken were starting to take effect. Slowly she bent and stretched her leg a few times then sighed.

"Leg still troubling you?" enquired Grey a tenderness in his tone.

"A bit."

"From the look of pain on your face earlier, it's more than a bit," commented Jake, moving to sit on the floor in front of her.

"Ok," she confessed. "I'll not lie. I'm sore tonight, but I'll be fine in the morning."

Jake rested his hand on her knee, "You're stubborn, li'l lady."

"That's what's got me this far," she stated. "Oh, Grey, Becky saw my scars earlier. Just in case she says anything. She was really sweet about them."

"Thanks for the warning," he answered then to change the subject asked, "What's your plans for the next couple of days?"

"That's up to Jake," replied Lori. "Although it will include a trip to the Metropolitan Museum of Art."

"Oh, will it?"

"Yes, it will," she stated firmly. "I love that place, but I didn't think Becky was ready for it so I've not had my fix yet."

"I was thinking of going with the guys to the Empire State Building in the morning if you've no plans," admitted Jake.

"Fine by me," agreed Lori.

"Rather you than me," declared Grey. "I don't do heights. This place is high enough for me."

"It has to be done," laughed Jake. "I've never been that high."

"What? Never?" teased Grey playfully. "I beg to differ, Mr Power. I remember a certain night in Baltimore…."

"Shut the fuck up, Grey," growled Jake. "Lori, doesn't need to hear about that."

"It's OK, Grey. I know he's been there," said Lori, running her fingers through Jake's hair. "We've all got stories we could tell, but are best left in the past."

As their glasses emptied, Lori announced she was worn out and headed to bed, leaving the two friends to chat over the last of their wine. Both musicians watched her as she left the room, limping heavily. She paused in the hallway to pick up her cane then made her way carefully down the oak staircase.

Once he was sure she was out of ear shot Grey said, "She's a wonderful girl, Jake. Look after her."

"I intend to," replied Jake sleepily. "Grey, I love her."

"I can tell. You guys are great together. There's a special chemistry there."

"I hope so," sighed Jake, finishing the last of his wine. "Time for bed."

There were more than a few tears from Becky the next morning as she said goodbye to Lori and her three Silver Lake uncles. At her insistence, Jake carried her down to the garage and promised that she could come over for a BBQ on Saturday and that he would play in the ocean with her. That was enough to stem the flow of tears long enough to get her into the truck and strapped into her car seat. Clutching her doll, she waved as Grey pulled out of the garage into the bright sunlight. Back upstairs Rich and Paul were getting ready to head off to the Empire State Building. Both of them were nursing hangovers and had decided a walk down to 34th Street would be the best cure. Planting a kiss on Lori's cheek, Jake promised they would be back for lunch.

With everyone gone, Lori decided that she was going back to bed for a couple of hours. Her own head was a little muzzy, a combination of the wine, champagne and painkillers she'd taken the night before. Another couple of hours of sleep would help. As she snuggled down in the soft mattress, she reflected over the last few days. Having friends around had been good for her. Inside, she felt more like the old Mz Hyde than she had since her accident. The ghosts of her past hadn't risen to haunt her as she had feared. She had faced several demons, although so far she had avoided the scene of the crime. Feeling content within herself, she closed her eyes and drifted off to sleep.

It was Jake's gentle kiss that wakened her some time later. He was stroking her hair and smiling down on her as she opened one sleepy eye.

"Good afternoon, sleeping beauty," he whispered.

"Shit!" she exclaimed. "What time is it?"

"Almost two," he replied.

"Lunch," she muttered. "I had meant to order in some food."

"Calm down, li'l lady," soothed Jake, as she sat up. "Rich has gone out to find a deli. He'll bring back lunch for all of us. Are you ok?"

"Fine," she replied. "I must have really fallen into a deep sleep."

"You must've needed it," he answered, helping her up.

"I guess. Let me jump in the shower quickly. I'll be up in a few minutes."

"Take your time, Lori," he said. "The guys aren't planning to leave until about four. Plenty of time."

"Ok. I won't be long."

It was nearer five when Rich and Paul finally gathered up their bags to leave. As he handed over the keys to his truck, Jake made his friend promise to take it easy, not to take it over sixty five and to watch his paintwork in the city traffic. As the elevator door closed on the two musicians, Jake wrapped his arms around Lori and kissed her on the forehead.

"Finally," he sighed. "We're alone."

"Will be kind of quiet here without them all," she mused. "It's been a busy week."

"Tell me about it," laughed Jake, hugging her tight. "Do you feel up to going for a walk?"

"Let's head over to the park and see where we end up," suggested Lori. "As long as we don't end up at the toy store!"

They meandered through Central Park hand in hand in the late afternoon sunshine. Several joggers trotted past them as they made their way towards Fifth Avenue. Occasionally Jake stole a glance down at Lori as they walked. Every so often they would stop to rest on a bench or a rocky outcrop and watch the world go by. Lori guided Jake through the park to show him the Alice In Wonderland statue that Becky had so excitedly told them about over dinner. They then sat on a bench for another spell watching the model yacht fanatics' sail their craft on the pond. As the day slipped towards dusk, it began to grow cooler and a welcome gentle breeze wafted over them. Suitably rested, they exited the park onto Fifth Avenue.

"Where to now?" asked Jake, as he looked up and down the busy avenue.

"Hail a cab," instructed Lori glancing at her watch. "I've an idea and we might just make it on time."

"Yes, ma'am."

A few moments later a yellow cab pulled up at the kerbside. Ever the gentleman, Jake helped Lori in before sliding in beside her.

"Rockefeller Plaza," requested Lori.

Jake looked at her quizzically, but she just smiled. A few short minutes later the cab stopped alongside the Rockefeller Center's Observatory entrance. Allowing Jake to pick up the fare, she then led them into the building. Much to her surprise, the queue for tickets to the Observation Deck was short considering the time of day. With two tickets and a map clutched in her hand, they followed the line through to the elevators. It was busier through here, but the lines were moving and they waited patiently with all the other tourists. Within fifteen minutes they were at the head of the line and first into the next empty elevator. As they stepped out of it a few moments later, Lori breathed a sigh of relief. They had made it just in time. Taking Jake's hand, she led him across the Observation Deck to watch the sun set over the city. It was a beautiful clear evening and the view was as breath-taking as she remembered it. She let Jake go up to the top level on his own while she enjoyed a quiet moment, gazing out over Central Park, trying to locate her own building off to the left of the Natural History Museum. When Jake came back down to join her, they moved to the opposite side of the observation area and gazed out over lower Manhattan.

"Good call, Mz Hyde," he complimented, as he stood behind her with his arms wrapped round her shoulders. "The view's stunning at this time of day."

"It is, isn't it?" she agreed wistfully. "Do you want to take the ferry tomorrow and visit the Statue of Liberty and Ellis Island?"

"We could do if you're feeling up to it."

"Don't fuss, Jake. I'll be fine."

It had grown dark and the sun had fully set by the time they were back at street level. Smelling food from the dining area in the courtyard reminded them both that they hadn't had dinner. Deciding not to venture any further, they wandered through the plaza in search of somewhere to eat. They checked out the menus at a few places before selecting the gourmet burger bar on the grounds that it looked less crowded.

Just as she was about to take a bite out of her burger, a silver haired man approached the table, "Well, well, well the elusive Lori Hyde."

Dropping her burger onto the plate, Lori whirled round sharply, "David!"

Rushing to her feet, she hugged the stranger tightly, then turned to face a rather bemused looking Jake.

"David, this is my friend, Jake Power," she introduced shyly. "Jake, this is David Chandler, my accountant and financial conscience and mentor."

The two men shook hands, both silently noting the other's strong firm handshake.

"Will you join us?" asked Lori, taking her seat again.

"I've already eaten," explained the older man. "But I'll join you for a quick drink if that's ok?"

"Pull up a chair," welcomed Jake warmly.

As he sat down, David asked how the week in the city had worked out.

"Busy," admitted Lori. "Jake has been in the studio all week with the band. I've been looking after his friend's little girl. I did manage lunch with Maddy midweek."

"That creature will get you into trouble one day," cautioned David, failing to mask his obvious dislike of Maddy.

"I can get myself into enough trouble without her help," laughed Lori, in an attempt to lighten the atmosphere.

A waitress took another drinks order from them, then David asked, "And how are you recovering, Lori? Honestly now."

"Slowly," she confessed, without looking up from her plate. "I just need to be more aware of my limits."

"Yes, you do," agreed Jake. "This is one stubborn lady, sir."

"Oh, don't I know it!" David replied, with a twinkle in his eyes. "I've known her for almost thirty years. She's never been anything else. Drove her poor father crazy."

"David!" exclaimed Lori shrilly, "No stories, please!"

"No promises," he replied, winking at Jake. "Now I do have some paperwork at the office that needs your signature. How long are you in town for?"

"Another two days," she replied. "Courier it over and I'll look at it."

The accountant nodded, then asked what their plans were before they returned to the beach. He offered a few suggestions of alternative things to do, then glanced at his watch before declaring he would need to run. "I'm meeting Olivia outside St Patrick's. She'll nag if I'm late."

"Give her my regards," said Lori fondly. "You'll both need to come to Rehoboth sometime. The sea air would be good for you."

"Too hot and crowded for me in summer," he muttered. "Maybe in the fall if you are still there."

"I'll hold you to that."

"Pleasure to meet you, Jake. Take good care of her," said David, smiling over at Lori.

"I intend to, sir."

With a wave, he was off and heading towards the door.

"He's a character," remarked Lori a few moments later. "David was my dad's closest friend and advisor. After Dad's death, he became my financial advisor and conscience."

"He manages your affairs?"

"Yes," she replied before adding, "He manages my business affairs, holds the purse strings. I joke that he's my Jiminy Cricket. All my expenditure from the trust goes through him. Anything into four figures gets his approval."

Jake laughed at the thought of her having to ask permission to spend her own money.

"What's so funny?"

"I just got a mental picture of you asking for an allowance," he smirked.

"Oh, I get a very generous monthly allowance," she replied. "And he doesn't touch anything I personally earn. I'm not good with the big numbers though. I'd be lost without him."

"Glad to have met him."

"I'm glad you met him too," she confessed. "After the accident, it was David who sat with me in the hospital. Him and Maddy. One of them was always there. Every day for the first three weeks. They both put their lives on hold for me."

"I'm glad you weren't alone," said Jake, not wanting to think of her lying battered and broken in a hospital bed.

"Me too," she said quietly.

Lori was quiet during the rest of the meal and in the cab on the way back to the apartment. Once back in the house, she seemed to shake off her dark mood. While Jake went into the kitchen to fetch them a drink, she put on some music in the living room and lit a few candles, creating a soft romantic atmosphere. She was standing gazing out of the window when Jake came through with some wine for them both. Not wanting to disturb her, he sat on the floor, leaning on the couch watching her. Standing there with her arms wrapped round herself, she looked small, frail and a little lost. Her blonde hair was glinting with gold highlights in the flickering candle light. Eventually something broke her daydream and she turned to cross the room. She was suddenly aware of Jake watching her and she smiled.

"You ok, li'l lady?" he asked, his voice inexplicably husky.

"Yes," she replied, coming to sit on the couch behind him. "I think so."

"You looked to be miles away there."

"Well, I'm back now," she said, kissing him on the nape of the neck. "And I wouldn't be anywhere else."

"Same here," he replied, turning to face her.

With a gentle passion Jake lifted her round to sit across his lap and then he slowly began to kiss her across her throat then down her décolletage. She allowed him to remove her top and to continue to deliver light feathery kisses across her breasts. Beneath her thighs, she could feel his jeans straining against her. As Jake reached up to unfasten her bra, she put a hand on his.

"Not here, please," she whispered. "Let's go downstairs."

There was no second invitation required as he easily scooped her up into his arms and carried her down to the master bedroom. Gently he sat her on the end of the bed and knelt before her as she slowly undid his shirt buttons. As Lori slipped the well-worn cotton shirt off his well-muscled shoulders, she kissed his chest, gently biting at his nipples. With a smile that said "two can play at that game", Jake unfastened her bra, discarding it carelessly on the floor. With a moist tongue, he licked her breasts, then blew a cold breeze on them, causing her nipples to harden instantly. Before Lori could protest, he removed his jeans and shoes in a swift, fluid series of movements. Wearing only his boxers, he stood over her and slowly, sensually slid her jeans down, pulling her shoes off with no thought to unfastening them. His eyes barely registered the scars on her thigh as he lifted her to remove her fine lacy underwear. Nervously, hands trembling, Lori reached out to slide his shorts down over his slender hips. For the first time they were naked in front of each other. As though she weighed no more than a feather, Jake lifted Lori into his arms, holding her facing him and supporting her buttocks in his hands as she wrapped her legs around his hips. He barely registered the small wince of pain that crossed her face.

"Are you sure?" he whispered, following the question with a caress of his tongue along the edge of her ear.

"Yes," murmured Lori softly.

Jake laid her down in the centre of the bed, kissing her breasts, then caressing her entire body with tender kisses. Pausing only to roll on a condom that he had optimistically left in the nightstand drawer the night before, he swiftly moved to straddle her. Cupping her silky smooth buttocks in his hands, he slowly entered her, feeling her moist and ready for him. Initially Lori seemed tense, then as he began to move in long, slow strokes he felt her relax. He quickened the pace, moving rhythmically but taking care not to hurt her. Their lovemaking was gentle but passionate. Jake was terrified that he was hurting her; scared she would break under him. Lori's nerves and apprehension melted away with each gentle stroke and in perfect harmony they climaxed together. She shuddered slightly as Jake's orgasm shot through him and his fire flooded into her. As Jake withdrew, she let out a sigh, more purr than sigh, and sank back onto the soft pillows. He kissed her hard then slipped out of bed.

Alone in the bedroom for a few moments, Lori savoured the lingering fire inside her. In the background, she could hear Jake moving around in the bathroom. Closing her eyes she let out a contented sigh. It had been a long time….

A few minutes later, Jake returned to bed, bringing their wine glasses down from the living room newly replenished. Lori had moved over to her regular side of the bed and had pulled on a T-shirt. Taking the glass from him, she said, "Thank you."

"For the wine?" he enquired, with a cheeky grin.

She blushed, but remained silent.

"I didn't hurt you, did I?" asked Jake softly, as he slid back into bed beside her.

"No," replied Lori with a smile.

"I was so scared that I'd hurt you," he confessed, before taking a sip his wine.

"I'm not that fragile," she giggled, touched by his concern.

"Glad to hear it," replied Jake, kissing her on the forehead. "I love you, li'l lady."

"Love you too."

For the next two days they played tourist across the city. They took the ferry from Battery Park to Ellis and Liberty Islands; they visited Ground Zero on their return and then the following day Lori introduced Jake to the Metropolitan Museum of Art. Her passion and love for the museum rubbed off on him as she showed him her favourite exhibits. The sheer scale of the museum amazed him and, when she led him through the Egyptian exhibit to the Temple of Dendur, he was stunned into silence by the fact that a whole Egyptian temple was standing there before him. His childlike enthusiasm and excitement filled her with even more love for him. When they finally left the museum, they sat on its front steps, listening to a street entertainer and watching the world go by on Fifth Avenue. Once Lori felt rested, she led him down the street to St Patrick's Cathedral. Again he was entranced by the gothic architecture and the vibrant brilliance of the Cathedral's recently restored stained glass. Lori sat quietly in a pew while Jake toured the building. Sitting quietly in the serene atmosphere, she offered up a prayer of thanks to whatever deity was listening. Life felt restored after her long dark, troubled months.

When they left St Patrick's, Lori said she felt up to the walk down to the theatre district and that she had somewhere in mind for dinner. Slowly they meandered down Fifth Avenue, then zig zagged their way across to Broadway. Jake became aware that at the walk/don't walk signs Lori tensed up but he kept quiet. Eventually they reached the buzz of Times Square and passed through onto 44th Street towards a former church that had been converted into a bustling restaurant. For a Tuesday evening, the place was bustling but the young waitress quickly found them a table in the front section nearest the door.

"Pizza," muttered Jake, as he surveyed the menu. "Pizza?"

Lori laughed that beautiful musical laugh that he adored and declared, "I like pizza."

"Hmmph," he said, feigning anger. "I'm having chicken parmigiana. I've seen enough pizza!"

"You can have anything you fancy," replied Lori, closing the menu. "But I'm having a pepperoni pizza and a cold beer."

Jake laughed at the determined look on her face, "And I wouldn't dare to dream of depriving you of it, Mz Hyde."

After their meal was over, they took one last short walk through Times Square then hailed a cab to take them back to the apartment. Both of them had had their fill of the city and were ready to return to the beach. When they arrived back at the apartment, Lori began fussing about packing up some bits and pieces she wanted to take back with them. Jake had already packed his bags and his guitars lay in their cases in the hallway. While Lori muttered and clattered about in her studio workspace, he took his acoustic guitar out of its case and sat in the dining room playing quietly for himself. A new melody was forming in his head and he passed the time by messing around with a few variations of it. Eventually, shortly before midnight, Lori had packed up the items she wanted and added two art folders, plus a large canvas bag to the pile of luggage already gathering in the hallway.

Next morning they both slept late then made love leisurely before conceding that it was time they made a move to depart. After a late breakfast of coffee and bagels, Jake asked what car he was to take the bags down to. Lifting a set of keys from the dish on the hall table, Lori said, "Silver Mercedes in bay 16."

"Mercedes?" he echoed, eyes wide in disbelief.

"Yes. The silver one in bay 16," repeated Lori, stifling a giggle. "Don't panic. I'll drive the first stint."

The silver e-class coupe sat in bay 16 exactly as she had said. It was the first Mercedes Jake had ever been in and he was a little nervous at the thought of having to drive it part of the way back to Delaware. All of a sudden he was missing his truck.

It took him three trips up and down to the garage before he had all their luggage stowed away in Lori's car. With the last of the bags safely locked in the trunk, he went back upstairs to collect Lori. He found her standing in the living room, locking up the French doors to the terrace.

"Ready to go home, li'l lady?" he called cheerfully.

"Sure am," she replied with a smile. "I need to taste that ocean air."

"Let's go then, Mz Hyde," said Jake, putting his arm around

her waist. "Are you sure you've got everything?"

"No," she laughed. "But if I'm missing anything I know where it is."

"Come on. Let's go home."

Getting back behind the wheel of her own car felt good to Lori. She had owned the car for a couple of years and had missed driving it. With a wave to the garage attendant, she pulled out into the sunlight. With long practiced skill, she drove smoothly through the manic New York traffic and had soon navigated her way to the Holland Tunnel. Part of her was sad to be leaving the city behind as she drove through the congested tunnel, but the other half of her was desperate to get back to their quiet life at the beach. As they approached the first toll booth on the New Jersey Turnpike, she muttered something under her breath.

"You ok?" asked Jake. "I'd take the middle toll booth. Line's shorter."

"I meant to get an EZ Pass before we left to save hassle," explained Lori, heading towards the middle line. "Can you fish in the glove compartment, please? There should be some dollar bills in there."

"No worry. I've got some here," said Jake. "I remembered the tolls from the ride up and made sure I kept some change for the way back."

"Mr Organised," teased Lori taking the cash from him. "Thank you."

Once clear of the turnpike toll, they settled back to enjoy the drive. The roads were quiet, making it easier for Lori. She set up the car's cruise control, turned up the stereo and flashed a quick smile at Jake.

"Where do you want to change over?" he asked, feeling a little less anxious about driving her precious car.

"We could stop at New Castle for a late lunch. That's a little over half way. We could swap there?" she suggested.

"Sounds like a plan," agreed Jake.

They drove on in silence for a few more minutes. From his view from the passenger seat, Jake noticed that the further away from the city they got, the more relaxed Lori looked. There had been times over the last few couple of days while they had been out and about that she had seemed tense and edgy and then a few moments later she would appear completely relaxed. He suspected it had to do with her accident, but while they had been in the city he hadn't liked to ask. Now felt like a better time to attempt to ask her about it.

"Can I ask you something, Lori?"

"Sure. No promises I'll answer, though," she joked playfully.

"Did you lay your ghosts to rest on that trip?"

"Some of them."

"And the ones relating to your accident?" he pressed softly. "Did you lay them to rest?"

"A bit."

"Lori," he began suddenly lost for the right words. He had rehearsed the question in his head for the last five miles to get it word perfect and now it was gone. Instead, he asked simply, "What happened?"

She stared silently straight ahead at the clear highway in front of them. He thought for a moment that she wasn't going to reply. After, what to Jake felt like an eternity, Lori began to speak slowly and haltingly, "It was midweek. Just before Christmas. December 22nd to be exact and I had gone out shopping. I had a few last minute gifts to pick up. I'd had a breakfast meeting with David at Rockefeller Plaza then I'd set off down Fifth Avenue. I remember it was raining. I had just crossed 46th street, then decided to cross back over Fifth Avenue to go to the book store. I could hear sirens coming towards me. Lots of sirens. There was a school class trip coming up the street towards me. I believe they were heading to St Patrick's. We were all crossing at the same crosswalk. There was one little girl tagging along at the back of the group. She was the last to cross. I was behind them all. The sirens were coming along the street at my back and, as she stepped into the road, I caught sight of a black motorcycle coming round the corner from my left. I jumped out to push her out of its path. I reached her in the nick of time. The bike hit me. One of the police cars chasing it hit the little girl."

Lori paused. A single tear ran down her cheek. She never took her eyes off the road.

"I was thrown in the air by the force of the impact. I remember the hot pain in my leg as I landed. The cold, wet feeling of the hardtop on my face when the world stopped moving. I could see under the police car. The little girl lay staring straight at me. I can still see her blank stare when I close my eyes. I knew instantly she was gone."

A second tear rolled down her cheek. Silence filled the car for a few moments before she continued, "After that, all I remember hearing was screaming. I don't know if some of the screams were mine. Someone dialled 911. Ambulances arrived. I must have passed out because the next thing I remember vaguely is the paramedics working on me. I blacked out before they moved me into the ambulance and the rest I'm not sure of. I came to in Mount Sinai hospital after the first major surgery with David and Maddy beside me. That was two days later. They'd both been there the whole time."

She paused again. "If I hadn't pushed the girl out of the way the motorbike would have hit her. Maybe she would have lived. Maybe she wouldn't. I'll never know if I helped to kill her or not. The police were chasing the bike guy for armed robbery. He wasn't badly hurt. He's due for trial soon. He's already been tried for the robbery and convicted. Now he's facing trial over the girl's death and my injuries. The paperwork David sent over yesterday was my final statement for the case. That signed statement means I don't need to attend court. I couldn't face that."

Wiping her tears away with one hand Lori said, "So now you know. Apart from my leg, I fractured my pelvis, my right wrist and collarbone. I was a grazed and bruised wreck from hitting the ground so hard. It wasn't a pretty sight for a while."

"Oh Lori," began Jake quietly. "I don't know….."

"Jake," she interrupted sharply. "There's nothing you can say. Just don't ask me to tell you about it again, please. It's too hard. Too painful. Too many ghosts."

"We crossed at that cross walk yesterday," Jake realised, suddenly remembering that she had seemed to freeze for a moment before following him across the street.

"I know," replied Lori with a weak smile. "And stepping off that kerb beside you was the toughest thing I've done for a long time. I wanted to tell you. I just couldn't blurt this out in the middle of the street."

"You're one hell of a woman, Mz Hyde," complimented Jake. "I won't mention it again. I promise."

"Well, now you know how I ended up in this state," she said, recovering her composure.

"Who else knows the full story?"

"David, Maddy and Mary," replied Lori. "A handful of police, lawyers and doctors."

"Explains why those guys are so protective towards you."

"I guess," she sighed then, spotting a sign post, commented. "Only twenty miles till we stop. You ready to drive my baby?"

"Shitting myself," declared Jake honestly. "There's more buttons on there than the bridge of the Enterprise!"

"You'll be fine," reassured Lori warmly. "I trust you."

When he got behind the wheel after their lunch stop Jake's nerves had settled. Calmly Lori told him how to adjust the seat to the right position for him and save the settings, gave him a quick tour of the dashboard and steering wheel controls then sat back and relaxed beside him. Sliding the car into drive he pulled carefully out of the parking lot and back onto the highway. Nervous of the cruise control and all the electronic gadgetry, he asked Lori how to turn it all off. After a few miles he began to relax and Lori noticed that the tension in his shoulders visibly decreased.

"So," she began with an impish grin. "Do I get to drive your truck?"

"If you want," he replied with a hint of reluctance. "That is, if it has survived Paul driving it home."

Lori laughed before adding, "You're safe for now. It's a stick shift, so I can't drive it just now."

"Let me know when you're ready to give it a try."

Eventually the Rehoboth Beach water tower came into sight. They were almost home. Lori opened the windows and let the salty sea air fill the car. Without a word they smiled at each other, silently agreeing it was good to be home. When they had stopped for lunch, Lori had called ahead to Mary to check if they needed to bring anything in or if she had stocked up the refrigerator. The housekeeper was delighted to hear Lori's voice and reassured them that all they needed to do was to bring themselves. She promised to wait at the house until they got there. As they drove through town, both of them drank in the familiar sights, sounds and smells. It was after four before Jake finally pulled up in the driveway in front of the beach house. With a sigh of relief, he noticed that his truck was parked safely in its usual spot under the tree with Mary's car parked alongside. As they both climbed stiffly out of the Mercedes, the front door opened and the small housekeeper rushed out to greet them.

"Welcome home!" she called cheerfully.

"It's nice to be back," admitted Lori, giving Mary a hug. "How are things?"

"Not good," sighed Mary. "I'll tell you all about it later. I've just made a pot of coffee."

"Music to my ears," declared Lori heading indoors.

"Hi, Mary," called Jake from the far side of the car, flashing her a smile.

Much to his surprise, the older woman came round to hug him, "Nice to see you back too, son."

"Thanks. I've missed the ocean."

"Not a city lover?" she asked with a smile.

"It's ok for a visit," replied Jake, following her into the house.

All three of them sat out on the deck with their coffee, enjoying the late afternoon sun and between them Jake and Lori filled Mary in on how the trip had gone and the sights they had seen. Both of them reassured her that Lori had not pushed herself too hard. As he drained the last of his coffee, Jake excused himself to fetch Lori's luggage from the car. Once alone, the two women began to chat about how Rehoboth has been while they had been out of town.

"Mary," said Lori softly, touching the housekeeper on the arm. "What's wrong?" I can tell you're worried. Is it your sister?"

The older woman nodded and began to weep, "She's back in hospital. The tumour was malignant. The doctors are doing further surgery on Friday."

"Why didn't you tell me? You should've called me, Mary," scolded Lori, her voice filled with concern.

"I didn't want to bother you, honey," said Mary, wiping away her tears. "You've been so good to me. I wanted to be here when you got home. Needed to know you were ok."

"Oh, Mary," sighed Lori, hugging her tight. "I'm so sorry about your sister. Remember your family comes first not me."

"You're almost family to me," said Mary. "I worry about you

too."

With a smile Lori thanked her, then said she should be at the hospital or with her sister's kids.

"I know I should," agreed Mary. "I just wanted to see you safely home first."

"Mary, no arguing. Take whatever time you need here. I'll be fine."

The housekeeper nodded, "I'm scared, Lori."

"I know. I wish I could tell you it will all be ok," said Lori softly. "If there's anything I can do, you only have to ask."

"Thank you," whispered the older woman, tears welling up in her eyes. "If it's ok with you, I'll wash the cups then go. I'll call you on Friday to let you know how things go."

"Leave the cups," stated Lori firmly. "Go home, Mary. Be strong for your sister. You know where I am if you need anything."

"Thank you," she whispered, rising to leave. "I'll see you soon."

A few minutes later, Jake came back out onto the sun deck and announced that her bags were in the bedroom and her studio stuff had been left in the lounge for now.

"Mary looked upset as she drove off," he commented casually.

"Her sister's still in hospital. It doesn't sound good," replied Lori. "I've told her to take some time off."

"You're too soft," he said with a smile. "Feel up to a walk along the beach?"

"Sounds good," agreed Lori. "I'm stiff after sitting in the car for so long."

The beach south of the house was deserted. It felt good to have sand underfoot again as opposed to the hard city sidewalks and to hear the waves crashing ashore. As they walked, a breeze got up and they could see storm clouds gathering ahead of them. Still lacking balance in the soft sand, Lori had resorted to her crutches for their stroll. Jake silently suspected the change back to her crutches was an attempt to hide the pain she was in. An occasional grimace crossed her face as they meandered along the shoreline. Jake knew better than to suggest they turn back before she was ready, however the first drops of storm rain made the decision for them. Before they made it back to the shelter of the house, the heavens opened, soaking them both to the skin. Dripping, they dashed into the sun room out of the storm, just as the first rumble of thunder boomed overhead.

"Jeez, where did that come from?" laughed Jake, stripping off his wet T-shirt.

"A great welcome home that was," giggled Lori. "I'll fetch you a towel."

Tossing him a towel from the kitchen, Lori limped down to the bedroom to get changed out of her own wet clothes. She pulled on a T-shirt and jeans, rubbed her hair dry, then wandered back through to the sun room. Jake was sitting on the couch searching the TV channels for a news broadcast to see if there were any severe weather warnings on the way.

"I brought you a dry T-shirt," said Lori. "It's one of mine, but it should be ok."

She tossed him a black T-shirt.

"Thanks," said Jake pulling it on over his damp hair. "I hate to say this, but I need to go back to my place. Do you mind?"

"No. Yes," stammered Lori. "What about dinner? Mary's left us her special chicken pasta to heat up."

Kissing her gently Jake asked, "Can you give me a couple of hours? I'll come back for dinner, but I'm not staying the night."

"Be back for eight," said Lori, trying hard to hide her disappointment. "Dinner will be waiting."

"I'll see you then," he promised, kissing her once more.

The truck's windscreen wipers struggled to clear the rain that was hammering down as Jake drove back to his apartment. Lost in his thoughts, he nearly missed his turn off. It took him two trips to get his gear back into his small apartment and Jake was soaked through again by the time he was done. He had dumped his holdall in the living room before gently laying his guitar cases down on the couch. The apartment smelled stale so he threw open the sliding doors that led to his tiny balcony. Outside the rain was gradually easing up. It felt like he had been away from here forever. The apartment might not be Upper West Side material, but it had been his home for a long time. During the last week it had been so easy, so natural to slip into Lori's luxurious world; stepping back out of it was proving to be harder. With a sigh, he opened his holdall and sorted out all the laundry in a pile on the chair.

"How very rock and fucking roll," he muttered to himself as he put the first load of clothes into the washing machine.

When he had unpacked the last of his gear, Jake decided to take a shower and try to lift his flat mood with some hot steamy water. As he stood under the hot power shower jet a few minutes later, he felt the last of the city dust wash away. He sang to himself as he washed his hair, finding new lyrics to go with the melody he had been playing with the night before. All too soon the water started to cool down and he stepped out of the shower dripping all over his tiny bathroom floor. Wrapping a towel round his waist, he wandered, still dripping, through to the kitchen to fetch a beer. A glance at the clock on the microwave told him he had an hour left before Lori expected him for dinner.

As he pulled on a clean pair of jeans – his only remaining clean pair- Jake thought back to Lori's revelation about her accident. In her position, he hoped he would have acted the same. But to watch a child die in front of you – how did you begin to pick up the pieces mentally after that, never mind recover from the physical injuries? She had spoken so candidly. Her emotions had very obviously been raw. Even the simple act of crossing at the same crosswalk with him the day before. When he had written the lyrics to "Stronger Within" about her, little had he realised just how true they were. Slipping on a white shirt he marvelled about how caring a person she was in such a relaxed natural way. Without a second thought she had opened her home to him and the rest of the band, taken a week out of her life to look after Becky without being asked and been the perfect hostess throughout. In fact, she was always the same, he realised. Rarely had he seen her flustered- apart from their initial meeting. Lady Luck had been shining down on him the day she brought Lori into his life. "Lady Luck," he mused thinking back to the new piece of music that was forming in his head. "That might just work as a title."

Grabbing a pair of sneakers, Jake decided that as the rain had stopped, he would walk back along the beach instead of taking the truck. He slipped his wallet into his pocket and his phone, deciding to pick up some wine to go with dinner. Yes, Lori the perfect hostess would already have a bottle prepared, but he felt it was the right thing to do. Just as being with her felt like the right place to be.

Along at the beach house, Lori was having a not dissimilar experience. Slowly she had unpacked her bags, hanging up the few clean items of clothing and sorting the laundry into two piles – light and dark. She returned her toiletries to the bathroom, deciding to take a quick shower before dinner. Travelling always made her feel grubby and the feeling of the hot water gliding over her washed all those miles away. It had felt good to be driving her car again, but she was sore from sitting for so long. The hot jet of water helped ease the tension from her neck and shoulders. As she shampooed her hair, her mind wandered back to Jake's question about her accident. Subconsciously her left hand moved to finger her scars. Now he knew all the scars weren't just physical ones. In a weird way it had been a relief to tell him. It was not an easy tale to tell, but it was all out in the open and she was glad she had told him. It meant they could move on with no secrets between them.

Once out of the shower and wrapped in a towel, Lori wandered back through to the bedroom in search of something to wear. Her favourite faded jeans lay over the back of the chair so she opted for them and a baggy white shirt. Having brushed out her long wet hair, she scooped up the first bundle of laundry and carried it through to the utility room. With the washing machine happily churning away, she began to prepare dinner. Mary's chicken bake was one of her favourites. While the oven heated up, Lori set two places at the dining room table and lit two small votive candles. Much as she loved her New York apartment, it was good to be home; much as she had loved having a house full of guests, and love and laughter, she was glad that tonight it was just her and Jake. Having set out two of her favourite crystal wine goblets, she fetched a bottle of red wine from the rack in the hall cupboard. With practiced ease, she removed the cork and set the bottle down on the table to breathe.

Shortly after eight Lori heard the sun room doors slide open.

"Lori!" called Jake, closing the door back over with its distinctive squeak.

"In the kitchen," she called back.

Following the delicious aroma of dinner, Jake wandered through the house, noting the set dining table with a smile. When he saw Lori standing by the sink, rinsing the salad leaves and heard the rumble of the washing machine, he couldn't help but laugh. "Were we both down to the last of the clean clothes?"

"Great minds," she giggled. "Don't tell me you went home just to do your laundry!"

Jake blushed and handed over the bottle of wine he'd brought, "I might have done."

"Maybe we both need to go shopping," she laughed, passing him the salad bowl to take through.

"I hate shopping," muttered Jake, taking the bowl through to the table.

Still giggling, Lori asked him to bring the pasta dish out of the oven for her. She was anxious about carrying things like that in case she tripped and burned herself. Her confidence in moving about the house without her cane was growing, but her balance was still fragile, especially when she was tired. Jake more than happily dished up their meal while she poured the wine.

"Welcome home, rock star," she declared, raising her glass to him.

Jake laughed, "Someday I hope."

"Well, rock stardom is closer than it was a week ago," said Lori warmly. "How do you feel about it all?"

"I'm not sure," he admitted, staring down at his dinner. "I love performing and writing music. Being in the studio was amazing. But fame scares me. I'm not good at the people bit off stage."

"I may be wrong, but I think Maddy has big plans to push you guys. I've seen her do this before," said Lori. "And I've seen her succeed. You're under her wing now and she doesn't like to fail."

"I guess," agreed Jake. "Rich and the others are stoked about it. Grey sees it as his best option of a good life for Becky. I don't want to let them all down."

"I get it," admitted Lori, pausing for a sip of wine. "It's one of the reasons I retired as Mz Hyde. Just remember who you are on the inside. At the end of the day, it's a job. Put the uniform on and play the game."

"That's a good way to look at it," he conceded with a smile. "So what's next for Mz Hyde now she's out of retirement?"

"I've a new commission," Lori stated proudly. "I checked my voicemail just before you arrived. More album artwork."

"Anyone big?" Jake asked curiously.

"Now you know I can't say yet," she scolded playfully. "When I can tell you I will. Client confidentiality and all that important stuff."

"Not even a clue?"

"No!"

Despite her protests, Jake insisted on clearing the table and stacking the dishwasher when their meal was over. There was just enough wine left for half a glass each so, while Jake was busy in the kitchen, Lori took their glasses through to the sunroom and turned on the TV, flicking through to one of the rock music channels. She was trying to stifle a yawn when Jake came through to join her.

"You need an early night, li'l lady," he said softly.

"You might be right," she admitted sleepily. "The sea air has hit me."

"Nothing to do with ten manic days in New York then?" teased Jake.

"They might have something to do with it," she giggled. "But they were fun."

"Ok, here's the deal," began Jake. "I'm heading home in a few minutes. I'll be back by early afternoon tomorrow, but only if you agree to get to bed as soon as I leave and rest until lunchtime tomorrow."

"And if I don't?" challenged Lori with mischief glinting in her blue eyes.

"I won't let you take me shopping."

Lori laughed and hugged him. "Deal. If I take it easy till lunchtime, you'll come with me to the outlets tomorrow afternoon?"

"Deal," he agreed reluctantly.

After Jake left to walk home a short while later, Lori was as good as her word. As she headed off to bed, she lifted her laptop and her sketch book. There was nothing in the deal that said she couldn't do a little work while she was "resting". Climbing into her big familiar bed, all thought of work left her. Jake had been right – she was worn out. Within minutes she was sound asleep, snuggled down deep in her crisp white cotton bedding.

There was a cool breeze blowing in off the ocean as Jake walked home along the cold sand. "Fame and fortune," he thought as he meandered along just out of reach of the waves. Was he ready for them? That was the million dollar question and he suspected that Lori was right- it was out of his control. The boundary line had been crossed and that scared him. Keeping an eye on the waves washing in at his feet, he thought back to all the gigs and festivals he had been to over the years where he had longed to be the one up there in front of the crowd. Maybe it was the right time to step up out of the crowd and take centre stage.

It was the dull ache in her leg that finally wakened Lori next morning. She bent and straightened it a few times, then surrendered and reached over to the nightstand for some painkillers. A glance at the clock informed her it was ten thirty. It had been a long time since she had slept so late and so soundly. Jake had been right – she had been worn out. Stiffly she got out of bed to visit the bathroom and to fetch a drink of water to wash the pills down. Having gone through to the kitchen to make herself some coffee, she returned to bed with her mug and switched on her laptop. Sipping the coffee slowly, she checked her emails, deleting the junk and marking the business ones that needed a response. Eventually she found the one she had been expecting. The voicemail she had listened to the previous day had informed her to expect the details via email and there they were on the screen in front of her - the details of her commission from Jason Russell; the artwork commission for Silver Lake's album. Keeping quiet until she had the rough proofs ready for the band's approval was going to be a challenge, but she was sworn to secrecy.

Among the emails she had tagged as "business" were details of two other potential commissions. She read over the details for both of them, checked her calendar to work out the scheduling and figured, if she could extend one of them by a week, she could accept them as well. The more work she had decreased the chance of letting slip about the Silver Lake project.

Once she had amended the acceptance emails to her satisfaction and sent them to David to approve the financial aspects of the deals, Lori went back through to the kitchen to fetch herself a late breakfast. The painkillers had finally kicked in. After such a good night's sleep, she felt steadier on her feet than she had since the accident. With a hot coffee in one hand and a toasted cinnamon bagel in the other, she returned to bed to finish up her emails.

Beside her, her mobile phone chirped, signalling a new message.

"Hope you are being a good girl. J x"

Smiling, she texted back, "Still in bed Lx"

A second chirp and she was rewarded with a smiley face and "see you at 3 J x"

Figuring she had about three hours to herself, Lori shut down her laptop and picked up the sketch pad. Thinking back to the tracks she had heard the band rehearse in New York she was struggling to determine a theme. The memory of Jake playing "Lady Butterfly" struck a chord. It was a start. She already had the butterfly she had designed a few weeks ago. An idea of how to morph it into a "rock butterfly" began to form and she started to sketch. Once she became engrossed in the task at hand she lost all track of time. The pencil outline began to take shape and Lori was soon lost in adding detail to it.

A chirp from her phone brought her back into the real world

"Be there in 5. J x"

"Shit", she muttered texting back. "Still in bed L x"

"What? At this time of day? J x"

Abandoning her artwork in the midst of the bed covers Lori got up as quickly as she could and threw on her favourite sun dress. She was still brushing her hair when she heard Jake's truck pull into the driveway. Its door banged shut as she slipped her feet into her white Converse. Lori was only just starting to tie the laces when she heard Jake call her name.

"In the bedroom," she called back.

"Hi," called Jake, poking his tousled head round the door. "Are you really just up?"

"Yes," said Lori bluntly. "I was sketching and lost track of time."

"Ah, working? That may make our deal void," he teased as he stepped into the room.

"No way," laughed Lori. "You just said I had to rest and stay in bed. I did."

"Ok," he relented with a smile. "You win. Anyway, I need to go shopping. There's a photo shoot set up for Saturday!"

"Explain," instructed Lori as she reached for her cane. "I thought we were having a BBQ on Saturday?"

"Slight change of plan," began Jake sheepishly. "Rich called this morning. He got a call from Jason. He's coming down here this weekend with a photographer. He's got a record company to take us on and they need photos. If they need photos, I need some new clothes!"

Lori laughed, "So much for hating shopping, Mr Power."

"Harrumph," he grumbled. "If we're going, let's get it over and done with. I do hate shopping but this is an emergency."

Still giggling, she lifted her car keys and followed him out to the driveway. He was all set to get back in his truck when she tossed the Mercedes key fob to him, "You drive."

"You sure?"

Lori nodded and opened the passenger side door. "I'm still sore. Be gentle with it though."

"Yes, ma'am," he said, actually inwardly happy to be getting back behind the wheel of the Mercedes.

As they drove out of town, they debated on where to start

their shopping expedition. The first priority after discussion was jeans, then sneakers of some sort and finally some new T-shirts. Having established the basics, Lori tried to fathom out what kind of "look" he was going for.

"How the hell should I know?" snapped Jake then quickly added, "Sorry, Lori. This is stressing me out."

"Why?" she asked softly. "It's only a few photos. Where are they going to shoot them?"

"Ah, I meant to talk to you about that too," he began, blushing slightly. "We wondered if we could use the beach house as a base, then maybe go out on the lake or down onto the beach?"

"And if I say no?"

"Then we use my one bedroom apartment that right now looks like a laundry room!"

When she had finished laughing at his stress and anxiety over it all, Lori agreed that they could base themselves at the house.

"Maybe I'll even dust off my own camera."

"I hate getting my photo taken," declared Jake, as he pulled off the highway into the "Seaside" parking lot at the outlets.

"Calm down, rock star," she said quietly. "It might be fun."

"Easy for you to say," he muttered.

Easy their expedition wasn't! Three stores in and Jake had yet to give anything more than a cursory glance. When they reached the jeans outlet, Lori offered up a quick prayer that this store would prove to be more successful. Once inside, she changed tactics and left Jake to browse on his own while she checked out the ladies section. She had a couple of T-shirts and a zip through hoodie over her arm by the time he wandered over with three pairs of jeans and a handful of T-shirts.

"I need to try these on," he said, sheepishly. "Will you come with me?"

"Sure," replied Lori, relieved that he was finally getting as far as the changing rooms. "Let me pick up a couple of pairs to try myself."

Ten minutes later they stepped back out into the afternoon sun with two bags. It took them another two hours to finish the shopping marathon by which time Lori was hungry and thirsty. The mission had been accomplished though and Jake was now the proud owner of enough clothes to last him for a while plus three new pairs of sneakers. Lori too had treated herself and, despite the stressful start, had enjoyed the whole traumatic event.

"You done?" she asked, as they left the last shoe store.

"I think so," declared Jake. "I've maxed out my credit card."

With a weary smile, Lori said, "Well, in that case, let me buy you dinner. I'm starving."

"Deal but let's drop the bags back to the car first," suggested Jake.

"I'll wait here and you can take the stuff back to the car," she compromised, handing him her bags.

"Ok. Don't wander off."

While Jake jogged back across the parking lot, Lori slipped back into the nearby men's store. They had been admiring a leather jacket in there and Jake had looked great in it when he had tried it on but had put it back. Now, after his credit card comment, she guessed it was the price tag that had swayed his decision not to purchase it. She only just made it back to the spot where he had left her on time, now clutching one more bag.

"Did I forget one?" asked Jake as he walked up to her.

"Not really," she said. "I slipped in the store while you were away. A gift for you."

"You didn't need to buy me this!" Jake protested as he looked in the bag. "It's way too much."

"Nonsense," replied Lori sharply. "Now let's go and eat. I need to sit down for a while."

Applebee's was the nearest restaurant and they were soon seated at a window table with a cold soda in front of them as they browsed the menu. The waitress who had shown them to their seats and talked them through the long list of specials could hardly take her eyes off Jake. When she returned to take their food order, she seemed flustered and nervous. Both of them had to repeat their order twice and just as Lori was about to ask if she was alright, the girl blurted out, "Are you the singer with Silver Lake?"

Dazzling her with a smile, Jake replied, "Guilty as charged."

"I loved your Surfside gig," she gushed, then flushed scarlet. "Could I have an autograph?"

"Sure," said Jake warmly, still smiling at her. "What do you want me to write?"

Her hand was shaking as she passed him her pen and a bit of paper, "To Cali."

"Is that all?" he teased.

Quickly he scribbled, "To Cali. Hurry up with my dinner order. Jake Power" then handed it back to her.

"Thanks!" she gasped. "I'll get dinner to you as soon as the kitchen can get it ready."

"Cali," called Lori as the girl turned away. "Bring your phone back with you. I'll take a photo of you both."

"Thanks! I will!"

Once the young waitress was out of earshot Jake asked why she had offered to take a photo.

"Because she'll live on the high of it for a while. She'll share it on Facebook and Twitter and you will increase your fan base," explained Lori. "Remember, it's all a game."

"I guess," muttered Jake, still shy at being recognised in public.

"Play along. Make her year," coaxed Lori softly.

When the waitress brought their meals out, miraculously managing not to spill them, she handed Lori her phone. Her delight at being photographed with Jake was written all over her face. Burying his own nerves, Jake put his arm around the girl's shoulders and smiled at Lori. Three photos later and Cali left them in peace to enjoy their meal.

On the way back to the house, Lori asked, "Was that so hard?"

"I guess not," admitted Jake grudgingly. "But she's a sweet girl."

"You'll probably find that most of your fans are sweet people," said Lori. "The vast majority of Mz Hyde fans, I've met have been really polite and genuine."

"Maybe you've just been lucky."

"Perhaps," she conceded "But you need to get used to this or find a coping mechanism."

With a sigh, Jake had to agree with her.

His coping mechanisms were being stretched to their limits by the middle of Saturday afternoon. A photo shoot was Jake's idea of hell, he had quickly determined. They had had a pleasant start to the day- coffee and croissants on Lori's sun deck where Jason had introduced the band to their photographer for the day, Matt. While the band had discussed business with Jason, the photographer had set up on the opposite side of the deck. He had brought a plain white backdrop and some photography umbrellas and lights. From the back of his truck, Matt had produced an ornately carved church pew to use as a seat cum prop. Rich had been the first up to pose for some solo shots. He was a natural in front of the camera. Paul then quickly established his identity as the band's joker. Grey went for the serious "Daddy" of the band persona, then it was Jake's turn and the only role left was band "heart throb". Just as he had almost got himself psyched up to pose, Matt announced they were heading over to the lake to do some group shots. With a look that pleaded for help, Jake kept his eyes on Lori as he followed the others out to the truck. A few seconds later she heard her phone chirp and she read the message from Jake "Get me out of here! J x"

"Hang in there, rock star," she replied.

It was two hours later before the Silver Lake entourage returned from the lake and, when she saw Jake's miserable expression, Lori just wanted to reach out and hug him. As they all bundled back onto the sun deck she called out, "Anyone ready for a beer?"

The deafening chorus of "yes" was all she needed to hear.

"Jake," she called. "Can you give me a hand?"

Glad to be free to spend a few seconds with her, he quickly followed her into the kitchen.

"You ok?" she asked, wrapping her arms around his waist and holding him.

"Just," muttered Jake. "It was ok out at the lake. Less intense."

"What's left to shoot?"

"The individual stuff of me then Matt wants to do some shots down on the beach nearer sunset. Something about dusky light.

We should be done around eight," explained Jake.

"Are they coming back tomorrow?"

"Christ, I hope not!"

Laughing Lori said, "Try to relax a bit. Now help me with these beers. I put some in that blue cooler. Can you carry it out?"

"Sure," he said, lifting the box effortlessly. "I'm really sorry about this invasion. We've kind of taken over your whole house."

"It's fine," she said softly. "Now get those beers out there before there's a riot."

"Yes, ma'am," he joked with a smile.

Back out on the sun deck, the mood was lifting as the band took a well-earned break. Someone had lit the BBQ coals and Rich had gone off to get some burgers and chicken. The photographer had accosted Jake and they were deep in conversation beside the BBQ. Lori was relieved to see that he was still smiling and looking more relaxed. All the furniture had been moved about and the only free seat was the pew in the photo set. She wandered over and took a seat there with a beer, quietly watching the others. It was hot out and she was glad of a bit of shade for a while. Catching sight of her sitting on her own, Jake excused himself and came over to join her.

"Penny for those thoughts, li'l lady?" he asked, draping his arm around her shoulder.

"Sorry, I was miles away," she apologised, snuggling closer to him. "I was thinking about work. I'm still trying to get a plan together for one of my commissions."

"I guess this isn't helping much," he commented before taking a chug at his beer.

"Actually, it is," replied Lori smiling. "Don't look, but Matt's coming this way and he looks armed and dangerous."

Jake looked up to see the photographer approaching, carrying two cameras. His stomach lurched at the thought of having to pose for his solo shots.

"You guys look great sitting there," said Matt kneeling down before them. "Try to ignore me."

Both Jake and Lori heard the camera fire a few times. She could feel Jake begin to tense up beside her. Whispering in his ear, she said, "Imagine him naked."

"I'd rather imagine you naked," he whispered back under the

pretence of kissing her neck.

"Later," promised Lori softly. "If you behave."

"Beautiful shots, guys," called out Matt, interrupting their moment. "I'll mail them to you later."

"Thanks," said Lori, flashing a smile at him. "I guess I'd better move and let you get on."

"That would be good."

"Lori," called Jake, "Stay beside Matt, please."

"OK, just for a minute or two," she promised. "It's only a camera. It won't hurt you."

"Easy for you to say," he muttered under his breath.

"Matt," said Lori, as she stepped carefully out of the set. "I have an idea to help here."

"What?"

"Let him play his guitar. It's in the sun room."

"Lori," declared the photographer. "You're a genius!"

Her idea proved to be inspired as less than an hour later Matt was more than happy with the results of Jake's solo shoot. Once he had his beloved acoustic guitar in his hands Jake's nerves melted. Grey had stepped over realising that his friend was struggling and he put in a few requests for Jake to play. Lori too suggested a few songs. In the midst of this impromptu performance, Rich returned, fetched his own guitar from the house and joined in. While Paul and Grey took care of the BBQ, they all enjoyed listening to the two musicians jam together in the late afternoon sun. When Matt announced he was done, Jake continued to play on for his own amusement.

"Ok, food's cooked," called Paul, placing a plate of burgers in the centre of the table. "Let's eat!"

As they all sat about eating and joking Matt seized the opportunity to capture some candid shots. Eventually, patience wearing thin, Grey cornered him and said bluntly, "Sit the fuck down and eat with us."

There was a round of applause when Matt set his cameras down safely in the shade and joined them for some food and a well-earned beer.

"What's the plans for the beach shots?" Jason asked, helping himself to the last of the burgers from the plate.

"Well, I thought we could go for a more relaxed look. A few

shots in the sand dunes. Some in the waves. Maybe a few with a football or a Frisbee being thrown about," explained the photographer between mouthfuls of food.

"We could toss a ball about a bit," agreed Rich "But no more posing, please."

"OK, let's try it with a football game," agreed Jason sounding far from convinced by the idea. "Anyone got a ball?"

"I do," confessed Grey. "There's one in the back of my truck."

"Grey," asked Lori. "When's your mom bringing Becky over?"

"In about an hour. They were going to dinner first," replied the bass player, fishing in his pocket for his keys.

"I'll clear up here and listen out for them while you guys go down to the beach," said Lori, stacking the empty plates. "I'll bring her down when they get here."

"Thanks, Lori."

Ball in hand, like a bunch of overgrown teenagers, Silver Lake headed off the deck and down onto the beach. It was after six and the day's tourists were more or less all packed up for the night. A couple of lone fishermen were still spaced out along the shoreline. Instead of getting his camera out straight away, Matt left the case wrapped in a towel and joined in the game, as did Jason briefly. The band's competitiveness gradually emerged and as the game got more serious the shirts came off and the tackles got rougher. This was the imagery that Matt had been searching for – Silver Lake relaxed and at play and finally oblivious to his camera. As the band's stamina wore out, he got a few natural, relaxed shots as the guys sat or lay in the sand. Soon it was only Jake and Rich still tossing the ball. With an impish grin, Rich launched a long throw towards the water. Already in his bare feet, Jake sprinted after it kicking up sand as he ran into the waves to catch the ball. He caught it by his fingertips as he lost his balance and disappeared headlong into a wave. The guys howled with laughter as Jake got bowled over and emerged dripping but still clutching the ball triumphantly. Matt never missed a moment of it.

"Daddy!" came the cry as Becky came running down the beach towards them. Lori, too, was making her way across the sand somewhat tentatively. She had left her cane in the sun room and was suddenly hit by nerves as she felt the soft sand under her bare feet.

"Wait there," called Jake, tossing the ball to Rich.

She paused where she was, grateful that he had picked up on her discomfort. In a few long, loping strides, he was at her side and had put a wet supportive arm around her waist.

"Be careful, li'l lady," he cautioned warmly, before kissing her gently.

"You look more relaxed," observed Lori with a smile. "And a bit wetter"

"It was fun," laughed Jake. "It's been a long time since we've thrown a ball about. It was good for the soul."

"As long as it worked for the photographer."

"Right now I don't care," he declared, grinning like a teenager.

Slowly they made their way over to where the others were now sitting on the sand. Becky was clambering all over her dad, trying to get him to come and play with her. When she saw Jake arrive with Lori, the little girl turned her attention to "Uncle Jake" and soon had him chasing her round in circles a few yards further along the beach. Carefully Lori sat on the sand beside Jason, who was watching this relaxed scene unfold with complete fascination. Turning to Lori, he said quietly, "Your friend Maddison was right. There is a special magic with these guys. I feel very privileged to witness this."

"Maddy's seldom wrong."

"I'll be honest. I doubted her this time, but I feel I was wrong," Jason admitted, his English accent sounding very out of place in the all American beach setting. "You are the key to this though, Mz Hyde. They come alive around you."

Lori blushed, "They're my boyfriend's friends. They're my friends. That's all. No magic."

"Perhaps," he mused before adding. "How's your work project coming along?"

"I think I've made a breakthrough today," she replied. "The deadline won't be an issue."

"What project?" asked Jake, dropping down on the sand with a dull thud.

"That new commission I was struggling with. The big project," replied Lori, deliberately keeping her answer vague.

The group sat and chatted till the sun had gone for the day, then, before it was fully dark, headed back up the beach to the house. Both Jason and Matt declined Lori's offer of a drink, saying they had some editing to do back at the hotel. After a quick debate, they agreed to meet at the hotel for lunch the next day to preview the day's work. With a time agreed, they bade the band goodnight. Jake walked them out, then returned to the sun room and sank down into the couch with a huge sigh, "Thank Christ that's over."

"It wasn't so bad," commented Paul as he opened a beer.

"It was torture!"

"Well, it's all over now," soothed Rich handing him a beer. "I saw a sneak preview of some of the shots. They looked great."

"I guess we'll find out tomorrow," stated Grey. "Becky, leave Rich's guitar alone."

"She's ok," said Rich, watching the little girl gently finger his acoustic guitar. "Becky, do you want to help me play?"

"Yes!" she squealed with delight.

Rich lifted the guitar over, allowed the little girl to climb up into his lap, and then showed her how to strum the strings as he played a few basic chord changes. The tenderness of the scene wasn't lost on any of them. Grey might be her father, but Becky had captured all of their hearts and had her Silver Lake uncles wrapped round her little finger.

Draining his beer, Paul declared he was heading into town to catch up with a few friends. With promises not to misbehave and not to be late for their lunch meeting, he left via the sun deck to walk back along the beach. A short while later Grey too, took his leave, taking a sleepy Becky with him. After the little girl had hugged them all goodnight, Jake fetched another round of beers for Rich, Lori and himself.

"Here's to rock 'n' roll," toasted Rich dramatically.

"Long life and happiness," toasted Jake, raising his bottle.

"Fame and fortune," added Lori with a wink.

All three of them laughed and agreed they would settle for long life and happiness and if it brought fame and fortune with it, then that would be a welcome bonus. When his beer was done Rich decided to head into Rehoboth to catch up with Paul.

Finally, Jake and Lori were alone. Glancing round the room and through towards the rest of the house Jake realised the full extent of the band's takeover of Lori's home. Their gear was everywhere. He knew without looking that the spare bedrooms also had clothes from earlier in the day strewn all over them.

"I'll get the guys to come back after lunch tomorrow to collect their gear," he promised.

"Don't worry about it," reassured Lori warmly. "It's been a long day. Let's go to bed, rock star. Then added slightly anxiously, "You are staying, aren't you?"

"For as long as you want me to," said Jake kissing her passionately. "I couldn't have got through today without you. Thoughts of having you all to myself were what kept me going."

"Nonsense," whispered Lori. "You were great today once you relaxed a bit."

Before she could say anything else Jake scooped her up into his arms as though she weighed little more than a feather and carried her down to the bedroom. He laid her down gently on the bed then, despite her protests, slowly began to undress her. When he had slid her out of her long skirt, unbuttoned her cotton top and discarded her silky underwear, Jake showered her body with kisses, starting with light feathery kisses across her collar bones then down between her breasts to her belly button. As he kissed down the length of her scars, he felt her tense up under him. With a gentle bite at her big toe, he moved from the bed to strip off his own clothes, dropping them carelessly onto the floor. A few short moments later he lay down beside her, gently tracing patterns with one long, slender finger across her breasts and stomach.

"That tickles," she squealed, giggling girlishly.

"Shh, let me explore," he breathed softly.

Moving to straddle her, Jake gently sucked on her nipples, biting them teasingly in turn. Turning his focus to her narrow hips, he ran his tongue over her hip bones spending just a little longer following the silvering scar on her right hip. Beneath him Lori let out a low moan of ecstatic pleasure. Jake entered her in one swift, hard movement. Instantly he could feel how ready to receive him she was and this fired his passion. Thoughts of this precise moment had danced around in his head all day and now that the moment was finally here, he couldn't hold back his hunger for her. With a few hard, fast strokes he climaxed. Lori had gasped as his orgasm triggered her own. With her back arched, she thrust her hips up towards him hungry for more. Spent but still entwined in her Jake held her tight for a few moments nuzzling her neck and gently nibbling her earlobe. His hair spilled over his shoulders and face like a golden curtain protecting them both in their intimate world. With a final intense kiss Jake withdrew and knelt up to face her. Lori sank back into the soft feather pillows and smiled up at him. A look of pain was written in her eyes that her smile was trying to mask.

"Did I hurt you, li'l lady?" asked Jake softly, concerned that he had been too forceful, too rough.

Lori shook her head, not trusting herself to speak.

"Are you sure?"

"I'm fine," she assured him. "It was wonderful."

Still not convinced Jake decided not to pursue matters. He slipped out of bed to dispose of the used condom. As soon as the bathroom door was closed, Lori closed her eyes, blinking back tears of pain, and reached down to rub the screaming muscle that ran down the front of her thigh. When she had arched her back and thrust her hips towards him she had felt the weakened muscles tear. "The price of pleasure," she mused inwardly as she massaged the tender area. Hearing Jake turn the handle of the bathroom door, she rolled over to face his empty side of the bed. With a satisfied smile he slid under the light summer duvet, kissed the tip of her nose and wished her good night. Wrapped in each other's arms, with Lori's head resting on his chest, Jake was asleep within moments.

Turning off the coastal highway into the Hampton Inn parking lot, Jake scoured the row in search of a space and a familiar truck. Spotting Grey's truck, he pulled in next to him. It was another blistering hot day and it was a relief to step into the air conditioned foyer. There was no sign of the other members of Silver Lake. Hooking his sunglasses into the neck of his T-shirt, Jake walked over to the reception desk.

"Good afternoon, sir. Can I help you?" asked the young dark haired girl behind the desk.

"Hi, I hope so," began Jake, flashing her a smile. "I'm due to meet Jason Russell here."

"Of course. His party are in the conference suite. I'll show you up," she replied.

When he entered the conference room, Jake was relieved to see his fellow band members were already there.

"Ah, the late Mr Power!" joked Grey. "That's another twenty in the pot, Jake."

"Sorry, guys. Overslept," confessed Jake taking a seat beside Grey at the table. Across from him Rich and Paul were reclining back in their seats with their sunglasses still on.

"Late night, guys?"

"Yeah," muttered Rich hoarsely. "I'm never drinking again."

"Never say never," cautioned Jake, trying not to laugh.

Paul groaned quietly.

"OK, now we are all here," began Jason formally. "Let's run through the shots from yesterday. Matt's done a great edit on them."

A buffet lunch was spread out on the table and, as Jason started the slide show on the whiteboard, Jake helped himself to a sandwich. He genuinely had overslept and had skipped breakfast in his hurry to get to the meeting. As he munched on a pastrami sandwich, the first results of the photo shoot appeared on screen. Half an hour later they had run through them all.

"Well?" said Jason, leaving a final group shot from the beach on the screen. "Thoughts?"

"Christ, I look old," muttered Grey sourly.

"Not as painful as I'd expected," admitted Jake. "They capture what we're about I guess."

Neither Rich nor Paul made any comment.

"I personally agree with Mr Power," said Jason. "Plenty for us to use for promotional material and for the album. Now to the promo plan."

Over the next two hours, the band listened to their manager's plans and proposals. As the Englishman outlined the draft timeline of events, Jake could feel it all rolling out of control. Their familiar Silver Lake routine had become a thing of the past overnight. Now it was being shaped into a slick business and hopefully a successful rock band. There were a few gigs that the band were committed to during July and August that Jason took careful note of. Without a second thought, he wiped all planned "wedding band" appearances from their calendar declaring that those days were over. Eventually they had a plan agreed, with a few rough edges to be fixed. Drawing the meeting to a close, Jason casually asked if they all had valid passports. Only Rich possessed a passport.

"Get that sorted this week, guys," said Jason bluntly. "If I need you to travel you need to be ready to go."

"Are you likely to want us to go overseas?" asked Paul tentatively.

"At some point," replied Jason, sounding slightly exasperated with them. "I've a few more calls to make but there may be an opening later in the year on a tour. When I know more I'll fill you in but get those passports in order."

"So what now?" asked Grey, like the rest of them suddenly feeling in way out of his depth.

"You've a radio station gig in Milford in two weeks. Rehearse. Add in a couple of the new tracks, but not all of them. Don't change things around too much just yet. I'll be in touch during the week," said Jason checking his watch. "I need to check out of here shortly. I've a flight to catch."

During the drive back into town, Jake reflected on the afternoon. He felt as though he had been existing in a parallel world for the past three hours. After Jason had left the meeting, the four of them had stayed on and worked out a rehearsal schedule for the week ahead. They were all in agreement that it was starting to feel like something big was about to take off; they all confessed to being a little daunted by it. The thought of potentially travelling overseas had rattled Paul, who confessed to a fear of flying. Before they left the conference suite, they agreed amongst themselves that if it all got too much they would pull the plug on the deal. Now, as he turned off towards the beach house, Jake wondered how much was too much.

Having parked in his usual shady spot, he wandered round the side of the house to the sun deck. All the furniture had been put back in the correct place and Lori was sunbathing, stretched out on the lounger. She had her earphones in and never heard him approach. Unusually, she was wearing a bikini and wasn't hiding under a long skirt or a sarong. Tiptoeing round Jake silently knelt beside her and kissed her full on the mouth.

"What the…." she screamed shrilly.

Laughing helplessly Jake collapsed down onto the deck.

"You scared the crap out of me!" yelled Lori, visibly shaken by his sudden appearance at her side.

"I'm sorry, li'l lady," he apologised, trying hard not to laugh. "You're even more beautiful when you're angry."

"I'll get my own back for this," she threatened with a hint of a smile appearing. "Now how did the meeting go?"

"Let me grab a glass of water and I'll fill you in," said Jake getting to his feet. "Want anything?"

"Water would be good."

When he returned with the two red solo cups filled with iced water, Jake set them on the table, then stripped off his T-shirt and kicked off his shoes before settling down on the deck at her side to tell her about the plans and proposals. She listened carefully and had to agree that things were picking up speed. If the plan fell into place Silver Lake were going to be flat out for the next few months.

"Has Jason given any indication about what you've to do with your day jobs?" she asked.

"Not really," answered Jake, sipping his water. "He was talking about setting up some local promo, acoustic stuff for Rich and I during August. We've all given him the dates we are free. Paul and Grey are back at work tomorrow. It's a weird in limbo feeling. Almost as though we can reach out and touch this, but that it's not quite real yet."

"I know what you mean," said Lori sitting up and swinging her legs round so she was sitting on the edge of the lounger. "Oh, Matt came round while you were out. He straightened this place up for me. I've tidied up indoors too, but I wasn't sure what belonged to who. It's all in the spare room opposite the bathroom for now."

"The photos from yesterday actually looked pretty cool," admitted Jake blushing slightly.

"They do," agreed Lori with a grin. "I talked Matt into leaving me a copy of them."

"Did he give you the ones he took of both of us?"

Lori nodded, "I downloaded them onto my laptop. I'll share them with you later."

"I feel like a swim," declared Jake getting to his feet. "Fancy coming down to the beach?"

"Maybe later," replied Lori. "I'm happy here for now."

"Sure?"

"Sure."

"I'll go and get changed," said Jake with a grin. "I'm not going in wearing my jeans today!"

As he wandered off into the sun room, Lori lay back on the lounger. A walk on the beach sounded good, but, as soon as she stood up, Jake was going to be able to tell she was limping badly today. The heat from the sun was easing the muscles in her thigh, but she had had to resort to painkillers twice so far. Wearing only a pair of bright orange swim shorts, Jake stepped back out onto the deck.

"Won't be long," he promised, kissing her on the top of the head.

"I'll be right here anyway," replied Lori, settling her earphones back in her ears.

She was grateful he hadn't asked what she was listening to. In order to get a feel for the Silver Lake album she had emailed Jim Marrs to ask for his help. He had obliged by sending her through four of the unfinished tracks. They were still a bit rough around the edges, but she was impressed with what she was hearing.

The beach was busy when Jake walked down the hot sand.

Looking back up towards the boardwalk, he could see a haze of coloured sun shades and there were lots of folk in the ocean enjoying the waves. He wandered further down the beach in search of a quieter spot. A few hundred yards down there were only a couple of fishermen sitting watching their rods. He wandered into the shallows, then, watching for a good wave, dived into the surf. The solitude of swimming in the ocean felt good and soon all the stresses and worries about the band were washed away. A strong swimmer, he swam out to sea for about fifty yards, then headed back towards the shore. He repeated another loop, then headed back towards the shore again. Watching the waves around him Jake bided his time for the right wave, then body surfed back in to the beach. As he slid onto the shore, he could feel the rough sand graze his stomach and thighs. He rolled onto his back and let the next wave crash right over him. Before another wave got him, he picked himself up and jogged back along the sand to the house.

The sun deck was deserted when he returned, but Lori had left a towel over the back of one of the chairs for him. As he rubbed himself down, Jake thought he could hear voices in the sun room. With the towel draped across his shoulders, he stepped inside to find Grey and Becky sitting watching TV.

"Hi, where's Lori?"

"Gone to put some clothes on," said Becky, jumping up to hug her favourite Silver Lake uncle.

"Think I embarrassed her by arriving unannounced," confessed Grey, blushing at the memory of arriving to find a bikini clad Lori reclined on the sun lounger.

"Ah," nodded Jake. "I'll go and check on her."

He found Lori in the bedroom. She was attempting to fasten her halter neck sundress but her trembling hands were fumbling with the neck ties.

"Here, let me help," said Jake taking the two cord strands and tying them neatly into a bow. "You ok?"

"I guess," she replied softly. "Grey caught me by surprise. I think he was more embarrassed than me."

"Neither of you have anything to be embarrassed about," said Jake hugging her. "He's seen plenty of pretty girls in bikinis before."

"You know that's not what I meant."

"I know and he's sitting through there feeling like shit about it," answered Jake softly.

"I better go back through," said Lori kissing him gently on the chest. "Yuck! You're all salt and sand."

"Let me jump in the shower. I'll be through in ten minutes."

Picking up her cane, Lori limped through the house towards the sun room. Taking a deep breath, she paused in the doorway, then said as naturally as she could, "Can I get you guys a drink?"

"Can I have some lemonade, Lori?" asked Becky, staring straight ahead at the cartoon on TV. "In the Elmo glass?"

"Of course you can, honey," Lori replied. "Grey, what about you?"

"Lemonade's good. I'll come and help you," he offered.

Once they were alone in the kitchen, he started to apologise for arriving unannounced. Lori stopped him, "It's me who should apologise. I was just embarrassed about being caught in my bikini," she paused then added quietly. "And about the mess on my leg. I'm not good at letting folk see it."

"Genuinely, I never noticed," said Grey warmly. "But you've got a fabulous figure, Lori."

"Grey!" she exclaimed flushing scarlet.

"I'm sorry," he laughed. "Jake's a lucky guy."

"I'm getting the lemonades before you say another word."

"OK, I lied a bit. I did notice your scars but so what?" he said, fetching the glasses off the draining board for her. "It's only marks on your skin. No worse than some of the ink you see on folk these days."

"I need to try to stop being so self-conscious about it," sighed Lori as she lifted the jug of lemonade from the fridge. "But it's hard."

"I understand," sympathised the bass player warmly. "I see the cane's back. You ok?"

"Just having an off day," she replied evasively. "It'll be fine again in a day or two."

Lori and Grey were sitting out on the deck with a bowl of potato chips between them when Jake finally sauntered through. He was wearing only his pale ripped jeans and the sand burn from his body surfing was plain to see across his well-muscled stomach. The others teased him about body surfing like a big kid then both confessed to being jealous as they couldn't do it. In the midst of their laughter Grey explained the reason for his visit – he had dropped by to collect the gear he had left behind the day before.

"I need my jeans for work tomorrow," he confessed. "The thought of going in to work sucks. I just want to be back out on stage."

"Well, we've two weeks before that happens," said Jake. "And a hell of a lot of work to do to get the new set list ready."

"We'll be fine," assured Grey casually. "We always are."

"Yeah, but we've got Lord Jason watching over us now," joked Jake only half kidding. "No more jamming and flying by the seat of our pants."

"No matter how hard we rehearse there will still be plenty of that."

In the two weeks running up to the Milford radio rock festival Silver Lake worked harder than they ever had before. They pulled together two new sets at the management's request – a full electric set and a one hour acoustic set. Emails flew backwards and forwards between the band and Jason, setting up various radio station appearances throughout July and August plus an extra gig at the state fair at the end of July. The record company were planning to release the first single from the forthcoming album in time for the Labor Day holiday with the whole album to be out by the middle of October. While the band rehearsed and rehearsed and rehearsed Lori spent her evening's working on their artwork. During the day when Jake was more likely to be about, she focussed on her other two commissions then at night, after he left, worked on the Silver Lake piece. All three were taking shape on schedule.

Two days before the Milford concert, Jason phoned Rich to say he was sending down someone to act as tour manager and to cover for him as band manager for the foreseeable future. When Rich started to protest that they didn't need extra help, Jason cut him short, saying it was a done deal and that they already knew the person he had hired. It came as no surprise to learn it was Maddy.

Around the same time Lori got a text message from her friend. "Dinner tonight? M x"

Immediately Lori replied "Where and when? L x"

"Sushi place Rehoboth at 8. Bring the boys. M x"

Shortly after eight Jake and Lori walked into the sushi bar, both scanning the room looking for Maddy. She spotted them before they saw her and came running over to hug Lori.

"You're looking great!" cried Maddy squeezing her tight. "And no canes!"

"No cane today," echoed Lori delighted to see her friend. "Some days are steadier than others."

"And Jake!" squealed Maddy hugging him affectionately. "Looking as hot as ever."

"Cut it out, Maddison," he cautioned playfully, kissing her on the cheek. "Are we the first to arrive?"

"Yes," replied Maddy, leading them over to the table. "Grey called to say he'd be late."

As they took their seats, a waitress brought over the wine that Maddy had already ordered.

"Can I have a soda instead?" asked Lori. "I'm driving."

"Of course, honey," said her friend. "Tonight's on Jason so have what you want."

At that moment Rich and Paul arrived to join them and, after more hugs and greetings, they were soon all seated round the table.

"I took the liberty of ordering a selection for us all to share," explained Maddy as the waiter brought several dishes to the table.

As they ate, they discussed the plans for the weekend's rock festival. It was quite a small local event running across the whole weekend. Silver Lake were scheduled to play the headline slot on Saturday night, but apart from the set, Maddy had lined up two one hour interview slots for the afternoon. It was going to be a long day for all of them. Apologising profusely for being late, Grey arrived in the middle of the discussion and was quickly brought up to speed.

"Does anyone have any questions?" asked Maddy when she was finished her download.

"Do you have a pass organised for Lori?" asked Jake.

"It's ok," interrupted Lori. "I'm not coming. I said I'd watch Becky."

"Oh," exclaimed Jake looking surprised. "I had wanted you there."

"Next time," countered Lori with a smile. "I promise."

"State Fair?"

"Definitely," she promised. "Maddy will arrange passes for that, won't you?"

Her Goth friend nodded. "State Fair should be a better show. I'm not comfortable with the set up for this weekend, but we're committed to playing so let's make the best of it."

"What's bothering you about it?" asked Grey curiously.

"Can't put my finger on it," muttered Maddy, shaking her head. "Just a gut feeling for now. I'll be glad when it's over though."

By late afternoon on Saturday they were all sharing Maddy's
unease. The two interviews had gone well during the early part of
the afternoon. The first had been with the radio station sponsoring
the rock weekend. Jake and Rich had taken their acoustic guitars
along to the makeshift studio and played three numbers much to
the delight of the DJ who was interviewing them. The second
interview was for a music magazine who were doing a special on
up and coming bands. This time Grey and Paul took a lead in
answering the questions. When they were done, the band
wandered through the site, stopping at a burger stall to get
something to eat. Already the crowd was growing restless. The
band on stage were being jeered by a large group down at the
front and Jake's concern grew when he saw two beer bottles fly
onto the stage. Feeling more than a little anxious, Silver Lake
retreated to the safety of the backstage area, their fears left
unspoken among them. They found Maddy pacing restlessly up
and down.

"Where were you guys?" she demanded sharply.

"Getting a feel for this place," replied Grey bluntly.

"And grabbing a bite to eat," added Paul, sipping on the last of
his soda.

"And how does it feel to you?" asked their manager directly,
her kohl rimmed eyes boring into them.

"Angry," stated Jake, his own concerns written clearly all over
his face. "That crowd could get ugly later on."

"They're ugly now," muttered Rich under his breath.

"That's my fear," sighed Maddy, running her hand through
her spiky hair. "Not much we can do at this late stage though.
Stay back here till it's time to go on. I don't want any of you out of
my sight."

At eight o'clock sharp, the compere announced Silver Lake
and the band ran out onto the stage to a resoundingly warm cheer
from the crowd. As Jake stepped up to his mark, he was relieved
to see some extra security personnel had been brought in and
there were plenty of them now manning the barrier at the front of
the stage. With a nod to Rich they started their set. Three numbers
in and Jake paused to talk to the crowd for the first time, "Good
evening, Milford!"

A roar went up from the crowd.

"I can't hear you! I said good evening, Milford!" he bellowed with a grin.

A huge roar came hurtling back at him, making him laugh.

"Looking good out there tonight, folks. We're going to play something brand new for you now. This is a track off our new album that's due out in a couple of months. This is "Flyin' High"!"

After the strong drum opening, Grey and Rich launched into the hard and heavy riff. As Jake began his guitar part, he felt a sharp hot sting at his right knee. The force of it sent him stumbling backwards, but he quickly recovered his balance and his composure to start his vocals on cue. The fiery pain in his knee intensified as he sang. It took all of his concentration to maintain his focus. During his mid-song guitar solo Rich moved over to him and mouthed "You ok?"

"No," he mouthed back between gritted teeth. He could feel blood running down his calf, hot and sticky and it was pooling in his boot.

When the song ended, he signalled to Rich to keep things going as he hobbled to the side of the stage looking for first aid help. Maddy was standing there white as a sheet.

"What happened?" she asked, staring at the blood soaking through his jeans.

"Not sure," admitted Jake shakily. "Feels like I've been shot."

"I think you were," said a roadie bluntly.

"I'm ok," insisted Jake. "I just need something to put on it."

"Here," said the roadie, tossing him a roll of gaffer tape. Jake smiled and nodded to the guy as he tore off a length and wrapped it as tightly as he could round his thigh, to act as a tourniquet.

As he turned to go back out on stage, Maddy yelled, "Jake! You can't go back on!"

"Yes, I can," he growled as he hobbled back out to join the rest of the band.

Miraculously Rich and Grey had held the set together with an impromptu guitar duel. Seeing Jake return to the stage, they slickly launched into the next number on the set list. The roadie, who had given Jake the tape, ran out with a bar stool before the end of the song. Gratefully, Jake sat down, as a second roadie brought out his acoustic guitar, and lowered the mic stand. From his vantage point, he could see the security guards handing a young guy over to two police officers. The kid looked vaguely familiar.

"Ok, Milford," called Jake, trying to ignore the fire burning at his knee. "We're going to slow this down a bit. This is for the representatives of the local police department."

Appropriately Silver Lake played an acoustic version of Bon Jovi's "Wanted Dead or Alive", much to the crowd's amusement. With their cheers still ringing in his ears Jake followed it up with "Lady Butterfly." His pain was clear for all to see, but he sang the acoustic number with his usual calm passion for the song.

With the two acoustic numbers completed, Rich stepped forward and said simply, "Last one. No arguing."

Jake nodded and accepted his electric guitar back from the roadie. He remained seated, not trusting that he wouldn't faint if he tried to stand up.

"Folks, this is the last one for the night before we hit the emergency room. We'll leave you with "Highway to Hell.""

The second they hit the last note, Maddy ordered the lights to be killed. In the darkness Rich and Grey, guitars slung over their backs, rushed over to help Jake down from the stool and off the stage. In the background they could hear the crowd cheering and crying for more.

"What happened?" asked Grey as they sat Jake down on a transportation case at the side of the stage.

"Some bastard took a shot at me!" replied Jake, suddenly feeling very light headed and nauseous.

"Let's get you to the emergency room," declared Maddy shrilly. "Will I call 911?"

"I'll drive him there," stated Grey, handing his bass to Rich. "You guys pack up the gear. I'll call you when I get him to the hospital."

"I'm coming with you," said Maddy, "Someone call Lori."

"No," said Jake sharply. "Don't worry her. I'll be fine. I'll call her myself from the hospital."

Heavy traffic leaving the festival site slowed their progress and it eventually took Grey almost half an hour to make the short journey to the medical centre. Climbing up into Grey's truck had aggravated the wound and, as they drove down the highway, Jake could feel the blood oozing down his leg into his boot. The adrenaline rush from being on stage was wearing off and the reality of what had actually happened was beginning to hit home. He began to sweat and to shake uncontrollably. As they had been leaving the site, two police officers had approached them, but Maddy had suggested they follow them to the emergency room and speak to Jake there. The police car had followed Grey throughout the entire journey. When they finally reached the hospital, Grey abandoned the truck as near to the front door as he could then ran round to help Jake down from the cab. With Maddy charging on ahead of them, he half carried his bleeding friend into the waiting area. At the desk Maddy was already giving the nurse Jake's personal details. Seeing Grey struggling with the weight of his friend, two orderlies came over with a gurney and soon they had whisked the injured guitarist through to a cubicle. Both Grey and Maddy made to follow them, but the nurse called them back.

"I'll let you know when you can go through," she said firmly. "I suggest you take a seat or grab a coffee from the machine down the hall."

Reluctantly, they took a seat. The bass player sat hunched forward with his head in his hands; Maddy sat fidgeting with her nails and then her earrings.

"I hate hospitals," muttered Grey without shifting his gaze from the tiled floor.

"Same here," agreed Maddy with a long sigh. "They remind me too much of Lori's accident."

"You were there?" asked Grey, looking up for a moment.

"After they brought her in. She had me listed as an emergency contact in her wallet. I was home for the holidays," began Maddy shuddering at the memory of the phone call that had informed her that Lori had been badly injured in a road traffic accident. "Rough time for all of us."

"I'm sure Jake'll be ok," reassured Grey quietly. "He was kind of pale when they took him through."

"Tough guy for keeping on playing," Maddy observed. "Oh, here's the police coming."

The same two police officers from the festival site were

walking down the hallway towards them. They questioned Grey and Maddy for a few minutes, but, as neither of them had seen what had happened on stage, they were of little help. The officers confirmed that a teenage boy had been arrested at the scene and that he had been in possession of an unauthorised firearm.

"I'm going to get a soda," declared Grey getting to his feet as the two officers left. "Want anything?"

"Coffee, please. Black. No Sugar," replied Maddy.

They had just finished their drinks when a young nurse came over to say they could see Jake. She led them down the corridor, past several curtained off cubicles to the second last one from the end. Holding the edge of the blue curtain back, she allowed Maddy and Grey to enter. Jake was sitting propped up on the narrow bed, his leg elevated on a pillow.

"You ok?" asked Grey, clapping his friend on the shoulder.

"Yeah," replied Jake sounding a bit groggy. "I've been lucky. The bullet's gone right through. It's just a flesh wound. It's ugly."

"So what are they planning to do to you?" quizzed Maddy anxiously.

"They need to x-ray my knee to make sure there's no fragments inside and no bone damage," Jake explained. "Then they'll stitch me up and I should be good to go."

"What a relief!" sighed the band's manager, sinking down onto the hard plastic chair beside the bed.

"Have the police been in?" asked Grey.

Jake nodded, "I couldn't tell them much. I never saw anything. I just felt a sting at my knee as we started to play "Flyin' High". Hurt like hell."

"I'll bet" sympathised his friend, relieved that Jake was alright. "Do you want me to call Lori?"

Jake shook his head, "Not yet. She's not expecting us for a couple of hours yet. We should be clear of here before then. If we get held up, I'll call her."

"Your shout," acknowledged the bass player. "I'd better call Rich though."

"OK," agreed Jake with a grimace, as a fiery bolt of pain shot through his knee. "Can you ask him to take my truck back to my place?"

"Sure."

"Mr Power," called the nurse cheerfully as she entered the cubicle. "Time to take you through to radiology."

She helped Jake down from the bed and into a wheelchair. Seeing his friend in a hospital gown with his boxers on display brought a smile to Grey's face. Noticing it, Jake cautioned, "No photos of this look!"

"Not even one?" laughed Grey, reaching for his phone.

"No!" stated Jake sharply before adding, "Do you have any spare jeans in your truck? They've destroyed mine cutting them off?"

"I'll check. They'll be too big for you though."

"Beats going out of here in my shorts," laughed Jake as the nurse wheeled him away.

It was after midnight before they finally left the hospital. Jake had been issued with a set of crutches and advised not to put any weight on his injured knee for a few days. The x-ray had shown there were no bullet fragments, but that there was a small chip out of the top of his tibia, just below his kneecap. The doctor informed him he had been incredibly lucky that the injury hadn't been more serious. A few millimetres over and it would have shattered the whole knee joint. He had sat calmly while the triage nurse had put in six stitches to close the ragged flesh wound and had then been discharged, armed with a course of antibiotics and painkillers. Fortunately Grey had found a pair of shorts in the truck and a belt so Jake was at least able to leave with his modesty intact.

There were still lights on in the beach house as Jake clumsily made his way inside with both Grey and Maddy fussing around him. Hearing the commotion Lori appeared through from the sunroom, cautioning them to be quiet as Becky was asleep.

"What happened?" she exclaimed, the colour draining from her face when she saw the crutches. "Jake?"

"I'm fine," he said through gritted teeth. "Let me sit down and we'll explain."

"He's not fine," announced Maddy glaring at the injured musician. "He's been shot!"

"Shot?" echoed Lori, looking from one of them to the other as she tried to make sense of the scene in front of her.

"Maddison," growled Jake, his patience worn thin, "Let me tell it, please."

Once he was settled on the couch in the sunroom with his injured leg propped up on a pile of cushions, Jake calmly told Lori about the gig and the shooting incident. In typical Jake fashion, he played down the potential seriousness of it and seemed more annoyed at having to cut the band's set short than about the injury. As she sat on the couch beside him, Lori held on tightly to his hand, eyes wide in horror at what she was hearing.

"You could've been killed," she said softly when he was finished his account of the evening's events. "All of you could've been killed."

"Exactly my point!" chipped in Maddy sharply.

"Well, I wasn't. The police have got the guy. He's been arrested. It's dealt with. Done," dismissed Jake with a yawn. "I'll be fine in a few days."

As Lori started to protest, Grey cut in, "Jake's right. It was a scary gig, but we survived. If one of us had been hit with one of the bottles that were flying around earlier that could've been just as serious. We got lucky tonight."

"I guess," agreed the girls in unison.

Noticing for the first time that there was no sign of his daughter, Grey asked where she was.

"She was tired, so I put her to bed in the spare room at the end of the hall. She's fast asleep."

"Thanks for looking after her, Lori," said Grey with a smile. "I'd better lift her and get her home."

"Why don't you stay too?" she suggested. "It seems a shame to waken her. The other room is made up."

"If you're sure."

"Of course," insisted Lori, stifling a yawn. "Maddy, what about you? Do you want to stay over?"

"No," replied the band's manager, suddenly returning to her usual business like self. Getting to her feet, she added, "I'll get a cab back to the hotel. I've a few calls to make about this fiasco and I need to get hold of Jason to fill him in. I'll drive back out tomorrow at some point."

"I'll call you a cab," offered Lori, sensing that her friend meant to work through most of the night.

"No need," said Grey. "I'll run you back out to the hotel."

"Thanks," sighed Maddy, lifting her bag onto her shoulder.

"I'll see you guys in the morning. Jake, make sure you follow the doctor's orders."

"Yes, boss."

"Grey," called Lori as the bass player was leaving the room. "Let yourself in when you get back. We'll probably have gone to bed."

Nodding, he said, "Sure. See you both for breakfast."

As they heard the truck's engine roar into life outside, Lori hugged Jake tightly, tears welling up in her eyes and spilling down her tired cheeks. He reached up and stroked her long blonde hair whispering, "I'm fine, li'l lady. No need for tears."

"I know," she sniffed tearfully. "But what if the guy's aim had been better?"

"Let's not think about that," he replied. "It's only a flesh wound and a small bone chip. I'll be fine in a day or two."

She kissed him gently then helped him to his feet. Stifling a giggle, she watched him fumble with the crutches, wobbling on one foot until he found his balance.

"No wonder you fell that day I met you," he muttered. "How do you drive these fucking things?"

"Takes practice," she answered. "And trust me, I've done my fair share. Go slowly until you find the rhythm."

"Harrumph," he grunted as he navigated his way slowly through the house.

Next morning they all slept late, except Becky, who crept through the house to the sunroom to watch cartoons. When Lori entered the kitchen, she could hear the Sponge Bob theme tune filtering through. Having set up the coffee pot, she limped through to the sunroom and found the little girl sitting cross legged on the rug in front of the TV with her American Girl doll sitting beside her.

"Do you want some cereal, young lady?" asked Lori.

"Yes, please. Can I eat it in here, Lori? I won't spill it. Please!"

"Just this once," agreed Lori unable to resist the child's charm. "I'll bring it through."

Having sorted out some cereal and a glass of strawberry flavoured milk for her youngest house guest, Lori set about making bacon and French toast for the rest of them. From down the hallway she could hear Grey going into the bathroom and, from further through the house, she thought she heard Jake moving about too. A knock at the back door startled her and she opened it to find Rich and Paul on the back step.

"What's this? A Silver Lake breakfast meeting?" she joked as they piled into the kitchen.

"We smelled the coffee," teased Paul.

"Help yourself," she offered. "There's some bacon and French toast ready too."

The two band members didn't need a second invitation and were both tucking into a full plateful of breakfast when Grey came in. She had just passed him a coffee and a plate of breakfast when the door opened again and Jake hobbled in unsteadily on his crutches.

"Morning," he said, surprised to find the kitchen full of his friends. "Did I miss the invite to this party?"

"We came by to check if you were ok," replied Rich, helping himself to more bacon.

"I'll live," declared Jake, sitting down and slowly bending his damaged knee. "Hurts like hell right now."

"Have you taken the pain meds I left out?" asked Lori with concern, pouring him a mug of coffee.

"Yes. They've not kicked in yet though."

"Maddy called me first thing," announced Rich. "The radio station want us to come in on Monday afternoon to do an interview. If you're up to it, we could do a couple of acoustic numbers too."

"Sounds like a plan," agreed Jake, helping himself to some bacon and French toast from the plate in the middle of the table. "I feel bad that I couldn't finish the set last night. We let those fans down."

"Are you for real?" exclaimed Paul. "You got shot!"

"I need to talk to you about that," began Rich quietly. "I got a call from Linsey."

The penny suddenly dropping Jake said, "That's who that kid was! That kid's Brad Green from school. I knew I'd seen him before."

Rich nodded, "His mom called Linsey after the police brought him home."

"Did he say why he did it?" asked Lori looking confused.

"They are still trying to figure it out. Linsey said the woman was distraught about it all."

"I'll bet," said Jake. "Can you get her number for me? I'd like to talk to her."

"Better than that. There's a meeting at the school set up for first thing on Monday, if you feel up to it," explained Rich. "So are you going to take it easy today?"

"Not got much choice," confessed Jake, stretching his leg out and wincing at the shot of hot pain that the movement triggered.

"Right," declared Grey, getting to his feet. "We're leaving you in peace for the day. Paul, call Maddy and tell her to leave these guys be for the day."

"You don't have to rush off," protested Jake as they all got up to leave. "I'm not sick."

"Grey's right," said Rich. "I've got your guitars in the back of the truck. I'll bring them in, then I'm out of here."

After the others left, Lori chased Jake through to the sunroom with strict orders to rest on the couch. Handing him the remote control, she declared she was going to do some work for a couple of hours. From her drawing board in the study, she could see into the sunroom and kept a watchful eye on him as she attempted to focus on the Silver Lake artwork in front of her. She already had the first draft of the album cover completed, but Jason had requested a few additional companion designs for the merchandising. It was the first of these she turned her attention to. Soon Lori was as engrossed in her work as Jake was in watching CSI on TV.

First thing on Monday morning Rich arrived to chauffeur Jake for the day. After faithfully promising Lori that he would take good care of him, they set off. During the drive across town towards the school where they were due to meet Brad and his parents, Jake sat in virtual silence. As he stared out of the truck's window, he wished Lori were with him instead of Rich. The thought of facing the student who had taken the shot at him filled him with a degree of dread, but both the police and the school principal had requested he attend this informal meeting to discuss the incident in light of the boy's known anger and behavioural medical issues. His knee was throbbing despite the painkillers he had swallowed before leaving the house. Beside him, he was aware that Rich was saying something, but he wasn't listening.

"Jake, did you hear me?"

"Sorry," he apologised. "I was miles away."

"I was saying not to feel pressured here not to press charges," repeated Rich. "I know that kid's got issues, but you could've been killed. Any one of us could've been killed."

"I know," agreed Jake rubbing his knee. "But no one was killed. In the grand scheme of things this is only a minor wound."

"One that has scarred you for life," pointed out his friend bluntly. "Plus, there's the emotional trauma to consider. How are you going to feel the next time we've to play live or play at an outdoor festival?"

"Shit scared regardless of whether the kid's in jail or not."

"Well, I guess that's true," acknowledged Rich turning the truck into the school grounds.

Both of them could see the police car parked outside the front of the building. Deciding this was an exception, Rich pulled into one of the handicapped spaces next to the door, then rushed round to help Jake out of the truck.

"I'm not a fucking invalid," growled Jake, as his friend fussed over him. "I can manage, thank you."

"Well, at least let me get the fucking door for you," retorted Rich, slamming the truck's door closed.

"Sorry, Rich," apologised Jake, as he adjusted his balance on the unfamiliar crutches. "I'm all over the place with this."

"It's ok, buddy. Sorry for snapping back," said Rich clapping him on the back. "Let's get this over and done with."

When they entered the principal's office a few minutes later they were greeted warmly by both the principal and the police officers from Milford. The student and his parents had yet to arrive. The principal, Dr Jones, fussed over Jake making sure he was seated comfortably, offering him another chair to rest his injured leg on.

"I'm fine sitting here, thanks," said Jake calmly, laying his crutches on the floor at his feet. "Just don't ask me to stand up in a hurry."

The more senior of the two officers asked how long he expected to be on crutches for.

"About a week, according to the emergency room," began Jake with a hint of resignation in his voice. "But we'll see. I'm not very good at driving them."

"What's the prognosis on your knee, sir?" asked the other officer.

"There's a small chip off the bone, but it's mainly a flesh wound. Now it's all stitched up it looks quite minor," replied Jake trying to play the matter down. "It could've been a lot worse."

Their conversation was interrupted by a knock at the door and the school secretary ushering the boy and his parents into the office. After the usual polite introductions they were soon all seated round the principal's desk, staring at each other, no one sure what to say first. Brad sat with his head bowed, staring at his hands, which were folded in his lap.

"Mr Power," started the boy's mother breaking the awkward silence. "I can't apologise enough for what's happened. I just don't know what came over Brad."

"That's what we'd all like to know," muttered Rich sourly under his breath.

"Can I ask a question before we go any further?" asked Jake calmly.

"Of course," answered Dr Jones. "I think you're entitled to ask what you want."

"And this is all informal and off the record?" asked Jake, looking directly at the two police officers for confirmation.

"Yes, it is," replied the senior officer. "For now."

"Ok then," said Jake looking straight at his assailant. "All I want to know is why you took a shot at me?"

A strained silence filled the room. The boy's father nudged him in an attempt to encourage a reply. Still the boy stared down at his trembling hands.

"Can you all leave us alone for a few minutes?" requested Jake, glancing round. "This is maybe something Brad and I need to discuss privately."

Reluctantly and after a few expressions of concern, the others stepped outside, leaving Jake alone with the troubled teenager. His heart was pounding and his palms were sweaty, but Jake guessed this was his best chance of finding out the truth. As the door closed, the boy looked up and stared at Jake.

"Well," began Jake softly, keeping his tone as calm and warm as he could. "Why, Brad?"

"To balance things," replied boy still staring straight into Jake's eyes.

"I don't follow."

"Your partner. The artist," the boy spoke stiltedly. "She limps to the left. You belong as a pair. You were out of balance. Now you're not."

"And now I limp to the right?" summarised Jake, following but not comprehending the boy's flawed logic.

Brad nodded and went back to staring down at his hands, only now he was trembling uncontrollably.

"You realise you could've killed me or someone else? Or yourself?"

He nodded, then said, "My dad taught me to shoot when I was younger. I never miss. If I'd wanted to kill you, I'd have aimed higher."

The confession sent chills rattling down Jake's spine.

"That doesn't make me feel any better," he admitted with a weak smile. "Why did you feel the need to hurt me at all?"

"I already said. So you balance with the artist. She hurts."

"Yes, she does," agreed Jake sadly. "Where did you get the gun from?"

"From my dad's desk."

"And it wasn't locked up?"

The boy shook his head.

Jake sat and watched him for a few moments, thinking through the little the boy had said. Knowing the limited amount he did about Brad's medical background and, in a warped way, following the logic, he got it. He could actually see how this all came about from the boy's twisted perspective; could understand how it made sense in Brad's mind.

"You know it was wrong, don't you? Illegal. Not to say dangerous," said Jake.

"Yes, Mr Power, and I'm really truly sorry. Mom explained two hurts, don't make it last. Don't make it right."

"Make what last?" asked Jake somewhat confused.

"The relationship. I know I shouldn't have done it. Sometimes I don't think straight like normal people do," he said, a tear rolling down his pale freckled cheek. "The artist and you belong together. She's beautiful. I'm sorry I hurt you. Probably hurt her too. Can you forgive me?"

"Actually, I think I can," said Jake, surprised to hear himself saying the words. "I'm not going to press charges against you. I'm going to ask Dr Jones not to kick you out of school, but I do expect you to turn up to my classes next semester."

The boy stared at him wide eyed. "You mean it?"

"Yes, I do," said Jake smiling at him. "Now I'm going to ask the others to come back in. Are you ok with that?"

"Yes, Mr Power," replied Brad, roughly wiping away his tears. "And thank you. I don't know what to say."

Stiffly Jake got to his feet, fumbled his crutches into position under his arms and limped his way over to the door. When he opened it, he saw the others all sitting in the waiting area. In unison they all looked up as Jake made his way unsteadily over to them.

"I've spoken to Brad," stated Jake calmly but firmly. "I kind of get it now. He's apologised for the incident and I don't want to press any charges against him."

They all stared at him in disbelief, Rich looking particularly surprised by his friend's statement.

"I'll leave it up to the rest of you to discuss what, if anything, else needs to be done. I've told Brad I expect to see him in class next semester," continued Jake. "And, Mr Green, I'd strongly advise locking your firearms away in future."

"Mr Power," said the police officer. "Can we talk about this please?"

Nodding Jake moved over to the side and spoke quietly to the two officers for a few minutes. The rest of the group could not quite hear what was being said, but from Jake's facial expression he wasn't backing down.

"Well, Mr Power," concluded the senior officer. "I take your point and I think you're being very generous here. I just hope the boy appreciates it."

"So do I," sighed Jake, as the three of them re-joined the group standing anxiously outside the principal's office. "Rich, are you ready to go?"

"Sure, if you are," replied his friend. "Dr Jones, I'll call you later."

"Jake," called Dr Jones. "I'll call you later. Take care of yourself and thank you."

"Thanks, sir."

As the two musicians were getting into the truck, Brad's mother came running out of the building after them.

"Mr Power," she called, tears in her eyes.

Jake was sitting in the passenger seat and was just about to pull the door closed when he heard his name being called.

"Mrs Green," he greeted the woman warmly.

"Thank you," she gasped, a sob catching her voice. "I know what he did was so very wrong, but Brad's not a bad kid at heart. He's just wired up a bit wrong. I am so so sorry."

"I know he's not a bad kid. I actually kind of followed his logic. Everyone deserves a second chance," replied Jake, aware of Rich's stare boring into him. "I meant what I said. I expect to see him in my classes next semester."

"I don't know how to thank you enough."

"Let's draw a line under this," suggested Jake generously. "However, if Brad ever decides to come and see the band play live again, please tell me first so I can have him at the side of the stage where I can keep an eye on him."

"Thank you," she repeated. "I'd better go back in. The police are talking to my husband about the gun not being locked up safely."

Jake nodded and reached to pull the door closed, "Tell Brad I'll see him in class."

"Thank you, Mr Power."

"It's Jake, Mrs Green."

"Thank you, Jake."

As Rich pulled out of the parking lot, Jake swallowed another couple of painkillers, then sat back in the seat with his eyes closed. Mentally, he was drained; physically he was in agony. They were on the Coastal Highway heading out of town before either of them spoke. It was Rich who finally broke the silence, "You did the right thing back there. I didn't think so at first, but I think you made the right judgement call."

"So do I," agreed Jake, screwing up his face as a hot fiery spike of pain shot through his knee. "He's a very mixed up kid, but he knows it. His logic is seriously flawed, but, in a warped way, I could see where he was coming from."

"And where was that?" asked Rich curiously.

"That stays between Brad and I," replied Jake quietly. "The matter's closed as far as I'm concerned. Time to move on."

"If you say so," said Rich shaking his head. "You never cease to amaze me, Mr Power."

With a smile, Jake settled back in the seat and closed his eyes, silently praying that the painkillers would kick in before they reached the radio station.

It was cramped in the radio studio with the presenter, his producer and all four members of Silver Lake present. Both Rich and Jake were set up with their acoustic guitars. Rich was jammed right in the corner, perched on a tall stool while Jake had been given a lower, softer seat. His injured leg was resting on an upturned plastic crate with a folded up sweatshirt on top as a makeshift cushion. The pain meds had finally kicked in but there was still a hot throb in his knee. All four of them sat silently waiting for their cue while they listened to the hourly news bulletin followed by a classic Weigh Station track dating back to Jake's teenage years.

"Now ladies and gents, we have some surprise guests in the studio for you," began the DJ. "Silver Lake have stopped by. These guys headlined for us last Saturday night and were literally blown off stage mid set when a shot was fired from the crowd injuring vocalist Jake Power."

The band exchanged glances and Jake could feel the urge to giggle mounting inside them all. He stared down at his guitar strings trying to maintain his composure.

"Good afternoon, boys. And an extra special welcome to Jake. How's the leg?"

"It's ok I guess," said Jake suddenly tongue tied at being the centre of attention. "I was incredibly lucky. It's only a flesh wound with a little bit of bone damage."

"So tell the listeners what happened out there on Saturday night."

"Well, we'd just started our fourth number, a new one for us, and I felt a hot stinging pain in my right leg around my knee. I kind of reeled backwards a bit, but didn't realise I'd been shot. Not at first anyway."

"But the incredible thing is that you tried to play on," the presenter prompted.

"I did my best, but had to surrender after three numbers. My boot was filling with blood and I wasn't feeling so great."

"Now Rich," said the DJ. "You were right beside Jake when the shot was fired. Did you see anything?"

"Not a thing," began Rich honestly. "I saw him stagger back, but my first thought was that he'd tripped. He made it through the vocals, but when I managed to ask him if he was ok, he said no. Grey and I held it together with an impromptu guitar and bass duel while Jake went off stage for treatment."

"Was there a first aider there?"

"No," laughed Jake. "A roadie threw me a roll of gaffer tape. My jeans were soaked in blood. I wrapped a length of tape round my thigh as a tourniquet and hobbled back out there."

"Security had pulled the guy out of the crowd by this point," added Grey. "And the police took it from there."

"So will you be out of action for long, Jake?"

"We'll be back out there at the State Fair a week from Saturday. I should be good by then and at least have ditched the crutches," answered Jake. "Worst case scenario I'll sit it out on a stool. I feel bad for letting the fans down on Saturday, so we want to make it up to them as soon as possible."

"Now you've brought your guitars into our humble studio and I believe you're going to play two tracks from your forthcoming album. When's the album out?"

"We're hoping for late September," said Paul, speaking up for the first time. "The first single from it will be out for Labor Day weekend."

"And is that one of the songs you're going to play for us this afternoon?"

"No," said Jake. "We're keeping it under wraps for another week or so."

"So what will you be playing for us?"

"Flyin' High," began Rich, "Which is the song we were playing when Jake got shot then we'll do Lady Butterfly."

"Ok folks, you're listening to 103.6 and this is Silver Lake, acoustic style!"

Playing the two numbers in the compact studio was a bit like playing in someone's bedroom, but, ever the professionals, Rich and Jake carried it off. Playing seated with his leg up on a box felt all wrong, but Jake put thoughts of his personal discomfort to one side, playing and singing to perfection. As the last notes faded out, the DJ said, "A huge thank you to Silver Lake for coming in today. We wish Jake a speedy recovery and we'll see and hear the boys at the State Fair a week from Saturday."

There were thunder clouds rolling overhead as they drove north towards Harrington. Sitting in the passenger seat of Lori's Mercedes, Jake began to fidget. It had been a long hard two week run up to the State Fair. There had been several radio appearances up and down the Delaware coast, plus another interview and photo shoot for a magazine. All those calls and emails Maddy had fired off following the incident in Milford were beginning to pay dividends and people were starting to sit up and take note of Silver Lake. Before the end of the first week, despite the advice from his doctor to the contrary, Jake had dumped the crutches. The stitches had been removed a few days later and the scar didn't look too bad, all things considered. His knee still felt stiff and was more swollen than usual, causing him to limp, as Brad had intended. Before they had left the house he had strapped it up and was praying he would make it through the show. At the final rehearsal the night before, the band had amended the running order, taken out two of their harder, heavier numbers and bulked the acoustic interlude up to four songs. If Jake sat down for those four songs, it should give him enough of a rest period to make it through the final four demanding numbers.

"You're kind of quiet," observed Lori. "You ok, rock star?"

"I suppose," he sighed, staring out of the window at a passing truck.

"Talk to me, Jake," she said, glancing over at him. "Something's eating at you?"

"I'm scared," he confessed quietly, without looking at her.

She had suspected as much and was relieved to hear him confess it. The feelings were wholly understandable.

"Security will be far tighter here than at Milford. Maddy's seen to that," began Lori calmly. "You'll be perfectly safe."

"Christ, I hope so," he sighed, running his hand nervously through his hair. "What if I freeze up out there? What if I can't do it?"

"Don't talk like that," she scolded softly. "You belong on stage, Jake. You come alive out there."

"I've never felt under pressure like this before a gig. Never felt so scared."

Their conversation was interrupted by a call coming through on his cell phone. Hauling the handset out of his pocket, he caught the call just as it was about to cut to voicemail.

"Good morning, boss," he greeted, feigning cheerfulness.

From the driver's seat Lori could hear her friend ask if they were on their way yet.

"We're about twenty minutes away from Harrington. A half hour at the most."

Lori didn't catch what her friend said next.

"We'll be there well before the sound check at two," he promised. "Yes, I've got the parking pass. Yes, I've taken my pain meds. Yes, I've strapped my knee up. And yes, I've got my guitars. Anything else on your Jake checklist?"

Lori giggled at his obvious frustration at being mothered by the band's manager.

"Yes, Lori is driving," he continued. "And before you ask, she's had her pain meds too. Oh, and we're both wearing clean underwear and we brushed our teeth before we left the house."

Lori could clearly hear the string of expletives her friend was yelling down the phone.

"See you soon, Maddison," he growled, as he cut the call. "Christ, she's worse than my mom was."

"Don't be too hard on her," giggled Lori. "She's just trying to get this right and to look out for you all."

"Well, she's trying too hard," he muttered sourly, before smiling quietly to himself at the memory of the tirade of abuse he'd just taken.

As they approached Harrington, the venue for the State Fair ground was remarkably well sign posted. Turning off the road onto a dirt track, an event organiser stopped them to check their passes, then directed them to the "artiste parking lot" which to both Jake and Lori looked like a cornfield. As Lori parked the car at the end of a row, Jake messaged Rich to say they had arrived. The guitarist came straight back to say he was on his way to help Jake with his gear. As both of them climbed stiffly out of the car, they exchanged glances and started to laugh. Grabbing her cane out of the back, Lori limped round to open the trunk.

"What are you two laughing at?" called Rich as he ran towards them.

"Ourselves," giggled Lori. "At the state of us trying to get moving after sitting in the car for an hour."

"I always thought you made the perfect pair," joked Rich. "Now you limp as a pair."

"Very funny," grumbled Jake, echoes of Brad's warped logic filling his head. "Here, take these," he added, passing two guitar cases to his friend.

"How is the knee today?"

"Stiff but I think it'll hold out," said Jake, lifting his acoustic guitar out of the car.

Lori handed him his backpack, lifted out her own tote bag, then locked up the car. "Don't worry about me, boys," she teased playfully. "I'll just limp along quietly at the back here."

"Sorry, Lori," apologised Rich, giving her a hug. "Are you ok today?"

"Thanks for asking. I'm fine," she replied, flashing him a mischievous smile. "One small flesh wound and he gets all the attention."

"She's right," called back Jake. "I've no right to complain here."

"I guess not," agreed Rich. "Let's go. Maddy's stressing because you guys are late."

"Hey, we're not late. She brought the time forward by an hour and never told me."

"Yeah, sorry about that," confessed Rich blushing. "I was meant to call you and I forgot."

Rich led them through a maze of motor homes, buses and trucks to the motorhome Maddy had hired for the occasion. She had been adamant that they needed some private space for the day and the band hadn't argued with her. When they finally reached it, Grey and Paul were in the middle of an interview with a local journalist. Upon seeing Rich and Jake arrive the journalist, ever the opportunist, directed his next question to Jake, "And how do you feel about getting back out there?"

"A bit nervous, but the show has to go on. There's fans expecting a whole Silver Lake set and I'm not about to let them down again," he replied, suddenly feeling very exposed.

"Will you last the pace tonight? I see you're still limping a bit."

"I hope so. We've tweaked the set a bit to make it easier on me physically, but we're here to play a rock show and that's what we intend to deliver."

"Thanks for your time, guys. Have a great night," said the journalist, wrapping things up quickly as he saw the band's manager approaching with a thunderous look on her face.

"See you out there," called Rich as they watched the journalist scurry away behind the adjacent motorhome.

Staggering slightly as her spike heels tangled in the grass underfoot, Maddy called shrilly, "Nice of you to finally get here! Sound check's in half an hour!"

"Plenty of time," stated Grey calmly. "Stop stressing, woman. You're making me nervous!"

She shot him a dark look and was about to snap but then thought the better of it. Instead, she hugged Lori and muttered, "Maybe you can keep them under control better than me."

"Unlikely," admitted Lori. "But you do seem a bit on edge. Is everything ok?"

"Jason's arriving in time for the show. I just want it to be right. Spot on," she explained. "He's bringing someone with him but wouldn't say who."

"Relax, Maddy," said Lori softly. "The boys won't let you down. Now show me where we've to put our things."

"In here," replied her friend, stepping up into the motorhome. "Do you want a coffee?"

"Sounds good," called Lori, negotiating the steep steps carefully.

Between the sound check and interviews, the hours vanished, leaving the band little time to get nervous. Thunder clouds still lurked overhead, but the storm looked to be moving west and the local radio station forecast a dry evening for the State Fair with temperatures in the mid-seventies Fahrenheit. Just after five, as arranged, a buffet was delivered to the Silver Lake motorhome and, while the band and crew were helping themselves, Jason arrived on site. His early arrival almost tipped Maddy's stress levels off the scale, especially when she saw that his "guest" was the female lead singer from the west coast band Molton that Lori had completed art work for recently. The Englishman casually introduced her as "Tori" and left her to help herself to a plate of food while he had a quick catch up with Maddy outside.

"Hi, Lori," purred Tori as she sat next to her on the narrow couch. "Long time no see, honey."

"It's been a while," agreed Lori. "I thought you guys were on the road out west?"

"We have been but we had a few unplanned days off. Jason rescheduled some of the shows till next week. Promoter issues or something. He's been talking non-stop about these guys though, so I grabbed the chance to check them out for myself."

"You'll not be disappointed," promised Lori with a smile.

At that moment Jake hobbled over to join them, not instantly recognising Tori. As he sat down opposite the girls, he realised who she was and was suddenly struck dumb.

"You must be Jake," said Tori warmly, reaching out to shake his hand. "Jason told me what happened. You ok to go out there tonight?"

"Ready as I'll ever be," spluttered Jake nervously. "Just hope I make it through the set."

"Go for the sympathy vote," she suggested. "It'll get the crowd on your side and they'll cut you some slack."

"We'll see."

"Want a loan of my cane?" joked Lori, offering him her walking cane that had been lying discretely at her feet.

"You're good, li'l lady" he said with a smile. "Besides, you need it more than me."

"I guess," she laughed.

"Oh, I heard about your accident, Lori!" gushed Tori. "I hadn't realised you were still in recovery."

"Well, it's been seven months, so this might be as good as it gets."

"That's a rough deal," sympathised the singer awkwardly. "Oh, Jason's looking for me. Need to go. See you back stage."

Completely star struck, Jake watched Tori glide out of the motorhome with Jason on her arm.

"Enjoying the view?" teased Lori, nudging him in the ribs.

"I can't believe I just met her!" he exclaimed. "I downloaded their album last week. She's got an incredible voice."

"She has," agreed Lori. "Among other assets."

Jake laughed, then declared it was time for him to get changed for the show. Grabbing his back pack from the floor, he went to the bedroom at the back of the motorhome to change. He had decided to go for a black look for the night, but it was a struggle to get his tight black jeans over the strapping on his knee. Leaving his shirt unbuttoned for now, he slipped two painkillers into his pocket as a precaution. If he started to struggle out there he could take them at the start of the acoustic interlude and hope they would kick in by the end of it. Swallowing two more, he went back out to join the others. As it got closer to show time, he began to pace nervously. Grey had gone off to find a quiet corner to call Becky, who was staying with his mom for the night. Rich and Paul had wandered off, when Maddy wasn't looking, to check out the size of the crowd. Shortly after seven thirty Maddy rounded them all up and herded them towards the backstage area. Lori had been all set to go and join Jason and Tori in the VIP enclosure when Jake reached out to stop her.

"Come up to the side of the stage tonight, li'l lady," he said. "Please?"

"If you're sure."

He nodded, "I'll feel better if I can see you're safe."

A few minutes after eight, the lights went out, cloaking the audience and the stage in darkness. Slowly the bass rhythm started, then Paul came in on drums, followed by Rich then, in an explosion of lights, Jake took centre stage. His hands were shaking so badly he could hardly play his guitar part of the intro and it was a relief when he could grip the mic and begin his vocals. At the side of the stage, Lori held her breath until she saw he had fully settled into the song. Beside her, Maddy put a protective arm round her and smiled. The crowd were going wild. After their second number Jake's nerves vanished and he stepped up to the front of the stage to gaze out at the crowd.

"Good evening, Delaware!" he roared. "You look beautiful tonight!"

A huge roar went up.

"We're about to play something new for you. This is from our new album and will be our first single release from it. This is Dragon Song."

With a quick nod over to Rich, the two guitarists launched

straight into a riff that Lori recognised from their time in New York. The two guitarists stood back to back then Jake spun round to the mic and began the vocal with more power to his voice than she had heard him sing with before. Judging by the crowd's reaction they were loving this new song. Between verses Jake fully found his stage presence, bounding from one side of the stage to the other, playing first with Grey then with Rich and finally ending the song standing up on the edge of Paul's drum riser.

A few numbers later he slipped off to the side of the stage to switch guitars and to grab a bottle of water. Behind him, one of the crew ran out with a stool and lowered the mic stand. As Jake limped back on stage to a thunderous cheer, he discretely swallowed the two painkillers that had been in his pocket. Having taken another long drink from the water bottle, he sat it down at the back of the stage before coming forward to take his seat. It was a relief to sit down for a while. His knee was screaming at him.

"You still with us?" he asked, grinning at the fans. "Time to slow things down for a moment. This is a song you might have heard us play before. This is Stronger Within."

The gentle strains of the acoustic melody drifted out over the crowd. His haunting vocal sent chills tingling down Lori's spine as she stood in the wings mesmerised by her man. Much to Jake's amazement when he started the first chorus most of the audience sang with him. The thrill of them singing his lyrics filled him with pride. When he reached the second chorus, he said, "Sing it for me, Delaware" and let the audience carry the song. Any lingering doubts about whether he wanted to pursue this rock star dream melted away as the crowd sang their hearts out for him.

By the time he reached the last acoustic number he could feel the painkillers taking effect. As he played the opening chords of Lady Butterfly he looked over at Lori and winked. She gave him the thumbs up sign and he nodded. It was enough to reassure her that he was ok.

All too soon it was time to start their final number. Stepping up to the mic to address the crowd for the last time Jake called out, "You've been a beautiful audience tonight. Thank you. From the bottom of our hearts we thank you. We're going to leave you now with Flyin' High!"

The band gave their final number every last ounce of their

energy, each one of them pouring their heart and soul into it. As the last notes faded away Jake yelled out, "Safe journey home, folks. Until next time. Good night."

The lights went out on the stage and the fireworks display to mark the end of the State Fair began, filling the sky with a fantastic array of coloured lights and thundering booms. Limping heavily Jake stumbled off stage straight into Lori's arms. Sweat was pouring off him, but neither of them cared as he kissed her passionately before hugging her tight. The intimate moment was interrupted by Paul slapping Jake across the back, "See you back at the motorhome, lover boy!"

He swept past them and walked away with his arm around Maddy's waist. Around them the stage crew were already starting to dismantle the set.

"You ok?" asked Lori, resting her head on Jake's chest.

"I am now," he sighed, his heart still pounding. "I was so scared out there at first. I felt so exposed at the front of that stage."

"You were awesome," whispered Lori. "Just as I knew you would be."

"You're biased," he teased. "It was some set, though. When the crowd started singing my lyrics back to me. When they carried that whole chorus themselves. Shit, that blew me away."

"Come on, rock star," laughed Lori. "Let's go and find the others."

On their way through the backstage maze several of the organisers and other performers from earlier in the day congratulated Jake on his gutsy performance. Eventually they reached the Silver Lake motorhome and found Maddy outside pacing up and down impatiently.

"Thought you'd got lost," she snapped sharply.

"Maddy," cautioned Lori, shooting a dark look at her friend. "We just needed a minute or two."

"I suppose," she relented. "Jason's waiting for you to get back here, though."

"Well, we're here now," declared Jake bluntly, stepping up into the motorhome.

A cheer went up from the rest of the band as he entered. Playing along, Jake gave a theatrical bow, then collapsed onto the nearest sofa. Someone passed him a beer and he drank deeply from the bottle before saying, "That was incredible out there tonight. Fucking amazing!"

"Couldn't agree more," said Jason from behind him. Tori was standing quietly beside the Englishman watching the boys. "How would you like to take this show on the road?"

"Say what?" said Rich his eyes wide.

"Next week. Three shows. Support act for Tori and her band," said Jason plainly. "You'd leave Tuesday, play Wednesday, Friday and Saturday, then fly home on Sunday."

Looking from one to the other the four members of Silver Lake could hardly believe what they were hearing.

"Where?" asked Grey, like the others not daring to believe what he had just heard.

"Phoenix on Wednesday, Sacramento on Friday and Seattle on Saturday," answered Tori with her honeyed tone. "We'd love to have you guys out there with us for these last three shows."

Nodding to each other, but no one daring to be the first to speak, the band silently agreed among themselves. Eventually, after what felt like an eternity, but in reality was only a few seconds, Rich said, "We're in."

"Welcome aboard," laughed Tori, obviously relieved that the band had agreed to join the tour.

Next morning when Lori awoke the space in the bed beside her was empty. During the drive home the night before, Jake had still been in a state of shock at Jason's offer. The finer details were still being worked out, but with Maddy on the case, he was confident it would all fall into place smoothly. After the band had agreed to play, Tori explained that the previous support act had been thrown off the tour. She didn't elaborate as to why and no one dared to ask. Silver Lake would be the second act on stage each night and would have forty five minutes to show what they could do. The opening act on each of the three nights would be a band local to the area. When they had arrived back at the house both of them had fallen straight into bed, worn out by the day's excitement and the long late night drive home. Getting out of bed, Lori wandered through the house searching for Jake. The coffee pot was on and the crumbs on the counter suggested he had had some breakfast already. Pausing to pour herself a coffee, she wandered through the sunroom and out onto the deck. It was already warm outside, the storm clouds from the day before long gone. Jake was standing at the edge of the deck looking over the shrubbery and out towards the ocean, sipping his coffee.

"Morning," said Lori as she sat down at the table. "Couldn't you sleep?"

"Morning, li'l lady," he replied, turning round and coming to sit opposite her. "My knee kept me awake."

"Did you take something to help?"

"Just coffee," he answered, then added quietly. "I wish you were coming to Phoenix with us."

"We talked about this last night," began Lori. "I've work to finish off here. I can't afford to take a week out just now."

"Can't you push your deadlines out?" he asked.

"Can you postpone the show dates?" she countered with a smile.

"*Touché*, li'l lady," he nodded. "Is this really happening? Did I get shot again last night and this is all a dream?"

"It's real alright," reassured Lori. "It's a huge break for the band."

"Don't I know it," agreed Jake. "The dream's coming true, isn't it?"

Lori nodded. "If you want it to."

"I want it. The four of us want it. If you hadn't asked Maddy down here for the Surfside weekend we'd still be playing local bars and weddings not stadiums in Sacramento."

"I'm not taking any credit here for your success. The band has worked hard for this. You deserve it," said Lori with a proud smile.

"Yeah, if I'd left you lying on the sand that day," joked Jake playfully. "None of this would be happening."

"I'm glad you didn't."

After a frantic couple of days all the arrangements were made, the instruments packed up, their bags packed, flights, transfers and hotels booked. The band squeezed in a rehearsal on Monday afternoon to finalise the shortened set. All too soon it was Tuesday morning and time to head off to Philadelphia for their flight to Phoenix. In true rock star style, Maddy had booked a limo for them to travel to the airport. It was scheduled to pick Jake up at nine thirty. Both he and Lori had been up early; both silently dreading saying goodbye to each other. His back pack sat on a chair beside the kitchen table and during breakfast, Jake had checked its contents at least three times.

"I'm sure I've forgotten something," he muttered as he zipped the bag up yet again.

"Relax," said Lori. "If you've forgotten something I'm sure Maddy can source a replacement. You're not going to the middle of nowhere. Phoenix does have stores you know."

"I guess," he agreed. "I'll call when we get there."

"You better," teased Lori. "And every day you're gone."

"I will, mom," joked Jake. "So what's your plan for the week?"

"Work," stated Lori. "I need to be finished up on two of the projects by Friday. Mary's coming over tomorrow. Grey's mom is dropping Becky off here on Friday at four."

"How did you get roped into babysitting?"

"Grey called yesterday and asked if I'd mind having her to stay. His mom had already arranged to go away for the weekend with her church group," Lori explained. "I'm looking forward to having Becky here."

Jake burst out laughing.

"What's so funny?" asked Lori pouring them a fresh cup of coffee.

"This crazy rock n roll lifestyle!" he laughed. "The lead singer's girlfriend can't be at the gig because she's babysitting the bass player's daughter so his mom can go on a church outing!"

"Just proves we're still normal people with normal lives," giggled Lori, seeing the humour in the situation. "Oh, and I've got a physical therapy assessment too."

"Want to throw in a trip to the dentist?"

"That's the following week," she giggled.

"I shouldn't laugh," confessed Jake. "I've got a doctor's appointment next week about my knee."

The crunch of tyres on the gravel outside and the toot of a horn signalled the limo's arrival. Together they walked out to the front door. The limo driver came up and took Jake's two holdalls to stow in the trunk. Taking Lori into his arms, Jake held her tight, drinking in the smell of her shampoo and her perfume, trying to imprint her in his memory. With a slow, lingering kiss, he said, "I love you, li'l lady."

"I love you too," she whispered. "I'll be right here when you get back on Sunday."

"Promise."

"Promise," she said, kissing him again. "You'd better go. If you miss this flight Maddy'll kill you."

"You're not wrong! See you Sunday."

With one backward glance, he was climbing into the back of the car and was gone.

Life at the beach house fell into an easy, if quietly dull, routine over the next few days. With minimal distractions Lori threw herself headlong into the task of finishing her commissions almost as soon as the limo was out of sight. By some miracle she had kept her Silver Lake work secret and it was this she turned to first. Jason had already contacted her to chase up the merchandise graphics. She had sent him what she had but, true to form, he came back asking for more- at least another two to use on T-shirts. The State Fair gig had given her some fresh inspiration after hearing Dragon Song played live. With a mental picture of Jake's dragon tattoo and the Celtic knots the band favoured, she set to work combining the two concepts. A grumbling from her stomach brought her back to the real world several hours later. Glancing at her cell phone, she was surprised to discover it was late afternoon. Not wanting to lose her train of thought entirely, she went into the kitchen and grabbed a glass of juice and a bag of potato chips. Within a few minutes she was back focussed on the design in front of her. The next thing to disturb her concentration was the cricket chirp from her phone. It was getting dark outside and she was genuinely surprised to discover it was after eight o'clock. She had worked away the entire day. The message, as she had suspected, was from Jake. "Arrived at the hotel. Flight was good. Paul shit scared. Will call tomorrow. Love you J x"

"Poor Paul. Worked all day. Miss you. Love you too. L x" she quickly messaged back.

"Don't work too hard. J x" came the quick response.

"Don't play too hard. L x"

The smell of fresh coffee wafting through the house wakened Lori the next morning. As quickly as she could Lori got out of bed and hurried through to the kitchen. Mary was standing at the sink washing some dishes.

"Good morning," called Lori from the doorway. "Why does my coffee never smell as good as yours?"

"Lori!" cried Mary, her delight at seeing her obvious. "Oh, you look fabulous! No cane?"

"Not indoors unless it's a really rough day," replied Lori hugging her housekeeper. "I still need it if I'm out. How's your sister?"

"Not great," confessed Mary, her eyes welling up with tears. "Not great at all."

"I'm so sorry, Mary. I had hoped when you called to say you were coming over that things were getting better."

"It's not going to get better," said the older woman, tears flowing freely down her cheeks. "She's terminal."

"Oh, Mary. I am so dreadfully sorry," replied Lori, feeling her own eyes filling up. "Should you be here?"

"Lori," Mary began, wiping her eyes with a Kleenex. "I came

to hand in my resignation."

"No, you don't need to do that," Lori protested. "Can't we talk about this? Work something out?"

The older woman motioned for Lori to sit down. She poured two mugs of coffee and sat at the table opposite her. Slowly stirring in the sugar and half 'n' half, Mary said, "I need to leave, Lori. I can't keep taking your money and not work for it. My pride won't let me."

"This isn't about the money is it?" asked Lori sharply. "The money doesn't matter. Lord, I've enough of it."

"I know, honey," said Mary warmly. "But look at you. You're not the fragile little bird that I came here to look after. You're back on your feet. You've got Jake. My work here is done."

"But what if I need your help?"

"If you need me for something specific then of course I'll be here," promised Mary with a smile. "But when I finish up today it is for the last time. I need to be there for my sister and her family and I don't know how long she has."

Nodding slowly Lori whispered, "I understand."

"And you won't try to stop me?"

"No," promised Lori. "Your family comes first. I'm just being selfish."

"OK, now that we've agreed, what do you want for breakfast?" asked Mary forcing a smile. "I didn't see any dinner dishes so I'm guessing you skipped at least dinner yesterday."

"Caught," whispered Lori somewhat sheepishly. "I was working until it was late."

"I'll make you some bacon and French toast," stated the older woman firmly. "You need to eat, girl!"

Knowing it was pointless to argue, Lori sat back and drank her coffee, allowing the older woman to fuss over her for a while. Once breakfast was finished, Lori showered and dressed then returned to her drawing board. She had one section of the last Silver Lake piece to finish, then she could email the designs through to Jason. This commission had grown considerably as the project progressed and she only hoped he appreciated her efforts. If it had been for any other band, she would have re-negotiated the terms of the contract but she had long since decided that the extra pieces on this one could slip under the radar just this once.

By early afternoon she was done and, as she signed the drawing with her usual flourish, Mary called through to say she was leaving. As they hugged their farewells in the kitchen, the tears flowed freely down Lori's cheeks, "I'm going to miss you."

"Me too," admitted the housekeeper. "I'll keep in touch and you promise you'll call if you need me."

"I'll call, I promise," said Lori hugging her tight. "Thank you for taking such good care of me."

"You did the hard work yourself," replied Mary. "Now I need to go."

Lori nodded and watched tearfully as the housekeeper left through the back door. Suddenly a feeling of complete and utter loneliness swept over her. Memories of how fragile she had been when she arrived in Rehoboth in the spring; memories of Mary cajoling her and encouraging her; the memory of the first night Jake had crashed out on the couch – that one made her smile. Taking a deep breath, she wiped her tears from her cheeks. With a heavy heart, she went back through to the study to finish submitting her designs. As soon as the last one was scanned and mailed, she fired off a quick email to David to tell him that Mary had resigned and to arrange a hefty payment as a thank you. With her work up to date for the day, Lori decided it was time for a walk along the sand to get some exercise and some fresh air.

A breeze blowing in off the ocean was keeping the beach from being unbearably hot. Lori had put on her bikini and tightly fastened a broad sarong around her hips to cover her thigh. Deciding to err on the side of caution, she took both her canes with the wide base plates securely in place. Feeling the sun on her back as she walked eased away the day's tensions, and she was soon smiling to herself. It was a beautiful afternoon and she wished Jake were there to share it with her. Right on cue her cell phone that she had securely tucked into her bikini top, began to ring.

"Hello," she called brightly as she answered the call.

"Hi, li'l lady," came Jake's warm voice. "How's your day been?"

"Emotional. Mary resigned. I'll tell you about it when I see you," she began. "I was just thinking about you. I'm down on the beach. It's gorgeous."

"Lucky you," he said. "We've just arrived at the venue. It's huge!"

"Is it sold out?"

"More or less as I hear it. About sixteen thousand. It's all a bit scary if I'm being honest. The State Fair is as big a crowd as we've played to and that wasn't a quarter the size of this."

"Once you're out there, you'll be fine. How's your knee?"

"It's ok," said Jake, a little evasively. She could hear Maddy yelling in the background. "Look, I need to go. I wish you were here."

"Me too," she replied. "Have a great show tonight. I'll talk to you tomorrow."

"Love you, li'l lady."

"Love you too."

On Friday morning Lori made the drive out to the medical centre for her appointment with Jo. It had been a couple of weeks since her last physical therapy session and Jo had been insistent that this session be held out at the medical centre instead of the house stating that she wanted to run some tests. Even being close to the medical centre made Lori nervous, but she tried to remain calm as she walked across the parking lot and into the air-conditioned building. Following the overhead signs, she eventually found the right department. Jo was standing talking to another therapist as she walked in.

"Hi, Lori," she called. "I'll be with you in just a minute."

While she waited Lori wandered over to read a bulletin board rather than take a seat.

"Sorry about that," apologised Jo coming over. "You look great. How's the leg?"

"Good actually," said Lori. "Still the odd bad day, but I can cope with that."

"Right, let's get you through to the gym. Did you bring gym clothes like I asked?"

Lori nodded and Jo escorted her through to the changing rooms. Once she had changed and completed a gentle warm up routine Jo put her through a rigorous series of stretches, resistance and balance tests. It took the physiotherapist almost an hour to satisfy herself as to Lori's range of movement and fitness.

"Ok, we're done," she announced at last.

"Thank God for that," gasped Lori. "I'm about done. That was tough going."

"No pain, no gain, Mz Hyde," declared the therapist, passing her a cup of water. "You did great."

"So what's the verdict?" Lori asked, sipping the ice cold water.

"Well, I think my work is done," stated Jo with a smile. "You've made great progress and I don't feel there's anything else I can do here."

A look of disappointment descended on Lori's face. She hesitated before replying, "So is this as good as it's going to get?"

"I'm not saying that, Lori," explained Jo calmly. "All I'm trying to say is that the therapy sessions aren't adding anything. If you keep pushing yourself the way you have been then you could see more improvement."

"But I could be stuck with the cane?"

"You could," admitted the therapist. "How often do you feel that you need to use it?"

"If I'm out on my own. If I have to walk any distance or stand for a while. Pretty much most of the time I'm out of the house," answered Lori quietly. "I'm scared of falling."

"That's understandable," agreed Jo, sensing her fear. "When's your next appointment with John?"

"In three or four weeks."

"Here's my suggestion then," began Jo. "See how you get on until then. Once John's examined you, if he thinks you would benefit from more therapy sessions, we can set them up."

"Sounds fair I suppose," conceded Lori trying to find a smile.

"Good," said Jo looking at her watch. "Would you like to grab a coffee before you head off? I'm due a break before my next client."

"That would be good," smiled Lori. "Let me get changed first."

A short while later the two women were sitting in the medical centre's coffee shop with two large coffees and Italian pastries on the table in front of them. It was surprisingly quiet with only one other table occupied. As Lori bit into her pastry, Jo asked after Jake and the band.

"They're in Sacramento tonight," said Lori with a proud smile. "They got three support slots with Molton out on the west coast.

He'll be back on Sunday night."

"That's a far cry from Surfside and Milford," laughed Jo.

"It sure is. They played to about sixteen thousand in Phoenix on Wednesday night. I think it freaked them out a bit."

"How's Jake's knee?" asked the therapist. "He was lucky it wasn't a lot worse from what I've heard."

"It's ok as far as I know. It could've been a whole lot worse," Lori agreed with a sigh.

They chatted idly for the next few minutes, then Jo spotted her next client arriving and apologised that she would need to go. Lori sat on at the small table finishing her coffee. In her bag, her phone chirped. Quickly she grabbed it and, as she'd hoped, it was a text message from Jake.

"Miss you. J x"

"Miss you too. L x" she typed quickly.

"Will call in a couple of hours. Radio show this morning. J x"

"Look forward to it L x"

Despite the lure of the "sale" signs Lori resisted the temptations of the outlets as she drove back into town. She had calculated that she had less than four hours until Becky arrived to stay for the weekend and she still had a few hours' worth of work to finish off on her second project. The design was finished, but she had some intricate calligraphy to add. Uninterrupted, she hoped to have it done in about three hours. When she arrived home, she parked her car next to Jake's truck then went round the back, entering through the back door. Pausing only to grab a sandwich, Lori headed straight through and sat at her drawing board. Calligraphy always posed a challenge for her. Carefully, she drafted out the wording on a spare piece of paper. It took her a while to get the angle and the balance of the pen right, but once she was settled into her rhythm, the lettering flowed smoothly. The detailed capital letter took a bit more practice, but soon she had a feel for it and was confident enough to sketch it out on the finished design. She had just finished the outline when her phone rang.

"Hi, Jake," she called cheerfully. "How are things?"

"Crazy!" he replied, sounding tired. "This is a crazy rock circus. Not what we expected at all."

"It's going ok though?"

"Show was great in Phoenix. Tonight's looking good. Slightly smaller crowd," he replied. "I don't know how these guys do this for months on end."

"Well hopefully you'll find out soon."

"I don't think I could cope," he laughed. "Has Becky arrived yet? Grey's missing her."

"She's due here around four. Still a couple of hours yet. I've some work to finish off before she gets here," replied Lori glancing at the time. "How's the knee?"

"Puffy and sore. I'll need to tape it up for tonight. We arrived at the venue a few minutes ago, so I'll deal with it after our sound check," said Jake.

"When's that at?"

"In half an hour," he replied. "I have to go, li'l lady. Time to re-join the crazy train."

"Ok. I'll talk to you tomorrow."

"I'll try to call about the same time. We've a tight schedule tomorrow to get up to Seattle so, if I don't get a chance to call, I'll call from the airport before we fly out on Sunday."

"Be careful," she said softly. "Love you."

"Love you too, Lori. Say "Hi" to Becky for me."

"Will do."

And then he was gone.

Crazy train. Crazy rock circus.

The words echoed round in her head as she pondered what kind of tour Silver Lake had joined. Resisting temptation to call Maddy, Lori returned to her calligraphy. Time was running away from her and she still had a fair amount to finish off. One of the letters didn't quite sit right and she had to disguise it and re-do it at a slightly different angle. The progress was slow as her mind kept wandering back to thoughts of Sacramento and Silver Lake and crazy rock circus trains. Just before four o'clock she applied the finishing touches and set the design aside for the inks to dry before she scanned it into the computer. Now that her commission was almost done, she emailed Maddy to check up on Jake and the band. Almost instantly she got a reply – "Don't worry. They are having an educational experience. Some more than others. I am keeping an eye on them."

"And that's meant to help!" Lori mailed back.

"Jake safe and missing you. He's not looked at another girl. He's been tucked up in bed early each night with an ice pack and pain meds. He's barely even had a beer all week. Relax. M x"

"Thanks." she mailed back, wondering if she could believe her friend.

The crunch of tyres outside announced the arrival of her small house guest. She could hear the little girl's excited voice chattering then a firm older voice suggesting that she may want to calm down a little. Becky was just reaching up to knock the front door when Lori opened it.

"Lori!" she squealed, flying into her arms and hugging her tight. "I've missed you."

"I've missed you too, honey," said Lori then turning to face the older woman who was coming up the steps. "Hi, you must be Grey's mom."

"Hi and you must be Lori. I'm Annie," replied the older woman. As she stepped up onto the porch Lori could see the strong resemblance to Grey, especially across the eyes. "I've heard all about you from this little miss."

"I'll bet," agreed Lori. "Come on through. Would you like a juice or a coffee?"

"Coffee would be great," replied Annie "And can I use your bathroom?"

"Of course. Down the hall to the right," directed Lori. "Becky, take your things into the bedroom at the end of the hallway."

Pulling her small pink wheeled suitcase behind her, Becky ran off down the hallway. As ever, her American Girl doll was tucked under her arm. With a smile Lori went through to the kitchen to fetch the coffee and some apple juice for the little girl. She had just poured the coffees when Annie entered the kitchen.

"You have a beautiful home here," she complimented.

"Thanks. It was the family holiday home when I was little," Lori explained. "Could you give me a hand here, please?"

Annie lifted the two mugs of coffee while Lori took the juice through to the sun room. Becky was already stationed in front of the TV and thanked Lori for the juice.

"Let's go out on the deck," suggested Lori.

"Oh, this is stunning!" gasped Annie as they sat outside a few minutes later. "I'd love a view of the ocean."

"It's why I came back here," confessed Lori. "Have you heard from Grey today?"

"He called just as we were getting ready to leave. Sounds like some tour they are on!"

"Jake called earlier. I got the same impression," said Lori, concern evident in her voice. "I checked with Maddy. She said they're ok."

"I'll be glad when he's home," admitted Grey's mother. "After what happened to Jake the other week I worry so much when they are playing."

"Me too."

"You've certainly made a big impression on Becky," commented Annie warmly. "And thank you for agreeing to have her over this weekend."

"She's adorable and good company. We had fun when we were in New York the other week. It's nice to see her relaxed and happy after what happened to her mom."

"She's been great about that," agreed Annie. "I always got the feeling she was scared of Sandy. It's a very un-Christian thing to say, but she's better off without that girl."

Lori smiled, but resisted the temptation to comment. Instead, she asked Annie where she was going for the weekend.

"Atlantic City," confessed the older woman with a girlish giggle. "Once a year a group of us from church go for the weekend. We save up our quarters all year for the machines. We love it!"

"Good for you," laughed Lori, picturing the bus load of senior citizens hitting the casinos.

"So have you any plans for the weekend?"

"Not really," admitted Lori. "We might go shopping tomorrow and I thought we could go into Rehoboth for dinner and a stroll along the boardwalk. Maybe go to the arcade for a while."

"Not the beach?" asked Annie with a hint of surprise to her voice.

"Maybe on Sunday. I'm not too steady on my feet on the sand."

"Oh, of course!" blushed Annie. "Sorry, I didn't mean…."

"It's ok," interrupted Lori with a smile. "I assumed Becky or Grey had said."

"Grey said you were recovering from a leg injury," replied Annie. "I'm guessing it was a serious one?"

Lori nodded, then said quietly, "Yes, it was," then added, "It's kind of how I met Jake. He rescued me after I fell while walking on the beach one day."

"Ever the hero is Jake," commented Annie with a smile. "He has a heart of gold that boy."

"He sure does," agreed Lori softly.

"Oh Lord, look at the time!" exclaimed the older woman. "I'd better be making tracks."

Lori and Becky went out to the front porch to wave goodbye to Annie then turned to go back indoors.

"Ok, honey," said Lori closing the door. "I have a little work to finish off. Can you watch TV for half an hour until I'm done?"

"Can I help you?" asked Becky hopefully.

"Well," began Lori thinking on her feet. "You could do your own drawing for your daddy while I finish mine?"

"And sit at your desk?"

"The little desk," conceded Lori. "I'll clear you some space."

When they went through to the study, Lori tidied away some of the books from the smaller desk, found a spare drawing board and set the little girl up with a large sheet of paper, some pens and some coloured pencils. As Lori sat back down at her own drawing board, Becky declared that she was going to draw her daddy and her Silver Lake uncles on stage. The little girl worked studiously on her drawing, while Lori scanned and mailed her work to the agent. As Becky was still engrossed, she decided to check her emails to see if there was any feedback from Jason about the Silver Lake pieces. There were two emails from him – one asking her to tweak one of the merchandising designs and another asking for an additional design to use as a belt buckle and badge. He had given her a deadline of Monday morning. There was no way she could meet that and she fired back an email saying the changes and the new design would be with him by noon on Wednesday. She also quickly sent a text to Jake saying that Becky was with her if Grey wanted to call.

"How's that drawing coming along?" she asked as she switched off her laptop.

"It's not finished yet," replied the little girl seriously, without looking up,

"Do you want to work on while I make dinner?" Lori suggested, moving over to admire the little girl's efforts.

"What's for dinner?"

"Is lasagne alright?" Lori asked hopefully.

"Sure," replied Becky before innocently adding, "Mommy used to make it."

"I can't promise it will taste exactly like hers."

"That's good. Her's was kind of yucky."

With a smile Lori left the little girl to her artwork and went through to the kitchen to prepare their meal. Three quarters of an hour later as they were just sitting down to eat, Lori's cell phone rang. She didn't recognise the number but she guessed it was Grey.

"Hello," she greeted cheerfully,

"Hey Lori. It's Grey. How're things?"

"Hi. I thought it might be you. We just sat down to dinner. How are things in sunny Cali?"

"Hectic," he laughed. "Rich and Paul are loving this crazy lifestyle. Jake and I are a bit out of it. Our party days are behind us. He's icing his knee before the show. Is my princess there?"

"Of course," said Lori, passing the phone to Becky. "It's your dad."

"Daddy!" shrieked the little girl down the phone.

She chattered away to her daddy about staying with Lori and doing a piece of "art" for him coming home, then passed the phone back to Lori, "He wants to say goodbye to you too."

"Ok," said Lori taking the phone back.

"Lori, she sounds great," said Grey. "Thanks for having her this weekend. Now don't spoil her."

"As if I would do that," laughed Lori, winking at the little girl. "We're going to watch a movie with some popcorn after dinner. We'll be thinking about you guys."

"I know one guy that's thinking about you," replied Grey with a laugh. "Need to run. Maddy's yelling again. See you on Sunday night."

"Tell Jake I love him," said Lori.

"You can tell him yourself. He's here," said Grey as she heard him pass the phone to his friend.

"Hi, li'l lady. Twice in one day. My lucky day," he joked.

"Did your sound check go ok?" she asked. "Grey said you were icing your knee. Is it ok?"

"It's fine, Lori. Stop worrying. We're all set for tonight. Need to go. Maddy's yelling."

"I can hear her," said Lori. "You better run. Love you, rock star."

"More like crock star," he laughed. "Love you too."

As he ended the call, she could visualise Jake smiling at her. Suddenly Sacramento and Sunday seemed a long way off.

In preparation for Becky's visit Lori had bought half a dozen kiddie DVDs, unsure of which films the little girl had seen or would like. With the dishwasher loaded up and the kitchen tidy, Lori suggested they put on their pyjamas, make some popcorn and curl up in the sun room with a film. Soon they were both stretched out on the couch watching a Disney classic. It was a film Lori remembered seeing at the cinema with her parents when she wasn't much older than Becky. The little girl cuddled in close to Lori, fingering Lori's hair subconsciously as she watched the animated film. When the first film was done the little girl pleaded to be allowed to watch a second, but, checking the time, Lori said no. Instead, she suggested that Becky go and brush her teeth then she would come and read her a story.

"I didn't bring any story books," said Becky sadly.

"It's ok. There's some of mine here from when I was a little girl," said Lori warmly. "I looked them out and put them in your room."

A few minutes later Becky was safely tucked up in bed, her doll tucked in beside her and Lori was sitting reading Dr Seuss' "One Fish Two Fish". They both giggled as Lori got tongue tied over the rhymes. When the story was done Becky asked for another one. This time she chose "The Cat In The Hat". After a third story Lori declared that she had overdosed on Dr Seuss and that it was time to put the light out.

"Night night, honey," she said, kissing Becky on the forehead. "Sweet dreams."

"Night Lori," replied the little girl sleepily before adding, "Night night Daddy too."

Around the same time several thousand miles west Silver Lake were waiting to go on stage. The first support act, four local kids from Sacramento, were just finishing their set. In the corridor behind the stage Jake had been pacing up and down restlessly while Paul was crouched down by the fire exit. The drummer had partied with the guys from Molton the night before until Maddy had hauled him away as the sun was rising. He had kept a low profile for most of the day, disappearing after the sound check only to be tracked down just before show time with the Molton crew. Now he was sitting shaking in the corner looking grey and haunted.

"You ok to do this?" asked Jake sharply.

"Yeah," replied Paul sourly. "I won't let you down."

"You fucking better not," growled Jake, staring into his dilated bloodshot eyes. "As soon as we're off stage, you are going straight back to the hotel with me. No drug parties tonight."

"I promised Tori I'd be there," muttered Paul, getting unsteadily to his feet.

"She won't notice your absence," hissed Jake, his face a mask of fury. "I don't know what shit they gave you or you took earlier, but there's no place for it in this band. You know the fucking rules!"

"We second that," added Grey and Rich, coming through from the dressing room.

"Ok. Ok," agreed Paul, swaying slightly. "I won't go."

Maddy was waving them through with a thunderous look on her face. As they walked past her, she put an arm out to halt Paul. "Don't fuck up out there. Don't let these guys down!"

"Yes, ma'am," he mumbled, with a salute.

As they stepped out on stage to rapturous cheers from the crowd, Paul seemed to come alive, bounding behind his drum kit, while the others began the first guitar riff. After the first three numbers Jake switched to his acoustic guitar and settled himself on a stool in the centre of the stage.

"You still with us out there, Sacramento?" he called, gazing out over the arena.

A huge roar came back at him from the crowd.

"We're a long way from home, guys, but you've made us feel very welcome. Thank you. Now we're going to calm things down for a few minutes. Let you catch your breath. This is Stronger Within."

As he began the gentle intro, the crowd went wild. Feeding off the audience's adoration he played his heart out through the song and through Lady Butterfly.

Another change of guitar back to his favourite electric and they lit the place up with Dragon Song followed by a rendition of Led Zeppelin's Immigrant Song before finishing with Flyin' High. Their work for the night was done and Paul hadn't missed a beat all night. They left the stage to an enormous roar from the crowd and chants of "Silver Lake, Silver Lake, Silver Lake Lake Lake."

"Awesome, guys!" screamed Maddy as they filed past her. "Incredible set."

"Get him to fuck out of here," stated Jake, pointing to Paul, as his furious mood began to erupt. "Lock him in his fucking room if you have to, Maddison!"

"Hey, Jake, calm down," protested Paul, slurring the words.

"If you ever turn up wasted again for a gig you're out!" roared Jake, his temper finally snapping. "We've worked our asses off to get this far and you're not fucking this up for us! Now get the fuck out of my sight."

Screwing the towel he had been using to dry himself off into a ball and throwing it into a corner, Jake stormed off through the corridors and back to their dressing room, leaving the others staring after him.

"He's right," said Grey coldly as he followed his friend.

It took all of Maddy's tact and diplomacy to get the four guys into the minibus together and safely to the hotel for the night. As they went their separate ways to their rooms she went with Paul. Although she didn't agree with Jake's outburst, she had to concede he was right. They had been lucky that Paul had held it together and she intended to tell him just that.

Alone in his room Jake turned on the TV then lay down on the bed staring up at the ceiling. His usual post show adrenaline high was long gone. Instead the fire of his anger towards Paul was still smouldering. There was no place in Silver Lake for drugs. They all enjoyed a few beers and the odd shot, but there was a long standing agreement about substance abuse. All four of them had experienced what drugs could do. He wasn't going to allow Paul to be lured back into that dark world. They'd both been there together before.

A soft knock at his door brought him back to the present and when he looked through the spy hole he could see Maddy standing in the corridor.

"Come in," said Jake opening the door. "Want a drink?"

She shook her head, "I just wanted to check you'd calmed down. You were pretty fired up back there. I don't think I've ever seen you angry like that before."

"Sorry about that," he said, sitting down on the edge of the bed and running his hands through his hair. "I won't tolerate that kind of shit. Paul knows the score."

"Paul was way out of line," agreed Maddy, sitting on the only chair in the room. "I've spoken to him. He is genuinely sorry. I've also had words with Molton's manager."

"If Molton can function that way, that's up to them, but we have a zero tolerance to drugs," said Jake. "I've lost too many good friends that way over the years. Both Paul and I have been down that road before. I won't stand back and let any of the guys go down that way, especially not Paul. Never again."

"It's in the contract you all signed too," commented Maddy. "Jason only deals with clean acts. A bit of weed he can turn a blind eye to but nothing like the shit these guys were doing. I'll take responsibility for keeping Paul clean."

"So how come Lord Jason got us involved here?"

"A friend asked him to help Tori and the guys out. Simple as that," she replied a hint of regret in her voice. "Anyway, I just wanted to check you were ok. Tomorrow's going to be a long day. Car's picking us up to head to the airport at seven thirty. Flight's at ten twenty."

"I'll be ready," promised Jake with a yawn.

"I know you will," smiled Maddy getting to her feet. "And clear the air with Paul before we reach the airport. We're not taking this to Seattle with us."

Jake nodded.

"Get some sleep, Jake."

Next morning they were all assembled in the hotel lobby hanging about, waiting for the limo to arrive. Every one of them still looked half asleep, especially Paul, who was reclining on one of the leather sofas. Sensing this was as good a moment as any to clear the air, Jake wandered over to talk to the errant drummer.

"Paul," he began calmly.

"You here to yell at me some more?" asked the drummer.

"No, I'm here to apologise," replied Jake wondering where the conversation was heading.

"No need. Someone had to chew me out. I'd rather it was you than Grey," confessed Paul forcing a smile. "I got caught up in the whole after show party thing. No excuses. I fucked up. It's kind of freaked me out a bit."

"How come?" asked Jake, looking down curiously at his friend.

"I remember you yelling at me after the show last night, but that's all I remember about yesterday. I've no idea what I took after the first line of coke," the drummer confessed quietly. "And I feel like shit."

"Don't you remember the set?"

Paul shook his head. "Don't tell the others, please."

"I won't," agreed Jake, recognising the look of fear with mixed shame on Paul's face. "Come on, car's here."

As they walked towards the door together Jake added, "You played a blinding set last night. Christ knows how!"

The two friends were laughing together as they stepped out into the hazy early morning sunshine. It was a sight Maddy was relieved to see.

The girls enjoyed a lazy pyjama morning in front of the TV watching cartoons, then around noon, Lori declared that it was time to get dressed. Becky started to protest, but Lori was firm with her and said if she didn't get dressed then they couldn't go shopping.

"Where are we going?" asked Becky.

"I thought we could take a run out to the outlets for a while," answered Lori, hoping that this idea would please the little girl.

"Is there a toy store out there?"

"I don't think so," replied Lori. "But there are lots of stores with stuff for little girls."

Her charge thought about this for a moment or two, then, with a huge smile, declared, "Let's get dressed and go!"

Before they set off Lori made them both a sandwich, then promised her little friend that they would go out for dinner. This idea seemed to meet with approval. The drive out to the outlets was uneventful and Lori was fortunate enough to find a slightly shaded parking space under a young tree. Hand in hand, she led the little girl across the parking lot towards the first row of stores. Remembering Grey's caution about not spoiling her too much, Lori tried to show restraint as they shopped. She bought her a couple of T-shirts in one store and a sundress in another. When they reached the Converse outlet Lori couldn't resist going in. Like most of the stores they were having a huge sale and she had soon picked up a couple of pairs for herself and some for Jake. Becky had wandered off towards the kids section.

"Lori!" she squealed, coming running over with a shoe in her hand. "Can I get these, please? They've got Dr Seuss on them like in the story!"

Smiling at the little girl's excitement she said, "Let's see if they have your size, honey."

Together they checked through the boxes until they found a pair in the right size. Lori also spotted a white pair with multi-coloured tongues and asked Becky if she liked them.

"They're like yours only with a rainbow!" she giggled. "We could both get matching ones. Please, Lori!"

"We could," laughed Lori, checking the pile of boxes for her own size.

By the time they left the store, they were weighed down with shoe boxes.

"OK, miss," declared Lori. "Time to go back to the car."

Her leg was beginning to ache and all the bending to tie shoe laces in the shop hadn't helped, but she tried to hide her growing discomfort from the little girl.

"Are we going to dinner now?" asked Becky hopefully.

"It's a bit early," replied Lori. "But why don't we head back into town and we can see how we feel when we get there."

"Ok," said Becky running on ahead to the car.

With the bags carefully stowed in the trunk and Becky strapped securely into the back seat, Lori headed back into Rehoboth. The traffic was heavy and they sat in a jam on the outskirts of town for almost half an hour. In the back of the car the little girl had dozed off, her head over to the right resting on her shoulder. Eventually they reached the centre of town where Lori toured around for a while searching for a parking space. After a few minutes she spotted a truck backing out of a spot just a few spaces up from the boardwalk. As soon as she stopped the car's engine, Becky stirred and stretched sleepily.

"You wait here while I feed the meter," said Lori as she climbed out of the car. She kept a supply of quarters in a plastic box in the centre console compartment and lifted out a small handful.

It only took her a minute or two to add in enough coins to safeguard them for about three hours. She figured that would give them plenty of time for dinner and a stroll along the boardwalk to the arcade.

"It's a bit early for dinner, miss. Do you want to go down onto the beach for a while first?" suggested Lori, as she helped the little girl out of the back of the car.

"Can I?" she asked, rubbing sleep out of her eyes. "Daddy said you might not be able to take me onto the sand."

"I'll be fine as long as I'm careful," assured Lori with a smile. "We won't go far. How about I buy you a bucket and spade and you can build me a castle?"

"Yes!" cried Becky, jumping up and down with excitement.

Having purchased a bright yellow bucket complete with spade and rake, Becky ran ahead of Lori onto the beach. Somewhat anxiously, cane in hand, Lori slowly followed the little girl. She hadn't planned on being down on the sand and hadn't slipped the wide base plate for her cane into her bag. If she put any weight on it, the slender stick sank into the soft sand. After what felt like an eternity, Lori reached the spot where the little girl was happily playing.

"Can you sit down and play with me?" asked Becky as she scooped damp sand into the bucket.

"No, honey. I'll stand here for now. If I sit down I might get stuck," replied Lori, feeling a little embarrassed. "How about I take a photo of you and your castles to send to your dad?"

The little girl posed for a photo then went back to building another castle while Lori sent the photo off to Grey. Soon she had built a ring of castles around Lori. When it was finished, the little girl jumped over them and joined her in the centre of the circle.

"Ok, miss, are you ready for some dinner?" asked Lori shortly after six o'clock.

"Can we get pizza?"

"Sure, if that's what you want," agreed Lori. "Pack up your things and we'll go and get pizza."

Together they walked slowly back across the sand and safely up onto the boardwalk. They put the sand toys in the back of the car, then headed across to the restaurant. It was the same place that Jake had worked in for all those long months and Lori felt a little guilty about going in. After a short wait for a table, a waiter showed them to a booth and handed them the menu.

"What kind of pizza do you prefer?" asked Lori.

"Pepperoni," replied Becky without hesitation. "Daddy used to bring me in here when Uncle Jake made the pizza."

"Good choice. Now how about some cheese fries to go with the pizza?"

"Yes, please!"

When the waiter returned with their drinks Lori placed the order. The waiter had given Becky a kids' pack and she was busily colouring in when Lori's phone chirped in her bag. As expected, it was a text from Grey to thank her for sending the photo.

"Pleasure. Don't tell Jake. We're having pizza at his favourite place for dinner. L x"

"He will never forgive you," came the reply quickly followed by "He's guesting with Molton tonight. He's stoked about it!"

"Wow! Go, Jake! L x"

Silver Lake played a blinding set to a capacity Seattle crowd. All the issues and dramas of the night before were long forgotten and each of them played as though their life depended on it. Despite the pain from his knee, Jake worked the stage and had the crowd eating out of the palm of his hand. When the band performed their acoustic interlude, the Seattle fans somehow knew all the lyrics. Hearing them sing swelled Jake's heart with pride. All too soon though Silver Lake were playing the closing section of Flyin' High and their set was over; their tour complete. They left the stage to a thunderous cheer from the crowd- their best reception to date. While the others went to shower and relax, Jake hung about at the side of the stage, pacing restlessly while he waited for his cue to join Tori for their duet. They had run through the song a couple of times at the sound check, but he still had butterflies the size of pterodactyls in his stomach. While he watched and waited, Maddy appeared at his side. She put a protective arm round his waist and whispered to him to relax. Eventually he heard Molton finish the number before he was due out on stage. From the wings, he saw Tori, in a skimpy leather dress and spike heels, step up to the mic and scream, "Seattle, we love you!"

The crowd went wild.

"I want to invite a very special guest out here now. Let me hear you scream for Mr Jake Power from Silver Lake! Jake, get your ass up here!"

Trying not to limp, Jake ran out onto the stage as the stadium erupted around him.

"Lover's Child, ladies and gentlemen," screamed Tori.

The performance was over in a blur. Jake remembered all the lyrics and with some encouragement from Tori, took the lead during the middle verse. As their duet came to an end, the female rock goddess commanded, "Let's hear it for the beautiful and talented Jake Power!"

His vocal battle with Tori was declared a resounding triumph, judging by the cheers from the crowd. Having taken an overly theatrical bow, Jake bounded off stage. His only regret about the whole experience was that Lori hadn't been there to share in his moment of glory. Maddy was the first person to greet him as he came backstage.

"Fantastic!" she squealed hugging him tightly. "You were awesome out there."

"Thanks," gasped Jake. "I need some water. My throat's killing me."

"I'm not surprised," commented Silver Lake's manager. "I hope you don't mind. I recorded that on my phone. I was going to mail it to Lori."

"Send it to me too," said Jake, accepting a bottle of water from one of the backstage personnel. "That was an incredible experience."

"I will," promised Maddy. "Now grab a quick shower before we go out to celebrate. The guys are waiting for you."

"We're not partying with Molton are we?"

"No. I've booked out a restaurant for a late private dinner," she assured him with a smile. "Now go and get cleaned up!"

As she sat on the porch, Lori listened to the cicadas singing in the trees over by the lake. She had lit a few citronella lanterns to keep the mosquitoes away and their flickering light was comforting. It had been a long day and she was worn out trying to keep Becky entertained. From the moment she had got out of bed that morning the little girl had been asking for her daddy. To keep her mind off the subject, Lori had taken her back down to the beach, had tried to teach her how to paint, watched two Disney movies and, finally, had lit the BBQ just so they could make smores. Now that the guys were due back at any moment, the little girl was curled up fast asleep on the couch hugging her doll. Lori had put the fleecy blanket over her and come outside to wait. She hadn't spoken to Jake all day, which worried her slightly, but he had sent a few text messages. The last one, a couple of hours ago said, "Landed. In baggage hall, Home soon. J x"

The two painkillers she had taken were starting to take effect and she bent and stretched her leg a few times to ease out her tired muscles. Almost as soon as she had sat on the sand earlier with Becky, she had known it was a bad idea, but the little girl had been so insistent that she play with her that she hadn't been able to resist. Now she was wishing that she had said "no" a little more firmly. Gently, she rocked back and forward on the old creaking chair. She was just beginning to doze off when headlights lit up the dark road and a car pulled into the driveway. As the back door opened, Lori was already down the front steps and almost at the car. A very weary Jake tumbled out and, with a huge relieved smile, wrapped his arms round her and held her tight. He buried his face in her hair, breathing in the very essence of her. Behind them, Grey and the driver were lifting out Jake's bags and piling them up in the driveway.

"Welcome home, rock star," said Lori, as she began to kiss Jake.

"Christ, I've missed you," he whispered hoarsely.

"Likewise," said Lori, smiling between kisses.

"Come on, guys," called out Grey. "Save that for when I've gone home!"

"Sorry, Grey," giggled Lori, moving to stand beside Jake, his arm securely around her waist. "Are you coming in for a while?"

"No," said Grey shaking his head. "I'll scoop Becky up and this guy's promised to drop us both home."

"She's asleep in the sunroom," explained Lori. "But her bags are sitting in the hallway. She's been packed and ready to go since first thing this morning. I think she missed you."

"You go get Becky," croaked Jake "And I'll get her things."

For the first time, Lori noticed that Jake had lost his voice. The extra huskiness made him sound even sexier than usual, but it sent a ripple of concern through her.

A few minutes later, the sedan reversed out of the driveway, leaving Jake and Lori alone in the dark. He pulled her into his arms again and kissed her gently but passionately, then just hugged her tight for a few moments.

"Let's get your stuff inside," suggested Lori softly. "Do you want a drink?"

"Just water," he whispered hoarsely, rubbing at his throat.

"Ok," she said, kissing his cheek. "I'll be in the kitchen when you're ready."

While Jake took his luggage down to the bedroom and put his guitars in the sunroom, Lori fetched his glass of water and a juice for herself. She raided the medicine shelf in the pantry looking for some throat lozenges, finally finding a packet with three left in it. Sitting them next to Jake's glass, she sat down at the table, waiting for him to come through. When he finally wandered in, he flopped down onto the wooden chair with a sigh of relief.

"It's good to be home," he said, with a smile.

"It's good to have you back. I've missed you," Lori admitted, reaching out to touch his hand. "How was it?"

"Wild. Amazing. Scary," he said huskily. "The duet with Tori was out of this world. Think that's what's killed my throat."

"Not so good. You'd better get it checked out."

"One step ahead of you," replied Jake. "Maddy's sorted out a doctor's appointment for tomorrow at noon. Throat and knee getting checked out. I'll be fine. I've just strained it a bit. The dry air on the plane didn't help either."

"I guess not," Lori agreed. "You look tired,"

"There's not been much sleep for the last few days. I hate

strange hotel beds," he admitted, popping one of the throat sweets into his mouth. "Tell me about your week."

"I'll tell you as we get ready for bed," suggested Lori, with a yawn. "It's hard work entertaining Becky here. I'm worn out."

As they lay wrapped in each other's arms, Lori told Jake all about her week, about Mary leaving, about her physical therapy session and finally about entertaining Becky for the weekend.

"I can't believe you took her for pizza," he grumbled, with a sleepy smile. "Traitor."

"It was great pizza. We loved it," defended Lori.

When she glanced over at him, Jake had fallen asleep. Gently, she snuggled in close to him and drifted off to sleep.

Next morning when she awoke, Jake was still sound asleep beside her. As quietly as she could, she showered and dressed, then wandered down to the kitchen to start breakfast. She had just poured her coffee when she heard a car in the driveway. By the time she reached the front door Maddy was standing on the top step.

"Good morning. Did you smell the coffee?" greeted Lori warmly.

"Hi, stranger," said her friend with a hug. "I brought Danish to go with that coffee."

"Come on through. I was just about to take mine outside," explained Lori. "Jake's still asleep."

"Lucky him," laughed Maddy. "Jason wakened me with a 4am business call. As I was up, I thought I'd come over for breakfast."

"Has Jason sent the artwork on to you?" asked Lori quietly, as they reached the kitchen. "Fetch plates for those will you, while I get you a coffee."

As she lifted two plates from the cupboard above the stove, Maddy answered, "That's what he called to discuss. He loves them. I've to share them with the band to get their views before we make a final decision. Your usual high standard, Mz Hyde."

"Thanks," said Lori, blushing slightly. "Come on out to the deck, then you can tell me what's been going on for the last few days."

Over two mugs of coffee each and a sinful Danish pastry, the band's manager filled her in on the details of the three concerts and all the interviews and the parties. She went to great lengths to reassure Lori that Jake had kept his partying to a minimum. Rich and Paul on the other hand had made up for him, especially Paul. As her friend spoke, Lori realised she softened her tone whenever she mentioned the drummer and that there were more tales of his antics than the others.

"Am I sensing a new man in your life?" Lori teased, as she tore off a small piece of her pastry.

"Pardon?" said Maddy, flushing as scarlet as her spike heeled shoes.

"Paul," stated Lori. "Is there something blossoming there?"

"Perhaps," laughed Maddy. "He's good fun. He likes to party. He's very like me in a lot of ways."

"Be gentle with him, Maddison," cautioned Lori warmly. "They are all very new to this circus that you thrive in."

"I know," laughed her friend. "But they are fast learners."

"Who's a fast learner?" asked a husky voice from behind them. "Good morning, ladies."

Lori turned round to see a freshly showered Jake standing in the doorway wearing only a pair of ripped faded denims. His half dry hair hung about his shoulders.

"How's the throat?" asked Maddy sharply.

"I'll live," he said quietly, coming out to take a seat at the table.

There were some pastries left and Lori offered him the bag. Taking one, he asked, "What brings you out here so early, Maddison?"

"Business and pleasure," she replied curtly. "Keep an eye on the time. You don't want to miss that appointment."

"Plenty of time," he said, as he bit into the custard filled pastry. "I don't need to leave for forty five minutes."

"In that case, I'll make a fresh pot of coffee," suggested Lori, starting to get to her feet.

"No. I'll make it," insisted Maddy. "You two catch up."

Before either of them could protest, the band's manager disappeared into the house.

"I missed this place," sighed Jake, stretching.

"You were gone less than a week!" exclaimed Lori. "How're you going to cope if you're gone for months on end?"

"That doesn't bear thinking about this morning."

"If you guys were half the success Maddy's been telling me about then you had better think about it," said Lori seriously. "Did you know she was soft on Paul?"

Jake smiled and nodded. "Seems the feeling is mutual. They party very well together."

"I can imagine," laughed Lori then changing the subject asked, "Do you want me to come out to the doctor's with you?"

"No, thanks. I'm going on my own. If you stay here, it's easier to fend off Maddy. She's not coming either, despite what she may think."

"Have you told her?"

"Told her what?" asked Maddy reappearing with a fresh pot of coffee.

"I was just saying to Lori that I'm going to the doc's on my own," stated Jake firmly. "I've a few errands to run on the way back."

Maddy started to complain, but Lori put out a hand to stop her, "Let him be. He's a big boy. He can go by himself."

"Mmmm," she muttered. "If you both insist."

"We insist," said Jake and Lori in unison.

"Ok, I'm not arguing with both of you," conceded Maddy grudgingly.

Much to his annoyance, Jake was late for his medical appointment. He got caught in traffic and arrived at the medical centre ten minutes after his allotted time. Fortunately, the receptionist was understanding and admitted the clinic was running behind schedule. She passed Jake a clipboard with some forms to be completed and instructed him to take a seat. Forms were not his forte and he had barely completed his personal details when he heard his name being called. As he handed the clipboard back to the receptionist, she advised him to take the third door to the left.

Knocking the door gently, Jake opened it and stepped warily into the doctor's office, clutching the sheaf of paperwork. A young female doctor sat behind the desk. She looked up when he entered.

"Mr Power?" she enquired, with a welcoming smile.

"Jake, please," he said hoarsely, laying the paperwork down

on the desk. "Mr Power makes me feel old."

"Jake, then," she replied. "I'm Lucy Novak. Pleased to meet you."

"Likewise."

"Now, what can I do for you today?" asked Dr Novak.

Briefly, Jake explained the problem with his throat and what he thought had triggered things, then he told her about the recent injury to his knee and the lingering pain and swelling.

"Let's start with your knee," suggested the doctor. "Would you mind slipping your jeans off and climbing up on the couch for me?"

As Jake wriggled out of his sneakers and his jeans, the doctor admitted she had read about the incident at Milford.

"Yeah, it was a pretty scary experience," Jake admitted, as he sat up on the narrow couch. "Not one I want to repeat."

"Must've been hard going out on stage the next time," she observed.

"That was the next scary experience," he joked, trying to make light of it. "It does make you think every time you step out there though."

"I'll bet," agreed the doctor. "Now let's see what you've done to this knee."

The doctor examined him thoroughly, putting the joint through its full range of movement. She got him to do some resistance exercises and stretches, then declared she was done.

"Well?" he asked, as he pulled his jeans back on.

"I'm sure it's just residual soft tissue damage. There's some swelling but, if you've been running about on stage and overusing it, that's what is likely to be causing it. Try to rest it as much as possible for the next few days. I'll give you some anti-inflammatory drugs for it. You should ice it too. Try to sit with it up if you can," replied Dr Novak. "Now let's take a look at your throat."

Again she examined him thoroughly, checking his glands and his ears as well as his throat. She asked him about his normal vocal range, his warm up routine and if he ever did a cool down routine after a show. Jake did his best to talk her through his usual pre and post show ritual and she nodded approvingly.

"At least you've tried to be sensible with it," she

complimented. "I suspect you've strained it. A bit of over use if you're not accustomed to doing three shows in quick succession. Rest your voice totally for forty eight hours, preferably seventy two, but I can appreciate that's not easy. No talking at all. Not even a whisper. Avoid alcohol, caffeine, smoking and all the usual irritants. Drinking hot water with honey stirred into it will help too."

Jake nodded reluctantly, accepting her advice with resignation.

"No singing at all for at least a week," she continued. "When's your next show?"

Jake shrugged to indicate he didn't know.

"I want to see you again next week to check you out before you sing another note. I'll also make enquiries about more suitable vocal warm ups. I've a friend who is an opera singer, so he should be able to recommend something."

Jake nodded and smiled.

Dr Novak smiled before adding, "And you might want to invest in a notebook and a pen."

Her attempt at humour was rewarded with a withering look.

"Don't look so worried, Jake. We'll get you back out there singing your heart out soon enough. You did the right thing coming straight in and not trying to force it."

He shrugged resignedly.

"Ok, so rest the knee. Rest the voice," she instructed, printing off the prescription for the drugs for his knee. "And I'll talk to you next Monday. Same time."

Jake nodded as he accepted the prescription and gave her a wave as he left the office. On his way back to the truck, he dropped into the centre's pharmacy to collect the prescribed drugs then made his way outside. The thought of not being able to speak at all for three whole days filled him with dread but, the fear of permanently damaging his voice terrified him. "Just as things were starting to come together," he thought miserably. Before he pulled out of the parking lot, he sent a text message to Lori and Maddy. "I've to rest knee. Got meds for it. No talking at all for 3 days. No singing for at least a week. Dr again next Mon. J x"

As he was about to pull out of the space Lori messaged back, "That will be tough for you. Will be worth it in the end. Love you.

L x"

"Love you too. J x"

During the drive back into town, Jake modified his plans. He had originally intended to drop into his apartment to check on it then head back out to the beach house. Now he decided to do things in reverse. He would go back and see Lori then hibernate at his apartment for the next three days. If there was no one there to talk to then that might make his vow of silence easier to handle. On the way back, he stopped at the food store and stocked up on enough supplies for three days plus a large jar of Manuka honey. It was mid-afternoon when he finally swung the truck into its usual spot under the tree in Lori's driveway. Slamming the door shut in frustration, he walked round the back of the house, expecting to find her out on the sun deck. The deck was deserted and the patio doors closed. He opened the back door and wandered through the kitchen, finally finding her at her drawing board, focussed completely on the drawing in front of her. At the sound of his feet on the wooden floor, she looked up.

"Hi," she said softly. "I wasn't sure if you were coming back over or not."

Reaching for a pen and a scrap of paper he wrote, "Came for a hug. Going back to my apartment. Will be easier I think. I'll be back for dinner on Thursday."

He passed her the note.

"Your writing is awful!" she laughed as she deciphered his scrawl. "I figured you might do that. Did the Dr say if you'd done any permanent damage?"

"She didn't seem to think so," he scribbled on the back of the first note.

"That's a relief," she sighed, as she got to her feet.

Silently, he put his arms round her and held her tight. The thought of being separated from her for another three days was nearly as painful as not being able to talk. Jake stroked her hair, feeling tears of anger and frustration pricking at his eyes. Gently, while he still had a slender hold over his emotions, he kissed her on the top of her head. Drinking in her perfume, he kissed her again, then reached for another bit of paper.

"Love you. Going now. Will text you later."

Nodding, she said with a sad smile, "I'll talk to you on

Thursday."

With a weak smile, he hugged her again, then turned and left. He didn't glance back as she hoped; he didn't want her to see his tears.

As soon as Jake opened the door to his apartment, a stale smell assaulted his senses. Before going back down to the truck for the rest of his bags and his guitars, he threw open all the windows and let the ocean air flow through the place. It took three trips up and down but, eventually, he had all his gear piled in the middle of the living room. Turning the key in the front door lock felt like a jail cell slamming shut on him.

Within a few short hours, Jake had straightened up the place, done all his laundry, checked over his guitars, restringing two of them, and drunk about two pints of warm water with honey added. The anti-inflammatory drugs had helped his knee, sparing him the incessant ache. The clock on his phone informed him it was just after nine. Late enough, he decided and headed off to bed. Before turning out the light, he sent messages to his fellow band members explaining that he was in hibernation for three days and not to call or come over. He prayed they would understand his need to be alone. He also sent a short message to Lori then switched the phone off. As he lay staring up at his plain white ceiling, sleep refused to come. The deafening silence of the apartment was terrifying. He tried to ignore the dark voice whispering in his mind, tried to ignore its taunt of "your dream is over." Jake could feel his own fears beginning to gnaw at him. Being centre stage in each of those three arenas had been the best experience of his life. Hearing the Seattle crowd singing his songs back to him had been incredible. Even the ill-fated duet with Tori was a memory that would live with him forever. If he couldn't sing like that again in front of a crowd, then he honestly didn't know how he would cope. The rational part of his brain scolded him for being overly melodramatic, but he was genuinely scared. Eventually sleep came, a sleep filled with haunted dreams of a devil slicing out his tongue and condemning him to a life without song.

Tuesday and Wednesday were the two longest days of his life; two of the darkest days of his life. Having made the conscious decision to shut out the world, his phone lay switched off, his laptop shut down on the coffee table and his entertainment centre remained unplugged. He passed the time silently reading a Stephen King tome he had picked up at the newsstand in the airport in Sacramento, shortly before boarding the flight to Seattle. Time was measured by his drug schedule and hot water laced with honey routine. Most of the food he had bought lay in the refrigerator untouched, his appetite having deserted him. Sleep, too, deserted him. By late on Wednesday afternoon, he could feel the walls closing in on him. His beloved acoustic guitar sat in its case in the corner of the living room gently calling out to him. As the sun set and the light in the room became an orange glow, a dark, haunting melody began to fill his head. Try as he might, Jake couldn't ignore it. After two hours, his creative side succumbed and he undid the catches on the guitar case then slowly lifted the instrument out. Still locked in his silent prison, Jake sat and worked on the piece until the small hours of Thursday morning. Satisfied at last with the piece of music, he decided to record it onto his laptop. Pressing the power button, Jake slowly felt his world returning to him. Once he had everything all set up, he recorded the new melody, then recorded the accompanying riff that had evolved as the evening wore on. Finally, he recorded the bridge. The song was still wordless but his confidence that these would come in time grew as he played the track back to himself. Now that the PC was powered up, Jake decided to open his emails. His inbox was crammed full of unread mails – most of which were advertising junk. Before this infuriated him further, he tweaked his junk mail filters, then returned to his inbox. There was one email from Maddy that caught his attention. The subject heading was "Silver Lake album and merchandising artwork." He opened the message, scanning the details about a band meeting scheduled for Friday to discuss the attachments. Jake opened the first of four attachments to reveal the three draft designs for the album cover, each significantly different. Instantly his eyes were drawn to the distinctive signature on the drawings. He opened the other three attachments and found a variety of other designs tagged as t-shirt proposals and miscellaneous. One proposed album design caught his eye - a dragon, with its wings spread out nestled inside an intricate Celtic knot. The twist of its tail reminded him of the Celtic trinity that was in the band's logo. When had Lori found time to complete this portfolio? Why hadn't she told him? Suddenly, he desperately wanted to talk to her, but it was four o'clock in the morning. Smiling for the first time since Monday, Jake reached for his phone and turned it on. A barrage of text alerts pinged through – he ignored them for now. Quickly he typed, "Love the designs. Love the Celtic dragon knot. Love you. J x". He hit send.

There were more than fifty messages on his phone and, as he read his way through them, Jake realised that more than thirty of them were from Lori, each sounding more concerned and worried than its predecessor. Like an oncoming freight train, it hit him that perhaps he hadn't been the only one struggling for the past three days. Guilt washed over him, drowning out the last of his self-pity. With a heavy heart he read over the other messages from Grey, Rich, Paul and Maddy. There were two from a number not in his contact directory; a number that looked vaguely familiar. He opened the first –"Hello, son. Give me a call." The second read "Son, I'm in Annapolis until Monday morning. Can we meet up? Dad."

It had been five years since he had last seen his father. They had never been close, never shared any common ground. His father had been in the air force, based out of Dover for most of Jake's childhood, and had retired more than ten years before. Since then he had spent his time sailing and delivering yachts, mainly in and around the Caribbean. The last time Jake had seen him had been at his mother's funeral. His parents had divorced shortly after his father retired, but they had remained close until cancer finally killed Jake's mother slowly and painfully. Her funeral was the last time he had seen any of his family, apart from his younger sister. He kept in irregular contact with her, but rarely heard from his two older brothers. Both of them had followed their father into the air force. Jake had always been made to feel that in that respect he was the family disappointment. He wondered why his father had reached out to him now. Why was he wanting to see him after all this time? What harm could it do to meet him for dinner or lunch?

"Hi," he began to type. "Can do Sunday. Let me know where and when. Will bring a friend. Jake." He sent the message before he had a change of heart.

Suddenly he felt tired- physically and emotionally. He switched off his laptop, set his phone to mute and headed off to bed. For the first time since before the short tour, he slept undisturbed for more than ten hours.

It was mid-afternoon before Jake finally awake. The sound sleep had done him the world of good. His knee felt good; his throat felt normal. His voice he was still scared to try. With a stretch, he dragged himself out of bed and into his tiny shower. Once out of the shower, he checked his phone for messages. There were two. One from his father, saying he would get back to him when he had booked a table. The other was from Lori. "Glad you like them. Love you too. See you later. L x"

"Will be over in an hour, J x," he replied.

Quickly he threw on his favourite ripped jeans, a red checked shirt, dragged a brush through his wet, tangled hair then stuffed his feet into his battered Converse. Having thrown a few spare clothes in his gym bag, Jake grabbed his laptop, his guitar and his keys. With a smile, he unlocked the door and stepped out into the narrow hallway, ready to face the world again.

On his way over to the beach house, he detoured out to the food store. As he drove, he cranked the volume up on the truck's stereo, filling the cab with the greatest hits of Guns n Roses. It took the last remaining shreds of his will power not to sing along in his usual fashion. Swinging the truck into the driveway a short while later, he turned the volume down to a more acceptable level. Without a thought to his knee, he jumped down from the cab and loped round the side of the house. As he had hoped, Lori was dosing in the late afternoon sun out on the deck. Carrying the huge bouquet of flowers he had bought at the store, Jake tiptoed across the deck. Trying to hide the bouquet behind his back, he bent down to kiss the sleeping artist.

"I'm sorry," he whispered gently. The first words he had dared to utter. "I've been a selfish jerk for the last few days."

"Jake!" she exclaimed, throwing her arms around his neck. "I love you, rock star."

"Love you back, li'l lady," he said, presenting her with the flowers, then added, "Peace offering."

"They're gorgeous. You didn't need to bring flowers."

Jake smiled. Her glowing smile was reassurance enough that he had been forgiven for being so self-centred.

"I'd better put them in some water," said Lori, getting up. "Want a juice?"

"Please. Anything but hot water and honey," he replied with a grin.

"So how's the throat feeling?" asked Lori, when she came back out with two glasses of apple juice.

"A bit tight but ok," replied Jake quietly. "I'm scared I strain it."

"That's understandable," she said, sitting beside him on the sun lounger. "I've spent the last few days fending off Maddy and the boys. They've been worried about your isolation stint."

"Sorry," he apologised sheepishly.

"Well, don't be surprised if they all decide to join us for dinner. I've stocked up on burgers just in case. Maddy and Paul were over last night for dinner. Rich was here for breakfast, then

Grey dropped by with Becky just after lunch," said Lori. "They all know you're going to be here for dinner."

"Should I send them a message?"

"Are you staying tonight?" asked Lori, hopefully.

"If you'll have me."

"Text them, then light the BBQ."

After a flurry of phone messages and a fair amount of muttering while trying to get the BBQ lit, Jake had everything under control. It was hot in the late afternoon sun and having stripped off his shirt and draped it over the back of a chair, he lay down on the sun lounger and closed his eyes. Lori had stepped back inside to change from her shorts into a long skirt. Small tendrils of smoke wafted across from the grill. In the background, Jake could hear the waves crashing in on the beach. Lying back on the lounger he drank in all the sounds and smells of the day. It struck him just how quickly life could turn around, as he reflected back to twenty fours earlier when he had felt so low. In his pocket, he felt his phone buzz. In the sunlight, he struggled to see the screen, but it was another message from his father.

"Table booked for lunch at 2 on Sunday at the restaurant at the marina. Hope this ok. Dad."

"See you then," he replied, still curious as to why his father wanted to meet up.

At that moment, Lori came back out onto the deck carrying some plastic cups and paper plates. As she set the things down on the table, she asked, "Have you figured out who's joining us?"

"All of them. They were all in the Turtle," replied Jake. "They're walking over now."

"Fine. Can you bring out the cooler? I've filled it with juices and beers and some ice. It's in the kitchen."

"Yes, boss," he teased, slipping his phone back into his pocket. "I'd maybe better have a honey drink before they get here. I don't need them ribbing me about it later."

"Go easy on yourself," cautioned Lori, her tone tender. "Not too much talking yet, just in case."

Less than an hour later, the burgers were sizzling on the grill, Maddy and Lori were bringing salads and relishes out from the kitchen, Becky was contentedly watching TV and the four band members were all catching up with each other, as they sprawled across the sun deck. Rich had taken charge of the BBQ, ordering Jake to stay clear of the smoke. Happy to relinquish the cooking duties, Jake had gone back to the sun lounger without a word of complaint. Once all the food was out, Lori came and sat beside him. He draped a protective arm around her shoulders, kissed the top of her head and whispered, "Love you, li'l lady."

"Love you too, rock star," she purred, resting her head against his bare chest.

Within a few minutes, Rich was dishing up burgers and they were all scrabbling round the table for rolls, salad and relish. No one was standing on ceremony and the relaxed atmosphere gave it the feel of a family meal.

"You could almost have had that meeting here, Maddy," declared Rich, between mouthfuls. "Save us all getting to the hotel for the crack of dawn."

"Today's for fun not business," she retorted sharply. "Besides Jason's dialling in from London for the meeting hence the early start. Be thankful it's not earlier."

"Jake," called out Paul, dripping ketchup down his shirt from his burger, "Did you write any new material while you were in exile?"

"I'm working on something," he confessed. "No lyrics for it yet."

"Very funny," groaned Grey. "When did the witch doctor say you could sing again?"

"Not till after I've seen her on Monday. Maybe longer than that," answered Jake. "I'm not prepared to take any chances. I don't fancy taking another vow of silence either."

"Tough three days?" Paul enquired, raising an eyebrow.

Jake nodded.

"I emailed a friend from college," began Rich, helping himself to a beer from the cool box. "He's in musical theatre. His suggestion was to change your warm up routine. He said he'd mail me some info for you."

"Thanks. Doc was doing the same. She mentioned an opera type technique."

Laughing uncontrollably, Maddy gasped, "I can just see it now if I have to tell Jason that Silver Lake are doing La fucking Traviata!"

Shortly before eight, Maddy and Paul rose to leave, declaring that they were going back into town for a couple of hours. The others declined to join them, but Rich said he would walk Grey and Becky back along the beach. Within a few short minutes, Jake and Lori found themselves alone out on the deck, in the fading light of the day. Lori had lit the citronella lanterns to keep the bugs away and, as it grew darker, she lit another couple of outdoor candles. While she was on her feet, she began to tidy away the discarded plastic cups but was interrupted by Jake. "Leave those a minute. I need to talk to you."

"You've no idea how good that sounds," she giggled, then noticing his serious expression said, "There's nothing wrong is there?"

"No," he assured her, as she came to sit beside him. "I need you to do something for me."

"Anything," she replied. "Within reason."

"Will you come with me to Annapolis on Sunday?"

"Sure, but why? It's a two hour drive there."

Gazing down at his feet, Jake said simply, "My dad's invited us to lunch."

"Your dad?" echoed Lori, sounding surprised. He had never talked about his family other than to say his mother had passed away a few years before.

He nodded, then added, "He contacted me the other day out of the blue. Wants to meet up this weekend. I haven't seen him in five years."

"Of course I'll come, but are you sure you want me to?"

"I don't want to go on my own," he confessed quietly.

"You've never really spoken about your family," commented Lori softly. "Tell me to but out, but, did you have a fight with him? Five years is a long time."

"No fight," sighed Jake sadly. "We just never saw eye to eye about life. With Mom gone there was no need to see him or my brothers. I keep in touch with my young sister kind of. We exchange emails every few weeks."

"So where are your brothers and sister?"

"Lucy lives just outside of Philly. She's a grade school teacher. Married to a lawyer. They have two boys," he explained awkwardly. "I've two older brothers. They both followed my dad into the air force. I'm not sure where they are based."

"And you've no idea what your dad wants after all this time?"

"No idea," admitted Jake. "But we'll find out over lunch on Sunday. He's expecting us at two."

From his tone of voice and his body language, Lori knew it was hard for him to talk about his past and his family. She didn't want to pry or push him for more answers. Instead, she reached out to hug him and said, "Well, we'll find out together."

"Thanks, li'l lady," he said with a relieved sigh.

As they sat listening to the sounds of the ocean, their casual conversation inevitably turned back to the band and Jake finally asked her about the design portfolio she had prepared.

"No freebies this time," she joked lightly. "Jason has paid me well for my blood, sweat and tears."

"But when did you find time to work on it all?"

"A lot of late nights after you'd leave and a lot of early mornings," she confessed. "I got a rough copy of four of the tracks you recorded in New York and worked the themes from the lyrics. When I heard Dragon Song was going to be your first venture into the singles market, I came up with the Celtic dragon design incorporating the knot. The smaller pieces are all extracts from the three main cover proposals."

"You were working on two other commissions though, were you not?"

Lori nodded, "I finished them off last week. They were smaller scale projects. One's actually the new stage backdrop for Molton."

"Do we get one of those?" Jake asked hopefully.

With an impish grin, Lori replied, "If you commission one."

"*Touché*, li'l lady," he laughed. "I'll speak to Maddison about it at tomorrow's meeting."

"Come on, rock star," she suggested, getting up from the lounger. "You've an early start tomorrow. Time for bed."

With the candles all blown out, they headed indoors, hand in hand.

As they lay side by side, Jake rolled over to face her, propping himself up on one elbow.

"I'm not sleepy," he whispered.

"Neither am I," she replied softly, reaching out to trace the outline of his dragon tattoo. "You could always make mad passionate love to me."

"Well the witch doctor didn't list that as one of my banned activities," he teased, reaching across to run his finger over the swell of her breast through her nightshirt.

Allowing herself to relax under his gentle touch, Lori let Jake slide the nightshirt over her head. He reached down to remove her underwear, then raised one eyebrow, "No panties, li'l lady?"

Lori giggled, then reached out to remove his boxer shorts, "No shorts, rock star?"

With a playful push, Jake shoved her over onto her back then pinned both her hands down with one of his. He kissed her hard on the mouth, then traced gentle kisses down her throat, down between her breasts, then down to the soft folds of her femininity. Teasingly, he licked small patterns along her hip bones, causing her to moan pleasurably. His long, loose hair tickled her stomach.

"Jake, please," she pleaded, her voice husky with need.

"Patience, li'l lady," he breathed, as he released her hands, then continued to deliver soft feathery kisses down the velvety smooth insides of her thighs, down her calves, along the arches of her small slender feet before gently nibbling each of her toes in turn. Ignoring the painful protest of his right knee, Jake knelt across her, slipped on a condom, before cupping her buttocks in his hands then entered her in one swift hard thrust. Their lovemaking was short and intense. The instant she felt him hard inside her, Lori felt the first waves of her orgasm wash over her. Forcefully, Jake thrust deep inside her, bringing them to a mutual climax, sending waves of ecstasy flooding through them both. Still entwined, they lay together for a few moments, both breathing heavily.

"I'm glad the witch doctor didn't forbid that," sighed Lori. Her sigh of contentment reminded him of a cat's purr.

"Likewise," agreed Jake, as he slid away from her and rolled onto his back.

Sleep evaded him and, as he lay awake in the small hours, Jake watched the sleeping beauty by his side. Her hair was spread all over the pillow and she had curled up in an almost foetal position. The soft cotton sheet was barely covering her. Carefully, he pulled it up and covered her bare shoulder. She stirred slightly in her sleep, nestling deeper into her soft feather pillow. In the first light of dawn, Jake knew that she was the person he wanted to spend the rest of his life with. This beautiful creature, who had literally fallen at his feet, was truly his soul mate.

Silver Lake's management meeting had started by the time Jake entered the conference room at Maddy's hotel. He saw that a video link had been set up and that Jason's face was filling the large screen at the end of the room. Helping himself to a juice, Jake apologised for being a few minutes late.

"Twenty bucks in the pot," said Grey bluntly.

With a resigned smile, Jake nodded, then took his seat at the table.

"Ah, the late Mr Power," joked Jason from the screen. "How's the voice? And the knee?"

"Hi, Jason. The knee's ok. I can't test the voice until I've seen the doctor on Monday."

"Keep me posted on that, Maddy," instructed the Englishman. "Now, back to the business of the artwork. Have you all discussed your preferences?"

This question prompted a thirty minute debate on the various designs before they all reached an agreement on the Celtic dragon knot design. In the midst of the debate, Jake enquired if they could add a stage backdrop to reflect the album artwork and, after a brief discussion, it was agreed that there was budget to fund this. Maddy was instructed to take an action point to email Lori confirming what designs had been selected and to request a further design for the backdrop. Deciding to push his luck, Paul asked if he could have a couple of drumheads designed to match the album art and that too was swiftly agreed and added to the list.

"Good. Progress. I like it," stated Jason firmly. "Now that that has all been agreed, let's talk about your schedules until the end of the year."

The four band members exchanged glances.

"Maddy, correct me if I'm wrong. Dragon Song is out on 1st September followed by the album three weeks later. Provisionally. Both need promoting. I've emailed a list of radio station promo events. I've tried to keep them local – well within two hundred miles of Delaware and to evening and weekend slots for those further afield. I appreciate you all have day jobs to consider for now. That is a situation you will need to give some thought to around December time."

"Why?" asked Rich. "Are you confident that we can afford to resign by then?"

"Mildly optimistic, Rich," commented Jason with a smile, "But I recognise your concerns. Would you each be able to get a leave of absence for, say, three, maybe four weeks late November into mid-December?"

"We can ask," replied Grey. "What do you have lined up for us?"

"A support tour of the UK with Weigh Station."

Four stunned faces stared at Jason's image on the screen.

"How many shows?" Jake asked, ironically being the first member of the band capable of speech.

"Six so far, but it may extend to eight or even ten depending on ticket sales. I'm hoping we can add an extra night in London and perhaps Birmingham too. If the schedule works, we may take in Dublin in Ireland. That would take it to ten shows. I'll email through the proposals and you can check with your employers and legal people. I need an answer by the end of next week," Jason explained. In the background they could hear his phone ringing. "I need to take this. Talk soon."

The screen went blank.

"Is he serious?" asked Rich, in stunned disbelief. "Support act for Weigh Station on their home tour?"

Maddy nodded, "As far as I can fathom out, they liked what they overheard when they were in New York at the same time as you. Their team contacted us. There's still a lot to work out. All the legal side, but there is a deal there waiting to be done. The tour is on sale already with no named support act. Ticket sales are looking good. The venues are smaller than the big stadiums you played with Molton but I've been to most of them."

"More fucking planes," muttered Paul, staring nervously at the band's manager. "You know I hate flying."

"Paul, it's not much further to London than it was to Seattle," said Rich bluntly.

"We've a few days to chew this over," said Jake quietly. "I'm not committing to anything until I've seen the doctor on Monday."

"Sounds fair," nodded Grey. "I need to think about Becky too. I'll need to have a talk with my mom."

"Right, here's the plan," stated Maddy, her tone leaving no room for further debate. "I need to go back to New York until Tuesday. Let's meet here on Wednesday, same time as today, and we can make a decision then."

Silently, the four musicians nodded their agreement, all scarcely daring to believe the deal on the table.

Sunday dawned grey and misty over the Delaware shore. Temperatures were soaring, setting records for the month of August, and, as Lori made breakfast, the TV weather forecasted over a hundred degrees for the next two days. She was glad they had agreed to take her car to Annapolis since its air conditioning was better than that in Jake's beloved truck. Sitting at the table with her coffee, Lori wondered what the day was going to bring. Since Jake had come back from the band meeting on Friday, he had been quiet. She knew he was still trying to rest his voice as much as possible, but she could tell he was pre-occupied, partly with the Weigh Station tour options but more so with Sunday lunch. They had agreed to leave at eleven to give themselves plenty of time to get to Annapolis. The route map online had indicated it should take them two hours and ten minutes, but neither of them wanted to get lunch off on the wrong foot by being late. She was just finishing her breakfast when Jake wandered in.

"Morning, li'l lady," he said with a smile. "Are you ready for this?"

"As I'll ever be," she joked. "Did you tell your dad who you were bringing?"

"I just said a friend. He's probably decided I'm gay and assumed it's a guy I'm bringing," muttered Jake sourly, as he poured himself a coffee.

"Jake," cautioned Lori softly. "Don't assume. Go to lunch with an open mind."

"I'm trying," he replied. "I just don't know what to expect. Five years is a long time."

"Plenty of time for you both to have mellowed," she observed. "Now I'm going to get dressed. Try to relax."

"Wear something pretty."

"Don't I always?"

Lori was putting the finishing touches to her makeup when Jake came through to get ready. She had decided to wear the same sea green maxi dress that she had worn for her birthday dinner.

"You look stunning," complimented Jake with a smile.

"Thank you," she replied, as she began to brush her hair.

"Don't tie it up, Lori," he said softly. "Leave it down."

"Your wish is my command, rock star."

She sat and watched Jake dress in a pair of smart black chinos and a black shirt.

"It's a heatwave out there and you're going dressed as Johnny Cash?" she questioned.

Jake nodded, then proceeded to tie his own sun bleached hair back into a ponytail securing it with a leather cord.

"Will I do?" he asked, as he pulled on his black leather boots.

"You look great. Every inch the rock star," she teased, with an approving smile.

"Let's get this show on the road."

After an easy drive across the state and into Maryland, they arrived in Annapolis just after one o'clock. Despite the assistance from the car's sat nav system, it took them another half an hour to locate the correct marina. During the drive, Jake had been quieter than usual and fidgety. He had channel hopped up and down the radio stations before settling on a local rock station. Both of them had been surprised when the DJ announced that his special studio guests on next Sunday's show would be Silver Lake. With a mutter, Jake declared that he had maybe better study the schedule for the promotional events that Maddy had emailed out. The DJ then played one of the tracks from their original CD and, as the song came to an end, they pulled into a parking space at the marina.

"I hope I still sound like that when I'm cleared to sing again," he commented as he climbed out of the car.

Stiff after sitting in the car for so long, Lori struggled a little getting out from the passenger side. Noticing, Jake rushed round to give her a hand.

"You ok, li'l lady?" he asked, as she steadied herself on her feet,

"Just stiff. I'm fine," she reassured him, then noticing a tall silver haired man striding towards them, asked, "Is that your dad coming?"

Jake nodded, then, forcing a smile, waved.

"You made it then!" called Jake's father, as he approached

them. "Nice car, son."

"Hi, Dad," said Jake warmly, wrapping a protective arm around Lori's waist.

"Good to see you, son," replied the older man, before asking. "Are you going to introduce me to this beautiful young lady?"

"Dad, this is Lori Hyde, owner of said car," began Jake nervously. "Lori, this is Colonel Ben Power."

Lori reached out to shake the colonel's hand, "Pleasure to meet you, sir."

"The pleasure's all mine, Miss Hyde," he said, kissing the back of her hand flamboyantly.

Now that she was up close to the older man, she could see a strong resemblance between him and Jake. They had the same twinkling hazel eyes and, apparently, similar wit and charm.

"Let's head over to the restaurant and in out of this heat," suggested the colonel.

As they started to walk across the gravel car park, Lori was careful not to trip. She was aware her limp was more pronounced than usual and, until her leg muscles eased after sitting in the car, she felt as though she was leaning heavily on her cane.

"So, Miss Hyde," began the colonel. "How did you meet my wayward son?"

"We met on the beach," replied Lori. "I had taken a tumble and Jake very kindly helped me home."

"A gallant start to the relationship," he declared, causing Jake to groan in embarrassment. "I noticed your cane. I take it you are still recovering from that tumble?"

"Not exactly," replied Lori, with a glance at Jake for reassurance. "I was involved in an accident last Christmas. It's that I'm recovering from."

"Ah, I see," said Ben, having the good manners not to pry any further. Instead, he turned to Jake. "I heard that you got wounded in action recently, son."

"How did you hear about that?" quizzed Jake, genuinely surprised.

"One of the crew from the yacht was at the show," explained his father, as they reached the restaurant door.

Politely he held the door open for his son and Lori, who both thanked him, as they entered the cool restaurant. A young waitress swept straight over, "Colonel Power, lovely to see you. We have your usual table ready."

"Thanks, Mandy," he said, flashing her a dazzling and very Jake-like smile.

Once they were seated at a window table, over-looking the marina, and had placed their drinks order, Ben commented, "First Power male to get wounded in the line of duty."

Lori giggled before adding, "And hopefully the last!"

"Have you fully recovered, Jacob?" asked his father, the paternal concern evident in his voice.

"Don't call me that," muttered Jake, scowling at his father then, taking a deep breath, added, "I'm fine. It was only a flesh wound. Chipped the bone a little. Not a big deal."

"Sorry, son," apologised his father awkwardly. "As I hear it, you kept on playing?"

Jake nodded, "Yes, sir. For a few more songs at least."

"Maybe you've more guts than I've given you credit for," he observed calmly.

Turning to Lori, Jake said, "Dad's never got over the fact that I didn't want to join the air force."

"That's a bit harsh, Jake," she said softly.

"No, he's right," interrupted his father. "To an extent anyway. So how is the music business?"

"It's a tough gig," answered Jake. "But we've had a turn of luck, thanks to Lori."

"Are you in the music business too, Miss Hyde?" asked Ben curiously.

"Not exactly. I'm an artist. I do the artwork for album covers, merchandising. That sort of thing," she replied.

"Must pay better than making the music judging by your car parked outside."

"Art's not my only line of work," continued Lori calmly, her tone almost business-like. "I own Hyde Properties of Manhattan."

"Property?"

"Yes. I have a portfolio of apartment blocks and office space," she replied, as though that were the most natural thing in the world. Out of the corner of her eye, she could see Jake begin to smirk. Nothing impressed his father more than money.

"So art's more of a hobby?"

"No, the property side is the hobby, Colonel Power. I take my artwork very seriously."

Before the conversation reached dangerous territory, the waitress returned with their drinks and asked if they were ready to order.

"Yes, thanks, Mandy. I'll have my usual," said Ben, flashing her another flirtatious smile.

"I'll have the flounder, please," said Lori, closing the menu.

"Crab cakes for me," said Jake, as he passed his menu back to the waitress.

"Will I bring a salad bowl to start?"

"Please, Mandy."

Taking a sip from his glass of juice, Jake decided to cut to the chase, "Dad, why did you invite us here? It's been over five years. Why now?"

"Well, to be honest, I got a scare when I heard you'd been shot," admitted the older man. "If anything were to happen to your brothers, the air force would tell me. If it was Lucy, her husband would call. I realised if it was you, no one would know to call. I guess, I want to build some bridges."

"Dad, it's been a long time," began Jake. "I'm almost thirty five years old, and you want to establish a father/son thing now?"

"I'm prepared to try if you are."

"And you won't try to judge me?"

"Jake, you're a grown man. I'm just asking for a second chance to get to know you."

Looking his father straight in the eye and not daring to glance at Lori, Jake nodded slowly, "Ok, I'm prepared to give this a go if you are but I'm not Peter or Simon. Don't expect me to be like them."

"Jacob, you've never been like them."

This time, Jake let the use of his full name slip.

To ease the tension, Lori raised her glass, "A toast to new beginnings then."

"A fresh start," agreed Ben, grateful that she had intervened.

"New beginnings," added Jake forcing a smile. He took a sip from his glass, then asked, "So, where are my older brothers these days?"

"Both still in the air force. Pete's out at Fairfield air base.

Simon just transferred to Langley last year. Both doing well."

"Are they still married?"

"Pete's divorced from Beth. They have two girls. I guess the girls must be about four and eight by now. Simon's just divorced wife number three. No children that I'm aware of."

"Simon always did like the girls," commented Jake, with a grin.

"You missed Lucy," continued Ben. "She was here yesterday with the boys. She said to say "Hi." I asked her to stay until today, but she had to rush home. Always rushing somewhere that girl."

Turning to Lori, Ben asked, "Do you have any family here?"

"No, sir. My parents both passed away a few years ago. I was an only child. I've a few cousins scattered around but I'm not good at keeping in touch."

Over lunch, with the ice melting between the two Power men, they chatted about Ben's sailing adventures, Jake's three recent concerts with Silver Lake and the plans for the band for the future. Much to Jake's surprise, his father said, if they were ever playing near where he happened to be, he would like to hear them. As the waitress brought their coffees, Lori asked, "Where do you sail to next?"

"We leave here tomorrow night, then we are heading up the coast to Long Island. There's a series of races up there that we do every year. After that, we'll bring the boat back here," replied the colonel, as he added sugar to his coffee.

"When you come back, perhaps you could visit us over in Rehoboth," suggested Lori, not daring to look at Jake.

"Perhaps," he replied non-committedly. "I'm hoping to pick up a delivery trip or two toward the end of the season."

"Consider it an open invitation," said Jake, smiling at Lori. "Bridges to build and all that."

"True," agreed his father. He paused for a moment, then added, "To be honest, son, I expected you to tell me where to get off earlier."

"I was tempted," admitted Jake, his eyes twinkling mischievously. "But Lori would never forgive me if I didn't give you a second chance."

"Then, Lori," declared Ben, somewhat theatrically, "I owe you a debt of gratitude."

With the check paid, Ben asked if they felt like a walk through the marina to see the yacht. Both of them were more than happy to go for a stroll before sitting in the car for another two hours for the drive home. Stepping out of the air-conditioned restaurant into the heat of the day was like standing in front of a hot oven with its door open. As they strolled down towards the pontoons, Jake rolled his sleeves up and unbuttoned his shirt. Once down on the floating pontoons, he put a steadying arm around Lori's waist and whispered, "Don't want you falling in, li'l lady."

They passed several other people as they made their way through the maze of yachts and motor cruisers, all of whom called out to Ben or waved. Eventually, they reached the end of the main pontoon and the colonel guided them down a narrower one towards a huge white yacht.

"She's not all mine," he admitted, with a hint of pride in his voice. "But I own a half share of her. Do you have time to come aboard for a drink?"

"Sure, Dad," said Jake, before turning to Lori. "Don't panic. I'll lift you up on deck."

"Thanks. I was wondering how I was going to climb up there," she replied, with obvious relief.

"Don't fret, princess," added Ben, flashing her a classic Power smile. "We'll see you safely aboard."

With a well-practiced manoeuvre, the colonel climbed on board and opened up a section of the guard rail. As he reached down to take Lori's hands, Jake lifted her up. Both of them held onto her until she had regained her balance, then Jake passed her cane up to her. Taking care not to jar his knee, he too climbed up, gratefully accepting a helping hand from his father.

"Shoes off, folks," declared Ben firmly. "Only deck shoes or bare feet allowed."

Having slipped their shoes off and set them to one side, Ben led them towards the cockpit and invited them to take a seat. At the sound of voices on deck, a young man came up from below.

"Hi, skipper," he greeted Ben. "I wasn't expecting you back yet."

"I brought my son to survey the premises," he explained. "Steve, this is Jake and his friend Lori. Jake, this is the guy I was telling you about who watched you get shot."

"Pleased to meet you both," mumbled Steve, suddenly somewhat star struck. "That was some gig."

"Memorable to say the least," joked Jake. "Scarred me for life."

"Join us for a drink, Steve," offered Ben warmly. "What can I get everyone?"

While his father went below deck to fetch the drinks, Jake slipped off his shirt.

"I told you black was a bad idea," giggled Lori, as he sat down beside her.

"Ok, you were right," he conceded, laying the folded shirt beside him.

Reappearing with a small cooler full of soft drinks and beers, Ben stared at his son's tattooed torso. Passing a can of soda and a plastic cup to him, he said, "That's some art gallery. You only had the sword and that dragon the last time I looked."

"And you never approved of them," stated Jake.

"They're awesome!" gushed Steve. "Must've hurt like Hell."

"Some did," admitted Jake, with a grin. "Mainly the ones over my rib cage."

"Is that the music to Stronger Within on your arm?"

"Well spotted," he laughed. "Do you play in a band or anything?"

Steve shook his head, "I play a bit of guitar but I'm not that good yet."

"Well, if you're ever in Rehoboth look us up and we'll give you a few lessons. Rich and I both teach music," Jake offered.

"You teach?" echoed Ben, sounding surprised.

"Yes," replied Jake. "Remember, I graduated college and got my teaching diploma. I teach music at a local high school. I've also taught guitar from home too over the years."

"I never knew."

"You never asked."

"*Touché*, son," he conceded, sitting down on the opposite side of the spacious cockpit.

Somewhat nervously, Steve turned to Lori and asked, "You're Mz Hyde, aren't you?"

"Most days," she replied warmly.

"And Stronger Within was written for you?"

"Yes, it was," answered Jake. "As was Lady Butterfly."

"Can I get your autographs, or photos or something?" blurted out the younger man, causing them all to laugh.

"Relax, Steve," said Ben, clapping the boy on the back. "This is just my son and his girlfriend."

"It's alright," interrupted Lori. "Jake needs to get used to this fan bit."

"She's right," agreed Jake, looking embarrassed. "I'm useless at it."

Shaking his head, Ben watched the young man scamper back below deck in search of his phone and something to be autographed. "If I'd known this was the effect you two would have on my crew I'd have thought twice about bringing you on board."

They were all still laughing when Steve returned with his phone, a piece of paper, a copy of Silver Lake's CD and a couple of pens. Ben played photographer, taking several shots of his young crew member with Jake, with Lori and with both of them. In between shots, Lori picked up the piece of paper and expertly doodled a quick basic Celtic knot design with dragon eyes and tail. She signed it with her usual Mz Hyde flourish, then passed it to Jake to autograph. He scribbled a message to Steve then signed his name below Lori's. Carefully, he opened the CD box and slipped out the slim booklet and signed his name across one corner of the front cover, before adding another personalised message to the back.

"Thanks!" exclaimed Steve, admiring his Mz Hyde original. "I'm going to frame that."

"You wouldn't be the first," laughed Jake. "Rich has one of Lori's doodles on a Hooters napkin framed and hanging proudly in his bathroom."

"Is that where he put it?" giggled Lori, remembering the look on the guitarist's face when her identity had been revealed.

"I'm feeling left out here," joked Ben, joining in with the banter. "Will you draw something for me?"

Steve ran to fetch another piece of paper and Lori quickly sketched a basic yacht, decorating the hull with music notes, then signed it and passed it to the colonel. Smiling, he handed it over to Jake, "You too, son."

A short while later, they both apologised that they would need to make a move. They said goodbye to Steve then Ben walked them back through the marina to the car. Making the first awkward move, Jake hugged his father, "Don't be a stranger."

"I'll do my best, son," he promised. "And thank you for today. Who knows, maybe one day the four of you will all get together with me."

"Who knows, Dad," replied Jake. "I'll call Lucy but I'm not sure about the others. There's a lot of unfinished business there."

"Speaking to your sister is a start."

Turning to Lori, the colonel gave her a huge hug, "It's been a pleasure, Lori. I'm glad he's finally found someone," then added, "And I'm glad you're not a guy."

"I told you!" laughed Jake loudly. His father looked at him quizzically. "I said to Lori that you'd have assumed I was bringing a guy along."

Ben blushed and hung his head in embarrassment, "Well, with that long hair and those tight jeans, who can blame a man?"

Dr Novak's waiting room was empty when Jake walked in and the doctor herself was standing chatting to the receptionist. At the sound of the door squeaking open, they both turned round.

"Hi," said Jake, suddenly feeling very self-conscious. "Am I early or something?"

"Not at all, Jake," assured the doctor warmly. "I had a couple of cancellations earlier in the morning and got right up to date. You're bang on time."

"Makes a change," he said, trying hard not to laugh.

"You're sounding much better," observed the doctor. "Come on through and we'll see how you're doing."

He followed her along the corridor and into her neat and tidy office. Closing the door behind them, the doctor commented, "No hint of a limp today either."

"I've been a good boy all week," he joked, taking a seat at the side of her desk.

"Glad to hear it," she said, as she sat down. "Now, how did the week go?"

Quickly, he filled her in on his three days in silent, solitary confinement, then detailed exactly what he had done since Thursday. She nodded approvingly when she learned he had managed a full seventy two hours of complete vocal rest.

"I'll start with your knee," she said when he was done. "Up on the couch. Can you please slip your jeans off?"

Having taken his boots and his tight jeans off, Jake sat up on the couch and let her manipulate his knee. It was still tender to the touch along the scar line, but the swelling from the previous week was long gone.

"I'm happy with that," said the doctor then added, "I meant to say last week, nice ink on your calves."

"Thanks," said Jake, blushing slightly. "Just part of the personal art gallery."

"You've more?" she asked then said, "I see there's one on your forearm too."

"Just a few," confessed Jake, getting down from the couch. "Let me get my pants back on and I'll show you, if you like?"

"I'm curious now," giggled the doctor. "Is this going to make my tiny circle of stars look pathetic?"

Having fastened his belt, Jake unbuttoned his shirt and slipped it off. The doctor stared in amazed admiration at the five large tattoos.

"That sword on your back is fabulous," she complimented.

"Thank you," said Jake, putting his shirt back on.

"Any plans for any more?"

"Never say never," he replied. "The music notes were the last one a couple of months ago. If the right design comes up, I'd think about it."

"Once your fans see those, I'm sure there will be plenty copies done."

"No doubt," he conceded with a resigned smile

"Back to business," stated the doctor softly. "Let's take a look at your throat."

As before, she looked down his throat, in his ears and palpitated the glands at his neck. When she was done, she asked if he had tried to sing. Jake shook his head.

"I want you to run through a few of your normal warm up exercises for me."

Taking a deep breath, Jake began with a few gentle scales, gradually moving up the octaves of his range. He then repeated the exercise in reverse, going smoothly down the octave. It sounded normal.

"Sounds alright to me so far," said Dr Novak. "But I'm not fully aware of your range prior to last week. How does it feel to you?"

"I don't want to push the top notes just yet," commented Jake calmly. "Otherwise, it felt ok. A bit huskier than usual, maybe. Throat's still a bit tight from not being used."

"Run through them again, then try actually singing as you would on stage," instructed the doctor. "But don't force it."

Jake did as he was asked then couldn't decide what to sing. He felt foolish standing in the doctor's office singing, but Dr Novak insisted.

"I wish I had my guitar," he muttered.

"What about the song you've got tattooed on your arm?" suggested the doctor, in an effort to help matters.

Jake nodded and, closing his eyes, he began to sing the first verse and chorus of Stronger Within. As he sang, he could feel the tension melt from his shoulders. His voice was still there. After the chorus, the doctor stopped him "I'm guessing you don't always sing so melodically. Try something harder. More challenging. Just a verse or a chorus."

Nodding, Jake took a deep breath and launched into Flyin' High. Again the doctor stopped him after a verse and a chorus. "That's some contrast in style!"

"The fans like the occasional softer track," he said quietly.

"And how does the throat feel?"

"Out of practice, I guess," he replied. "It's not sore and the tightness has eased now I've warmed up a bit."

"Good," replied Dr Novak. "I spoke to my friend and he's given me a few web links to vocal tuition sites he uses. He suggested you use those to learn the basics of the technique. He also said it was fine for me to pass on his phone number and email address. If you want to talk to him and run through a few exercises, he's more than happy to help."

"Thank you," said Jake, accepting the sheet of information from her. "I have been doing a bit of research myself. I think I've found the stuff he's talking about, but it would be good to talk to him about it."

"Well, he's in New York until the end of the month. Call him," suggested the doctor. "His name's Tony."

"I will. So am I good to go back into rehearsals and performing?"

"Take it slowly. Build things back up gradually. If you can, don't use either extreme of your range for another couple of weeks. When's your next performance?"

"We've got a series of radio station promo events over the next month. If all goes to plan, we go out on tour in November," he explained.

"Give me a call in a couple of weeks to update me. Any problems before then just drop in. I'll see you without an appointment if need be."

"Appreciate it. Thanks, doc," said Jake warmly. "Am I ok to start running again on that knee?"

"Gently at first. Any sign of swelling and I want you to stop and rest it for a further week."

"Deal."

"Then you're good to go, Mr Power," she said.

As soon as he was back outside, Jake called Lori and Maddy to let them know he was back in business. He then sent a message to the band, suggesting they meet up later for a rehearsal. A few text messages later plus another call to Lori, it was arranged that Silver Lake would meet up at the beach house at seven. With the truck's stereo blasting out Weigh Station's latest offering, Jake headed back into Rehoboth. He stopped off at his apartment to pick up two electric guitars, his practice amp and a spare mic then drove back out to the beach house. Lori was at her drawing board when he came in the back door, clattering his guitar cases off the door frame. Hearing him cursing under his breath, she shouted hello.

"Back in a minute," he called, as he disappeared back out to fetch the rest of his gear from the truck.

A few moments later, he came through to the study, came up behind her and kissed her on the nape of the neck.

"Mmmm, what was that for?" she purred.

"Just because," he replied, softly kissing her again. "And to say thanks for letting the band come over here again tonight."

"Not a problem. Becky and I will watch a movie while you boys rehearse," she replied. "Now, I hate to say this, but I'm working. Go play with your toys in the basement."

"Is that our backdrop?" asked Jake, peeking over her shoulder at the partially finished design on the board.

"If you give me peace to work on it for a while, it might be," she replied, sharply. "Maddy wants it for your meeting on Wednesday."

"No pressure then?" he laughed. "I'll leave you to it."

"Thanks," she said, turning her focus back to the design in front of her.

Half an hour later she could hear Jake starting his warm up exercises. Despite the lack of tune to them, it was nice to hear his voice again. With a smile, she re-focussed on the task at hand. The design was gradually taking shape. What she hadn't told Jake was that Maddy had ordered two designs for Wednesday. It was an unreasonable timeframe, but, if she could at least have them drafted, it should be enough for the band to make a decision as to which one they preferred. She had already completed a couple of draft drumheads for Paul and mailed them on to Maddy and Jason.

Eventually Jake's warm up was complete and she heard him tune up his guitars. So much for peace and quiet, she thought as she surveyed her work. The concept tied in with previous work she had prepared for Silver Lake but she wasn't entirely happy with it. As she listened to Jake practice a fresh idea started to form in her mind. Casting aside the half-finished design, she started to sketch out an alternative backdrop. This one felt right and, as her passion for it took control, the design seemed to burst forth from the page almost drawing itself. She was still immersed in her creative world when Jake came back upstairs.

"You still working?" he asked, surprised to find her still bent over the drawing board.

"Yes," she replied, without looking up,

"Want me to fix dinner?" offered Jake.

"Please. There's some chicken breasts in the refrigerator and some fresh pasta."

"Ok, I'll see what I can come up with."

If nothing else, Jake's stint at the pizza place had taught him basic cooking skills and, by the time Lori wandered through from the study, he had prepared chicken Parmesan and was boiling some pasta to go with it.

"Smells great," she complimented. "Are we eating in or out?"

"Out. We've been indoors most of the day."

Lori had only just finished setting the table and fetching them both a juice when Jake carried their dinner out. It was still hot outside, despite the hour. The record breaking heat wave hadn't broken yet but, at least, there was a gentle breeze wafting in off the ocean. The chicken was delicious. Lori hadn't realised how hungry she was until she had sat down at the table.

"This is fabulous," she complimented, warmly. "You should cook more often, rock star."

"Thanks," he replied, with a smile. "I don't mind cooking. It beats starvation!"

A few moments later, Lori spoke again, "Jake, there's something I want to ask."

"What?" he asked, looking concerned.

"How would you feel about moving in here?"

The question caught him off guard and he stopped in his tracks, a forkful of dinner half way to his mouth, "Are you serious?"

Lori nodded, "You spend more than half your time here anyway and I don't like the times when you're not here. It feels right."

"I'd like that," he said softly. "I've been thinking the same thing, but didn't want to say anything. I'm not sure I'm ready to give up the lease on my apartment yet though."

"I'm not asking you to," said Lori. "Lord, I'll pay your rental if need be but I'd like you to be here more."

"I'm not taking your money," Jake said firmly. "But I'd love to live here with you."

"That's settled then," she said with a smile. "When do you want to move your stuff in?"

"I guess half of its here already," he acknowledged, sheepishly. "I'll collect my clothes tomorrow or Wednesday."

"I've already cleared space in the closet for you," she confessed, her cheeks flushing scarlet.

"Confident, weren't you?" teased Jake with a laugh.

"Optimistic."

Raising his half empty juice glass, Jake said, "Here's to us and happy days."

"Happy days."

When their meal was over, they both worked together to clear the table and tidy the kitchen. As she stacked the dishwasher Lori said, "I've been thinking about the basement."

"The basement?"

"Yes. I had originally planned to convert it into my studio, but there's not enough natural light. How would you feel if I converted it into a proper rehearsal space for you guys? Sound proof it a bit," she suggested.

"Hey, that's too much, li'l lady," he protested.

"Not really. I had a chat with Maddy and the construction bit is cheap. You've already got all your own equipment. Maddy said some of your stage gear could be moved here too, if need be or she can arrange equipment hire as needed."

"You two have this all worked out, haven't you?"

"Yes," said Lori, reaching to hug him. "Also, if you decide to teach guitar again, you could use it as a teaching space."

"There's no point in saying no, is there?"

"No," said Lori, kissing him on the cheek. "It's all lined up. I just need to tell Maddy when to start."

"Then I'm not going to say no," said Jake hugging her tightly. "I'm going to say, I love you, Mz Hyde."

"Love you too," she whispered, as he kissed her on the top of her head.

Glancing at the time, Jake joked, "Don't you have work to do? I need to head downstairs. The boys will be here any minute."

"I do, but I need to entertain Becky. I'll do an hour later on. I made a breakthrough earlier."

"Will you be done by Wednesday?"

"Only if you give me peace all day tomorrow," she admitted. "If I get an early start, I should be done by late afternoon. Plenty of time to get the images through to Maddy and Jason."

"I hear you, li'l lady," acknowledged Jake, as they both heard a truck pull up outside.

As August moved into September, life around the beach house took on a new routine. True to his word, Jake had moved the rest of his clothes and his belongings in. The work to finish out the basement as a proper rehearsal studio had been completed. Silver Lake had been kept busy with promotional radio station events, meaning that Jake was away every weekend and a couple of times during the week. The band had agreed that for the midweek events Jake and Rich would represent them and at the weekends all four of them would go. The new school term was fast approaching and a few of the dates had to be rescheduled as they clashed with school commitments. Once Dragon Song, their first single, was released there were press interviews to give too. While the band and Jake were fully occupied with all the promotional work, Lori threw herself into her own work by accepting two new commissions from two diverse musical groups.

With the band's album launch imminent, Maddy engaged Lori to help design the launch material. It had been decided to host a launch party in Rehoboth, at the hotel where Maddy was based. The date was set for the third Saturday in September. In the days leading up to the event, tensions were running high as the band's manager went into organisation overdrive. Rich and Jake were delighted to have a full workload of classes all day Thursday and Friday which left Grey and Paul bearing the brunt of their manager's full on "party planning." After a bit of gentle persuasion, Lori had convinced Jake to invite his father and his sister to the launch. Much to his surprise, they had both accepted.

The big day dawned clear and sunny, still mild for late September. It had been arranged that Silver Lake would meet at the hotel at eleven for a photo shoot with the record label and their management team. All the other invited guests were to be there for one, with the official "launch" set for two thirty. The band would then play a one hour set at five. At the rehearsal on Friday night, anything that could go wrong did - from broken strings to power outages. Jake had arrived home downbeat and anxious about the whole affair. When he drove into the hotel parking lot just before eleven, Lori could tell he was still nervous.

There were press photographers gathered outside the front door and, spotting Jake and Lori arriving, they swarmed round the car.

"Ready, rock star?" asked Lori, as she prepared to step out of the car.

"As I'll ever be, li'l lady," he replied, forcing a nervous smile.

Calmly, they both climbed out of the car, excused themselves past the photographers and, amid a flurry of flashes and camera whirs, they walked smartly across to the front door. Several of the photographers were shouting on Jake by name. As they reached the safety of the doorway, Jake turned and posed for photos with Lori for a few brief moments. When they entered the foyer, Maddy was the first person to greet them. Looking pale and decidedly off colour, she chastised Jake for posing for the press.

"Relax, Maddison," he cautioned, as he took off his sunglasses. "Is everyone else here?"

"Yes. They're through in the function suite. Get your ass in there," she snapped. "I need a private word with Lori."

Grabbing Lori by the arm, she guided her friend towards the ladies room. Having checked all the cubicles were empty, she turned to face Lori and burst into tears. It was a sight Lori had never seen before.

"Maddy," said Lori softly, reaching out to hug her friend. "What's wrong?"

"I've been so stupid," sobbed Maddy. "I need your advice. I need to tell you something."

"What have you done?"

Before Maddy could reply, she darted into one of the empty cubicles and was violently sick. When she came back out to face Lori, she was even paler, but she had the tears under control.

"I'm pregnant," she stated then began to sob again.

"Oh, Maddy, is that all?" said Lori, relieved that it wasn't anything more serious.

"All? This is a disaster!"

"Is it?" asked Lori calmly. "Have you told Paul?"

Maddy nodded, "I had to. I've been so sick all week. He thinks its fabulous news. He's so excited."

"And you're not?"

"I don't know. I never saw myself having children. They don't feature on my life map," admitted Maddy, wiping her face with a tissue. "But now it's happened, I'm not so sure. What should I do?"

"How many weeks are you?"

"About seven or eight I think. I've not been to the doctor yet," answered her friend. "I'm more worried about how I'm going to get through today."

"Pass it off as stomach flu or food poisoning," suggested Lori calmly. "I'll cover for you as best as I can."

"Will folk believe that?"

"No reason why they wouldn't," replied Lori with a smile. "But, if you hide in here all morning, folk will worry. Fix your make up and we'll go back out there together."

"What if Paul says something?"

"Talk to him," said Lori. "Now come on, you've a launch party waiting for you."

The two women slipped out of the ladies room a few minutes later and casually mingled in with the other music industry guests. Dr Marrs had Jake cornered with a photographer while Rich and Paul were posing by the bar, with two beautiful record company employees. One of the management representatives had Grey backed into a corner near the window, trying to convince him to promote one line of bass guitars. No one appeared to have realised that Maddy and Lori had been absent. Eventually, Jake made his escape and came over to Lori with a broad grin on his face.

"What're you looking so pleased about?" she asked, as he slipped a protective arm around her waist.

"Dr Marrs wants me to do guest vocals on an album he's working on," he said, with a wink. "Weigh Station are putting out a deluxe edition of their album in time for the UK tour and want me to sing on one of the additional tracks."

"Nothing less than you deserve, rock star," congratulated Lori.

"Me? Sing with Weigh Station?" he said, shaking his head. "I can't believe it!"

"Well, you better try to believe it," stated Lori. "Look around you. This is all for you guys. The Silver Lake dream is real."

"Thanks to your intervention," he said, kissing her gently. In the background someone was calling his name. "Better circulate, li'l lady. Can you keep an eye out for my dad and Lucy?"

Lori nodded and watched as Jake confidently walked back towards Jason and the group of record company executives. Out of the corner of her eye, she could see Maddy hovering near the door talking to Dr Marrs. As she headed back out towards the foyer, she felt someone touch her elbow.

"Mz Hyde?"

"Yes," she responded, turning round and finding herself face to face with a young woman. There was something vaguely familiar about her, but Lori couldn't place it.

"Hi. I'm Lucy," introduced the young woman with a smile so like Jake's that she needed no introduction.

"Jake's sister?"

"Yes," she giggled. "For my sins."

"Nice to finally meet you. Jake'll be so pleased you're here," said Lori warmly. "He's busy just now, though. Can I get you a drink?"

"That would be good," agreed Lucy nervously. "I was to meet Dad here, but he called to say he's running a little late. I was already here so he said I should come down and find you."

"I'm glad you did," said Lori, lifting a glass from the tray of a passing waitress and handing it to Lucy. With practiced ease, she scooped up a second glass. "Let's step out into the foyer."

There were two empty chairs beside a small table near the door and Lori directed a rather nervous Lucy towards them. As they sat down, Jake's sister said, "I came down by myself and checked in early. I've left my husband home with the boys."

"How long are you staying?"

"Just for tonight," she replied. "Dad's staying over too, when he finally gets here."

The two young women sat and chatted for a few minutes, gradually getting to know a little about each other. Lucy admitted that Jake had emailed her and told her a bit about Lori but not much.

"What else do you want to know?" asked Lori, feeling at a disadvantage. "There's not much to tell."

"I don't know," admitted Lucy with a girlish giggle. "You're the first of his girlfriend's I've ever met! Crazy isn't it? How long have you been together?"

"About five months," replied Lori. "We met on the beach."

"Oh, he told me that part! He said you'd broken your leg or something like that," gushed Lucy, then spying Lori's cane resting against the chair, she flushed scarlet and muttered, "Oh, I'm so sorry. Foot in mouth again."

"Lucy, its ok," assured Lori quietly. "I had an accident last Christmas. When I met your brother, I could barely walk a hundred yards on crutches. I still can't stand or walk very far without a bit of support, hence the cane. If anyone had told me a year ago that a bad femur break would leave me like this, I would've sworn they were lying."

"I never realised," replied Lucy, staring down into her glass, as she tried to hide her embarrassment.

"Hey, don't look so sorry. This is a party," declared Lori. "I've more or less comes to terms with things. It took a while though, and Jake's help."

"Dad told me you're an artist," commented Lucy, subtly changing the subject.

"Your brother told me you're a teacher," countered Lori playfully.

"Yes. I teach third or fourth grade most years," replied Lucy. "I hear Jake's teaching too at long last."

"Music," added Lori, with a hint of pride. "At a local high school."

Before either of them could say anything else, Jake came striding out of the main function suite, a worried look on his face. As soon as he saw Lori, he smiled, obviously relieved to have found her then he realised who she was talking to. At the sight of his young sister, his whole face lit up. With tears in her eyes, Lucy got to her feet.

"Hey, baby sister," said Jake, sweeping her into his arms. "You made it. And you've met Lori."

"Long time no see, Jake," greeted Lucy, tears gliding down her cheeks. "God, I've missed you."

"Don't cry, Lucy," he whispered, wiping her tears away.

"My big brother, the rock star," she sighed, as more tears flowed freely. "Mom would've been so proud. She always had faith in you."

"I wish she was here," he confessed quietly, then, regaining his composure added, "Where's the old man?"

"Behind you," came the reply, as Colonel Power arrived to join them.

"Dad!" exclaimed Jake. "Glad you made it."

Father and son exchanged hugs then Jake apologised that he would have to get back to circulating, but promised he would catch up with them as soon as he could get free. He paused to give Lori a quick kiss and then he was gone. A few moments later, Maddy came over and asked Lori to come back through. Lori was relieved to see her friend looking a bit better and less nauseous. She insisted that Lucy and Colonel Power came through to join the official party. Both of them were a bit hesitant at first, until she reminded them that Jake wanted them there. The socialising and posing for photos continued for what felt like an eternity. Every time Lori tried to get a few moments with Jake, someone pulled one or other of them aside. The official speeches to launch the band's album were blessedly short. Once the formalities were over Jason gave a final vote of thanks and hoped that they would all stay to hear Silver Lake perform a selection of the new album's tracks.

Through in the dining room, the hotel had laid on a sumptuous buffet and Colonel Power insisted on fetching plates of food for both Lucy and Lori. He had only just returned with a plate for himself when Jake came wandering over.

"You guys ok?" he asked, helping himself to a sandwich from Lori's plate.

"We're fine, son," assured Ben, between bites. "Do you have a minute to join us?"

"Literally a minute," laughed Jake, stealing a prawn bite from his sister's plate. "I need to go and warm up shortly."

"What's the plan for after the set?" asked Lori.

"Good question, li'l lady," said Jake. "Maddy's not wanting to do a big band meal. Jason's running off to catch a flight. Not much of a rock and roll party planned. Do you want to go and grab a meal somewhere? Rich and Grey might want to tag along."

"Works for me," agreed Lori, glancing at Jake's family. "Or we could go back to the house? You'd get more privacy there."

"True," nodded Jake. "I'll let you decide. I need to go and warm up. I just hope the room we've got back there is sound proofed! You don't need to be hearing that!"

"I know," giggled Lori, remembering the vocal exercises he had been practising since getting his voice back.

"Be good till I get back," he said, kissing her gently. "Oh, can you check on Maddy? Paul said she'd gone upstairs."

"I'll go up in a minute," promised Lori, trying to disguise her concern for her friend.

It was almost a relief to get away from the crowds on the ground floor, as Lori walked down the corridor towards Maddy's room. She had sent her friend a message to let her know she was on her way up. Reaching the room, Lori knocked on the door. She could hear her friend moving about inside and, finally, she opened the door. From the streaks of mascara on her cheeks, it was clear she had been crying again.

"Oh, Maddy," said Lori, hugging her. "Are you ok?"

"I feel like I'm dying," replied her friendly weakly. "Why now? Why today of all days?"

"It's ok. I spoke to Jason earlier and he was more worried that you got "food poisoning" from here than anything else. The boys have been great. They've got your back," reassured Lori calmly. "Is there anything I can get you?"

"Oh, I don't know," sighed Maddy, flopping down on the bed. "I wish this was food poisoning. At least then it would be over in a few days."

Clearing a space on the settee, Lori sat down. "Have you managed to eat anything?"

Maddy shook her head.

"How about getting room service to send up some toast. I believe it's meant to help," suggested Lori.

"Ok. Call them. I'll try anything," said Maddy. "I need to be back down for five. I promised Jason. He wants to formally announce the Weigh Station UK tour just before the set."

"You've still got about an hour. We'll get you back down there for five somehow," promised Lori, lifting the phone to call room service.

Forty five minutes and a slice of dry toast later, Maddy was feeling a little better. She fixed her make-up, re-spiked her hair, and then turned to face Lori.

"Will I do?" she asked, forcing a smile.

"Vampirically stunning as ever," assured Lori.

"Ok. Show time."

The function suite had been cleared and the small stage pulled forward. Silver Lake's stage equipment was dwarfing the space they had available to them. In Maddy's absence, the band had changed the plan and asked the hotel staff to clear an extra area in front of the low stage to allow them to move around a bit more. When the two girls walked in, Jason was the first person they met.

"I was beginning to think I'd lost you, Maddison," he stated bluntly. "Are they ready back there?"

"Of course," replied the band's manager sharply, praying that the band were waiting for their cue to come on.

Choosing this an appropriate moment to escape, Lori headed through the crowd to where Jake's father and sister were standing. They were chatting to a journalist from one of the local newspapers when she reached them. When he saw and recognised Lori, the journalist turned to question her. Dismissively she said, "Later." Taking this as his cue to leave, he moved on quietly.

"I hope he wasn't annoying you?" commented Lori, watching him weave his way through the crowded room. "They can be very intrusive."

"He was rather in your face," admitted Lucy. "But we never told him much other than who we were."

"Keep it that way," suggested Lori with a smile. "They're like leeches, if you give them the hint of a story."

Before she could add anything more, the lights were dimmed and Jason stepped out onto the small stage to a polite round of applause.

"Thank you for your patience," he began. "Don't worry. No more speeches. Just one big announcement for the night before the boys take to the stage. It's been confirmed that Silver Lake will support British rock legends Weigh Station throughout their British tour in November. Further details will be announced over the next few days."

A cheer went up from the crowd of media and invited guests.

"And without further ado, I give you Silver Lake!"

The four band members walked out to a thunderous cheer and a barrage of photography flashlights. Without a pause, they launched straight into Dragon Song. Jake stood centre stage looking every inch the rock star, as he sang the powerful lyrics. As the last notes faded, the band started an old favourite from Guns N Roses then went straight into another high impact heavy track from the album. When their third number was done, Jake reached for a bottle of water, then stepped back up to the mic.

"Good evening, folks. I hope you can still hear me," he said, with a mischievous grin. "I'm guessing we're a bit louder than the usual entertainers around here."

The hotel staff, who were lined up along the back wall, whistled and cheered.

"We're going to slow it down a bit for a moment," continued Jake, accepting his acoustic guitar from the stage hand. "This is one that is close to my own heart. Stronger Within."

Every time she heard the first gentle chords of the song, it reminded Lori of the very first time Jake had played the song in the sun room. The contrast in his singing style seemed to catch his father and sister off guard, as they watched totally mesmerised while he sang the haunting melodic lyrics. Everyone in the room, who knew the meaning of the song, knew he was singing solely to Lori. Some of the guests and the younger hotel staff members joined in on the chorus. Lori stole a glance at Jake's father as the song reached its ghostly end and saw that there were tears in his eyes- tears of pride.

"Thank you," said Jake, humbly bowing his head to the crowd. "If you know this one, feel free to sing along."

Lady Butterfly proved to be just as popular with the crowd and they sang every word with him. Even Jake's sister joined in with the final chorus.

After a return to their harder rock style for two more numbers, Jake announced, "This is our final number. We'd like to thank you all from the bottom of our hearts for coming today. Tell your friends and family to buy the record or, if you want to see us play live again soon, get yourself a plane ticket to the UK. We'll leave you with Flyin' High."

All too soon the last notes were fading away and the small crowd were pleading for more. The four band members exchanged glances and nods before Jake raised his hand for silence. "OK. We hear you. Unrehearsed so this could fail epically. Immigrant Song!"

Rich led the intro and, as Jake had said, unrehearsed Silver Lake dived headlong into the rock classic. His passion for the song and for entertaining the audience shone through. If there were any nerves at tackling the high notes, they didn't show. The crowd lapped it up, all of them in awe at the power in Jake's vocals. It was a show stopping ending to their short set and the perfect encore.

"Thank you and good night," called Jake grinning broadly. "Safe journey home, all."

And with those few words, Silver Lake left the stage to the cheers and whistles of the audience. Lori spotted Maddy waving to her from beside the stage and indicating that she should check her phone. Quickly she slipped it from her bag and, as expected, there was a message from Maddy. "Come up to the conference room now. Bring Jake's family with you." Putting the phone back into her bag, Lori turned to the colonel and Lucy, "Are you ready to meet the rest of the guys? Jake wants us to go backstage. Well, upstairs in this case."

"Yes!" squealed Lucy, her eyes gleaming with excitement. "I can't believe how good they were! And that's my big brother out there?"

"Have you never heard him sing before?" asked Lori, smiling at Lucy's obvious pride in Jake's performance.

"Never like that," she replied.

"I've never…." began Ben Power, still bordering on the over-emotional. "Was that really my son up there?"

Laughing Lori said, "Yes, Colonel, it sure was. Do you still wish he'd gone into the air force?"

"Hell, no!" declared Colonel Power. "No, ma'am. That was incredible!"

"Well, tell him that, dad," suggested Lucy, glancing at Lori. "I think Jake needs to hear it from you."

"Come on. Let's go and find them," said Lori, shifting the weight off her left leg, as she felt the familiar ache begin to creep in.

One of the stage crew was acting as minder outside the door to the conference room. He recognised Lori at once and opened the door to allow the three of them entry. Inside the room, the conference table had been moved and there were leather sofas around the outside of the room, a small bar at one end and few occasional tables. It was obvious that this was where the band had warmed up prior to the set from the scattering of personal belongings that littered the room. Jake was sprawled out along one couch with a towel over his face. His bare arms were gleaming with sweat. Grey was reclined on another chair, chatting on the phone while Rich was playing a game on his. Over in the corner, beside the bar, Maddy and Paul were deep in conversation. It was Rich who looked up first and, spotting Lori, reached out to kick the sole of Jake's foot, "Visitors."

Lifting the towel from his face, Jake sat up. His young sister flew straight into his arms, "That was awesome! You were amazing!"

"Why, thank you," he said, giving her a hug. "You'll need to come to a proper show. That was just a bit of fun."

Spotting his father standing next to Lori, Jake stood up and walked over to him. "Well?"

The older man smiled and hugged his son, "That was incredible. I'm proud of you, son."

Laughing loudly, Jake declared, "Jeez, I've waited thirty five years to hear you say that, dad!"

"I never knew you could sing like that," continued his father, the emotion of the moment putting a catch in his voice. "Your mom would be so proud of you. I wish she could've been here to see all of this."

"Me too," agreed Jake, with a sad smile. "But I think she might have heard us wherever she is. It was kind of loud in that small room."

"It sure was," nodded his father, smiling proudly.

"Let me introduce everyone," said Jake. "In the corner, we have Paul, our drummer, and Maddy, our manager. On the phone is Grey, bass, and Rich, playing games rather than guitar."

"Guys!" called out Jake, causing everyone to look up. "I'd like you to meet my dad, Colonel Ben Power, and my kid sister, Lucy."

Once the chorus of "hellos" and "pleased to meet you" died away, Jake asked what the plan was for the rest of the evening. They debated the options for a while, made a couple of phone calls and arranged to go out to dinner in Rehoboth. With the table booked, they had less than an hour to get there. Both Maddy and Paul declined the dinner invitation.

"Grey, what about you?" asked Jake, tossing his towel at him.

"I'll stay for dinner but I need to pick up Becky from my mom's," he replied, before turning to face Jake's dad and adding, "This is the side of rock n roll that folks don't see. My mom's got church in the morning so I need to fetch my daughter by ten."

"So no sex, drugs and rock n roll?" joked Lucy.

"Not for me tonight," sighed Grey with a wink.

Once the band had got themselves cleaned up and changed into their "street" clothes, they said their goodbyes to Maddy and Paul and headed out to the parking lot. Enough time had passed and the hotel staff had cleared the vast majority of invited guests through to the bar area and restaurant. The foyer was quiet, allowing the band to slip out more or less unnoticed. It took them twenty minutes to drive back into town. It took longer to find a parking space, followed by the inevitable hunt for quarters to feed the meters. With the Mercedes and Grey's truck safely parked and the meters fed, the group made their way into the sushi restaurant. Dinner was a relaxed affair with conversation focussing more on teaching than music. Fortunately, none of the guests from the launch party were in the restaurant, so the band were able to enjoy their meal in peace. As the waitress cleared away the empty plates and bowls, Jake's father asked them what the plan was next for the band.

"Well," began Rich. "We've more promotional work for the next couple of weeks for the album, then we need to rehearse for the British tour. We've no shows booked here until early next year, as far as we've been told."

"So what about school?" enquired Lucy, "Is it time to quit your jobs?"

"That's the next step," answered Jake. "But it's a huge leap of faith to make."

"I've spoken to the principal about getting six weeks unpaid leave," said Rich. "We should find out next week if it's been agreed."

"And if it's not agreed?" persisted Lucy, cutting to the chase.

"I'll quit," stated Jake without hesitation.

Rich nodded, "Same here. This is too big and too close to

throw away."

"What about you, Grey?" asked Lori softly. "Have you made a decision yet?"

"Kind of," replied the bass player slowly. "The boss has said I can take the time off, but he won't guarantee my job will still be there when I get back. It's a tough call."

"This time next year we'll all be millionaires," joked Rich. "And we'll look back at this decision and wonder what the fuss was about."

Realising the time, Grey apologised that he was going to have to go.

"Can I catch a lift home?" asked Rich, fishing in his pocket for his wallet.

"Sure," said Grey, pushing his chair out from the table.

"Put your wallet away, son," said Ben. "I've got this."

"Thank you, sir," said Rich shaking the colonel's hand. "It's been a pleasure to meet you. And you too, Lucy."

"Loved every minute of it!" gushed Lucy enthusiastically.

"Till next time, folks," called Grey warmly. "Jake, I'll catch you tomorrow."

"Night," called Jake then turning to his family asked, "What do you guys want to do?"

"It's getting late," said Ben. "And I've had a long day. I think I'll head back to the hotel. Are you free tomorrow? We could do lunch before I drive back to Annapolis."

"Why not come out to the house tomorrow morning?" suggested Lori.

"Sounds good to me," agreed Lucy, with a yawn. "I'd better go back to the hotel too. I promised I'd call Robb before eleven."

"I'll drive you back," offered Jake.

"No, we'll take a cab," insisted his father. "It's time for you and Lori here to catch up. She's hardly seen you all day."

"If you're sure?"

"I'm sure."

Colonel Power called the waitress over and asked her to call them a cab, then the four of them stepped outside to wait together. As the car drew up at the kerb, Jake said, "Thanks for coming today. It meant a lot."

"Thanks for inviting us," said Lucy, hugging him tight. "I've loved every minute of it."

"It's been an experience," agreed their father. "I'll call when we're leaving the hotel in the morning. We'll aim to be with you by eleven."

"Perfect," said Jake, putting his arm around Lori's waist. "Gives you a couple of hours at the beach before you head off, if the weather's ok."

When they arrived home, while Jake was putting his guitars away, Lori fetched a bottle of wine and poured them both a glass. Limping heavier than she had for a while, she carried the glasses through to the sunroom, where Jake was sitting flicking through the TV channels. He reached for the glasses as she lowered herself onto the couch beside him.

"You ok, li'l lady?" he asked softly. "You seem to be struggling tonight."

"Too much standing about today," she confessed with a sigh, as Jake handed her the wine glass.

Raising his own glass, he said, "Here's to the success of the record."

"To success," echoed Lori, raising her own glass. Having taken a sip, she commented, "Your dad seemed to enjoy the launch."

"Yeah," agreed Jake with a smile. "I can't believe he said he was proud of me. That blew me away."

"I like your sister. She's sweet."

"Lucy's adorable. Very like my mom was," replied Jake softly before adding, "Have you heard from Maddy since we left the hotel?"

Lori shook her head, "I'll call her in the morning."

"Paul's worried about her," admitted Jake, trying to gauge if they both knew the same secret. "I haven't seen him this stressed out for a long time."

"I'm sure she'll be fine."

"At least Jason bought the food poisoning line."

"Paul told you?"

Jake nodded, "He's terrified, but stoked by the news."

"She's terrified too," said Lori, relieved that he knew and that she could finally talk to someone about it. "I hadn't a clue what to say to her!"

"Paul confided in me last night," explained Jake. "She kept

disappearing, then chewed us out when things didn't run smoothly. She was all over the place."

"They'll sort it out, I'm sure," sighed Lori. "I just hope she can stop being so sick. She'll need to see a doctor. What'll happen about the tour?"

"I guess she'll still come," answered Jake, with a shrug of his shoulders. "If not, Jason will find us someone else. He had already said he might use a British based tour manager to support Maddy. Someone that knows the UK's ropes better than she does. We'll find out in about eight weeks I guess."

"Well, knowing Maddy, she'll still be working when she's in labour," muttered Lori snuggling in beside Jake.

As she cuddled into him, Jake checked the TV guide and selected a movie to watch. He put his arm around Lori's shoulder and settled down to watch an action thriller. Within half an hour of the start, Lori had dozed off and was sound asleep, with her head resting on his shoulder. Torn between watching the film or taking her to bed, Jake decided to watch the film. His mind kept wandering from the plot back to the events of the day. Getting on that tiny stage in front of less than two hundred people had been tougher than playing to twelve thousand. Knowing that the most important person in his life plus his father and sister had been out there had piled on the pressure. Up until the point when his dad had told him how proud he was, Jake had wished his old man had stayed away. Just hearing those words of praise had melted years of pent up angst. He had been genuinely surprised that Lucy had driven down too. When they had been kids, he had always been closer to her than his older brothers. She was four years his junior and had always idolised him while she was growing up. Compared to Peter and Simon, he was the cool older brother with the long hair, leather jacket and guitars. Seeing her enthusiasm and passion for the day's events proved that that hero worship thing wasn't buried very deep.

With a yawn, Jake realised it was late and that he had lost the thread of the plot in the movie. Reaching for the remote, he killed the power to the TV. Beside him Lori was snoring softly, her long golden blonde hair cascading down over her shoulder like a silk cloak. Asleep, she looked so peaceful, with an air of fragility about her. Gently he scooped her into his arms and slowly stood up. She stirred slightly at the movement, but, with her head resting on his shoulder, she remained asleep. Carefully he carried her through to the bedroom and laid her down on the bed. Deciding against removing her dress, he pulled the cotton sheet over her. Watching to see if she stirred, Jake stripped off his own clothes and slid into bed beside her. Propping himself up on one elbow, Jake lay watching her, coming to the conclusion that he was the luckiest man alive to have her by his side. Eventually his eyelids began to droop and he too settled down to sleep.

Sun was streaming in the window and across the bed when Lori finally woke the next morning. Stretching sleepily, she realised that something didn't feel right. She pulled back the covers and saw she was still fully dressed. The memory of falling asleep in front of the TV filtered back through. Beside her the bed was empty. All the warmth was gone from the space where Jake had slept, suggesting he'd been up for some time. Wiping the last remnants of sleep from her eyes, Lori wandered through to the bathroom.

Freshly showered and dressed in slim fitting jeans and a black vest top, she went through to the kitchen, following the aroma of freshly brewed coffee. Jake was standing barefoot by the sink having a glass of water. From his attire and the sweat pouring off him, he had just been for a run.

"Morning, sleepy," he said with a grin.

"Morning," she replied. "Good run?"

"Best for a while," he declared, wiping the sweat from his brow. "I ran up towards town for a change. Up beyond the far end of the boardwalk and back. It's beautiful out there today."

"Any word from your dad?"

"He called a few minutes ago to say they were just checking out and heading over. They'll be about a half hour," Jake explained. "I ran out to the store first thing and got fresh bagels and pastries. I wasn't sure what to get, so I bought a variety. Hope that's ok."

"Perfect," said Lori, pouring herself a coffee. "You go jump in the shower and I'll get organised here. I'd better call Maddy too."

Her friend's phone rang out, then cut to voice mail. Having left a brief message asking her to call back, Lori went to set the table for brunch out on the sun deck. It was still a nice temperature to eat outdoors, but she appreciated that days like this were numbered as they moved through autumn. Over the past week, the town and especially the beach had been quieter. She preferred it like this – warm enough to be out and quiet enough to enjoy it. As she brought out the plates and plastic cups, she heard cars in the driveway. From indoors, Jake called, "They're here!" By the time Lori made her way to the front door, Jake was ushering his sister and father into the hallway.

"Morning," called Lori brightly. "You found us then?"

"Jake's directions were spot on," said Lucy, giving her a hug. "Oh, and we stopped off and picked up a cherry pie. I hope that's ok."

"You didn't need to bring anything," scolded Lori, accepting the box from the colonel.

"We couldn't come empty handed, my dear," he stated.

"Go on out to the deck while I put this in the kitchen," Lori suggested, before asking Jake fetch them all a juice.

When she came out to join them on the sun deck, Lucy and Colonel Power were admiring the view of the ocean.

"This is a prime spot you have here, Lori," said Ben, as he came to sit at the table. "Beautiful."

"Thanks. It was the family holiday home. After my accident, I decided to relocate down here," explained Lori, also taking a seat. "Best decision I ever made."

"Do you never miss the city?" asked Lucy.

"Not really," admitted Lori. "We went back for a week or so in June and it was nice to be there, but it was nice to come home too."

"You've still got a place there?" asked Ben.

"Lori nodded, "An apartment on the Upper West Side."

"Will you go back there for the winter?"

"I doubt it," said Lori. "But never say never. We need to go back for a few days next month. Jake's back in the studio for a weekend."

"You are?" Lucy squealed. "What are you doing now?"

Looking a little embarrassed, Jake replied, "I've to record some vocals for a track for Weigh Station."

"Oh, your room used to be covered in posters of them! Remember?"

"I'll never forget," muttered their father. "Left a hell of a mess on the walls when I tore them all down."

All of them laughed and Jake confessed to feeling a bit overwhelmed about being asked to tour and sing with his idols.

"Will you get to guest on stage with them?" asked Lucy.

"Maybe," he admitted. "How good would it be to play with them in London?"

"Well, you never know," said Lori with a smile.

The relaxed conversation continued for the next couple of hours over brunch. Lucy insisted on helping with the food, leaving Jake and their dad to chat. As the two girls prepared a selection of filled bagels, they too chatted and got to know each other a little better. Lori found herself warming to Jake's little sister. She talked animatedly about her two young sons, commenting on how much they would love the beach and the ocean. When they took the plates out to the table, the two men were talking NASCAR, a common passion for both of them from the comfort of their armchairs. Shaking their heads, the girls continued to chat amongst themselves. Keen to know more about Lori's work, Lucy quizzed her about the designs she had done and her plans for the future. Guardedly, Lori explained about the two projects she was currently finalising but she said she had nothing else lined up.

"Don't let her fool you," said Jake, butting in on their conversation. "She's a workaholic!"

Lori blushed, then confessed, "I do tend to get absorbed in it once I start. But, in my defence, I'm no worse than him when he starts to write."

"That's true," conceded Jake, with a smile.

"Well, this has been lovely," said Colonel Power. "But I have to head off. Time to get back to ship. We're heading out tonight about seven."

"Where to this time?" asked Lucy, checking her watch.

"We're delivering a yacht to St Lucia then flying back unless we can pick up another delivery trip while we're out there," he replied. "Oh, I was meant to ask. Do you have any souvenirs from the launch that I can take back for Steve?"

Jake thought for a moment, then disappeared into the house. He came back out smoothing out a crumpled piece of paper and clutching a pen.

"Will this do?" he asked. "It's my copy of the set list from yesterday."

"Sure. That kid would accept anything as long as you've touched it. He kept that plastic cup you used for three days after you left!" laughed Ben.

Shaking his head in disbelief, Jake scribbled a message along the bottom of the set list and signed it. He passed it over to his dad then gave him two guitar picks that were in his pocket.

"Thanks, son," said his father. "He's a good kid."

With a flurry of hugs and promises to keep in touch, Ben and Lucy said their farewells, Lucy somewhat tearfully, and then they were gone.

"It was great to see Lucy again," declared Jake, as he watched her reverse carefully out of the drive. "I'm glad you and her got along so well."

"I'm just glad you've made peace with them," admitted Lori, giving him a hug.

"Me too," he agreed. "Right, time to come back to earth. I promised Grey I'd help him tow a car into the shop then I've papers to grade."

Laughing Lori said, "Oh the rock and roll lifestyle!"

"Well, what are you planning to do, Mz Hyde?" he challenged playfully.

"Laundry."

Once she had the first load of laundry on to wash, Lori poured herself a coffee and tried to call Maddy again. The phone rang out, but it was Paul who picked it up.

"Hi Lori," he whispered.

"Hi. I was looking for Maddy," said Lori. "I've been worrying about her."

"You and me both," he sighed. "She's sleeping. It's been another rough day."

"Oh, poor Maddy. She was so fragile yesterday. So unlike herself."

"I know," agreed the drummer sadly. "I'll get her to call you when she wakes up. No promises though."

"Ok, don't stress her about it," replied Lori. "But try to convince her to see a doctor."

"I'm trying. Believe me, I'm trying."

"Are you ok?" asked Lori, suddenly concerned at how flat the usually cheerful drummer was sounding.

"I'm ok. Just worried," he assured her. "And excited. And scared."

"Well, you both know where we are if you need us," said Lori warmly. "Maddy's like family to me. She was there when I needed her."

"Thanks, Lori. Means a lot."

"Ok. I'll talk to you later."

By the time Jake got back, the laundry was done and was in the dryer and Lori was sitting sketching out on the deck. An idea for a new venture had slowly been developing at the back of her mind ever since she had drawn the Celtic dragon for Silver Lake. It had struck her that it would make a nice pendant and, when she had had a few minutes to spare, she had begun to expand on the idea. The page in front of her was full of Celtic themed doodles.

"Hey, li'l lady," called Jake from the doorway.

"Hi. Did you get Grey sorted out?" she asked.

"Eventually. First tow rope snapped. Scared the crap out of me. We got there at the second attempt. I'm going to get cleaned up. I'm covered in oil."

"Lovely," she sighed, as she returned to the design in front of her.

It wasn't long before Jake was back outside beside her, armed with the book bag he used for school.

"Better do my homework assignment before dinner," he said grudgingly, opening the bag and taking out a pile of essays.

Closing her notebook over, Lori said, "I'll go make dinner and leave you in peace."

"Stay for a while," suggested Jake softly. "I'm not really hungry yet. Too much cherry pie earlier."

"If I'm not disturbing you, I'll stay," she agreed, picking up her pencil again and opening the book back at the page she had been working on.

Together they sat working on their respective projects for more than an hour, barely communicating with each other. It was the chill of an early evening breeze blowing in from the ocean that brought them back to reality. Much to his surprise, Jake had enjoyed reading his students' essays on what music inspired them and why. His class' tastes were quite diverse and some of the reasons that the kids had given were heart wrenching. He was relieved to discover that none of the essays featured Silver Lake. Since both he and Rich had returned from the summer break, both staff and students had been playfully teasing them about their rock star status. More than once he was quizzed by the kids in his classes about the incident in Milford, with numerous requests to see his gunshot scar. It all served to reaffirm his belief that teenagers were ghouls, but he had obliged on every occasion, noting their disappointment that it didn't look more impressive.

With a shiver, Lori closed over her sketchbook and declared, "I'm going in."

"Let me finish these off and I'll be in," said Jake, lifting the second last essay from the pile. "Almost done."

When he finally wandered back indoors, Lori was in the kitchen folding the laundry she had just removed from the dryer. The warmth from the clothes was gradually removing the chill from her hands. Smiling at watching her perform such an everyday task, Jake stood behind her and wrapped his arms round her waist.

"Are you happy, li'l lady?" he asked softly.

"Yes," she replied without hesitation. "Are you?"

"Couldn't be happier," replied Jake, kissing the nape of her neck.

"Glad to hear it," she purred, as he continued to kiss her neck.

"Do you want me to run out and bring something back for dinner?" he offered.

"There's still salad and shrimp left from lunch. It would be a shame to waste it."

"Sounds good to me," Jake agreed. "Do you want me to sort it out while you finish what you are doing?"

"No," said Lori. "You can take this lot down to the bedroom and fetch some wine while I fix dinner."

"Deal, li'l lady," he said, with a final kiss to her neck. "Love you."

"Love you too, rock star."

After Jake left for work on Monday morning, Lori tried to get hold of Maddy again. Her phone went straight to voicemail. Guessing that her friend was on a call, she left a message, then settled herself at her drawing board to finalise one of her designs for an up-and-coming country rock band from Kentucky. The remit had been for cowboy boots and western style saddles and felt a bit too cheesy for her liking, but the client was the one calling the shots. She had to admit that it had been fun re-producing the intricately tooled designs characteristic of the culture. In some ways, it wasn't dissimilar to the Celtic knots that she loved to work with. The design she was finalising was a detailed oak leaf pattern. The shading work was complex as she worked to create a 3-D effect. Totally engrossed in the challenge at hand, she lost all track of time and was startled back to reality when the door opened, announcing Jake's arrival home from school. She glanced at her watch and was stunned to discover it was after four o'clock.

"Lori!" he called, dropping his bag on the kitchen floor. "Are you there?"

"In here," she called back. "You ok?"

"Yes and no," he said, striding through.

"What's wrong?" asked Lori, noting the worried look on his face.

"Paul called. Maddy's in hospital. She collapsed last night and he had to call 911."

"Is she ok?" asked Lori, the colour draining from her face.

"She's going to be fine, but they've admitted her for a few days," explained Jake calmly. "Paul said it's something called HG. It has a fancy Latin name that I don't remember. She's on an IV and they've given her meds to try to control the sickness. Baby's ok too."

"Thank God," sighed Lori. "When can we see her?"

"He's cleared it for you to see her anytime. I assume you want to go now."

Lori nodded. "Let me grab my bag."

As they were driving out towards Beebe's maternity unit, Lori remembered Jake had had good news too.

"Oh, that," he said nonchalantly. "The principal has given Rich and I the six weeks off on one condition."

"That's great news!" exclaimed Lori. "But what's the catch?"

"He insists the band plays a set at the school Christmas social. We've agreed but I just hope Grey and Paul are up for it," revealed Jake, trying hard not to laugh. "London one week, then school gym hall the next!"

"The kids will love it," giggled Lori, seeing the funny side of it.

"I'm not sure Dr Jones will when he hears us."

"Well, there is that," she acknowledged with a laugh. "I'm sure Maddy will manage to turn it into a good publicity stunt too."

"You can bet on that," he agreed.

Hand in hand, they walked across the car park and into the medical centre, following the signs towards the maternity wing. In her hurry to get there, Lori had left her cane at home and she was trying to ignore the panicky feeling that was rapidly rising in her chest. Subconsciously she must have been squeezing Jake's hand tight. Leaning towards her, he whispered, "I won't let you fall. Stay calm."

"You know me too well," she said quietly.

When they arrived at the maternity unit, they went to the nurses' station to find out what room they were looking for. A mature, rather matronly, nurse gave them directions and said she would call through to say that they were on their way round. Paul was waiting for them in the corridor when they reached the room. His usually cheerful face was pale and there were dark shadows under his eyes. Giving him a hug, Lori asked how Maddy was.

"A good bit better," he replied. "The nurse is just fixing her IV. She hasn't been sick for almost three hours."

"Is that good?" asked Lori anxiously.

He nodded, "Better than she has been for over a week."

Behind them the nurse came out and said they could go in.

"You go on in, Lori," said Paul. "I'm going to grab a coffee. Jake, do you want to come?"

Jake nodded, glad to have an excuse not to go in to see Maddy just yet. Women's health and baby issues always made him uncomfortable. Hospitals made him uncomfortable.

"We won't be long," he said to Lori. "Promise."

"Ok. Bring me one back, please," she answered, as she opened the door to Maddy's private room.

The small private room was noticeably cooler than the corridor, thanks to a large fan sitting on the bedside locker. Maddy was propped up on a pile of white pillows, her face almost as white. When she saw Lori, she smiled weakly, then burst into tears. Without hesitation, Lori rushed over and hugged her friend, holding her tight until the sobs subsided.

"Come on now, no more tears," soothed Lori softly. "You'll be right as rain in a few days."

"Oh, God, I hope so," sighed Maddy, slumping back against the pillows. "I feel like shit. I've never felt this bad. Not even the worst three day hangovers felt this bad."

"Three day hangovers?" quizzed Lori, with a smile. "You've never confessed to those before."

Maddy managed a weak laugh, "There's been a few over the years, darling."

"Can I get you anything?" asked Lori, as she moved to sit on the chair beside the bed.

"No, thanks," replied Maddy. "Paul was going to bring me back some juice. I asked him to fetch my phone and my laptop too."

"I suspect he might accidentally forget those."

"He better not," said Maddy. "I need to call Jason and tell him the truth. The doctor hopes this will settle quickly, but it could go on for weeks apparently. I can't take any chances with some of the stuff I'm working on. Jason's going to have to draft in some help here."

"Stop even thinking about work," Lori chastised. "Think about yourself and the baby for now."

"It's all I've done all day."

"Well, keep doing that," suggested Lori. "Take a break. Paul can call Jason to explain and you can talk to him when you get out of here."

"Perhaps," Maddy agreed, with a sigh. "It's funny. At the launch I wasn't sure I wanted this baby. Something changed last night. I got really sick and lost a little blood. When I saw that, I realised that I really do want this baby. I remember going back through to tell Paul how I felt. Next thing I know, I'm in the back of an ambulance on my way here."

"That must've been scary," said Lori softly. "Did you hurt yourself when you collapsed?"

"I've a bruise the size of a dinner plate on my thigh," her friend confessed, pulling the covers back to show off her large dark purple bruise.

"Ouch," sympathised Lori, before playfully adding, "I still win for thigh damage though."

"You sure do," agreed Maddy, remembering the state her friend had been in the first time she'd visited her after the accident. "You never talk about it. How is your leg now?"

"Still not brilliant some days, but I can cope like this," said Lori, running her hand over her thigh.

"Does it still cause you so much pain?"

Lori shook her head "It's more of an ache like a bad toothache. It was sore yesterday after standing about so much at the launch party."

"Have you come to terms with the scars?"

"What is this?" laughed Lori, dodging the question. "Twenty questions? I came to see you, not to talk about me."

"You never answered me," stated Maddy, staring at her directly.

"Not really," confessed Lori. "They aren't as angry as they were but they're still there. An omnipresent reminder."

"Good job you never did like short skirts," Maddy joked, trying to lighten the mood. "Lord knows what I'll wear when I get fat!"

"A pregnant Goth," giggled Lori, trying to visualise her friend with a big, round baby bump. "You'll have to give up your corsets."

"Don't remind me," Maddy sighed. "And my spike heels. Will I still be able to wear them?"

"I have no idea," admitted Lori. "I certainly won't be wearing them. I can't wear heels anymore."

"Oh, I forgot!" gasped Maddy. "Sorry."

When the boys returned a few minutes later, the girls were still giggling about Gothic maternity clothes. Jake passed Lori her coffee cup, then hugged Maddy, "You ok, boss?"

"I've been better," she admitted. "And I might not be the boss for much longer. Depends what Jason has to say when he hears the news."

"I'll call him later," promised Paul, sitting on the edge of the bed and taking her hand. "And you'll still be the boss."

"Too late today. Call him early tomorrow morning. He's in London so remember the time difference. They're five hours ahead, honey."

"First thing tomorrow," promised Paul.

"Oh, I never told you Rich and I's news," said Jake, with a grin. "We've been granted six weeks leave, but there's a catch."

"What's the catch?" asked Maddy, as Lori stifled a giggle.

"We've agreed to play a set at the school Christmas social," confessed Jake grinning.

"A school dance?" asked Paul, his eyes wide open.

"Yup. A school dance."

The two girls giggled at Paul's disbelief.

"Oh, the publicity possibilities are endless," sighed Maddy. "That's great that you've got the leave though. Gives more flexibility for the tour. Maybe Jason can get you some extra shows."

"Maybe," nodded Jake. "Rich was emailing him. The school need both of us back by December 15th."

"When's the school social?" asked Paul with a look of dread.

"The Saturday before Christmas. He wants us to do a full set."

"Oh the joy!" sighed the drummer. "But, if it gets you guys the time off, I'm in. Might be fun."

Their conversation was interrupted by a knock at the door and the arrival of a nurse.

"Sorry, folks, you'll need to leave for now. The doctor wants to see Maddison then she needs some rest."

"It's time we were making a move anyway," said Lori. "I'll run out to see you tomorrow afternoon. If you need me to bring anything, let me know."

"My phone and my laptop," stated Maddy bluntly.

"More than my life's worth," replied Lori, giving her a hug. "I can do a sketchpad and some colouring pencils?"

"Harrumph," muttered Maddy.

"Take it easy, Maddison," said Jake, blowing her a kiss.

As they walked back to Jake's truck, Lori confessed to him that she hadn't eaten since breakfast. Shaking his head, he suggested they stop off in Rehoboth to get some dinner then drop by his apartment to pick up the mail. The traffic was quiet as they headed back into town. Jake proposed they park outside his apartment building, then walk along the boardwalk to find somewhere to eat.

"I've never been to your apartment," Lori commented, as he pulled up outside the building in Laurel Street.

"You must have!"

"No," she said, shaking her head. "Never."

"It's not much to brag about," he confessed. "But it was home for a long time. Lot of memories up there. Come on. I'll show you Casa Power."

Caringly, he put an arm around her waist and kept pace with her as she negotiated the steep stairs up to the apartment. It had been a couple of weeks since he had dropped by, so he was unsure how much mail would've built up. With a mutter, as the key jammed, he unlocked the door, forcing it over the small mountain of mail.

"Come on in," he said, stepping over the letters and flyers.

Almost hesitantly, Lori entered his tiny hallway. The air was stale and there was an unloved air about the place.

"Go on into the living room," said Jake, pointing to one of the three doors. "I'll be in when I've picked this lot up."

The small living room was spotlessly clean and sparsely furnished. Jake's old sloppy couch dominated the room, his stereo and TV sat silent. On the cream walls, there was a variety of photos and framed posters. She smiled as she spotted a college, or perhaps senior high, group photo among a montage in a frame. Dropping the mail on the couch, Jake came up behind her.

"Want the guided tour?" he asked. "It will take all of thirty seconds."

He opened the door beside where she was standing to reveal a bright airy bedroom. The large bed was neatly made up with blue and white checked covers. One wall was lined with bookshelves. Jake excused himself, as he squeezed past her to reach up for some of the books.

"Lori, can you grab a bag from the bottom of the closet?"

She slid open the closet door and picked up a small blue sports bag.

"Will this do?"

"Perfect. Thanks," he said, taking the bag from her. "I was talking to Rich and Linsey earlier. She's not read this series so I said I'd loan them to her."

Noticing there were still clothes in the closet, she asked, "Do you want to bring any of these home?"

"No, it's ok," replied Jake. "They're mainly old stage gear. I just can't bear to part with them."

"Ok," said Lori, sliding the door closed.

"So what do you think so far?" he asked, piling the books into the bag. "Palatial, isn't it?"

"Where's the kitchen?" she asked, then looking round, added, "And the bathroom?"

"Kitchen's off the living room. Bathroom's off the hall. Take a look," he said. "I'll be done here in a minute."

Carefully, she wandered through the tiniest galley kitchen she had ever been in then found an equally compact bathroom. Both were clinically clean.

"So how does Casa Power measure up?" he called to her.

"It's a perfect apartment for one person," she answered.

"There were three of us here at one point a few years ago," he shouted through. "Just after we formed the band. Rich got kicked out of his place. Paul had been sleeping on his floor for about a month, so they both moved in here with me. It was meant to be only for a week or two."

"How long did they stay?" she asked, giggling at the thought of the three musicians crushed into the small apartment.

"Six months," replied Jake. "And Paul brought his drum kit!"

"Tight squeeze?"

"You could say that," admitted Jake, still smiling at the memories. "Ah, they were crazy happy days. Paul stayed another six months after Rich moved out."

"I always thought it was Grey you were closest to," Lori commented.

"Now it is but back then it was Paul. We kind of shared a dark time together and got each other through it," he explained, a tinge of sadness in his voice. Changing the subject, he asked, "Where do you fancy for dinner, li'l lady?"

"Anywhere," declared Lori. "I'm starving."

"How about the fish place that's off the boardwalk before you get to the Turtle?"

"Perfect," Lori agreed. "Have you got everything?"

"Have now," he replied, stuffing the mail into the sports bag. "Let's go."

As they sat eating their meal a short while later, Lori said, "I have two questions, rock star."

"Shoot," said Jake, with a mouth full of crab cake.

"Where did you put the drum kit?"

Laughing, Jake explained that it had been set up under the window in the living room, but, that back then, there had been one less armchair in the room.

"Second question," she began a little nervously. "What dark times did you share?"

"That's ancient history," said Jake calmly. For a moment or two, Lori didn't think he was going to reply, then he continued, "All four of us enjoyed a joint and the odd line of coke back then. For a while Paul and I enjoyed it a bit too much for too long. Plus some other shit too. Pills. Meth. I was a wasted mess for a few months around about the time my mom died. I couldn't handle her being sick. After her death, I got my act together. Wasn't easy. I've been clean for over four years. No relapses. Paul too, until the Molton gigs. He had a relapse out west for a day or two."

"Maddy told me about that," replied Lori, reaching out to touch his hand. "As you said, ancient history."

"You're not mad at me? Not disappointed in me?" he asked, gazing into her blue eyes.

Shaking her head, Lori said, "No. Why should I be? It's in the past. And I've experimented too on occasion. Probably around the same time and you can blame Maddy for that. She still dabbles."

"I noticed," said Jake, remembering the after show party in Phoenix. "I've seen that shit kill too many people. Seen first-hand how it can destroy families. There's no room in my life for it anymore. Hasn't been for a long time. I just wish my mom could've seen that I cleaned up my act. I let her down. One of my biggest regrets."

"Let's leave the past where it belongs," whispered Lori, squeezing his hand, then changing the subject asked, "Is it next weekend you need to be in New York?"

"Friday night," replied Jake with a smile, his eyes gleaming with excitement. "I've to be in the studio all day Saturday and maybe a few hours on Sunday. Why?"

"I'll need to let David know we are coming up to the apartment. I also want to arrange a couple of meetings of my own. I might as well schedule those for while you are in the studio."

"I thought we talked about you coming to the studio too?" said Jake, sounding disappointed.

"I am," she assured him. "But I still need to do some business while I'm there. One of my meetings is with Weigh Station."

"The whole band aren't going to be there."

"Dan will be, and their manager," she replied. "It's really the management I need to see, but Dan wants in on the discussion."

"Who else are you meeting?"

"Can't say. Secrecy clause," said Lori, with a wink. "And don't even think about trying to get me to tell you."

"As if I would," laughed Jake, releasing the last of the ghosts from the past. "My last class is before lunch on Friday so we should be able to head off around two."

"How about I drive you to school in the morning and pick you up after class?" suggested Lori. "That'll save a bit of time. If we can get to the city before five, I can meet David before dinner."

"Sounds like a plan," he agreed. "And you can fight with the Friday afternoon Manhattan traffic, li'l lady. My nerves couldn't handle driving through that shit."

All too soon it was Friday morning and Lori was driving Jake to school. They had packed up the car the night before, after they had visited Maddy in the hospital. The band's manager was still much the same and, to her great annoyance, the doctor was insisting on keeping her in over the weekend. Her condition was improving gradually but she still couldn't keep any solid food down. Despite her protests, Paul was refusing to bring her laptop to the hospital, but he had relented and brought her cell phone. This had gone some way towards placating her. As Lori stopped the car outside the school, Jake asked what she was going to do with her morning.

"I have an appointment in town, but I'll be back here around one," she replied evasively. "If I'm going to be late, I'll call you."

"If you can get here for twelve thirty we could have lunch with Rich and Linsey before we head off," suggested Jake, as he got out of the car.

"I'll see what I can do," promised Lori before adding, "What's going on with them? Has he asked her out yet?"

Jake nodded, "I'll fill you in later."

"Have a fun morning!" Lori called, as she pulled away from the kerb.

It had taken her a few weeks to pluck up the courage to make the appointment at the tattoo parlour. She had forgotten about the butterfly design she had drawn at the start of May until she came across the sketchbook on her desk. After deliberating for a few more days, she had gone into town to see Danny to discuss the design with him. Much to her surprise, he had recognised her and remembered the butterfly she had shown him all those months before. They had chatted for almost an hour about the design and how long it would take to do. The tattoo artist had suggested it would look best inside her wrist. Eventually, she had made the appointment for Friday and, now that she was driving towards it, Lori was nervous. Danny had told her to park around the back of the shop and to bring him a skinny latte from the coffee shop. Having parked the car and bought two coffees, Lori headed towards the small tattoo parlour. The diminutive ink artist was watching out for her and opened the door as she approached, relieving her of the small cardboard cup holder containing the two hot coffees.

"My sincere apologies, beautiful lady," he said theatrically. "I had forgotten about your disposition."

"I can carry a cane and two cups," she replied, with a smile. "Just."

The tattoo artist smiled and showed her into the shop. It was empty inside, but Danny said his partner was due in soon.

"I've everything set up," he continued, sipping his latte. "Which throne would you prefer, princess?"

Remembering that Jake had chosen the middle one that was the one she opted for. As she sat down, Danny asked, "And how is our budding rock star?"

"In school this morning then we are heading to New York for the weekend."

"Anything special planned?"

"He's got some vocals to record on Saturday and I've a couple of business meetings. It'll be mainly work," she explained quietly.

"What line of work are you in?"

"Art," she replied. "I did the album artwork for Silver Lake and I've worked with a few others."

"Understatement of the year, princess," stated Danny bluntly. "Or should I say Mz Hyde?"

Lori smiled, "Only when I'm working."

"I've tattooed my fair share of your designs on clients over the last few years. I'm honoured to be inking you."

"I'm just any other client and it's a tiny piece of work for you," said Lori, flushing with embarrassment.

"Ah, but once you start, princess," he teased with a wicked grin. "You'll be back for more."

"Let's see how this goes first," she giggled nervously. "I decided on the left wrist by the way."

"Your wish is my command," he replied, as he lifted the first antiseptic swab from the tray. "Sit back and relax. Don't flinch. If you need me to stop, say. If it's too uncomfortable, we can take a break. And we're agreed it's to be on the inner left wrist and no more than an inch and a half by two inches?"

Lori nodded, took a large mouthful of her coffee, then settled back to try to relax. As she drank the rest of her coffee, Danny worked swiftly to draw the outline of her butterfly from the transfer. Once he was convinced she was completely satisfied with the position and dimensions, he began to ink it in. Much to her relief, it was less painful than she had anticipated, despite the delicacy of the skin in the area. When the outlining was complete, Danny asked if she needed a break for a minute or two.

"I'm ok, thanks," she replied, before draining the last of her coffee. "It's not as bad as I expected."

"It never is, princess," he said, with a smile. "And I suspect you, personally, tolerate pain better than most." He nodded towards her cane that was leaning against the chair.

"Perhaps," conceded Lori, with a sad smile. "Not one of my better claims to fame, though."

"I guess not," agreed Danny. "But if it works to my advantage. Are you ready for me to start again?"

"Ready when you are."

Carefully and silently, the tattoo artist worked to fill in the shades of blue and highlights of yellow. He paused once to change tattoo gun and, before Lori realised, he was finished. Gently, he cleansed the area again and applied a warm, damp cloth over the design. When he lifted the cloth, Lori finally saw the butterfly in all its glory. The level of detail he had managed to incorporate was fantastic. She was delighted with the finished article.

"Can I take a photograph of this one?" asked Danny hopefully.

"Why?" she asked curiously. "You asked Jake the same thing and he refused."

"I'd like to enter it in my catalogue of work and maybe into a competition or two, but I'll understand if you decline," he explained.

"Then no photos, Danny," Lori said softly. "Sorry."

"Ah, maybe next time," he laughed, as he covered the design with a dressing and taped it in place.

"You seem confident I'll be back."

"You will. I guarantee it," he said with a wink. "Jake'll be back too. He's already sent me a couple of ideas he's playing with."

"Well, who knows, we may come in together next time," she said with a giggle, as she reached for her bag.

Having settled the bill, Danny gave her a folder with the aftercare instructions and a receipt, then he handed her a small tub of cream.

"Use this on it, princess," he instructed. "Just in case, Jake has run out of it."

"Thanks, Danny," she said, putting everything into her bag. "I'd better go. I've to meet Jake for lunch."

He walked her over to the door and held it open for her. "Till next time, Mz Hyde."

"Bye, Danny," she called, "And thank you."

The lunch bell had just sounded, as she parked the Mercedes in the visitor's section of the school car park. Quickly, she sent a message to Jake to say she had arrived, then pulled on her jacket to hide the dressing over her wrist. As she was walking towards the main building, her phone rang.

"Hi, li'l lady," called Jake cheerfully. "Where are you?"

"Almost at the main door."

"I'll meet you at the school office," said Jake. "I've some paperwork to turn in. I'll be two minutes."

"Where's the office?" she asked.

"Inside the door, turn left, then right."

"See you there."

Lori had just finished explaining to the school secretary why she was there when Jake came striding along the corridor. His face lit up in a huge smile when he saw her.

"Sorry. A student stopped me as I was leaving the department," he apologised, giving her a quick hug. "Let me hand these in then we can catch up with Linsey and Rich. They've gone on ahead to the canteen."

Before she could reply, he turned to the school secretary and handed over the pile of papers he had been clutching, "That's the last of the permission slips, Annie. Rich will be down with the full list this afternoon to allow you to sort out the transport."

"Thanks, Mr Power," she said, taking the forms from him.

"It's Jake," he corrected, flashing her a smile. "Have a great weekend, Annie."

"You too, Mr Power."

The school's cafeteria was packed when Jake showed Lori

through the heavy double doors. A buzz of student chatter filled the air and there seemed to be people carrying lunch trays going in all directions. The chaos scared Lori a little, but Jake put a gentle arm around her waist and guided her through the maze of students towards the table where Rich and Linsey were eating lunch. With a sigh of relief, Lori took a seat as they both greeted her warmly.

"What do you want to eat, li'l lady?" asked Jake. "I'll go get lunch for both of us."

"Whatever you're having," replied Lori, feeling wholly overwhelmed by the surroundings. "I'm not that hungry though."

"I'll surprise you," replied Jake. "Are you guys needing anything else?"

"Can I get a bottle of flavoured water?" asked Linsey. "I forgot to pick one up. Any flavour will do."

"Rich?"

"I'm good, thanks," replied his friend, as he bit into a toasted sandwich.

Jake turned and disappeared into the chaos towards the serving counters.

"Is it always like this?" asked Lori, staring round wide eyed.

"It is busier today," admitted Rich. "The students get the chance to perform during Friday lunch break for a maximum slot of fifteen minutes. More of the kids hang around to hear what's going on."

"So who is performing today?" asked Lori, noticing the corner was set up with a microphone and a stool. There were two acoustic guitars on stands behind the stool.

"One of Jake's students," said Linsey. "Poor kid looked terrified the last I saw of him."

"I can imagine this is a tough crowd to please," observed Lori, remembering some of the harsh criticisms of her own school days.

"Generally, the kids really support each other," commented Rich. "The punishment for any heckling is that you have to perform the following week. It works."

"Do staff ever perform?"

"Occasionally," replied Rich. "Your man's on amber alert to step up there today."

At that moment, Jake returned with two trays of food and a

bottle of water sticking out of his pocket. "Tony will be fine without my help," he said, as he sat down and passed the water to Linsey.

"What's he playing?" asked Lori curiously.

"Stairway to Heaven," Jake replied. "It's his first time up there so we felt one long number was best. I ran through it with him at morning break. He was great."

As they ate their sandwiches, they chatted about the plans for the weekend. Linsey was going with Rich and Grey to Wildwood, NJ to do a radio show while Jake was tied up at the studio. They also planned to visit Maddy if she felt up to it.

"Mr Power," said a nervous voice from behind them. "I can't do this."

Both Jake and Lori turned to face a shaking young boy. He looked to be about fourteen with very short dark spiky hair that he was running his hands through nervously.

"Tony," began Jake warmly. "You were fantastic at break. Once you get up there, you'll be absolutely fine."

"My hands are shaking. I don't think I can play," said the boy, his eyes silently pleading for help.

"Have you done the vocal warm up?" asked Jake, taking the last bite from his sandwich.

The young musician nodded. "Right before I threw up, sir."

Pushing his chair out from the table, Jake got up and put both his hands on the boy's shoulders, looking him straight in the eye, "I'll help you with the guitar part but I'm not doing any vocals, Tony. I've not warmed up and I'm working this weekend."

"Thanks, sir," sighed Tony, the relief written all over his pale face.

"Give me five minutes to finish my lunch," said Jake. "I'll meet you over there."

"Thanks."

As the slightly less nervous student headed back into the crowd, Rich said, "You're too soft on him."

"I remember being scared at his age," said Jake, biting into an apple. "He just needs to work on his confidence."

True to his word, five minutes later, Jake excused himself from the table and walked over to the microphone. From out of the crowd of students, Tony stepped forward and picked up one of the guitars. He exchanged a few words with Jake then settled himself on the stool, adjusting the microphone to the correct height. Jake pulled over a chair and positioned it behind and to the side of where Tony was seated. He lifted the microphone from the stand, turned it on and addressed the student body, "Without further delay, people, please welcome Tony Martinez to the stage."

There was a resounding cheer from the boy's fellow students.

"Stairway to Heaven, folks," said Jake, before putting the microphone back in the stand.

Quickly he sat down, lifted the other guitar and settled himself to play. With a quiet count, he counted Tony in and allowed his nervous student to play the first few bars on his own before he subtly joined in. As Jake had suspected, as soon as he started to play Tony's nerves disappeared, as he focussed on the music. The boy had some talent and a reasonable voice for someone so young. Gradually Jake played a little softer to allow his student to shine in front of his peers until, by the middle of the song, Tony was flying solo. The boy finished the performance with confidence and received a huge round of applause.

"Well done," said Jake proudly, as he replaced the guitar on its stand.

"Thanks for helping me, Mr Power," replied the boy, all signs of nerves long gone.

"Any time," said Jake. "Now I need to run. I'll see you on Monday and we'll do more work on your playing. Check out those You Tube links over the weekend."

"Yes, sir," promised Tony. "Good luck in New York."

"Thanks. I'll tell you all about it on Monday."

Having said their farewells to Rich and Linsey, Jake and Lori made their way out of the school just as the bell rang to end the lunch break. Several students called out greetings to Jake as they walked to the car. Unlocking the Mercedes, Lori commented, "You were great with that boy back there."

"He's a good kid," replied Jake, as he slid into the passenger seat. "There's potential there if he puts the work in."

They had barely driven five miles when Jake enquired, "Were you at Danny's place this morning, li'l lady?"

"Why do you ask?" replied Lori, without looking away from the road ahead.

"I can smell the ink and the antiseptic cream he uses," said Jake with a grin. "Confess your sins, Mz Hyde."

With a giggle, Lori said simply, "Later."

Spotting the edge of the tape at her left sleeve, Jake continued to tease her, "I know where."

"You do?"

"Left wrist," he laughed. "I can see the tape from here."

"Correct," giggled Lori. "He says you've been mailing him about another design for you."

"I might have been."

"Well, he seems pretty confident that we'll both be back," she declared.

"He may well be right," agreed Jake, still curious to know what was hidden under the taped dressing. "What time are you meeting David tonight?"

"He promised to be at the apartment by five thirty. We should be done for seven," Lori replied. "Do you want to go out for dinner after that?"

"We could. Let's play it by ear," said Jake. "I'll go for a run while you're catching up with him. Stretch my legs round Central Park for an hour. Probably the only chance I'll get over the weekend."

As soon as she exited the Lincoln Tunnel, the traffic ground to a virtual halt. They had made good time on their journey up to that point, but it took them almost an hour to negotiate the Manhattan traffic. Weaving expertly in and out, taking alternative routes up town, Lori could sense that Jake was relieved that it wasn't him in the driving seat. It was almost five o'clock before she swung the Mercedes into the underground garage, bringing the car to a halt in her allotted parking bay. Turning off the engine, Lori let out a long sigh of relief.

"Well, we made it," she declared, with a yawn. "I'd almost forgotten how bad it gets out there late afternoon."

"I'm just glad it was you driving and not me," admitted Jake, opening the car door. "That traffic scares me shitless!"

"I could tell. Your turn on the way home though, rock star," she declared, as she stepped stiffly out of the car. "There's David's Jaguar. He must be early."

The older man was in the lounge on the phone when Jake and Lori clattered into the hallway. While Lori had packed one small holdall plus her workbag, Jake had two holdalls and two guitars, plus his gym bag. Dumping their stuff at the top of the stairs, Lori headed straight into the kitchen to make some coffee. When she got there, she discovered David had beaten her to it and there were three mugs sitting beside a freshly made pot. Declining a cup, Jake fetched himself a bottle of water from the refrigerator. He helped Lori to take the coffees through to the lounge, then went to take their luggage downstairs. Lori fetched her workbag and brought out her laptop, along with a pile of paperwork as David finished his call.

"You made it in one piece, then," he said, giving her a hug. "You're looking radiant, Lori." Then, spotting the dressing on her wrist added, "Another injury?"

"No," she replied with a smile. "A tattoo. I only had it done this morning."

"Tattoo?" he echoed in surprise. "I'm not sure your father would've approved."

"He'd have had a holy fit!" laughed Lori, imagining her father's reaction.

"Each to their own," said David warmly. "Where did your young rock star go?"

"He's gone to get changed. He's going for a run in the park," replied Lori as she switched on her laptop. "Gives us peace to get the formalities dealt with."

They were both focussed on the computer screen when Jake entered the lounge a few minutes later. He had tied his long hair back and was in vest and shorts. Fiddling with his iPod, he said, "I'll be about an hour."

"Alright," replied Lori smiling at him. "Be careful. Don't get lost."

With a wave, he was gone. As he watched the younger man leave, David noticed the tattoos on his arms and legs and looked at Lori disapprovingly.

"What?" she asked, under the scrutiny of her advisor's dirty look.

"Every inch the rock star," muttered David.

Laughing, Lori said, "Don't panic. I'm not about to go that far. He has more on his back and his ribs. It's his way of expressing himself."

"He's like a walking art gallery," David declared bluntly. "No doubt he has piercings too."

"Just the one ear," giggled Lori. "He's not as bad as Maddy."

"I suppose," he agreed reluctantly. "Now about these figures, young lady."

For the next hour, they talked nothing but business- facts, figures, contracts and twelve month plans. These meetings were too intense for Lori and it took her all of her time to concentrate on what her advisor was telling her and to focus on the commitments he was recommending. Hyde Properties was doing well and the expansion David was advising her on was well thought through. There were three new contracts relating to the property side of things for her to sign and, after questioning a few clauses, she signed all three. He had several investment updates on her own personal finances and complimented her on the commercial success of her artwork commissions over the last few months. They had just concluded their meeting when Jake arrived back, breathing heavily and dripping with sweat. He waved at them and went through to the kitchen for a drink, then called out that he was going for a shower.

"Is it serious between you two?" asked David, putting the completed files back in his briefcase.

"Yes," smiled Lori. "He moved in with me a few weeks ago. Life's good just now, David. I'm happy for the first time in a very long time."

"I just don't want to see you get hurt, Lori," he said softly. "Granted, Jake seems like nice guy."

"He is," assured Lori. "Despite the rock star bit, Dad would've liked him. He's been good for me. I don't think I would've recovered as fully without him being there for me."

"You do seem happy, my dear," David conceded. "How is your health? Are you still getting physical therapy for your leg?"

"No. I finished that a while back. Dr Brent was pleased with me when I saw him earlier in the month. He still doesn't think they will remove the internal fixation. You know the rod and pins and stuff. He's not convinced the bone would be strong enough. I can live with that though," she explained quietly, reluctant to discuss her recovery with him.

"But you're still relying on your cane?"

Lori nodded, "I'm ok without it around the house most days but, if I'm out, I do still need it. I've tried without it, but I get so scared that I'll fall. I guess it's partly psychological, but the medical advice was to keep using it when I'm out and about. I've come to accept things. More or less."

"And your young man doesn't mind it?"

"No. He understands completely. I've told him the whole story."

"No secrets, then?" said David, putting a hand on her knee. "It must be love."

"I do love him," said Lori, blushing a deep shade of red.

"Then I'm happy for you."

Closing his briefcase and slipping his phone into his pocket, David declared, "Now, I need to make a move. I'm meeting Olivia for dinner."

"Say hello to her from me. Maybe next time we can all go to dinner together?" suggested Lori.

"Perhaps. How long are you here for this time?"

"We'll be leaving on Sunday afternoon. Jake has school on Monday," she replied. "I might come up for a few days at the end of November. Jake's going to the UK with the band. I haven't decided yet."

"Are you not going overseas with him?"

Lori shook her head, "No. He's working. I don't want to interfere. I might fly over and meet him at the end of the tour. We'll see."

Having said goodbye to David and waited to see him safely into the elevator, Lori went in search of Jake. She could hear water running and the gentle strains of his singing coming from the en suite bathroom. It made her smile to hear him splashing and singing to himself, oblivious to his audience. When he finally came out of the bathroom with a towel wrapped round his hips, she gave him a round of applause.

"Encore!" she called playfully.

"No chance, li'l lady. Need to save my voice for tomorrow. I've a feeling it's going to be a long day," he said. "Now, about this new ink of yours?"

Trying not to giggle, Lori held out her wrist and allowed Jake to gently ease off the paper tape and dressing. She held her breath as he saw the small butterfly for the first time. He inspected it closely, moving her wrist from side to side and flexing it slightly, nodding all the while in silent approval.

"That's beautiful," he said finally. "Possibly the best piece I've seen from Danny. But most importantly, do you like it?"

"I love it," said Lori, relieved that Jake liked it too. "I wasn't sure how you'd react to it."

"It's tasteful. It's discrete and it's beautifully designed. One of yours, isn't it? The one we showed him when I got my music inked?"

Lori nodded.

"I thought so. Follow the aftercare regime to the letter and it will heal in no time. I've got some of Danny's magic cream in my wash bag."

"He gave me some," said Lori. "He wasn't sure if you had any left."

"Use it well then," he said, kissing her wrist below the design. "I think he's right. You'll be back. There's that special tattoo lover glint in your eyes."

Laughing, Lori declared, "We'll see."

It felt strange heading back to the studio next morning without the rest of Silver Lake being there. As he sat in the back of the cab beside Lori, Jake's mind was running over the music and lyrics for the track he was to work on. It still didn't feel real that he was about to record vocals with a band who had been his idols for so long. Over dinner the night before, he had expressed his nervous excitement, much to Lori's amusement. It was another dream come true moment that was actually about to happen.

"I still feel like I'm going to waken up in a minute and we'll be back at the beach," he said to Lori, as the cab pulled up outside the studio.

"No, this is as real as it gets," stated Lori, as she passed the fare to the driver.

"Let's grab a coffee before we head in," suggested Jake, as they stepped out onto the pavement.

Armed with their coffee cups, they made their way up to the lounge a short while later. A small group of people were sitting on the settees watching the TV. Both of them recognised Dan Crow, Weigh Station's singer, instantly and Lori assumed the others were the people she was due to meet with. Dr Marrs came into the lounge at their back.

"Mr Power, you made it and on time," said the producer, clapping Jake on the back. "And you brought the stunning Mz Hyde with you."

"Morning, Jim," said Lori, with a grin.

"Jake!" called Dan, getting up to greet them. "Great to see you. Thanks for agreeing to do this."

"It's a pleasure," assured Jake, reaching out to shake his idol's hand.

"And you brought your guitars too?"

"As requested."

"Right," declared Dr Marrs. "Let's get this show on the road. Dan, can you explain the changes to Jake while I go and finish setting up?"

"Changes?" echoed Jake anxiously.

"Another guest artist pulled out really last minute. Royally pissed me off," began Dan. "You get to do his tracks too."

"Tracks?"

"Yes. Two of them, with guitar tracks too. Time's going to be tight, but Dr Marrs here tells me you're a slick worker. It might take us all night, but we'll get all three done," said the Weigh Station singer with confidence. "Lori, I'll be back to join your meeting in an hour."

"Fine," acknowledged Lori, setting her work bag down on the large table. "I'll get the boring finance bit done while we are waiting for you. I've another meeting here at two so I'm in no rush."

"Gentlemen," called Dan to the three men sitting on the couch. "Play fair with Mz Hyde till I get back up here."

"Lori," said Jake, still looking a little overwhelmed. "I'll catch up with you later."

She nodded, then said, "Go and play and have some fun. Relax."

"Easier said than done, li'l lady."

Lori's meeting with Weigh Station's management, and eventually Dan, when he returned nearly two hours later, was a challenge. As requested, she had prepared a portfolio of draft designs for them, based on the detailed criteria that had been emailed to her. None of them could reach agreement on what designs they wanted to use. If one liked a design, another wanted to add in features from one of the other designs. When Dan joined them, his personal preference was for the one design that didn't tie in with the management's views. Normally Lori would compromise and re-work the design, if they reached a consensus, but the timescales here and her current workload did not allow for that. It went against her nature and general work ethic not to alter the designs on offer if asked to do so, but she knew she had to stand her ground.

"Mz Hyde," began Laughlan, the band's manager with a broad Scottish accent. "If you could add in the features from this one to the background here, I feel we could resolve this here and now."

"And is the deadline still Monday?" asked Lori bluntly. "That's a complete re-work and is going to take considerable time. I can't promise to do that in one day."

"This is Saturday, my dear. By my count, it gives you three days," he countered forcefully.

"I have a full diary of meetings today," replied Lori, trying to maintain an even tone of voice. "I have commitments booked in for tomorrow morning. I plan to travel home tomorrow afternoon. I can re-schedule my Monday diary, but it still only leaves me one day to complete this commission for you."

Slouching back in his chair and appearing not to be paying any attention to proceedings, Dan spoke up, "I say we email the designs on offer to the guys in the band. If they agree on one of the existing designs, then there's no need for re-work. I still prefer the Gothic cross theme. It links with one of the three new tracks. I'm pretty confident the boys will want to go with it."

"Fine. Email them, then get them on the phone," declared the manager angrily. "I'm going outside to get some air. I'll be back in twenty minutes."

The three "suits" left the lounge together, leaving Lori and Dan sitting at the table. Much to her surprise, he threw back his head and laughed.

"I'm glad you're finding this funny, Dan," she said quietly, giving him a hard stare.

"I'm not laughing at you, gorgeous. I'm laughing at them," he explained. "Every meeting has been like this for months. Let me make a few calls but I'm pretty sure we'll be going with the cross."

"I hope you're right," sighed Lori, gathering up the papers in front of her.

"Give me a few minutes, Lori," said Dan, pulling his phone out of his jacket pocket.

"Take as long as you need. I'll be right here."

An hour later, much to Lori's relief, the management, Dan and, via phone and email, the other band members agreed to go with the Gothic cross design and no re-work. After the trials of the morning, Lori was delighted to shake hands with them all to bring proceedings to a close. She remained at the table as they all trooped out of the lounge, moving on to their next fraught debate. Sitting, feeling drained, with her head in her hands, Lori hoped and prayed that Jake's studio session was going better.

Downstairs in Studio A things were running along smoothly. The plan had been changed due to the addition of the two extra tracks, but the vast majority of the tracking had already been done by Weigh Station, back in a studio in the south of England. It only took three takes to get a vocal track recorded for the original song that Jake had been due to guest on. While Dan was in the lounge at the management meeting with Lori, Dr Marrs let Jake familiarise himself with the other two tracks. He was to record a guitar track for both and a vocal on one. Neither of them were tracks that he felt a connection with, even after hearing them a few times. When Dan returned to the studio, the two of them worked together for a few hours, gradually ironing out the issues that Jake was having with the tracks. It was late afternoon before they stopped for a break.

"Ok, boys," said Dr Marrs, checking the time. "Be back in here for four thirty. We'll get set up while you guys grab some food."

Jake excused himself, laid his guitar back in its case and went upstairs to the lounge in search of Lori. His earlier nerves had long since vanished and he had been so focussed on the additional tracks to be learned that he had almost forgotten that she was in the building. When he entered the lounge, it was empty. A wave of disappointment washed through him as he realised he wasn't going to see her. Quickly he pulled his phone from his pocket. There was an unread message waiting for him.

"Change of plan. Second meeting now at a hotel. Will see you back at home later. Love you. L x"

"What hotel? J x," he replied, concerned that she hadn't said where she was headed.

He was on his way back to the studio, with a takeaway sandwich from a nearby deli, when she finally replied. "In a cab on the way home. Are you winning? L x"

"Still a few hours to go. Don't worry. I'll be late back, Love you. J x"

When he re-entered the studio, the Weigh Station management guys were nowhere to be seen. Dan was sitting on a stool playing with an acoustic guitar, while Dr Marrs and the two technicians were eating Thai food out of small white waxed cardboard cartons.

"Did you find the lovely, Mz Hyde?" asked Dan, without

looking up.

"No. She had already left," answered Jake, picking up his guitar.

"I'm not surprised," commented Dan, putting the guitar back on the rack. "The suits were rough on her this morning. She's a tough cookie though. Held her ground. Stood up to Laughlan. I was impressed."

"She's stronger than she looks," agreed Jake, with a grin. "Don't be fooled by the limp and the cane."

"I noticed the cane. I don't remember that from the last time she did some work for us."

"She's recovering from an accident," explained Jake, deliberately keeping his answer vague. "When did you work with her before?"

"We go back a long way!" laughed Dan, before adding. "I think she was still in college when we first worked together. Last time I worked with her, she helped me source two guitars for my collection. Must be about eighteen months back."

"She never said," replied Jake. "But then she never discusses her clients with me."

"A true professional," acknowledged Dan with a wink. "Time to get back to work. With a bit of luck we might be out of here by midnight."

Midnight came and went and still Dr Marrs wasn't satisfied with things. They had the vocal nailed by nine thirty, but the two guitar tracks were proving to be a challenge. He sent the technician down to the store in the basement in search of some different guitars to try. Together they worked on the first track and got a couple of variations recorded to the producer's satisfaction just after midnight. Having found the set up and the guitar that fitted with the sound he was looking for, he suggested they work on and finish the last guitar track. At some point, someone went out for pizza for them and also a case of beer. Usually Jake wouldn't drink when he was playing, but, partly for the sake of being polite, he downed a couple of beers before he went back into the studio to record the last track. He could see Dr Marrs and Dan in the control room with a bottle of whisky and began to wonder if they were settling in for an all-night session.

"From the top, Mr Power," called the producer.

Perhaps it was luck, or perhaps the beer had relaxed him a little, but Jake nailed it at the first time of asking. He was all ready to pack up when Dan asked if he would play on and improvise a short solo that they would integrate into the track. Not wanting to let his idol down, Jake played on for another hour, then declared he was done.

"You've been fantastic today, Mr Power," congratulated Dr Marrs. "A true professional. Thank you."

"Thanks", said Jake, blushing slightly at the praise as he fastened his guitar cases. "It's been a pleasure."

"If these tracks mix ok, how do you fancy doing them with me on the tour?" asked Dan, whisky bottle in hand. "Not every night, but maybe at a couple of the shows?"

"Would love to," said Jake, trying hard not to sound too keen.

"Good. We can work it out when we hit the road next month," said Dan.

"Right. I'm out of here," declared Jake, picking up his bag and his guitars.

It was after three o'clock in the morning before the cab dropped Jake off at the apartment. He had been nodding off as he sat in the back seat and it took the last of his energy to pay the fare and stumble into the building. The concierge came out to help him with the guitar cases and then wished him good night as the elevator doors closed. Jake tried to be quiet as he entered the apartment, but failed miserably as the strap broke on one of the guitar cases causing it to clatter down onto the wooden floor. He fetched himself a drink of water, then wandered down to the bedroom. Lori was sound asleep in the centre of the large bed, her hair trailing across the pillow like a golden web of silk. He watched her sleep, as he slowly drank the glass of water, then undressed and slipped into bed beside her.

Several hours later, Jake wakened alone in the bedroom. Checking the time on his phone, he discovered it was nearly noon. As he lay on his back, staring up at the ceiling, thinking back to the previous day, he thought he heard voices upstairs. Realising Lori had company, he decided to shower and dress before going up to join them.

Upstairs in the living room, Lori was chatting to an old friend over coffee and donuts. It had been over a year since she had caught up with Lin, her Oriental friend from college. Lin ran her own jewellery design business and Lori had invited her over to show her the designs she had been toying with. They were both still laughing like schoolgirls when Jake wandered in.

"Morning," called Lori cheerfully. "Jake, this is Lin. We were at college together. Lin, this is Jake."

"Ah the rock star boyfriend!" squealed Lin. "Delighted to meet you."

"Likewise," replied Jake, sounding almost shy.

"Did you get finished last night?" asked Lori. "Or do you need to go back to the studio today?"

"I'm done. We finished the early hours of this morning. Dr Marrs seemed happy enough with what we got," answered Jake. "I'm going to grab a coffee. Can I get you ladies a refill?"

"Please," they both said in unison.

As Jake walked through to the kitchen, Lin turned to Lori and whispered, "You never said he was so hot."

"Lin!" exclaimed Lori, before dissolving into a fit of embarrassed giggles.

"Well, he is!"

"I guess," agreed Lori, still laughing.

Returning with the coffee pot, Jake refilled their cups, then turned to head back into the kitchen in search of some breakfast.

"Jake," called Lori. "There's donuts through here. Please eat some of them and save us from ourselves."

Turning back, he said softly, "I didn't want to intrude on your meeting."

"We're done with the business bit," stated Lin, shutting her laptop down. "Your girlfriend has talent."

"I know," agreed Jake, winking at Lori and causing her to blush.

"For designing jewellery," finished Lin bluntly. "I'll take these designs and get my team to work on them. Happy to try the LH range for the fee we agreed."

"Jewellery?" asked Jake, looking at Lori somewhat bemused.

"Just a few bits and pieces I've been playing with. Lin's going to test the waters for me and see if there's a market for it," explained Lori. "Another string to my bow."

"Ok," nodded Jake. "Another art form I guess."

"Exactly," agreed the girls together.

"Time I was making a move," said Lin a few minutes later. "I'll email or call during the week with an update for you. Lovely to meet you, Jake."

"Likewise," he replied, flashing her one of his Power smiles.

"I'll see myself out," stated Lin bluntly. "Tel Maddy I said hello when you see her next."

"I'll be seeing her tomorrow, hopefully," said Lori. "Come down to the beach for a visit."

"Maybe in the spring," agreed her friend. "For now, goodbye to you both."

As they had agreed, Jake was in the driving seat on the journey back to Delaware. Once he was out of the tunnel, he relaxed a little more and cranked the volume up on the stereo. Beside him, Lori sat watching the familiar scenery go by. They chatted about the highs and lows of their weekend then Jake told her that Dan had mentioned about guesting on stage with Weigh Station.

"That's fantastic!" she exclaimed, genuinely pleased for him. "Things are really taking off, aren't they?"

"It's just happened so fast," commented Jake, with a hint of disbelief in his voice. "The album's selling well. The tour's coming up in about six weeks. We're going overseas to play. It's all a dream come true, but it's like the scariest roller coaster ride ever."

"Do you want it to stop?"

"Never!" exclaimed Jake before adding, "Well, not for a while. I've dreamed about this for twenty years. I've worked hard with the guys for more than five years. I want to see how far we can take this."

Lori smiled at the passion and enthusiasm ringing through his voice. She had a sudden vision of a teenage Jake practicing guitar in his bedroom, dreaming of playing with Weigh Station and now here he was staring the reality of it in the face.

"Will you come to the UK with us?" Jake asked a few miles further down the road. "I want you to be a part of this."

"Maybe," replied Lori. "I don't want to be there for the whole tour. You don't need the girlfriend hanging about. Where's the last show?"

"As far as I know we're finishing with two nights in London," said Jake. "I think it's the third and fourth of December."

"I'll meet you in London then," agreed Lori. "And we can fly home together."

"It's a deal, li'l lady."

Next morning, when the alarm clock went off at five thirty, the rock star life seemed a million miles away. It felt like a cool morning so Jake dressed in sweat pants and pulled on an extra T-shirt before he set off for his morning run. He left Lori curled up asleep as he headed out to run along the beach.

There was a stiff breeze blowing in off the ocean and the waves were crashing onto the shore. As he ran, Jake's mind drifted to the coming weeks. Both he and Rich had three weeks of school left, then there were roughly two weeks of rehearsals before they would pack up and head across the Atlantic. As he ran, he looked out over the ocean. It would be his first trip to Europe; it would be the first trip to Europe for all of them. Even preparing for the concerts was a dramatic change from just a few short weeks ago. The management company had them surrounded by technicians and stage crew - a far cry from hauling their own gear in the back of the truck and setting up the stage themselves. It definitely did not feel natural to have someone tune his guitar for him. As he ran, he made a decision - no one other than him would touch his beloved acoustic guitar. It might seem childish but it suddenly seemed important to him to retain something that was wholly his.

When he arrived back at the beach house, Lori was up and in

the kitchen making breakfast. He greeted her with a sweaty hug and a kiss.

"You taste like the ocean," she protested, pushing him away.

"I thought you liked the ocean," Jake teased, kissing her again.

"I do," she agreed. "But not like this. Go jump in the shower."

"Yes, li'l lady," he called before adding, "Why are you up so early?"

"I've a call with Jason at eight about a new piece of work," she explained. "I need at least two coffees before I can cope with that man in the morning."

"That I can understand," he agreed. "Are you going to see Maddy today?"

"That's the plan, if she's up to it. I'll call her around lunchtime," replied Lori, pouring her first coffee of the day. "What's your schedule like?"

"School then the band are rehearsing at six."

"Here?"

Jake nodded, "Just for a couple of hours."

"And, I suppose, you'll all want dinner?"

"We'll sort something out later. You don't need to feed us all, li'l lady."

The phone rang at precisely eight, just as Jake was heading out the door to school. Lifting a freshly poured mug of coffee, her third, Lori answered the call, "Good morning, Jason."

"Good afternoon, Mz Hyde. Apologies for the early start for you."

"Not a problem. How's London?" she asked, as she set the mug down on her desk and took a seat.

"Grey and wet," replied the Englishman. "Have you seen Maddison?"

"Not since Thursday night," Lori answered. "I was going to call her this afternoon."

"You know she's pregnant," stated Jason bluntly.

"Yes," replied Lori, unsure as to how to respond.

"Delighted for her, but it screws up the plans somewhat. Music management and touring isn't the world for babies."

"She's got a few months to go," said Lori calmly. "No reason why she can't work up until a few weeks before the birth. Most women do these days."

"I suppose," he conceded reluctantly. "Now down to business. About this new band I've signed."

Their discussion took over an hour, as Jason described what he would like her to consider for the latest band he had signed to the firm. She made various notes and listened intently to his detailed requirements. On the face of it, Lori was happy with the project plan and then they got down to talking money. The Englishman liked to drive a hard bargain, but recent experience, of the multiple add-ons to the various commissions, caused her to challenge back firmly. Their monetary debate raged for a further half an hour before the Englishman gave in.

"I'll have the lawyers draw up the contracts and email them to your man in New York."

"That would be good, Thanks," she replied, taking careful note of the final figure they had agreed on."

"I had meant to ask before," began Jason. "Are you going on the road with Jake and the boys?"

"No," she replied quickly. "But we talked about the possibility of me joining them in London. I've commitments here to keep me busy till the end of the year so I can't afford to take several weeks out just now."

"Sounds fair," he responded. "I was hoping you'd join them at some point. You seem to be their Svengali. Jake especially is more alive on stage when you're there, but I understand."

"They need to do this their way," said Lori firmly. "I'll come to London, but that's it."

"Understood, my dear. Now I need to run. I'm late for another call. Ask Maddison to call me if you see her today."

"Will do, Jason," replied Lori. "Pleasure doing business as always. I'll look forward to the contract and the info files by the end of the week."

"Till next time, my dear."

And the line went dead.

As soon as the call was over, Lori switched on her laptop and spent the next hour reviewing her calendar and checking emails. She blanked out the first ten days of December, marking the third and fourth with the Silver Lake shows. Including this new commission, she had three projects on the go, two of which had deadlines in November. As she stared at the dates on the calendar screen, she realised she could travel to the UK earlier if Jake really needed her to be there. Perhaps she could surprise him by turning up a day or two early.

The chirp of a message alert brought her back to the present and she reached for her cell phone. It was a message from Maddy.

"Finally out of hospital. Back at the hotel now if you want to come over. M x"

Quickly she replied, "Fabulous. Will be over after lunch. How are you? L x"

"Much better. Not been sick since Thursday."

"Great news. Do you need me to bring you anything? L x"

"Just yourself. M x"

Huge drops of rain began to fall as Lori walked from the car into the hotel. The stiff breeze hadn't dropped all day and the wind was tugging at the bouquet of flowers she was carrying. Clutching them tightly, Lori prayed they would survive till she made it indoors. With a sigh of relief, she stepped in out of the inclement weather a few moments later. Taking extra care not to slip on the damp foyer floor, she headed straight towards the elevator. As she reached up to knock Maddy's door, the door opened and Paul stepped out, almost standing on her in the process.

"God, I'm sorry, Lori," he apologised, reaching out to steady her, as she stumbled slightly. "You ok?"

"I'm fine. Don't panic," said Lori giving him a hug. "Where are you off to in such a hurry?"

"Ultimately, your place," he admitted. "I have some errands to run before rehearsal."

"I'll see you later then," she replied, as she stepped into the hotel suite.

Maddy was sitting at the desk in front of her laptop when Lori entered the room. She was also on the phone. Wondering why she wasn't surprised to find her friend working already, Lori sat down on the couch, laying the flowers down on the table. From the edgy tone to her friend's voice, she sensed the call was not going smoothly or to her liking. Still looking pale, Maddy smiled over at her and indicated she would only be a couple of minutes.

Sure enough, she ended the call two minutes later.

"Working already?" chastised Lori, as her friend turned to face her.

"I need to catch up," explained Maddy. "And Jason's being a complete pain in the ass."

"Ah, he caught up with you," Lori observed, with a nod. "I had a call with him this morning about my next commission."

"He doesn't want me to fly to the UK with Silver Lake next month. I've told him I'm going, unless I'm declared medically unfit to travel," she explained, running her hands through her spiky black hair. "He's also hiring a UK based tour manager."

"He was talking about that weeks ago," Lori pointed out. "And you know that it makes sense all round. Relax, girl. Anyway, I didn't come here to talk shop!"

The pale Goth laughed as she came over to sit beside her on the couch, "You're right as always, honey."

"So, what has the doctor said?" asked Lori, her concern obvious in her voice.

"They did an ultrasound and everything's fine. From that they worked out I'm just over ten weeks pregnant. I've to take the anti-sickness meds for another ten days and see if I'm ok without them after that. Apart from that, I've to eat sensibly and get plenty of rest," explained Maddy, her hand subconsciously rubbing her tummy.

"Did they say what caused you to be quite so sick?"

"Hormones," she replied, then a smile crept across her face. "If I tell you something you can't tell a soul. Not even Jake."

"What?"

"The scan showed its twins," giggled Maddy.

"Twins!" squealed Lori, hugging her. "Oh my God, Maddy!"

"I know. I found out on Friday and I've been dying to tell you, but Paul said no. I don't want it to be public knowledge until after the tour at least."

Shaking her head, Lori sat and smiled at her friend in stunned disbelief. Maddy was the last person in her circle of friends that she could imagine as a "mommy" but, seeing her sitting there so thrilled at the prospect of having twins, just blew her away.

"Changed days, Maddison," she replied eventually. "What happened to the party animals we were?"

"You had your accident, introduced me to a rock band, I fell for the drummer and got pregnant," stated Maddy with a giggle. "That about sums up the last ten months in one sentence."

"Ten months," mused Lori. "Amazing how quickly life changes."

"For the better I hope."

"In some respects," agreed Lori, subconsciously running her hand down her thigh.

"Oh shit, I'm sorry…." stumbled Maddy. "Me and my big mouth."

"If I hadn't had my accident, I wouldn't have moved down here and I wouldn't have met Jake and you wouldn't have met Paul. Things, even the bad bits, happen for a reason."

"I guess," agreed Maddy, then spotting the edges of the butterfly on Lori's wrist said, "Do you have something to tell me about, girl?"

"New York?"

"Your wrist!" corrected Maddy sharply.

Pulling back her sleeve, Lori showed her butterfly tattoo to her friend, who nodded approvingly.

"Stunning piece of work," complimented Maddy. "I never thought you'd get any ink done."

"Things change as you just said yourself."

"*Touché*"

After they had been chatting for over an hour, Lori could sense her friend was starting to tire. They had talked about the weekend in New York and eventually returned to talking about work and the tour. When Maddy asked if she was coming with them, she gave her the same answer she had given Jake and Jason. Maddy promised to mail her the full itinerary as soon as it was finalised. As her friend tried to stifle a yawn, Lori said she would need to go. Having arranged to meet up later in the week, Lori left to drive home.

Rain was still pelting down as she left the hotel soaking her through by the time she reached the Mercedes. Originally, she had planned to go to the food store on the way back to buy something for dinner but the torrential rain changed her mind. Instead, she headed straight home, deciding to order in some food later for dinner instead. Jake's truck was in the driveway when she pulled up and, as she walked into the house, she could hear him warming up in the basement. She knew that his new vocal warm up routine had helped to strengthen his voice and was really helping him, but there was no denying that it wasn't pleasant to listen to. Cringing at the almost operatic scales echoing up from the basement, she went through to the sun room and switched on the TV to one of the many rock music stations. Much to her amazement, the song that was playing was Silver Lake's Dragon Song. The video looked to have been filmed out west as it was live concert footage. Seeing Jake on the screen made her smile.

"Jake!" she yelled. "Come up here!"

Thinking something was amiss, he came bounding up the steps from the basement into the sun room then stopped dead in his tracks.

"It's us!" he said, gazing wide eyed at the screen. "That's Seattle."

"You sure?" asked Lori, moving over to stand with her arm around his waist.

"Positive. That's the shirt I had on for that show."

Together they stood and watched the rest of the video. Beside her, she could feel Jake tense up as he watched himself on the screen. When the video was finished, he wrapped his arms around her and held her tight.

"That's the first time I've seen myself on TV," he said, burying his face in her rain damp hair. "That was kind of weird."

"You looked great on screen."

"You're biased," he muttered. "I wonder if the others have seen it."

"Ask Maddy to get a copy of the video for you. Maybe there's more footage from the show," suggested Lori.

"I'll ask Paul when he gets here," said Jake, kissing her on the top of her head. "I'd better get back downstairs to finish my warm up before they get here. How was Maddy?"

"Fine. Still tired," replied Lori. "But she's back working as usual. She was on the phone to Jason when I arrived."

"Glad she's ok. Maybe Paul will start focussing a bit better now. He's been all over the place for the last couple of weeks."

"I wouldn't bet on it," laughed Lori, remembering how harassed the drummer had been as he had left the hotel.

Grey was the first to arrive for the rehearsal, early as was his usual style, and with Becky in tow. He apologised for having to bring her along but Lori quickly shushed him, saying she would be delighted to entertain her for a few hours. He was soon joined by Rich and, a little late, Paul, who was greeted with calls of "Twenty dollars in the pot!" While the band rehearsed, Lori and Becky went down to the bedroom where, at the little girl's request, Lori painted Becky's nails. She allowed the little girl to choose whatever colour she wanted and was soon painting the tiny fingernails hot fuchsia pink. After some encouragement from Becky, Lori painted her own to match. While their nails were drying, they curled up together in the sun room to watch TV. Despite the soundproofing, the vibration from the rehearsal could be felt through the house. Occasionally, Lori could make out exactly what they were playing or could hear Jake's vocals. Filling the house with music and friends made the place feel more like a home - made her smile. After the band had been rehearsing for about an hour and a half, Lori left Becky watching TV and carefully went down the steep steps into the basement. Her timing was perfect, as they had stopped to debate a change to the proposed set list for the tour.

"I was going to run into town for some food," called Lori from the bottom step. "Who wants what?"

"Pizza," joked Paul, winking at Jake, who groaned theatrically.

"Anything but fish," said Grey, as he tweaked the tuning on his bass. "Actually pizza's not a bad call."

"Fine by me," agreed Rich. "Jake?"

All eyes were on him when Grey played the emotional trump card, "Becky loves pizza."

"Ok. Ok," he yelled, with a defeated look in his eyes. "I guess I can eat pizza just this once."

His fellow band members gave him a round of applause.

Laughing, Lori declared, "Pizza it is. I'll take Becky with me. We'll be about a half hour."

True to her word, she was back at the beach house thirty minutes later with three large pizzas and three portions of cheese fries. As she set the boxes down on the dining room table, Lori called out as loud as she could to be heard over the rehearsal, "Food's here!"

Within minutes they were all seated round the dining room table enjoying slices of pizza. The band's debate around their set list continued throughout the meal. As the discussion wore on, Becky climbed up onto Jake's knee, snuggled into his chest, thumb in her mouth, and promptly fell asleep. After a while, Lori got up to clear away the empty boxes and asked if anyone needed a drink.

"I'd better get Becky home," said Grey, getting to his feet. "I'm easy about the changes. Just let me know what I've to play."

"Same here," added Paul, checking the time. "I'd better get back to the boss. I'll call you guys tomorrow."

After the bass player and drummer had left, Rich and Jake continued the debate while Lori cleared everything away. With the boxes out for recycling, she returned to the table with three beers.

"Are you guys open to a suggestion?" she asked, taking a seat between the two musicians.

"Go for it, Lori," said Rich, opening his beer.

"Have two sets. Rotate them. No huge differences, but just a bit of variety. Gauge what the fans respond well to."

"Fair idea, li'l lady," nodded Jake, looking over at Rich. "I'm liking it. That way we can please all of us."

"Works for me," agreed Rich, feeling a little sheepish that they hadn't thought of that option themselves.

The three of them sat on at the dining room table compiling the two lists, trying to balance out the harder songs with the acoustic numbers that seemed popular with the audiences. Each version started and ended the same, so it was only the middle twenty minutes that they were flexing about. When they had finally agreed on the two versions, Jake fetched his laptop and emailed the proposed lists to Grey and Paul.

"I'd better head home," said Rich, once the email was sent. "Thanks for dinner, Lori."

"Pleasure as always," she replied with a smile.

As they listened to Rich's car roar out of the driveway, Jake took the empty beer bottles through to the kitchen, then both he and Lori headed off to bed. Lying wrapped in each other's arms in the darkness, Jake said, "I'm looking forward to this trip. It's all starting to come together. Three more weeks of school, two of rehearsal time, then we fly out to Dublin."

"Dublin?" questioned Lori. "Is that not Ireland?"

"Yes," he replied. "We got word that two dates in Dublin have been tagged onto the start. We fly out on November 19th."

"That's not so far off really, is it?"

"Scarily close," he said, hugging her tight. "And the first London show's on my birthday."

"Maybe they'll sing Happy Birthday to you on stage."

"Now that would be quite something, li'l lady."

Plans and preparations for the tour filled the hours for all of them throughout the remainder of October and the first two weeks of November. As the days wore on, Maddy felt better and threw herself into the organisation. With her usual professional efficiency, she arranged everything from the purchase of additional equipment right down to their stage clothes. There were various aspects to the plans that the band themselves would never have thought of. It was a steep learning curve for them all. Eventually though all the plans were in place, the rehearsals complete and departure only a day away.

While Maddy had been busy organising the band, Lori had linked in with her regarding her own travel arrangements. She had confirmed to Jake that she was only coming to the two London shows at the end of the tour but, with Maddy's discrete help, she arranged to travel a couple of days earlier and surprise him in Glasgow. With all her own plans confirmed, Lori returned her focus to her own work commitments. Taking almost two weeks out of her schedule at the start of December made her deadlines tight but she was confident of bringing everything in on time, ahead of time if she could.

The night before Silver Lake were due to leave, they agreed to meet for dinner. A table had been booked at the local steakhouse and they were expected there at seven. As she sat at the dressing table fixing her hair, Lori tried not to think about having to say goodbye to Jake next day.

"Penny for your thoughts, li'l lady?" he whispered behind her. He was already dressed for dinner and had come through to check if she was ready to leave.

"I was thinking about tomorrow and how I hate saying goodbye," she replied, putting the final pin in place.

"I've been trying not to think about that bit," he confessed. "But in two weeks' time you'll be there for my birthday."

"That's true," she conceded with a wistful look. "Ok, I'm ready."

"You look stunning as ever," complimented Jake, admiring the long dark forest green dress she was wearing.

"Thanks. You don't look so bad yourself, rock star."

They were the last of the party to arrive at the restaurant and, as they made their way to the table, Grey called out, "Forty dollars in the pot. You're both late!"

"Sorry, folks," apologised Jake. "We couldn't get parked."

"Excuses. Excuses," muttered Grey with a grin. "Forty bucks, Mr Power."

Maddy got up from her seat at the table and came over to hug them both. She was wearing a short black dress and her trademark spike heels, but, as she hugged Lori, her friend could clearly see the outline of her growing baby bump.

"You're not going to hide that for long," whispered Lori as they embraced.

"Don't I know it," said Maddy, smoothing her dress down.

Once they were all seated and the waitress had brought their drinks order, Rich proposed a toast, "Here's to the first overseas Silver Lake tour!"

"The first of many!" added Jake clinking glasses with his fellow guitarist.

"And short flights," joked Paul, causing a ripple of laughter round the table.

Reaching out to put a calming hand on Paul's wrist, Maddy said, "It's only three flights, honey. Most of the travel's by bus."

"Praise the Lord," sighed the drummer.

The easy, relaxed banter continued as, in turn, they all voiced their hopes and fears for the coming weeks. When dessert was served, Rich asked Lori when she was joining them.

"London on December 3rd," she replied, not daring to glance at Maddy.

"And we can't convince you to fly over any sooner?" asked Grey, with a twinkle in his eyes.

"No, you can't," she stated before adding. "This will be my first overseas trip since my accident. Lord knows how many alarms I'll set off at security!"

"I hadn't thought of that!" sniggered Maddy, remembering the metalwork hidden in her friend's thigh.

"You'll be fine," reassured Jake, putting his arm around her shoulders, realising she was nervous about the trip.

All too soon dinner was over, the bill was paid and they were all standing outside the restaurant ready to go their separate ways. Business–like as ever, Maddy reminded them all of their pick up times and warned them not to keep the driver waiting. As they said their goodbyes to Lori, there were lots of hugs and kisses and promises to text or call. Lori said goodbye to Maddy last. She hugged her a little longer and a little tighter than the others.

"Be careful, Maddy," she said quietly. "These guys can look after themselves. You need to look after you this time. No risks."

"I know," promised Maddy. "I'll be sensible. I promise. The boys will take care of me."

"They better or they will have me to answer to," joked Lori. "I'll see you in a couple of weeks."

Slowly Jake and Lori walked back to the car in silence, hand in hand. Jake was just pulling out of their parking space when Lori finally spoke, "Look after Maddy for me, Jake. Don't let her push herself too hard."

"I'll try," he said warmly. "That's the first time I've seen her looking pregnant."

"Her bump's really starting to show," agreed Lori.

"Do you think we'll have kids?" asked Jake sounding serious.

"I hadn't given it any thought," replied Lori, caught off guard by the question. "I'm not sure this battered body of mine would cope."

"Don't panic. I just wondered that's all."

"If it's meant to be, it will be."

In bed a couple of hours later, their lovemaking was tender and gentle, both of them keen to ensure it was perfect. When Jake entered her, he moved slowly, teasing her to orgasm before allowing himself to come. Still inside her, he held her and whispered how much he loved her and how much he was going to miss her. Sensually she kissed him, reassuring him it would be no time at all until they were back together to celebrate his birthday. Wrapped in each other's arms, they drifted off to sleep.

Rain was lashing down and a cold wind was howling when Silver Lake stumbled out of the taxis outside their Dublin hotel. The night flight from Philadelphia had been uneventful, but none of them, apart from Maddy, got any sleep. Now, as they gathered their bags together, they were all sluggish with jet lag. The taxi driver said something to Jake in his fast lilting Irish accent, but the musician had no idea what.

"Beg your pardon?"

"Are you the group who will be playing at the Olympia tomorrow night?" he repeated slowly.

"Yes," replied Jake with a yawn.

"I've got tickets for the show. I'm taking my boy along."

"It should be a good night," said Jake, forcing a smile. "I'll watch out for you."

Once they were checked into the hotel and had found their rooms, Maddy suggested getting some rest for a few hours. There were interviews set up for three o'clock that afternoon in the hotel bar and she warned them all to be awake and on time. Jake's room was on the third floor, between Rich and Grey and across the hall from Paul and Maddy's room. He locked the door behind him, abandoned his bags in the middle of the floor and collapsed onto the king size bed. The next thing he knew, the phone beside the bed was ringing loudly. Still half asleep, he lifted the receiver, "Yes?"

"Jake, wakey, wakey," called out Maddy brightly. "You've got an hour to get cleaned up and down to the bar. And you missed lunch."

"What time is it?" he muttered, as he tried to focus his eyes.

"It's just gone two," stated the manager sharply. "Now get your ass in gear. I'll see you downstairs."

A lukewarm shower went some way to waking him up. With the towel wrapped round his waist and his hair dripping, Jake investigated the room's coffee maker and made himself a strong cup of coffee. He rummaged through his suitcase for a change of clothes and drank the coffee as he dressed. A thundery migraine was beginning to pound at his temples and he knew it was triggered by a lack of sleep and food. He paused to send a quick text message to Lori to say they'd arrived, then left the room in search of the bar and his fellow band members. With a little help from reception, he found the bar and was soon seated at a table with the rest of the band. In her usual efficient manner, Maddy had ordered soup and sandwiches for those who missed lunch and coffees for everyone. While Jake and Grey, who had also slept late, ate their meal, their manager went off to meet the three journalists that they were scheduled to meet. As she re-entered the room, Maddy's harsh New York accent rang out loudly.

"Guys, this is Brendan, Mike and Rob," she introduced. "Plus Luke who's here to take a few photos."

Silver Lake managed a half-hearted greeting as the journalists pulled over extra chairs to join them. Maddy remained standing and, once the others looked settled, declared she had a few calls to make and would be back in an hour.

"So what do you all think of Dublin?" asked one of the journalists as an ice breaker.

"To be honest, it is kind of early to say," began Rich. "We only flew in this morning and most of us have been asleep since. The drive in from the airport was nice."

"Is this your first overseas tour?"

Jake nodded and added, "For all of us it's our first trip to Europe too. We're really excited to get the opportunity to play for you guys."

"Now, Jake, you sang on the recent Weigh Station album. How did that come about?"

"We met them briefly when we were recording our own album. I guess they liked what they heard. I was invited to guest on one of the new songs on their deluxe edition of their record. When I got to the studio in New York, there had been a change to the plan and I was asked to appear on three. I only sang on two of them."

"Do you think they'll invite you out on stage with them?"

"Maybe. We'll see how the tour goes," replied Jake, deliberately keeping his response vague.

For the next forty five minutes, the three reporters fired a broad range of questions at them, ranging from trivial things like their favourite foods and music to the more technical details of their music and choice of equipment. They were asked about the three stadium shows they had done with Molton and about the various smaller festivals they had played in the past.

"Is it true one of you got shot on stage last summer?"

"Jake was," answered Grey, sipping a fresh cup of coffee.

"Can you tell us what happened?"

"We were playing an open air show near home and a few songs into the set I felt a sharp sting at my knee and I staggered back a bit. I didn't realise at first what had happened and kept playing," began Jake. "Blood started to soak through my jeans and was running into my boot. I went to the side of the stage to get help while these guys kept playing. I taped my leg up and managed another three songs before we wrapped it up."

"You played on?"

"Yeah," admitted Jake, with a sheepish grin. "The fans had paid good money to hear us. I didn't want to let them down. I had to try to carry on for them."

"And there was no permanent damage done?"

"Just a two inch scar on my knee," he confessed. "But it does make you think about how vulnerable you can be out on that stage. Going out the next time, just a couple of weeks later, was tough."

"But you're over that now?"

Jake nodded, "Playing live is what we all live to do. Can't let it scare me. Life's too short."

Out of the corner of his eye, he saw Maddy returning. The three journalists spotted her as well.

"Final question," began one of them. "What can the fans here and in the UK expect from Silver Lake?"

"A damn good time," laughed Rich. "We've put together a strong set and we just hope you enjoy it as much as we do."

"Thanks for your time, guys."

"Can we just get a few more photos?" asked Luke, the photographer. "Just the band on their own."

Maddy allowed them a few more minutes, then stepped in and wrapped things up. As she watched the four members of the media depart, she asked how it had gone.

"Fine," said Rich, with a yawn. "Nice guys. Honest questions."

"Good. Now, you're free until dinner at seven. Weigh Station have just arrived so we'll probably see them at dinner. I spoke to their manager and they're going to eat here tonight too," explained Maddy, then almost as an afterthought added, "Oh, Jake, there's a radio interview tomorrow morning that you've to go to with Dan."

"Ok," agreed Jake. "I don't want to end up being the mouthpiece of Silver Lake though."

"Don't worry," reassured Maddy. "These guys have another media slot in the morning too. You'll all get your fair share of the limelight."

"Well, if we've a couple of hours to spare, I'm going for a walk," said Grey standing up and stretching. "I need to stretch my legs and get some air."

"I'll come with you," offered Jake, thinking that some fresh air would clear away his headache once and for all. "Give me five minutes to grab a jacket."

"Don't be late for dinner, boys," warned Maddy, as she headed out to the foyer with Paul.

"Rich, what about you?" asked Jake. "Fancy a walk?"

"Not just now. I'm going back upstairs for a while. Think I'll watch a movie. See you at dinner. Don't get lost out there."

The rain had eased up when Grey and Jake stepped out of the hotel, but a cold wind was still whistling down the street. Neither of them knew where to go. Grey had picked up a tourist leaflet from a stand in the hotel's reception area and suggested they set off in search of the venue, the Olympia Theatre. It only took them a few minutes to find the theatre, striking looking with its red and cream olde worlde façade.

"Not quite the stadium in Seattle," commented Grey, taking a photo of the building with his phone.

"It's kind of neat," said Jake, with a grin. "Fits with the charm of this place."

"As long as the crowd has plenty of charm," said Grey, putting his phone away. "Feels strange being so far from home."

"It'll be fine," replied Jake, glancing round the immediate area to see what else they could visit. Spotting a couple of pubs nearby, he suggested, "Let's try the local poison."

"What?"

"Is Ireland not famous for Guinness?"

"So I read in the magazine on the plane," answered Grey then pointing to a bar across the street added, "Let's try that place. One won't do any harm, will it?"

"Only one way to find out!"

One pint turned into two before the two friends headed back to the hotel. They arrived in time to meet Weigh Station in the foyer. The headliners were posing for photos after an interview and called on Grey and Jake to join them. A handful of fans were also hanging about hoping for photo opportunities. The two members of Silver Lake happily signed a few autographs and posed for a few photos.

"Jake!" yelled Dan. "Get your ass over here."

"What's up?" asked Jake, as he strode across towards his idol.

"Jake, meet Dermott our host for the next two nights," introduced the Weigh Station front man. "He's the promoter for the shows here in Dublin."

"Pleased to meet you, sir," said Jake, shaking the small red haired man's hand.

"Pleasure's all mine," he replied with a softer Irish accent than they'd heard all day. "If you need anything while you're here, let me know. Anything at all."

"Thanks," nodded Jake. "Now if you'll excuse me. I need to freshen up before dinner."

While Weigh Station were still meeting and greeting the group of fans, Jake and Grey slipped off towards the elevator almost unnoticed. As Jake swiped the key card in his door, he heard Maddy call out behind him. Turning round she thrust her phone into his hand and said, "Lori's on the other end."

"Hi, li'l lady," he called brightly. "I was just going to call you."

"Beat you to it. I called Maddy to check she was ok after the flight."

"She's just fine," reassured Jake, winking at the band's manager. "She's taken it easy all day. We all have. That flight was a killer. No sleep."

Lori laughed, then asked what the plan was for the rest of the day.

"It's almost time for dinner, then I'm having an early night. I'm dying here. Migraine and jet lag," admitted Jake. "Tomorrow's going to be a full day. The venue looks amazing from the outside. Really old fashioned. Can't wait to see inside it."

"I'd better not keep you late for dinner. Let me know how the show goes tomorrow. I'll be thinking about you all."

"Wish you were here, Lori," he whispered softly. "Seems a long time till you fly over."

"You've only been gone one night," she giggled. "I'll talk to you tomorrow. Call after the show. Love you, rock star."

"Love you too, Mz Hyde."

Ending the call, he passed the handset back to Maddy.

"You'll see her soon," said Maddy quietly. "Now, are you ready for dinner?"

"Almost," replied Jake. "Let me drop off my jacket and freshen up. I'll be five minutes."

"Knock our door when you're ready. We can all go down together."

Dinner proved to be a rowdy affair as the restaurant manager had seated both bands and their entourage in the one section of the dining room. The Weigh Station party also included several invited guests plus four lucky fans, the winners of a radio competition. Under the ever watchful eye of their manager, the boys from Silver Lake were on their best behaviour and politely declined several offers of more beer or wine as the meal progressed. Weigh Station had invited along a filmmaker to document the tour for a proposed DVD release. Shortly after ten thirty, Jake excused himself apologising that jet lag had caught up with him and that he was headed to bed. He walked out of the restaurant to a few pleas from the party behind him to stay. The camera man followed him and asked if he could spare a few minutes. With a yawn, Jake agreed and stood outside the elevator while the filmmaker set up his camera.

"Jake, tomorrow's the first of Silver Lake's shows with Weigh Station. How are you feeling right now about it?"

"Right now I just want to sleep. Grey and I walked down town to take a look at the venue before dinner. It hit me then just how big a deal this is for us. The US audiences, especially on the east coast, know us, but this is unknown territory. It's a whole new crowd to convert into Silver Lake fans," replied Jake. "I just hope they like what they hear and tell their friends."

"What's your initial impression of Dublin?"

"Cold, wet and windy," Jake joked. "The people seem friendly. Can't understand a damn thing they're saying though!"

"Thanks, mate," said the filmmaker, shaking Jake's hand. "Appreciate that. I'm Scott by the way."

"Pleasure," replied Jake with another yawn. "Now I really need to get some sleep."

"Can I ask one more favour?"

"You can ask," said Jake, pressing the button to call the lift.

"Can I interview you guys backstage tomorrow before and after the show?"

"Fine by me, but clear it with Maddison," he agreed. "If it's ok with her, we'll talk to you anytime."

"Thanks. I will."

"Night, Scott," said Jake, stepping into the open elevator. As the doors closed, he thought the young film maker looked like one of the students he had left behind at school. So young, keen and eager to please.

After a sound sleep and a morning of interviews and more photos with Dan Crow from Weigh Station, Jake finally arrived at the theatre for the sound check. The road crews had worked hard setting up the stage. While Weigh Station completed their sound check, Silver Lake warmed up backstage. The theatre was as quaint inside as out and the backstage area was a rabbit warren of small dressing rooms. Wherever they went there seemed to be people scurrying about with cables or coffees or lists. The management company had put a new British stage crew in place for Silver Lake so they spent a fair amount of time explaining how they wanted to be set up for the gig. When they finally got out on stage, they were mesmerised by the beauty of the small auditorium. At capacity the theatre held just less than two thousand, but it was incredibly ornate. There were two balcony levels plus small private boxes to either side of the stall area. The carving between levels and the ornate ceiling with Victorian plaster cornicing made them all feel as though they were performing inside a birthday cake. There were a few minor glitches during sound check but no major debacles and the four of them returned to the dressing room quite calm about things. As usual Maddy was buzzing about checking and double checking everything. She had authorised Scott to film whenever the band were happy to be filmed so he too was wandering amongst proceedings, camera in hand. As Jake was getting changed for the show, there was a knock at the door.

"Have you got five minutes?" asked Scott hopefully.

Jake was stripped to the waist, but had luckily just fastened his favourite black ripped jeans.

"Two minutes," he agreed, reaching for his black shirt.

"That's some art work!" said Scott. "Want to talk me through those?"

"Some other time," said Jake. "It's a long story."

"Do you ever go out on stage with your shirt off?"

"What kind of video are you shooting here?" teased Jake, causing the younger man to flush red with embarrassment. "No, seriously, I've taken my shirt off a few times at summer outdoor gigs but never indoors."

"I'm sure your female fans would love a closer look at that tattooed body," commented Scott, with a wink.

"I'm sure they would but not tonight," stated Jake, putting his shirt on. "There will be no messing about tonight. Strictly business out there. Need to create a good impression."

"What's your pre-show routine?"

"Pretty much what you've seen," answered Jake warmly. "Sound check. Something light to eat, warm up, get changed, then more or less get on with it."

"And after?"

"Wait and see," said Jake, checking the time. "Need to make a move."

With Scott still in tow, Jake went back to join the rest of the band. They were gathered in the one dressing room. All of them were twitchy and restless, anxious to be out on stage. When Maddy saw the film maker in their midst, she chased him out, promising that he could come back later. She shook her head as he left the dressing room looking dejected. With one eye on the clock, the band waited to be called through to the side of the stage. Five minutes before show time, Maddy led them all out of the dressing room.

From the side of the stage, they could hear the buzz of the capacity crowd. The house lights dimmed and the crowd roared and cheered. Show time! Once out on stage, all nerves vanished as

Silver Lake launched straight into Dragon Song followed by two of the heavier tracks from the album. The audience were quickly on side and were singing along enthusiastically.

"Hello, Dublin!" yelled Jake, as he gazed out at the sea of faces before him. The crowd cheered. "I can't hear you! You still with us, Dublin?"

A roar came straight back at him.

"This is a special show for us so thank you for coming out tonight. This is our first show outside of the United States."

A huge roar erupted from the crowd.

"Now we are going to slow it down for a minute or two," continued Jake, accepting his acoustic guitar and settling himself on the stool that had magically appeared. "This is Stronger Within. Sing along if you know this one."

The gentle first few chords of the song drifted out across the hall. When Jake began to sing, the crowd sang along with him. It totally amazed him that the Irish crowd were so familiar with his lyrics. When the song ended, he started to play Lady Butterfly straight away, not trusting himself to speak to the audience for fear of his emotions catching in his voice. As the final notes of Lady Butterfly soared high over the audience they cheered wildly.

"Thank you," called Jake, smiling. "You guys are amazing. Totally blown away by you."

Behind him, the band began to play the ACDC rock classic, Highway To Hell. In between the next two numbers Jake whispered to Rich and Grey about an impromptu set change. They agreed and Grey stepped back to alert Paul to the change of plan.

"Ok, guys!" called out Jake, sounding a little out of breath. "We're going to try something just for you. Something totally unrehearsed."

Out of the corner of his eye, he saw Maddy at the side of the stage frowning at him. He winked at her then turned back to the audience, "This could crash and burn, but we're going to try one we hope you all know. Sing along and help us out if you know it. This is Whiskey In The Jar."

The crowd went wild. Their enthusiasm for the popular rock song helped to carry Silver Lake through it virtually error free. All too soon they were starting their final number – their favourite finale song, Flyin' High. The set had been the quickest forty five minutes of their career and as the last notes faded away, Jake called out one final time to the audience, "Thank you! You've been awesome. Till next time. Stay safe."

All of them were trying to talk at once as the post show adrenaline surged through them. Trying to keep them under control, Maddy ushered them back to the dressing rooms and clear of the immediate backstage area. Once they were safely back in the dressing room, she hugged each of them in turn.

"Jake, that set change was inspired!" she squealed, hugging him tight, her baby bump hard against him.

"Thanks. It felt like the right thing to play once we were out there."

"I'm just glad we made it through it," stated Grey, grabbing a bottle of water. "It's been a LONG time since we last played that one."

"More than two years," added Rich. "Was a great shout though, Jake."

"So are we keeping it in for tomorrow night?" asked Jake with a cheeky grin.

"Hell, yeah!" cried Grey. "They loved it!"

Nodding Maddy declared, "You've made fans for life out there tonight."

Once he'd got showered and changed, Jake said he was going back to get a glimpse of Weigh Station. Before Maddy could stop him, he had slipped out of the room and back towards the stage. Standing at the side of the stage, watching his heroes, Jake transformed into "Jake the fan" instead of "Jake the rock star" who had commanded the same stage an hour before. As he stood discretely out of the way, Weigh Station's manager spotted him and came over to congratulate him on their set. Having mumbled a humble reply Jake was then asked about performing two numbers with Weigh Station the next night. It was the dream ending to a perfect night and, as he watched Dan strut his stuff in front of his adoring fans, he wished Lori was there to share the moment with him.

Twenty four hours later, Jake was standing on the same spot, waiting for his cue to step out on stage. He had run through the two songs earlier on at the sound check and was anxious that he would forget the words or fluff the guitar part. Silver Lake's set had been another amazing experience, possibly even better than the night before. Now the adrenaline rush was wearing off and nerves were creeping back in.

"Dublin!" screamed Dan into the mic. "I'd like you to welcome a good friend of ours out on stage now to sing with me."

The crowd roared expectantly.

"Give a huge welcome to Mr Jake Power from Silver Lake!"

The crowd went wild as Jake loped out on stage, plugging his guitar in as he went. A roadie brought out a second mic stand already set up for him.

"Ok Dublin, this is one of our new tracks. This is Broken Bottle Empty Glass."

Taking a deep breath, Jake listened for his cue to come in on guitar, then stepped up to the mic and began to sing the hoarse throaty lyrics. It was a different style to his Silver Lake vocals, but one that was fun to perform. As he reached the chorus, Dan and the entire audience joined in. During the mid-song guitar break, he stepped back towards the drum riser to allow Weigh Station's lead guitarist, Mikey, to take centre stage. Dan stepped back with him and reached over to whisper, "Awesome job. You lead on the next one."

Jake only had time to nod before the solo ended and he was back out at the mic for the final verse and chorus.

"Folks, I've asked Mr Power here to sing it out for you on Sunset After The Storm. Let's hear it for Jake Power!"

The intro to the song was soft and haunting, with the vocal almost whispered, before it exploded into a frenzy of fast paced lyrics. The guitar part was easy after the complexity of the vocal. Making a show of letting Jake hold court on the Weigh Station stage, Dan sat on the edge of the drum riser, allowing the younger man the freedom of centre stage. As the song drew to a close, Dan came forward.

"Give it up for Jake Power!"

With a theatrical bow to the crowd, Jake walked off stage feeling on an all-time high. All his Christmas's had come at once. In the wings, the rest of Silver Lake had gathered to watch and all rushed round him, congratulating him on an amazing performance. Weigh Station's manager clapped him on the back and declared him to be sensational. As the headline act continued their set, Jake tried to make his way back to the dressing room. He had one mission on his mind – to phone Lori. Eventually he reached the door and, after politely excusing himself and promising to be back shortly, Jake found himself alone in the tiny room. His bag was hanging on the back of a chair and he reached into it to retrieve his phone.

It only rang twice before Lori picked up.

"Hi," she said softly. "I was just thinking about you."

"Hi yourself, li'l lady," he replied, suddenly lost for words.

"What time is it over there?"

"No idea. Around ten thirty I think," began Jake. "Tonight's been incredible!"

"Did you duet with Dan?"

"Just off stage," he laughed, still buzzing from the experience. "I hope someone's videoed it so you get to see it. I can't describe how amazing it felt! I've played on stage with my heroes!"

Laughing with him, Lori said, "And I'm sure it won't be for the last time."

"I hope not," said Jake. "I hope this happens every night. The crowd loved it."

There was someone knocking at the dressing room door yelling his name.

"Lord, I wish you were here, Lori," he breathed softly.

"Soon, rock star," she promised. "I'll catch up with you in just over a week. It's not so long."

"Feels like forever right now."

"So where are you off to next?" asked Lori.

"We fly to Wales tomorrow, then play in Cardiff the following night. No idea what to expect there."

"More of the same, I'd guess," she replied.

"I'd better run, li'l lady. Someone's beating on this door. I'll talk to you tomorrow."

"Looking forward to it already."

"Love you."

"Love you too, rock star."

Ending the call and slipping the phone into his pocket, Jake opened the door to find Paul standing there with a beer for him.

"The boss wants us to be ready to leave in five minutes," he said, handing the bottle to Jake.

Accepting it, he replied, "Ready whenever she is."

"She wants to be clear of here before Weigh Station leave. They just came off stage," explained Paul then added, "I think she really just wants to get to bed."

"OK. Let me gather up my gear," said Jake, taking a quick swig from the bottle. "I'll be out in two minutes."

A small crowd had gathered round the stage door and when Silver Lake stepped out to head towards the minibus that was waiting to take them back to the hotel, they were quickly surrounded by fans. As the venue's security personnel tried to clear a path for them, the four members of the band obligingly signed autographs and posed for numerous photos. Every fan they spoke to was so grateful for their few moments of the band's attention. The warmth and affection stunned them all and, as they finally made their way onto the minibus, it was the sole topic of conversation.

"Get used to it, boys," said Maddy as the minibus drew up outside the hotel. "Looks like there's a few more folk here. Try not to get too caught up. The hotel has a late dinner waiting for us."

"Yes, boss," joked Jake, with a salute.

He was the first to step out onto the pavement and was immediately surrounded by four young female fans. Smiling, he signed autographs, posed for more photos then politely bade them goodnight. Another two fans were waiting right by the door, but they seemed satisfied with a wave and a "hello". At last Silver Lake were safely back inside and heading for the dining room. The hotel staff had excelled themselves and laid on a buffet style supper that catered to all tastes and preferences. It was after one o'clock before they finished their meal. The long day had taken its toll on Maddy and she was the first to leave the table, saying she was heading off to bed.

"Guys, we have a late check out tomorrow. The bus is picking us up at five to go to the airport. You've nothing lined up for tomorrow. Just make sure you are all back here and packed up for four," she instructed with a yawn. "I'm going to sleep until then. This being a baby carrying manager is tough going."

"Night, Maddy," they all called after her.

Paul walked out to the elevator with her then came back to join the others for a night cap. The four of them sat chatting for a while, then Jake said quietly, "We've done it, guys, haven't we?"

"Done what?" asked Paul, looking confused.

"Crossed that line," said Jake. "No more bar gigs. No more make-ends-meet jobs. This is it."

"He's right," agreed Grey, the realisation hitting him. "Silver Lake are on the international rock road map."

"Here's to it being a hell of a long road!" declared Rich, raising his glass.

The next eight days cemented the feeling that they had finally broken through to the next level. As the tour wound its way through Cardiff in Wales, onto Birmingham, Manchester and Newcastle in England, the band continued to attract fans in every city. Their confidence on stage grew and as they crossed the border into Scotland *en route* to Glasgow all of them believed that this was as good as it got. Adjusting to the late nights, hours of travelling, interviews, sound checks, more interviews and finally their performance had been easy; second nature to them all. When they had arrived in Cardiff, they had been introduced a new member of the team – Gary York, their British tour manager. Almost instantly they had gelled with him and welcomed him into the Silver Lake "family". Gary's arrival made life easier for Maddy as it left her free to focus on the band's wellbeing while he dealt with the venues, travel and basically anything she delegated to him.

At each of the shows Jake had been invited out to perform with Weigh Station. It still had not truly hit home that he was performing as a musical equal alongside his teenage heroes. They were playing in Newcastle before the Weigh Station manager shared a confession with him. As he had been waiting for his cue to go on, the burly Scotsman had passed comment to Jake about saving Dan's skin. When Jake asked how he had done that he was shocked to hear, "Dan can't sing Sunshine After The Storm live." His idol's weakness had given him those extra five minutes of fame every night but it also made him stop to think about how fragile fame could be.

Back at the beach house, Lori had been busy finishing off her two commissions and packing for her overseas trip. The house had seemed quiet and empty without Jake and the rest of the band about. She had kept her phone by her side day and night waiting for the all too brief calls and short text messages. The five hour time difference made it harder for them to find a good time to talk. Even when they had snatched a few minutes, Lori was careful not to let slip her travel plans, in case Jake figured out she was travelling earlier than he suspected. Once she had completed her commissions, she had emailed Maddy to finalise the travel details. A few hours later she got a detailed email back confirming that she would be collected at the airport, taken to the same hotel as the band were booked into but would be given a room on a separate floor. Once the band were safely at the concert hall, a driver would be sent to fetch her and they would smuggle her into the venue in time for the sound check. On paper it all looked easy and Lori was just hoping that luck would be on her side and the surprise would work.

The day before she was due to leave, Lori was busy packing when her phone rang. It wasn't one of her contacts, but the number looked vaguely familiar.

"Lori Hyde," she answered brightly.

"Hi, Lori. It's Lucy," replied the familiar voice of Jake's young sister.

"Lucy! Hi. How are you?"

"Busy. Busy," laughed Lucy. "School. Boys. House. You know how it is."

"Stops you from getting bored," said Lori. "It's quiet here with your brother away."

"I can imagine. No singing or guitar solos in the small hours," she giggled nervously. "That's kind of why I'm calling. I need to ask a huge favour."

"Sure. What can I do?" asked Lori, curious to know what Lucy was about to ask of her.

"Simon called me the other night. He's going to be in the UK on a visit to an air force base and said he was going to spend a few days in London. I mentioned that the band were going to be playing there. Long story cut short. I've talked him into trying to catch up with Jake. Can you help me to arrange it?"

"Yes," said Lori instantly. "I'll need to sort out a pass for the show with Maddy but I'm sure we can do something. I'm flying out to meet them so I'll be there too. Give me his number so I can get in touch with him while I'm over there."

"I've already given him your number and your email address. I hope that's ok, Lori," confessed Lucy. "I'll mail you his details."

"It's fine. I'll speak to Maddy and sort something out. What have I to tell Jake though?"

An awkward silence hung in the air, both of them fully aware that the two brothers hadn't parted on good terms.

"Can you play that one by ear?" asked Lucy finally. "It's been a long time since they've seen each other. Things have moved on."

"Alright," agreed Lori with a sigh. "I'll work something out, but no promises that Jake will agree to see him. Now can you do us a favour?"

"If I can."

"We fly back into Philly on Dec 6th. I was going to leave my car at the airport while I'm away, but I don't fancy driving all the way back here when we land. Can we spend the night with you?"

"Of course!" Lucy squealed. "We'd love to have you guys stay over."

"Thanks. Not a word to Jake about this either," cautioned Lori. "I haven't run it past him yet."

"We can have a late birthday celebration for him," suggested Lucy excitedly.

"Don't plan anything yet. He's bound to be wiped out after touring and the flight back."

"I suppose," agreed Lucy. "At the very least we can have a nice dinner and a birthday cake. The boys would love that."

"Sounds perfect."

"I need to run, Lori. Thanks for your help. You'll get on fine with Simon. He's a lot like Jake only with less hair," she laughed. "And less tattoos!"

With a laugh, Lori said, "If you send me his details, I'll call him as soon as I've got the arrangements made with Maddy. Pity you can't come too."

"I know. Maybe next time. See you soon, Lori."

"Bye, Lucy. See you on the 6th."

As soon as her packing was complete, Lori checked her emails for the message from Lucy. It was waiting in her inbox as promised and Lucy had even attached a photo of Captain Simon Power. He did indeed look a lot like Jake, only his hair was a regulation military cut and looked to be greying at the temples. She quickly typed up an email to Maddy, asking her to arrange an additional backstage all areas pass for both London shows. A few moments later she got a reply from her friend asking simply, "Who for?"

With a sigh, she realised she was going to have to trust Maddy with this secret too. Instead of mailing her back, she quickly dialled Maddy's number.

"Maddy," came the prompt, but sharp reply. It sounded complete chaos in the background.

"Hi. Is this a bad time to call?" asked Lori then added, "If Jake's in earshot don't let on this is me on the phone."

"They're in the middle of the sound check. Can't you tell?"

"I hear them," said Lori, recognising Jake's voice in the background. "Just a quick call about those passes."

"Yes, Mz Hyde. Who are you trying to smuggle backstage? You know I'll need full name."

"You can't breathe a word of this. I've not fully set it up yet. They're for Jake's brother, Simon Power," explained Lori briefly. "He's in the UK and is going to be in London for a few days. Lucy's talked him into seeing Jake. I don't think they've seen each other for at least five years."

"Ah! So this could be an unpopular guest?"

"God, I hope not!" sighed Lori, part of her already regretting agreeing to this reunion.

"I'll get them arranged and give them to you to keep. On your own head be it, girl!" warned Maddy playfully.

"Thanks. You're a star. How are things?"

"Great. Tour's been fabulous so far. Gary is a godsend. You'll adore him. Audiences have been amazing."

"And you? How's the baby bump?"

"Very noticeable!" declared Maddy, rubbing her swollen belly as she spoke. "Most folk have realised I'm pregnant, but that's all."

"When are you planning on telling them the truth?"

"After the final show," Maddy promised.

Lori could hear Jake yelling in the background.

"Is he ok?" she asked with some concern. "He sounds really angry."

"He's fine, but I'd better go. Looks like a technical glitch. Add in some pre-show nerves too."

"OK. I'll see you the day after tomorrow, Maddy."

"Counting the hours. Safe journey, darling."

As she drove into the multi-storey car pack at Philadelphia International Airport, Lori was feeling anxious. Over the years she had travelled the world and flown more miles than she cared to count. However, this was her first flight since her accident and she was inexplicably nervous. She parked the car, then lifted her wheeled case out of the back. Despite attempting to pack light, the bag was awkward to manoeuvre but she managed to wrestle it out of the trunk and set on its wheels. Her carry-on bag slung over her shoulder and her cane gripped tightly in her hand, she carefully made her way across to the terminal building. With her luggage checked in, she made her way towards the elevator to the first floor. There was a long line at security and the signs warned travellers to remove coats, jackets, belts and shoes. With a bit of a struggle, she managed to get her shoes unlaced without falling and piled everything into two grey plastic trays. When the security guard called her through, as expected, she set off the alarm.

"Can you please step to the side, ma'am?" asked the burly guard.

"Of course," replied Lori, suddenly aware of all the eyes of her fellow travellers on her.

"I need to pat you down, ma'am," stated the guard.

Lori nodded, then said, "It's the surgical rod and screws in my leg that set it off. I have a letter from my doctor with my passport."

She handed her passport and the medical letter over, thankful that she had kept them in her hand instead of placing them in the plastic tray. The guard read over the letter and her passport details matched the personal details in the letter. He then excused himself until he referred to a senior colleague before returning.

"Thank you, Miss Hyde," he said, passing the documents back to her. "Have a safe flight."

"Thank you."

Her two trays of belongings were causing a backlog on the conveyer. Quickly she lifted her things and, carrying her shoes in her hand, limped over to the nearest row of seats. She sat down with a sigh and put her shoes back on, relieved that she was through security. Her nerves began to settle and she realised that it was the security x-ray that had been making her anxious. There were still over two hours until her flight was due to depart so Lori decided to go and get something to eat. Since her last visit to the airport, there had been a few changes to the layout, but she soon found a gourmet sandwich bar that looked appealing. She never liked to eat a big meal before flying so a deli sandwich, potato chips and a bottle of apple juice proved to be the perfect meal deal. When she had finished her light dinner, Lori wandered slowly back along the concourse, browsing in the duty free shops and then the Hudson News stand where she bought some magazines, a bar of Hershey, some gum and water for the flight. By the time she reached her departure gate there were only thirty minutes until the flight was due to be called. She took a seat near the window and idly flicked through one of the magazines until the boarding announcement.

Despite being at the gate promptly, Lori was one of the last passengers to board the plane. She had reserved an aisle seat in the business class section so she could stretch her leg out a bit more if need be but she was pleasantly surprised to find the two seats beside her were vacant. As she glanced round, she saw there were quite a few empty seats. Delighted at having the extra space to spread out, she settled herself for a long night on the plane. No matter how many night flights she had taken, Lori still struggled to sleep on a plane. Across the aisle from her, there was a couple and their teenage son. The boy had been given the aisle seat directly opposite her.

Right on schedule, the plane took off and, a few minutes later, the cabin crew came round with the drinks trolley. As was her usual custom, Lori ordered champagne and a can of Sprite. Having poured half of the small bottle of champagne into the clear plastic tumbler, she offered up a silent toast to a safe flight. For the next hour she sat reading the magazines she had bought. One of them was a popular rock magazine that had a feature article on the Weigh Station tour. She had picked it up on impulse purely to see if there was any mention of Silver Lake in it. There was a brief mention of them, but there some good photos of the stage back cloth she had designed. It made her smile. When she was finished reading, Lori realised the boy opposite had been trying to read it over her shoulder. Closing the cover, Lori passed it over to him, "Do you want it?"

"Thank you," he replied shyly. "I was trying to see the Weigh Station bit."

"Likewise," said Lori, noting his Scottish accent. "Are you going to see them tomorrow in Glasgow?"

"Yeah," he replied with a huge grin. "I've had my ticket for weeks. Just hope the jet lag doesn't kill me."

After a few minutes, he added, "How did you know about the concert? You don't look like a Weigh Station fan."

Lori laughed, the same magical laugh that Jake fell in love with all those months before. The boy stared at her, a confused look on his face.

"What's so funny?" he asked.

"Nothing," said Lori with a smile. "But tell me, what does one of their fans look like?"

"I don't know," he began, looking embarrassed. "Long hair, tattoos, black T-shirt, ripped jeans."

"Those I can do," she teased playfully.

"Are you going?" he asked hesitantly.

"The only reason I'm on this plane," she replied, with a wink.

"You're kidding me on!"

"Seriously," she replied. "Maybe I'll see you there."

"You're really going to the exhibition centre tomorrow night?"

"Yes then on to both London gigs."

"Wish I was," he sighed. "I'm David, by the way."

"Lori," she said, as she took a sip from her drink. "Enjoy the article."

The boy opened the magazine at the Weigh Station feature and sat engrossed in it for a few minutes. While he was reading, Lori lifted her small sketch pad from her bag and began to doodle. Her mind was thinking about a section of the backdrop that she wanted to change. One of the photos in the article had reminded her of it. She began to re-draw the lower right hand corner, adding in her preferred detail.

"There you go," said David, interrupting her concentration as he passed back the magazine.

"What did you think?" she asked curiously.

"Not much new in it. Like the new photos," he replied. "I got the new version of their last album yesterday. You know the deluxe one with the bonus tracks with the guest musicians."

"Have you listened to it yet?"

"I played it last night. I really liked one of the new tracks."

"Which one?"

"Broken Bottle Empty Glass," he replied, craning his neck to see her sketch. "What are you drawing?"

"Just doodling," she replied evasively.

"That looks a bit like the stage set thing," stated David bluntly. "Well, a wee bit of it."

"I guess it does," agreed Lori nodding.

"Are you really going to those gigs?"

Lori nodded.

"And you're really a Weigh Station fan?"

"More of a Silver Lake fan," she confessed. "But I do genuinely like Weigh Station."

"Are Silver Lake any good?" asked David. "I know it's their singer on the new Weigh Station stuff. He sounds alright."

"Jake has a fabulous voice," replied Lori, more defensively than she intended. Her new friend quickly picked up on this.

"Is he a friend of yours?"

"Yes," she replied softly.

"You're Lori Hyde!" exclaimed the teenager loudly, causing his parents to look up to see what was going on. "Mz Hyde?"

"Sometimes," answered Lori warmly. "Jake's my partner."

"You did that stage set design, didn't you?"

"Yes, among other things."

"Wow! I'm so glad I met you. My friends won't believe me when I tell them," he gushed.

Beside him, his father muttered something about not harassing the young lady.

"It's alright, sir," interrupted Lori politely. "I started the conversation by offering your son my magazine to read."

"Don't let him pester you," said the boy's father.

"Dad!" protested David, flushing red with embarrassment.

"You're not pestering me," assured Lori, with a warm smile. "Travelling solo can be lonely. I'm glad of the conversation."

"Can I see your drawing?" asked David boldly.

"Sure," said Lori, passing the small sketchpad over.

"That's great," he complimented, passing it back to her. "Why isn't the band's actual one like that at the corner?"

"It's not what they asked for," she explained. "When I saw the photo in the magazine of the finished backdrop, it still bothered me that that corner could be better. I guess, I'm more of a perfectionist than I thought."

"Do you do stuff for Silver Lake too?"

"Yes," replied Lori. "A few bits and pieces."

Carefully, she tore the page out of the sketchpad, signed it and gave it to David, "There you go."

"What? For me?"

"If you want it," said Lori, pouring the last of her champagne into the tumbler. "I know you'd rather a VIP pass for tomorrow night, but I can't fix that."

"Thanks," he said, with a huge smile. "My mates will be so jealous."

"Guess I'd better give you the magazine too," said Lori.

"Will you autograph it, please?"

Obligingly, Lori wrote a short message to David, thanking him for his company then signed the front cover.

"Awesome!" he sighed contentedly

Again his father spoke something quietly into his ear.

"I don't mean to be rude," began Lori, "But I'm going to finish my drink and try to get some sleep."

"Same," agreed David. "We've both got a long day tomorrow."

By some miracle, or perhaps it was the champagne, Lori managed to get almost four hours sleep on the flight. The dull, crampy ache from her leg wakened her less than an hour before the plane was due to land. Her new friend across the aisle was sound asleep. Very slowly she eased herself into a standing position, then, holding on to the seat backs, limped her way towards the lavatory. As she began to move and put weight on her weak leg, the pain began to ease off a little. Once locked inside the tiny cubicle, she stood with her hands on the edge of the small basin, flexing and straightening her leg in an effort to ease off the remains of the muscle cramps. After a few minutes, Lori began to feel it improve. She took a minute or two to use the facilities and to freshen up before returning to her seat.

The stewardess was serving breakfast and Lori only just made it back to her seat before the passageway was blocked by the trolley. Gratefully she accepted the tray of breakfast and a cup of coffee. Across the aisle David was still asleep, but his parents were wide awake and chatting. His dad clambered over him and out into the aisle to fetch one of their bags from the overhead locker, wishing her "good morning" as he stood beside her.

"Morning," replied Lori sleepily.

"Thank you for being so patient with my boy last night," he continued. "I don't know who you are but it's a long time since I've seen him so excited and happy."

"He's a nice kid," replied Lori. "It was a pleasure to talk to him."

"Trust me, it isn't always a pleasure," joked the man. "He said you're going to this concert tonight. Do you really like that God awful heavy metal music?"

"Yes," said Lori, with a sleepy smile. "My partner's the lead singer with the support band. I've also worked with the headliners."

Shaking his head in disbelief, the man just smiled.

"I hope your son enjoys the show," continued Lori. "I'll speak to Jake later and see if he'll give him a name check. Don't say anything. I'm not sure he'll be able to do it."

"Thanks. He'd appreciate that."

As the plane began its descent into Glasgow, Lori looked out of the window at the beautiful hills and lochs they were flying over. This was her first visit to Scotland and the scenery was breath-taking on this clear winter morning. On schedule, the plane touched down smoothly and the captain welcomed them all to Glasgow and wished them a safe onward journey. The sleepy passengers made their way quietly through the terminal building towards immigration. Much to Lori's surprise, she was first in line for non-EU passport checking and within a few minutes she was in the baggage hall with her fellow passengers waiting patiently for the luggage to start coming round the carousel.

"Excuse me," said a voice behind her. "Would you like me to lift your bags off for you when they arrive?"

"Oh, David, that would be great! Thank you," gushed Lori, her relief at his offer written all over her face. "I was wondering how I was going to do this."

"Just let me know when you see your bags."

"It's just one. It's black with a bright blue bow tied to the strap," she replied.

"Ok," nodded the boy.

He stood in awkward silence beside her as the luggage started to trundle round. Almost every bag, whether holdall or suitcase, was black. Soon Lori spotted her suitcase coming towards them and pointed it out to the teenager. She stood back out of the way as he easily caught the bag and swung it round, setting it down on its wheels beside her.

"Thank you," said Lori, giving him a hug. "It's been a real pleasure to meet you. I hope you enjoy the show tonight."

"Me too," he said shyly. "And thanks again for the drawing and the magazine."

"My pleasure. Take care," she said, as she lifted the handle of her bag and made her way towards the exit.

Once through the automatic doors, Lori scanned the arrivals hall for the mystery person who was due to meet her. There was no one with a sign saying either "Hyde" or "Silver Lake" but she spotted a young man rushing into the arrivals hall wearing a Silver Lake T-shirt under his open puffy winter jacket. He saw her looking at him and waved. Slowly she made her way towards him. As he reached her, he was out of breath.

"Lori?" he panted hopefully.

"Yes," she replied. "And you are?"

"Gary," he gasped, shaking her hand. "Also known as Maddy's gofer."

With a laugh, Lori said, "I pity you. That girl will run you ragged. Nice to finally meet you, Gary."

Taking her suitcase from her, he said, "Nice to meet you too. How was the flight?"

"Good, thanks. I even got some sleep," she replied. "I'd kill for a decent cup of coffee, though."

"I'm afraid that'll need to wait until we get you to the hotel. Time's a bit tight this morning," he began. "The plan is to sneak you up to your room while the guys are doing an interview for the local paper. I've left Maddy trying to keep them all together."

"Ok, let's go then," said Lori. "Do you have a car outside?"

"No, but we can grab a taxi at the front door."

The chill morning air hit her as she stepped outside the terminal building a few moments later. It felt colder than the US had felt the day before and she shivered despite her own thick winter jacket. The taxi rank was immediately opposite the entrance and Gary soon had her bags in the boot and both of them settled in the back seat. It was only a fifteen minute ride from the airport to the riverside hotel where the band were staying. As the taxi pulled up at the entrance, Gary quickly called Maddy to check the coast was clear.

"We're good to go," he said with a conspiratorial wink. He passed the fare through to the driver then helped Lori out of the car. "Keep your hood up just in case."

"Why do I feel like I'm doing something wrong?" she giggled, as they entered the foyer.

"Not a word until we are in the lift," he cautioned.

Once they were in the small lift and on the way up to the second floor, Lori began to giggle uncontrollably. Seeing the funny side Gary couldn't resist her laughter and joined in.

"Will you be alright in your room for a few hours?" he asked. "We don't want to ruin this at the last minute."

"I'll be fine," assured Lori warmly. "I'm going to try to get some sleep."

"Good idea. You're in for a long day," he observed, as the lift stopped and the doors opened. "This way."

Her room was along the corridor to the right and, when Gary opened the door, she saw that she had a stunning view out across the river outside. Checking the time, he said, "I'm really sorry to abandon you so soon. I'll call room service and get them to send up some breakfast for you and that coffee."

"Thanks," said Lori, as she slipped her jacket off. "What time do I need to be ready?"

"I'll send someone to fetch you about three o'clock," said Gary. "That way you should arrive as the guys are almost finished their sound check. It's only two minutes from here to the exhibition centre. If you need anything before then, call Maddy or room service."

"I'll be fine," stated Lori. "You'd better go before they realise you're missing. What's your cover story?"

"Toothache," he confessed with a laugh. "I told Maddy to tell them I'd gone to look for an emergency dentist."

"Sneaky, boy," she giggled. "Thanks for your help with this. I'll buy you a drink later on to say thank you properly."

"I'll look forward to it. Need to go. Your breakfast will be here soon."

Lori wandered over to the window and surveyed the view of the River Clyde and the city beyond it. The cerulean blue sky was cloudless. It was a crisp, clear winter's day, not what she had been expecting at all. In her bag she heard her phone give a chirp and she walked stiffly over to fetch it. The message was from Maddy, "Glad you made it. Don't have time to come up just now. Will see you later. M x"

"Looking forward to it. Does J suspect anything? L x"

"Nothing. M x."

The next six and a half hours seemed to drag by as Lori confined herself to the hotel room. After a delicious breakfast and the best coffee she had enjoyed for a while, she lay down on the bed to rest. Her brain was racing with thoughts – the excitement of being there; of knowing she would see Jake in a few hours; of the thought of seeing the show. She must have drifted off to sleep for a couple of hours as a knock at the door roused her. When she looked through the spy hole, it was a member of the hotel staff with a lunch tray for her. Quickly she opened the door to let the girl in.

"Thanks," she said sleepily, as the girl slipped back out of the room.

When she checked the contents of the tray, Lori realised that Maddy must have had a hand in her lunch as all her favourites were there. Discovering that she was ravenous, Lori sat down at the desk to eat and admire the view. Once her meal was over, she took a shower, then opened up her suitcase to decide what to wear. Wrapped in a towel and with another smaller one round her hair, Lori carefully selected her tight black jeans, vest top and a chunky black sweater. She wanted to arrive looking her best, but was concerned she would look out of place. As she dressed and dried her hair, she could feel her excitement mounting at the thought of surprising Jake. Carefully, she applied her makeup, using a little extra concealer to hide the dark circles under her eyes. By the time she had dried her hair and finished getting ready it was almost three o'clock. Her leg still felt stiff and achy after the uncomfortable night on the plane so she took two painkillers then put the packet in her handbag.

A sharp knock at the door startled her. She glanced through the spy hole and saw Gary standing in the hallway.

"Hi," she said warmly as she opened the door.

"Hi," he said abruptly, looking and sounding a little frazzled. "Are you ready?"

"Yes," replied Lori. "Let me lift my bag and my jacket. I didn't expect you to come back for me."

"There's a few technical glitches at sound check. I slipped out, claiming to be going to speak to the centre manager. We need to hurry though, as I do need to speak to the guy urgently."

Leaving him standing in the corridor, Lori lifted her bag, cane and jacket, then almost as an afterthought, the swipe card to get back into the room. As before, Gary had a come by taxi, but this time he had left the driver waiting with the meter running. When they climbed in, he instructed the driver to return to the exhibition centre. Within five minutes the car had stopped at the same spot it had started from less than a quarter of an hour before. The harassed tour manager helped Lori out, paid the fare, then strode on ahead into the building, leaving Lori to follow behind as quickly as she could.

"Through here," said Gary bluntly, opening a "restricted access" door. "Go straight to the end. Turn right. Maddy should be down there."

"Thanks, Gary. I appreciate this."

"Harrumph," he muttered, as he rushed off in search of the centre manager.

Lori followed his directions and arrived at an open plan area with tables and chairs and the band's belongings scattered all over the place. As she approached, she could hear Maddy's shrill New York accent. Quietly she walked up behind her friend then cleared her throat. Hearing the noise, Maddy turned round and only just stopped herself from squealing, "Lori!" Giggling quietly the two girls hugged and whispered their greetings. Lori was amazed at how big her friend's baby bump had grown in just over a week. Still whispering, Maddy said, "If you go through that door at the left, then follow the corridor down you'll reach the stage. I warn you, it's been a tough sound check and no one's in a good mood."

"I guessed from how harassed Gary was when he picked me up," said Lori. "Should I wait till they're done?"

"No," said Maddy, shaking her head. "On you go. I'll be along in a moment. I just need to double check on something first."

"OK," agreed Lori heading towards the door.

Out on the stage Silver Lake were slowly getting through the sound check. They had struggled with an issue with the electrics that had shorted out some of their cabinets. Safe in the knowledge that Gary and Maddy would get it sorted, they had continued with the rest of their standard routine. Things were still not going well though- broken guitar strings, split drum skins and feedback issues from Jake's microphone.

"Jesus H Christ!" he yelled, hauling the microphone from the stand. "Trash this fucking thing!"

"Calm down, Jake," said Grey in his usual laid back manner. "Gary's getting it sorted."

"It's completely fucked, Grey," screamed Jake in exasperation.

One of the crew scurried out with a replacement and removed the faulty mic from Jake's hand before he hurled it out into the empty concert hall.

"Right, from the top," said Rich calmly, tweaking the tuning of his guitar slightly.

The empty hall filled with the opening section of Dragon Song and this time the microphone worked, allowing Jake to run through the first verse and chorus of the song. As Rich launched into the mid sector guitar solo, Jake turned round to look to his right. A small movement off stage had caught his eye. At first Jake thought he was seeing things, then he realised that Lori was standing there. He stopped playing, still not fully comprehending what he was seeing. Sliding his guitar round his back, he walked over to the side of the stage, half expecting the mirage to vanish.

"Hi," whispered Lori softly, as he wrapped his arms around her.

"How? When?" he spluttered, nuzzling into her neck. "Am I dreaming?"

With a giggle, Lori kissed him and said, "You're not dreaming, rock star. I thought I'd surprise you."

"Lord, am I glad to see you, li'l lady," he sighed, his previously foul mood melting away as he held her close. "I've missed you."

"Me too," she whispered. "Now, do you not have work to do, rock star?"

"Sure do," he admitted with a sigh of exasperation. "It's not been an easy day so far."

"So I heard. If its ok, I'll sit here till you're done," said Lori, pointing to the stool he used during the acoustic interlude.

"Fine by me or you can come out on stage? Sit on the drum riser if you want," he suggested.

"Here will be fine," she assured him, with a warm smile. "You'd best get back out there. Rich is staring at you."

"Ten minutes," he promised as he walked away, smiling and

feeling relaxed for the first time that day.

As he reached the centre of the stage, Rich asked, "Is that Lori?"

"It sure is," replied Jake, grinning broadly.

Thanks to a few more technical glitches ten minutes turned into half an hour. During that time Gary returned with the centre manager and two local electricians, who worked to fix the issues. Eventually the band and management were happy and Gary told them to wrap it up.

"Lori!" called Jake from the stage. "Come over here, li'l lady."

As she walked out onto the huge stage, the enormity of the empty hall struck her. When she reached Jake, he put his arm around her waist, "Like my view from the office for the night?"

"It's ok just now, but I'd be terrified to stand here in front of a crowd," she confessed. "Can you do me a favour when you are out here later?"

"I'll try," agreed Jake, hugging her tight. "Depends on what it is."

Quickly she explained about the boy on the plane the night before and about how helpful he had been in the baggage hall.

"Ok, what's his name?" asked Jake, relieved to know that someone had been on hand to assist her. The thought of her travelling alone had been worrying him.

"David," Lori answered. "He was a sweet kid. Kind of shy. Polite. Nice family."

"I'll do my best, but I'm not promising anything," he said, leading her off stage. "I still can't believe you're actually here."

"Well, you'd better believe it, rock star."

When they arrived back at the dressing room, there were a few chaotic moments as everyone greeted Lori and while she confessed that Maddy had known all along that she was arriving today and about how Gary had collected her that morning and smuggled her into the hotel while they were giving an interview in the hotel's bar. She was relieved that they all seemed genuinely happy to see her.

"Ok, guys," said Jake getting to his feet. "I'm taking this li'l lady out of here for an hour. I'll be back in plenty of time to warm up."

"Jake," began Gary sharply, "I'm not too keen on that idea."

"Tough shit," stated Jake bluntly. "I'll be back on time. Trust me."

"Let them go," said Maddy, intervening. "He'll be fine."

"Can you at least stay in the complex? There's a bar/grille at the far end. Go there if you need some time together," suggested Gary, failing to hide his exasperation. "The doors aren't open to the public for another two hours or so."

"Maybe. We'll be back by five thirty."

"Have you both got your security passes?" asked Maddy calmly, resting her hand on her bump.

"Yes, boss," said Jake with a wink. "See you in an hour."

As they walked through the concourse where the merchandising stalls were being set up and the centre's staff were having a team briefing, Jake suggested to Lori that they take a walk outside.

"That would be good," Lori agreed. "Some fresh air might help to keep me awake."

"What time did you leave yesterday?"

"I left the house just after lunch to drive up to the airport. I got in here around eight this morning, I think. It's been a long day, but I'm fine."

"Did you get any sleep?"

"A few hours on the plane, then a couple at the hotel," she said before adding, "Don't fuss. I'm fine."

"As long as you're sure, li'l lady. Now how about a walk around the building then we can come back in and grab a coffee and something to eat at that place Gary mentioned?"

"Sounds good," agreed Lori, taking his hand. "I'm just happy to be here."

It was dark outside when they slipped out of the building, but the floodlights were on, lighting the way for them. Hand in hand, they meandered slowly round the large exhibition centre, their hoods pulled up to ward off the cold. They kept their heads down as they walked past several small groups of fans, who were already gathering for the show. Jake led her past the huge trucks that transported all the gear for Weigh Station, then pointed out the smaller truck that their gear went in. There were three large tour buses parked nearby and again, Jake pointed out the silver coach that was theirs. He explained that they would be in the hotel for the night, but would travel to London overnight on the bus the following night. Apart from an interview in the morning, the band had most of the next day free. Seizing the chance to play tourist, Lori suggested that they go into the city to see a bit of Glasgow after the interview.

"I suppose we could," he agreed. "Let's wait and see how your jet lag is tomorrow."

When they reached the centre's main doors, they both showed their security passes to the guard, who opened one of the doors and let them in out of the cold. Behind them a dozen or more eager Weigh Station fans were clamouring to be allowed inside. Listening to the fans cheers, Jake and Lori looked round and found that they had re-entered near the bar/grille, but it didn't look as though it was open. Jake knocked on the door, then showed his pass to the man who appeared on the other side.

"When do you open?" he asked, shouting through the thick glass to be heard.

"Not till six, pal," replied the man in a broad Glasgow accent.

"Any chance of letting us in early? I need to be backstage by five thirty," asked Jake hopefully.

"Just the two of you?"

"Please," said Lori with a smile. "We just need a drink and something light to eat."

Noticing that both of their security passes were "band - access all areas," he relented and opened the door. "Can you please sit at one of the tables away from the glass? I don't want folk hammering the door in trying to get in here to meet you."

"Of course," agreed Jake. "Really appreciate you letting us in early."

"Aye, well, your young lady looks frozen and you both look as though you could do with some peace and quiet for a while," he replied, showing them to a table near the bar at the rear of the room. "What can I get for you both?"

"A chicken salad would be good," said Jake, taking his jacket off. "And a bottle of water, please."

"Miss?" asked the Scotsman.

"The same only can I have a black coffee too?"

"Of course you can. I'll be right back. Make yourselves comfy."

At five thirty on the dot both of them returned to the Silver Lake dressing rooms. The relief at Jake having been true to his word was written all over Gary's face while Maddy just winked at both of them. Planting a kiss on the top of Lori's head, Jake excused himself, saying he was going to go and do his vocal warm up somewhere quiet and out of earshot. The rest of the band were all lazing about, killing time until it was time to get changed. Taking her jacket off, Lori went over to sit beside Maddy for a catch up. Her friend was reclined along a low settee and, from the angle she was lying at, her baby bump made her look as though she had swallowed a basketball. Rubbing her swelling belly gently, she reassured Lori that she was absolutely fine; that she was taking plenty of rest and was eating properly. Now that the morning sickness was long gone, Lori had to admit her friend looked the picture of health.

About an hour before show time, the dressing room door opened and Dan Crow from Weigh Station came striding in.

"I heard a rumour that the beautiful Mz Hyde had come to join the party," he called out loudly.

"Good evening, Dan," called Lori, without getting up from her seat. "Good news travels fast."

"Welcome aboard, Mz Hyde," he declared, coming over to give her a hug. "When did you get in?"

"This morning," she replied, stifling a yawn. "It's been a long day."

"I'll bet," agreed Dan. "Get that man of yours to bring you to the side of the stage when he comes out with us later on."

"Thanks. I will," nodded Lori.

"Lovely to see you here, Lori. These guys have missed you," said the older man softly. "Better get back to my boys. See you after the show, beautiful."

By seven thirty Silver Lake were pacing around the dressing room like caged lions. All of them had completed their pre-show rituals and routines and were ready to step out on stage. Eventually Gary and Maddy agreed it was time to make a move out to the side of the stage to await their cue. As soon as they were out in the connecting corridor, they could hear the audience cheering and chanting. Jake gave Lori a brief hug and whispered,

"Time to head into the office, li'l lady."

"Don't work too hard," she teased.

She could see through the doorway that the house lights had dimmed, the stage was cloaked in darkness and the crowd were cheering and whistling expectantly. Paul led the band out onto the stage, darting on ahead to get behind his drum kit by the time the others were in position. With the lights still out, Silver Lake launched into the opening riff of Dragon Song. The crowd went wild as the lights blazed bright and Jake stepped up to the microphone. From her position at the side of the stage, Lori observed that all of them were playing with a new found confidence and professionalism. Silver Lake was now a finely tuned machine.

After Dragon Song, Jake yelled out, "Good evening, Glasgow!"

The crowd cheered back.

"I can't hear you!" he screamed. "Good evening, Glasgow!"

The roar from the crowd was deafening as the band launched straight into their next two hard, heavy and fast songs. As had now become the usual routine after the first three numbers, Jake switched to his acoustic guitar and perched himself up on a tall, wooden bar stool.

"You still with us?" he asked, gazing out at the capacity crowd. "Time to catch our breath. Slow things down a bit for a minute or two. If you know the words, feel free to join in."

The haunting melody of Stronger Within flowed out over the appreciative Scottish crowd and, when Jake began to sing, the whole exhibition centre sang with him. From the side of the stage, Lori stood captivated by the sight of four thousand rock fans singing word perfect with her rock star.

"Ok, over to you guys," said Jake, letting the crowd sing the chorus on their own for him.

"That's just beautiful," he declared with a smile.

As the last notes faded away, Jake said, "Glasgow, you've stolen my heart. That was amazing."

The fans cheered and whistled.

"Ok, maybe you can help me out with the words for this next one," he said nodding over to Rich.

The two of them had worked on this song earlier, but were still anxious at attempting to play Flower of Scotland to the Scottish crowd. There was no need for nerves as the audience soaked up the song and sang it strongly for the band. After a verse and a chorus Jake brought the focus back to their own music.

"That was fun. Thank you," he said, bowing his head in recognition of the crowd's vocal support. "This next one is Lady Butterfly. I'd like to thank a young man in this crowd. He helped Lady Butterfly out at the airport this morning. David, this one's for you."

Lori scanned the crowd and finally spotted David right down at the front, just left of centre stage. She could see from the stunned look on his face that the "thank you" had made his night. Jake glanced over at her as he started the song and she tried to point the boy out to him. As he played and sang, he worked out which kid it was. When the song was over, he switched guitars again, but held onto the pick he had used on Lady Butterfly. While Rich launched into the intro to ACDC's Highway to Hell, Jake reached out to David and, with the help of one of the security guards, was able to pass the pick to him and mouth "thank you." It was a simple gesture that warmed Lori's heart.

All too soon the band were finishing their final number, Flyin' High, to a thunderous roar from the crowd.

"Thank you for coming out tonight, Glasgow. You've been amazing. Till next time," called out Jake waving, to the crowd.

The band flicked a few guitar picks out into the audience, Paul threw them his used drumsticks and they left the stage having won over a whole new legion of Scottish fans. With cheers and chants of "Silver Lake, Silver Lake, Silver Lake, Lake Lake" ringing in their ears, the band made their way back to the dressing room.

An hour later and Lori and Jake were back at the side of the stage watching Weigh Station, waiting for Jake's cue to go on. His guitar was already on a stand at the back of the stage. Both of them could see Lori's young friend gazing up at his idols, lost in their music. The moment wasn't lost on Jake, as he realised it wasn't so long ago that he had been that fan standing in the crowd.

"Tonight's going to live with that kid for a while," he mused with a smile.

"And me," replied Lori grinning at him.

Hugging her tight, he listened for his cue from Dan. Sweat was pouring off the older singer, causing Jake to wonder if the tour was starting to take its toll on him.

"Glasgow!" roared Dan with a wide grin. "I'm going to bring a very special, very talented young man out on stage. I want you to give him a huge Glasgow welcome."

On cue, the crowd went wild.

"Let me introduce you to the incredible Jake Power!" announced Dan as Jake ran out to pick up his guitar.

Watching Jake perform alongside his heroes brought home to Lori just how much his confidence in himself and his ability had blossomed since she had last seen him perform. His performance of Empty Bottle Broken Glass was the best of the tour so far and the fans went wild when Dan let him take the lead on Sunset After The Storm. When the second song was finished, Dan clapped Jake on the back before stepping back up to the mic, "The one and only Mr Jake Power, folks! Give it up for Jake one last time!"

With what was becoming his routine theatrical bow, Jake left the stage and Weigh Station launched into one of their popular rock anthems. Still with his guitar slung over his back, Jake led Lori back to the dressing room.

"That was fantastic," she declared, just before they entered the crowded communal dressing room area. "You looked like you were lapping it up."

"I was," he confessed with a grin. "I love singing those two numbers. Hard to believe there's only two shows left."

"Two big ones to finish with."

"That is very true, li'l lady," he agreed. "I'm going to grab a quick shower. Will you be ok out here with the others?"

"Of course. Go and cool down and get cleaned up," said Lori, opening the dressing room door.

"Love you, li'l lady," he said, as he turned to go towards the other dressing room further along the corridor. "I'll be back soon."

The rest of Silver Lake, plus Maddy and Gary, were in the midst of being filmed by Scott, the documentary maker. After a lengthy email exchange, Maddy had convinced Jason to hire the young filmmaker to do a Silver Lake film in conjunction with his Weigh Station project. Since he had been commissioned to work with them, it had made it easier for the two managers to curb his enthusiasm.

"Lori!" called Paul loudly as she entered the room. "Come and meet Scott. He's going to make us all movie stars!"

"Hi Scott," she replied, with a wave. "Give me a minute. I need to make a call."

She could feel Maddy's eyes following her as she went over to the far side of the room and rummaged through her handbag for her notebook. Quickly she found the number that Lucy had emailed to her and prayed that Captain Simon Power was available. She had debated all day about when would be a good time to call and she realised that, no matter when she called, she was going to be nervous about the reception. The phone rang out and, just as she thought it was going to cut to voicemail, a familiar yet deeper voice answered, "Simon Power."

"Hi, Simon," she began, trying to remain calm. "This is Lori Hyde. Lucy asked me to call you."

"Ah, Miss Hyde, I've been expecting to hear from you. I take it you are now in the UK?"

"Yes. I flew in this morning," replied Lori. "I just wanted to check that you still want to meet up in London."

"Have you told my baby brother?" he asked directly.

"Not yet," she confessed. "I wanted to talk to you first."

"Don't fret. I don't want to cause trouble," he assured her, sounding eerily like Jake. "I felt it might be the right time to build some bridges."

"There's only one way to find that out, I guess," she agreed softly. "I've arranged access to both London shows for you. Lucy couldn't tell me your plans."

"I've been hearing great things about his band," continued Simon then confessed, "I bought their CD a few weeks back after I saw Lucy. She was so enthusiastic about meeting you all at the launch party with the old man."

"It was a great day," agreed Lori. "And you're more than welcome at both shows."

"How about I meet up with you before the first one?" Simon suggested. "My last business engagement finishes at two. I can be there for around four thirty."

"That should work. Why don't you call me around four and we can arrange an exact meeting place either at the arena or nearby? I'm not sure of the guys' itinerary for the day," she said. "To be honest, I'm so jet lagged, I don't know what day it is."

"Haven't you slept since flying in?" There was warmth and concern in Simon's voice. "You must be exhausted."

"I grabbed a couple of hours this morning, but I'm still in the exhibition centre at the show so bed is still a way off."

"You have my sympathy," he laughed. "How did it go tonight?"

"It was incredible," she said, pride filling her words. "I don't think you'll be disappointed when you see them."

"Believe me, I'm looking forward to seeing it for myself. I've let this thing with Jacob fester for too long."

"Don't call him that to his face or it could fester a while longer," she cautioned softly.

"He always did hate his name," mused Simon. "I'll call you the day after tomorrow, Miss Hyde."

"It's Lori," she corrected. "I look forward to meeting you. Captain Power."

"Simon, please," he said. "I need to go. I'm at an official banquet. Duty calls. Sleep well tonight, Lori."

"Thanks. I'm sure I will."

"Night."

As she slipped her phone and notebook back into her bag, Maddy crept up behind her and asked, "Who were you flirting with, Mz Hyde?"

"I was calling Jake's brother," she confessed, her voice barely more than a whisper. "He's meeting me in London the day after tomorrow at four thirty. I hope you got those passes."

Maddy slipped her a small envelope, "In there. Access all areas, both nights, as requested."

"Thanks. Just pray this goes ok," said Lori, stowing the envelope safely in her bag.

"It'll be fine, honey," reassured Maddy. "Now how are you holding up? Can you stay awake for another couple of hours?"

"Get me a strong black coffee and I'll try," said Lori with a weary smile. "What's the plan?"

"The boys haven't had dinner yet," stated Maddy. "We are booked into an Indian restaurant nearby I believe. Gary organised it all."

"I guess I can do dinner," agreed Lori. "I have no idea what time my brain and body think it is!"

"You'll be fine tomorrow after a good night's sleep," laughed Maddy. "Let's get you that coffee."

The Indian restaurant in the city's West End had stayed open especially to accommodate Silver Lake. On the minibus ride from the exhibition centre, Gary explained that he had eaten there a few times, promising they wouldn't be disappointed. An elaborate buffet was waiting for them when they arrived. The smell of the warm aromatic spices caused Lori to realise she was ravenous. Once they were all seated around a large circular table and had placed a drinks order, the band slowly filtered up to the buffet to fetch their meal. With a tired smile, Lori asked Jake if he would mind fetching her a plate of food.

"Who was that kid you thanked tonight?" asked Grey, between mouthfuls of Lamb Jalfrezi.

"The boy I met on the plane last night," answered Lori. "He was sitting across the aisle from me and we got chatting. He also helped me with my luggage this morning when we landed."

"You did well finding him in that crowd," Rich observed.

"As long as he went home happy," said Jake, biting into a chunk of naan bread.

"I think they all went home happy tonight" commented Gary. "Your Flower of Scotland was a truly naff idea, but you pulled it off. Good job you're good lookin' Mr Power. The ladies would forgive you any transgression!"

Laughter echoed round the table while Maddy quickly filled Lori in on the fact that the British music press were setting Jake up as the latest heavy rock heart throb. This tickled her sense of humour causing her to giggle uncontrollably.

"What's so funny, li'l lady?" demanded Jake, trying and failing to feign anger.

"Nothing," she replied with an innocent look.

"Glad to hear it," he replied with a wink, then added, "You know, I still can't believe you're here. Maddison, I need to have words with you about keeping secrets."

Maddy blew him a kiss across the table.

Their easy banter continued throughout their late night meal. By the time they were ready for dessert, Lori had pulled her chair closer to Jake's and was resting her head wearily on his shoulder.

"How about we get you back to the hotel?" Jake whispered to her.

"Would you mind?" she yawned. "I can hardly keep my eyes open."

"How long have you been up for?"

"I have no idea. About thirty six hours I guess, but I have had a few hours' sleep."

"Gary," said Jake. "Can you get us a cab, please? This li'l lady is wiped out."

"Sure," said Gary getting to his feet. "I'll get the owner to call one."

He went over to the restaurant's bar and asked them to phone for a taxi to go back to the hotel. When he returned to the table, he said, "Two minutes. You got enough cash for the fare?"

"Eh, not sure," confessed Jake. "I can't get used to this funny British money."

"Here's ten pounds. It'll be less than that."

Gently Jake helped an exhausted Lori to her feet, bade the others goodnight and, guided her out of the restaurant, with a supportive arm around her waist. Their taxi was already waiting outside. The cold, crisp night air revived Lori enough to keep her awake for the short ride back to the hotel. Within ten minutes they were both in the lift on the way upstairs.

"Your room or mine?" asked Jake only half joking.

"Whichever one is closer," replied Lori yawning before adding, "Mine."

"OK," agreed Jake.

When they entered Lori's room, he commented on the fact it was identical to his. While Lori got herself undressed, Jake slipped back to his own room to grab his belongings. It only took him a few minutes to grab what he needed and return to Lori's room, but it was long enough for her to have crawled into bed and fallen sound asleep.

When Lori woke next day a watery winter sun was filtering through the curtains. The space in the bed where Jake had been was empty and long cold. On the pillow there was a note scrawled on the hotel stationary, "Didn't want to wake you. Will be back by 11.30. Love you. J x"

Rubbing the last remnants of sleep out of her eyes, Lori looked at the time. The bedside clock said 11.15. Every inch of her was aching and her stomach was rumbling. Sitting up slowly, Lori carefully swung her legs round and sat on the edge of the bed for a moment or two. With a yawn, she got to her feet and stumbled into the bathroom to shower, praying that the hot water would help ease off her aching limbs. She was still standing under the deliciously hot jet of water when she heard her name being called.

"I'm in the shower," she yelled back.

She could hear the bathroom door opening, then saw Jake's head appear round it through the steam of the shower screen.

"Have you eaten yet, li'l lady?" he asked.

"Not yet. I'm starving," she confessed. "Can you order me some breakfast while I finish up in here?"

"Will do. You ok?"

"A bit sore but more awake than yesterday. Give me five minutes."

The hotel had just delivered a tray of coffee and croissants when Lori came out of the bathroom a few minutes later. While Jake poured her a coffee, she brushed the tangles out of her hair, then came to sit beside him on the bed, wearing one of the hotel's fluffy white towelling robes.

"How did the interview go?" she asked between bites of hot buttery croissant.

"Fine," replied Jake. "I was struggling with the guy's accent. Plus, he was talking so fast."

"I noticed that at the airport," commented Lori. "So what's the plan for the afternoon?"

"I'm easy," said Jake with a smile. He was secretly thinking he could quite happily spend the rest of the day in bed making love to her.

"We could do a bit of sightseeing and I need to buy you a birthday present," replied Lori. "What are the others doing?"

"Maddy and Paul are going to the art gallery. Rich and Grey went off with Gary. I'm not sure where to. We've all got orders to be back here no later than five thirty. I think the plan is to have dinner here, then sort ourselves out and get back on the bus."

"Let's do the shopping first, then we can see where we end up," suggested Lori, draining the last of her coffee. "I also need to get gifts for Lucy and her family."

"Why?" asked Jake, raising one eyebrow and looking at her curiously.

"Oh!" exclaimed Lori looking sheepish. "I spoke to Lucy the other day. We are dropping in to visit her on the way home from the airport."

"We are?"

"Is that ok with you?" she asked hopefully. "I just couldn't face the thought of driving for over two hours after an eight hour flight."

"It's fine," he assured her warmly. "I haven't seen my nephews for a while. I take it we are spending the night with her?"

Lori nodded.

An hour later a taxi dropped them off in the city centre. During the journey from the hotel, Jake had quizzed the driver about the best places to shop and he'd given him directions to three malls, all more or less in the one area. He had assured Jake that they couldn't get lost. The pedestrian precinct that he dropped them at was bustling with lunchtime shoppers; office workers making the most of their precious lunch hour.

"Left or right?" asked Lori, looking up and down the busy street.

"Left," decided Jake, taking her hand. "You sure you're up for this?"

"Stop fussing. I'm fine."

Slowly they made their way down Buchanan Street marvelling at the beautiful architecture mixed in with the modern shop fronts. Most of the store names were familiar brands, typical of any city centre. Near the bottom of the gently sloping street, they found the city's jewellery arcade, a short covered stretch of prestigious jewellers. They wandered leisurely through it with Lori admiring the gold and diamonds while Jake admired the watches.

"Would you like a watch for your birthday?" she asked, as he paused in front of yet another display of timepieces.

"I don't know," he replied, shrugging his shoulders. "The last person to buy me a watch was my mom. I think I was sixteen."

"Time you had a new one, then," she teased.

He pointed to several different ones that he liked, all of a similar style. Once she had a clear idea of what one she was going to buy, Lori suggested he look in the shop across on the opposite side for some Celtic jewellery for his sister. With Jake occupied, Lori entered the watch store to make her purchase. A few minutes later they met up again outside, both of them clutching small bags.

"I got Lucy some earrings. The girl said Rennie Mackintosh was the popular choice. They just look like earrings to me," said Jake, handing her the small gift bag. "And I got my brother-in-law a hip flask with a thistle engraved on it."

"Sounds fine to me," declared Lori. "Let's shop for the boys then we can grab a coffee."

"Let's head up the street a bit first," suggested Jake.

For the next half an hour, they meandered back up Buchanan Street, browsing in various shops before finally entering the mall at the top of the hill. Both of them decided they were making this overly complicated and opted for T-shirts for the boys with "Glasgow" across the front and a Highland cow picture printed below it. Along the way, Lori had picked up a few bits and pieces for herself, mementos of her first trip to Scotland. With their shopping complete, they went for a late lunch at a coffee shop. Over a sandwich, they debated what do to do with their remaining few hours in the city. Lori commented that she would quite like to visit the Kelvingrove Art Gallery, if time allowed.

"Suits me," agreed Jake, as he ate the last bite. "Paul mentioned there was a rock memorabilia exhibition open. Might be kind of fun to check it out."

When their taxi pulled up outside the ornate Victorian red sandstone building both Jake and Lori were stunned into silence at its splendour. While Lori paid the fare, Jake stepped back across the grass to take a photo of the building with his phone. Inside was as stunning as outside and, having picked up a map and realised they had less time than they had anticipated, they decided to visit the rock memorabilia exhibit in the basement first. The small hall was busy with students, but they took their time to browse the articles on display. Pointing to one of ACDC's guitars that was displayed under a spotlight, Lori whispered to Jake, "I bet that's on loan from a private collector in New York."

Sure enough, when he read the small label, it was and he looked quizzically at Lori, who just smiled and winked.

"One of your acquisitions?" he asked quietly.

"One of my private collection," she replied. "I'd forgotten David had me authorise the loan of some pieces for this tour."

"You have a private collection?"

"Call it an investment," answered Lori with a smile.

"Any more of yours here?"

"I'm not sure. If I spot any I'll tell you," she promised.

As they made their way out of the hall a few minutes later, a group of teenage boys wearing Weigh Station T-shirts came towards them.

"Hey," said one of them spotting Jake. "You're him, aren't you?"

"Jake Power?" asked his friend.

Taking a deep breath and forcing a smile, Jake nodded, "Yes, I'm him."

"You were pure brilliant last night."

"Thank you," replied Jake blushing slightly. "Glad you enjoyed the show."

"Can we get an autograph and maybe a photo?"

"Sure," agreed Jake. "If you're quick. We're on a tight time schedule here."

The three boys started to debate who was taking the photo and who had a pen when Lori intervened.

"Here's the loan of a pen and I'll take the photos," she said, offering them a ballpoint pen she had found at the bottom of her bag.

Once Jake had signed various scraps of paper that the three boys produced out of their pockets, he posed for photos with them. Lori took them as quickly as possible using each of the boys' phones.

"Thanks," they all said.

"Pleasure," said Lori, putting her pen back in her bag.

"Have a great day, guys," said Jake as he led Lori towards the lift back to the upper level.

Once in the lift, Lori complimented him on remaining calm and friendly.

"I still struggle to put the public face on when I'm not on stage," he admitted, as the doors opened to let them off on the first floor.

"Just be yourself," said Lori taking his hand. "Come on, the Salvador Dali painting I want to see should be down this way."

They spent the remainder of the afternoon browsing the museum's art collections and its historical artefacts. There wasn't enough time to see everything however, and by four thirty Lori confessed she was struggling. Taking this as their cue to leave, they headed back to the exit. Jake asked at the information desk if they could call them a taxi to take them back to the hotel. While they waited for the car to arrive, Lori searched in her wallet for some cash to slip into the donation box by the door. It didn't take long for the taxi to arrive and within a few minutes they were back at the hotel. Silver Lake's tour bus was now parked at the side of the building. When they walked through the foyer they found Gary pacing up and down, waiting for them.

"Afternoon," he said brightly. "We were beginning to wonder where you two were."

"Worried you'd lost me?" joked Jake.

"A bit," admitted the tour manager. "Where did you get to?"

"City centre, then the art gallery," Lori replied. "That place is stunning."

"It's quite something. Maddy's been raving about it since they got back."

"What's the plan?" asked Jake. "I see the silver bullet awaits us."

"Dinner at six then out of here by eight and off down the M6 to London," Gary answered.

"How long will that take?" asked Lori.

"About eight or nine hours. We might stop part way. I'll leave that up to the drivers," replied Gary before turning to Jake. "Rich brought two of your guitars onto the silver bullet earlier. Said he wanted to work on something with you."

"Yeah, he mentioned something about that this morning," nodded Jake. "Right, we're going upstairs. We'll be down for six. When do you want the bags brought down?"

"We'll sort that after dinner."

Once back up in the privacy of their room, Lori slipped her shoes off and lay down on the bed. From the strained look on her face, Jake could tell she was in pain. Without asking he fetched her a glass of water, then asked where her pain meds were. She directed him to her toiletries bag and a bottle of Vicodin.

"The strong stuff?" he asked, as he handed her the pills. "Are you sure you're ok?"

"It's the damp, cold weather, I think," she replied as she swallowed two of the pills. "The doctor warned me that I might suffer a bit more in winter. He wasn't joking."

"You should've said earlier, li'l lady," scolded Jake softly. "I don't like to see you in pain."

"I'll be fine once these kick in," she assured him, forcing a smile. "I've enjoyed every minute of today."

"Same here," agreed Jake. "Now you stay right where you are. I'm going back to my room to check I've not left anything behind. So many hotel rooms and venues. I'm getting paranoid about losing my gear."

"Trust me, I'm not going anywhere," she declared as she failed to stifle a yawn. "Pass the TV remote though before you go."

Less than ten minutes later, Jake was back, carrying a T-shirt, a pair of shoes and a book. Shaking his head, he dumped the stuff into his open holdall.

"There's always something," he muttered, as he rounded up the rest of his belongings from around the room.

"Just don't leave me behind," joked Lori.

"Never," he said with a grin. "But I don't think you'll fit in the bag."

"Very funny, rock star!"

As he stuffed some T-shirts into his bag, he commented, "You're looking a bit better already, li'l lady."

"Thanks," she sighed, rubbing her thigh. "I think the Vicodin's kicking in."

"Is there anything you need me to pack for you?" asked Jake, fighting with the zip on his bag.

"No. Thanks. I'll sort it out after dinner. It's just my toiletries to go in, I think," she replied. "I don't spread my stuff about the room as much as you do."

Jake looked at her with one eyebrow raised.

"I've lost too many things in the past, like shirts, shoes and the odd book," she confessed with a giggle. "I try to keep everything in my bag or at least beside it now."

"Very funny, li'l lady."

As she climbed carefully aboard the tour bus, Lori felt as though she truly had stepped into the rock star world. A horseshoe of sumptuous black leather couches and a large chrome-edged glass coffee table dominated the lower lounge area of the coach. Beside it was a galley kitchen and a toilet next to the stairs that led to the upper deck. Rich and Grey were already on board and she heard them chatting upstairs. Carefully she made her way up the narrow staircase coming out into another very similar lounge, where the two musicians were lying sprawled along the settees. Behind her Jake brought their bags up and headed through a narrow door to the sleeping quarters.

"Let me show you to your coffin," he teased.

He led her through to a narrow corridor with curtained off sleeping bunks.

"We're the second set on the right," he explained. "Maddy was quite insistent about which bunk I took when we picked the bus up in Wales. I guess she knew you were coming by then."

"She knew before you left home, Jake," laughed Lori, pulling back the curtain. "Doesn't look too bad."

"It's not so bad once you're in there," he agreed. "You take the bottom one and I'll be right up above. Maddy and Paul are opposite. Rich and Grey are the first two top bunks. Gary is the bottom one on the right."

"What about the film maker guy?" asked Lori, glancing round.

"I'm not sure if he's with us tonight," Jake replied. "I think Scott said he was on the Weigh Station bus. I hope he is!"

"He's not so bad," said Lori softly. "Just a bit keen."

"I guess," acknowledged Jake, as he stowed their bags in the lockers under the bunk. "There's another lounge area beyond that curtain and another toilet at the left."

"Ok, now what?" asked Lori.

"Let's head up the front for a while till we set off. Rich and Grey usually play the play station for a while in the rear lounge."

Soon they were settled on the longer of the two couches in the small front lounge. Jake had plugged his iPod into the docking station before he sat down. Casually he put his arm around Lori's shoulder with a contented sigh. Taking advantage of their few minutes alone, Jake began to kiss her tenderly across the throat, then he lifted her up to sit on his lap. He gently bit her lower lip before kissing her hard and deeply. Lori responded to the bite by returning his kisses with as much passion. Running her fingers through his long tousled blonde hair, she murmured between kisses that she loved him.

"God, how I've missed you," he sighed as he held her tight. "If only those bunks were a bit bigger...."

"Not tonight, rock star," she whispered, nibbling his earlobe. "Way too public!"

Laughing at her prudishness, Jake kissed her again before agreeing with her.

Deciding to take advantage of his relaxed, good mood, Lori reasoned that this was as good a time as any to tell him about Simon.

"Jake," she began. "I need to talk to you about tomorrow night."

"What about it?"

"I've got a guest coming to the show to see you. I just haven't been sure when was a good time to tell you," Lori answered, her voice growing quieter and quieter.

"Spit it out, li'l lady," he suggested. "Who is it?"

"Simon."

He stared at her in stunned silence. "My brother?"

"Yes."

Quickly she explained about the rest of the phone call from Lucy then about her own brief phone conversation with his older brother.

"I'm to call him tomorrow around four to arrange exactly where I'm to meet him," she finished.

"And this is all my little sister's idea?"

Lori nodded.

"And she's sure Simon isn't coming to cause trouble?"

Lori nodded again, "He told me he was looking forward to seeing you. I don't know what happened between you two, but he said it had festered for too long."

"And you're meeting him at four thirty?"

"Yes," she replied. "And you're not mad at me, are you? I've been worrying that this is a bad idea. Worrying that you'd be angry."

"I'm not mad at you, li'l lady," he said softly, kissing her gently. "I don't think I could ever get mad at you."

"You're sure?"

"I'm sure," he promised. "He's probably right. It's time we cleared the air."

"When did you last talk to him?"

"At my mom's funeral," replied Jake. He paused, seemingly lost in the memory, before continuing. "He took a side swipe at me for being a junkie waste of space. An embarrassment to the family. Both him and Peter had a go at me about my drug habit. I was mostly clean by then. I was in a rehab programme, but they wouldn't believe me. Nothing I tried to say to convince them that I was clean mattered. I didn't want a scene so I got in the truck and drove off. I haven't seen or spoken to either of them since."

"I never knew. You don't need to see him if you don't want to. I've not promised him anything."

"I'll see him. I'll listen to what he has to say. If I don't like what I see or hear, I'll walk away again."

"And you're definitely not mad at me?"

"No," he said with a smile. "If you don't like him, you can walk away too."

"That's easy for you to say," laughed Lori, lightening the mood. "It could be physically challenging for some of us!"

They were still laughing when Gary stepped into the lounge to declare they were about to leave and that the rest of them were having a drink downstairs. Gently Jake helped Lori to her feet and hovered around her protectively until she had safely negotiated her way down to the lower deck. As she sat beside Maddy, Grey passed her a plastic cup with some white wine in it.

"We've a no glass rule," he explained. "Ever since the first night on here."

"Who broke or cut what?" she asked, glancing round trying to identify the guilty party.

"Jake broke a tumbler and I stood on a sliver of glass later on in my bare feet," replied the bass player. "One cut and a lot of blood later, glasses were banned on Silver Lake tour buses for life."

"Ouch," she sympathised.

Once everyone had a cup, Gary proposed a toast, "To the last stop for now."

"To a good night's sleep," added Maddy.

"You'd better make the most of those, girl," joked Grey, remembering the endless sleepless nights he had endured when Becky was a baby.

"While we're in a toasting mood," said Paul, winking at Maddy. "I've got another toast to make."

All eyes were on him.

"Here's to Maddy and I having twins."

His fellow band mates stared at him disbelievingly. The stunned looks on their faces made Lori laugh.

"Here's to twice as many sleepless nights," she giggled, hugging Maddy beside her.

The next few minutes, as the bus rolled out of Glasgow, were little short of chaotic as they all congratulated the parents-to-be. Eventually Jake managed to sit down beside Lori and whisper in her ear, "You knew, didn't you?"

She smiled, sipped her wine, then nodded, "But I was sworn to secrecy."

The party atmosphere continued for another hour or so, then Rich suggested to Jake that they go upstairs to continue work on the new material they had been writing. Taking his drink with him, Jake promised Lori that they wouldn't be too long. Paul challenged Grey to another round of the driving game they had been playing on the play station, leaving Gary alone with the two girls.

"Twins?" he said, shaking his head. "That explains the size of that baby bump, Maddison."

Resting her hand protectively across her stomach, Maddy

laughed. "I'm sorry. I'd have liked to have told everyone sooner, but, if Jason had found out, he might not have agreed to me coming out on the road. I wasn't missing this tour for anything."

"I see where you're coming from," he agreed. "You know he's trying to set something up for January/February time?"

"Where's he planning on sending them?" asked Lori curiously.

"Sorry, can't say," said Gary somewhat officiously. "Not till it's all confirmed."

"Somewhere warm for the winter," hinted Maddy. "But I'll be staying home. I'll be too huge to move by then."

"So what are your plans for after this tour, Gary?" asked Lori, sipping her wine.

"I thought I might come back to America with you guys for a few weeks. Tour about a bit. See New York. Stuff like that."

"You need to come to the band's special Christmas show," suggested Lori. "Have they told you about it?"

"No," he replied. "Please enlighten me."

"Rich and Jake made a deal with the principal that if he was authorising their six weeks leave that they had to come back and play a set at the school Christmas social."

The young manager threw back his head and laughed, "You're pulling my leg?"

"No," said Maddy. "Full set."

"That could be fantastic for publicity."

"I think they want to keep it low key," said Lori.

"We could invite Scott along to film it," suggested Maddy. "It would make a great end to the DVD."

"Perhaps," agreed Gary. "A school dance? After the crowds they've played to here, they're really going to play in a gym hall?"

"Yup," giggled Lori. "I can't wait to see it."

"That settles it," declared Gary, refilling his plastic cup. "I'm booking my flights over. I need to be at that gig."

"Well, you're more than welcome to stay with us a few days," invited Lori warmly. "And, if you're needing somewhere to stay in New York, let me know. I can probably help you out there."

"Thanks. Appreciate it."

"Ok, boys and girls," said Maddy. "I'm heading to my bunk. I need to get some sleep. Keep the partying down to a riot and I'll see you all when we get to London."

"Night, Maddy," said Lori, watching as her friend got awkwardly to her feet.

Left alone, Gary topped up Lori's plastic cup with some more wine.

"Just a little," she said, stopping him before he poured too much. "Doesn't mix well with the pain meds I took earlier."

"You ok?" he asked, screwing the top back on the bottle. "Jake mentioned that you'd been in an accident a while back."

"I'm fine," she assured him. "The last couple of days and the cold, damp weather have just caught up with me. I'll be fine in the morning, I hope."

"Well, if there's anything you need to help, just ask," said Gary awkwardly.

"Thank you, but I'm fine. Honestly. Unless you can magic up a new thigh bone without pins and screws in it," joked Lori to lighten the atmosphere. "The one I've got is a bit of a wreck."

"Sorry. I can't manage that, Mz Hyde."

Changing the subject, she asked what the itinerary looked like for the next day.

"Good question," replied Gary stretching out along the couch, filling the gap left by Maddy. "We should be in London for breakfast. The guys have interviews at the hotel in the morning. I think the first one is at ten. We'll be at the venue around two. Sound check at three. Light meal around five then show time."

"And what have you planned for Jake's birthday?"

"Pardon?"

"It's Jake's birthday tomorrow. Didn't you know?"

"Shit. I'd forgotten," muttered Gary. "Guess I'm sourcing a cake and booking dinner for after the show. Shit. I can't believe I forgot."

"Has Maddy sorted anything?"

"She might have. I'll need to go and ask her," he said, getting up from the couch. "I'll be right back."

Left alone in the bus' downstairs lounge, Lori felt quite out of place. She could hear Jake and Rich playing upstairs and she could hear the drone of the play station game the others were playing. Stiffly, she got to her feet and headed over to the stairs. Very carefully, conscious of the movement of the bus, she climbed to the upper deck in search of Jake. When she reached the top and stepped out into the lounge, both Grey and Paul looked up from their game and invited her to join them.

"I was looking for Jake," she said as she sat down beside them.

"I'd leave them a few more minutes, Lori," suggested Grey quietly. "Sounds like they're almost done back there."

"I'll wait here. I'm not fighting with those stairs again tonight," said Lori bluntly. "They terrify me."

"Bad day?" asked Grey, nodding towards her leg.

She nodded. "A Vicodin day."

"That bad?"

"It'll pass," she answered quietly. "Had you guys remembered its Jake's birthday tomorrow?"

"Sure," said Paul, looking up from the game. "Maddy's got that all worked out. She's booked dinner for after the show somewhere."

"I thought she'd be organised," said Lori, silently relieved to hear that a celebration had been arranged.

"I don't think it's anything major," added Grey. "But there's a big Weigh Station party the last night."

"I figured there would be," laughed Lori, remembering previous end of tour parties she had attended. "I hope I feel human by then."

"You'll be fine by then, li'l lady," said Jake, who had just come through the door from the sleeping quarters. "Can I get anyone a drink? I'm going down to fetch a beer."

"Can you bring up my wine?" asked Lori. "I left it on the table."

By the time Jake came back upstairs with the wine and some beers, Rich had come back to join them. There was no sign of Gary but Rich said he'd gone to bed. It still felt weird to Lori to be relaxing with the band on a bus. She was so used to their gatherings being at the house. Jake settled down beside her with his arm casually draped across her shoulders. The five of them chatted until it was after midnight, telling stories of their trip, discussing their hopes for the future and also playfully teasing Paul about becoming a father.

"Right. I'm calling it a day," declared Grey with a yawn. "I need my beauty sleep, boys and girl."

"See you in the morning!"

"I'm ready to turn in too," confessed Lori.

"Time we were all calling it a night," agreed Jake, helping her to her feet. "Big show tomorrow night."

Cocooned in her bunk in the dark a short while later, Lori felt as though she was trapped in a coffin. Before settling down, she had taken another painkiller, not a strong one this time, and the ache in her leg was finally fading away. Knowing that Jake was in the bunk above her made her think of sleepovers she had gone to as a child, where her friend had had bunk beds. The memory made her smile. It made her wonder what Jake's childhood had been like and how the relationship with his family had disintegrated so badly. She offered up a silent prayer that things would go smoothly when they finally met up with Simon in a few short hours. She must have drifted off to sleep, despite the feelings of claustrophobia, because the next thing she knew, Jake was gently shaking her awake.

"Good morning, sleepy," he said, kissing her tenderly. "We're about forty five minutes out. Coffee's on. Time to get up. The small lounge up front is empty. Might be easier to get dressed in there."

"What time is it?" she murmured.

"Around seven," he replied. "How're you feeling this morning? Did you sleep?"

"I'm fine. Pain's settled down again, thank God," replied Lori, as she carefully climbed out of the bunk. "I slept, but I felt like a vampire in there. It's like sleeping in a casket!"

Laughing as he helped her to her feet, Jake said, "It is a bit, but you get used to it."

"I'll let you get used to it," she muttered. "I'll get used to hotel rooms."

Laughing, Jake hugged her tight and whispered, "I love you, li'l lady."

"Love you too, rock star," she said, snuggling into his chest. "Happy birthday by the way."

"Thank you," he replied, kissing her again. "Now go and get ready."

When they checked into the hotel later that morning Jake had to concede that this was preferable to the tour bus. While Lori sorted out their things in the room that was to be home for the next three nights, Jake went downstairs to join the rest of the band in the hotel's bar/grille. Walking in to join the interview, late again, he painted on the public face and joined them at the table.

"That's another twenty," hissed Grey under his breath.

Before the interview was over, Jake spotted Lori enter the restaurant and take a seat a few tables away. The journalist noticed that he kept watching the other table and, when he realised who Jake was admiring, asked if Lori would perhaps talk to him about the album artwork.

"I'll ask her," agreed Jake, slightly angered that the journalist was even asking. "But I'm not sure if she'll do it."

As soon as the Silver Lake interview was complete, Jake excused himself and went over to ask Lori if she was prepared to give a short interview. At first she was a little hesitant, but, when Jake said he was heading off to do another interview for a music magazine, she agreed to talk to the journalist. Kissing her gently on the top of the head, Jake promised to meet her for lunch. He wandered back over to give the anxious reporter the good news then left for the next meeting with his fellow bandmates. A waitress brought a fresh round of coffee as the music journalist took a seat opposite Lori.

"Thanks for agreeing to do this unarranged," he said shaking her hand. "I'm Baz by the way."

"Pleased to meet you," Lori replied, forcing a smile.

"So how come you're here with Silver Lake?" he asked directly. "Business or pleasure?"

"Strictly pleasure until you sat down," she joked, before adding, "Jake's my partner. I flew in to catch the last couple of shows. Moral support and all that jazz."

"But you did the stage design for Weigh Station too, didn't you? A foot in both camps, Mz Hyde?"

"Yes. I guess you could say it's the Mz Hyde show," she giggled as she took a sip of her coffee. "I did the most recent artwork for both bands and both backdrops."

"We thought we'd seen the last of Mz Hyde about three years ago after the "Molton On Fire" cover work. What persuaded you to come back out of retirement?"

Lori thought for a few moments before answering, "A change

of circumstances. I retired Mz Hyde because I felt I'd achieved what I'd set out to do. The whole rock 'n' roll scene isn't really me and I'd done my fair share for about five years. It felt right to take a break from it. Move on while I was at the top of my game." She paused to drink another mouthful of her coffee. "Late last year I was involved in a bad accident. It made me re-evaluate things. I moved out of New York while I was in recovery. I was more or less confined to the house for a while and I began to sketch again to pass the time. When I met Jake, I did a small design for him as a gift and, in the process, rediscovered my love for designing. That was about six months ago and it's all snowballed from there."

"So is Mz Hyde back to stay?" asked Baz.

"For now," she replied with a smile. "I've a few projects in the pipeline for the start of the year. I've also designed a small jewellery collection to test the market. A friend is promoting that for me in New York."

"How did you meet Jake?" asked Baz, hoping to gain more material for his Silver Lake piece.

"Too personal," stated Lori with a calm stare.

"Sorry," he apologised, trying to mask his disappointment.

"Have you been to any of the shows on the tour so far?"

"Just one. I met up with them in Glasgow. I'm looking forward to seeing them play tonight when I'm not quite so jet lagged."

"And Weigh Station?"

"I only saw part of their set so I'll catch the whole thing tonight or tomorrow," she replied. "What I saw was fantastic."

"What can the fans expect tonight?" asked the journalist.

"From me?" laughed Lori. "Nothing." Still giggling, she added, "From the bands, they can expect a good night out. Almost three hours on stage between them. I have no idea if Weigh Station have anything special lined up, but tomorrow's the last night of this leg of their tour so who knows. Dan likes to surprise his fans."

"And when can we expect to see something new from you?" asked Baz as a closing question.

"Early next year. I've done the cover work for a country rock band and I think the album is due out mid-February."

"Thanks for your time, Mz Hyde," he said warmly. "That was an added bonus for the day."

"Not a problem," said Lori, relaxing a little now that the interview was over. "I was just going to be hanging around here anyway. That's one thing that never ceases to amaze me. The amount of hanging about waiting for something to happen that goes on. Are you coming to the show?"

"Tomorrow night," he replied. "My girlfriend and I got the VIP package. We'll be right down the front with any luck."

"Enjoy," she said, getting to her feet and lifting her cane. "It's been nice meeting you."

"Likewise, Mz Hyde," said Baz, taking note of her cane.

"Its Lori today," she corrected. "I'm off duty. See you around."

Calmly she walked out of the restaurant towards the foyer, aware of the journalist's eyes following her. With time to kill before her lunch date with Jake, Lori went back up to their room and got out her laptop. She hadn't checked her emails since she had arrived so she spent a while going through them, then typed up a quick message to Lucy to let her know she was due to meet Simon in a few hours. With her inbox back in order, Lori got out her sketchpad and began to doodle. Before she realised, she had drawn a delicate trellis of flowers and it crossed her mind that it would make a pretty tattoo. Fingering the outline of her butterfly, she wondered if she would add to her own ink collection. The thought triggered another and she began to think about what else Jake could add to his personal art gallery.

All thoughts of tattoos and art were long gone by late afternoon. As planned, they had all travelled to the arena straight after lunch. She had barely seen Jake all afternoon as the Weigh Station team asked him to join their sound check before Silver Lake's own rehearsal. At four o'clock she had called Simon as arranged but his phone went straight to voice mail. Quickly she left him a short message to say she would meet him at the TGI Friday's next to the arena and that a table had been booked in the name of Hyde. Fifteen minutes later she picked up her jacket and bag, sent a quick text to Jake to say where she was going and, having checked she had her security pass and Simon's, she slipped out of the arena complex. Already it was dark outside despite the flood lighting. As she made her way round to the front of the building, she could see the square outside was already filling up with Weigh Station fans. There were a few ticket touts offering tickets to those who were milling around. She reached the restaurant just before four thirty and was about to open the door when a tall gentleman reached out and opened it for her.

"Thank you," she said.

"Pleasure, ma'am," he replied in a familiar voice.

She looked up and found herself looking into the unmistakable face of Simon Power. The resemblance to Jake was uncanny.

"Captain Power?"

"Miss Hyde?" he said, with a smile so like Jake's that her heart skipped a beat. "We meet at last."

"So it seems," she replied. "Let's move inside. We're blocking the doorway."

Once inside, Lori spoke to the young hostess about her reservation and they were shown to a booth in the middle of the restaurant. Lori took her jacket off and folded it on the seat beside her. Across the table, Simon was doing the same. Both of them felt awkward and a bit unsure as to what to say. The waitress came over to take a drinks order.

"Can I have a white wine spritzer, please?" asked Lori, deciding she needed a little something to settle her nerves.

"I'll have a beer. Bud if you have it," added Simon, flashing a

"Power" smile at the girl.

"So what's the plan?" he asked Lori as the waitress walked away.

"Cut to the chase, why don't you?" she said with a nervous giggle.

"Well?"

"I left the band finishing up their sound check. Jake said he would try to slip out and come over here for about five. He'll need to be back over there before six though. If this goes well then you come back with us," replied Lori calmly. "He might struggle to get out. It's quite crowded out there already."

"I noticed," said Simon. "I kind of feel out of place. I didn't know what to wear. I don't know what to expect. It's a long time since I've felt nervous like this."

"What you're wearing is fine," assured Lori warmly. "You can't go far wrong with jeans and a sweater."

"You're not what I expected."

Lori looked at him curiously, then asked why.

"You're more petite than I imagined," replied Simon somewhat awkwardly. "You don't look like an artist or a property tycoon."

"So what do I look like?" she teased with a mischievous smile.

"A beautiful petite woman. My brother's a lucky man," he answered softly.

"Ah the Power charm and flattery runs deeps," she declared as the waitress arrived with their drinks.

"Sorry. Nerves," he apologised, taking a swig from his beer.

"It's ok," she assured him. A cricket chirp from her bag alerted her to a text message. When she checked her phone, it was from Jake. "On my way J x". Putting her phone bag in her bag, Lori said, "Your brother's on his way over."

"So what's this rock star lifestyle that my baby brother's leading like?"

"Hectic. Chaotic. Loud," laughed Lori, feeling the tension melt a little. "Well from what I've seen anyway. He's done at least two interviews today. There's been two sound checks, as he joined in with Weigh Station, and he's still to warm up properly before the show. Then it's show time."

"And today's his birthday?"

"It sure is," she smiled. "We're having a small celebration after the show."

"I remembered," said Simon quietly. "I even brought him a gift."

"What did you get him?"

"I got a set of dog tags made up for him. I hope he likes them."

"Closest to the air force he's likely to get," giggled Lori. "I'm sure he'll appreciate the thought."

"We'll see," sighed Simon, sipping his beer.

With the ice broken between them, they both relaxed a little as Lori asked what had brought him to Britain. He was limited in what he could disclose but the answer seemed to satisfy her curiosity. Simon went on to explain that he had taken four days leave to allow him to spend some time exploring London before he headed back to Virginia. Just as Lori was beginning to wonder where Jake was, he came rushing in and slid into the booth beside her.

"Sorry," he apologised. "I got caught by a group of fans outside. I still can't get used to that."

"As long as you were nice to them," said Lori, giving him a hug.

Before Jake could greet his brother, the waitress arrived to take their food order.

"Are we eating here or back at the arena?" asked Lori.

"Let's have a snack here," said Jake. "Gives us more time to catch up and a little privacy."

"Fine by me," agreed Lori, as she turned to the waitress. "Can I have some nachos, please?"

"I'll have a mineral water and a chicken salad," said Jake. "Simon?"

"Loaded skins and the chicken strippers, please," requested Simon. "And another Bud."

Once the waitress was out of earshot, Jake turned his attention to his older brother, "So how's life treating you? Been a while."

"I'm good, thanks," replied Simon awkwardly. "Changed days. You're on the mineral water and salad and I'm ordering a second beer. Oh, and happy birthday, little brother."

"Thanks," said Jake with a warm smile. "Relax, Simon. The past's in the past. Let's leave it there."

"Suits me," agreed Simon, as he fished in his jacket pocket for Jake's gift. "I brought you a present."

He handed Jake a small metal tin with the air force insignia stamped on the lid. With a quizzical look at his brother, Jake opened the box, then laughed out loud as he lifted out the customised dog tags. He was genuinely touched by the effort his brother had gone to as he read the inscription – Power, Jake, rock star #1, O Negative, Delaware. On the reverse the air force insignia had been replaced with the Silver Lake logo.

"That's awesome, Simon," he declared, with obvious delight. Jake slipped the chain over his head and tucked the tag into his shirt, shivering at the chill of the metal and the chain. "Thank you."

"Glad that you like it," said Simon, relieved that his gift had been well received.

"Well, are you up for this show tonight?" asked Jake, stealing a sip out of Lori's wine glass.

"I don't know," admitted his brother. "I've not been to a rock show in about twenty years, if not longer."

"I'll look after you," said Lori. "We can both watch from the side of the stage."

"Do I need to get you ear plugs to cope with the noise?" teased Jake mischievously.

"Very funny," laughed Simon. "To be honest, I'm looking forward to it. I was listening to your album on my iPod last night."

"You have an iPod?" asked Jake, astounded at this revelation.

"Yeah, but there's not much heavy rock on there," confessed his brother.

"We'll soon sort that," stated Lori, glad to see the two brothers enjoying each other's company.

Once their food arrived, the three of them, now wholly relaxed, chatted casually about the tour, life at the beach and life in general. Simon was curious to hear about how they met so that tale was also told.

"Sounds like you've had a long road to recovery, young lady," said Simon warmly as he finished off his beer.

"It's been an interesting journey," replied Lori quietly. "Jake, you'd better keep an eye on the time."

It was almost six and Jake agreed that they should be making a move. Simon insisted on paying the bill then the three of them headed back towards the arena. The doors still weren't open to the public and the square outside was now crowded with excited fans. Keeping his hood up and head down, Jake led them round to the side entrance he had used earlier. He phoned on ahead to Gary to get him to meet them at the door. When they reached the side door, there was a small group of fans waiting. Patiently Jake posed for photos and signed autographs, promising to watch out for them all in the audience later on. When they eventually got into the building and back to the dressing rooms, Maddy was pacing up and down.

"Cutting it fine tonight, Mr Power," she snapped.

"Chill, Maddison. Plenty of time," he said, giving her a hug. Turning to Lori and Simon, he said, "I'll catch up with you shortly."

"Where's he off to?" Simon asked Lori as Jake disappeared through a nearby doorway.

"He's gone to warm up," explained Lori, taking her jacket off and dumping her things on a nearby table. "He had a problem with his voice a while back and now sticks to a strict vocal warm up routine. It's not pretty to listen to but its working so far."

"How long does that take him?"

"Over an hour every night," said Lori. "Now let me introduce you to a few folk."

Quickly she introduced Simon to Maddy then to Grey and Rich. The two musicians were tinkering with their guitars and generally just jamming with each other. Both of them greeted Simon warmly, making him feel welcome.

"Maddy, where's Paul?" asked Lori, realising the drummer was missing.

"Taking a nap," replied Maddy, pointing to what Lori had mistaken for a pile of jackets on a couch at the far end of the room. "He's not feeling so hot. Man flu."

"Aw, poor baby," sympathised Lori, as she sat down across from her friend.

"He'll live," stated Maddy bluntly. "So Captain Power, how did the big reunion go with your brother?"

"So far so good, ma'am," answered Simon, as he sat down

next to Lori.

"Maddy," began Lori. "Simon's coming out with us after the show. I take it that won't cause a problem?"

"Not at all. I booked for a few extra people just in case. Jason's due to show up in a while."

"I thought he'd be here by now," said Lori then explained that Jason co-owned the band's management firm and called the shots about most things Silver Lake.

Time ticked by until shortly after seven then the whole band regrouped in the dressing room. Paul crawled out from under the pile of jackets and declared he felt much better. When Jake came striding back in, dressed all in black, Lori noticed he was still wearing the dog tags. Once they were all assembled, the lights went out and Gary appeared carrying a large candle lit birthday cake in the shape of a guitar. There was a rowdy chorus of "Happy Birthday" and in the midst of the celebrations, Jason walked in.

"OK, guys," called Gary loudly a few minutes later, bringing them all to order. "Showtime. Let's move it on out."

Standing at the side of the stage, Lori could feel Simon fidgeting beside her. The house lights had been dimmed for a few minutes and the crowd were cheering with wild anticipation. With a final glance over at Lori, Jake ran out onto the stage, the last of the group to do so. The lights went up and Silver Lake launched headlong into Dragon Song, their set opener. Instead of watching the band, Lori was watching Simon. His reaction was the same as his father's and sister's had been. He was hypnotised by the polished confidence and talent of his young brother. He stood in stunned silence until after the acoustic interlude, drinking in the whole experience. When the stage hand brought Jake's stool back off stage, Lori signalled to him to bring it over so she could sit for a few minutes.

"You ok?" asked Simon, putting a concerned hand on her shoulder.

"I'm fine. Just getting a bit uncomfortable," she replied.

Out on stage Jake had glanced over and noticed her taking a seat. He returned his attention to the audience and stepped up to the microphone, "So are you still with us, London?"

The sell-out crowd roared back at him.

"I can't hear you!"

A thunderous roar surged back at him.

"OK," acknowledged Jake, adjusting his guitar. "If you know this one, feel free to sing along."

Before Jake could begin his guitar solo intro, Rich stepped forward and addressed the crowd, "Change of song, folks," he began, conscious that it was the first time he had spoken to the audience on the tour. "It's Jake's birthday."

The arena went wild with whistling and cheering.

"Will you help us to sing Happy Birthday to him?"

While Jake stood shaking his head and grinning, the band played and fifteen thousand rock fans sang Happy Birthday just for him. At the side of the stage, he could see that the crew plus Lori and Simon were also singing along. It was a moment in time that would live with him forever.

"Thank you," he called out when the song ended. "Thank you very much. That was quite something. So very special."

One fan down on the barrier at the front of the stage called out, "I love you, Jake!"

"Why thank you," he replied, obviously flustered. "I love you too."

And with that, the band started the final section of their set with Highway To Hell. All too soon they were playing the closing notes to Flyin' High. They left the stage to a thunderous roar from the London crowd. A small section of fans down near the front sang out another round of Happy Birthday to Jake and were rewarded with a bow and a wave.

At the side of the stage, Lori got down from the stool and turned to Simon.

"Well?" she asked, a smile lighting up her face.

"Jesus Christ, that was amazing!" he declared, his eyes filled with wonder and admiration. "Was that really my kid brother out there?"

"It sure was," she laughed.

"My mom would've been so proud of him if she'd still been with us," said Simon with a sad smile. "She always believed he'd be a star."

"Moms are like that," agreed Lori, giving him a hug. "Let's go and catch up with him."

Back in the dressing room it was the usual chaos as the band all tried to get drinks and cleaned up, all of them talking at once. Jake was standing off to one side with his shirt off, drinking a bottle of water, when Simon and Lori came in. His brother's bear hug caught him by surprise, spilling water all over both of them.

"That was quite some show, Jake," said Simon sincerely. "What happened to my scrawny kid brother?"

"He cleaned up his act," joked Jake, downing the rest of the water. "But show's not over yet. I'm out with Weigh Station in a while."

"Weigh Station?"

"Yup," he replied with a grin. "Just for a couple of numbers."

Lifting a clean shirt and another bottle of water, Jake led his brother and Lori back out of the dressing room; back to where they had been standing at the side of the stage earlier on. Out on stage Weigh Station were charming their home crowd and were seemingly unable to put a foot wrong. It was hot beside the stage and Jake stood with his shirt in his hands, waiting for his cue. He had one arm draped protectively across Lori's shoulder as he drank down the bottle of water. On his other side, he could feel his brother tapping his foot in time to the music. Time ran away with him and before he could pull on his T-shirt, Dan was announcing him out on the stage.

"Shit," he muttered, tossing the shirt to Lori.

Still stripped to the waist, he walked back out to join Dan, picking up his guitar from the technician as he went.

"Looks like the birthday boy is feeling the heat tonight, folks," commented Dan with a devilish wink. "Ladies and gentlemen, the one and only Jake Power."

Before he had time to get any more embarrassed, the band began his first number. Refocussing his attention Jake powered his way through Broken Bottle Empty Glass then almost brought the house down with his rendition of Sunset After The Storm. As he sang out the last note, Dan came up behind him, then called out, "Please give it up for the under-dressed Jake Power!"

A mix of cheers and wolf whistles filled the arena as Jake took a bow and ran off stage. Behind him, he could hear Dan crack another joke at his expense, then Weigh Station began the next number on their set. Lori and Simon were both laughing when he reached them. Giving him a huge hug, Lori handed him his shirt.

"I'll put it on after I've taken a shower," he muttered, still embarrassed. "Half of London's seen me half naked now anyway."

Jason was standing in the corridor between the stage and the dressing room. He too had seen Jake's performance. As they reached him, he said, "Smart move to win over more female fans, Mr Power."

"It wasn't intentional," admitted Jake, gradually beginning to see the humour in it. "Lesson learned about being ready for your cue."

"No, seriously," said Jason, clapping him on the shoulder. "It was an inspired move."

"Perhaps," muttered Jake then changing the subject asked, "Are you joining us for dinner?"

"Yes, I am," declared the Englishman. "Go and get cleaned up. I'll see you when you're better dressed."

Maddy had excelled herself with her choice of restaurant for Jake's birthday dinner. She had booked the band and crew into a local oriental restaurant. The owners had agreed to stay open late to cater for the Silver Lake party. It was the first time the band and road crew had had the opportunity to share a meal together. The crew had clubbed together to buy Jake a present. While they waited for their meals to be brought out, the band and crew presented a very surprised Jake with a variety of gifts, ranging from a novelty alarm clock right down to a custom made guitar, presented by Jason on behalf of the management team. Their generosity overwhelmed him and, when he was called upon to make a speech, Jake was lost for words.

"I don't know what to say, guys. Thank you doesn't begin to cover it," he said humbly. "This is too much. Thank you."

He lifted his glass of champagne to propose a toast, "To all of us. To a great tour. To a great final show tomorrow night. To rock and fucking roll."

The party gave Jake a rousing cheer, then sang Happy Birthday again as the waiters served their meal. At the table where the band were seated, Jake was sitting between Lori and Grey. His brother was directly across the table from him.

"Glad to see you're better dressed now, Mr Power," commented Jason from the far end of the table.

"Am I ever going to live this down?" asked Jake, blushing anew at the memory of stepping out onto the stage stripped to the waist.

"You've done it before," commented Grey between mouthfuls of rice.

"I know, but that was at an outdoor summer beach gig," laughed Jake. "And I wasn't the only one. We all stripped down to our shorts that day"

"I remember," reminisced Grey. "It was a hundred degrees out on that stage."

"It'll be all over YouTube by morning," joked Rich, winking at Lori. "And the kids back at school will be following our every move."

"Shit," muttered Jake, shaking his head at the thought.

"Personally speaking," began Maddy, "I think you should do it every night. Did you see the female fans' reactions?"

"And some of the male fans," teased Lori.

"Hey, leave the kid alone," said Simon, trying hard not to laugh. "It's his birthday after all."

"Why?" asked Grey with a scowl. "Jake-baiting is our favourite past time!"

And so their banter continued.

Eventually the restaurant owner spoke to Maddy and apologised that they really had to close up. When she checked the time, it was after two o'clock in the morning. With the minibus ready outside and the bill paid, the Silver Lake entourage spilled out onto the pavement. As everyone got on board the bus, Jake hugged his brother, "Come back to the hotel with us."

"No. I'll get a cab and head back to my own hotel," said Simon warmly. "You and Lori need some private time, birthday boy."

"Are you joining us tomorrow? Today? Oh, whenever it is?" asked Jake hopefully.

"If you want me to."

"Great. Be at the hotel for midday. We can take it from there. Bring an overnight bag. It'll be a late one tomorrow."

"See you later, Jake," said Simon with a nod towards the bus.

"You'd better go. Your ride is ready to leave."

Wrapped in each other's arms safely curled up in bed, alone at last, Lori kissed Jake tenderly.

"I never gave you your present," she whispered softly.

"I thought that was what you just gave me," he said, kissing her back "You mean there's more?"

"Stay there," said Lori, carefully stepping out of bed and limping over to her open suitcase. She picked out a small gift bag and came back over to the bed. Sitting naked on top of the covers, she passed the bag to Jake, "Happy birthday, rock star."

Sitting up Jake opened the bag to reveal a beautifully wrapped box, complete with silver and blue ribbons. He pulled off the bow, tore off the paper and opened the box to reveal a Tag Heuer watch. Very carefully he lifted the charcoal grey and silver watch out of the box and turned it over and over in his hand, admiring it.

"Lori, this is way too much," he protested softly.

"Nonsense," she replied. "Put it on."

"I don't know what to say."

"Don't say anything. Just put it on," she said with a smile. "No excuses for being late now."

"I guess not," he said, as he fastened the watch round his wrist. "Thank you, li'l lady."

"Glad you like it," she replied, as she slipped back under the covers. "Now you'd better get some sleep. What time are you needed today?"

"Not sure," he said, trying to recall the schedule for the last day. "Ten thirty I think."

Sleep then. It's gone four."

The gentle melody of her cell phone ringing wakened Lori from a deep sleep. For a moment she was confused as to where she was. There was a cold empty space in the bed where Jake had been and she realised she had slept through her alarm call. Reaching out she grabbed her phone and answered the call just before it cut to voicemail.

"Hello," she said still sounding half asleep.

"Lori, it's Simon," came the familiar voice. "I'm downstairs in the lobby."

"Shit," muttered Lori, sitting up. "What time is it?"

"Midday," he replied, then added. "Did I waken you?"

"Yes," she admitted. "But I'm glad you did. Give me half an hour and I'll be down."

"Will I get us a table in the bar restaurant place?"

"Sounds like a plan," agreed Lori. "I'll be as quick as I can."

"Don't rush. I'll see you down here when you're ready."

"Half an hour," she promised, already climbing out of bed.

When she came out of the shower ten minutes later, Lori could hear voices in the room. Listening at the closed bathroom door, she recognised Jake's voice, but wasn't immediately sure of the other one. Wrapped in a towel, Lori also realised that the two towelling robes were lying on the bed. There was nothing for it, she was going to have to go into the room. As she opened the bathroom door, holding on tightly to the towel, she prayed it was someone she knew who was there with Jake.

At the sound of the door opening, Jake turned round.

"Lori!" he exclaimed, his eyes wide with surprise at her state of undress.

Simon was sitting on the chair at the far side of the room next to her open suitcase. Mustering as much dignity as she could, Lori walked across the room.

"Sorry, boys," she said quietly as she limped over to her suitcase. "I wasn't expecting company."

"I should've waited downstairs," said Simon apologetically. "I'm so sorry, Lori."

"Just look away till I get my clothes out of that bag," she said, trying not to sound as embarrassed as she felt.

Quickly she lifted the clothes she had set aside for the day and turned to retreat to the sanctuary of the bathroom. As she moved past Simon, the edge of the towel caught on his knee, peeling back to reveal most of the scarring on her thigh. He glanced up at Jake and flushed scarlet with embarrassment.

"I shouldn't be here, Jake," he said, getting to his feet. "Let's go back downstairs."

"Stay where you are," said Lori, her tone sharper than she intended. "I'll be five minutes."

She could hear their muffled conversation through the closed bathroom door as she wriggled her way into her jeans and top. Her damp skin was making it impossible to dress in a hurry. Finally, she was dressed and was brushing out her wet hair when there was a gentle knock on the door.

"Lori, can I come in?" asked Jake.

"It's not locked," she replied.

He slipped in and closed the door gently behind him. "I just wanted to check you were ok."

"I'm fine. Embarrassed but fine," she answered, continuing to brush her hair.

"I'm not sure my brother is," he said with a smile. "He's mortified."

"Why? Has he never seen a woman in a towel before?" she asked, trying to inject some humour into the situation. "It's no big deal if we don't turn it into one. And, yes, I know he saw my scars."

"You sure you're ok?"

Lori nodded and took a deep breath, "At least I only walked out half naked in front of two people unlike someone we could mention."

"Very funny, li'l lady," he said with a grin. "Hurry up. I need to be finished lunch by two."

On the way down in the lift, Simon apologised profusely for embarrassing Lori. No matter how many times she assured him that there was no harm done, he continued to look upset by the incident. As they waited for their lunch order to be brought out a few minutes later, Lori reached across the table and touched his hand. "Simon, please stop apologising. Relax," she said warmly. "I know you saw the scars on my thigh. Trust me, you never saw the half of them."

He looked her straight in the eye and replied, "As long as you're not angry that I saw more of you than I should have."

"Let's forget it ever happened," she suggested.

Changing the subject, Jake asked what the two of them were going to do while the band completed their sound check and a meet and greet session alongside Weigh Station for a handful of VIP fans.

"Hang about and wait, I guess," said Simon as the waitress arrived with their lunch.

"We could do some sightseeing?" suggested Lori. "As long as we're back at the arena for six we should be ok, shouldn't we?"

Jake nodded as he took a bite out of his panini, "Just make sure you have your passes and Gary's phone number."

"I've got them," said Lori. "So, Simon, what do you fancy doing for a couple of hours?"

"Your choice, young lady."

"Well," began Lori. "I would like to see the British Museum. I never made it there the last time I was in London."

"Fine by me."

Six o'clock had come and gone and there was no sign of Lori or Simon arriving at the arena and Jake was growing anxious. He had tried to call both of them several times, but their phones had gone straight to voicemail. Watching the dressing room door, he paced restlessly up and down. After a few minutes Maddy sent him to warm up, promising to send Lori through as soon as she arrived. Reluctantly, he agreed, knowing that he had to warm up properly before the show. In the small rehearsal room he went through the motions of his warm up routine, trying to maintain his focus on his voice and his breathing. His mind was racing, imagining all kinds of horrors that could have happened to them.

The squeal of the door opening behind him startled him back to reality.

"Sorry," said Lori quietly as she stood in the doorway. "Maddy said you were worried."

Jake turned to face her, relief flooding through him. In two quick strides, he was beside her and had pulled her into his arms.

"I was worried," he whispered, his face buried in her hair.

"I'm sorry," she apologised. "We decided to venture back on the underground. No phone signal down there. I wanted to get changed, so we dashed back to our hotel, then came straight here. It took us fifteen minutes to get into the building."

"You're here now. That's all that matters," said Jake. "Stay till I finish my warm up, please."

"Is this punishment?" she joked, sitting on the only seat in the small room.

"No," he said, trying to look and sound stern. "That comes later."

Trying not to giggle, Lori sat quietly as he ran through the last few vocal exercises and scales. Happy that he was in good shape, Jake took her by the hand and led her back to the main dressing room. There were only a few minutes left before show time and his fellow band mates were pacing about like caged animals, anxious to get out on stage. A large bottle of champagne sat open in the middle of the table. Seeing Jake eyeing it up, Rich explained, "Dan sent it through for us. Do you want one?"

Jake shook his head, "I'll wait till later."

"Lori?" offered Rich, lifting an empty glass.

"Please," she replied. "Just a half glass though."

From his reclined position on the couch, Simon said, "Sorry, we were late, Jake. My fault entirely."

"No harm done," replied Jake, still keeping a protective arm around Lori's waist. "Did you have a good afternoon?"

"Loved it," declared Lori with a smile. "But then you know how much I love museums."

"I guess I should be glad you made it back here at all," joked Jake.

"We did stay till closing time," she confessed. "But I bought you a present."

Slipping out from his grasp, she went over to the chair where she had left her bag and tossed a white T-shirt to him.

"It's the Rosetta Stone," she explained as he held it up.

Nodding approvingly, he said, "I'll wear it later, li'l lady. Thank you."

He tossed it back over to her and, while she was folding it neatly, he called over to Simon, "Do you fancy watching from out front tonight?"

His brother sat up and replied, "Yeah, I'd love to."

"I spoke to our film maker, Scott, earlier," explained Jake. "He's going to be filming from the pit right down at the front tonight. He'll take you with him, if you're up for it."

"I'm up for it," Simon declared, getting to his feet.

"Well, you'd better get your ass out there," said Maddy, manoeuvring herself out of the chair. "Come on. I'll help you find him. Gary, keep an eye on the clock."

A few short minutes later, Gary rounded them up and led Silver Lake out of the dressing room for the final show of the tour.

When they reached the side of the stage, they were surprised to find Jason already there with Weigh Station's front man. As they tried to have a hushed conversation, the house lights went out and it was time for Silver Lake to step out on stage. One of the stage crew had thoughtfully left a spare stool in the wings and Lori settled herself on it to watch the show. She had brought her camera with her and was hopeful of getting a few shots of the band in action. Behind her, Dan leaned forward and said, "That boy has so much talent. He'll headline the next time he's on that stage."

"I hope so," said Lori, turning to smile at him.

"Look after him, Mz Hyde," he added warmly.

The first notes of Dragon Song filled the air and conversation became almost impossible as the band gave one thousand percent to the London crowd.

Out on stage Jake felt relaxed and in control. He was trying to ignore the voice in his head that said this was the final show. Focussing on his playing and his vocals, he determined to chill and enjoy the moment. When the spotlights panned out across the audience, he was awestruck by the sight of the thousands of fans singing along with him. Down among the security personnel and press photographers he could see Simon shadowing Scott. When it came to the acoustic interlude, he quickly settled himself on the wooden bar stool, stealing a quick look over at Lori in the wings.

"Ok, folks, are you still with us?" he asked, turning his full attention back to the crowd. "Time to calm down for a minute or two. Catch our breath."

The crowd cheered.

"The next two songs are special to me," began Jake. "They were written for a very special person in my life and I'm delighted she's here tonight. If you know the words, please help me sing them for her. This is Stronger Within."

The London crowd sang both acoustic numbers word perfect along with Jake as he knew they would. As he switched back to his electric guitar, Jake called out to them, "That was beautiful. Thank you. You guys are amazing."

All too soon the band were wrapping things up with Flyin' High and as the last notes faded out over the arena, Jake thanked the London fans, "You've been brilliant. Thank you for making tonight special. Till next time. We'll love you and leave you."

As Paul hurled his used drumsticks out into the crowd, the others flicked a handful of guitar picks out into the sea of fans then waved them goodbye, savouring every last second out on the arena stage. Jason was the first to congratulate each of them as they came off stage. Knowing that Jake would be back in a few minutes, Lori stayed where she was, allowing the band to celebrate the success of the show together. From her perch on the stool, Lori watched the road crew slickly clear all the Silver Lake gear off stage and a second crew uncover the Weigh Station equipment and set up their mics. She could just make out Simon and Scott down in the pit in front of the stage. It wasn't easy to mistake Simon as at six foot four he towered over the filmmaker. Before Weigh Station were even in the wings, Jake was back beside her. Still sweaty and without having changed his shirt, he hugged her tight.

"You were fantastic out there tonight, rock star," she said between kisses.

"Just doing my job, li'l lady," he replied with a mischievous grin. "That crowd are lapping it up tonight."

"You planning on keeping your shirt on tonight?" she teased.

"Too damn right I am!"

Their conversation was cut short by the arrival of Weigh Station beside them. As Dan prepared to go on, he turned to Jake and said, "You up for three numbers tonight?"

"Three?"

Dan nodded, "Watch for your cue, young man."

As the older singer charged out on stage to a deafening roar, Jake was left wondering what the third song was to be. He glanced nervously at Lori, who just shrugged. Hand in hand, they watched the Weigh Station set, occasionally spotting Simon and Scott at the far side of the stage. All too soon Dan was stepping forward and introducing Jake. Accepting his guitar from the technician, Jake sprinted out on stage to a huge cheer from the crowd.

"Nice to see you're better dressed this evening, Mr Power," joked Dan then he turned to the audience. "For those of you who missed it last night, Mr Power here, forgot to put his shirt on before he joined me up here."

There was an immediate rowdy chorus of wolf whistles and shouts of "Get it off!"

"Not tonight," said Jake, shaking his head.

A chorus of boos surged back at him.

"Are you really going to disappoint these young ladies down at the front?" challenged Dan playfully as he pointed to a group of girls wearing Silver Lake T-shirts.

Realising he had no choice, Jake handed his guitar to Dan and pulled his T-shirt off over his head. The audience went wild as he tossed the sweat soaked shirt down to the group of screaming Silver Lake fans.

"Ok, now that my esteemed friend is appropriately dressed, it's time for Broken Bottle Empty Glass!" roared Dan, trying hard not to laugh.

Feeling slightly self-conscious, Jake stepped up to the microphone and, for the final time, sang the gently hoarse lyrics of Broken Bottle Empty Glass. He turned the last chorus over to the crowd and both he and Dan stood back in awe of their fans. Sunset After The Storm almost raised the roof off the arena a few minutes later and again the fans sang every word. With the last notes dying away around him, Dan stepped up to the front of the stage, "London, give it up for the talented Mr Jake Power!"

Obligingly the crowd roared back to show their appreciation.

"Now time for a bit of end of tour fun," declared Dan. "We've travelled up and down the country for the last ten days with these guys and couldn't have done this without them. Please give a huge London cheer for our good friends in Silver Lake!"

Much to Jake's surprise, his three fellow band members joined them on stage, Paul armed with a tambourine in place of his drumsticks.

"Sometimes, folks, we all need "A Little Help From Our Friends"," declared Dan loudly.

Totally unrehearsed, both bands jammed their way through The Beatles song in true Joe Cocker style. With a few discrete nods and hand signals, they pulled it off successfully, to the delight of the crowd. With an arm around Jake's shoulder, Dan called out, "A round of applause please for our special friends Silver Lake!"

Having taken a bow, Silver Lake left the stage for the night to a resounding cheer. In the wings, Lori was waiting for Jake, grinning and trying not to giggle. He put an arm around her waist and bent to kiss her, careful to keep his guitar from hitting her. Sweat was dripping off him and she curled up her nose at the smell.

"You need a shower, rock star," she teased. "And a new shirt."

With a laugh, Jake nodded his agreement. "I really liked that shirt."

"Not as much as those young ladies do," giggled Lori.

"Harrumph," he muttered as they walked slowly away from the stage.

By midnight the end of tour/after show party was in full swing at a private club near their hotel. Both bands and crews were relaxing among record company and management executives, friends, family and invited guests. Silver Lake had commandeered a table in the corner of the room and the champagne was flowing. Paul and Simon had already moved on to shots and it was shaping up to be a messy night for them. Over at the bar, Jason had cornered Jake and Rich and the three of them were deep in conversation.

"So, Simon," called out Lori, leaning across the table to be heard over the music. "What was it like down with the crowd?"

"Incredible. The atmosphere was fantastic. I'd love to have been out in the middle with all the fans," he admitted. "Next time!"

"A far cry from your air force banquet from the other night?"

"Ever so slightly," he laughed.

Eventually Jake managed to make his escape from Jason and came over to sit beside Lori and Maddy.

"I can't believe that's it over," he said, pouring himself some champagne.

"Good job," replied Maddy, stifling a giggle. "Before you run out of shirts!"

"Very funny, Maddison."

"That looked kind of serious over there with Jason," commented Lori. "What was going on?"

"He was asking if we were ready to give up our day jobs yet," replied Jake.

"And are you?" she asked curiously.

"We can talk about that later," said Jake quietly. Turning his attention to his brother, he asked, "Have you been converted to rock 'n' roll, Simon?"

"I sure have," declared Simon raising another shot to his brother. "Mom would've been so proud."

"Thanks," said Jake with a sad smile. "Go easy on those. These guys are pros when it comes to partying."

"Let's take a walk," suggested Lori, getting to her feet. "I'm getting stiff sitting."

Before they were quarter of the way round the room, Jake and Lori were stopped by a photographer. Smiling, they politely posed for him, then continued round to the Weigh Station corner. Out of the corner of her eye, Lori spotted Scott approaching with his camera.

"Bandit at three o'clock," she whispered to Jake.

The young film maker soon stopped them and asked if they would spare him a few minutes.

"You never give up, do you?" teased Jake. "Ok, you've got two minutes, young man."

"What's been the highlight of the tour?"

"Good question," commented Jake, buying some time to think about his answer. "Tonight was pretty special. Last night when the crowd sang Happy Birthday was quite something. It's all been an amazing experience."

"So, what's next?" asked Scott.

"We've a special gig to play back home the Saturday before Christmas," replied Jake with a smile. "Then we'll see where we end up at the start of next year."

"Any hints on that? There's been a few rumours flying round back stage."

"No," stated Jake bluntly.

"Is playing with your shirt off going to be a feature of your performance going forward?"

"No way!" Jake declared. "Unless it's a hundred degrees in the shade I'm keeping my shirt on my back."

"Thanks, mate," said Scott, pausing his filming. "Lori, do you have a few words for me?"

"Seeing as you asked so nicely," she replied. "I guess I can spare you a couple of minutes."

"I'll go on over to see Dan," said Jake, giving her a kiss. "Come over when you're through with Stephen Spielberg here."

Once Jake was out of earshot, Scott started the tape and asked Lori what her highlight had been.

"Would it be wrong to say my visit to the British Museum today?" she giggled.

"No," acknowledged Scott. "But it wasn't the answer I was hoping for, Mz Hyde."

"Seriously, that's been the highlight of the trip," she replied. "I love museums. However, seeing the guys on stage has been amazing. I hadn't seen them play live since the album launch. There's a new edge to their performance. A new level of self-assurance. Of confidence. Seeing Jake out there holding his own with Weigh Station was fantastic."

"How do you feel when he performs the songs he wrote about you?"

"Honoured. Kind of embarrassed too," admitted Lori. "Hearing the fans sing along with those songs in particular was beautiful."

"Thanks, Lori," said Scott. "I appreciate your time."

"Pleasure," she said with a smile, "Now, if you'll excuse me, I need to circulate."

Taking her time, Lori made her way through the party guests towards the Weigh Station table. She could see Jake sitting beside their lead guitarist, Mikey, talking animatedly with his hands. It made her smile to see him so relaxed in the company of his musical heroes- now an equal amongst them. Despite all the years of work for various bands, she never truly relaxed at these functions and tonight wasn't proving to be any different. Part of her felt self-conscious about her cane; part of her didn't like being on display as the artist. Tonight she just wanted to be Jake's girlfriend; tonight was about him and the rest of Silver Lake.

"Why, it's the stunningly beautiful Mz Hyde!" declared a theatrical voice beside her. It was Dan, more than a little the worse for wear.

"You're hallucinating," she countered with a warm smile.

"Let me fetch you a drink, darling," he offered.

Knowing it was pointless to even attempt to refuse, she watched as he poured her a glass of champagne.

"Thank you," she replied, as he presented her with the glass. "Some party."

"This is tame, darling," said Dan, surveying the room. "Everyone's still standing and the police haven't been called yet."

"So what's next for you?" Lori asked, sipping her champagne.

"A month off over Christmas then we're touring Europe in February. Wish we could take your man with us," he replied, swaying slightly. "Those guys have impressed me from day one."

"Jason has plans for them," she said. "I've not been privy to what they are but I suspect they won't be working as teachers for much longer."

"Teachers were never like that when I was in school," he laughed.

Jake had spotted her and moved over to join them. Putting a protective arm around her waist, he asked, "Can you still remember school, Dan?"

"Just," admitted the older man. "I'll concede it was a long time ago and confess that I wasn't a regular in class latterly."

"Can I say something," began Jake, sounding a little nervous. "I just wanted to say thanks for the last few days. I've been a fan of yours for a long time and this has been like all my Christmases come at once."

"You can sing with us anytime," said Dan sincerely. "It's been a pleasure being out there with you."

"Thanks," replied Jake, suddenly star struck and lost for words.

"Thanks for the drink, Dan," said Lori, stretching up to kiss the older man on the cheek. "We'd better head back to our own guests."

Above them the seatbelt and no smoking signs were lit. Their fellow passengers were still making their way onto the plane behind them. It had been a long two hour wait in the departure lounge and beside her Jake was fidgeting. This was the first time the two of them had flown together and his childlike nervous curiosity made Lori realise that he hadn't been on that many flights. All four members of Silver Lake had been the same in the terminal building- in and out of the duty free shop; in and out of the newsstand; in and out of the men's room. Now that they were all safely seated in the business class section of the plane she could see they were all fidgeting nervously. It made her smile. As before Lori was seated at the aisle with Jake on her right and Grey at the window. Across the aisle, Paul was at the window with Rich in the middle and Maddy at the aisle.

"I hope the guitars are ok in the hold," muttered Jake, as he flicked through the airline magazine.

"They'll be fine," assured Lori softy. "Relax."

"I can't believe that we're on our way home," he said, taking her hand. "It doesn't seem any time since we left."

"I'll be glad to get home," admitted Lori, sounding weary. "The damp weather has been killing me and I miss my own pillow."

"I've missed the ocean," confessed Jake with a sigh.

"You'll see it tomorrow. You'll need to make do with the Delaware River today, rock star," she teased. "How long will it take to get to Lucy's from the airport?"

"About forty five minutes, I'd guess. Maybe a half hour, if the traffic's quiet."

Once the plane had taken off and had reached their cruising altitude, the cabin crew came through with the drinks trolley. Despite it only being late morning, both Jake and Lori ordered champagne. Beside them, Grey had fallen asleep. They ordered an orange juice for him, just in case he wakened thirsty. With their drinks poured into the regulation airline plastic tumblers, Jake proposed a toast, "To the future and many more tours."

"To a safe trip home," toasted Lori.

She realised that with all the packing and getting sorted to leave for the airport that she hadn't asked Jake what his decision was about school. In her heart, she knew what it had to be but she wanted to hear him say it.

"What does Jason have planned?" she asked. "You never told me."

"He's wanting us to tour again at the end of January," explained Jake with a grin. "In Australia and New Zealand then a final show in Tokyo."

"Who with?" she asked.

"An Australian band called Bodimead," Jake replied. "I checked them out on You Tube. Sound ok."

"I've heard of them," said Lori. "But I don't really know much of their stuff. Have you agreed to do it?"

Jake nodded. "Will you come?"

"We can work something out," she promised. "I've got work commitments lined up right through till mid-March."

"We've not got the schedule yet anyway. There's still a lot to work out. Grey doesn't want to leave Becky again so soon. I don't know if we can get her to come out with his mom or his sister. Paul's worried about leaving Maddy. She's already said there's no way she can come."

"What about school?"

"Rich and I talked about that. We'll see out the end of term until Christmas then finish up. He's already set up a meeting with the principal for first thing on Monday."

"This is it, isn't it, rock star?" said Lori with a smile.

"I guess so," agreed Jake, the realisation slowly sinking in. "We've done it. We're an international rock band. I still can't believe it. I keep expecting to waken up and I'm fifteen again playing guitar in my bedroom to Weigh Station albums with my dad yelling at me to turn off the "God damn racket"!"

The rest of the flight passed quickly and without any dramas. Even Paul managed to remain calm, although Maddy claimed he was still hungover from the end of tour party. A couple of hours before they were due to land Grey wakened up and soon he was deep in conversation about music with Jake. Meanwhile the two girls sat chatting across the aisle. Sitting in the one position for so long was causing both of them discomfort for differing reasons.

When the stewardess came round for the final time, Lori asked for some water and discretely swallowed two painkillers. Only Maddy noticed, but Lori shot her a look that told to say nothing. Her friend silently mouthed, "You ok?" and Lori nodded. Eventually the plane began its descent and they were all trying to spot familiar landmarks as they flew over Philadelphia, over the Phillies stadium and the dockyards before landing smoothly at the airport.

"Welcome home, rock star," said Lori, squeezing Jake's hand.

Within a few minutes the plane had taxied to the gate and the doors were open. Making sure they had taken everything with them, the Silver Lake party slowly made their way into the building. The painkillers had kicked in and Lori managed to keep pace with Jake as he charged on ahead. When they reached the escalators that would take them down to passport control, she paused. He put a steadying hand round her waist and, on the count of three, they stepped onto the moving staircase together.

"Thanks," she said, smiling up at him. "I'm still a bit nervous of these."

There were no delays at immigration, and soon they were waiting patiently in the baggage hall with their fellow passengers. Jake and Rich were both pacing, anxiously awaiting the safe arrival of their precious guitars. Slowly the luggage began to emerge out of the chute and make its way round. Patiently Maddy and Lori sat at the side and waited while the four guys rounded up their suitcases, holdalls and instruments.

"You ok?" asked Maddy, when she was sure the boys were out of earshot.

"I'm fine. Just tired and sore. It's been a long few days and the British weather didn't agree with me," replied Lori, rubbing her thigh. "All the standing about hasn't helped either. What about you?"

"My back's sore," confessed her friend. "It's only going to get worse. I've an appointment at the clinic next week to get checked over. I'm exhausted. I think I'll sleep for the next three days at least."

"I think we all will."

After almost an hour the band had collected all their luggage and guitars. Much to everyone's relief everything looked to have survived the transatlantic journey intact. *En masse* they headed for the exit that led to the arrivals hall. As they walked through the automatic doors, Lori caught sight of a small blonde child, then heard the familiar shriek of "Daddy!" as Becky came hurtling towards Grey. Behind the barrier, they could see Grey's mother standing waving. With tears in his eyes, the bass player swept his little girl into his arms and hugged her tight.

"I've missed you, Daddy," she said as she cuddled into his neck. "Grammy said we could come here to surprise you."

"I'm glad you did, princess," he replied. "I've missed you too."

Still clinging tightly to Grey, Becky shouted hello to the others. Her delight at having him home was clear for all to see.

"Hi," said Annie, Grey's mother, as they reached her. "Good flight?"

"It was fine. Bit of a delay in the baggage hall, but no dramas," replied Grey, giving her a hug. "Jump down, Becky."

Once they'd all greeted Grey's mother and Becky properly, Rich said, "I guess it's time we went our separate ways."

"There should be a limo outside for us," said Maddy with a yawn.

"My car's in the car park," said Lori. "We're stopping at Jake's sister's house for the night."

"So what's the plans for the weekend?" asked Grey, still holding Becky's hand.

"Why not come out to the house for lunch on Sunday?" suggested Jake. "That gives us all a few days to recover."

"Sounds like a plan," agreed Rich.

"Right," nodded Jake. "Till Sunday, guys."

Having said their goodbyes, Lori led the way to the car park. As they went up in the elevator, she rummaged in her bag for the car park ticket and her keys. After a quick debate, they agreed she would drive to Lucy's but that Jake would drive them home next day. It took a bit of re-organising and squeezing of bags to get all their luggage into the car.

"Did you not leave with two bags?" she observed as Jake put his guitar cases on the back seat. "How come you've got four now?"

"I don't know. I bought some stuff and we got gifts from folk every night. It just kind of multiplied," he confessed, closing the car door. "You sure you're not too tired to drive?"

"I'll be fine," she promised, getting behind the wheel. "As long as you can direct me."

"I'll try. It's been a while since I've been there."

Much to Lori's relief, the early afternoon traffic on I-95 was light, making it easier for her to relax and watch out for road signs showing the exit towards Media. Beside her, Jake was lying back in the passenger seat with his eyes closed.

"Don't fall asleep on me," she cautioned, as she reached to turn on the stereo. "Once we get off the highway, I have no clue where we are going."

"I'm not asleep," he muttered. "Just a bit of a headache after the flight."

"There's some Advil and a bottle of water in my bag," offered Lori.

"Don't mind if I do," sighed Jake, reaching round to lift her bag out of the back seat.

It took them about half an hour to reach the outskirts of Media and, once they left the highway, Jake directed her along Baltimore Pike, past the local mall and the hospital before telling her to make a right at the Wawa building. Once off the main road, he directed her along a picturesque tree-lined road, then told her to turn left at the crossroads that lay up ahead.

"It's the third driveway on the left, Lori," he directed. "Lucy's house is at the far end on the right."

Slowly she navigated the Mercedes up the long, narrow tree-lined driveway before finally parking in front of a beautiful modern colonial style house. As soon as the car came to a halt, the front door of the house flew open and two small boys came hurtling out, yelling, "Uncle Jake! Uncle Jake!"

"Guess they remember me," observed Jake, as he opened the car door.

Lori sat and watched as the two boys threw themselves at Jake, almost knocking him off his feet. As she opened the driver's door to climb out, she saw Lucy coming out to greet them.

"Boys!" she scolded sharply. "Be gentle."

"They're fine," said Jake, giving her a hug. "I can't believe how big they're getting."

"Tell me about it," replied Lucy with a smile.

While brother and sister had been greeting each other, Lori had manoeuvred herself out of the car and come over to join them.

"Hi, Lucy," she said, hugging the young woman warmly. "Thanks for having us over. I couldn't have faced that drive home right now."

"Delighted to see you both," replied Lucy. "Boys, help your Uncle Jake with the bags."

The two small boys scampered after their uncle as the two girls made their way into the house. Once inside, Lucy said to Lori to go straight through to the kitchen.

"Coffee?" she asked, as Lori took a seat the large pine kitchen table.

"Oh please," sighed Lori wearily. "It might help to waken me up a bit."

"How was your flight?"

"Flight was fine. It's just been a busy few days. I'd only just got the jet lag sorted and then it was time to fly home."

"Too many late nights?" joked Lucy, passing her a Winnie the Pooh mug.

"Or early mornings," laughed Lori. "Depends on how you look at it."

"Simon called yesterday," said Lucy, as she joined her at the table. "He was suffering a bit."

Lori burst out laughing, "I'm not surprised. He partied hard on Tuesday night."

"Who partied hard?" asked Jake, as he strolled into the kitchen.

"Your brother."

"Whew! He sure did," agreed Jake, remembering the state his older brother had been in as they had taken him back to the hotel. "I bet he was suffering yesterday."

"He was," said Lucy, getting up to fetch him a coffee.

"Lucy, where do you want me to put our bags?" Jake asked. "I've dumped them in your lounge room for now."

"Leave them there till you've had your coffee," she replied. "Your room is at the top of the stairs and round to the right, next to the bathroom. I'll show you later."

"Ok," acknowledged Jake, gladly taking a seat beside Lori. "When's Rob due home?"

"He promised to be home by five thirty," replied his sister. "I thought we'd eat around six if that's ok with you guys."

"We'll eat anytime," grinned Jake. "Our schedule has gone right out the window for the last couple of weeks."

"Yeah, Simon said you went out for dinner at midnight the other night."

"Music business hours," joked Jake, adding half 'n' half to his coffee. "We can't eat a full meal before a show, but we're starving after we're done. It's crazy."

"Add in jet lag" said Lori. "And you just eat when someone puts food in front of you."

"MOM!" screamed a voice from the family room. "Josh won't change the channel."

"Excuse me," said Lucy. "Time to referee the angels."

As Lucy marched across the kitchen and into the family room to straighten out her sons, Jake put a hand on Lori's knee.

"I'm glad you arranged this, li'l lady," he said softly. "Lucy's so like my mom was. Reminds me of home when I was a little kid."

"Her boys are cute," said Lori, putting her hand on his. "The older one is very like her. What do you want to do about giving them their gifts?"

"Let's wait until Rob gets home. He's quite strict with them. Best wait till he's here," suggested Jake, keeping his voice deliberately quiet.

They sat in the kitchen in silence for a few minutes enjoying their coffee and the fact that they didn't have to keep an eye on the time or be any place specific. The pace of their world was slowly returning to normal. From the family room, they could hear Lucy laying down the TV rules, followed by a shrill protest form Josh, her younger son. Once peace and harmony had been restored, she returned to the kitchen to join them.

"Sorry about that," she apologised. "They get an hour of TV before dinner and always fight about who gets to watch what. It's the same every day. Oh, and they want Uncle Jake to play Lego with them."

"Once I've finished my coffee," he agreed.

"Lori," began Lucy. "If Jake's ok to wait with the boys, would you come to the food store with me?"

"Sure. I could do with stretching my legs for a bit."

"How is your leg?" asked Lucy, her voice filled with motherly concern.

"Pretty much the same," admitted Lori, her hand subconsciously going to her thigh. "It's not enjoyed the cold, damp weather or flying. Sitting for too long is worse than being on my feet for too long."

"You sure you're up for a trip to the store?"

"Yes," replied Lori with a smile. "I need to move around to loosen it off a bit."

It was already getting dark when the two girls left the house. The boys had dragged Jake into the family room to play with them, despite his mock protests about being too tired to build Lego. Once Lucy had reversed her SUV out of the driveway, she explained to Lori that she had ordered a birthday cake for Jake but had forgotten to collect it. The food store was only a five minute drive from the house and looked to be quiet as they parked close to the front door.

"I just need to grab a few bits and pieces while we're here," said Lucy, as she pulled out a small shopping cart. "What do you guys like for breakfast?"

"Coffee and whatever's going," replied Lori. "Don't go to any trouble for us. Please."

"Look, it's not every day I have a famous artist and a rock star for a sleepover."

Giggling at her excitement, Lori suggested she buy some cinnamon raisin bread since she was so insistent on spoiling them and some maple cured streaky bacon for Jake.

"Is there anything you need while we're here?" asked Lucy. "If you see anything, just toss it in the cart."

"I'm fine," assured Lori. "We'll probably stop off at the Giant on the way home tomorrow."

Once Lucy had toured the shop and picked up her essentials plus the bread and the bacon, she led Lori back over to the bakery counter. The glass display cabinet was full of brightly coloured cakes coated with thick butter cream icing. Beside the cabinet was a smaller display of character themed cupcakes. While Lori gazed incredulously at the display, Lucy spoke to the assistant about collecting her pre-ordered cake. There was a bit of confusion while they searched for the order, but, after a few worrying moments, the assistant brought out a box with the correct cake inside. Lucy called Lori over to check it out before they sealed the box. It was a large square cake with a photo of Jake onstage in the centre and she had requested Royal icing instead of buttercream.

"He'll love it," declared Lori with a smile, knowing he would be genuinely touched by the effort his sister had gone to.

"Did the band get him a cake on his actual birthday?" asked Lucy, as she sat the box carefully on the lower level of the shopping cart.

"Yes," Lori replied. "They gave him one shaped like a guitar before the show. I'm not sure who ate it though. I never got a slice."

"Well, there's plenty of this one to go round."

When they got back to the house, there was a black BMW in the driveway beside Lori's car and, as they entered via the front door, all they could hear was the boys giggling and squealing. Having hidden the cake in the laundry room, Lucy led Lori through to the family room. There was Lego scattered all over the floor and both boys were clambering all over Jake, tickling him as he lay in the midst of the small coloured bricks.

"Help," he groaned with a boyish grin. "These gremlins are killing me."

"Where's Rob?" asked Lucy, surveying the scene with a smile.

"He's gone upstairs to change and he said something about fetching some beers," replied Jake, as he attempted to sit up.

Lucy nodded, then turned to Lori, "Guess it's wine o'clock then?"

As the girls went back towards the kitchen, Lucy called back over her shoulder, "Uncle Jake used to be really tickly behind his knees, guys."

"Thanks, sis," groaned Jake, amid fresh squeals from his two nephews.

Laughing at his distress, the girls returned to the sanctuary of the kitchen where Lucy busied herself getting the wine glasses out of the cupboard.

"Red or white, Lori?" she asked. "It's a fillet of beef for dinner. Just in case that influences your choice."

"Red would be good," replied Lori. "Do you need a hand with dinner?"

"No, you're fine," assured Lucy warmly. "I set the table earlier and everything else is in the oven. Sit down and relax. You're our guest."

Before Lori could reply, Lucy's husband, Rob, came striding into the room. He wasn't what she had expected. Rob was almost as tall as Jake with short dark hair going grey at the temples and had obviously played football in his earlier years from his solid frame that had gone to seed somewhat over time. He looked to be a few years older than his wife. When he saw Lori standing in the middle of the kitchen, he smiled and said, "You must be Lori. I'm Rob."

"Pleasure," said Lori, shaking his large hand.

"Nice to finally meet you. Lucy's been so excited about you both coming to visit," he continued. "I hear that Jake has the boys wound into a frenzy."

"They're just having fun, honey," said Lucy quietly. Lori noted that her entire tone of voice had changed in the presence of her husband.

"Is the beer in the basement?" Rob asked, as he opened the drawer in search of a bottle opener.

"I put some in the small refrigerator in the garage," replied his wife. "If you want more then it's downstairs."

While Rob was out in the garage, Jake managed to make good

his escape from his nephews. He wandered into the kitchen, pulling his T-shirt down and fixing the belt on his jeans.

"You losing your clothing again?" teased Lori, as she gave him a hug.

"I've been beaten up by two gremlins," he said with a relaxed smile. "Lucy, your kids need their nails trimmed. I'm scratched to bits."

"Sorry," apologised his sister. "Rob's gone to get you a beer. That'll help to anaesthetise it."

At that, Rob re-appeared with four bottles of beer. He set two down on the counter and put the other two into the fridge. With two swift, well-practiced movements he had both bottles open and passed one to Jake. By now Lucy had poured two glasses of red wine and passed one to Lori.

"What'll we drink to?" asked Lucy.

"Health, wealth and happiness," suggested Rob.

"A good night's sleep," countered Lori, raising her glass.

"Happy days," compromised Jake, raising his beer bottle towards his sister and brother –in-law.

"Happy days," echoed the others.

"We've brought some gifts for you guys," began Lori, setting her glass down on the table. "Is it ok to fetch them just now?"

"Sure, but you didn't need to bring anything," said Rob.

"Jake, the bags are on the top of the red holdall," directed Lori. "Can you fetch them?"

"I took your bags upstairs," commented Rob. "I'll show you where I put them."

The two men disappeared upstairs while Lucy suggested they go and take a seat in the family room. Both boys were sitting huddled over the Lego box, working together to build something. Setting their wine glasses down on the large square glass topped coffee table, the two girls sat side by side on one of the two-seater couches. Lori laid her cane down at her feet, laying it lengthways along the couch to prevent anyone tripping over it. Seeing his mum come to sit down, Josh clambered up onto her knee.

"Can Uncle Jake stay with us for ever?" he asked, staring seriously at his mother with big round brown eyes.

"No, honey. He's only staying tonight, then he has to go home with Lori," replied Lucy, cuddling her younger son.

"But he's good fun," protested Josh. "I want him to stay."

"Well, he can't stay," stated his mother firmly. "Uncle Jake has got to go to work. He can't stay and play all the time."

"Aw," muttered Josh sourly.

"Maybe you could visit us sometime," suggested Lori, reaching over to rub his shoulder. "We stay at the shore. You could come for the weekend."

"The shore is only for vacation," stated the small boy bluntly. "No one lives there all the time."

Trying not to laugh at the seriousness of his expression, Lori whispered, "We do, but don't tell anyone else."

Before Josh could reply his father and uncle came into the room and sat down. Jake had three plastic bags in his hand as well as his beer. He opened the first bag and brought out two boxes, "Rob, Lucy, these are for you to say thanks for letting us stay tonight."

He passed the boxes over to his sister and her husband then brought out two Silver Lake tour T-shirts. "And there's these if you would like them."

"Thanks!" squealed Lucy, holding up the large black T-shirt.

"We didn't know what to get for the boys so they've got a gift bag each," explained Lori, as Jake handed his nephews a bag each. "It's just some things we picked up in Glasgow and London."

"You shouldn't have," said Rob, as he opened the box containing his silver hip flask. "Wow! That's awesome!"

All of them watched as the two boys emptied their bags over the floor, then screamed in delight at the contents. Both of them had more or less the same range of gifts. Apart from the gifts Lori had picked up for the boys, Jake had added drumsticks from both Silver Lake and Weigh Station, autographed photos from both bands, T-shirts, baseball caps, guitar picks and backstage passes from London.

"You've spoiled them," said Lucy, hugging both Lori and Jake. "And I love my earrings. They're stunning."

"Glad you like them," said Jake. "I chose them."

"You did?" she asked, eyes wide in surprise.

"He did," confirmed Lori, sipping her wine. "I was in a different jewellers buying his birthday present."

"Oh, I almost forgot!" gasped Lucy, putting the box with the earrings down beside her glass. "We have a birthday gift for you, Jake."

She went over to the display cabinet, opened the cupboard and brought out a blue shiny gift bag. Instead of handing the bag to Jake, she gave it to Sam and Josh to present to their uncle. Suddenly acting all shy, the two boys passed the bag over then rushed to stand by their mother while he opened it. With a wink at the boys, Jake looked into the bag. Slowly, teasing them, he pulled out a black zipped hoodie and two T-shirts, one white, one black with the store logo on the chest.

"Just what I need!" he declared enthusiastically, "Thanks."

"It's not much," apologised Lucy, a hint of sadness in her voice. "But I had no idea what to get you."

Trying hard not to laugh, Lori said, "Jake needs all the T-shirts he can get."

"Why?" asked Rob, looking bemused.

"Very funny, Mz Hyde," said Jake with a smile. "The first night in London I had taken my shirt off after our set. I was standing with Lori and Simon watching Weigh Station and had my clean shirt in my hand. I got so engrossed in the set I forgot to put my shirt on, almost missed my cue and ended up out on stage stripped to the waist. The next night, Dan, the singer with Weigh Station gave me a rough time about having a shirt on. I had no choice but to strip it off and toss it into the audience."

Lucy threw back her head and laughed, "Oh, the ladies must have loved that!"

"As long as someone did," laughed Jake. "The girls that caught my stinky T-shirt seemed happy enough."

All of them laughed.

"What's it like stepping out in front of a big crowd?" asked Rob, draining the last of his beer.

"It's a buzz. It's scary. It's fantastic," gushed Jake. "I love it. Don't get me wrong, I get nervous before we go out there but, once you're on that stage, it's an awesome feeling."

"Was it big arenas you were playing in the UK?" asked Lucy, curious to hear about the tour.

"Not really," replied Jake. "It varied from about a thousand right up to about fourteen thousand in London."

"Where was the best place you played?" asked Rob, as Sam

clambered up to sit on his knee.

"Tough question," sighed Jake, glancing over at Lori. "Glasgow was special because Lori was there. Dublin was amazing, probably because it was first. Having fourteen thousand folk sing "Happy Birthday" to me in London was quite something. I guess London wins."

"What's next?" asked his sister.

"Well, we've to play a set at the school on the fifteenth," answered Jake. "Then early next year we're heading to Australia, New Zealand and Japan with an Australian band if it all goes to plan."

"Wow!" stated Lucy. "This has really taken off, hasn't it?"

Jake nodded, "It's been a bit of a roller coaster ride. I keep thinking it's a dream and I'm going to wake up."

"Is there money in it yet?" asked his brother-in-law bluntly.

"We've not met the accountant recently, but yes," replied Jake with a grin. "We're starting to see the fruits of our labours."

"You'd do it for free," declared Lori with a giggle. "I've seen you on that stage."

"Probably," he conceded with a grin. "Hearing the fans singing along with you, and singing your lyrics back at you is an incredible experience. You can't put a price on that."

"Is there any video footage of the tour?" asked Lucy hopefully.

Glancing at each other, Jake and Lori burst out laughing.

"Hours and hours of it!" giggled Lori. "There was a young documentary filmmaker following them. Every time you turned round Scott was there filming it. He filmed all the performances, I think. Simon was helping him the other night."

"He was?" asked Rob sounding surprised.

"He just carried some cables and a spare battery or two," joked Jake. "Lucy, as soon as I get a copy of the footage, I'll get it to you."

"Thanks," she said with a smile. "Now, I reckon dinner's about ready. Rob, will you give me a hand please? Boys, go wash your hands and get to the table."

"Yes, mom," they both said, racing towards the downstairs bathroom.

"Can we help?" offered Jake, as he helped Lori to her feet.

"No need," assured Rob. "Go on through to the dining room."

After a delicious meal, Lucy asked the boys to help clear the table so she could serve dessert. Throughout the meal the two boys had been begging their uncle to play his guitar before they went to bed. While Lucy cleared the plates away, Jake ran out to the car to fetch his acoustic guitar. Leaving it propped up in the corner, still in its case, Jake took his seat again just as his sister and her sons came in carrying the birthday cake and singing "Happy Birthday." Rob and Lori joined in as Jake sat back smiling and shaking his head.

"Make a wish," said Lucy, as she placed the cake in front of him.

With one breath, Jake blew out all the candles and made his silent wish as he did so.

"Thanks," he said quietly, gazing down at the photo on the cake. "And you remembered about the icing too."

"I just hope it tastes as good as it looks," said Lucy, passing him the knife.

When they had all eaten a generous portion of cake, Jake asked his nephews, "Do you still want me to play my guitar?"

"Yes!" they both screamed at once.

"Only for ten minutes, boys," stated Rob as he checked the time. "You have school tomorrow, remember?"

"What do you want me to play?" asked Jake as he went over to the corner to fetch his guitar.

"Something you play on stage," said Sam.

"Something loud!" grinned Josh mischievously.

"Ok," began Jake, as he adjusted the tuning and tried to figure out what to play. "Josh, I can't play too loud as I don't have my electric guitar or any of the amps we use on stage. Sam, I'll play one of the songs we do, but it's a quiet one."

As Lucy brought through the coffee from the kitchen, Jake began to gently play "Stronger Within." Hearing the acoustic melody in the confined space of the dining room sent shivers through Lucy and, when Jake began to sing, she could feel tears of emotion welling up in her eyes. She stood behind her husband, with her hands on his shoulders, mesmerised by the sight of her brother playing and singing in front of her. The boys both sat in stunned silence, totally entranced. Neither of them had seen anyone play the guitar up close before and were fascinated by it.

"That was beautiful," acknowledged Rob when the song was over. "Really something."

"Play another one," said Josh, clapping his hands.

"One more. Then it's bedtime," agreed Jake.

This time he opted to play a more familiar song and played Led Zeppelin's "Stairway to Heaven". Lori had never heard him play it before and she sat as enchanted as the others. As he played, Jake glanced over at her and she nodded her approval. When the song ended, the boys pleaded for a third one, but their dad said no. With sad, tired faces the two little boys hugged Jake and Lori and said good night as Lucy took them up to bed.

Stirring his coffee, Rob said, "I'm beginning to understand why Lucy was so blown away at your album launch."

"Thanks," replied Jake, realising that was praise indeed from his brother-in-law. Casually, he sat picking out a melody that had been forming in head over the last few days.

"I don't know how you do it," added Rob. "I've not got a musical bone in my body."

"A lot of years of hard work," said Jake.

"Why don't the band ever play "Stairway to Heaven"?" asked Lori, sipping her coffee. "That sounded fabulous."

"We've played it before. A long time ago," replied Jake. "Who knows, it might find its way back in someday."

Carefully, he put his guitar back in its case, feeling a bit embarrassed at playing in his sister's house. To him, it felt a bit like showing off.

When Lucy came back downstairs half an hour later, she was disappointed that he had put the guitar away.

"Thanks for playing for the boys," she said warmly. "It was all they could talk about as I put them to bed."

"Pleasure. I'd play all night given half a chance."

"I remember," laughed Lucy. "And it used to drive Dad wild. Was that the same guitar Mom gave you when you turned eighteen?"

Jake nodded. "The very one. My most treasured possession."

They sat around the table for another hour or so reminiscing about Jake's misspent youth, telling more tales about the tour and the end of tour party. Just after nine, Lori yawned, then declared that she was struggling to keep her eyes open.

"Lord, I'm forgetting how tired you two must be," apologised Lucy.

"It's been a long day," admitted Jake, realising he too was tired. "Are you both working tomorrow?"

"I'm not," said Lucy. "But I'll be up early to get the boys out to school and kindergarten. When do you need to leave?"

"Before lunch," replied Jake, getting up from the table. "No doubt we'll be up at the crack of dawn though with the time difference."

"Well, if you're first up, put the coffee pot on," suggested Rob, only half joking.

"Night night, folks," said Lori sleepily, allowing Jake to help her up. "Thanks for dinner."

"Sleep well," replied Lucy softly.

By five a.m. both Jake and Lori were wide awake, their body clocks telling them it was mid-morning. Both of them had slept soundly in the soft, comfortable bed and now lay wrapped in each other's arms, listening to hear if anyone was moving around. Gently Jake fingered Lori's long blonde hair, enjoying the fact that, if he chose to, he could lie there all day. It had been an intense few weeks and, now that the rock'n'roll rollercoaster had come to a temporary stop, he realised just how tired he was. Sitting around having a laid back family dinner the previous night had been the perfect way to wind down. As he lay beside Lori, Jake silently reflected on how much the band had achieved in such a short space of time.

"Penny for them?" whispered Lori softly.

"Eh?"

"You were miles away there."

"I was just thinking back over the last few months and how far we've come so fast. It'll be nice to slow things down for a few weeks before it all starts up again," he replied. "I still can't quite believe what we've achieved this year."

"We've both come a long way, I guess," mused Lori.

They heard the distant "cheep" of an alarm clock signalling that someone else was probably awake.

"I'm going to get some OJ," said Jake, getting out of bed. "Want some?"

"I'll come down in a few minutes," Lori replied. "Don't bring juice up here. I'd hate to spill anything."

"Ok," nodded Jake, as he opened the bedroom door.

Once down in the kitchen, Jake poured himself a large glass of orange juice and, having swallowed half of it in two thirsty gulps, he then began to make a pot of coffee. He hadn't bothered to pull on a shirt and was standing at the sink in his shorts when his elder nephew walked in.

"Wow!" exclaimed the voice behind him. "You're all pictures, Uncle Jake!"

Trying not to laugh, Jake turned round. "Morning, Sam. You ok today?"

The little boy nodded, still staring in fascination at his uncle's tattoos.

"Can I get you some juice or some cereal?"

"Milk and Cheerio's, please," replied Sam still staring. "How come you're all pictures?"

"They're tattoos," explained Jake with a grin. "A friend drew them with special ink that goes into your skin."

"Doesn't it wash off?"

"No," replied Jake, as he searched for a bowl and the cereal. "It stays forever."

"Did it hurt?"

"Some of it did," admitted Jake, finally finding the bowls. "It stings a bit when it's getting done."

At that Lucy came in, closely followed by Rob and a very sleepy looking Josh.

"Mom, look!" cried Sam excitedly. "Uncle Jake's covered in pictures!"

"They're scary," whined Josh, cuddling into his mother.

"I'm guessing they haven't seen anyone with tattoos before," deduced Jake, pouring milk into Sam's cereal for him then passing him the bowl.

"I've never seen tattoos like that for real," Rob confessed, almost as wide eyed as his son. "That's some collection."

"You've had some of those a long time," said Lucy, sitting her younger son at the table. "I remember you getting the first one. Mom had a holy fit when she saw that sword on your back."

"I can imagine," said Rob.

"The face on your leg is scary," stated Josh, scowling at his uncle. "So is the man on your shoulder."

"They're only drawings, honey," reassured Lucy, passing Josh a bowl of cereal. "Is Lori awake yet?"

Jake nodded, "She'll be down in a minute or two. Takes her a while to get moving in the mornings some days."

Right on cue, they could hear Lori making her way down the stairs. She had left her cane in the bedroom and couldn't disguise her limp as she entered the kitchen.

"Good morning," she said brightly, as she sat down beside Sam.

The boy was staring at her then, feeling brave, he asked, "Why do you walk funny?"

"Sam!" scolded his mother. "Don't be so nosy!"

"It's ok," said Lori, taking a deep breath. "I had an accident, Sam."

"What happened?"

"I got hit by a motorcycle when I was crossing the road. I broke my leg badly and it hasn't healed properly," she explained briefly. "So I limp now when I walk."

"I'm sorry," said the boy, staring down into his cereal bowl.

"Didn't you look before you crossed the road?" asked Josh seriously.

With a wistful smile, Lori replied, "I did, Josh, but the man on the bike didn't stop at the red light."

"Enough questions, boys," said Lucy sternly. "Eat your cereal."

"Right," declared Rob, finishing his last mouthful of coffee. "I'll see you guys another time. Have a safe drive back down to the shore."

"You'll need to visit us sometime," offered Lori warmly. "And thanks again for letting us stay here last night."

"Not a problem. We'll maybe take a run down in the spring. Too cold for the beach in winter."

"You're welcome any time," said Jake.

"Thanks," replied Rob brusquely before adding "Lucy, I'll be late home. Don't wait dinner for me."

Without waiting for a reply, he was gone out the back way through the garage.

"Ok, boys," snapped Lucy, clapping her hands. "Go and get dressed for school and brush your teeth."

The boys didn't need to be told twice and both quickly scampered off up the stairs. Pouring herself a coffee, Lucy sat down at the table with a sigh.

"Sorry, it's a bit chaotic in here at breakfast," she apologised. "And I'm sorry if the boys made you feel uncomfortable, Lori."

"Don't worry about it," replied Lori, forcing a smile. "I'm getting better at answering those awkward questions. It's easier when kids ask though than when it's an adult."

"It must be hard," sympathised Lucy with a sad smile. "Sounds awful."

"It's a taboo subject," stated Lori plainly.

"Let it go, Lucy," cautioned Jake quietly.

"Sorry," she apologised then changing the subject said, "I need to leave before eight to take the boys to school and kindergarten. I'll be back around nine. Will you still be here?"

"If you want us to be," replied Jake.

"I thought maybe Lori and I could go to the mall for an hour or so before you leave. A bit of girlie retail therapy," suggested Lucy hopefully.

"And what am I meant to do?" asked Jake, a mischievous grin spreading across his face.

"Oh, I don't know," giggled Lucy. "The breakfast dishes will need washed and the family room needs vacuumed. That's if rock stars remember how to do chores?"

"Mom taught me well," laughed Jake. "I'm sure I can figure it out."

"Lori?" asked Lucy hopefully.

"Sure, why not," she agreed. "But we do need to head off before lunch."

The beach house stood in darkness in the fading light of the afternoon when Jake finally turned the car into the driveway. One hour at the mall had turned into two and then Lucy had insisted they stay for an early lunch. Traffic on the Coastal Highway had been backed up due to an overturned truck and their two hour drive had taken almost four. It had been a relief when the Rehoboth water tower came into sight signalling that home was only a few short miles away.

"Home sweet home," sighed Lori, as Jake switched off the engine.

"Feels like I've been away forever," he said as he opened the car door.

"You've been away less than three weeks," replied Lori. "Can you give me a hand, please?"

"Sure," he said, rushing round to help her.

As Jake helped her out of the car, he could see pain etched across her face. Over the past week, he had seen that look too often and his concern was growing.

"Don't yell at me, li'l lady," he said softly, as he put a supportive arm around her waist. "But I'd be happier if you called your doctor and made an appointment to see him. I can see you're struggling here."

With a heavy sigh, Lori surprised him by replying, "I'll call him in a few minutes. I missed my last check-up. I'm sure I've just overdone things over the last few days."

"I hope that's all it is," said Jake. "I hate seeing you in pain, Lori."

"I'll be fine," she assured him, as she unlocked the door. "You go and fetch the bags and I'll get the coffee pot started."

It took several trips back and forth but, by the time Lori had poured two freshly made mugs of coffee, Jake had brought all their luggage into the lounge, including his guitars. While the coffee had been brewing, Lori had taken two Vicodin to ease the growing pain in her leg. Much as she hated taking the strong pain medication, she hated suffering the pain even more.

"Right, li'l lady," said Jake picking up the two mugs. "You're going to lie down in the sun room for a couple of hours. No arguments."

"I'm not arguing," conceded Lori, sounding depressed. "Let me bring the mail and my laptop through though."

Almost as soon as she was settled on the couch with her leg supported by cushions, Jake handed her the phone.

"Call the doctor."

Without argument, Lori dialled the all too familiar number and asked to be put through to Dr Brent's secretary. Gentle classical music played in her ears as she waited to be connected. After several minutes her call was transferred.

"John Brent speaking," came the familiar voice.

"Hi. It's Lori Hyde," she said. "Times must be hard if you're answering your own calls."

"Good afternoon, Lori. I was beginning to think you were avoiding me. You missed your last appointment."

"Technically, I cancelled it," replied Lori. "But I'm calling to make another one. Sooner rather than later if possible."

"Let me check the schedule," said the doctor. "How have you been?"

"Fine up until about a week ago," she admitted, then she briefly explained about her trip to Britain. The doctor asked her a few questions about the type and location of the pain she was experiencing. He quizzed her about what pain medication she had been taking.

"Can you come in first thing on Monday?" he asked. "I've a clinic starting at nine thirty, but it's full. If you can be here for nine, I'll see you before it starts. From what you're telling me it sounds as though you've just overdone it on your trip. It doesn't sound like an issue with the internal fixation, but we'll get some x-rays done to rule that out. In fact, can you go and get them done first. I'll tell the department you'll be there for eight thirty."

"OK, I can be there for eight thirty on Monday," agreed Lori resignedly.

"Great. Now take things easy over the weekend. Go back to your low level pain management routine. Even if you feel ok, follow the regime until I see you."

"Should I try to stay off my feet?"

"Take plenty of rest. When you are sitting down, keep your leg up and supported," advised the doctor. "I'd be wasting my breath to put you on bed rest, Mz Hyde."

"I guess you would," acknowledged Lori with a laugh. "I'll be sensible though. I need to be ok for next weekend."

"Why? Where are you off to?"

"I'm going to a high school Christmas dance with Jake," she confessed.

"No dancing for you, young lady," he cautioned her.

"I was never much of a dancer before my accident," she giggled. "So I'm not likely to start now."

The doctor laughed. "Ok, take it easy over the weekend, Lori, and I'll see you first thing on Monday. If the pain gets too much, do you still have Jo's number?"

"Yes."

"Call me on that if you are really struggling."

"Thanks, John. I appreciate it."

While she had been chatting on the phone, Jake had been sorting through the large pile of mail he had retrieved from the mailbox. There were a handful of letters for him, a large pile of letters for Lori and an even larger pile of junk mail. As she put the phone down, he passed the letters over to her.

"You sort through these while you drink your coffee," he suggested. "I'm going to take my guitars downstairs, then unpack the bags."

"Leave the bags. We can unpack later."

"Rock tour's over, li'l lady," he joked. "I've got laundry to do!"

Before she could protest, he left her alone in the sun room and disappeared through the house. Jake knew, if he left her alone with the mail and her laptop, she would soon become engrossed in catching up and take a longer rest than if he hung around talking to her. Having taken their bags down to the bedroom, he fetched two laundry baskets and sorted the dirty clothes out as he unpacked. The bag with his used stage clothes was crammed full and, as he unzipped it, the smell of stale sweat was overwhelmingly revolting. Before touching the other bags, he took the first basket through to the utility room and loaded up the washing machine.

"If the fans could see me now," he thought, as he walked back down to the bedroom to fetch the rest of the laundry. It felt good to be doing "normal chores". The same feeling he had had earlier as he vacuumed his sister's family room; a good leveller after his time spent centre stage.

He left most of Lori's unpacking for her, but, in true Lori organised fashion, she had made it easy for him to identify her laundry. It was all neatly folded in a bag marked "Laundry" and zipped into a separate section of her suitcase. Deciding not to even attempt to unpack the rest, he left her case sitting open on the small two-seater couch in the bedroom.

The basement looked bare, with most of the band's equipment still missing. Paul's practice drum kit sat silent in the corner and all the guitar stands stood empty. Lovingly, he placed his own instruments back into the storage rack where they lived. When he lifted the new electric guitar that Jason had presented him with, he smiled at the memory of his birthday. Since then he hadn't had the chance to play with his new "toy". Now seemed as good a time as any.

Up in the sun room, the pain medication had kicked in and Lori was feeling a lot more relaxed. There had been a few household bills in the mail to take care of but she had dealt with most of them over the phone. As she powered up her laptop, she could hear Jake playing down in the basement. She didn't instantly recognise what he was playing, but guessed that it was something he was still working on. While she caught up with her emails, both personal and business, she enjoyed listening to him practice. He had run through the unfamiliar piece a few times, then cranked up the volume and entertained her with his renditions of a few rock classics. Shutting down the laptop, Lori lay back to listen to the music, accompanied by the gentle hum of the washing machine. It felt good to be home.

She must have dozed off because the next thing she knew Jake was gently shaking her and, when she opened her eyes, the sunroom was in darkness.

"Sorry to wake you, but I didn't know what you wanted to do about dinner," he said, kissing her tenderly.

"What time is it?" she asked sleepily.

"Almost seven. I was going to go into town and pick up some Chinese."

"Sounds good," she agreed, as she rubbed the sleep from her eyes. "Want me to come with you?"

Jake shook his head. "You stay where you are. I won't be long."

Before she could argue, he was getting to his feet. "And don't touch the laundry either," he warned. "I have that under control."

"Am I allowed to turn on the TV?" asked Lori with a sleepy smile.

"Only via the remote," replied Jake, passing her the remote control. "Don't bother setting the table either. We can picnic in here."

"I get the hint," she said. "I'll stay here till you get back."

"Good. I won't be long."

Once she heard the truck pull out of the driveway, Lori slowly got to her feet and wandered through the house to the bedroom. She smiled when she saw that Jake had tried his best with the unpacking, but was relieved to see that he had left her bag for her to attend to. Lifting her bag of toiletries out of the open suitcase, she limped through to the en suite bathroom to freshen up. On her way back through to the sun room, Lori paused to fetch a bottle of wine and two glasses, then went back to the kitchen for plates and cutlery. She set them down on the coffee table then settled herself back on the couch. Leisurely, she flicked through the TV channels in search of something worth watching before eventually settling for one of the rock music channels. Silver Lake's "Dragon Song" had just finished when Jake returned with their meal.

"You just missed yourselves on there," commented Lori, as he came striding in.

"Good," he muttered, "I don't like seeing myself on TV. I'm dreading watching the DVD footage Scott has stockpiled."

"He's coming to the school, isn't he?"

"I believe so," stated Jake, setting the food down on the large square footstool. He eyed the wine and plates suspiciously, then commented, "I thought I told you to stay where you were, li'l lady?"

"I needed the bathroom and picked these up on my way back," Lori explained. "I'm not an invalid, Jake. Besides, if I lie here all weekend I won't be able to move at all by Monday!"

"I hear you," he conceded, then added softly, "Just be extra careful."

"I will. Now what's in those boxes? I'm starving."

As they ate their meal, they watched the local news on TV, attempting to catch up with the events they had missed over the last few days. Jake sat on the floor, leaning against the couch where Lori was reclining. Both of them enjoying the relaxed intimacy of sharing each other's meal. After the buzz and midnight meals of late, it felt strange to be eating at a civilised hour.

"Rich called while I was out," began Jake, as he cleared away the empty food containers. "He asked if it was ok to bring Linsey over with him on Sunday. She wants to see you about something to do with the dance. I told him it was fine."

"We'll need to go food shopping tomorrow," observed Lori, pouring them a fresh glass of wine.

"I'll need to go," corrected Jake, firmly. "You can write me a list."

"I give in!" she conceded with a laugh. "OK, I'll write you a nice long list."

"If you rest all day, we can maybe go out for dinner tomorrow night," proposed Jake by way of a compromise.

"Deal," agreed Lori immediately. "Am I allowed to sit at my drawing board tomorrow? I have some work I need to finish off."

"Only if you have a long lie in the morning."

"Deal number two."

Saturday turned into a lazy day for both of them. When they finally awoke, Jake fetched them both breakfast that they ate in bed. A storm was brewing outside and rain was lashing off the windows. Instead of heading out for a run as planned, Jake fetched his laptop and Lori's sketchbook and they both spent the morning together in bed, working quietly. Occasionally they would exchange a few words, but they were both individually engrossed until almost lunchtime. It was Lori who gave in first and declared she was going for a shower. By the time she had showered and dressed, Jake had hauled himself out of bed, dressed and made them both a sandwich for lunch.

"Sorry," he apologised as she took her seat at the table. "There was only tuna."

"I like tuna," replied Lori with a smile. "So what's the plan for the rest of the day?"

"Food shopping then we can see if you feel up to going out for dinner in town."

"I wrote you a list," said Lori. "But no doubt you'll phone to check it several times. Would it not be easier if I came with you?"

"Yes, but you are staying right here, li'l lady," he said firmly. "Rest is what you are going to do."

"I spent weeks resting. Months! I'm sick of resting!" she protested sharply, tears stinging at her eyes.

"And you'll rest until Monday when you see John Brent," added Jake, feeling her frustration. Reaching out to take her hand, he added, "You need to take care of yourself."

She let out a long sigh and nodded slowly as a tear of frustration and fear slid down her cheek.

Despite her reluctance to stay at home for the afternoon, Lori enjoyed a productive few hours at her drawing board. Instead of looking at any of her commissioned projects, she decided to try to complete some of the jewellery designs she had been playing around with. The designs that she had given to Lin had sold well and her friend had requested another small collection. With her iPod plugged into the docking station in the study, she worked away to a selection of rock tunes. The pain in her leg had eased off a bit while she had been sitting, but as soon as she put any weight on it, she was aware of the throbbing ache.

"I'm back!" called Jake as he clattered in through the back door shortly after four. The water was dripping off his shoulders and hair. "It's insane outside!"

"Still raining?"

"Monsoon style," he called. "I'll be back in a minute. More bags to bring in."

When he finally came through to see her, he was soaked through.

"Are you sure you want to go out for dinner?" he asked as he stood dripping in front of her.

Trying not to laugh at his bedraggled state, Lori said, "Well, I had been looking forward to getting out of here for a couple of hours."

"Lori," he began to protest, then, seeing the wave of disappointment cross her face, he paused. "OK. We'll head out to the steakhouse. I just hope we can park right beside the door, near to the canopy."

"Thanks," she said warmly. "Now, am I allowed to help you put the groceries away?"

"No," he replied. "But you can come through and keep me company while I put them away."

"Fine," she agreed, getting slowly to her feet. "But I am making a fresh pot of coffee."

"No argument on that one, li'l lady," he said with a grin.

There were only a handful of cars parked at the steakhouse when they arrived a couple of hours later, so, much to Lori's relief, Jake had no trouble parking near to the entrance. The rain had eased off, but it was still coming down steadily. Having helped Lori out of the car, Jake kept a protective arm around her as they walked into the restaurant. They were swiftly shown to a table at the window by a young waiter, who looked vaguely familiar to Jake. When the young man returned with their drinks order and began to rhyme off the day's specials, he realised the boy was one of his senior class.

"How's school been?" asked Jake with a wink.

"Dull without you, Mr Power," replied the student, looking a little embarrassed. "How was your break?"

"Hard work," admitted Jake honestly. "We only got back on Thursday. Still a bit jet lagged and tired."

"Are you coming back to school? Some of the kids are saying you and Mr Santiago both quit."

"We'll both be back in class on Monday," replied Jake. "If you've not finished that assignment I set, you'd better get a move on with it."

"Yes, sir," said the boy. "I'll be back in a few moments for your food order."

Taking a sip from her wine, Lori giggled, "You were cruel to tease him about assignments."

"Perhaps," agreed Jake with a mischievous grin. "But he does have stuff to prepare for Monday. I set the piece myself before we left. Six weeks is more than enough time to complete it."

"Slave driver," giggled Lori.

During the drive home a couple of hours later, Jake asked Lori if she would listen to some of the new material he had been working on. Without hesitation, she agreed but suggested he bring his guitar up to the sunroom rather than playing for her in the basement. As they drove back along the lakeside road towards the house, Jake explained that he had been writing material with Rich on tour for a second album. So far they had about eight ideas, all needing a lot of work, but the bare bones were there to build on. The plan, he said, was to speak to Jason and the record company about recording locally around the time Maddy's twins were due so that Paul could be close at hand.

"Is there anywhere local?" asked Lori as he turned into the driveway.

"Here," Jake replied as he switched off the engine. "We might need to record the vocals elsewhere, but Rich reckons we can do the guitar tracking, drums and bass right here. Would you mind?"

"Not at all," she answered without pausing to think. "It sounds like a logical plan. If you sell it right, Jason should go for it."

"I hope so," said Jake, helping her out of the car. He noticed her wince as she put weight on her weaker leg but said nothing.

With only the two small table lamps lit, the normally spacious sun room felt small and intimate. Having fetched a bottle of wine and some glasses, Lori settled herself on the couch, silently relieved to have the weight off her leg again. Part of her was sure it was her imagination, but the pain and discomfort had grown more noticeable over dinner. Banishing it to the back of her mind, she focussed on Jake, who was sitting on the smaller couch adjusting the tuning on his acoustic guitar. His long blonde hair was falling over his face, hiding his features from her gaze.

"Most of these aren't acoustic tracks," he commented, as he ran his hand through his hair.

"Well, fetch an electric guitar and your practice amp from the basement, rock star," suggested Lori.

"Hmm, think I will," he muttered, setting his acoustic guitar down against the wall.

Quickly, Jake ran downstairs and returned with the guitar that the management had given him for his birthday and also a small square amp. It took him another few minutes to settle himself and tune up before he eventually began to play. The confidence and power of the opening riff took her by surprise and was a far cry from the Jake, who had played "Stronger Within" in the same spot only a few short months before. With a heart swelling with pride, Lori listened to half a dozen half-written new songs; some more complete than others. All of them building on the previous album's content. Switching guitars, Jake played two new acoustic tracks for her. Both of them sounded delicate and haunting after the raw power of his electric performance. His vocals sounded different too, and she could hear the influence of the two Weigh Station tracks he had sung on tour coming through. It added a different vibe to the music that she wasn't convinced was a Silver Lake sound.

Carefully, he put the guitar down, then looked at her, eyes silently appealing for approval.

"Well, li'l lady?" he asked, coming over to sit on the floor beside the couch.

"They're all rough around the edges, but I love them," she replied, reaching out to run her fingers through his hair. "Just be careful. Remember, you're Jake Power not Dan Crow."

He looked at her almost with an air of confusion.

"The two acoustic melodies are beautiful," began Lori softly. "But the vocal sounds too Weigh Station and not enough like Silver Lake. Don't confuse the two."

"I hadn't thought of them like that," confessed Jake, nodding his head. "I hear you, li'l lady. They are all still very much a work in progress."

"And they're great," she assured him. "Just don't lose sight of who you are. It's Silver Lake your fans want to hear. Its Jake Power the fans want. But, that said, you've got to feel the love for it too."

"Wise words, Mz Hyde," he acknowledged, as he moved to kiss her tenderly. What started as a soft gentle kiss gradually grew in passion and, within a few moments, they were hungrily kissing each other.

Taking care not to hurt her, Jake moved up to sit beside her on the couch. Slowly he unbuttoned the shirt she was wearing and caressed her breasts with light feathery kisses. With a few careful movements, he had helped Lori to slip out of the soft cotton shirt and had removed her lacy bra. Feeling exposed, she eased his T-shirt over his head and soon he was embracing her skin to skin. She could feel the bristly hairs on his chest teasing her nipples as he kissed her neck then nibbled her earlobe.

"I want to make love to you right here," he murmured, as he undid the belt of her jeans.

Lori relaxed back on the cushions as he carefully slid her jeans down and tossed them carelessly onto the floor. Her Disney princess socks made him smile as he teased them off her dainty slender feet. Swiftly he stood up and pulled off his own black jeans and socks. As he was about to remove his boxers, Lori sat up and firmly pushed his hands away from the waistband. In all his tattooed splendour, Jake stood still while she slowly slid his checked boxer shorts down over his slender hips. His erection betrayed the sexual urgency of his desires as he pulled down her flimsy white lace panties. Slowly Lori spread her legs, allowing Jake to slip into position between the soft skin of her inner thighs. She felt herself tense up a little as a wave of pain swept down her leg. Trying desperately not to cause her any discomfort, Jake entered her in one swift hard move. With long, slow strokes he teased her to the brink of orgasm, fully aware of her moistness and obvious hunger for him. Lori moaned softly, almost purring, in anticipation of the ecstasy that was building within her. With a few quick hard, fast thrusts Jake sent her spiralling into orgasmic oblivion. Moaning his name with a deep throaty growl, Lori surrendered to the full force of her feelings as she felt Jake find his sexual release within her.

Supporting his weight on his hands and knees, Jake delivered another cascade of light kisses across her breasts. Playfully he bit her erect nipples hard then ran his tongue down her smooth taut stomach. Beneath him, Lori groaned and instinctively arched her back, thrusting her hips towards him, as her body craved more attention. Sensing her readiness, Jake could feel his manhood, still wrapped within her feminine softness, harden and respond to her carnal desires. This time their lovemaking was hard and fast. As another orgasm swept over her, Lori shuddered and moaned pleasurably, all too aware of the searing pain burning in her leg.

"I love you, rock star," she purred, as Jake gently withdrew from her.

"Not as much as I love you, li'l lady," he sighed, kissing her tenderly on the forehead.

Before she could object, Jake had stood up and scooped her up into his arms. Skin on skin, he carried her through the house to the bedroom. Very gently, he laid her down on the bed then stretched out beside her, gently running a finger down the length of the scar on her thigh.

"I didn't hurt you, did I?" he asked, his voice suddenly husky.

"I'll live," whispered Lori quietly.

Sitting up, looking concerned, Jake asked again if he'd hurt her.

"No," reassured Lori with a forced smile. "You didn't hurt me. I was sore before you touched me. For those wonderful moments, I forgot the pain."

"Oh, Lori," he sighed, as he lay down beside her and pulled the duvet around them. She wriggled over closer to him and lay her head on his bare chest.

"Jake, you could never hurt me," she whispered softly. "Now hold me. I need a hug."

They were still wrapped in each other's arms when Lori awoke next morning. Slowly, trying not to disturb Jake, she moved over to her own side of the bed to check the time. A watery winter sun was filtering through the gauzy drapes, casting a ghostly light around the room. Feeling her move, Jake stirred and opened one sleepy eye.

"What time is it?" he muttered through a yawn.

"About nine," replied Lori, lifting her phone. "When are the others arriving for lunch?"

"Around twelve" answered Jake stretching like a cat. "Time for a run along the sand before I cook lunch."

"You're cooking?"

"I thought it might be easier for you," he said. "Nothing fancy. Chicken Parmesan, pasta and some garlic bread. A green salad bowl on the side."

"Sounds fabulous," replied Lori with a sleepy smile.

"Means you get to rest a bit more too," he added.

"Please, don't say anything to them," said Lori sharply. "I

don't need a fuss today. I've had a sore leg for a year. Let's not draw any more attention to that fact."

"Ok, li'l lady. Calm down," he soothed softly. "I won't say a word. You ok though?"

"Sorry," she apologised, tears welling up in her eyes. "I'm just a bit anxious about what John's going to say tomorrow. I don't think I can cope with another setback."

"Do you want me to come with you?" offered Jake.

She shook her head. "You've got your meeting at school. I'll be fine. I'm just being paranoid."

"If you're worrying about going, I'll come with you."

"No. I'll be fine," she said, with what she prayed was a confident smile. "Now if you're going for a run, you'd better make a move. I'm going for a shower."

Music and the relaxed notes of friendly conversation were filling the beach house by early afternoon. Maddy had been the first to arrive, roaring into the driveway in her Mustang. Both Jake and Lori were surprised to see her arrive on her own, but she quickly explained that Paul had driven up to Philadelphia to collect Gary and Scott from the airport. Traffic permitting, he hoped to be back around four and would bring the guys straight out to join them. While Jake busied himself in the kitchen preparing lunch, the two girls retreated to the sunroom. Within a few minutes Grey had arrived with Becky then Rich pulled up with Linsey in tow. Soon the three girls were relocated in the lounge while Becky sat happily watching cartoons in the sun room. The three members of Silver Lake were all in the kitchen helping Jake with lunch.

"So how was the tour?" asked Linsey, as she settled herself on the couch beside Lori.

"Tiring," said both Lori and Maddy in unison.

"It was fabulous," added Lori. "I'm not sure what the fans would say if they could see the guys just now though."

"Good job Scott hasn't arrived with his camera," laughed Maddy, casually resting a hand on her expanding baby bump.

"Rich told me about him," said Linsey. He's going to film the school show, isn't he?"

"That's the plan," replied Maddy. "Just be careful what you

tell him, honey."

"Don't scare her," cautioned Lori softly. "He's adorable. Just don't tell him anything too personal about you and Rich."

"Thanks for the warning," said Linsey nervously. "Oh, Lori, can I ask a favour about Saturday?"

"Sure."

"The seniors are in charge of decorating the gym hall and are planning to do a piece for Silver Lake. Would you be able to come into school for a few hours to help get them started?"

"I'd be glad to," agreed Lori warmly. "When?"

"Are you free tomorrow?" asked the art teacher hopefully.

"I have an appointment first thing, but I could come in after that. I'm not sure when I'll be done. Probably mid to late morning."

"Perfect. I'm free for an hour before lunch. We can talk through a few ideas, grab some lunch and if you could spare the kids some time after lunch that would be brilliant."

"Fine. I'll drop Jake off so I can hang around till school's done and drive home with him," agreed Lori. "Give me a note of your cell number and I'll call when I know a more definite time."

"Thanks," said Linsey, breathing a sigh of relief.

The girls chatted casually for a while until Jake called to say he was serving lunch. Soon they were all seated round the dining room table, dishing up chicken and pasta and pouring juice.

"Did you keep back any chicken for Paul and the boys?" asked Lori, noticing the dish of chicken breasts was almost empty.

"Yes, li'l lady," replied Jake. "There's a second dish in the oven as we eat."

"I didn't expect them to fly over so soon," commented Grey, as he helped Becky to cut up her chicken.

"Gary called on Friday to say they'd grabbed the first flights they could get," explained Maddy. "I know they both wanted to be here well before Saturday."

"Where are they staying?" asked Rich, tearing off a piece of garlic bread.

"I've booked them into the hotel beside me," Maddy explained.

"How long are you going to camp out there for?" asked Lori curiously. "You've been there for months!"

"Not much longer. Paul and I are going to rent a house near here. We've a couple to look at this week. One's on the far side of town, out towards the outlets. The other one is near here. It's on the far side of Silver Lake. I don't want to be too far from the medical centre, just in case."

"Have you seen the doctor since you've been back?" asked Lori.

"Friday afternoon. Everything's fine. She reckoned I'm about twenty weeks. I've to go back in four weeks," answered Maddy. "Although Lord knows what size I'll be by then!"

"You look like you swallowed a big meatball," said Becky, with a cheeky grin.

Everyone laughed at the little girl's observation.

"Honey, it's one heck of a size of meatball," commented Maddy, as the twins both kicked furiously.

"Well, technically it's two meatballs," added Jake, flashing her one of his smiles.

Their casual banter continued throughout the meal. Initially Linsey had sat quietly among them, but, as she relaxed, she too joined in the animated conversation. The relationship between Rich and Linsey was still in its infancy and she still felt shy around the band. Once the main course was over, she rose to help Jake clear the plates. Grey too got up to lend a hand. While her daddy was in the kitchen, Becky took the opportunity to disappear back into the sunroom, lured by the call of the cartoon channel.

As the adults were finishing off their leisurely lunch with coffee and cheesecake, they heard Paul's truck pulling up outside, closely followed by the back door opening, sending a blast of cold salty air shooting through the house.

"Hello," called Paul, as the three of them entered the kitchen.

"In the dining room," Jake called back.

A few seconds later, Paul came through, pulling off his beanie hat. A rather weary looking Gary and Scott followed him.

"Hi, guys," greeted Lori with a smile. "How was your flight?"

"Early," muttered Gary with a yawn. "Thanks for inviting us over."

"The more the merrier," replied Jake, getting up from the table. "You both hungry?"

Both of them nodded.

"Grab a couple of chairs from the kitchen till I fetch you some food," instructed Jake. "Beer?"

Lunch stretched into early evening as Paul and the two new British arrivals ate their meal. This was Scott's first visit to the USA and he was enthusing about the drive down from the airport and the sights he had taken note of. His enthusiasm was infectious. Soon they were all debating what their favourite local landmark was. Arguing over which one signalled their arrival in town.

"When I used to come here with my folks for the summer it was the first road sign that says beaches. Then I would watch for the water tower," reminisced Lori.

"The outlets," declared Linsey. "They're my landmark."

"No, I'm with Lori on the water tower," added Jake.

"So what else is there around here?" asked Gary, as he finished his last mouthful of chicken.

"Miles and miles of sand and ocean," said Jake. "It's quite a sleepy town in winter. In summer the place is jumping with tourists."

"Well, I'm sure you'll soon show us both around," said Scott before adding, "Any decent nightlife?"

"There's a few bars in town," said Paul, with a wink to his band mates. "Enough to get you in trouble."

Their conversation was interrupted by Becky coming back through from the sunroom. She clambered up onto Grey's lap and whispered in his ear.

"This young lady is tired, guys," said the bass player. "We're going to call it a night if you don't mind. What's the rehearsal schedule for next week?"

"Tuesday night?" suggested Jake, glancing over at Lori for approval. "Say six thirty?"

"Fine by me," said Rich. "How about I bring food over with me?"

"Perfect," agreed Paul, nodding.

"Ok, I'll be here Tuesday," promised Grey, getting to his feet and hoisting Becky onto his shoulder. "Thanks again, Lori."

"It was all Jake's hard work today," she replied. "But I'll take the thanks. Night, Becky."

"Night, Lori," murmured the sleepy little girl.

"Night, all," said Grey, as he headed for the door.

"We'd better go soon too," said Linsey quietly. "I've got some prep work to do for tomorrow."

After Rich and Linsey left, Lori went through to the kitchen to make a fresh pot of coffee for the others. Maddy followed her through to offer her assistance. She had noticed the pained look appearing on her friend's face and, as she entered the kitchen, she caught Lori swallowing down two painkillers.

"When are you seeing a doctor?" Maddy asked softly. "I can see you're in real pain."

"First thing in the morning," replied Lori, filling the water reservoir for the coffee maker.

"Are you ok?"

"I'm fine. Just sore. It's a pain like bad toothache. Not the same kind of pain as when everything was healing," explained Lori quietly, not wanting the others to over-hear her. "I'm scared though that it's something serious."

"Like what?" asked Maddy with genuine concern.

"I don't know. A problem with the metalwork. An infection," answered Lori, with a resigned sigh. "It's so close to the anniversary of it all that I just want to move on from hospitals and doctors and pain meds."

Giving her friend a hug, Maddy soothed, "I understand, honey. If you need me, we're here for you. All three of me."

Her turn of phrase made Lori giggle and lightened the mood again. The fear of what the doctor was going to find slid to the back of her mind once more.

Next morning that fear was foremost in Lori's mind as she drove towards the medical centre. She had dropped Jake off at school for his meeting with the principal, promising to call him as soon as she was out of the doctor's office. They also agreed to meet for lunch when she came into school to help Linsey with the school dance art project. Once she was alone in the car, her mind started racing and filling with "what if's". All weekend she had resisted the temptation to Google her symptoms but, as she navigated her way through the breakfast time traffic, Lori wished she had. Ironically the pain in her leg had eased considerably over night, but a part of her wondered if she was just growing accustomed to it.

When she entered the medical centre she made her way to the X-ray department and was met by a friendly, motherly radiographer who was expecting her. Instantly the woman put her at her ease as she escorted her through to the take the x-rays. It didn't take long to complete the series of films.

"Alrighty, that's you done, Mz Hyde," she declared cheerfully. "Dr Brent is waiting for you round in his office. Do you know the way round?"

"Yes, thanks," replied Lori as she got to her feet.

Slowly she walked through the building towards the doctor's office. The waiting room was empty, as was the reception desk. John's office door was open slightly. Lori knocked gently on it and entered the all too familiar room.

"Good morning," he said, getting up from his seat to come round the desk to greet her. "How are you?"

"Hi," she replied nervously, forcing a smile. "I'm ok. A bit scared."

"Understandable," he empathised. "Take a seat."

He watched her closely to see how she moved as she sat down, then returned to his own seat at the desk.

"Did you get the x-rays done?"

"Yes. I went there first. Just as you told me to."

"It'll take them a few minutes to email them over. Now, tell me again, in detail, about when this pain started, what you've done differently. Anything different that you've done in the past couple of weeks."

Calmly Lori explained about her trip to the UK, about the flights, attending the shows, the long days and the late nights. The doctor listened closely and made several notes as she spoke.

"When you were watching from the side of the stage, were you standing all that time or sitting down?" he asked.

"A mix of both, but when I was sitting, it was on a wooden stool. You know, like a bar stool," she replied. "Why?"

"Just a thought," he began. "Were your feet dangling or supported? Did your feet reach a spar on the stool without over stretching?"

"I'm not sure. Both nights in London my feet were dangling, as you put it, I think," she answered, frantically trying to visualise the scene at the side of the stage. "I also sat on a high cocktail stool for a while at the end of tour after show party but my feet were definitely supported then."

"Give me a moment while I look over these x-rays," he said, turning his attention to the PC in front of him.

Lori watched anxiously as the doctor scrutinised the x-rays on the screen. She could see he was zooming in on part of the image, but from his facial expression, she couldn't tell if he liked or disliked what he was seeing in front of him. Eventually, after what felt like an eternity, he turned the screen towards her.

"The good news is there is nothing major showing up on here. The internal fixation is all still in place apart from one screw that has split. Now that can happen for various reasons and shouldn't in itself pose a problem," he began, pointing to the broken screw on the screen. "Is that about the level with the site of the pain?"

"I think so," replied Lori hesitantly, trying to gauge how far down the length of her thigh that particular screw was.

"Pop up on the couch for a minute," requested the doctor. "I want to take a look and see if we can confirm this."

Fortunately, Lori had had enough sense to wear a long skirt instead of trousers. She sat back on the narrow couch and pulled her skirt up. Knee high length brightly coloured striped socks adorned her feet and lower legs. When he saw them, John Brent raised an eyebrow at her and smiled.

"I like stripes," she confessed with a nervous giggle.

Slowly and gently, the doctor palpated the length of her thigh, gently applying light pressure to try to determine where the precise point of injury was. As his hand reached the midpoint, Lori flinched. He noted that there was more heat in this area, but it was hard to determine if there was any swelling.

"That seems to fit with where that troublesome screw is," he commented. "Does it fit with where the edge of the stool was when you were sitting on it?"

"More or less, I think."

"Ok. I think I have an explanation of the problem here," said John calmly. "I want to email your surgeon from Mount Sinai and send him the x-rays to confirm a couple of points. Just as a precaution. He may have a different opinion to mine here and want to take an alternative course of action."

"So what are you thinking?" she asked quietly, inwardly dreading the answer.

"It's been a few months since we took any x-rays so I can't be certain, but I'm guessing that screw snapped as the bone was healing over the summer. I also suspect that, at that point in the bone shaft, the bone is still healing. The x-rays suggest that. I would have hoped it would have fully healed by now. Remember though, there was significant trauma in that area. It was the point of impact in the accident. By sitting on the bar stool with the weight of your leg unsupported, I suspect that you've put extra stress on that weak area of partially healed bone. In short, I'm confident that the problem now is a stress fracture of your femur."

Tears welled up in her eyes and Lori could feel her throat tightening.

"Don't look so scared," said John softly. "It's a setback, but it's not the end of the world, Lori."

"So why do you want to refer to Dr Hartson if you're sure that's what the problem is?" she asked, sounding totally defeated.

"I want his professional opinion," replied John. "I want to ensure he's happy to leave the broken screw where it is. The bone's still well aligned so I would rather not touch the screw either to replace or remove it. He may decide differently. I just want to double check. We need to ensure whatever we decide to do is the best for you and your long term recovery."

Lori nodded slowly as a tear slid down her cheek, "So what

now?"

"This is the tough part, I'm afraid," he began. "You need to go back to using your crutches for a few weeks. You need to be non-weight bearing on that leg to allow that bone to heal completely. When you're sitting you need to ensure your thigh is fully supported. No more perching on bar stools, Mz Hyde."

"How long will it take to heal?"

"The million dollar question," he sighed. "Judging by your recovery time so far I would estimate eight to twelve weeks. Now you won't need to be non-weight bearing that whole time, but I do want you to stay on crutches until it is fully healed. No pushing it this time."

"How long will I need to be non-weight bearing for?"

"That also depends on the rate of healing and the level of pain. Initially I'd say about four weeks."

"So what am I allowed to do?" she asked, wiping away another tear. "Am I confined to the house again?"

"Not at all," he replied quickly. "Just be sensible about what you do, Lori. Once the bone has healed a bit more I'll send you to one of the physical therapists. Keep up with some gentle stretching and non-impact exercise for now. And I mean gentle."

"Can I still drive?"

"Your car's an automatic, right?"

Lori nodded.

"Then you should be ok to drive. Just be careful if you've had to take any strong pain medication," he answered. "Stick to your low level pain meds routine for the next four weeks. If you play by the rules, you shouldn't need to resort to the strong stuff."

"What about flying?"

"How long a flight?" asked the doctor.

"The band are going to Australia and New Zealand towards the end of next month. Jake wanted me to go with him," she explained.

"Leave that thought with me for now," said John. "I'll see you back here on Jan 7th and we can talk about it then."

"Ok," agreed Lori with a heavy heart.

"Come on," said the doctor with a warm smile. "I'll take you round to see Jo just now to get you sorted out with some crutches."

"Thanks," she muttered, as John helped her to her feet. "Great Christmas present."

As they walked slowly across to the physical therapy department, the doctor asked how things were going with the band. Briefly Lori filled him in on the success of the album and the UK tour dates. She then explained about the school show lined up for the weekend.

"That's where I'm headed after here, if that's still ok?" she said as they reached the physical therapy waiting room. "I'm to support an art project along a Silver Lake theme this afternoon."

"No reason why you can't still go if you feel up to it," he replied with a smile. "Jo will be with you in a minute or two. I'd better get back to my clinic. Any problems give me a call. If not I'll see you at ten on January 7th."

"I'd love to say I'll look forward to it," she joked feebly. "Have a lovely Christmas if I don't see you."

"You too, Lori."

Across town, Jake and Rich were sitting outside the principal's office waiting for Dr Jones to call them in. There was a student already in the office along with their parents. Raised voices could be heard coming from behind the closed door. Politely the secretary had instructed the two music teachers to sit and wait. After a few minutes, Jake began to grin.

"What's so funny?" asked Rich looking confused.

"Us sitting here like two naughty kids," laughed Jake.

"I guess," agreed Rich, with a smile, seeing the humour in it. "Think we'll get expelled?"

Before Jake could reply, the principal's door opened and Dr Jones bade farewell to the student and their parents. As the family headed towards the exit, he beckoned Jake and Rich to come in.

As Jake shut the door behind them, Dr Jones said, "Welcome back, gentlemen. How was your trip?"

"Fantastic," replied Jake, taking a seat.

"But hard work too," added Rich. "Long days and late nights."

"Glad to hear it went well. The school has been buzzing as the kids followed your shows on YouTube and various other social media sites," declared the principal with a hint of pride. "Even the staff are excited to have our two rock stars back." He paused, then added, "I'm guessing you're not back for long though."

"That's what we are here to talk about," admitted Rich. "Things are really taking off and the band needs more and more of our time."

The principal sat nodding as he listened to their plans for the start of the year.

"We'll see out the next two weeks till the end of term," Jake said. "But we have to move on after Christmas."

"And I wish you all the best of luck," said Dr Jones sincerely. "You've not said anything I hadn't anticipated. I've two supply teachers lined up for January to cover your classes."

"Thanks, sir," said Rich. "We would like to make an offer to help you though."

"Shoot."

"Poor choice of words, sir," joked Jake, remembering his previous visit to the principal.

"Apologies, Jake."

"I'm teasing you," laughed Jake. "What we want to suggest is that we keep in touch with the school and when we're in town with some free time on our hands that we come back in to do some workshops. Free of charge, of course."

"Very generous of you and I'd be delighted to take you up on that. The kids will really benefit from it too."

"We want to give something back," added Rich.

"And to keep me on side in case you need to come crawling back looking for a job?" observed Dr Jones with a wink.

"Something like that."

"I'm sure we can work something out," he agreed. "Now speaking of working things out. Let's talk about this show on Saturday."

They spent the next half an hour filling the principal in on their ideas for the set for Saturday night. Both of them were keen that Silver Lake did not monopolise the whole evening and that the senior school still got their traditional Christmas social too. After a bit of debate, Dr Jones agreed that there would be a semi-formal drinks reception between six thirty and seven thirty to allow everyone to arrive and that Silver Lake would play for an hour or so until nine. That left an hour and a half for the traditional elements of the school social. The two musicians explained that they would get the stage set up after school on Friday then have a run through on the Saturday morning.

"We'd like to invite some of the students in for the sound check," said Jake. "If that's ok with you?"

"Fine by me. I will need to notify the parents that the event is being professionally filmed. I don't see it being a problem though."

"We'll make sure Scott doesn't film too much of the kids," promised Rich. "Unless any of them get parental consent to be interviewed."

"Leave that with me," said Dr Jones checking the time. "You had better get yourselves to class. The bell's due any second."

"Yes, sir," said Jake getting to his feet. "And thank you."

"Pleasure, boys."

Lori had been sitting alone in the waiting room for almost ten minutes before one of the physical therapists came out to fetch her. It had been a long, lonely wait. Several times she had reached for her phone to call Jake, but each time she changed her mind. If she heard his voice now, she would lose the fragile grip she had on her emotions. The news hadn't been as bad as she had feared, but it still wasn't good. The very thought of possibly facing more surgery scared her to the very core. Being forced to use crutches again, even for a few weeks, after working so hard to be free of them broke her heart.

"Sorry to keep you waiting, Miss Hyde," said a bright cheerful young male therapist. "Jo's been caught up with another patient and asked me to see you. Is that ok?"

"It's fine," said Lori softly, forcing a smile for the young man.

"Ok. Let's get you through," he said helping her to her feet. "I'm Billy, by the way,"

"Nice to meet you. Are you new here?"

"Yes, ma'am. I just graduated at the summer. Jo's my mentor. Dr Brent mailed round to say you've to be issued with crutches and given a basic rehab exercise schedule."

The graduate showed her into a cubicle then excused himself while he went to fetch her a pair of crutches. He was back in a few moments with a bright red metallic pair, still wrapped in cellophane.

"We got stock last week from a new supplier," he explained, as he opened the bag. "All of them are crazy colours. Is red ok for you? I thought it was kind of festive and a bit of fun. You looked like you needed something to make you smile."

Laughing, Lori nodded. "I can always put fairy lights on them."

"Not a bad idea," agreed Billy joining in the laughter. "Right, that looks to be about the correct height for you."

He handed her the red crutches, then asked if she remembered how to use them. Nodding, she got to her feet and positioned them carefully.

"Have you been non-weight bearing before?" asked the therapist, scanning over her case notes.

"No," admitted Lori, shaking her head. "Last time round I started off partially weight bearing."

"Let's take you through the basics then."

Billy had just finished running through the "driving instructions" and talking her through the basic exercise sheet when Jo Brent came dashing in. Her white tunic failed to disguise her baby bump.

"Hi, Lori," she called cheerfully. "Sorry I was busy when John brought you round."

"No worries, Jo," said Lori quietly. "Congratulations. John never said."

"Oh, this!" laughed Jo, rubbing her belly. "A little surprise! I'm due in March. Baby number three for us."

"Your bump's tiny compared to my friend Maddy's," observed Lori. "She's about twenty weeks with twins."

"Oh Lord!" exclaimed Jo. "I'm glad this one isn't twins. I feel huge already compared to the last twice."

"Jo, I've set Miss Hyde up with the rehab schedule. Do you want me to book her in for clinic?"

"Yes, Billy," replied Jo. "Twice a week from January 7th. Is that ok with you, Lori?"

"Whatever it takes," replied Lori resignedly. "I just can't believe this has happened."

"It's rotten luck," sympathised Jo warmly. "But you're starting your recovery period from a far stronger position this time. You'll be back on your feet in no time."

"John said eight to twelve weeks at least," she said staring at the floor. "It feels like a life sentence right now."

"I can imagine," agreed the therapist. "Especially after all you've been through to get this far."

"What a way to celebrate the first anniversary. Still broken," sighed Lori, feeling tears welling up in her eyes. With a deep breath, she pulled herself together. "Is there anything else I need to know or do for the next few weeks?"

"Rest. Healthy diet," recommended Jo. "And relax and enjoy the holiday season. Get Jake to run around after you."

"He'll smother me in kindness," admitted Lori with a sad smile. "Am I free to go?"

"I'll walk you out," offered Jo, as she watched her struggle to her feet. "John said you were still ok to drive, didn't he?"

Lori nodded, "Thank God."

"Here, let me take your bag and your cane till you get used to walking with those pretty red festive sticks," offered Jo kindly. "Billy, I'll be back in a few minutes. You write this up while I'm gone."

Sitting alone in the car, watching Jo walk back into the building, Lori felt her emotions flood through her. Tears flowed soundlessly down her cheeks as she sat with her head in her hands. Tears of anger and frustration; tears of hurt and fear. Gradually she calmed herself down, reasoned with her inner self that this really wasn't the end of the world and that, like all the other aspects of her recovery, she would get through this. A cricket chirp from her bag brought her back to reality. Reaching for her phone, she saw it was a message from Jake, "What did the Dr say? J x"

"Just leaving. Will tell you when I see you at school. Will call when I get there. L x"

Before she set off, Lori spent a few moments fixing her makeup in the tiny vanity mirror in the car. Her eyes were still red, but she hoped they would clear by the time she reached the school. As she started the engine the radio came on, tuned to the local rock station. They were playing "Stronger Within", a version Jake and Rich had recorded during an interview a few months before. Hearing Jake's beautiful, haunting voice filling the car made her smile as she drove out of the car park.

Jake was pacing up and down outside the school watching for her when she finally drove in through the gates. Without a second thought, Lori pulled into one of the handicapped spaces by the main door. Before she had turned off the engine, Jake was beside the car.

"I was worried," he gushed, as he opened the door. "Hey, you've been crying, li'l lady."

"Sorry," apologised Lori, trying to remain composed. "Is there somewhere we can talk privately? Somewhere with coffee?"

"Sure. There's an interview room next to the principal's office," answered Jake. "You're scaring me, Lori."

"No need to be scared, rock star," she assured him, as she reached round for her scarlet crutches. "Just a bit of a sorry tale to tell."

"Crutches?" he asked, stating the obvious.

"Yes," she replied with a forced smile, as she climbed awkwardly out of the car. "Red ones."

A few minutes later they were sitting in the small interview room. Jake had fetched them a coffee from the refectory and, having taken a large mouthful of the hot dark liquid to steady her nerves, Lori told Jake exactly what John Brent had told her.

"A stress fracture?" he echoed in disbelief. "From sitting on a stool?"

"John says it's the most likely explanation and it fits with when the pain began to feel worse."

"And how long will it take to heal?"

"Eight to twelve weeks he reckons," answered Lori. "I've to see him in four weeks and begin therapy again then. He's also going to consult the surgeon who operated on me after the accident to get his opinion. Until then, I'm to be non-weight bearing as far as possible."

"Oh, Lori, I'm sorry," soothed Jake hugging her. "I don't know what to say."

"There's not much to say," she replied, wiping away a tear.

"Hey, don't cry, li'l lady," he said, kissing away the teardrop. "We'll get through this together. You're not on your own this time."

"Thanks," she whispered, kissing him gently.

The bell to sound the end of morning recess rang loudly in the background.

"Do you want me to tell Linsey you've had to go home?"

"No," stated Lori emphatically. "I promised to help her out. I'm as well sitting about here helping out, as I am sitting at home on my own."

"If you're sure."

"Positive," said Lori firmly. "Can you take me up to find her?"

"Of course," agreed Jake. "Then I'll need to run. I've a class this period."

"Poor choice of words, rock star."

Spending time with the senior art class proved to be the perfect distraction. Lori and Linsey spent the hour before lunch working out a rough plan of the decoration required for the hall to promote the band. Deciding to aim big, Lori suggested splitting the class in half and have one half produce a mural to reflect a rock concert venue while the other half could do a back drop for the stage. If time allowed, they agreed they would produce some promotional posters to display round the school. The art teacher loved the ideas and suggested that she could get some of the younger students to help with the posters. With such a tight deadline, it was a challenging task to set the students. The two girls opted to work through lunch in order to be as prepared as possible for the afternoon class. When the lunch bell rang, Jake came to fetch Lori but was instead despatched to the refectory to fetch lunch for all of them. He returned a short while later and threw his own thoughts into the planning as they ate their lunch together.

When the students came tumbling into the art room after lunch Lori recognised a few of them from her previous visit, including Brad Green. He sat quietly at the back, listening closely as Linsey explained that Lori had been on tour with the band and had come to help them recreate a genuine concert scene for Saturday night. The class plied Lori with questions about the concerts she had attended in Britain and she did her best to keep her answers relevant to the task at hand. Eventually Linsey intervened, split the class and set them to work, with promises that they could quiz Lori later. Throughout the lesson, Brad sat silently designing a poster, unwilling to be part of the team events. As Lori toured the classroom, she complimented him on the design. He looked up and smiled briefly, then said quietly, "Thank you. I want to make sure it's perfect for Mr Power and you. To say sorry."

"Thanks, Brad. We appreciate it."

All too soon the bell signalling the end of school rang and the class had to pack up for the day. They had made really good progress – both the mural and the backdrop were outlined.

As the last student to leave closed the door, Linsey turned to Lori, "Thank you so much for today. I couldn't have done it without your help."

"It's been fun," confessed Lori, feeling calmer and more relaxed than she had for days. "Just the distraction, I needed after this morning. Do you need me to come in later in the week?"

"If you can spare the time and feel up to it that would be fabulous."

"I'll aim to come back in on Thursday," suggested Lori, as she spotted Jake hovering about outside the door. "What time?"

"Whenever you can manage," said Linsey. "All day would be wonderful."

"I'll see how I feel," replied Lori, rubbing her aching thigh.

The door opened behind them and Jake stuck his tousled head in, "Come on, li'l lady. Let's get you home."

"I'm coming. I'm coming," called Lori playfully, "I'll see you on Thursday."

There were still a few students milling about as Jake and Lori made their way slowly through the school and out to the car. A couple of the students tried to stop Jake for a chat but he politely dismissed them, claiming to be late for an appointment. When they reached the car, he watched closely over Lori as she slid herself into the passenger seat.

"Jake," she began, as he adjusted the driver's seat. "I forgot to ask. How did you and Rich get on with the principal this morning?"

"Great," he said, adjusting the rear view mirror. "We finish at the end of term. He also liked our idea of doing workshops when we are back in town. To be honest, he was expecting it."

"And he's still ok with you playing on Saturday night?"

"Yup. Sure is. Apparently the kids and some of the staff have been following the band on Facebook and Twitter and YouTube. I never even realised there was stuff out there," gushed Jake. "I had a look online earlier. It's incredible! I'll show you when we get home."

"The art students are all looking forward to it. I got bombarded with questions all afternoon. Even Brad Green spoke to me," she replied. "You've built up quite a female following out there."

"Stop it!" he laughed. "You're embarrassing me."

"Just telling the truth, rock star," she teased.

"You seem happier than you were earlier," Jake observed, relieved to see that the worried look had gone from her eyes.

"I guess I am," she agreed. "I've had time to put things into perspective a bit better. Time to calm down. Maybe I was pushing myself too hard and this is the warning to be more careful. As you said, we'll get through this. I've really no other option."

As planned, Silver Lake descended on the beach house for rehearsal on Tuesday. Rich was the last to arrive, armed with four large pizza boxes. Breaking with her usual dining rules for guests, Lori told them all to go through to the sunroom. While she settled herself on the couch with her leg supported on a pile of cushions, Jake fetched paper plates and napkins. All of them felt at home at the beach house and Grey made himself useful by fetching the drinks. Watching the boys fuss around her made Lori feel guilty, but Jake had explained to them about her trip to the doctors so they understood.

"I thought Maddy and Gary were joining us?" commented Grey, as he passed Paul a glass of juice.

"They'll be along in an hour or so," replied the drummer. "They were on a conference call with Jason when I left. Scott's coming too."

"With or without camera?" asked Jake.

"Without I hope," growled Grey, helping himself to a slice of pizza. "Kid's a pain in the ass with that damn camera."

"He showed me some of the footage," said Paul. "It's looking good. Actually, I was quite impressed. We looked ok. Not too ugly."

"Have any of you looked at the clips on YouTube?" asked Jake, as he sat down on the floor in front of the couch. "The kids at school are all talking about it."

"Maddy mentioned it," said Paul. "But I've avoided looking up to now."

"You should take a look."

"How many likes are there for the videos of you with your shirt off?" teased Lori, nudging Jake on the shoulder.

"Too fucking many," he muttered, cringing at the thought.

"If it helps our music, I'm all for it," declared Rich. "But, Jake, keep your clothes on this Saturday, please."

"Very funny."

Saturday dawned all too quickly and they wakened to find a light dusting of snow coating the town. Despite her protests, Jake brought Lori breakfast in bed, insisting that she rest all morning as it was going to be a long day. She had been at the school, helping Linsey all day on Thursday and most of Friday before finally admitting on Friday night that she was tired and sore. Having made this confession, Lori knew it was pointless to argue with Jake over resting for the morning before the show. Satisfied that she would stay in bed till at least noon, Jake kissed her on the forehead, then left to head over to the school for the sound check, promising to be back for lunch.

Seeing the town covered in clean, white, powdery snow suddenly made it all feel more festive. With only ten days until Christmas, Jake hadn't been feeling in the holiday spirit, but the snowfall was all it had taken to change that. As usual, he arrived slightly late at the school and, as he entered the gym hall, Grey called out, "Ah, the late Mr Power!"

The students, who were gathered in front of the low stage, giggled.

"Twenty bucks in the pot, Jake," laughed Grey then, with a conspiratorial wink at the students, added, "In fact make it fifty. It's Christmas after all."

"See the abuse I have to put up with," said Jake to the students as he pulled off his leather jacket. "Have the guys introduced themselves?"

The group of students shook their heads. All of them looked nervous and more than a little star struck now that they were in the presence of Silver Lake.

"Guys, come over here a minute," Jake called out cheerfully.

Grey and Paul jumped down from the stage, while Rich chose to sit on the edge. Quickly, Jake introduced the twelve students to the bass player and the drummer. He explained that both he and Rich had wanted them to learn a little about the work that went on behind the scenes to pull a performance together. Rich continued, that while this was Silver Lake's official sound check for the evening's set, it was also the ideal opportunity for them to learn and to help.

"Is there an assignment on this, Mr Power?" asked one girl nervously.

"No. Not from me," replied Jake, flashing her a smile. "We just wanted to share this with you guys. Partly as a thank you for all your hard work this semester and partly to help with your own performance skills."

"Right," called Rich, jumping down from his perch on the edge of the stage. "We'll split you into four groups. Each group will shadow one of us for the next half hour or so."

Between them the two music teachers split the students into groups then buddied them up with an appropriate member of the band. Both Grey and Paul had been briefed the night before as to what Jake and Rich wanted them to do. Jake took his group out of the gym hall and through the school to the music department. The first part of his "lesson" was on vocal warm-ups and he encouraged the three budding vocalists to practice his operatic pre-show routine with him. He explained that this was a much shortened programme and that he would go through a similar series of exercises for at least an hour before the show later.

"What happens if you don't warm-up right?" asked Jenny, as they headed back to the hall.

"You risk straining your vocal chords and doing permanent damage," replied Jake. "Trust me, tuning your voice is as important, if not more so, than tuning say a guitar. I've lost my voice once and I don't intend to do so again."

"When?" asked Kate, another budding vocalist.

"After the band supported Molton last summer," Jake answered. "Scary silent few days." He shuddered at the dark memories of his three days in the solitary confines of his apartment. "OK, guys, when we get back into the hall we need to check the guitars that I'm setting up for tonight. I'm setting up four so we can take one each."

When they returned to the gym hall, Rich was working with his group at one side of the stage. Grey had taken his trio up to the back of the hall while Paul was showing the three budding drummers how he liked his kit set up. The only space left for Jake was the small backstage area so he led his group through there.

Once they were happy that everything was tuned and set up as each of them preferred, Rich told the students to take a seat while the band played through three of the numbers from their proposed set list. There were a few stops and starts, but eventually, Silver Lake were satisfied with the sound and the set up.

"Kate, you're on," called out Jake from the stage. "And Todd, you come up too."

The two stunned looking students clambered up on stage, both of them trembling nervously. Rich handed Todd his guitar while Jake gave his to Kate and adjusted the microphone down to her level.

"Now we know you guys know Dragon Song but who knows the bass or the drum parts?"

One of the boys said he knew the bass part.

"Get your ass up here. Listen for Paul's count, then take it from the top," instructed Jake with a grin. "And the rest of you will be up here shortly so start to think about what you're going to play or sing with one of us."

Over the next forty five minutes all of the students got the chance to play with Silver Lake. Some of them begged for more than one appearance. All nerves disappeared as soon as the talented teenagers took to the stage. They selected a wide variety of songs to perform. All four members of the band were amazed by the confidence and talent that they displayed. Keeping a watchful eye on the time, Rich finally called a halt to the impromptu jam session.

"Thanks, guys," he said with a proud smile. "From the bottom of our hearts, thank you for that performance. It's been a privilege to share the stage with you."

"We've some gifts for you all," announced Grey, as he brought out a plastic crate from behind one of the cabinet speakers.

The band presented each of the students with a goody bag containing a selection of tour merchandise, autographed photos, CDs and guitar picks. Politely the twelve students thanked them for spending the time with them and some asked if they would pose for photos. Each member of the band was more than happy to oblige.

"Ok, folks," declared Jake eventually. "Time to wrap this up for now. As Rich said, thank you for letting us play with you today. We'll see you all tonight when you're better dressed."

"Before you go," called Rich. "Andy, Todd and Kate, can you wait behind for a moment, please?"

As the rest of the students filed out the door at the far end of the hall, the band invited the three remaining teenagers back up on stage. They were exchanging nervous glances, none of them sure what was going on.

"Don't look so scared," laughed Jake. "You're like rabbits caught in the headlights."

"Final task for you three," said Rich. "If you're up for it?"

"We're up for it," stated Kate quickly, without even consulting the two boys beside her.

"All of you?" asked Jake, looking intently at each of them in turn. "This is a big task."

"Yes, sir," replied the two boys in unison.

"Lose the "sir" bit," suggested Jake. "Now, how would you three feel about being our stage crew for tonight?"

"For real?" gasped Kate, eyes wide in amazement.

"For real," confirmed Rich. "We'll talk you through what we want you to do, but you three are the Silver Lake stage crew for tonight. Are you up for the challenge?"

"Yes!" they all shouted at once.

"Glad to hear it," muttered Grey. "If you'd said no then we would have to do it all ourselves."

"Don't listen to him," said Jake with a smile. "Be back here for six tonight. We'll talk you through the checks you need to do and answer any questions you have. As soon as we are off stage you guys are obviously free to party with the rest. We'll clear away all our gear tomorrow. You even get to help with that if you can spare the time."

"Any questions?" asked Rich, glancing at each of them in turn.

"Do we get lanyards saying "Stage Crew - access all areas"?" joked Todd.

"We'll see what we can do," smiled Jake. "Now go and get yourselves scrubbed up for tonight. We'll see you back here at six."

Chattering loudly among themselves, the three students made their way out of the hall, leaving the band to finish off the rest of their sound check. It took them another hour to be fully happy with the set up and to draw up checklists for their trainee stage crew for later on. All four of them had really enjoyed working with the music students and some of their youthful enthusiasm had rubbed off.

"What's our dress code for tonight?" asked Paul, as the band prepared to leave.

"All black?" suggested Jake, putting his leather jacket back on.

"Works for me," agreed Grey.

"Black it is then," stated Rich. "Are we going out afterwards?"

"Let's play that one by ear," said Jake, searching for his car keys.

"I'll see if Maddy feels up to it," Paul added. "We've not been out for a while."

"Would be good to take Gary and Scott into town," Rich added. "Show them the beach night life. We could go to the Turtle."

"Let's see how we feel tonight," said Grey. "Becky's staying with my mom so I'm up for a few shots."

"Ok, guys," said Jake. "I'm out of here."

"See you at six, Mr Power, and not a minute after," Grey cautioned with a wink.

While Jake had been at the school, Lori had been as good as her word and had stayed in bed until noon. As soon as she saw the clock change to 12:01, she manoeuvred herself out of bed and headed for a shower. Showering and washing her hair, while trying to keep the weight off her injured leg, was a balancing act fit for the circus, but she did her best and eventually stepped out of the shower and sat on the toilet seat to get dried. Frustration at her own weakness was creeping in but, after a few deep breaths, she pushed the negative thoughts to the back of her mind. Instead,

Lori thought ahead to what she was going to wear to the school extravaganza. Earlier, she had called Maddy, who had reliably informed her that Jason was planning to attend along with one of the record company executives. The two girls had debated what to wear and Maddy said she had managed to source a long black and red dress that partially disguised her baby bump. As she sat in the bathroom, Lori ran through her own party dresses in her head, trying to decide which one was most suitable. She had a dim recollection of buying a long dark green velvet dress and wondered if it was here or in her New York apartment. Wrapped in the towel, she headed back through to the bedroom to check the closet.

"Lori!" called Jake loudly, as he came in via the back door.

"In the bedroom," she yelled back.

She was still searching through her wardrobe when Jake came striding into the bedroom. She didn't need to ask how well the sound check had gone as he was still grinning and looked totally relaxed.

"You lost something?" he asked curiously.

"No," she replied, lifting down a hanger. "Just found what I was looking for. I had a panic that this dress was in New York."

"Don't recognise it," commented Jake, taking the hanger from her and hanging the dress on the outside of the bathroom door. "Have you had lunch yet, li'l lady?"

"Not yet."

"Good. I stopped and picked up some steak sandwiches. Come through and eat before they get cold."

"Can I throw some clothes on first?" she asked, indicating the towel.

"If you insist."

Over lunch, and in between mouthfuls of steak sandwich, Jake filled her in on the morning's activities. His enthusiasm and passion for the kids' achievements rang through his every word.

"You're going to miss teaching, aren't you?" observed Lori.

"Yes," he admitted without hesitation. "We'll be back to do workshops with them. I just hope we play well for them tonight. They deserve a good show."

"You'll be fabulous as ever."

"I hope so. It's a strange gig. I think I'm more nervous than I was in London," he confessed.

"A little nervous energy is a good thing."

A few short hours later, as she was trying to get ready, Lori decided that a nervous rock star was a challenge. Jake was showered and dressed an hour before they needed to leave and was pacing the house like a caged animal. At her suggestion, he went down to the basement to do some vocal warm-ups, but was back before she had finished getting dressed. He paced up and down the bedroom as she applied her make-up and brushed out her hair. In an attempt to focus Jake's mind on a task, she asked him to find her silver ballet pumps in the wardrobe. A few moments later he handed her two odd shoes, causing her to giggle helplessly.

"Relax, rock star," she said calmly. "Deep breaths."

"Sorry," he muttered, looking for the correct shoes for her. Finding them, he passed them over.

Carefully, she slipped her feet into the flat silver shoes, put her lip gloss and phone into her small silver evening bag, and then got stiffly to her feet, putting out a hand to balance herself on the dressing table. She positioned her festively red crutches, then asked, "Will I do?"

The dark green dress complimented her petite figure perfectly. It set off the blue of her eyes and the sun kissed golden highlights of her hair. Her natural beauty took Jake's breath away.

"You look stunning, li'l lady," he said, his voice hoarse with emotion.

"Thanks," she whispered, as she adjusted her balance. "Time to get this show on the road, rock star."

Jake held her coat for her as she slipped her arms through the sleeves, then grabbed his own leather jacket.

"Right, let's rock 'n' roll, li'l lady!"

Lori had only just got herself settled in the passenger seat of the Mercedes when Jake declared he had forgotten something and would be back in a minute. Watching him run back into the house, she shook her head. Never had she seen him so nervous before a show. He was back a few moments later, a copy of the set list clutched in his hand.

"Was that all you'd left behind?" she asked, as he handed her the sheet of paper.

"Yes," he answered, starting the engine. "How does it look?"

Quickly she scanned down the list of songs. "More or less the same as it did in Glasgow and London."

"Appropriate for school?"

"Perfect," she assured him. "Just remember not to swear if you're talking to your audience."

"Shit. I hadn't given that any thought."

Fairy lights illuminated the front entrance to the school and, as the lights twinkled, they added to the festive air of excitement. The car park had been cleared of snow but Jake still fussed round Lori as she walked carefully towards the entrance, anxious in case there were any patches of black ice. They were a little early but, from the number of cars in the car park, not the first to arrive. As they entered the warmth of the gym hall, the principal came striding over to greet them.

"Good evening, Jake. Miss Hyde," he said with a welcoming smile. "What do you think of the decorations?"

Since the band had departed, Linsey's team of artists had been hard at work. Behind the small stage the large backdrop was suspended on two wires and that, coupled with some clever shading, created a 3D effect. A long mural ran down one side of the hall creating the image of a large crowd of fans clamouring to be allowed into the private party.

"These worked out really well," replied Lori, nodding approvingly.

"They're fabulous!" declared Jake gazing round. "I hope that back drop's secure. We don't want it landing on Paul's head while he's playing."

"It's fine," promised Lori with smile. "Anyway, its light. Trust Linsey."

"Let me show you to the table we've reserved for your party," suggested Dr Jones smoothly. "We've an adjacent table for staff and another for invited guests."

There were a few members of staff already gathered at the tables, most of whom shouted a cheerful greeting to Jake.

"There's a drinks reception in the refectory shortly," explained the principal. "I hope you'll both be able to join us through there."

"Sure," agreed Jake, glancing at Lori. "I'll need to go and finish warming up about six thirty."

Spotting more guests arriving, the principal excused himself, leaving Jake and Lori to mingle with the staff. After a minute or two, Lori saw Rich and Linsey entering at the back of the hall. The art teacher waved and rushed over. She was enthusing about how fabulous the mural looked before she even reached their table.

"Nice to see you made it on time," teased Rich, clapping Jake on the back.

"He's a bag of nerves," laughed Lori. "Go easy on him, Rich."

Gratefully Lori lowered herself onto one of the chairs and propped her crutches up on the wall behind her. Jake sat next to her, casually draping his arm around her shoulders, then began nervously fingering her hair. With a smile, Lori put her hand on his thigh and whispered, "Relax."

Next to arrive was Grey, accompanied by Gary and Scott, who was armed with a large bag of camera equipment. As agreed, he had been in earlier and set up some cameras on stage to record the band. The school had agreed to him placing a couple around the hall and these were discretely mounted around the room near to the stage. Some of the students had also begun to arrive and were congregating in small groups at the far end of the hall, furthest away from the adults. Dead on the stroke of six, the three "stage crew" arrived at the table.

"Punctual," complimented Rich. "Good start, guys."

"We can't afford the late fine," joked Todd bravely.

"Very funny, kid," teased Jake. "Your checklists are on stage and back stage behind the curtain. Don't touch Scott's film equipment. Don't break anything. Don't unplug anything. One of us will be up to check on you shortly."

"Yes, sir," said Andy, saluting Jake and Rich.

"Get to work," laughed Rich, with a grin.

As the three students made their way towards the stage, Maddy and Paul arrived with Jason and two record company representatives, who introduced themselves as Eric and Cameron. Maddy looked striking in her long black dress. The soft folds of the fabric draped over her baby bump, but the red lace side panels still gave her figure a seductive shape. She had taken care with her make-up and had even added some sequins to the stars tattooed beside her right eye.

"You look stunning, Maddison," said Jake, as he hugged her.

"Love the dress," declared Lori approvingly, without making a move to get up, "It's perfect for you."

"Thank you," said Maddy, blushing slightly at the compliments.

"Mz Hyde," Jason said smoothly, bending to hug her. "Beautiful as ever. I heard you've had a set back to your recovery."

"Hi Jason," she replied. "Bad news travels fast."

"Maddison says it was caused by sitting on the stool at the side of the stage," he said disbelievingly.

"Apparently," acknowledged Lori. "Sitting for long periods of time with my leg unsupported has stressed the partially healed bone or so my doctor reckons. I'll live."

"I hope so," said the Englishman warmly. "I've more work to put your direction next month."

In the background, Rich noticed that the principal was inviting everyone through to the school cafeteria for drinks and *canapés*. Once he had escorted Lori through and was content that she was in safe hands, Jake excused himself to go and warm up. As he walked along the corridor, away from the reception, he could hear the buzz of conversation and was sure he could hear Lori's musical laugh.

When he returned to the hall an hour later, Lori, Maddy and Linsey were sitting with Jason and the record company "suits" at the band's table near the front of the stage. There was no sign of Gary or his fellow band members. Having checked that Lori was alright and exchanged pleasantries with a couple of his teaching colleagues, he made his way backstage in search of the others.

"How's it going back here?" he asked, as he slipped behind the curtain. "Are we nearly good to go?"

"A few more minutes should do it," said Grey. "This junior crew are fantastic. I think we should hire them."

Todd passed Jake his dark cherry red Gibson SG and asked him to double check the tuning.

"Spot on," nodded Jake, handing it back. "Well done. Are the others done?"

"All except your acoustic," replied the boy. "I was warned not to touch it."

"Smart move," said Jake, reaching over to lift it out of its case. "That acoustic and I go way back. It was a present from my mom for my eighteenth birthday. No one touches it but me. No offence intended. I'm just kind of funny that way about it."

"It's a beautiful instrument," admired Todd wistfully. "I hope to get one half as nice for my eighteenth."

"When's that?" asked Jake, idly strumming the guitar and fiddling with its tuning.

"December 30th," replied the boy. "But I seriously doubt if my mom will buy me anything. She doesn't bother much with presents."

There was an air of defeat about the boy's tone of voice and choice of words that touched Jake's heart. Todd was one of his most talented students with a natural ear for music. He made a mental note to stop by the music store on Monday after school to see what he could pick up for the boy. Every young musician needed a break now and again.

When the band were all happy with their pre-show set up, Kate was despatched to find the principal to inform him that Silver Lake were ready whenever he was. Once she was out of sight, Paul produced a Santa hat from his jacket pocket and put it on.

"You look like a fucking garden gnome," Grey stated gruffly glowering at the drummer.

"Just be thankful he didn't get us all one," laughed Rich, shaking his head.

"Where's your Christmas spirit, guys?"

"Still in a bottle in the bar," quipped Grey.

Kate re-appeared at that moment with the principal in tow, cutting short their banter.

"I'd just like to say thanks again for agreeing to do this for us," said Dr Jones looking round at the four musicians. "In all my years of teaching, it's the first time an international rock band has performed at the Christmas social. I hope it's not the last."

"Say that after you've heard our set," joked Grey "And dealt with the angry parents."

"I'm sure there will only be disappointed parents who missed out on being here," countered the older man with a knowing smile. "If you're ready, I'll go out and introduce you."

Without waiting, he turned on his heel and walked out onto the stage. Andy handed him a cordless microphone that the principal switched on as he reached the front of the stage.

"Good evening, everyone and welcome to our rocking Christmas extravaganza," he began. "I'd like to thank you all for coming this evening. I'd like to welcome our invited guests. There's too many people to thank everyone individually, but I would like to thank Linsey Bergman and the art students for decorating the hall and also Miss Lori Hyde for her artistic direction."

The students, teachers and guests all applauded politely.

"Now without further ado I'd like to welcome our very special guests out on stage. Please give a huge welcome to Silver Lake!"

Handing the microphone back to Andy, the principal retreated from the stage. The lights dimmed and Silver Lake quietly took up their positions. As soon as the stage lights went on, they launched straight into "Dragon Song". Two hundred eager students were standing in front of the stage spellbound. For the band, it made a pleasant change to have their audience so close to the stage and not to be divided from them by a row of security personnel. Due to a lack of space, their performance was less physical than the norm, but Jake poured his heart and soul into the vocal.

"Thank you," he said with a grin, as the song ended. "Not too loud for you?"

"NO!" screamed back the students.

"OK. Time to rock this joint!" roared Jake, as the band began their next song.

While the band played their next two hard and heavy rock numbers, Lori looked round at the crowd. There was a strange mix of emotions on display. The students and younger teaching staff were obviously loving it; the more mature members of staff and invited guests looked less impressed. If the band noticed, it didn't affect their performance. In the relatively small hall, the huge Silver Lake sound drowned everything out.

At the end of the third number, Jake switched guitars, accepting his acoustic from a rather nervous Todd. He declined the stool that Andy brought out. Having plugged the lead in, he moved to sit on the edge of the stage, lowering the microphone stand to the lowest setting.

"Change of tempo, folks, to let our more mature members of the audience recover," said Jake, with a wave towards the staff table. "I would normally sit on a stool on stage for this, but I discovered recently that wooden stools can be bad for your health."

A small round of applause came from Silver Lake's guests and he guessed, correctly, that Lori had gone scarlet with embarrassment.

"The next two songs were written for a very special person who's here tonight," continued Jake, gently strumming the guitar. "Lori, this is for you, li'l lady."

To Lori, "Stronger Within" and "Lady Butterfly" had never sounded better. The small audience listened in silence as Jake's haunting voice and delicate playing filled the hall. Perhaps it was the intimacy of the setting or just a reflection of how fragile she had been feeling all week, but Lori had to fight back her tears as the acoustic interlude came to an end. As Jake stood up, he turned towards her and blew her a kiss. She caught it, placed her hand over her head, then blew one back out to him.

Over the next thirty minutes, Silver Lake rocked the gym hall with a mix of their own songs and some rock classics that were a last minute change to the proposed set. Staff and students entered into the spirit of things and were soon all on their feet in front of the stage.

"Still with us?" asked Jake, grinning as sweat began to run down his forehead. "We're going to try a couple of extra numbers for you now. These are genuinely unrehearsed, so this could be a complete car wreck, but we've had a couple of requests for these tonight. For those older rockers out there, here's some Led Zeppelin for you."

"Immigrant Song" was the shortest song the band played, but, whether it was rehearsed or not, it came across as the most intense part of their performance and left no one in the room in any doubt about Jake's vocal ability.

"If you know the words to this one, join in," cried Jake, wiping the sweat off his face and running his hand through his hair. "Our token festive tune."

The staff cheered louder than the students as Silver Lake

played "Merry Xmas (War Is Over), the John Lennon and Yoko Ono classic. Soon they were all singing along, totally captivated by the band's performance. As the final notes died away, the band took their final bow to rapturous cheers and cries for more. Exchanging swift glances, the four members of the band silently agreed to two more.

"You're wearing us out," Jake joked. "Two more, then it's time for us all to party. This is one of my personal favourites. Sweet Child O' Mine."

The band followed the classic rock number with their usual set closing number, "Flyin' High". All of them gave the last song everything they had and left the stage to the triumphant cheers of their exclusive audience. As the stage lights dimmed, the speakers began to play more traditional Christmas social music and the principal announced that a buffet was being served in the refectory.

While Jason and Gary went to fetch some food for the table to share, Maddy declared, "I had my doubts about tonight but that was brilliant. Seeing those kids lapping it up was quite something. Amazing."

"It was something special," agreed Lori, sub-consciously rubbing her thigh. "Do the babies not react to the noise?"

"Yup," nodded Maddy, smoothing her dress down over her bump. "They're starting to squirm a lot. It feels weird in a nice way."

"Poor kids will be born with their ears ringing," teased Jake, appearing beside them.

"Probably," laughed Maddy rubbing her bump.

"Do you ladies want something from the buffet? The guys already went through, but I thought I'd check if you were ok," said Jake, resting a hand on Lori's shoulder.

"We're fine, rock star," replied Lori. "Jason and Gary already went to fetch us a plate."

"Good. I'll go grab myself something and be right back."

By the time Jake returned with his plate piled high with food, the others were already crammed round the table. Carefully, he squeezed in beside Lori, having taken a spare chair from the next table. It wasn't the band's normal after show party but all of them were relaxed and entering into the festive spirit of the occasion.

The music had started up and soon Paul had led Maddy up to dance. Staff and pupils were mingling on the dance floor, all genuinely having a good time. Looking rather shy, Kate came over and invited Jake up to dance. Flashing her one of his "Power" smiles, he took her hand and followed her out onto the dance floor. It struck Lori that that was the first time she had seen him dance. From where she was sitting, he looked to dance as well as he played guitar. Soon one of the other senior girls came over to ask Rich up to dance. Scott was discretely mingling with the dancers, filming the members of Silver Lake. The whole scene reminded Lori of her own school days and she smiled to herself as the music discretely slowed down as the evening wore on and the students paired off into couples.

She was contentedly resting her head on Jake's shoulder when Eric Clapton's "Wonderful Tonight" began to play.

"Come on, li'l lady," said Jake softly. "Humour me. We're going to dance."

"Jake, I can't," she began to protest.

"Trust me," he said, helping her up. "Leave the crutches. I'll hold you."

Keeping a tight hold of her waist and supporting her weight, Jake guided Lori over to a quiet corner of the dance floor.

"Stand on my feet," he said. "And let me dance for both of us."

"What?" she giggled, doing as he asked. "Oh, what the hell! A little weight on my left side can't hurt for a few minutes."

With his arms securely around her waist and her arms draped around his neck, they danced gently to the beautiful ballad.

"I asked them to play this," confessed Jake, whispering the words softly into her ear.

"Good choice," agreed Lori, gazing up into his hazel eyes.

"Lori," he began, his voice husky. "Will you marry me?"

She stared at him for a moment, tears welling up in her eyes for the second time that evening, then whispered simply, "Yes."

Tears in his own eyes, Jake hugged her then supporting her weight with one arm, he reached into his jeans pocket and brought out a delicate diamond ring. Slowly he slipped the ring onto her finger, then kissed her passionately, oblivious to their surroundings.

"I love you, li'l lady," he sighed. "I was so scared you'd say no."

"Ah," she sighed with a smile. "Everything from earlier on makes sense now. Your nerves. The mad dash back into the house."

Jake shrugged his shoulders and continued to dance to the dying notes of the song, forever now etched in his mind as their love song.

As the hall echoed to the sounds of Brian Adams "Everything I Do", Jake escorted Lori back to the table. Both of them re-took their seats and Jake casually draped his arm around his fiancée's shoulders.

"You guys looked cute out there," complimented Linsey. "Just like a pair of kids."

"It was our first dance," announced Jake with a mischievous grin.

"And our last for a while," added Lori, as she took a sip of her soda. "I never could dance."

"I know!" laughed Maddy. "Not even copious amounts of alcohol helped."

"Where's Grey?" asked Jake, noticing the bass player was missing from the table.

"On the dance floor," pointed out Rich. "With the head of the history department."

"Nice to see him having fun," observed Jake, watching the bass player dance. "Time he moved on."

All too soon, the principal announced that it was time for the last musical number of the evening. When she looked round, Lori realised that the four members of Silver Lake had vanished. Before she could turn to ask where they had gone, the stage lit up and Jake and Rich were centre stage with acoustic guitars, Grey and Paul behind them with tambourines and sleigh bells. On a count of three, they began to play an acoustic medley of Christmas classics starting with "White Christmas" and eventually ending with the whole audience singing along to "Jingle Bells."

"Merry Christmas, everyone!" roared Jake then added, "Safe journey home, all."

For a final time, the students and staff filled the hall with cheers and applause. This time the lights came on, signalling the end of the party. Slowly the students began to leave the hall, some of them pausing to say good night to the band, others still cheerfully singing "Jingle Bells".

As the Silver Lake party prepared to leave, they had a quick debate as to where they were moving on to. It came as no surprise to Lori when they unanimously agreed to meet up at the Green Turtle for a few drinks. Before they left, Rich went over to the staff table and extended an open invitation to his colleagues to join them at the boardwalk bar.

Snow was falling gently as Jake drove into town. He had the stereo turned down low and smiled as he watched Lori fingering her engagement ring.

"You do like it, don't you?" he asked somewhat anxiously.

"It's perfect," she replied, gazing down at her hand. It was a three stoned ring – a large emerald cut diamond flanked by two smaller emerald cut stones set in a white gold band. "How long have you been planning this?"

"A while," confessed Jake grinning. "I bought the ring a couple of weeks ago."

"But I was with you a couple of weeks ago?"

"True," he replied with a nod. "But you were pre-occupied at the time. I believe you were purchasing a watch."

Lori laughed, "You bought this in Glasgow!"

"I sure did," admitted Jake. "And managed to hide it from you until tonight. I never told a soul."

"What do you think the others will say when we tell them?"

"We'll find out soon enough," he said, pulling into a parking space around the corner from the bar on Wilmington Ave. "I've a confession, li'l lady."

"What?" asked Lori, as she unfastened her seatbelt.

"The Turtle are expecting us," said Jake. "I've arranged for them to stay open late for us. Private party."

"Confident were we?" teased Lori with a giggle of excitement.

"No, but definitely optimistic." He paused, then added, "The guys think it's just an after show party. The champagne and decorations might be a giveaway though."

"I love you, rock star," giggled Lori, reaching across the car to hug him.

Despite Jake's offers of assistance, Lori insisted on negotiating the stairs up to the bar on her own. She was pale and a little shaky as they walked into the bar room, but quietly assured Jake she would be fine in a minute or two. The manager rushed over to greet them with two glasses of champagne. Jake politely accepted both glasses, then allowed the bar manager to show them through to the function suite. The room had been decorated with silver and blue balloons. The ceiling was festooned with twinkling blue and white fairy lights. Lori stared round, eyes wide with wonder at the lengths Jake had gone to. Putting the glasses down on the nearest table, Jake reached out to hug her.

"Like it?" he asked, kissing the top of her head.

"Love it," she sighed, beginning to tremble with the emotion of it all.

"Come on. Let's sit down before you fall down, li'l lady," he said caringly.

They had just sat down at the table in the centre of the room and taken their first sip of champagne when the rest of the band, closely followed by the management, came clattering loudly into the room. As soon as they saw the decorations and champagne glasses set out on the tables, they stopped in their tracks.

"Are we celebrating something?" asked Grey, getting straight to the point as ever.

"Christmas," replied Lori with a glance up at Jake that said "Not yet."

"I'll celebrate Christmas!" declared Paul pulling his Santa hat out of his pocket and putting it back on.

Once they were all seated and the Turtle staff had poured everyone a glass of champagne, Jake decided he couldn't stay quiet any longer. A few of the teachers from the school were still making their way in but he had to share the good news with the band.

"Guys," he said, clinking his glass to get everyone's attention. Spotting Scott with his camera ready, he said, "Turn it off for a moment, Scott. Please."

Jake moved to stand behind Lori. "Guys, I've an announcement to make." He paused, feeling all of their eyes boring into him. "Lori's agreed to be my wife."

"Woo hoo!" screamed Maddy, rushing to hug her friend and spilling several glasses in her hurry. "Congratulations, darling!"

The next few minutes were chaos as they all congratulated the happy couple. Each of them hugged and kissed Lori. Most of them hugged Jake too. Champagne flowed. Someone started the music in the background and the party was soon in full swing.

It was well after one and the party was beginning to wind down. The champagne had been replaced by shots of tequila and most of the band were more than a little the worse for wear. In the corner, Maddy was resting against Paul, struggling to keep her eyes open. Beside Jake, Lori too was showing signs of fatigue. With his camera confiscated for the night by Grey, Scott had passed out across the next table, surrounded by empty shot glasses.

"One last toast," said Jake, slurring his words slightly. "Here's to all of us! Here's to Silver Lake's success! Here's to our happy ever after!"

"Here's to friends who are family," added Lori, raising her glass with a smile.

The story of Jake and Lori and Silver Lake will continue in

Excerpt from **Impossible Depths – Book 2 in the Silver Lake Series** - due to be published 2016

Bright sunlight flooded the bedroom when Lori finally roused herself from sleep on Sunday morning. Instantly she knew she had slept late, but if a girl couldn't have a long lie on her birthday, when could she? A single red rose lay on the nightstand beside the bed with a small white card tucked underneath it. On the card were a series of scribbled music notes and "Happy Birthday li'l lady. J x" written on it.

The night before both of them had worked on until after midnight, hence the need for the lie in. One of Lori's deadlines had been pulled forward causing her to work flat out for three days straight as she tried to cram two weeks' worth of work into four days.

Pulling on one of Jake's discarded T-shirts, Lori lifted her rose and went through to the kitchen to put it in some water before it wilted. A bud vase already filled with water was sitting on the counter and under it was another card. This time the card had the same music notes drawn on it plus a picture of a sun. Curious, Lori put the rose into the vase and wandered through to the sunroom. Silence was filling the house and she felt confident that she was alone. In the centre of the sunroom one of the small occasional tables had been moved into the centre of the room and placed on the centre of it was a vase with eleven roses and another card. More music notes and a champagne glass were drawn on this one and a small pile of sand had been drizzled on top. With a smile, Lori wandered outside and across the deck to the edge of the path in her bare feet.

She spotted Jake immediately. Without pausing to dress or to fetch her cane, she very carefully made her way across the warm, soft sand towards the picnic blanket and her fiancé. As she drew closer she saw he had a champagne brunch laid out for them. He was sitting on the sand with his back to her, facing the ocean and was playing his beloved acoustic guitar.

"Hi," said Lori softly as she reached the edge of the blanket.

"Happy birthday, beautiful," said Jake as he turned to face her.

Carefully, he laid his guitar in its case and got gracefully to his feet. In two long strides he was beside her and had wrapped his arms round her. "Happy Birthday," he whispered before kissing her tenderly.

"Thank you," replied Lori with a bright smile. "I never expected this."

"That was the general idea."

Taking her by the hand Jake led her over to the blanket, then helped her to sit down and get comfortable. While Lori settled herself, he popped the cork on the bottle of champagne, firing it towards the ocean. Bubble flowed over the rim as he poured them each a glass.

Passing her a half full glass, he said, "Here's to many more birthdays, li'l lady."

"To us," she toasted, raising her glass to his.

Coral McCallum lives in Gourock, a small town on the West coast of Scotland with her husband, two teenage children and her beloved cats.

https://coralmccallum.wordpress.com

https://www.facebook.com/pages/Coral-McCallum

https://twitter.com/CoralMcCallum

Printed in Great Britain
by Amazon